FURTHER
ADVENTURES

FURTHER
ADVENTURES

JON
STEPHEN
FINK

ST. MARTIN'S PRESS
NEW YORK

Library of Congress Cataloging-in-Publication Data

Fink, Jon Stephen.
    Further adventures / Jon Stephen Fink.
        p.   cm.
    ISBN 0-312-08787-X (hc)
    ISBN 0-312-09059-5 (pbk.)
    I. Title.
PS3556.I4755F85   1993
813'.54—dc20   92-21570
                                                CIP

First Published in Great Britain by Martin Secker & Warburg Limited.

First U.S. Edition: January 1993
10 9 8 7 6 5 4 3 2 1

To Dawn & Lenny

FURTHER
ADVENTURES

To Who It May Concern—

I was The Green Ray. Now it can be told the Story which many tried to silence many Refused to believe & many did not want to hear about. I Believe that there are Contracts which prove this Fact amid the Papers of the late Mr. Howard Silverstein of Westchester, New York. I do not know where those Papers could be Filed today or even if they still Exist but he was a V.I.P. and maybe all of them became Donated to his Alma Mater back East. I believe he graduated from Yale. Or Princeton. One of those two or Harvard. If they are not there then I do not know what to tell you please take my Word for it. My name was Ray Green.

To tell you the Truth I think that was the main Reason why the V.I.P.s of the Liberty Broadcasting Co. gave me the job on account of my Name. Many choices which change a person's Life happen on the spurt of the moment on account of Hunches & Mr. Silverstein had a Hunch about me because of my Name. Since he Rose Up from messenger boy to President of the Company by playing such hunches (you may Remember it was Howard Silverstein who took a gamble on the popular appeal of Spiller's High-Energy Buckwheat Breakfast Flakes & the rest like they say is breakfast food History) the other V.I.P.s took his Word for it & lapped up the Idea that I was the right man at the right time. I will always be very Thankful to him until the end of my Life which will be as soon as I finish writing this Note.

I would have told him my name was Franklin Delano Roosevelt if it was going to make a Difference because the year was 1938 & Good jobs were scarce on the ground. Especially jobs on the Air. Radio jobs being the ones cherished very high in New York i.e. besides the Stock Market which anyway did not feel itself since the famous Crash. It took a World War plus millions of Deceased to puff it back up to its old level of Success & there is a Moral

I

there I believe. Nor I do not mean to sound Unpatriotic but I claim in the Heart of everything Beneficial that is done you will find some kind of selfish Human motive & this makes a mockery of all Decent human efforts. I know this is True because I was The Green Ray who defended the Defenseless—punisher of the Criminal who fought to purge wrong & keep America Strong. I held Life & Death in my fingers & stared Evil right in the face so even if Ray Green went down in the final round The Green Ray lives on in 12 tough washable plastic statuettes Available Free inside every single specially marked box of Spiller's High-Energy Buckwheat Breakfast Flakes. Ask your Mom to buy some today!

I write this Note to tell you that I am not a Helpless Victim of a murder but I Believe there are many villainous people who will Rejoice when they hear the news of my Death. I write this Note to Explain why I decided to end my Life from my own hand.

I do not Believe that Death can be Worse than any of the things I have seen over the years but Especially it can not be Worse than the Events of the last 3 weeks & 4 days. People run from Death every way they can by Business or by Pleasure or a Combination a person can trick himself & believe he can put enough Distance between his footprints & Death's. Wake up in the morning and get out of bed Vertical it is a trick to make you forget how Life always has Death in it. You can not defy Gravity forever. Well I am not going to Trick Myself about this business anymore. I will call a spade a spade I will let all chips fall Wherever they may. AMEN.

I am not going to Hang Myself since there are not any Structures in my Apartment strong enough to hold my Weight. There is the exercise bar where I used to do my morning pull-ups but it is not Tall enough I would have to Hang with my Legs curled up which is a position I can not Maintain for all the necessary Time.

Also I Decided I am not going to swallow a Overdose of pills because the only kind of Medicine I have in the Bathroom is St. Joseph's Aspirin For Children which does not upset my Stomach. I believe I would have to Swallow about 30 bottles before they gave me any Lethal Effect nor I do not think that the Rexall Pharmacy will sell me so many at a single time without some kind of a Explanation.

So I decided I am going to make Good use of the Snubnose .38 Revolver which my Arch Foe handed me on a silver platter in my glove compartment. Out of the 3 Methods I know blowing my Brains out causes the most of a Mess but I have to say SO WHAT for also I know Mrs. Roderiguez will clean the place up when she comes in as usual on Thursday morning.

Now I run into Death's arms with my eyes wide open. Ray Green died by a Bullet from his Own Hand this is the Truth. Amen. Furthermore *I please ask* you should add this Note into the phony boloney Official F.B.I. File which that phony boloney bastard JOHN NEWBERRY wants to palm off is the True Picture of Events. He will tell you the Evidence in my File says everything about me but it is not even 10%. Nor I am not Afraid to spell out the real Facts & you can see how they all add up to the Truth. I will give you full Descriptions I hope you do not flinch. My Words should fall on his neck like a Heavy Ax. I Sincerely Hope that somebody exactly as Rotten as John Newberry but with a different Motivation (namely JUSTICE) will get that sonofabitch BUT GOOD!

I will not go on about this but I want to Die by Myself. Most of my Life that is the way I lived. Most of my Days have been very quiet Except for the ones between September 12 1938 & March 5 1946. Plus the last 3½ weeks. The 1st day I was The Green Ray before the great American audience was a carbon copy of the day that certain Events forced me out of Retirement. The Weather & everything. This is a Fact you can look up.

I am a little jumpy at the Moment since I do not Know what that scraping Sound outside my window is. Wait. I am going to check on it.

No it was not Who I expect here it was only the Loose cover coming off my Air Conditioner which aggravates me something Terrible since it is brand new from Sears and not cheap Merchandise either.

These are the Facts of September 12 1938. The 1st thing that Mr. Silverstein told me was nobody NO MATTER WHO is allowed to know the True Identity of The Green Ray. I had to keep it a Secret from my own Family even. I promised him I will do this to my Dying Day but he said for the term of my Contract was enough. Off the record he advised me if anybody else found out who was really The Green Ray i.e. this skinny Jewish kid from Philadelphia who was bald on top by the Unfair age of 19 then said Jewish kid etc. would find himself selling matches on a streetcorner pronto Tonto! Public knowledge of my Identity interferes with the mission of The Green Ray it hampers my ability to do anonymous unrewarded Good.

I agreed with Mr. Silverstein who also spoke on Behalf of Mr. P.K. Spiller who owned Spiller's Foods, Inc. the makers of Spiller's High-Energy Buckwheat Breakfast Flakes the Sponsor of our Program. I even asked Mr. Silverstein if I should change my name again my name Ray Green was a dead giveaway in spite it was a Fateful Coincidence but he made a Good Point that such a Obvious measure would arouse suspicion in the Public Mind.

Of course the producer Mr. Argyll knew of my Identity and the Engineer Mr. Burrows & his Assistant Leon Kern. Other persons who became connected to the show knew who I was & I brought this fact to Mr. Silverstein's Attention but he told me I could Relax about it these Individuals are hand-picked for Loyalty & we could count on their Honor to keep quiet. (I believe Leon Kern was Related to P.K. Spiller somehow so it would not be a big Surprise to me if he had to take a Blood Oath on top of just giving his word to Mr. Silverstein. At the time I only knew P.K. Spiller by his Reputation and when I met him face to face I will say at close range his Powers took effect & he made me act against my Will.)

My Life before September 12 1938 was dark & my Life from then until 1946 was light. I had a strong Voice for a man of my frame which fact Leon Kern made a Remark on this way—"He's all sticks & bones but he's got a hell of a loud voice!" After that it was Leon's job to remind me I should keep back from the Microphone even further away than anybody else in Radio History.

In that Radio Studio I came to Life like I never did before I Felt like I was just as live as the Electric wires that carried my Voice out of there & up into the Air & down into livingrooms all across America. And when I walked out of the Liberty Building after our First Episode I strolled around very light in the head. I heard a bunch of boys & girls talking about it in front of a Drugstore. A icy cold wind was cutting across Broadway but I walked right into it with my coat Wide Open. I was Invincible. Also Anonymous & above Rewards but I was walking with a Secret inside me my Secret Identity. I knew who I was plus I knew what a Good thing it was that nobody else did even if they did not realize how their Ignorance was Protecting them.

My whole Life changed. It was light all over.

The bright light of my Life faded out all the way (almost) in 1946 & when I came to again I was sitting in my kitchenette 40 Years later in my Apartment on Pecan St. in Mason, New Mexico. I had my pot of water boiling and I was just going to drop my onion in it then *blooey!* A Blackout! All the Electricity went out in a flash nor not just in my Apartment but the whole west side of Town. (I Discovered by Word of Mouth before it got Printed in the Newspaper that the cause of this Blackout was a prank by a couple of High School boys Billy Higgenbotham & Carl Kemp. It was Billy Higgenbotham who got microwaved to Death by trying to reheat his Big Mac on top of a 100,000 Volt transformer.)

I sat in my dark Kitchenette for a few Minutes I Waited for them to turn the Electricity back on. But the Blackout went on for a few Minutes & then some so I left my onion in the pot & went into the Bedroom to sit. I waited 2 More Hours & still no Electricity. The funny thing about Blackouts is how they quiver so Uncertain. In the middle of the Dark they tease you by the Promise if you wait it will return to Light and Power. With different people the Hope of things getting back to Normal fades at Different times. My Hope faded after 2 Hours and 10 Minutes which I Believe is somewhat longer than the National Average.

But the really funny thing about a Blackout is how it changes a person's Life completely. One minute your Life is normal—you have Light & Air Conditioning & the T.V. with a Baseball Game on it maybe & a person has Plans—to sit down & be Comfortable with a boiled onion for instance & a can of beer he will spend a Couple Hours watching the Game. And 1 Minute later it is all Upsidedown! The water is not Hot enough to cook the onion the Television is a dead appliance dead as a Fossil and the dark silence is everywhere. Then there is only the beer & the bedroom. The game is playing somewhere or maybe it is not. Maybe it has been Called on account of a shower of meteorites or a Anarchist Invasion. All of a sudden anything is possible. The dark Conceals a person from the world and it Conceals the World from a person. So a person can stew or a person can change his Plans.

I did not stew. I left my Apartment I walked around the Neighborhood. The dark was Everywhere and even though by my watch

6

it was only 9:00 P.M. it could have been any Time it could have been the Middle Ages.

I believe it was the Silhouettes by the fences & the ones running back & forth behind the Elementary School that gave me this particular Idea. Ring Around The Rosy I believe was not a Innocent children's game always but was in the Beginning a game they played to take away the terror of the Plague. The *ashes* in the song was in regard to the ashes of the burned Corpses I believe.

I heard Children shouting there in the school playground and I followed the Sound of their Voices because I could not hear the Exact words which they shouted i.e. the Purpose. I could not tell about the Words they called out but I Felt they were not calling out in Terror or in fear of Terror. It was playing. You know those Children hated like Hell to be in School during the day but now that they were not Supposed to be there they just Flocked In. Gangs of them & I Believe that fact has a Moral in it about the way people Act in unpredictable ways when the Circumstances change.

The Blackout changed all of the Circumstances all right the Normal World took a vacation. The West side of town was out for sure and for all I knew so was the rest of the town. The state. The whole Country. If it was not for the many transistor Radios in Mason which brought News of the local Emergency everybody would have thought that it was The End of one thing and the Beginning of something else. But the Emergency was not the Condition of that 100,000 volt transformer etc. it was the Condition which surfaced & sank then surfaced & sank again in everybody's Mind i.e. something in the world was Different now & nobody knew for sure that it was all going to be the same again when the Sun came up. The Balance of the World went in this minute it was too dark for this time of Night.

I Believe my step must sound like it has a Purpose because the kids in the playground there ran away when they Heard Me walk over. Only a couple of them did not run away maybe they did not Hear me since their Purpose was stronger than mine. They were a boy & a girl in the shadows there leaning between 2 bungalows. "Where's my kiss honeybun?" the boy said & I

7

thought it was not dirty it was Beautiful. I doubt it they had much practice at it like Adam & Eve on the 1st night of their Romance.

They made the dark Gentle around them there I thought & I thought if it was Safe enough for them to show their Love outside then the world was safer because it had their Kissing in it. I am guessing about this. Maybe they were not a boy & girl. Maybe they were short old people but so what is the Difference. I walked away from there & I imagined in my Mind what it felt like to say *Where's my kiss honeybun?* & how it felt to hear somebody ask me Likewise.

In this minute my feet Fainted in my shoes. When I looked around I did not see any local Landmark I did not Recognize where I was. But that was beside the fact of what I did Recognize. It is a Remarkable thing how a person can not see inside the Innocent things of this world the seeds of Doom. They are in everything like dust is in the Air like Death is in Life. No matter what a person does he opens the door to worldly Doom. I think this is Remarkable how a Normal person will ignore all of the Warnings!

This little stroll was the only time I went over 2 Blocks from my Apartment since January. And that was only down to the Rexall Drugstore for the baby aspirins. But look what I did I Wandered all the way over to the East 8th which is a Rotten part of Mason. So I turn around & walk a Block this way then I turn around & go the Opposite and all the time I am sniffing the Atmosphere like a dumb animal so I can zero in on the odors of the bakery on Rose Ave. which I could follow back to the right Neighborhood. All of a sudden it hits me the ovens in Bea's Bakery are Electric so they are knocked out so I was in Misery.

I sat down on a bus bench I had to catch my Breath & figure things out which was not easy. Maybe you can Locate this exact spot & go over my Exact steps for the Record. It had a Happy Valley Cemetery ad painted on it—A Real Nice Place To Spend Eternity & if I was paying Attention to the meaning of my surroundings I would take this as a Warning Message but I got very Distracted by my predicament so I did not Notice this. (Since also all of a sudden I could not think of my own Address!)

8

Something invisible was choking the Air something was pressing down. I heard Shouts but not playful ones anymore. The fun of it was finished. I heard footsteps but not strolling ones they were all Running by now—away or home. I Decided to go find them & join them before this Idea of dread came out of the Air & fell on me like a net and trapped me so I could not Move.

I did not want to Attract any rough Attention so I went slow with my back to the storefronts. I waited in the Shadows of the doorways until it felt safe again then I made it to the next one. I Pretended I was on a ledge 30 Storeys up & the moonlight on the sidewalk was the open Air. From one of these places I saw a woman very Terrified in the street running she had 1 shoe on & 1 off. I heard the roar of a big car it was a 1978 Cadillac El Dorado with NEW MEXICO PLATES BBS 312 which pulled up sharp in front of her. One wheel jumped the curb and she Doubled Back very quick & only animal Instinct driving her. A man tore out of the Caddy he made a Grab at her dress but she Jumped back too fast for him (he was portly I saw). She Belted him with her shoe & then she made a crazy dash out of his Reach.

By now the Caddy spun around & I saw it Skid after the running man & woman and it cut them both off a block away. The Driver heaved his door open and that frantic woman Socked him in the eye & tried to run for it again. She did not make it. Her left hip caught on the edge of the open door and that gave her pursuers time to Pounce.

I did not know what to do. I heard her Shout a curse she was spitting acid at them so then I heard her cry out for help. She did not say "help" but I knew what she meant by Instinct. She cried out in Mexican. I believe those men beat her up very bad they kept on shoving her into the door of the Caddy & in that moment I felt something Inside me snap. My stomach went Dizzy and I felt my hands faint but my feet did not faint when I took a step out of the shadows I crouched down & Coiled up like a cobra. I had to be sure that the 2 men did not see me. I swallowed hard and with all of my Courage I ran out of the doorway I ran away from there as fast as I could go.

I was ½ a block away when I heard her Cries again until a long

9

blast from the Caddy's horn Drowned them I think it must be the front seat pushing against it. And when the horn stopped Blasting I still heard the woman's cries. I thought she must be putting up a hell of a Fight just 1 woman against 2 men & a Cadillac. Then I recognized her Voice. I heard it before i.e. the same rage & helplessness. It was the Voice of Innocence crying in terror. Then I stopped in my Tracks. I ran back down the street toward her Cries and the 2 men grunting like Low Animals and I felt my dingle go stiff in my pants Because of the Excitement. But I did not stop & rearrange my Clothes I threw myself in between her cries & their fists.

The woman at first thought I had to be 1 More attacker and I believe even those 2 men did not know what I was Doing. Getting in on their act! The woman started Kicking me in the shins but as soon as I started shouting "Get your mitts off of her you bastards! You lowlifes!" and I got in a punch or two the Situation cleared up very fast.

I Believe that the Idea I could Identify their faces in a Police line up really hit those guys hard all of a sudden & the portly one cursed me in these words "You crazy old bastard!" Nor he did not loosen up his Tight Grip on the lady's throat at that time either. His friend did not say a word he hauled off & Punched me in my stomach so hard I doubled over like in a Comic Book. Nor I could not Breathe. "Put him in the car! Get him in!" he ordered after he hit me. And his friend Pushed me on the back seat also the woman on top of me Unconscious & drove off with us Prisoners against our will speeding into the dark in the Direction of the East 8th.

My 1st day in the Studio of the Liberty Broadcasting Co. started very similar. Only I was not Speeding into the dark but out of it i.e. out of the dark of the Holland Tunnel in the back seat of a taxi cab. Mr. Silverstein ordered it personal for my 1st day on the Job it had to pick me up at my Hotel & drive me down to make sure I was on time for the Broadcast of Episode 1. (I think back to this Episode in my Life because now I can Remember my Feeling in the back of that Cadillac—carsick. I felt the Exact same way in that taxi. I did not Reveal this Fact out loud because I was with Strangers I was at their Mercy & if I threw up then & there absolutely I believe it would make Everything Worse beyond my Imagination.)

Mr. Argyll introduced me to the other people of the Cast. Starting with Bernhardt Grym who portrayed the Voice of Police Captain O'Shaughnessy. He came to The Green Ray direct from his triumphs on the Yiddish Stage where he always played to a Full House even matinees. Bernhardt only played 2 different Roles that I know of. A Dybbuk (ghost) who is Tortured by being able to see but never Feel the joys & pleasures of the Physical World which is portrayed in the form of a lusty Rabbi. Or he played a Rabbi who is tortured by the Knowledge of how feeble & frail the Physical World is compared to Spiritual Enlightenment portrayed in the form of a lusty Dybbuk (ghost). He told Mr. Argyll that as a regular Rule he needed 2 Hours of silent Preparation before he performed so he got a private dressing room. But on the 1st day the cleaning lady revealed that in his 2 hours of silence Bernhardt drank down 3 entire bottles of Mogan David wine which he only did while working so he was not a lush strictly speaking. He had a good Explanation: the Mogan David helped him get out of his Dybbuk or Rabbi character and into Captain O'Shaughnessy. Since in 320 Episodes he never missed a Cue or muffed a Line Mr. Argyll allowed him to keep the room and even bought him a extra bottle of Mogan David every Christmas.

There was David Arcash who portrayed the Voice of The Green Ray's Arch Foe i.e. Criminal Mastermind Prof. Lionel Horvath. He was a sullen man with a low forehead who I believe took his Work home with him. He got married 6 Times to my Knowledge even twice in fact to the same woman which was not as you might think a Brave try to give Love another chance but it was a Extreme case of mistaken Identity which right after was made world famous in a special edition of Ripley's Believe It Or Not.

There were other people who came & went who have faces & Voices that blur all together in my Mind but there is one person who stays Clear. Annie LaSalle who portrayed the Voice of socialite and amateur sleuth Rosalind Bentley who was always in and out of trouble but mostly always in like Little Lulu. Captain O'Shaughnessy called her Miss Sherlocka Holmes as in "So what's this you discovered for us now Miss Sherlocka Holmes? Professor Horvath's shoe size maybe?!" Bernhardt Grym called her Ketzel which in Yiddish means kitten and it is Affectionate. Many times he offered to Demonstrate the value of his 2 hours of silence to her in his private room which she never Accepted.

I believe Annie LaSalle changed her Name like I did to boost up the chances of her Employment. I recall her Genuine name was not so musical being Vilma Gvodenovic which mouthful she Decided could only Hamper her rise to the Top. Peaches & cream she was so Beautiful with Shirley Temple curls etc. And with perfect manners and Grooming but there was something hard & broken in the Heart of her like a glass paperweight fractured & repaired & fractured & repaired each time weaker.

In spite of the fact I was the Hero of the show I also was the youngest person in the room. When I met Bernhardt Grym that day I offered my hand but he Ignored it and patted my head and said "Top o' the marnin' to ye Sonny Boy!!" In a nutshell that was the Attitude he took to me (The Green Ray)!

But I took it like a man. I opened my Script to Page 1 then Leon Kern showed me where to hold my mouth & then the Music came up! DA DOO DA DA DUM! DA DOO DA DA DOO! BA BOOM BA BA BA BOOM! If Niagara Falls could be a fanfare then it would sound like the Theme tune of The Green Ray . . . and then like always there was our Famous Intro: *"When the Hour of Darkness is upon us—when all Hope is gone—he blazes from the shadows to defend the defenseless! To punish the Criminal! He seeks to purge wrong to keep America strong! Spiller's Fine Foods, The Makers of Spiller's High-Energy Buckwheat Breakfast Flakes present . . . The Adventures of The Green Ray! Tonight . . . Episode 1: The Vault of Time!"*

Here are the beginning Sound Effects—a Dance Band playing a peppy two-step "Ain't I The Only One" and the noise of a big Party in full swing. Then the Sound of a door closing which muffles the party noise in the Background.

SEN. BENTLEY:	We can talk here in my study Captain O'Shaughnessy.
O'SHAUGHNESSY:	My apologies for this Senator. If I thought this could wait I . . .
SEN. BENTLEY:	No no not at all. I think my daughter's coming out ball will roll along nicely without her aged father in attendance. Please sit down. Cigar?
O'SHAUGHNESSY:	Don't mind if I do Senator.

Now the Sound of a match lighting up and O'Shaughnessy taking a couple of Puffs.

O'SHAUGHNESSY:	I won't beat around the bush. I'm here to tell you my boys will have your daughter under round-the-clock surveillance.
SEN. BENTLEY:	Rosalind? What for?
O'SHAUGHNESSY:	There's been another kidnapping.
SEN. BENTLEY:	Oh Lord! No!
O'SHAUGHNESSY:	Makes three girls in two weeks. Something's up and I don't like the smell of it.
SEN. BENTLEY:	You think Rosalind is in danger Captain?
O'SHAUGHNESSY:	I have a hunch. Here's a list of the names of the girls.

Now the Sound of a piece of paper being Unfolded.

SEN. BENTLEY:	Edwina Napper . . . Betty Jenkin . . . Melody Fitzwalter. They're all Senators' daughters. I see.
O'SHAUGHNESSY:	Look closer Sir. Counting backwards in the alphabet starting with "N"—for Napper—each initial is exactly 4 letters apart & the next one has to be a "B". B—for Bentley.

13

In the next breath the Scene moved to the Party again & the next Voice the Nation heard was mine but it was not the Voice of The Green Ray. It was the Voice of spoiled rotten but very Tragic orphaned playboy Peter Tremayne i.e. the disguised Identity of The Green Ray. Peter Tremayne enjoyed every privilege Wealth can buy plus Good Breeding also his manly charm he Learned from trips to London, England. He was always turning down Invitations including the Romantic kind from Rosalind Bentley. Deep inside he Returned her Love as I was able to Portray in many solitary moments in the form of Peter Tremayne's inner thoughts. I did this by the Help of Leon Kern who took control of the Echo on my Voice. Peter Tremayne did not dare & speak Out Loud about loving Rosalind for her own sake since his 1st Devotion was to defend the defenseless etc. and put the Happiness of his Personal life after. Also Mr. Silverstein pointed out such Behavior coming from a Crime Stopper was sissy.

PETER:	Oh well. All right Rosalind. Since it's a special occasion. One kiss. On my cheek.
ROSALIND:	There. I hope Daddy's watching. Where *is* Daddy?
PETER:	I think I saw the old man go into his study with a policeman. Maybe he's in trouble!
ROSALIND:	Daddy's on too many committees to be in trouble. Anyway let's not talk about him. I've got something serious to discuss with you.
PETER:	Oh what in the world's worth being serious about?
ROSALIND:	Well poor Edwina Napper for one thing. She's been missing for two weeks. Everybody's talking about it. And Betty Jenkin. Nobody's seen her since Tuesday at the club.
PETER:	Oh you know those two. Always pulling stunts. You call that serious?
ROSALIND:	I want to elope.
PETER:	All by yourself? Darling that just isn't *done*.

ROSALIND: With you silly.

PETER: Now who's being silly? Playboys don't elope. We just drink too much and lose at cards and break women's hearts.

But something Serious *was* going on behind the scenes but it was not in the character of Peter Tremayne to Reveal his inner thoughts to Rosalind. He was full of dark Suspicions which Mr. Argyll portrayed by organ music & a violin playing Eerie Melodies that cast a pall of Gloom over the Fade Out of the party. And when the music faded back in this time Annie LaSalle's Voice bubbled out of the gloom—

ROSALIND: Good night Father. Thank you for the most wonderful night of my life!

SEN. BENTLEY: You're very welcome darling. I'm so proud of you. If only your mother—

ROSALIND: I know. I feel in a way she is here. Oh I'm so happy tonight!

SEN. BENTLEY: I love you very much Muffin. Do you want me to leave the hall light on?

They laughed about that and the Sound Effect of the bedroom door closing led into the next Sound of Rosalind turning the pages of her Diary & thinking Out Loud.

ROSALIND: Dear Diary . . . Peter Tremayne was acting very queer tonight. He—

But those were the last Words she spoke before all of a sudden a pair of strong hairy hands Grabbed her & another hand Forced a wad of Gauze over her nose & mouth soaked in Chloroform.

ROSALIND: N-no! Mm-mm-mm!

Leon Kern Decided on a crash of thunder here he shook a big piece of Sheet Metal which sounded very Realistic to my ears.

The rain was still Pelting Down when the Scene changed to outside the Police Station and the Sound of car doors slamming.

PETER: You can't do this to me I know my rights! It's ridiculous! This is a farce!

FLATFOOT: Maybe it is maybe it ain't. Walk.

And inside the police station Captain O'Shaughnessy was waiting for the Flatfoot to bring in Peter Tremayne.

FLATFOOT: I got him outside Captain.

O'SHAUGHNESSY: Bring him in Officer.

FLATFOOT: He says he didn't do nothin'. And he don't know nothin' about nothin'.

O'SHAUGHNESSY: The jails are full of innocent men.

FLATFOOT: Uh . . . yes Sir. (*Off*) In here Tremayne.

PETER: Captain! This palooka ruined the best night's sleep I'd had all week. He just dragged me out into the rain and well if you're accusing me of anything I want my attorney here. This is America! This is Washington, D.C.!

O'SHAUGHNESSY: Calm down Mr. Tremayne. I just want to ask you a few questions. It's routine.

FLATFOOT: You want me to stay Captain?

O'SHAUGHNESSY: I think I can handle this by myself.

FLATFOOT: Right. I'll wait outside.

And the Flatfoot left so the room was Quiet. Peter Tremayne's Voice was quiet too and it was O'Shaughnessy's turn to be in the dark.

O'SHAUGHNESSY: Mighty fine piece of acting.

PETER: Thanks.

O'SHAUGHNESSY: I've been meaning to thank you for your help with the alphabet. I never

	would've thought to count up the initials of those girls' last names.
PETER:	I wasn't quick enough to save Rosalind.

And right on Cue the door burst open and Senator Bentley burst in and when he saw Peter Tremayne his anger Exploded like a Time Bomb.

SEN. BENTLEY:	Tremayne! Where is she? What did you do with her? Where's Rosalind?
O'SHAUGHNESSY:	Please Senator! This is police work!
FLATFOOT:	Please sir. If you don't mind.
SEN. BENTLEY:	I do mind! Get your paws off me. Grill him! Give him the 3rd degree! He'll crack! I know his type—all talk all big talk!
O'SHAUGHNESSY:	He'll talk all right—to me. I have to go by the book.
SEN. BENTLEY:	Arrest him! Look at Rosalind's diary. The last thing she wrote—

The Flatfoot had to wrestle Senator Bentley out of the Captain's office so he had a Problem of Loyalty but Mr. Argyll Explained that while he was in Uniform on duty the Flatfoot took his orders from Captain O'Shaughnessy & as soon as he Slammed the office door (Leon) Peter & O'Shaughnessy were Free to talk again.

O'SHAUGHNESSY:	You can't blame him Peter.
PETER:	No. He's right.
O'SHAUGHNESSY:	What?
PETER:	Arrest me.
O'SHAUGHNESSY:	Are you crazy? On what charge?
PETER:	Use your brains! Anything. How about—kidnapping?
O'SHAUGHNESSY:	So that's your plan is it?
PETER:	Yes. It's the perfect cover. Now I'm free to operate as—The Green Ray!

That was all I had to say & The Green Ray summoned all his Strength from the Theme Music which came up like a Volcano all drums & trumpets it held the Nation spellbound especially Moms for them to hear the Important Message concerning the digestive wonders of Spiller's High-Energy Buckwheat Breakfast Flakes.

Then the adventure continued as Promised & I landed very sly in the lap of a gang of foreign Anarchists by the names of Britzky & Zoharin—

BRITZKY:	It's all very simple Mr. Tremayne. One by one we kidnap the precious daughters of your V.I.P.s Your Senators & Congressmen—your Captains of Industry . . .
ZOHARIN:	You see you Americans are so sentimental. A father will do anything to get his little princess back. Blood is thicker than . . . oil!
PETER:	That's why you kidnapped Stanford Fitzwalter's daughter Melody. Why he owns the biggest—
BRITZKY:	Correct. Empire Oil Company. Even a society playboy like you can see that with the means of industrial power under our control it's only a matter of time before your feeble democracy crumbles like a sand castle!
PETER:	Yes. Quite. Even I can see that. But why?
ZOHARIN:	To strip this world of the lie of freedom! To rid your country of all of its masters!
BRITZKY:	The people will thank us.
ZOHARIN:	The masses will rise up!
PETER:	I wouldn't bet on it old man.
BRITZKY:	It's a shame you won't be alive to witness the glory of the new age Mr. Tremayne. A different fate awaits you here—in the Vault of Time.
PETER:	Vault of Time?
BRITZKY:	A bizarre name yes but it means this tunnel under the Potomac just 100 yards from the place your President docks his yacht. Where the past ends and the future begins.

ZOHARIN: Come on. We don't have time to waste. Good-
bye Peter Tremayne.

The door is chained & locked but Peter Tremayne is not Down-
hearted.

PETER: And hello Green Ray . . .

Another door unlocks & Opens Up. In this other dank Cell
elsewhere in the so-called Vault of Time the young rosebuds on
the thorny stem of American High Society suffer at the filthy
hands & filthy mouths of these cruel Foreigners. Unlucky for
Britzky & Zoharin they forget to Frisk the namby-pamby playboy
who they mocked—

PETER: Good thing those fiends never found my 2-way
Communicator! Green Ray to base! Green Ray
to base! Come in base!

The worried Voice of Captain O'Shaughnessy pushes through
the crackling Ether (a ball of cellophane).

O'SHAUGHNESSY: Yer comin' in loud & clear! Now where
th' Dickens are ye?
PETER: In a tunnel under the Potomac. The
entrance is 100 yards down from the
President's yacht! Hurry Captain! And
alert all F.B.I. units!
O'SHAUGHNESSY: F.B.I.? What's that you're saying?
Can't hear you—your voice is fading
away!

Now the Sound of trickling water starts to burst into a Flood.

PETER: Hold on . . . What's that? Water. The
                    room it's . . . being flooded!

Meanwhile the kidnapped Debutantes try to act brave & Defy
the will of their captors. This is not a easy Task for them since
they are Worn Down by days & nights in a room that is like a
deep freeze but without the frozen food or even the little light that
goes on when you open the Door.
They were finding out just how girls with nice Manners would
be treated under a Anarchy form of Government.

EDWINA: This is horrible! Horrible! They'll never let us
            go—never!
BETTY: What do they want us for? Why are we here?
            Don't they know who we are? Don't they know
            who our fathers are?
ROSALIND: That's it! That's why! All of our fathers are
            government men!
MELODY: What do they want to do? Keep us here until
            they run the world?
EDWINA: It would be horrible if they took over! There
            wouldn't be cotillions or catered receptions or—
            or—not anything!
ROSALIND: I won't *live* in a world without joy.
BRITZKY: Be quiet! No talking or I take away your privi-
            leges!
ROSALIND: What privileges?
BRITZKY: Staying alive! Ha ha haha (etc.)

But in a second Britzky is laughing out of the other side of his
face. At first all he sees is the glow of a Green Light like a green
Fireball Rolling toward him from the other end of the Tunnel
portrayed by a roll of kettle drums & strange flute fluttering. Then
right in front of him Britzky sees the fat figure of Zoharin stumble
& fall down paralyzed by the glow of the Green Light. When he
fell he croaked out one word—

20

ZOHARIN: Run!

—but Britzky did not need any Advice to blow but fast nor he did not need a Scorecard to tell him who he was up against.

BRITZKY: The Green Ray!

He squealed all right true to his weak Character & he ran away down the tunnel like dirty water down a Drain. I had to get to him before he got to the girls Because all down the Tunnel under the Sound of his cowardly pounding Footsteps I heard a steady tick-tick-tick. I took a Chance & tried that old Trick to get him to turn around all I needed was a single solitary Fraction of a second.

GREEN RAY: Britzky!

And he fell for it—

BRITZKY: Huh?

He just gasped & glanced back over his shoulder & I let loose with a Blast from my Green Ray Hand Beam I shot my green light right into his eyes with Perfect Aim . . . Britzky tripped over his big fat feet like he had 3 of them! One more second & I had my Gladiator Net around him so he was Whimpering

BRITZKY: Let me go!

& flopping around like a Doomed Fish on a boatdeck. Sure I was going to let him go! Right into the long arms of the Law! Tick-tick-tick there it was in my ears still going on. The bundle of Dynamite was somewhere in the shadows so I Acted fast I dived into the dark & got a grip on it and I threw it for a Touchdown to the other end of the tunnel. KA-BOOM! What a noise! The Explosion Leon made from only the echo machine & a 5 Gal. water bottle dropped off the top of a filing cabinet sounded as big as the Atomic Bomb in the Studio i.e. if we knew in those days what the Atomic Bomb made a Sound like. It Blew the door off the secret Entrance to the Vault of Time & when Captain O'Shaughnessy showed up with his squad of flatfeet The Green Ray had the whole thing under his Control.

BRITZKY:	Ach! Mein head!
O'SHAUGHNESSY:	Get him out of my sight . . . I guess this is one I owe you Green Ray.
GREEN RAY:	Forget it Captain . . . And remember Britzky—America isn't just a pretty place on the map. It's people—people of many races & colors & creeds all with one thing in common: the chance to better their lives & bring their children into a happier world. It's a government of the people—by the people—& for the people. It's a fire that burns inside every citizen in every walk of life and no matter how much cold water you try to pour on it you'll never extinguish it Britzky not you or anybody like you.

The Sound here was the roll of drums again and the blast of trumpets like a Volcano finally time for the final Theme Music of the Opening Episode of The Green Ray. I could not stand up. All I saw was Annie LaSalle's face glancing back over her shoulder with a smile aimed at everybody (or nobody) it flickered on & then off only once like a Neon Light. I closed my eyes so she was the Last Thing I saw the Last Thing I wanted to Remember of that day. Her tight gold curls around her pink cheeks like a Porcelain doll. But I did not want to stand up mainly because my dingle still was all stiff but I could not tell you from which Excitement. I sat there & they all left the Studio Bernhardt Grym then David Arcash then Mr. Burrows and Mr. Argyll and lastly Leon Kern. A long time later Leon said to me how he Thought it was very Moving when he saw me sitting there sort of paralysed after Episode 1. Such a Success so choked up with Emotion about it I did not want to leave nor I did not want the day to end and how he Felt the same way. I nodded yes I agreed with him. I told him how Good it Felt to know how somebody was getting to know me and my secret Personal Thoughts. That was a lie of course but I want to tell the Truth about it now to get the Record straight before my Voice is no longer Heard in the land.

Now I am reminded of those Past times and I Know how they were not Perfect & Golden nor I was not 100% happy then but I did not know then what I know now about how people act lower than the lowest beasts.

I have read Reports of what dying is from people who died & came back in the National Enquirer. They die completely and then come back into the World into their Body and they all say how they see their own Body underneath from a place beyond Pain beyond any Emotion. And in that State they Drift down a long Tunnel where they find a bright Light pulling them along. But their Body will not let them go or the will of the World will not let them go and they float back down heavy into the Pain & Emotion of their last Predicament. People get pulled back for some Purpose maybe just to tell others about how Death is & do not worry about it. It will be O.K. so concentrate on Life. This is a Medical fact.

I Concentrated on the Sound of the Voices of the men in the front seat. They talked very free because I Believe they Figured that I was unconscious or harmless so it did not matter if I heard a Word they said. That was a mistake. That gave me the Chance to get a picture of their Characters which gave me a good idea of the kind of Predicament I was in. Once I knew that I knew what I had to do because if I knew what was in their Characters then I knew what was in their Plans & so then I would be a jump ahead. I knew what I had to do at that moment & it was lie still since I was pinned to the floor of the back seat of a Cadillac with a fainted woman on top of me doing 50 M.P.H. and the wise course of action was playing possum. The first thing I Learned was their Names: Nilo (doing the driving the fat slob with a Voice like a diesel engine that needs a tune-up) and Perry (who fiddled with the tuning on the radio which was picking up mostly static and Country & Western music and his Voice when he sang along with it sounded like a cat trying to mate with a blender).

"Aw shut that off Perry. It's making my head hurt," Nilo growled at him. "Nigger kids broke off the damn antenna."

Perry kept on tuning back & forth he just ignored whatever Nilo said to him. "Perry come on now!"

"I'm tryin' to find out something on the blackout. If they fixed it yet," Perry explained himself.

"Look outside boy and tell me what you see." Nilo slowed the car down a little. A empty beer can rolled out from under the front seat & hit my nose but I kept quiet.

"Nothing," Perry observed very frustrated. "It's too damn dark."

"No streetlights?"

"No."

"No house lights?"

"Right Nilo. Don't make a big song & dance out of it. It ain't been fixed yet. So what's that make you huh? A damn rocket scientist?" Perry twisted the Radio knob and shut off the Radio and pushed himself back in his seat where he rocked back & forth full of Anger.

Nilo tried to make things right. "Means there's no electricity at the house."

"Guess so." Perry let out a little sigh which was the last breath of his little tantrum.

"Guess that ice cream I bought tonight'll be all melted."

"You got ice cream?" Perry's tone brightened up. "What kind?"

"Fudge Ripple. But it's probably melted now. That dry ice they pack it in don't last forever."

Perry almost was squealing from Joy. "You tricky bastard! Dry damn ice! Hell that stuff stays cold for good! Ice cream'll be all right. But the milk'll probably be bad."

"I finished the milk lunchtime," Nilo chuckled.

"How am I goin' to make a milkshake then?" It could have been that Perry just heard he had to get through Life without a Friend. "I want to make a Fudge Ripple milkshake when we get home."

This whining Voice annoyed Nilo which he showed when he stepped a little harder on the Gas & he took a corner too fast. The beer can hit me in my face again & I found out then it was not really empty when a Puddle of warm flat beer washed around my Chin but I knew if I opened my mouth I was Dead so I shut up about it & heard the Conversation in the front seat go sour.

Nilo said, "I had to give all the milk to the dogs. That's why."

"You can't give milk to dogs! They get diarrhoea! They're gonna get it all over the house!"

"I wouldn't a had to give 'em milk if somebody by the initials of Perry Peckerhead Peacock remembered to go down to the 7-11 & buy a bag of kibble!"

Perry sat straight up & so I thought he was going to sock Nilo in the jaw. "I bought the kibble last week. If we ran out of it & if Princess & Harley made diarrhoea all over the place it's you who's goin' to clean it up. Not me. That's all I'm sayin'." He did not sit back. Perry waited there for Nilo to Answer him.

"Back off Perry. I got other stuff I hafta think about."

Ditto I had some things on my Mind too. So this is what I had to face. Nilo was slow on his feet but not so dumb which I could tell by the way he outsmarted Perry at every turn—about the Blackout also on the Fudge Ripple. Perry was fast on his feet but in the Mental Department as the saying goes his elevator did not go to the top floor & this was his weak link.

Which did not Calm me down i.e. since Perry was so Stupid he could do something without Thinking (or even with Thinking but in his case what was the difference) & it turned out that is what Happened. I will say between the 2 of them Perry was crueler. Nilo Treated him like his Kid Brother but by my Observations I did not see Affection only some friendship of Convenience. It looked like it was going to end someday & not with a Whimper either I mean with a Bang. The way it turned out it ended with both.

My worst Fear in that time was not "How am I going to get out of this" I got out of Worse Messes before in earlier Episodes of my Life nor it was not finding out what Nilo & Perry wanted to keep us for. It was only the idea of those dogs Princess & Harley (which I pictured had to be Dobermans nor I was not off by much—they were German Shepherds) doing their dog plop all over that house in the East 8th mainly the empty back Bedroom with the torn & stained mattress on the floor where their Master Perry was going to Imprison us.

I was Thinking about that room and I am sure I had a sour look on my face so it was my Expression not my Inner Thoughts that made that woman on my back cry. I felt her tears on my neck & I turned a little I looked up and I saw all of a sudden that most of the Fight was knocked out of her. Her dark eyes were dead staring into my face & I could only see the shiny Surface of them. But she was trying to tell me something not in her Language or in mine. In the oldest Language that most people have Forgotten. It is the one from our time Before Words when people only had their simple Emotions & that was how they Understood things. What she wanted was I should make it better—to give her Hope that I was going to help her & not just lay there like a bump on the Earth.

When I had this kind of Conversation with her I was not 100% Sure about how this Adventure with Nilo and Perry was going to end up—maybe they were going to Repent and return us to our side of Mason or maybe it was on the cards I could Rescue us with some fast talking or just wait for them to fall Asleep. Even if they tied us up I knew how to get out of Ropes I did it many times before (twice in Night Of The Clown) & I Remembered how step by step I tried to Communicate all of this to her in some way & what I tried to do was bring her Hope out of hopelessness by a short cut I tried it by a smile & a wink. This did not do the trick.

Because her Language started to work on me. She did not know how to accentuate the Affirmative and eliminate the Negative. Her head was full of visions of what Nilo and Perry wanted us for and I saw those Visions in front of me in her eyes. Of her stripped down to her Lingerie. Of her bound Hand & Foot. Of her at their Mercy for the sake of cheap thrills.

Now I Concentrated on these Ideas while Nilo was steering the Caddy into a weedy concrete Driveway & he nosed it through a chainlink gate that hung open. Perry hopped out to shut it and lock it with a chain behind us and the Caddy slid into a tilting corrugated garage behind the house. The house of course did not have any Light in it but I saw enough I saw it was only a Stucco bungalow like you see street after street of out beyond the East 8th. When Nilo turned off the motor I could hear two dogs Whimpering & Barking inside and jumping up against the Back Door crazy to get out. I believed that was a bad Sign. Nilo glanced back over the seat at us and he said, "Everybody out. End of the line."

The rear door on my side flew open and Perry made a Rough grab for the woman and yanked her out by her arms her knees hit the Ground hard. "You ain't goin' to be no more trouble right Amelia?" he Warned her but she did not take it. She Spit in his face and Perry did not think about what to do he just did it— Punched her hard in the stomach and it was that fast: spit-punch it was a Reflex like her mouth & his fist had to be Connected by some tight string: spit-punch. She crumpled up against the car & he carried her in the back door the way a Groom carries his Bride over the Threshold. I would call him The Groom From Hell.

I watched this Happen from inside the car where I started to think that Nilo and Perry just forgot about me but no there was Nilo with his hand around my wrist like a Strict Teacher. "You walkin' or you want me to carry you in too?" I heard the diesel in his Throat idle and it idled Rough. I got out of the car & went into the house under my own Steam Because what was I going to do? Pole vault over the chainlink fence? I needed Time to think so I walked slow & I took the whole place in.

In the kitchen where every Drawer and Cupboard was open

Perry stood in front of the Refrigerator staring into the dark freezer he still had a Tight Grip on Amelia's arm.

"Where is it Nilo? Where's the Fudge Ripple?"

Nilo told him he was looking in the wrong place and Perry answered him that he did not want to play Hot And Cold with him just tell him where the damn Fudge Ripple is. Nilo opened up a plastic beer cooler & spooky clouds of Dry Ice poured out. It was some Top Secret Germ in there not a tub of Fudge Ripple. He lifted up a gallon Bargain Barrel of the Fudge Ripple and tossed it over to Perry. "Here Fido. Chowtime!"

This business Excited the dogs who looked like they tore the place up Hunting for food all day with wrappers & pieces of bread and a lettuce etc. Scattered everywhere. They jumped up on Perry when he caught the ice cream & I thought he was going to start barking too Fighting over the Fudge Ripple with Princess and Harley. And guess what he did—showing his teeth and barking back in their faces to make sure they knew in their own Language how the Fudge Ripple is not dog food.

"Let's leave him eat in peace," Nilo said. "You guys come with me." He could have been a Real Estate agent showing a newlywedded couple around their Dream House.

I believe we did not go with him because we Bent under his will but just to be out of Perry's company. Not that Nilo's company was more Inviting only it was more predictable so then I decided to speak up. "This is illegal what you are doing," I informed him.

He chuckled. "Tell me about it!"

So I did. "Who the hell are you people you think you can get away with this—kidnapping innocent people off the street?" I got worked up now & even though I wanted to stay calm & set a Good example for Amelia I could not keep my Emotions bottled up. "What do you want from us?"

"Shut up or you'll give yourself a heart attack you old fart." Nilo was not really interested in my Health nor he was not really interested in my Comfort when he pointed at a bulbous shape that looked like it just Oozed out of a corner of the room. "Sit down."

"On what?" I wanted to know.

"On that beanbag thing. It's a chair. Now sit in it and shut your mouth and we'll all get through this thing in one piece." His fist was raised he took a step toward me but I did not Flinch until Perry came in and I Decided to sit.

"What's goin' on?" Perry focused on Nilo and Nilo relaxed a little to show him that there was nothing to Worry About. Perry went back to the kitchen.

Nilo called at his back, "You got ice cream all over your damn chin Perry!" Then he said to me like he was my Dear Friend, "He likes Princess to lick it off. Disgusting ain't it?"

"Just Princess?" I was making Conversation. "Does the other dog get jealous?"

"Harley's a boy dog. What do you think? Perry's a homo?" As if I just Insulted his best friend & then I saw some aggravating Idea start to break into Nilo's mind. "What do I have to explain anything to *you* for?" He looked at his watch and then leaned into the kitchen doorway and in the softest Voice I heard him use so far he said, "Yo Perry. If you're done messin' with those dogs go and call Mr. Newberry. Tell him we got Amelia here but don't tell him—nah hell tell him we got this other problem here too."

Nilo came & sat on the window sill or anyway leaned his big Buttocks against it pressed his hands together and stared down at his shoes. Amelia did not say a Word and I got the picture that these men were not Strangers to her & her Vision of what they wanted her for was not based on dark Imagination. She went to sit down next to me and Nilo looked up real sharp. "I didn't tell you to sit." I put my arm around her shoulder. Nilo looked away and said O.K. but he made it sound like a Curse on her head.

Perry started barking again and this time he Sprang into the livingroom with Princess & Harley chasing him until he let them think that they Overpowered him so he fell on the floor Rolling Around there saying "You got me! I'm dead! I'm dead meat! I'm dead!" Nilo asked him what Mr. Newberry told him but Perry maybe didn't hear him or he had to finish his game with Harley and Princess.

Nilo did not have any Patience for this. "I'm talkin' to you Perry!"

Perry jerked up and in a second he had Harley in a armlock around his neck. "Gotcha! I'm not dead you bastard! I gotcha!" His grip was not Playful and the dog was Choking and twisting its head to get away and digging in his paws. "You give?" Perry wanted Harley to tell him. "All right." And he let go with Princess just watching it all from the other side of the Room. "Said sit on 'em till he gets here." He was talking to Nilo now but he was staring at the ceiling.

"Where's he at now?"

"Secret location. Said it'd be least a hour." For the first time Perry said something to Amelia in a Civilized tone of Voice. "You know why Greaser men all have mustaches?" If she knew why she was not going to say so he answered it himself. "So they can look like their mothers!" Perry's laugh sounded like Harley choking and it was the only Sound in that room.

"Look you finish wiring up those lights?" Nilo wanted to know.

Perry shrugged & he threw a Rubber Bone over to Princess. It bounced off the wall and landed between her front Paws where she Ignored it. "What's the point?"

"Point is the power ain't goin' to be off forever and when Mr. Newberry gets here I don't want to be trippin' over things in the dark like a fool!" Nilo tossed Perry the flashlight.

Perry sat up Indian style he got busy fixing the Wiring on a pair of lamps Shaped like fruit bowls. "Where's my needle nose pliers?" and he shined his flashlight around the room. There they were on the floor in front of Amelia's feet. "Kick 'em over Senorita." Amelia did not do it. Perry crouched down to pick them up and held them Close in front of her face and Menaced her with them making them open & close open & close then he went back to work on the Lamps.

Nilo checked his watch again & Yawned. I could smell the sour beer and dirty teeth on his Breath from 10 Feet away. "What do you do?" he asked me all Casual now.

I was going to make him Work for it all right. I did not say a thing.

Then he asked me again and he wanted the Respect of my Answer he put it very strong. "Tell us what you do huh?"

I only gave them one word. "Retired."

Nilo shifted on the window sill & it sounded like any second it was going to split apart underneath him. "Retired what?"

I bit my lip and shifted on my beanbag.

"Retired dog catcher? Retired garbage man?" Nilo was not really trying to guess just goat me.

Princess dropped the rubber bone at my feet.

"What did you do before you retired from it?" Perry asked me this time.

The dog pulled back and barked at me to get my Attention. I threw the bone & answered Nilo—"Doctor." I was not going to let a cheap bully feel Superior to me! But my Answer meant something special to Perry because for the moment he lost his Interest in the lampbase and swiveled around to join in the Conversation.

"You a Jew?"

Amelia squeezed my hand and I did not say anything back.

"Think we got a kike here?" he asked the room. Nilo laughed with the Sound of a laugh at a Dirty Joke. Perry had his teeth into something all right & he just fiddled with the shaft of the screwdriver & flicked the loose wires back & forth to give his Fingers something to do. "You a Kike Izzie? You a Jew bastard?"

I gave him my profile. "Kish mir in tuchas!" I was not going to tell him *anything*.

What happened after that I imagine now as if I did not see it from in that house but I saw it from somewhere in the Air over the East 8th. I Imagine I see the Lights coming on street by street a line of streetlights Flicking on cutting more pieces out of the dark. A rolling wave of Light and a surge of Power humming down the wires down the street under the crabgrass into the walls of that house spraying like a Fountain out of the bare lampbase Perry forgot to Unplug . . . The light swelled in the bulb and broke it and let out the smell of Electric smoke and Perry was on the floor with his hand clamped very Tight on that buzzing lampbase . . . his jaws locked together . . . blue smoke was curling through his fingers with those raw Volts belting into him.

Nilo tried to pull the plug to pull it out of the wall but in the dark now he only knocked over a table it fell between him and the socket. I did not need to signal Amelia what to do and I did not have to think about it either. She pulled the front door open so hard it Bounced off the wall and almost slammed shut again in my face when I got to it right Behind her. We ran out across the front yard and I heard Nilo shouting his head off in my Direction: "Come back here! Help! Help him! You have to! You're a doctor! He'll die goddamnit! He'll be dead!"

But I did not stop. I saw Amelia duck into somebody's backyard so I could guess that she knew how to Reach her best avenue of Safety. I fell over the handlebars of a bicycle that was just there lying on the front lawn and I had no Guilt about stealing it to use for my Escape. The house was on a hill and I Coasted down with no brakes and Nilo still shouting at me all the way. When I hit the bottom I pedaled for my Life.

How did this Country fall so far? How did it get this way for people to act so low hurting and disrespecting to feel Satisfied? The United States of America used to be a Lamp unto all the other Nations and then the American Way meant the Pursuit of Happiness not greed and Liberty not lust. All the Foreign masses who suffered in the mud yearning to breathe free lived with a hope in the world in the form of a place with standards of Public Decency. The public was Decent I Remember and I do not Believe my Memory is tricky about this. Tell me how a place like that turned into a place like this.

I pedaled that bike out past the end of the neighborhood which was also the end of Mason only the gas station after that and then only the Desert. I did not know where I was going I just pedaled with all of my strength to put Nilo & Perry & the dirty Events of that night behind me. But 1 big push on the pedals was 1 push too many & the rusty chain Snapped off the gears whipped against my ankle & I almost broke my Testicles on the bar under the seat. (I am 66 years of age and I still do not Know why they put a solid metal bar on a boy's bike and no bar on a girl's bike when it does not take a Ph.D. in Anatomy to see that it should be the other way around.) I had that Idea in my head and between my legs I had this Ache the size of a watermelon. I heaved the bike into the middle of the road where a big truck should run over it.

My ankle felt like a snake Bit into it and it bit harder & deeper on each step I took. But I could not stop making tracks Because my feet had a Mind of their own nor they did not want to be stuck in the middle of Nowhere in the wee small hours of the Morning. All of a sudden I Noticed that it was a different Sound under my shoes now—not the flat slap of them on Asphalt anymore but the soft dull pad of sand Underneath. In the Dawn's early light I saw how I was off the road I was in the middle of the Desert i.e. the middle of red sand red rock & tumbleweeds. A mackerel would feel more at home there than I did & I thought a mackerel would have a better chance of Survival.

The Sun always rises in the East this is a Scientific Fact so when the Sun poked its early rays up over the rim of the mesas I almost fainted from Relief. If I knew which direction was East then I knew which direction was West North etc. I was Calm for about a second Because then I realized how I did not know what Direction from there Mason was. I believe it was that moment when my Heart started beating faster from the Worry but I did not want to cry I wanted to laugh! What a thing after I made it through all of that horrible business with those apes Nilo & Perry then I end up lost in the Desert! What is it going to be now—40 years of Wandering before I get home to Pecan St.?

So I did not stand still when the Sun came up I went walking toward it while the Dark shrank to shadows under the rock ledges. And then the Sun rose up Fiery in front of me it was not a Sight I ever saw before it came Roaring into my eyes—the Air opened up & the same way the Sun was rising so was I floating up in clouds of Light—I had sharp gravel grinding in my chest & all of my Breath sucked out of me—my skin & bones dropping out of me nor my Body not have anything left for Gravity to pull down

& if I moved a muscle the Sun was going to suck me through a hole in the sky—if this is a Heart Attack I promise NO MORE FAT FOODS!—& I saw the Light of the stars pushing out everywhere it is not shining already—everywhere it is empty dark the Green Light of Stars wants to fill it—I heard the Voices of Angels without teeth it was the Sound of Air hissing & I breathed in I Floated higher & I looked down then I saw my Body lying in the Desert curled up like a sleeping Baby in the middle of the Desert— there was my own Face set apart from that dry dead place I saw how I am Singled Out in the World. It was very Beautiful to see this Sight. Also I saw which direction Mason was from there then I fell again. I came back out of the blue out of the thin Air I was coming back for a High Purpose.

My Purpose was not for my own Glory I say it was to bring back Hope to the World. A kind of Hope that mocks & ignores Human barriers the way the weather Mocks & Ignores the Borders of countries.

I was a little bit shaky on my feet when I stood up and looked around. I did not see anybody else anywhere. "Me?" I cried up to the sky in that empty place with my Voice echoing in the Air. "Who? Me?"

If all it was was just leaving my Body and floating up into the clouds of light at the threshold between Life and Death and Returning to the world & back into my body a changed person then I am sure all it would take to make me feel O.K. again is a little nap. But after the excitement of touching the edge of the Universe and learning about my High Purpose in the tangled web of all Human Life I had to walk 12 miles back to Pecan St. & *then* push my legs up 2 flights of stairs to my Apartment.

I was Exhausted from limb to limb. I felt punch drunk I was seeing double I did not know what I was seeing but by raw Instinct I made it Home. As soon as I got there I knew Something was Funny. The door of my Apartment was open & I knew for a Fact that even in a Blackout I would not exit without closing &

locking. I tiptoed up & I Nudged the door open by my foot a little bit more and I noticed other things that were not usual Sights in my livingroom—

A cigar was smoking in a cereal bowl they could not find a ashtray? The T.V. set was on the floor not on the Chinese tray where it always is—all of the drawers & cupboard doors in the kitchen were opened up—piles of my Clothes made a trail leading into my bedroom—

The cigar smoke rose up and stayed in the Air like smog which is holy Hell to my sinuses & I figured: there is Somebody in here who does not wish me well. It is a Fact that in situations like this victory goes to the one with surprise on his side. I heard the bedroom closet door creak open and I stepped into the Apartment into the open bedroom door. I screamed loud and ran at that closet door and bashed it hard with my Full Force. It swang halfway shut made contact with something Solid and it could have been the door all by itself screaming back at me! It slammed back on its hinges hit me flat in the Face—I fell backwards and all of a sudden a yelling screaming banshee Tackled me digging into my chest and clawing at my face—I shut my eyes not out of Fear of the sight of my Enemy but to Protect them if my glasses broke. I rolled over and this wildcat rolled with me did not let go and still Screaming with that cigar smoke breath in my face—I saw a fist curl above me & I guessed it was heading for my mouth so I jerked up and caught a sharp chinbone with my forehead—both of us fell back—I fell down on the Cushion of my green leather library chair & clung onto it like a drowning man in a stormy Sea—I heard a Sharp Crack when somebody else's head hit the T.V. on the floor. Then it was very quiet.

I looked over at the spread-eagled shape that was lying on my livingroom floor like another Pile of dirty Laundry and then— BOOM—I came to my Senses. My head cleared up and it hit me that it must be Thursday and I just Knocked Out my cleaning lady Mrs. Roderiguez.

I stepped over her to get some Water from the kitchen. She was Moaning but not Moving. I kneeled down with a cup of water— the Sparklets *not the ordinary tap water*—and one of her eyes Opened the one that was not Swollen shut. I did not even see her gnarled little hand shoot up like a Rocket and grab a hold of my hair. She pulled my face down she tried to Bite my Nose.

"You no lovemake me! You *man!*" she cursed me. "You old man!"

I pulled away and left her a Souvenir of a handful of my hair and I put 2 + 2 together: Mrs. Roderiguez a grandmother of large Proportions nor not a Weakling either! I know this woman 10 years—my own cleaning lady believed that I Attacked her Because I could not control my Sexual Desire.

"I no want you Cowboy!" she spat out at me. "Dirty dirty dirty!"

"Mrs. Roderiguez I'm very sorry. Believe me I didn't know it was you!"

"You criminal! Senor Ray! You make me hurt my head!" She rubbed the spot on her Skull that put a Dent the size of a Quarter in my 14″ Motorola and then Stooped to pick up my framed photo of Bernhardt Grym as the Mad Rabbi of Slovensk. The glass was cracked. "I no pay for this. You. You!"

I took the Frame from her. 'Look at this stinking mess," I said & I kicked some clothes from one Pile into another one.

"Cost you extra today Senor Ray. Cost you double. You made this estinkin' mess!"

I did not want to Argue with her right after the Wrestling and the Fistfight so I told her she could go home and I would pay her half the usual.

"I hurt my head," she reminded me & she rubbed the spot again to illustrate the point. We settled on her full pay of $17.50 cash. "You look esick," Mrs. Roderiguez notified me. She lit up her cigar & pulled on her plastic raincoat. "Go lie down Senor Ray. You must esleep it off," & so that was her Advice her Parting Words.

I closed the door behind her. "I feel terrific," I said to the closed door, "I never felt better in my life," nor I was not lying either. I did feel Terrific only a little bit Sore but very different anyway from how I looked. I saw my Reflection in the bedroom mirror. I saw I had a bruise on my Forehead but I did not even

36

feel it there until I saw it. (I believe that it is a matter of Record that many Soldiers in the field of battle suffer horrible wounds for instance bullet holes and exposed organs and they fight on Ignorant about their Condition so they become Heroes. Maybe it is only Survival this is my Guess.)

I sat on my bed I saw she put on clean sheets. Mrs. Roderiguez must have changed them before I attacked her. I love the smell of clean sheets & the cool Temperature. I felt the pillowcase cool on my cheek & I dragged my gaze around the Mess of my bedroom looking for my flannel pyjamas with the St. Bernards on them (my favorite ones with the Elastic not the String) so I could take my nap in Peace & Comfort. I got the Feeling I was going to Encounter exciting times ahead and not many more Chances for afternoon naps. I saw my St. Bernard p.j.'s on top of the pile of clean clothes in the blue plastic basket that was the only thing that did not get knocked over in that room. I willed my Pyjamas they should rise up out of the Basket & wrap themselves around me since I was too Tired to move too Tired to go over there & put them on. But that big Act of Will took all of my Power and I blacked out.

It was my telephone Ringing that Woke me up again. I felt like I was out for 5 Minutes. The party on the phone was Miss Petersen who was calling up to Remind me about my Doctor Appointment with Dr. Godfrey. I picked up my calendar with the sunsets on it to check and I saw that yes I did have this Appointment to hear the Results of my tests.

"My appointment isn't till Friday. What do you think—I'm an old man who gets lost and doesn't remember things like appointments anymore?"

I was trying her Patience something she did not have in a Generous amount. "Mr. Green it *is* Friday afternoon." She waited so this fact could sink into my thick skull.

"I know it is. I know it's Friday. I got it all written down right here in front of me." I read her the facts off the calendar. "Friday the 27th—Dr. Godfrey—3 o'clock. There. What time is it?"

"It's 3:25."

"I was out the door. You know—I'd be there now but I had to come all the way back up two flights of stairs to answer the phone!" It was a dumb Excuse and I knew but Under Pressure I Improvise.

"Do you want the Convenience Wagon to pick you up?" she asked me as if it really was what I was after all along.

The Convenience Wagon is like something out of the Black Plague. They should not put a horn on it but a bell and the driver should just stand outside your Apartment and shout "Bring out your dead!" Corpses sitting up go in the Convenience Wagon. Mrs. Calusco who is 92 years old across the street goes in it to visit the Hospital for her Treatment that keeps her sitting up. People who are Dead but do not know this Fact go in the Convenience Wagon and my guess is that someday some Reporter is going to find out that the Convenience Wagon just goes to a lime pit out in the desert and it just takes Corpses back & forth to pretend it is a Useful community service. To my shame I Admit this i.e. I used the Convenience Wagon ONCE and I told the driver (who was at that time a Hopi Indian about 5 minutes younger than the mummies he was carting Back & Forth to the lime pit) I told him to do some Shopping for me. Instead of Corn Flakes he brings back some brown kind of dry cereal that had a Laxative Effect on me like a Firehose.

"No, I'll walk," I advised her.

"You sure you remember how to get here?"

I Believe that her real Worry was the Effect of Mass Confusion my tardy behavior & no Guarantee of Delivery was having on her waiting-room Routine. For my Answer to her I hung up the phone but I did not leave in that time. I was not 100% Sure I wanted to go at all. So What if I did not know the time of day! So What if I even did not know Exactly what day it was! I visited the Cosmic Observation Deck and I re-entered Human Existence very strong with a death defying Purpose so what kind of bill of health would you call that? I was not even bushed anymore I was Revived

38

from my long (about 27 Hours) nap which did not get Interrupted by any dreams. (What did I need any dreams for anyway? Awake I had more surprises in my Life!) A bowl of Cornflakes & soapy water on a washcloth on my face and I was going to be ready for anything—for my Test Results from Dr. Godfrey even for my dose of Disrespect from Miss Petersen the Snow Queen.

I was not Afraid to hear the results of the Tests that Dr. Godfrey performed on me. Only before when he was doing them then I was afraid—the mystery substances in my Blood or in my pee even I could not believe that my pee could become my Enemy and betray some secret about my Heart. It is all Connected he told me. My Heart can not be doing something that my Kidneys do not know about etc. it is all Connected & it comes out in your blood & pee. I wonder if there is a Lesson in that fact. My old body changed from under me. After my Adventure in the Desert I wondered if my Body had changes in it which Dr. Godfrey did not know any test for. Maybe my Heart was on the other side of my chest now or where my kidneys used to be maybe I got turned Inside Out & back again like a rubber glove I felt so Different. I knew one thing for a fact: if Dr. Godfrey was going to tell me to lay off after I found my Purpose after 40 years of wandering then I was not even going to ASK for a Second Opinion. My Life was in my own hands the way my Death is *where it belongs*.

(These are the intimate Details of my Life here but not all the Worst of them so I do not want to withhold this. If I am going to reveal all of the ugly facts of my Predicament i.e. murders mutilations betrayals & so on then I will not withhold the Details that describe my Life at this time. I want to tell everything that happened to me step by step so it is the True Story so when I am finished there is no Confusion about What and Why.)

I got a very strange Idea in my Mind when I looked at Miss Petersen in Dr. Godfrey's waiting room. It was Different from the Idea that grew on me about Mrs. Roderiguez. I Believe it was the Color of Miss Petersen that did it which was White all over. Her skin is pale like talcum powder nor she does not have a tiny mole anywhere & her hair & eyebrows even those are just White. But her eyes are ice blue. Maybe she is 20 Years old maybe 19 but she combs her long hair straight down the same way it was I will bet when she was 10 or 8 or 5.

The strange Idea I got was she did not Remind me of anybody else she was a brand new person with no Experiences or Memories just a brand new Soul that dropped down out of the Air & formed in Dr. Godfrey's office. Or from the dew on the grill of the Air Conditioner but I know a Soul has to be more. The funny thing is she does not leave a Absence when she goes out of a room just a Clean Smell.

It is Different with Mrs. Roderiguez. She Reminds me of my Papa. To both of them Life is to suffer & if a person is not Suffering then a person does not understand Life. Mrs. Roderiguez has a Good Excuse for this point of view since she is 1.) a Catholic & 2.) a Cleaning Lady her entire Life so she works long for little besides $5.50 per hour. The Excuse my Papa had was he was a Civil Engineer & by him Human Nature ran in straight lines Beginning to End.

It was the straight lines inside him which pointed him to his job & his view of Life was also based on the Grid Pattern. The more a person tries to make his Life run in straight lines I believe the more Disgusted he will get. Here is why—nothing else in the world besides his Desire runs that way. Not Atoms or Bones or Radio Waves. Those are the Scientific facts. (I think I read in a magazine that the genius Albert Einstein did Research on this & he made the discovery that Outer Space is not straight it is curved so what other big Example do you need?) When a person lays down straight lines to follow the rest of his Life he is asking for trouble in my Opinion & by my sorry Experiences I claim he will be Doomed to disappointment at every corner.

On Thanksgiving Day in 1938 I went out & came home early in the Morning. By that time I had been the Voice of The Green Ray 11 or 12 weeks & true to my signed Word I did not tell my Family about what I was doing. I did not tell them even about 1 of my many Adventures not about drinking Mogan David wine with Bernhardt Grym nor not about foiling the plots of Foreign Anarchists. I was making a Good Income from it too so I was not careful about how I spent my money. I bought good looking Clothes for instance plus I spent a lot by sending Anonymous Bouquets of red roses to Annie LaSalle with a pretty note signed "Your Mystery Man" or "Your Secret Admirer" etc. (I always had a inner laugh when Annie practically swooned everytime those roses got Delivered. She believed that some Broadway actor or Millionaire was sending them to her but that is another Story . . .) I spent some money on a 24 lb. turkey which I placed on the kitchen table for my Mother to find.

"Where did that come from?" she wanted to know. (This Conversation was mainly in Russian which was my parents' Native Tongue but you will understand this better if I give you the translation.)

"From a big egg," I joked with her.

"Don't joke with me Reuven. Where did your father get such a bird?"

"He didn't get it. I got it. I'm a Yankee Doodle dandy! Happy Thanksgiving."

At that exact second in comes my Father with a little turkey that looks like the Runt of the litter next to mine.

"Look what Reuven bought for Thanksgiving Paul."

"Where did you get the money?"

This was not the first time that I ever heard my Father ask me this Question. Maybe I was full of the Joy of the Holiday or maybe I wanted to give him a Answer that was going to settle it once and for all so I Improvise, "I did some work for Uncle Jake."

My Mother's hand jumps up to her trembling mouth and Papa stands like his shoes are Nailed to the floor. He Sways a little bit and steadies himself on my Turkey before he can find words in any language that fit his rage shock & disgust.

Uncle Jake—or as he was known in police line-ups up & down the East Coast Jacob "Jack the Clap" Feigenbaum— was Mama's brother and he was a jailbird. He made his money like a lot of people because of Prohibition bootlegging beer & doing occasional Accountant work for certain Trucking & Laundry firms with shady Reputations. Until I opened my mouth nobody said his name in our house for 10 years.

41

"You bum!" my Papa finally hollered at me before his Voice seized up. Other words backed up in his throat like a log jam his face turned fiery red from the pressure of them.

My Mama is sobbing now. She slumps in a chair at the table she rests her head on the little turkey that Papa brought in. I did not have any Idea that my Story about working for Uncle Jake was going to cause such Heartache. It was terrible. But more Trouble was coming: my father picked up the telephone & he asked the Operator to get him the Police.

"You criminal," His voice cracked nor he could not look at me when he said it. Then he did look me in the eye. "Reuven you are going to tell the police where Jake is hiding."

This snaps my Mother to Attention. "No Paul! It's going to be trouble for Reuven too! Don't make him!"

"Don't worry ketzel. It'll make the authorities go light on him."

I could hear the Voice on the other end of the phone. "Hello? Sergeant French speaking. Hello?" I do not know what was more important to me in that Moment—do I keep up my Story and Protect my Secret Identity and live with the open sore of my loved ones disapproving me or do I tell them the Truth and win their Respect & then start the countdown of my own Destruction? Was it going to be days or only hours before everybody in Philadelphia knew who I was & then it would not be my Secret or my Identity anymore. Mr. Silverstein I believe would be Honor bound to deny that I ever was the Voice of The Green Ray and then in the Public's eye and in my Family I would be branded as a Liar on top of everything else.

"Don't try to understand what I do—and don't be afraid. I'm on the case!" It was a line from a Episode of The Green Ray— in my Predicament except for that my mind is a Blank.

My Mother grabs the phone out of my father's hand she hangs it up in a hurry as if the Voice on the other end of the line is a Evil Genie rushing down the wire into her kitchen. She clutches my father's hands to keep them away from the phone to Comfort him and calm him down.

He hunches his shoulders a little like somebody has socked him in the stomach (Me). "You're a mystery to me Reuven," he tells me and Exits since he can not stand being in my Presence anymore.

My two sisters Rachel and Esther come in now they huddle around my mother and all three of them look over at me then Burst Out crying. I do not wait around for the flood waters to Reach my Neck I make a quick Exit I slam the screen door behind me in Other Words just the kind of stunt that a no-goodnik Son pulls on his way to being the 2nd Skeleton in the Family Closet. *It isn't too late for him don't say it's too late!*

I walked & I walked in a Circle without knowing it until I saw my Turkey still with the red white & blue ribbon around it nesting in the Garbage can by the garage. I heard music playing a few streets away—Marching Band music it was Yankee Doodle Dandy. It was a Thanksgiving Day Parade of the mayor & a few Cadillacs and a few High School brass bands. It was noon & it was a silver chill in the air so I did not stand still nor I did not go back I fell in behind the band and I Thought all right my Mama & Papa want to believe I am a criminal in Uncle Jake Jack the Clap's filthy Footsteps. All right we do not have to Pretend that we know each other anymore. Where the band stopped a bus stopped & I just climbed in and rode it all the way to 30th Street Station where I did not stop either. My next stop was Penn Station & I kept going too all the way over to Bernhardt Grym's apartment. So I ended up on his sofa in a Tricky Situation that night. The direction of my life I believe where I Arrived & when I Departed was always on account of avoiding misery instead of pursuing Happiness.

"You're wandering." These are the next words my Mother speaks to me a few days later when we are sitting in a Hospital lobby waiting for Visiting Hours to start so we can visit my Father. "What are you doing with your life? Why can't you live like a person?"

I do not give her a Answer.

"Reuven—answer me. We'll sacrifice. Your father and I and Rachel and Esther will go without if you will stop wandering & go to medical school. Then you'll be somebody in the world. You'll be a doctor."

I do not Answer her Because she is saying this to me in Russian so I am starting to feel the heat from the Superior glances of 2 wiseguy doctors a matching pair of Ivy Leaguers with names like Whitney and Pillsbury who pass by us talking horses. She squeezes my hand to tell me *Look—that can be you in 8 Years* and I shudder & stare at the clock & at the numbers on the Elevator while they go Up & Down I close my eyes and Imagine I am Somewhere Else.

But NOT please God back in Bernhardt Grym's basement apartment which is where I go when I close my eyes—A square room quivering in dim yellow Light with him in the middle of it it looked like his Presence drained Electricity right out of the walls. That tall thin man in one of his black velvet coats with a bottle of Mogan David by the neck in each hand he Announced, "Dinner!" He was a Sight to make your eyes sore. All of his Clothes he stole from different Productions he was in (I believe he stole one of Mr. Silverstein's custom tailored Sports Jackets and he felt Entitled to it since The Green Ray being a Radio Show did not have any real Wardrobe to speak of.) I saw a dress with a bustle hanging up on the hatrack—I did not know if it was a Costume or a Trophy but I was going to get a good idea about that before the night was over. Most of his clothes were all black either Rabbi costumes or Dybbuk costumes which was all he had for Daytime Wear. His long coat opened up & I saw he was wearing very dirty long Underwear under it which did not break my Serious mood.

I told him everything about my Predicament with my Mama & Papa. So Bernhardt poured wine & drank & listened he bobbed his head and said "Mm" a lot he Absorbed it all. When I finished he flung the empty wine bottle across the room—it missed the top of my head by a Inch & it smashed on the wall Behind Me. Bernhardt did not Notice the noise or my Worry he Peered into the space a few inches off the side of the tabletop. He blinked a few times to come out of his Trance of Deep Thinking and he leaned across the table almost into my lap. "To live is to act," he boomed out at me, "to act is to live!" then he dropped back into his chair.

This got a Answer from somebody in the apartment above i.e. war drums pounding on his ceiling. Bernhardt stood up & took a bow to it. Now his Voice was rasping. "No my dear you must give yourself body & Soul to your part & be faithful to it then thou canst not be false to any audience." The rasping trailed off into wheezing then boomeranged back in a coughing fit that filled up his eyes from Tears.

While he was Coughing I tried to Contemplate his advice and connect it to my personal Situation but by the time he was just wheezing again it was still a Puzzle to me. "You don't think I ought to tell them the truth about what I'm doing?"

Bernhardt cleared his throat & nodded. "Yes."

I waited to hear what else he had to say but he was not going to say anything else. "You mean yes you think I ought to tell them or yes you don't think I should?"

He gulped wine from his glass. "No," he shook his head.

Maybe he was trying to give me some kind of Lesson of Drama but I was still in the dark about it. "No what?"

"I don't know anything. You shouldn't ask me questions. Look at my life." I got the feeling Bernhardt was lost in his own inner Thoughts but he pulled my eyes back to him when he looked at me & said, "Poor . . . little . . . bird . . . " nor he did not stop staring even when I yawned out loud.

The warm room & a glass of wine & my personal exhausted Emotions made me very Drowsy. I think I heard Bernhardt tell me he was going to "prepare" my "bower" so I could "slumber" & he Staggered over to the wall behind me. He yanked the Murphy bed down I saw it did not have any sheets or blankets nothing but Stains on it & 2 raw pillows. I was so Exhausted that I curled up on that mattress and I fell asleep as soon as he lay a wool blanket over me and whispered, "Good night sweet princey."

I do not remember how long I was asleep but it was not the clear Light of day that woke me up it was something Stiff poking me from behind my back. It was Bernhardt Grym naked in my bed rubbing me all over saying my Name again & again. I had to make a snap Decision before things got out of hand and he got the Wrong Idea about me that I was cheap & easy not to mention

45

I was not a Pansy. I Slammed my elbow into his ribs and he Released me from his Embrace. I grabbed the empty Mogan David bottle off of the table but my feet got tangled in the blanket and I fell flat on the floor.

Bernhardt leered down at me from the bed. "Spunk!"

I threw the bottle at him.

"My dear! Don't run away from a new experience!"

Boy did I run from that new Experience.

"You'll live to regret it," he warned me and bounced from the bed landing like a Vulture right next to me. "How can you act if you don't experience Life?"

"Stop it! Stop it!" Maybe I was screeching at that moment I do not know but the Pounding started again from the ceiling but this time Bernhardt did not feel the Desire to bow since he was closing in on me.

"My dear! My pretty dear! My little bird . . . This is a big moment for us now seize it!"

I did not want to Seize it I did not want to look at it I did not want to know it was there at all. I crawled under the table I was caged but I was out of his reach. He Prodded me with his cane he tried to get me to come out like a Cockroach from under a refrigerator. All of a sudden he just Gave Up. Threw his cane across the floor and he sat back on his hands. "Well," he said out of the silence, "I couldn't live with the Regret if I didn't try. If I had to keep my Feelings in. The regret of not doing haunts me harder than the regret of doing. Regret of holding still. It's a bottomless hole you fall into." He was not Shaky when he stood up he was like another person he was Elegant and calm like Franklin D. Roosevelt. Maybe it was a act I guess it was out of Embarrassment. He tucked the wool blanket around his waist and started to leave the room, "And so . . . to bed," he said and walked Straight Into the side of the Door. The Impact knocked him flat on his back on the floor next to the bed.

My Instinct told me go get out of there but I did not because a Feeling that was stronger than my instinct kept me there. I got a dishtowel from the kitchen & I wiped away the Blood from Bernhardt's forehead and I Covered him up with the wool blanket.

46

I sat there with him with his head on my lap until Morning. When he woke up he said, "I don't remember a thing my dear!" I open my eyes because my Mama almost pulls my arm out of the Socket Jerking me up from the Hospital bench to walk the Long Lonesome Mile with her to Papa's room. Of course she expects the Worst—she is going to come in on the stroke of the exact minute the Doctor is there shaking his head very sad & the Nurse dabs her nose on a Hankie & pulls the sheets up over Papa's cold gray blank face.

But we get to the room & no one is in it not even my Father & I see the pink flush of Alarm on Mama's cheeks *They didn't even leave me his body to say good-bye!* Then we hear the Noise of the toilet going flush and a second later my Father comes out in his pyjamas like he has just been caught raiding the icebox.

"I'm not supposed to get out of bed."

"You're not supposed to get out of bed," my mother scolds him.

"It's the Jell-O. I think they put something in it." He winces and grabs his back. "Help me."

He Leans on my Mother's shoulder and Limps back to his bed. He hardly notices I am standing there.

"How are you feeling Papa?" I speak up from the corner of the room.

"Yes are you feeling better Paul?"

His Answer is only for her. "I hate it here ketzel. I want to go home." She hugs him which sends a lightning bolt of Pain down his spine so she lets him go she does not Know what to do. He says something she does not hear so she lowers her ear to his mouth & he says again, "Did you bring cookies?"

She pulls out of her pocketbook a box of Lemon Cookies she made for him & ½ a dozen cold leathery Potato Pancakes in a paper Napkin. Now he is happy as a cherrystone clam.

"I miss those," he coos to her.

I tease him. "You've only been in here two days."

He notices me. "And two nights. The nights are the worst part." He is trying to make Peace with me or it is a white flag. "Reuven? Want one of these lemon cookies?" I go over & reach for the box.

47

He taps my wrist with his finger. "Take a cookie. Leave the box."
I do & he sinks into the huge pillows and with lemon cookie
crumbs all around his mouth he asks me a Serious Question: "Did
you tell the police where Uncle Jake is?"

I do not Answer him.

My Mother explains for me. "He's been away to think about it
tell him Reuven. How you've been thinking."

I have been thinking you bet—I was thinking I am their son
their first Child & they do not know who I am—If they can believe
that I am a Criminal if they can believe that I am a loser in Life
if I am anything besides a Medical student well then I will not
tell them the Truth. I will not tell them how my Life is so Different
under the Surface so Different from what they think it is from the
Evidence & so pure that if they Disowned me then J. Edgar
Hoover would adopt me for his Son! I will not tell them how top
V.I.P.'s and names they Revere put all of their Confidence in me
in the very Sound of my Voice—I will not tell them about the
Radio Studio (a Complicated and private place) or about how
Important people act with me in front of the microphones and
behind the Scenes. I will not tell them about the Privileges they
give me for instance why our Pantry is always stacked so beautiful
always by a wide range of Delicious breakfast cereals—I will not
tell them how I was picked out of the Millions to act as the Enemy
of phonies traitors conmen and spies the Fighter of prejudice
intolerance greed and lust and the Upholder of Decency—I will
not tell them how it is my Voice that rides the Airwaves from sea
to shining sea with only one Purpose: to Appear as the ray of hope
to the sick at heart when all Hope is gone! How I blaze from the
shadows to defend the defenseless to punish the Criminal! How I
seek to purge wrong to keep America strong and proudly present
them with the American Way of Life that they enjoy now Because
they Suffered for years being immigrants from Russia—I am all
they Hold Dear but they do not Recognize it in me so they do not
hold me dear—I do not say a word I keep my Feelings in. I Regret
how I kept them in the dark for so long until it was too late. I
Regret how I kept my word to everybody at the Liberty Radio
Network and did not tell the Truth to the people I loved.

48

"You're a disappointment Reuven." My Papa turns his face away. "What do you think you're going to accomplish from this direction?"

I do not say even a single Word to him.

He swivels his head back toward me to deliver his Judgement man to man. "You don't realize how fast it goes. I don't want to know what you do anymore. By me your life is over. Your life is finished."

"You'll live to be a hundred." Dr. Godfrey slapped me a good slap on my back. "You've got a heart like a horse."

"So did you find out what were my chest pains from?"

He flapped his hands. "I don't have the faintest idea."

"You did tests."

"Your tests came out fine. All negative."

"Negative is fine? I get pains in my chest."

"Gas," diagnosed Dr. Godfrey.

"All the men in my family die from heart attacks. All the women too."

"You've got a heart like a horse."

"What if there's something wrong with it you can't find?"

Dr. Godfrey lit a cigarette. "We'll have to let it go wrong. Then we'll know what it was. You don't have anything to worry about."

He was all Compliments about my general Physical Condition and not just for a man of my years (66) but he told me some of his Patients only ½ my age wear their bodies ragged by playing squash & jogging etc. He said if there was a slick way to do it he could make a small Fortune cutting me open & selling my big healthy Heart to some diseased old Texas millionaire. (I do not Believe that he had Anyone particular in mind this was one more old doctor joke ha ha.)

He put a Bandage on the cut on my forehead. "What did you do Ray—walk into a door?"

"Smack into it."

"Really?"

49

"O'Reilly."

"Get outa town. I was just kidding. I didn't think anybody did that in real life y'know just walked into a door."

"They do."

"Promise you won't try to walk through any more doors O.K.? You aren't the Swamp Thing."

"But listen. It didn't hurt when I did it. It didn't hurt till after. Is that normal?"

He pressed his Thumb hard on the bandage right into my cut. "Does that hurt?"

It hurt like Hell freezing over & from the other side of the room I told him so.

"Good. Normal," he shrugged. "I'll tell you what else you can do for me. Get outside more."

"I want to get a high colonic."

"How long since you went?"

"I'm like a block of concrete down there. Did you find out for me? Where I can go and get it?"

"You treat constipation with diet and exercise. Not enemas. Enemas are unnatural. You want to get your bowels sprayed out with a fire hose go talk to one of those hippy zippy witch doctors up in Taos."

"Listen to you. The enema expert."

"Get some sunshine. Get some exercise. Age is a mental thing. Live it up. Eat a bowl of prunes and play some shuffleboard."

What do I need Webster's Dictionary to define me what HOPE-LESS means? I know all the Measurements of it when I shut my eyes—it is blank space with no edges. I know the Feeling of it—time and no Future or the feeling of standing still on a Planet going in slow circles out of control falling into the Sun & when I Burn to ashes to Atoms to nothing my Absence will be less than nothing.

What kind of a cockamamie Life is this for me? Now I want some Answers! Where am I Supposed to go? Who am I supposed to ask about this? Dr. Godfrey?! I want to know a few Answers before I die!

There I was in another little room again with the Lights Off dark as a train Tunnel in there but I heard Voices just outside trying to get in through the cracks. *Don't come in don't come in don't come in here* I hoped & I Hoped that was the Last Thing I had to hope Forever but the lock clicked open & the light clicked on so the Green Room changed from my peaceful Haven into a steel trap.

"Why the hell didn't you answer me?"

I kept my eyes closed my head down so David Arcash's smooth Voice swirled around my head like smoke. I had Trouble thinking of the right word to say to him.

"Where's your manners Ray?" When he said my name it was Open Sesame his Voice pulled a Answer out of my mouth like a magnet.

"I apologize." And I covered myself, "For everything."

"Good." He let the door swing shut. "Where's your script?"

I lifted my leg to Show him I was sitting on it.

"You planning to read it through your ass on the air too?"

I pulled the Pages out from under me and Smoothed them out on my lap but I did not pay any Attention to what I was doing it was Mechanical and I believe that he Noticed some usual light was Absent from my eyes.

"Don't you know you're not allowed to lock the Green Room door? Green Room doesn't mean your room kid."

"I know."

"Or anybody's."

"I know that. I apologize."

"What's wrong with you?" He was not all Correction by his tone I believe he wanted to show me some Care.

I did not know if I wanted to answer him in full in the General or in the Specific since how did I know? maybe anything I was going to say he might use in Evidence against me someday. (This particular Worry is not a part of my business now—even if I

Admit I held back many things from many people in the Past I do not have any Good Reason I should leave out any Facts anymore. So now you will Read how I did not tell David Arcash the whole Truth about things but I beg you do not think of this Trait as a permanent flaw in my Character I do not want you to Doubt me. At that time because I was young my Hormones forced my thinking about my Future but now it is *different* I am forcing myself to think about my Past.)

I did not tell him how it was getting to be a Habit this sitting in the Green Room a hour or more in the dark 5 Days per Week especially when nobody else was in the Building after the finish of one of our dramatic Adventures. Then in there by myself I recollected who I was. After I spent all of my Energy being with those people being grateful to Mr. Silverstein and tight assed to Bernhardt Grym then being Dependable for Mr. Argyll and Available for Annie & acting interested in the Details of Leon Kern's Sound Effects . . . I Felt little Particles of me break off & drift away into the Air into space. In the Calm of the dark I attracted those Particles back & after a couple of Hours I wound it all up with a nice long look at myself in the Green Room mirror there I was again . . . I did not see the Point of telling any of this to David Arcash—too many Particles in a Secret like that escaping into the Air etc. so I would only have to start in the dark all over again nor I did not have enough time for that. I would walk out into the Studio & just be transparent just my Outline there behind my Microphone! "Nothing's wrong." I grinned up at him & I kept that grin like cement on my Face while I turned over the pages of my Script.

He tugged it out of my hands. "Don't try to con a professional Sonny. Don't insult me that way."

I opened my mouth. I closed my mouth. I held my breath. I let my Breath out very slow it sounded almost like the Feeble Squeak a balloon makes when you pinch the nozzle. I improvised. "Something did happen to me . . . "

"What?" he insisted but gentle (for him).

I did not have enough Energy to lie about it so I Plunged in. I told him about how my own Parents think I am a Criminal and how on account of that Fact I ended up in a tricky situation with Bernhardt Grym. He Listened to me he did not even Blink but in the middle of my Sentence about how Bernhardt knocked himself out by walking into a door David Arcash held up his hand like a Cop stopping Traffic.

"I get the picture," he nodded. His little mustache twitched. He patted the tight oily curls of his gipsy hair. "Listen to me now kid—" he broke off when the door behind him opened halfway. His Reaction was quick as a boxer he jammed his foot against the bottom of the door.

Bernhardt Grym poked his head in. "Who's in there with you Ray? Is that Annie?"

"No it's not Annie you cueball. Me and Ray have got some business to finish here so . . . " He started pushing the door shut.

"Well if you're rehearsing I'd—"

"Beat it Bernhardt will ya? Can't you take a hint?"

"Arcash! You can't barricade the Green Room! I want to rehearse my part with Ray!"

"I'll bet," David smirked.

Now I had both of them looking at me I guess it was my turn to say something. "It's our big scene Bernhardt. We were just at the climax when you—"

"Coitus interruptus!" It was Bernhardt smirking now.

"Cut out the Yiddish crap and leave us alone for 10 minutes O.K.? Have another bottle of Mogan David."

Bernhardt straightened himself & puffed out. "We're on the *air* in 10 minutes."

"Tell it to the Marines." David shouldered the door shut & locked it a message that Bernhardt Answered by Pounding his knuckles on it very Sharp & Defiant. David spun around & Belted that door even harder. His teeth showed through his tight lips when he faced me again. "You're not the only citizen here with problems! And I'm not going to lie down and let a punk kid like you cry-baby himself out of character and screw up the first regular radio work I've had since 1935!"

The words spat out of him like bullets so I wanted to Duck but they hit me rat-a-tat-tat & I went down: tears started boiling under my eyelids so I Covered my face with my hands. But that did not slow him down.

"I'm a heel for saying it? Sue me! O.K. I'm a heel and now I'm giving you a heel's-eye-view of the facts of life bub. The world's overflowing with sob stories. So many tears someday they'll drown the oceans. Big deal. You think the world'll stop going round & round if you & your little sob story disappeared tomorrow? You're not home with Mama and Papa right now. This minute you're in *here* get it?"

Another Knock on the door it was Lucy Least this time who was Mr. Argyll's secretary. "Five minutes please Green Room." We listened to her high heels click down the hall & the big Studio door opened & banged shut.

"If you want to screw up the show tonight do it right. Keep on stewing in your own juice. You don't want to be the Green Ray anymore? Fine by me pal. What do you want to be? A little punk kid crying into his milk on account of Mommy and Daddy don't wuv 'ou lots an' lots—O.K. presto! That's who you are! You want to be a guy who lets flea-bitten fairies roll all over you? O.K. it takes all kinds to make a world. But if that's who you want to be then you're going to run into another problem because after you screw up the show tonight I'm coming after you with everything I've got left."

I stood up to him with my eyes dry. "There's only one way this is going to end! You've run up a big tab at the expense of decent people and now you're going to pay up!" I was not Improvising it was the Climax Line of my big scene with him in that week's Episode which I knew by heart. I wanted to show him how I did not only know the lines but I knew the Emotion of them.

He answered me by his next line, "Listen to me Green Ray— or whoever you are—the prison hasn't been built that can hold me! And when I'm out I promise I'll keep you busy for the rest of your useless interfering life!" Then he shook my hand. "Good," was all he said then he said it again softer, "Good."

That was Good Enough for me so I said it too. "Good."

"About the other business—if you really have a problem about

54

someplace to live you can stay in my apartment till you locate yourself. Cheap rent."

I stuttered something like Thanks.

"Don't try to talk," David patted my back. "Save yourself for the show."

The Adventure of King Crime was a Dramatic turning point in the Life of The Green Ray—it was the first time I was pitted against the brilliant but insane Criminal Mind of the character Destined to be my ARCH FOE Professor Lionel Horvath . . . In this Case it was almost a success his Attempt to forge a Unholy Union of underworld bosses from every corner of the Great 48 & turning them into a Criminal Version of the AFL/CIO with more Muscle than the famous Mob (sort of a National League or Republican Party of crime) . . . with Guess Who as the King of them all.

It was not long before Peter Tremayne uncovered Horvath's mad Scheme and by pretending he was a bad golfer trying to find his ball in the Rough he led Captain O'Shaughnessy & his boys in blue to the Remote hunting lodge where the Mr. Big convention was going on. When the Police swooped in after the commercial message King Crime i.e. Professor Lionel Horvath i.e. David Arcash & his goons slipped through the Police net like green corn through a cow. Now it was the job of The Green Ray to track him down & bring him to Justice dead or alive.

I found him in a Mountain lodge where his goons tied up the old couple who Lived there & left them out in the woodshed. Leon blew into his Microphone very gentle & rolled a crumpled wad of Cellophane in his hand to Portray the Sound of a mountain wind Rising amid the pine trees. The Green Ray rescued the old couple in the woodshed & they told him what he was up against inside . . . Then Leon shut a little door on a little door frame and the Sound of the wind Stopped.

LOU: That's it Boss. Lefty and Pug they're upstairs
            and Joe an' Mack they're down here out back.
HORVATH: Where are Softy and Buck?

55

LOU:	Went to relieve some citizen of their auto. They're good boys. Be back any minute.
HORVATH:	Good. Till then we'd better lie low. I get nervous on the lam.
LOU:	Don't worry Boss. I checked nobody tailed us.
HORVATH:	You better be right . . . Hey! What was that?
LOU:	What?
HORVATH:	Keep your head down! There—that! I saw a green light flash out there.
LOU:	Where? I don't see nothin'. Must be the wind Boss.

Leon was wearing two old stiff leather bedroom slippers on his hands like puppets and they Creaked like old dry shingles when he squeezed them in half.

HORVATH:	Ssh! Listen! Somebody's up on the roof . . . Give me a gun.

Before I locked myself in the Green Room that time I got cornered by Leon Kern in his Sound Effects Booth. It was his corner of the Studio it was just a table with all of his Sound Effects laid out on it (he called them his "devices") & a chair behind a glass window in a Portable cork wall that screened him off from the rest of us. The Collection of his Devices changed every week. One at a time all of the common household Objects got to be Replaced by devices he invented & brought in. (I believe a Leon Kern invention which portrayed the Sound of a grenade launcher going off got adapted later on in the field of Dentistry but also I believe that Leon never did Benefit from this Invention himself except as the patient of the dentist who stole the Idea from him.) For The Adventure of King Crime besides the slippers & the wad of Cellophane Leon had a boxing glove a catcher's mitt a bunch of ice cream bar sticks some cheap china a slap-stick two long wood slats and a broken Radio.

I did not see Leon around much that day—very Unusual since what was Usual was bumping into his red cornfed face puffing around every corner of the Studio doing Errands i.e. Fixing this & that for Mr. Argyll. He was a Genius at fixing anything with gears wires tubes pulleys levers springs gaskets or sprockets a Trait which I think is there in the DNA of people born in places like Nebraska or Kansas just like the cornsilk hair pale skin & a Lifetime Supply of baby fat. Every time I saw him Leon had pie crumbs sticking to his blubbery lips (or for all I knew it was crumbs from a wide range of Breakfast cereals being a blood relative of P.K. Spiller etc.) and his Stomach went like a boiler the whole time. On account of that besides the cork wall Mr. Argyll made it a Rule that when we were on the Air Leon had to wear a rubber cummerbund made out of a truck tire inner tube — this was after the Occasion when the burbling from Leon's stomach broke the Mood of a tender love scene between Peter Tremayne and Rosalind Bentley which got louder during our inner thoughts which all were echoey. It sounded like we were courting in the engine room of a U-boat.

"Oh hullo Ray!" Leon made it sound like it was 10 years since we saw each other.

"Hi-dee-ho," I bounced back & I made it sound like it was only 10 minutes since we saw each other which it probably was but Leon held on to me he was in the mood for a Reunion.

"You in a big hurry huh?"

If I wanted to get past him (I did) the only way was by crawling through his legs (I did not) so I stopped and told him not a *big* hurry but—

"Oh. Where to?"

"Drugstore," I lied.

"You aren't sick are ya? We got that big scene tonight."

"I guess that's why I need some aspirin."

"I'm all ready for it."

"I want to collect my thoughts about it too."

"It's a big scene. The biggest so far."

Leon did not mean the same thing when he talked about the big Scene as David Arcash meant. For Leon the Big Scene was not the first fatal face to face showdown between Human Good Personified (The Green Ray) & Human Bad Incarnate (Professor

57

Lionel Horvath)—Leon meant all the fighting that came in the minute before. We were practically exactly the same age (19—even born in the same month December) but I Remember times when he sounded like a pesky Eager Beaver 9 year old and the undertone of his Voice told me he wanted me to Treat him that way. For 1 or 2 Minutes I pushed my Problems to the back of my Mind in the fog & shadows there they all crowded in—my Mama's disappointment my Papa's disgust my own picture of how I look to them like a hopeless Lowlife even if the whole Idea they have of me is based on a Misunderstanding and how am I going to act around Bernhardt Grym now probably Pretend it never happened so here goes another double life lie piling up . . . The Sound of all those Voices was not as loud as Conversation so I leaned around the cork wall & Glanced over the Devices on Leon's table. "So this is the scene of the crime."

Joy broke out all over him. "Catcher's mitt see? For punches to the bread basket." He slammed his pink fist into the mitt and went "oohf!" acting out a guy on the wrong end of a sledgehammer blow to the stomach. "I won't do the oohf's though that's you guys. Sorry. Just showing you."

"I get it."

"It's going to be the most exciting fight you ever heard I can tell you. Like the real thing."

"What are the ice cream bar sticks for?"

"When Lefty and Pug fall through the banister at the top of page 20." Then he picked up the boxing glove he put it on his hand. He gave me a Lopsided smile pulled his arm back & belted himself in the face. "Smack in the face!" My look of Surprise must have made him think he had to Explain this berserk behavior.

"Why can't you just—y'know smack your bare hands together for the sound of a sock in the jaw or something and—"

"I experimented with it Ray and that sound I just did was the most realistic." His nose was bleeding. 'Lookit," and he held the flat of his hand in front of my face with his fingertips touching my nose & out of Nowhere his other hand that was the size of a pancake griddle flew flat into it WHAMMO! I jumped away just from the Surprise of it back into the cork wall which fell over with me on top of it.

Mr. Argyll & Bernhardt Grym were the 1st bystanders on the scene. They thought that Leon belted me in the kisser for real.

"Are you all right my boy?" Bernhardt helped me get back on my feet by shoveling his hands under my rear end.

I brushed him away & I saw Annie watching the Hubbub from the door. "I'm all right. We're fine. It wasn't—"

"What's this about?" Mr. Argyll breathed out a ragged plume of cigar smoke that made him look like a Anger factory.

"He's all right," Bernhardt reported & squeezed my Behind.

Leon worked his mouth but only one word came out of it framed by the Blood Dripping out of his nose. "I . . . I . . . I . . . "

"It wasn't a fight. Leon was just demonstrating something to me and it flew off the handle Mr. Argyll."

"Put it back on the handle and pick that wall up. We'll be on the air and nothing'll be ready nothing'll be rehearsed. Don't fight me you people. Work with me don't work against me." Mr. Argyll recited this as if it was the Number One Rule from now on and he traipsed back to his office.

Annie was still by the door trading Professional secrets with Lucy Least. When she saw me look her way she gave Lucy a pearly smile and pirouetted out of the Studio in the swirling wake of Bernhardt Grym.

"I better get back to business," Leon mumbled & wiped his nose. "I got to arrange my devices in order," and he turned his back on me.

That was the Minute when I wanted to wake up again & start that day over when the Voices of my inner Drama roared back into my Mind's Ear when all the signs pointed in 1 Direction & that was where I went that was the minute when I locked myself in the Green Room with the Lights off for my own Good.

After the commercial Message I glanced over & took a look at Leon to see how he was doing he was doing all right. He still had little wads of Toilet Tissue stuck in his Nostrils which he put there to mop up his bloody nose so he was Breathing through his mouth but besides that he looked O.K. He leaned into the light of that bare bulb that hung over his table of Devices hunched over like a Concert Piano player starting a Movement. When we got back to the Criminal Infested hunting lodge Leon & everybody else was Ready for action.

The first Sound was a window cracking open & splinters of glass tinkling on the floor. (This was a bonus since Leon used the broken window in his cork wall for this Sound so this time a real broken window portrayed the Sound of a broken window so we were off to a Realistic start of our big Scene.)

My Voice echoed something terrible from Inner Thoughts of dread.

GREEN RAY: Sometimes the agents of Good have to be just as tricky as their foes.

Leon had those old slippers on his hands again so I Sneaked down the creaking attic stairs & at the bottom there I heard the muffled voices of Horvath's two goons Pug & Lefty on the other side of the door.

PUG: Hope the boss knows what he's doin' bringin' us here.

LEFTY: Aw use your smarts will ya? He's a professor ain't he? Nothin's gonna happen to us here.

And Leon threw back the little door so it snapped the hinges loose and I crashed through and took Pug & Lefty by a complete surprise . . . My Hand Beam stunned them for a temporary time but those gunsels were as big as bulls & that upstairs hallway was pretty Narrow—and one of the goons grabbed me from Behind while his pal laid into me with a few roundhouse Punches to my bread basket.

GREEN RAY: Oohf! Two against one is it?

Leon kept that catcher's mitt on & somehow he slid his other hand into the boxing glove & slammed them together!

LEFTY:	Oohf!
PUG:	Aargk!

I grunted from the Exertion of it & I threw them off me so they
hit the wall hard but they kept coming back for more—

GREEN RAY: You boys just don't know when to give up.

A right to the head! A left to the other head! A jab! A jab! My
fists fell like Righteous rain on their ugly mugs! I had them both
up against the banister and Leon was Sweating now with some of
the fight knocked out of him. The rotten old wood started Cracking
& he broke his ice cream bar sticks one by one.

GREEN RAY:	Where's Lionel Horvath?
PUG:	(*Choking*)Who's that? Never met the stiff.
LEFTY:	(*Also choking*)Tell him Pug! He means business!
GREEN RAY:	Play it smart fellahs. Talk.
PUG:	O.K.! O.K.! Downstairs—he's . . .

Leon stood up on his chair which was high enough to give that
broken Radio of his a good crash when it hit the floor. His eyes
were all on me Waiting to hear his cue . . . So I Released my
famous death grip on Pug & Lefty—but that was some kind of a
Mistake.

LEFTY:	Get him!

I just had time to flash my Green Ray at them I Blinded them
so they both Staggered into the banister & the banister cracked
apart with Leon busting those slats of wood in half with his feet
dancing from the chair to the table like a cross between Porky Pig
& Fred Astaire.

PUG:	Aah! Lefty!

61

LEFTY: Aaaaaah!

They fell nor I will not say I am Sorry how it turned out for
them. Leon threw down his broken Radio & it smashed on the
floor with the Sound of two very sorry goons. Leon was breathing
hard bobbing up & down & practically Drowning in sweat in fact
he looked like a giant ham basting in the Sound Effects Booth but
he flashed us the O.K. sign and I went down to meet Professor
Lionel Horvath face to face.

He was waiting for me all righty right there in the Dark of the
parlour he was waiting the way a piece of cheddar cheese waits
in the jaws of a mousetrap.

HORVATH: Well as I live and breathe—The Green Ray.
GREEN RAY: Horvath.
HORVATH: *Professor* Horvath if you don't mind.
GREEN RAY: Put that gun down—Professor . . . Don't you
              know there's just one way for this madness to
              end?
HORVATH: You convinced me.

The Sound of his gun hitting the floor and Horvath took a step
back into the Shadows. Even if The Green Ray was used to all
the Foul Tricks that criminals play the lying the brass knucks in
a fair fight etc. this time I figured that the Motivation of the
smartest criminal cookie of them all was he Realized by Logic
how there could only be one winner in a pissing contest against
America's Number One Crime Stopper . . . but Horvath had one
tricky trick left.

GREEN RAY: You're smart Professor. Captain O'Shaugh-
              nessy is . . .

Now the Sound of heavy shoes on the gravel out front.

GREEN RAY: . . . right outside.
HORVATH: Sure he is . . . Or maybe Softy and Buck got
              here first . . . Boys! In here.

62

JOE:	Right Professor.
MACK:	Check Boss.
LOU:	Boss—it's Lefty and Pug they're—
HORVATH:	Forget about them they're history.
GREEN RAY:	You inhuman monster.
HORVATH:	Escort our friend out to the car.

He had me 4 against 1 with maybe 2 More of his goons outside. Horvath picked up his Gun & I heard the Sound of it when he cocked the hammer & aimed it at me Point Blank . . . Then it was a familiar Voice shouting that changed everything.

O'SHAUGHNESSY: Don't try anything funny Horvath! You'll live to regret it!

Perfect all set up for the big Climax . . . Then Leon changed the Story right out from under us. O'Shaughnessy & his boys in blue are supposed to storm into the hunting lodge & shoot Hell out of those 3 goons i.e. Joe Mack & Lou while The Green Ray collars Horvath and drags him to Justice. We were all ready to Waltz through the fight scene like we Rehearsed it but if the rest of us were dancing the Waltz then Leon was doing the Fandango! The Tarantella! The Can-Can!

He shot off a Blank from his starter's pistol—BA-BOOM!— that got us going it sure did with all of us grunting & oohfing to Beat the Band while Leon beat holy Hell out of a bunch of china teacups just smashing them up and stamping on the Pieces.

JOE: Aah! Got me!

And that was Supposed to be the end of our big fight but Leon did not stop his smashing or his stomping—he was not even looking our way for his Cues anymore he went on throwing his Devices against the walls & floor in his Booth at top speed.

JOE: No—I'm O.K. Boss!

More oohfs & grunts since all of us are watching Leon now for some kind of Cue. Mr. Argyll raises his arms over his head and shakes his hands like a Chimpanzee just a useless Gesture but he sends Lucy Least to get the Message to Leon that the fight is over & now is the time for the Forces of Good to Triumph. When Lucy taps him on his shoulder from behind Leon raises his chair up over his head he crashes it down on the edge of his table. One of the bit players had the Brains to Improvise there & say "I give" before making a wheezing noise like he was expiring.

That was what we all felt like doing too but Leon was not Finished with his big Scene he still had two more Radios to smash up. He had them both Cradled in his big arms & he Climbed up on his table & let go of them 1 at a time. We had the Problem of trying to picture what Exact kind of violence was supposed to be going on in the mountain lodge but by that time I Believe all of the bit players got knocked out or shot dead & came back to Life so many times nobody was sure who they were Supposed to be anymore.

Except Leon who was portraying the Violent Capture of Professor Lionel Horvath. Now he was jumping up and down on the pieces of the two Radios & the tubes & wires spilled out of them like mashed organs and torn entrails. This Scared us but it did not choke Bernhardt Grym.

O'SHAUGHNESSY: Give up now! It's the Law!

And all of a sudden Leon shuddered & then he stood still like a big tree going to keel over. Nobody said a Word nobody wanted to set him off again so we Watched him very close & beady when he put on his boxing glove & started swinging his heavy arm Back & Forth and then all the way around in big circle whooshing by in front of his face—

I do not Know for sure what Bernhardt's motivation was maybe just to guess right & jump in & save the show but at the top of his lungs he Shrieked—

BERNHARDT: Get him!

And Leon's fist connected with Leon's jaw the blow of it knocked him back knocked him sideways he Reeled into the table and that flipped over so he fell flat on his back he hit the floor Unconscious but with his eyes open like a dead fish.

I jumped in to Rescue the moment.

GREEN RAY:	There's only one way this is going to end! You've run up a big tab at the expense of decent people and now you're going to pay up!
HORVATH:	Listen to me Green Ray—or whoever you are—the prison hasn't been built that can hold me! And when I'm out I promise I'll keep you busy for the rest of your useless interfering life!
O'SHAUGHNESSY:	Escort our fine friend to the paddy wagon boys.

During the final Commercial Message they wheeled Leon out of there on a Stretcher. The next day P.K. Spiller sent a Telegram he addressed it to all of us saying how The Adventure of King Crime was the most Satisfying Episode of them all—especially he made a Point about the big fight in the mountain bungalow how it was so Realistic about how it portrayed the capture and come-uppance of a Vicious antisocial criminal Mastermind and how it stood as a living Lesson to any of those types who Tuned In. He also sent each one of us a personal case of Spiller's High-Energy Buckwheat Breakfast Flakes for our reward.

I ponder which Episodes of my Past led me direct into this Predica-ment. Over & over I read True Accounts of how when a person is dying from a Disease or drowning in the Ocean he sees his whole Life flash before him (how then? *After?* ha ha)

Since I have my finger on the Trigger of this Snubnose .38 & I have a Sound Mind I am in control of things for a few minutes my whole Life is flashing very slow so I can see every Detail. But in this case I will not waste any time & unravel my whole Life Story only the Highlights & Lowlights of it i.e. the Episodes which stick out those are the Important ones which remain in my Mind.

Something I did not get around to doing I regret is I never changed the wallpaper in this room. Even if I only Rent so what? I am the Sad Sack who has to look at it every day the Beige & Burnt Orange lace doily Pattern crawling up & down my living-room walls the identical stupid Curly-Q's over & over the same cockeyed Design over & over again. I look at it & I think maybe that is how my Life is i.e. like this wallpaper. I regret it further-more because I have to look at it now in this Final Moment it is the last Sight I am going to see.

Also my belongings—my TV set my Radio my paperbacks & magazines etc. which so far I arranged the stacks in order of date. My collection of National Geographics together the same with my Scientific Americans & Life Magazines also my Saturday Evening Posts all going back to 1963 when President John F. Kennedy got shot. I saved all of the Memorial Issues & just kept going from there including my Playboys. (While I am telling the Truth the whole Truth & nothing but the Truth I will not leave out any Detail which ashames me. So I will say I DID NOT BUY PLAY-BOY MAGAZINE FOR THE INTERVIEWS I GOT IT STRICTLY TO LOOK AT THE PICTURES OF NAKED WOMEN ESPECIALLY THE FOLD-OUTS!)

All the rest of my Furniture is piled up against my front door I made a Barricade out of it. This Tactic gives me a little more time also a Warning when that bastard Newberry gets here. Any minute from the other side of my door my Past is going to catch up on my Future & there it is the Original meaning of Doom.

LET HIM COME IN! I WILL WAIT HERE VERY PA-TIENT! LET HIM FIGHT HIS WAY IN!

"Gimme the mustard will ya bub?" David Arcash tapped the counter in front of a scrawny bookworm who was just eating pie

& coffee so he did not need the Mustard. He slid the little jar into David's hand & he did not look up nor he did not say "Here's the mustard" he only gave up a weak little smile. This is the kind of thing which David enjoyed about eating lunch in a Manhattan automat the Manly Atmosphere.

'When I was 6 years old," I said, "I had a dream about going to Jupiter."

"When I was 6 I had dreams about 6 year old girls."

"You're not normal."

He raised his finger in the Air. "No! I'm not average."

"I'll say," I said. "So what's my dream make me? Below average?"

"I'm not Sigmund Freud. How should I know? I just hope you grow out of it soon."

"I did grow out of it. I was 6 years old a long time ago."

"Then how come it's still on your mind? Answer me that. How come you don't have girls on your mind?"

"I do. I don't talk about it is all."

"Do you do it?"

I acted nonchalant. "Not lately."

"So you don't do it and you don't dream about it and you don't talk about it. That's what I said. You're not normal."

"You're not Sigmund Freud. What do you know what's normal?"

"By trial & error. How else?"

I know I felt I knew a few Sincere reasons why I could trust David Arcash with my inner thoughts. He took me in to live with him when the strain of my Family on me got too much to bear— also he Revealed his own feelings very Honest (at first) which Males are not so free about with other Males (except Bernhardt Grym in my Experience but those are not Feelings exactly I think what he did comes under the title of Exposing Unnatural Urges)— also I wanted to test a particular Idea & Benefit by his Opinion since he was a Man of Experience so to say—also then it would be 1 Idea that was not just Rattling around like a Echo in my Mind but it was out in the world once and for all—if I said it out loud there it was: a Real thing at the Point of No Return & for

67

Better or Worse just telling somebody changed the balance of the world. Another reason—talk about a woman dissolves a Barrier between 2 equal men and I wanted to Enjoy some Manly Atmosphere with him that did not depend on lunch in the Automat.

"I dream about Annie."

If my secret gave him a Surprise he did not show it. "Nothing special about her. Broadway baby that's all she is. Dime a dozen. Dime a dance."

"No—uh-uh. You're wrong. On the surface maybe. O.K. I'll go along with it. O.K. all you see is the blonde hair & the face powder & that squeaky laugh of hers but underneath—"

"Calm down! Anyway what do you know about underneath with her? She's the Mona Lisa! She's Eleanor Roosevelt! What do I know?"

"You don't know from anything." My Voice cracked. "I know she isn't Eleanor Roosevelt. So what? I don't want her to be Eleanor Roosevelt."

"Let me tell you something about Annie LaSalle. She's looking for Daddy Warbucks and between you and me I figure she's got one on the line. *Some* rich geek keeps sending her dozens of roses I mean two three times a week since she started the show. You try competing with a guy like that and she'll squash you like a bug."

"You think things like flowers have some effect on her?"

"Gimme this gimme that. Gimme gimme gimme. That's her all over."

"Good."

"Get that glassy look off your face Ray. Piss up a flagpole you'll get more satisfaction."

"I want to tell you a secret O.K.?" I said. "Another one."

"Trust me."

"I send her those flowers."

This time David got a surprise & he showed it. A shred of pastrami dangled off his lower lip. "How—" he swallowed & then he started again. "How long for?"

"For 6 months."

He gave me a big smile I think in a way he was Proud of me

68

or it just Felt that way. "Putz! So putz—tell her! My God 6 *months?* How many roses is that?"

"Counting the extra dozen on her birthday that's 372 I think. If you mean individual flowers."

"How did you find out when her birthday was?"

"Why?"

"I'm curious. How?"

"I went into Lucy Least's office a few minutes before the show one time and told her Mr. Argyll wanted her in the studio pronto. Then I looked in the files. Easy. There's a medical one. Did you know that Annie has a little mole next to her bellybutton?"

"Oh really?" He did a bad job of acting interested. "Tell her why don'tcha? Don'tcha want to get anything out of it ever?"

"I can't tell her now! I'd look stupid. Also I think she'd feel stupid for believing it was some fancy shmancy tycoon all along."

"Oh. Right." He whistled Do-Re-Me I guess he wanted to change the Subject. "You ever been in a gym?" He squeezed my stringy arm. "Let me guess."

David led another Life in Brooklyn where he owned ½ of a Gym where local lightweight boxing Talent came to train plus he Fixed up Bouts for them which was a Sideline that kept the spare semolians rolling in. The name of it was The Golden Glove Gym painted up in red & gold right on the bricks over the front door. The Smell of the place hit me first hit me smack in the kisser a hot Breath of sweat & leather. I heard the Sound of scuffling feet & grunts of Exertion maybe the same Sounds people heard in Roman times what with all the Gladiators they had back then. Snorting like bulls plus smelling like them too.

But they were not bulls in there these Fighters were wiry ones with skin as tight as cellophane over a sirloin steak. "Light-weights," David pointed out. "You're about their size . . . Hi Sparky!" We strolled across the Gym to the ring which was only wrestling mats up on Risers with Ropes strung around them but it looked like the Real thing.

"How's it goin' Mr. Arcash?" Sparky was a tiny brownish man with a towel around his neck & a bucket of water in his hand. He did not have any teeth or any hair either he looked like a unwrapped Egyptian Mummy. "This some new talent?" He jerked his chin at me.

Before David had a Chance to crack wise he got a slap on his back that almost knocked him into the ropes. He had to hop on one foot to stop toppling over. "Pigmeat," he cursed.

A boom of a Laugh met him when he looked up into the Man-In-The-Moon face of the chubby Negro man planted like a tree behind him. "Dis' one of yo' pro-tee-jays Dave?" He twisted his Yankees cap backwards & hunched down into Boxing position.

"That's what I axed him," Sparky put in.

"Say hello to Ray Green. Ray this is Pigmeat & Sparky."

Pigmeat pulled my hands out straight to Examine them. "Sof' han's. Yo' ain't no fighter."

"I never said he was. Ray's a doctor. A Jewish doctor." David flashed me a wink when Pigmeat turned his back.

"Tha's good. Worl' need mo' doctors. Worl' never run outa cuts." Pigmeat clapped his hands like a Potentate. "Les have some fresh meat up here! Coogan & Tangledweeny!"

The carrot-topped kid Coogan came off the Punching Bag & the other one dark and lanky skipped his rope over to the Ring. "It's Tangherlini all right?"

Pigmeat showed us his wicked grin. "Tangherlini. Right. Ain't it jus' Atalian fo' tangled up weeny?" He boomed out a laugh like a Ocean breaker that rolled back into a soft chuckle. "Ah kin make that boy so mad!"

Coogan & Tangherlini squared up and Pigmeat hit the bell— they came out Fighting circling and jabbing . . . Pigmeat did not hold still either he was circling the Ring in big sidewise steps ducking so he could see the shape of every Punch.

"My flea circus," David whispered my way while the 2 boys batted each other & Pigmeat did Laps around the ring.

He happened to be right next to me at the second I was smiling over David's remark. "What's that Doc? You's so superior uh-huh. Smartass sheeny."

David kept his eyes on his fighters. "Hey Pigmeat. I'm just a smartass sheeny too."

"Nah. Yo' gots colored man's hair. Yo' daddy's a colored man."

70

"So's mine," I spoke up. "He's a sharecropper in Philadelphia."
I tap danced in a little circle. "Sho' nuff chile."

Pigmeat hit the bell. "Corners!"

The place emptied out after dark since the bare lightbulbs did not
do much to push out the gloom. David & Pigmeat discussed about
Business on the edge of the Ring & I wandered over to Punch the
punching bag since that was what it was there for. Sparky swabbed
the floor around me in lazy Figure 8s with a Comment for me like
"Nice weather" or "How's it hangin'" every time he came back
my way.

"Hey Ray!" David called me over. "C'mere I'll teach you how
to take care of yourself."

The punching bag hit me in the back of my head. So what. I
do not have eyes back there & if I did then I would have got a
Black Eye & I did not even get a Bump or not from that Bag
anyway.

Pigmeat pushed the Boxing Gloves on my hands. "Sparky a
little help here!" he shouted over my shoulder & David held up
his bare hands like a Surgeon scrubbing up so Manny got the
Message. "Put up your dukes."

I held my Gloves in front of my face the way I saw Coogan and
Tangherlini do it. Pigmeat aimed a few jabs left-right-left which
I Knocked away very smart since my Reactions were young &
quick. "Tha's th' stuff Killer." He pulled me out into the middle
of the ring where David was raring to go just Bouncing from one
foot to his other.

"O.K. I want a clean fight. No hittin' below the belt. No bitin'
scratchin' or kickin'. When you hear the bell come out fightin'."
Pigmeat climbed over the ropes out of the ring and called "Corners!"

"Is somebody going to say On Your Mark—Get Set—Go?"

"C'mon Ray. Take this serious."

"Sure. Whatever you want."

"Put up your dukes."

"On Your Mark. Get Set. Go!" Sparky blurted.

71

"Shut yo' face Sparky." Pigmeat rang the bell hollering, "Yeah yeah!"

I shuffled back into the middle of the Ring very light on my toes I bobbed up—David ducked down—he bobbed up & I ducked down.

"I feel like a duck in a shooting gallery." He did not laugh maybe it was the Mood he was in or maybe my Remark was not very funny. I was thinking about the way I looked then O.K. so what—all of my jokes are not Gems! Who am I supposed to be? Bob Hope? Anyway now this gets Serious—

"Let's see your stuff Killer. Show me what you got."

"What stuff? You know I don't have any stuff."

He jabbed at me. "Show me the Green Ray stuff."

"I need Leon for that." I blocked another jab. Another jab clipped my ear. "Hey! Cut it out!" I was laughing but it was not funny.

"Be a mensch. Don't let me knock you around Ray." He had a dark light in his eyes nor I did not see his Left come up & under my ribs.

"Oohf!"

"Show me what you're made outa."

I swung & missed. "I'm a lover not a fighter see?"

He danced away from me while I stood on the spot like a sundial.

"Who are you guys? Fred Astaire & Ginger Rogers?" Pigmeat bawled at us.

"You a lover? Then you gotta be a fighter too—right?"

"This is over." I backed off but David moved in on me he was not going to let me go he had me Cornered in the corner.

"You gonna let Annie do this to you too? She'll punch your heart right out." Jab. Jab. Pushing at my chest.

"Cut it out. You're not going to get me mad. I'm stopping." I let my limp arms my stringy arms hang down but David scooped up my hands so I just held them still where he put them.

"Show me your stuff." He Feinted left he Jabbed right. He was wearing out my eyes trying to follow him I did not know *what* he

72

was trying to do and Meanwhile I did not know what I was doing either.

"I don't want to play anymore." I let my gloves drop.

"Put up your dukes!" I heard Pigmeat's Voice.

Then David's. "Who's playing?"

A thunderbolt hit me flat in the face—I spun around & watched the floor come up at me at 100 Miles Per Hour. I woke up on my back on the mat my face all wet my head in David's cupped hands.

"Is it blood?"

"Is it blood?" Pigmeat mocked me he Mimicked my faint Voice.

"You're O.K. It's water."

"I taste blood."

"You bit your tongue."

"Is there a doctor in the house? HAA-AHH-HAH!" Pigmeat boomed over me at that Crack like it was the funniest joke he ever heard.

"You learned two very important things here Ray. First—never drop your dukes and second—you got a glass jaw."

I tried to say something I think it was maybe *I can't see your face* but David put his hand on my Swollen Lip.

"Don't thank me now," he said. He swiveled to look at Sparky. "Any ice left?"

"You bet Mr. Arcash."

"Good." David let my head hit the mat. "I need a drink."

I have read some interesting Stories in the National Geographic Magazine about tidal waves i.e. about their Causes and Effects. Some of the Effects have been Earth shattering for instance whole islands wiped off the face of the Map—the shape of coastlines changed—jungles buried underwater—1000's of villagers Drowned—etc. Huge Effects only mean one thing: Huge Causes (as the English scientist Isaac Newton discovered).

One of the main Causes of a tidal wave Scientists learned could be a Earthquake on the bottom of the Ocean. Picture that! The sand & rocks under the middle of the Ocean lurch like a broken card table or in the Case of a Volcanic Activity split open like a hot melon! The Energy of it the sheer Force of it pushes out the water Far & Wide so there is your Tidal Wave set in Motion—the glassy face of rolling doom. Picture some peaceful tropical Island there in its path stretched out in the hot sun then a little stir of damp breeze. The palm trees shimmy—a spray of dry white sand fans up from the beach because there is a wind now—& a roar is rising up from the deep water—the shallow water in the lagoon starts to hum—now over the reef the Ocean just Curls up this seamonster up on its purple haunches tumbles down Roaring so Loud it crushes rocks down to sand sand down to mud—the only Sound there is to Hear until deep water Buries everything Alive.

Scientists (and Insurance Companies I believe) call a tidal wave a Act of God & by me that is a pretty Good Description of the Cause & Effect of all my Feelings about Annie LaSalle.

I was not Calm enough to Concentrate on anything else especially my Portrayal of The Green Ray. The outside sign of my Condition was my wandering eyes they just followed anything in a room that moved—the Flightpath of a fly or a falling Speck of Dust or somebody's shoes shuffling by it did not matter what. This was a Problem for me since my Performance Suffered in what was supposed to be another very exciting action packed Episode called The Return of King Crime.

Leon Kern was the first person to tell me out loud that some kind of OOMPF was missing from my Style which Fact he told me during a scene between David & Annie which did not include or Involve me so I strayed over to Leon's side of the room. Leon said he had to multiply his Sound Effects to compensate for my lack of character what was wrong with me? "I've heard Lucy Least order a bowl of creamed corn with more nerve," Leon advised me with one eye on the action in the Studio. He rattled the little doorknob in the miniature doorframe on his desk. He opened the little door.

ROSALIND: This is a surprise. It's Dr. Denton isn't it?
HORVATH: Oh please. My name's Howard.
ROSALIND: If you want my father I'm afraid—

74

HORVATH: No it's . . . Actually it's you I want.

This was a pretty sneaky move by Horvath since he knew for a fact that Rosalind Bentley and Peter Tremayne 5 Minutes ago had a little tiff & Peter stomped off which was why I was in the Sound Effects Booth with Leon Kern. I did not have to be out behind my Microphone until right after the Message from our Sponsor.

While Bernhardt pretended that Captain O'Shaughnessy ate a bowl of Spiller's High-Energy Buckwheat Breakfast Flakes 1st thing when he went on Duty in the morning Mr. Argyll reminded me that I was supposed to be Convincing out there & I sounded like I was phoning my lines in from the planet Ming. For instance —

GREEN RAY: Captain — I can't wait to get my hands on
             Horvath.

I said that with the wrong Emotion in it I made it sound like I was falling in love with my Arch Foe. "You've got a big scene coming up Ray," Mr. Argyll warned me, "and if it doesn't inspire the youth of the nation I swear to Jesus — P.K. Spiller's going to blame *you*!'

The funny thing about Acting is there has got to be some real Emotion in it even if the Character is acting phonus bolonus. The feeling has to be a True one nor it does not matter if a person is portraying Abraham Lincoln or a little green man from Mars or the Nation's Number 1 Crime Stopper a person has to find a Genuine & Sincere Emotion to portray. I believe that people can tell the Difference and if they see there is nothing True or Sincere going on nobody will care how it comes out. Nobody will care about you if you are a phony boloney.

The Story that led me up to my big Scene went like this:

Professor Lionel Horvath swore to me that no Prison was built that could hold him and it turned out he was True to that Word. After his Escape (by submarine) from Alcatraz Island he Embarked on the biggest most bizarre caper in his perverted

75

criminal Career. He hired a lookalike gunsel to take his place in jail so he was free to live under a assumed Identity 3,000 miles away. His object was to grab Control of all of our City's services — the Water & Power ... the Garbage Collection ... the Sewer System ... the Port Authority ... the Subways ... the Fire Department ... the Police Department ... the Office of the Mayor and on and on ... Horvath could run the whole City like a giant toy Train Set just shut it down at the flip of a switch if he wanted to he was going to be Top Banana if nobody Stopped him. He was playing the game of Monopoly for keepsies & if he won there was not going to be any Competition from anybody anywhere anytime. Anyway that was how he Figured it was going to be with King Crime back on his Throne.

His method was simple. At his Command he had a small army of suicide Gigolos i.e. very handsome well-bred but selfish & spoiled young men who were in hock up to their eyeballs from gambling Debts & shady dealings. Horvath promised to square things for them if they did one little thing — marry the girl of the Mad Professor's choice who was a Daughter of some rich and powerful City father ... so 1 by 1 the High Society weddings were followed by High Society funerals of the Fathers of the Brides ... the Victims of a string of High Society fatal accidents.

Horvath saved the biggest Plum for himself. After he lost the tender heart of Rosalind Bentley he won the hand of Cornelia Deasy the daughter of our Mayor. But in the middle of their Wedding ceremony The Green Ray unmasked Horvath also his insane Plan.

BISHOP FEENY: And if any here can show cause why these
                 two may not be joined in matrimony let
                 him speak now or —

The Sound like a gust of wind tore down the Cathedral aisle on top of the very Astonished cries of the Wedding guests —

GUESTS: What is it? Aah! Ooh! What's that light?
                 That green light? (Etc.)

HORVATH: Oohf!

The Green Ray tackled Horvath & we crashed into the crowd!

BISHOP FEENY: Stop this! Who are you?
CORNELIA: Howard!
HORVATH: What's going on?

Horvath was just acting Innocent like he was just a Normal guy getting Attacked by a crazy masked person in a green suit & green cape for no Good reason on his Wedding day. I knew better I knew the whole Truth.

GREEN RAY: I think Your Worship if you look in this man's inside pocket you'll make a nasty discovery . . .

Nervous whispers from all the Members of the Cast who were not portraying the Voices of their usual Characters at that part of the Story—Bernhardt Annie the Gunsel actors plus Leon Kern. Pss pss pss.

HORVATH: This should satisfy you . . .

The Whispers stopped & he Reached inside his morning coat and pulled out—

CORNELIA: A gun!

I threw my Cape over his head—a shot echoed! We both went down Wrestling locked in a Violent struggle . . . In 2 Seconds I have him pinned.

HORVATH: I'll get you for this!
GREEN RAY: I don't think so . . . Horvath.
BISHOP FEENY: Horvath? But this is—

77

I told the Bishop all about Professor Lionel Horvath & read out what I lifted from his Pocket: a list of the Names of all those High Society newlyweds with a row of big black *check marks* next to the names of the influential Deceased . . . Marlin Shardlow—Water & Power CHECK! . . . Morton Kimmel—Port Authority CHECK! . . . Vance Seward of Sewage CHECK! . . . Toland—Archibald—Meacham   . . .   Subways—Garbage—Fire   . . . CHECK! CHECK! CHECK!

For my Courage & Public Service (not to mention the fact of saving the Mayor's dear daughter from a Life as Mrs. King Crime plus his own skin too) J. Edgar Hoover decided to Honor me at a Public Ceremony on the steps of City Hall. Now proper Homage was going to get paid to the acts of unrewarded anonymous Good wrought on Earth by The Green Ray.

I did not Feel I was Ready for it. I was still not 100% up to Concentration on my Lines nor my mood since I still felt some Interference from my Inner Thoughts about Annie. I tried to keep the picture of City Hall & Mr. Hoover & the Adoring crowd in my Mind I tried to hear how my Green Ray Voice was supposed to sound i.e. Righteous yet Humble but when my Cue came up I Pretended that the ceremony at City Hall was not for The Green Ray it was for me Ray Green it was a big Award for my portrayal of the Voice of The Green Ray & it was in the Presence of my dear Mama & Papa.

So Besides the crowd of Actors who did not need to say any more Lines e.g. Bernhardt David his Gunsels Bishop Feeny et all standing next to Annie I pretended I saw Mama & Papa in the Studio too watching me the Son they thought was a criminal was really a Radio Hero. There I was getting the key to the City for stopping crime & Inspiring the youth of the Nation to grow up doing unrewarded anonymous Good.

J. EDGAR HOOVER: Mr.—um . . . Green Ray . . . So many times in the past you have appeared on the scene in our hour of need & did what needed to be done and disappeared in a blaze of green light before

anybody had a chance to say thanks.
Before now we didn't know who to
thank—for restoring decency to our
streets for giving back some hope to
our hounded citizens. You have
inspired our children to strive to do
Good and so Green Ray you have
given us all a brighter future. It is now
my proud personal pleasure to present
you with the key to our City . . . Your
City.

A roar of Applause and cheering (I Believe some of it was a
recording of the crowd in New York greeting Charles Lindbergh
in 1927) the Studio was alive with it with Captain O'Shaughnessy
& Sen. Bentley with Rosalind & the whole crowd of them—Mama
and Papa . . .

GREEN RAY: Thank you Mr. Hoover sir & all of you in
Radioland. I accept this fine award on behalf
of the Spirit of Goodness that lives in every
human heart. I dedicate my Life to finding
that Spirit and raising it up—and trampling
down every vicious thug and hoodlum who
stands between us and our Liberty between
us and our pursuit of happiness!

And every one of them turned their eyes toward me at that
moment and they were Cheering again Cheering for me clapping
like crazy even Mr. Argyll grinning almost biting right through
his cigar on the other side of the Control Room glass. I looked
straight at Annie & she was in the front clapping & cheering—
the Music played out and her eyes shining and smiling at me. I
believe I caught a flicker of real Affection in her eyes for me how
could she fake every Hooray? No it was the Reflection of how I
felt about her & how she felt about me just then blushing up
through her flesh & bone I will say it came very Sincere from

79

Annie to Rosalind Bentley & out to me what else could it be? Just acting?

Yellow light from the control room window caught in her hair so it turned it dusty gold. She patted a loose curl back into place over her ear & giggled her Answer to some question or Compliment from Mr. Silverstein. Then I knew for a Fact how the Famous Portrait painter Rembrandt felt when he stood in front of a blank canvas he filled up before his eyes with one still single moment in the Life of a Beautiful face. Annie's bare neck just the size of my palm and her narrow back Half the Length of my arm. She gave a Blank Glance over her shoulder & there I was staring at her but she raised her eyebrows just a look of happy pretend Surprise you know like she just made her Entrance at the Surprise Birthday Party she was not supposed to Know About. She cupped her hand for a Stage Whisper, "Ain't . . . life . . . grand?" then the Vacuum left there in the second she turned her face away pulled her back. Playing like his naughty daughter Annie poked Mr. Argyll in his ribs such a flibbertigibbet!

David brushed by them. "Watch this one in the clinches," he jerked his thumb toward Annie.

"Don't I know it!" Mr. Argyll nodded he Wrapped both arms around his Ribcage.

Mr. Silverstein rested his hands on his hips. "Don't abuse the staff young lady," he frowned. "That's my job."

So Annie poked Mr. Silverstein in the ribs instead and all the men over there started Laughing big beery Laughs. The bosses just Adored her. I had a picture of the pair of us in my Mind hand in hand bridal gown and groomal suit with Mr. Silverstein giving her away to me & Mr. Argyll in the Pulpit & David for my Best Man.

David handed me a handkerchief. "You're drooling. Wipe your mouth."

I dabbed at my mouth. "No I'm not," I said & I bit my dry lips.

"You can't hide anything from me. I'm your pal. You live in my apartment. I go through your dirty laundry."

My throat closed up. "What's that mean?"

David shook his head put on $\frac{1}{2}$ a smile snorted "Jeez" & strolled away from me I guess to give me my chance. If I was going to climb into the Ring with Annie all he was going to do for me was ring the bell for Round 1. He strolled back. "She's going to some dinner tonight at her sister's in Far Rockaway." He walked me back to the Studio door & Encouraged me, "Go on. Ambush her. Who can identify you in Far Rockaway?" He leaned through the door whistling.

Annie hurried past me. "G'night Ray," was all she said and with the curtain of rosewater perfume she pulled behind her Clinging around my head I knew all of a sudden I only had 2 choices—

CHOICE NUMBER 1: Stay true to my Nature and lie down nor do nothing just "Wait & See" if Annie is someday going to admit out loud the same feelings for me that I have for her

Or

CHOICE NUMBER 2: Change my Character for the better and go on & make my move no matter what come heaven hell or high water

I went after her down in the next Elevator down to the Lobby. It felt like a month between floors but when the big brass doors opened up there she was buying a pack of Wrigley's from Stan the one-armed Cigar Man.

"Annie!" I waved at her but I think she did not see me in the Crowd that Swamped me from behind when another Elevator load of commuters spilled out into the Lobby. A thick-necked man bulled past her into the Revolving Door and behind his back she showed 2 rows of teeth of her clenched smile mocking Good manners. With that same monkey smile she elbowed some pimply

81

Junior Accountant out of her way her teeth Clenched until she made it through the door.

It was already dark on the street and umbrellas went up as cold drizzle came down. I ran through it down the sidewalk like a Notre Dame fullback until I saw the back of Annie's head show through a Break in the wet raincoats like a Highway flare on a foggy road.

I was knocked out of Breath when I caught up with her the Sound of my clomping feet sure Startled her because her hand jerked up to her throat. "Oh Ray! It's only you."

I felt like a masher. "Hey want a hot dog?" There was a Greek guy with a cart on the corner.

"I'm going to my sister's for dinner but don't let me stop you."

"O.K." I went over to the shivering Greek angling for time. "I could eat a horse."

"That's probably what you're going to get."

If the Greek heard her wisecrack he did not Care About it he held out his hand for my Dime. When he took it from me he gave me a Sly little look and made a kissy-kissy noise and the tip of his tongue Poked Out between his lips. I took this as a Good omen.

"I'd like it if I can walk with you a little ways." Oh no! It was Cowboy Gene Autry coming out of my mouth!

"If you can walk fast. I'm getting soaked."

"Sure." I chewed as Fast as I walked and I ate about half of my horse dog by the time we hit a red light at the end of the Block.

Annie raised the flat of her hand for a kind of Salute. "I can go down this way. Gotta get to—"

"Far Rockaway," I said with her.

"—by seven . . . " She screwed up her eyes I guess trying to Figure how I knew where she was going and what it Meant if I did.

I did not want to let her go then & I told her so. I saw the muscles around her mouth go tight & she Braced herself to listen to something she did not want to hear. "I see," Annie sniffed. She did not see the half of it but 10 minutes later she was staring down the snout of the whole snorting buffalo.

I told her how I Thought about her—how Deep and how Regular—I told her how I did not want to lose my Feelings by keeping them in I had to let them Loose—I said how I Felt scooped out like a halloween pumpkin when I Pictured this place without her in it and all of a sudden I Realized I felt that way all the time Before I met her—I told her she was my Dreamgirl which led me to tell her about my Imaginary voyage to the planet Jupiter & my own parents believing I am a criminal in league with Uncle Jake but now I can not tell them the Truth about things—what a Relief at last to say all this! to be with somebody who knows what I am doing Truly who I am Because I Care so much about her I do not need to Force myself to hush my Inner Thoughts—

The more I said to her the easier it was to tell her more as if I got shoved down a greasy chute nor I did not Worry if it was a Tropical Lagoon at the end or a fiery furnace—"If I never came out with it all I'd regret it for the rest of my life," I told her—more than I would live to regret telling her come what may & I started to Recite the sorry story of Bernhardt's funny ideas on the Subject of Hospitality but I stopped myself on Religious grounds also the picture of me pinned under Bernhardt Grym was not going to make me look very Attractive in her eyes—I told her I was sorry if this was a Wild Ambush but it did not come out of any Unnatural Urge—I wanted to tell her all the events in my Life that led up to it also it made a very Dramatic ending.

We were standing under a dripping awning with the rain hammering down around us in front of The Palm Bar & Grill. The doorway was marked by a Potted Palm outside it and in the lull in the seconds I was waiting for Annie to say something all I wanted to do was trade places with that waterlogged Tropical transplant. Annie listened to me with her face Turned Down just chewing her gum slowly slowly shaking her head. Beads of water hung off the fringe of her hair and Dripped off of her chin.

"Boy Ray. You sure don't pull any punches do you!"

I said, "I know I've put you on the spot. I'm on the spot too. We're both on the same spot."

"Getting soaked." She wiped a dewdrop off of her nose with the heel of her hand. She tilted her head so I could see her little

twisted smile part worry part Embarrassment. "I'm flattered,"
she finally said.

A little stir of a breeze the potted palm Shimmied.

"I'm involved with a man already." She kept her Voice flat
and on the level but turned her face away from me to say it and
when she turned back I probably was giving her a glass eyed fishy
stare. "Did you think I'd just be single?"

That sounded like a Trick Question so I let it fade in the noise
of traffic and scuffling feet.

"It's not the way you think it is," she informed me.

"How do I think it is?"

"You think if you tell me all this stuff how you feel for me and
private details of your life I'm going to see what a swell fella you
are & what a lucky girl I am & how stupid I've been all along
for not seeing that my Mr. Right was under my nose the whole
time. Then we kiss all lovey dovey find a love nest settle down
have a baby get old and die."

"Well . . . yeah. About."

"It isn't like that."

"Tell me what it is like then Annie."

"You don't want to know."

"Yes I do *too*."

"You'll be sor-rr-ry," she sang & teased me.

I kept quiet and stood back to show her I was Ready to listen.

"He's a much older gentleman."

"How older?"

"Oh . . . " she shivered she knew what she was going to tell me
was going to hit me Hard it was going to Knock the wind out of
me. "He's over 6o."

"Wowie." Oh my oh yes.

Annie forced out a heavy sigh her Breath bloomed in the Air
between us. "You want to hear any more?"

My tongue swole up like a meatloaf I was speechless . . . so she
handed me some more . . . The buffalo turned its snorty snout on
me!

"He's a real dreamboat. He singled me out of the entire restaurant when I was out for dinner one night. With my sister and

84

her hubby for their anniversary. I didn't notice him first off—not till he noticed me. He signaled me with his steak knife. Sort of waved it. The waiter thought he was trying to get his attention and J.B. told me that was why he sent the fizz over to us." Annie shrugged in Memory of it. "What did I care? It broke the ice. And after dinner he took us all out on the town. It was so extravagant Ray! I'm telling you—nightclubs—floorshows—a nightcap at some hoity-toity upstate German roadhouse. So it turns out he's a honest to Jesus tycoon. In the shipping business. His wife died seven years ago. No children. A real sob story I mean a *real* one. In the morning in the back of his limo he says to me I bring out certain feelings in him he thought he'd never feel again. He sobbed a couple of times on my shoulder. That got my waterworks going. In the front seat his chauffeur is bawling his eyes out too. Jeez! I didn't even know he could hear us all the way up there. I get weak knees for a guy who's strong enough to let go like that in front of a lady."

I did not say what was on my Mind then i.e. *Why didn't you fall for J.B.'s chauffeur in that case?* What did it mean when she stroked the White Hairs on his chest what was she Thinking about? What did it look like his veiny old onionskin skin his hands like roots with hers just as smooth as soap? Jesus H. Christ Annie! Your boyfriend can remember what Life was like *before the telephone!* Before the Model-T! Before Radio shows! Your boyfriend was born in 1877! People put nickels that old in *coin collections!* Besides all that what is he Different what is he Better than a boyfriend who has all his senses and a *future* to boot 40 maybe 50 years? 1979 *at least!* Maybe 1989 who knows?! Your boyfriend is going to be almost 110 years of age then what kind of a Life is waiting for him? I'll tell you what—the Convenience Wagon and a one-way trip to the lime pits. SO WHAT IS HE BETTER THAN I AM?

"He's tender to me. He leaves me alone when I want. I've got my own apartment & he doesn't have a key to it. He never lies to me or cheats on me and I know he could and how. He could get any chorus girl at Radio City if he wanted but he only wants me. He never expects anything back and he makes me feel secure for once in my life. He knows all about the rotten times I've had

85

with men and my past and everything. He doesn't care. He doesn't think about my past he just loves me up. I want to try being faithful for once."

"O.K. I get the picture." I was not going to talk her out of anything or into anything her heart was not up for Auction. "Can I buy you a cup of coffee?"

I Believe in spite of the Difficult Moments we just went through or maybe On Account of them Annie wanted to make Sure we were still friends. She looped her arm through mine she said, "I really *am* flattered you like me so much. I feel like you just handed me a Valentine's card. A month too early."

I answered her back with my undertaker's smile. "No—a month too late."

"Oh Ray. Cut it out now." She yanked me toward the bar & grill door but pulled up short by the palm tree. "If I tell you something will you keep it secret?"

"Not unless you want me too."

"Am I dumb or does that mean yes?"

"How could you be dumb? I don't fall for dumb bunnies."

"Good. O.K. Nobody else on the show can ever know about this you promise?"

"Not even if they torture me."

"This is just a secret between us. You know how ever since I started on the show somebody's been sending me a dozen roses every week?" A spray of sand fanned up from the beach . . . "And how I got a double bouquet on my birthday?" The water in the lagoon started to hum . . . "Don't tell anybody but you-know-who sends them by limo. My gentleman. J.B. Pierpont sends them . . ."

That sidewalk Shuddered & Heaved under my very feet! That seamonster reared up on its watery haunches it roared fell and crushed me under! So this is how it feels in the bull's eye of a Natural Disaster! Breath! Which way is the air?

I lunged up I pushed myself on Annie's lips I whispered her Name . . . She was making it all up about J.B. Pierpont ha ha ha Tycoon and Senior Citizen Romeo ha ha ha! Annie was just telling me her inner thoughts just what kind of Romance she was Hoping

86

for and *all along* here it was the same kind I was there to give her boy oh boy! Ain't Life grand?!

"Stop it! Stop it Ray! Are you crazy?" I Astonished her she was pushing me away. "What're you thinking of?"

I was Thinking of what to say to her after I let go. Do I tell her I am the Mystery Man who sends her flowers every week and so I know what she told me about her older gentleman is a Ridiculous Lie now she does not have to Pretend with me. Would she be overwhelmed by deep Emotions then and swoon in my arms or would she Despise me for the rest of her Life because I was another man who Tricked her who made her Reveal her naked Desires in public? Or maybe it is the easy way out to pretend it is all my Mistake it is just my own deep Feelings acting up that way Annie can keep her Pride & I can keep mine even if I am the only one who knows it. I let her go.

"You pig!" she screamed at me she Punched me too.

"I'm sorry." I backed away. "Ow. My eye. Annie? I'm sorry!"

I saw her Run Away from me & climb into a bus she was wiping her lips Back & Forth on the back of her hand.

The very second David switched on the light in the Green Room he saw my black eye in the mirror but how could he miss it when I Peeled that slab of raw steak off of my face. Nor I did not want him to miss it.

"You hamburger. Who did that to you?" My face was marble my heart was flint. It took David about 2 Seconds to guess Whodunnit. "She belted you? Annie did?"

I cradled the steak in my hand. "I need your advice."

"You need Pigmeat's advice."

"Seriously," I groaned.

"Seriously. Annie's a dumb twist. So now you know. Now you found out. There there. You'll recover. Now forget about it."

"I can't forget about it. It isn't finished in my mind. Would the Green Ray forget about it?" I showed him my shiner.

"She wouldn't've laid a glove on him. My advice to the lovelorn is forget about that squirrelly twist."

"She isn't squirrelly. She had a right to punch me."

87

"Looks like she's got a pretty good left too. My kind of female. What did you do—jump her?"

"I jumped her. I'm as bad as Bernhardt."

"Nah."

"Almost."

"Nah you need to practice 12 hours a day to get that bad. I'll tell it to you again. Annie LaSalle is very easy to please Ray she only wants one thing in her life: fame and fortune."

"I can give her more than that."

"Come off it. You can't even get a good table at a mid-town restaurant. Name one maitre d' who knows you're on the radio. Name one maitre d' who knows your name."

"It isn't all she cares about."

"You mean it isn't all you care about."

"I know what I mean."

"Oh—you'd never fall for a golddigger right? With all of your intimate experience and hands on knowledge of the opposite sex you can tell what a girly's after the minute she opens her mouth is that it?"

I let the steak drop on the floor & I shook my head very slow nor I did not Believe how David could punch me so far below my belt.

He picked it up for me and Tilted my head back he just gave my forehead a light touch. "I don't have any more advice about Annie. What am I anyway? Ask Aunt Eunice?"

"I'll ask Aunt Eunice."

"Don't waste the stamp. Eunice can't tell pee from lemonade."

"I've heard her get right to the heart of a problem not just lonelyhearts either. She solves all kinds for all kinds of different listeners."

"Yeah," David chuckled. "You know who writes her answers? Lamont Carruthers. Also the questions. He writes all of our shows too."

"Maybe you can boost me up in Annie's eyes. Tell her I'm dying."

"You don't need me to read you the news. You got two eyes and two ears. Annie is a Sound Effect with tits. She wants the

88

public attention. The star treatment. Just craves it. You say she's not just a dumb twist. O.K. I'll bite. So she's a smart twist. Now what?"

"I need a new plan."

I worked on my problem Scientifically I worked on it with all of my Psychological powers and it all boiled down to 3 Simple Steps:

Step 1:

QUESTION: What would The Green Ray do in this situation?

ANSWER: Let Peter Tremayne investigate.

Step 2:

QUESTION: What would Peter Tremayne do in this situation?

ANSWER: Seek the cunning counsel of Lamont Carruthers.

Step 3:

QUESTION: So what was I going to do?

ANSWER: Going to go up to the 14th Floor to knock upon Carruthers' office door.

So Aunt Eunice owed it all to Lamont Carruthers—So What so did I. Or not all of it in my Case in my Case Lamont Carruthers created the Adventures of The Green Ray but I created his Heart and Soul. But look how far Heart and Soul got me with Annie: a shiner short of a cup of coffee so now I needed some Expert Guidance to suggest where my personal Story could go from here. Who was it who found all the Clues before Peter Tremayne did? Lamont Carruthers! Who figured out all the twists and turns of complicated Mysteries that led to The Adventures Of The Green Ray? Lamont Carruthers! Who knew the true Motives of Rosalind Bentley the ones that made her Tick i.e. all the Feelings that

Annie had to sincerely feel to play her part Episode after Episode? Lamont Carruthers! Besides that who was the Brains behind Aunt Eunice who answered Complicated questions about modern Human Life I bet Lamont Carruthers knew a thing or two about womankind.

The elevator door opened before me and before me was the length & breadth of the 14th Floor & the Echo of that creaking metal was the only thing Stirring up there. (The 14th Floor was a good piece of Deception really since anybody who could count that high knew it was the 13th Floor in fact. What did people think people thought in the elevator when it went by 10—11— 12 . . . 14?! The builders just forgot to put the Unlucky Floor in? Or did they want it to look one floor taller from the sidewalk?) The hallway went off in 3 Directions with dozens of doors down each one all the same wood on the bottom half milky glass up above and gold numbers not Names. It did not make exact Sense i.e. the way the numbers went e.g. 1400 to 1422 went down one side one way and 1431 to 1455 down the other side the other way etc. and 1401 to 1421 up a few Stairs so after two dead ends I was lost & Exhausted & wandering around the 15th Floor now and down I went in the Elevator to start all over again.

This time when the door opened I saw a strange Sight—a guy at the water cooler he looked like a stork up on One Leg dipping his beak for a drink. When I got up close to him I saw he was in pretty Bad Shape for one thing he only had One Leg. Also cloudy blue eyes & his face all white stubble yellow sweat stains on his collar and at his feet i.e. foot was a Fuller Brush sample case. How he got past Stan the Cigar Man in the lobby was a mystery to me but what was it my Business? It was Hard Times all over so why should I make it harder on my fellow man even if he was a door-to-door salesman?

"Say—bub?" I got his Attention. "You haven't passed by 1421 in your travels by any chance?"

"It's easy to get lost up here," he observed and I observed he had a very polished Accent on him. "Are you a messenger boy?"

Of course I could not let a member of the General Public in on

90

the fact of my True Identity so I went along with his Idea of me. "Today's my first day. I'm just trying to find my way around."

"You say you have a message for 1421?"

"Uh-uh."

"Down the hall. First door on your left after you turn the corner. I've just come from there."

"Was Mr. Carruthers in?"

"Oh. Him." He picked up his Sample Case. "Be careful around him my boy. In days of yore when a messenger brought bad news—" he Swiped his finger across his Throat and gurgled. "Cut off the messenger's head."

"Good thing this isn't bad news then."

He turned his back on me mumbling. "You can leave it with his secretary. Miss Shapiro."

I looked back when I heard the metal door creak behind me but all I saw was the Elevator floor clock start down 14 . . . 12 — 11 — 10 . . .

"Dropping or picking up?" The U.S.S. Miss Shapiro moored at her desk turned her bow guns on me.

"Is Mr. Carruthers in?"

"About what is this concerning?"

"It's personal."

"Personal concerning whom or what matter?"

"Um—"

"What are you? The F.B.I.?"

I did not want to Reveal too much too soon so I just told her it was Business about The Green Ray.

"Oh. *That* hooey."

I did not Expect her to do a backflip when she heard those words Green Ray but a dark surprise hit my stomach when I heard her shrug off our Show being just hooey. "I'm Ray Green." I pressed out a Inviting smile & gave her one more Chance.

"Mr. Carruthers doesn't like to get involved with the actors Mr. Green." She offered me a frosty smile. "Anyway," the smile melted, "he's at lunch." She stretched a canvas cover over her Typewriter shutting up shop for the Lunch Hour.

"I don't think it's hooey. Why do you think The Green Ray is hooey?"

"Don't take it too personal." She took her handbag out of a drawer in the filing cabinet behind her desk. Miss Shapiro standing up was not much Taller than Miss Shapiro sitting down & when she stood next to me to switch off the office Light I was looking down on a bald spot the size of a yamulke. Until that moment I did not know that a woman can go Bald—all of the women I ever saw were hairy or wore hats. Miss Shapiro must be on the Fritz through & through so how much did her Opinion matter? Another thing—who portrayed the Voice of The Green Ray around here me or Miss Shapiro? I DID. Who knew more about the virtues of The Green Ray me or Miss Shapiro? I had 1st hand Knowledge & what did she have? One bald woman's Opinion—

"The world should be so simple. At exactly the right place at the nick of time a man in a green cape shows up flashing a green light & before you can say *mozel tov* the world is better than new. That's not like life. How're children going to grow up if they believe in something like that?"

We were walking toward the Elevator & Miss Shapiro stopped at the water cooler. While she was sipping I slipped in a Personal question. "Is that what you tell Mr. Carruthers?"

She wiped some water off of her chin. "Are you kidding? He doesn't ask. He doesn't ask to hear my opinion. He doesn't care. He doesn't get emotionally involved in his shows."

I pushed the Down button for her. "That's not how the shows sound to me."

"That's because you don't know him from Adam Mr. Green and I know him 6 years. He doesn't have feelings about your show or any show that I ever heard of." She tugged my sleeve Confidentially she lowered her Voice. "Mr. Carruthers doesn't vote. That's how much he cares about what happens. Not even for president. Not even for Franklin Roosevelt."

"But he didn't vote for Wendell Wilkie either."

Miss Shapiro stabbed the Down button a few angry stabs. "It's not the New Deal or the Old Deal he just doesn't care. He says we get the politicians we deserve. I say we must be doing something right to get Franklin D. Roosevelt and he's a man I thought Mr. Carruthers would sympathize with."

"How come?"

"Since they both raised themselves up from their handicaps. Instead of staying cripples they rose to the top of their profession." Ding-a-ling. "What do you mean Miss Shapiro?"

"F.D.R. had polio didn't he and Mr. Carruthers lost his leg in the Great War."

"Him?" I sang out. "Him?!"

Well I could not Stand Around counting my fingers and toes just waiting for the Elevator so I ran down the 13 flights of stairs and skidded across the Lobby. Stan the Cigar Man was not Surprised to see me in the same Situation two days in a row and he called me over.

"Your girl must be eating upstairs today kid. I ain't seen her come down."

"She's—oh I'm not looking for Annie now. Lamont Carruthers."

"Who the hell's Lamont Carruthers?"

"Tall geek," I panted, "with one leg."

"Yeah yeah." Stan scratched his beak & closed his peepers to Picture him. "Panatellas." His poached egg eyes popped open. "Carruthers huh? Tell him he owes me 35 cents from last week."

"You seen him go out yet?"

"Yeah a few minutes ago. Walked right past me. Hey y'know 35 cents is 35 cents. Y'know Ray?"

I look back at what Happened to me & where & when & so help me I can not tell when I was in the Right Place at the Right Time or when I was in the Wrong Place at the Wrong Time. Time is supposed to tell but so far Time has not told it has not told me Why. I am guessing here but maybe the things that Happen are just the things that have to Happen when you look at the state of my Mind (desperate) & state of my Body (exhausted).

I revolved out of the revolving door in the nick of time to see Lamont Carruthers heave his Fuller Brush sample case into the back of a taxi pull the door shut and I was close enough to see

93

his lips move he was telling the cabbie where he wanted to go—
if I could only read lips! I stood there Helpless like a toddler
watching his taxi cab Disappear into the Traffic.

I walked around the Block I walked around the City with no
Expert Guidance what else was I going to do? I did not feel the
cold of the Weather or hear the noise of the traffic only the Pressure
of the heavy clouds & the scrape & slap of my own shoes In &
Out of sidewalk rain puddles. Ugh. My mind went back to Annie
what did Annie think when her Mind went back to me?

When Annie pictured me I was just a Girl Crazy short pants
kid going around in a goofy swoon all of the Time and it was her
Bad Luck she got in the way of it.

When Mama & Papa pictured me I was a juvenile Fugitive
from Justice just living it up Cheap & Easy with a man they won't
mention his name who has the Morals of a cockroach already
riding for a fall into the pit of Shame and Regret.

When David pictured me I was a whiney glass-jawed Creampuff
who did not Possess the nerve or the verve to stay in the ring any
ring.

When Lamont Carruthers pictured me I was a dumb ham Actor
in the words of Miss Shapiro ALL HOOEY.

So what did I see in that Moment when I looked at my Reflection in the window of Al's Delicatessen in Times Square? I saw
my hair blow over to one side in the wind & over my head I saw
the clouds scampering I saw the skin of the sky peel away & show
the Sun beating away there in the ribcage of heaven—sunlight
barreled down the street Banged on the doors Rattled the windows—It peeled off the top layer of my Skin so I felt the razor
edge of the chill in the Air my throat felt it my lungs my liver
down deep in my kishkas I felt the world turning again. I was in
many places in one second—

With Pigmeat in the ring in the Gym spraying champagne foam
on David's face to bring him around after I K.O.'d him in the
final seconds of the 14th Round—He comes around his eyes roll
open & we Hoist him up to his feet. He throws his arm around
my shoulders he says, "You're O.K. Rayola!"

And with Mama & Papa at the dining room table with Rachel

and Esther allowed to stay up late because I was there with them—the good silverware and glasses—crackling skin on the roasted chicken potato pancakes and applesauce sour cream cinnamon cake a Special dinner.

And with Annie at the Stork Club with her wrapped around my arm since here I am to bring her what she truly Craves plus lots more besides—the crooner sings to her at our table—the crowd laps at our feet the Public Love her they Envy me—our picture in the morning paper—

This Idea came to me like the diamond bright Light of a newshound's flashbulb. All I had to do to make a big Splash in the news was go out and bring in a Wanted Criminal the Real Goods. I was going to be a Hero in my own Name that way and not have to Reveal to the public my true false identity i.e. the Voice of The Green Ray so I still kept the word of my Contract with Mr. Silverstein. How was he going to complain if private citizen Reuven Agranovsky got so fed up from hearing about the crime wave sweeping across our fair Nation that he stopped talking and *did* something about it? Something about the high cost of prostitution and gambling to the ordinary working man i.e. the Moral decay in low places the political corruption in high places the City fathers on the take and the greasy hoodlums on the make—*not* the colorful "Robbing" Hoods of song & story e.g. John Dillinger or the Barrow Gang who only did with a tommy gun the same thing that tycoons in skyscrapers did with a fountain pen OH NO I was going to net one of the gross errors of human Evolution a missing link a Caveman with a Gun in one hand and a Adding Machine in the other one of the lousy crumb bums who bled our Citizens dry with protection rackets and loan sharking one of the Termites who tear down every ideal America is built on a Louse living off the fat of the Land of Opportunity loitering on streetcorners heads up for the next Episode of Opportunity Knocks i.e. his next Opportunity to Knock some honest Citizen on the head and steal his daily bread . . . The crooked Union Boss who uses his locals' dues to put Italian shoes on the feet of some pink toed uptown Mobster: I wanted *him* . . . The crooked Lawyer who Convinces the Judge and Jury that his fat cigar smoking scarfaced client is just a honest hardworking Businessman in children's garments and anyway he was in Poughkeepsie at the time: I wanted *him* . . . The crooked Accountant who cooks the books and boils down a million bucks from the numbers racket bookmaking and rake-offs to $1,275.50 of Taxable Income less dependent allowances and misc. deductions so when he is finished the United States Treasury owes *him* hands over a fat *rebate* to the gangland gorilla in the white silk suit: I wanted *him* . . . I wanted Jack the Clap Feigenbaum I wanted to drag him kicking and screaming before the Bar of Justice if he wanted to give himself up or not I was going to bring in Uncle Jake.

How I did it:

I knew about the cold hard Fact that before Uncle Jake took it on the lam he made a deal with his only boy my only cousin Manny. The deal had two Purposes and in my Investigation I Discovered one extra—but 1ST it was to protect Manny and Aunt Sophie i.e. as long as they did not have any Knowledge of Uncle Jake's whereabouts or whatabouts it was no use anybody be he mobster or fedster trying to Force any info out of them . . . 2ND the deal was regular Money coming in which paid for food shelter clothes etc. plus Manny's college tuition to Insure his dream of becoming a Dentist . . . 3RD I found out that it was Protection for Uncle Jake from anybody hunting him down including Manny & Aunt Sophie.

Most of this I got from my Observations of kitchen talk between Mama & Papa scraps which maybe stuck in my Mind for no Good Reason at the time but I am sure now that because they were in there I came out with the Story about working for Uncle Jake the story that got me out of one mess & led me into worse ones. But I Remembered I heard about the In & Out of Uncle Jake's deal this was my Advantage when I started to think like Peter Tremayne.

"Once in 18 months Paul. That was the stinker's last visit to his own family." She hands Papa a plate to dry.

"He sends good money so you can't say Jake's a complete stinker."

"Sophie is almost at the end of her wits. I'm telling you. I talked to her on Sunday."

"By me Sophie passed by the end of her wits a year ago."

Mama purses her lips and stops with her hands in the dishwater. "Don't talk like that."

"I'm only saying now Sophie should live a life." Papa flips the damp dishrag over and dries the back of our big yellow serving dish.

"All she's got to go by from that stinker is a post office box."

A post office box? Ah-ha! Where?

Mama pulls the plug & wipes the sink with the dirty water draining out. "I'm only her sister-in-law so what do I know about it but I told her Sunday she should change her name from Feigenbaum. She should change it to Mrs. Post Office Box."

It is a Serious moment but they are laughing a little about it Mama with a tight smile that would look wicked on any other face & Papa with his cheeks puffing In & Out trying to hold back the full force of the naughty Laugh backed up in his throat.

"It's not funny," pronounces Papa & his next Laugh almost pushes his teeth out of his face bursting into the kitchen.

"No. It's *serious*." But it is no use now Mama has to hold herself up with her arms straight against the side of the sink she is shaking with Laughs that start in the middle of the marrow of her bones push up and out so fast so much only *some* come out of her mouth and the rest come out of her eyes in tears. "Mrs. Sophie Post Office Box!"

They both have tears from their eyes Spilling out now they hug each other crying with Laughs that way they say to each other *See what can go bad between two people? Nothing will go bad between us . . . See how another lovelife is just a soap bubble? But ours is the Rock of Gibraltar.*

Ah-ha! What Post Office Box? Where?

Manny got to be a dentist all right with his Office in the Bronx or Yonkers it is hazy now maybe Queens. I do not Remember if it was very hard to find him that part of it did not take a high level of Detective skill. Dr. Immanuel Feigenbaum, D.D.S. it said on the door I opened into a waiting room that was the size and temperature of a meat locker. I was the only joe waiting in there.

A Radio was playing on the desk of his nurse but she was not around so I tapped the brass button on the sill of her little wooden Hatch & right after I heard a toilet flush. I wondered if I set off some kind of new Electric toilet down the hall but my inner question got answered by the outward Appearance of Manny's nurse smoothing down her starchy white uniform. Besides the dress she looked like a young version of Aunt Sophie—blue-black hair thick eyebrows pale skin and wide full lips with a trace of mustache hair at the corners. From the nose down she looked like a Latin Lover. (Even though I can not imagine it I wonder if Miss Petersen looks like Dr. Godfrey's mother. I wonder if it is more Evidence of the Idea by Sigmund Freud that all men do is look for Replacements of their own Mother in their own Life?)

"Good-morning. Name of the appointment?" She opened the flat Appointment Book on her desk.

"My name is Reuven Agranovsky," I started telling her & I got as far as Revealing that the man she knew and Respected as Dr. Immanuel Feigenbaum I knew as Cousin Manny . . . yes on those very words Manny came into the waiting room with a pink paper party hat on his head & he was twirling a noisemaker.

"Happy days are here again the skies are bright & clear again so let's—" he was singing when he saw me but stopped when I stuck out my hand.

"Manny?"

He did not recognize me right off but he smiled and shook hands, "Next victim?" His secretary nurse came over to see how long it was going to take Manny to guess my face. He narrowed his eyes under his furry eyebrows. His smile Faded Away then Faded Back. "Reuven?"

"Bingo."

"My cousin Reuven," he pointed me out for Vicky. "What's this a surprise?"

"Not to me," I kidded him.

He dragged the party hat off of his head a little Sheepish. "Leftover from our office warming party."

"This office sure needs it." I tried to blow a smoke ring with my Bare Breath.

"Vicky did you tell the Super?"

"I told him yesterday. I told him and told him."

"The radiators only work on and off," Manny said. As if it needed more Explanation he went on, "They're off in here now. Come on into the Torture Chamber. I've got a good electric heater in there."

Vicky opened the door into Manny's operating room. Smoky daylight pushed in through the low window & lifted the dentist chair up in the Pool of Shadows. Manny sat on a padded stool with wheels which left me in the dentist chair.

"Put your feet up," invited Manny & he jack-knifed his string-bean legs back & forth with his feet glued on the floor so first he was by my head then my feet & then by my head again. "Want a check-up? On the house. Family discount."

I Decided it would be a fine way to milk him for the Info I needed I Believe it was exactly what Peter Tremayne would do i.e. lean back open my mouth & say ah-hh-hh.

"Swell. Now I can start practicing."

So we got the pleasantries out of the way so we could get down to the unpleasantries. In between the floating shreds of one-way Conversation I found out why it is called a Practice because that was exactly what Manny needed—he was the first one to Admit it. Before I could steer him around to the Subject of his father my Uncle Jake the Fugitive accountant Manny wanted to bring me up to date on his own Life Story. What he told me Riveted me to that chair. He never Graduated from dentist school he got kicked out of Cornell.

"Open please Reuven. Wider." Manny stuck a little mirror and most of his fingers into my mouth and clicked his tongue. "You have a cavity the size of Ebbet's Field in that molar. I can see half-way to China," he said. He dug into it with a needlenosed buttonhook. I yelped. "I know how to fix that."

I did not want to show Fear in front of Vicky so I let him work on me & tell me while he drilled hammered & drained my mouth how he got the boot from Cornell by performing Experiments in the area of Orthodonture which 25 years later was going to be a Boom Industry in dental care. But in those years the Science of dental Appliances was in its Infancy so the top Professors at Cornell did not recognize Manny's Vision of the Future. Maybe they also did not enjoy forking over $10,000 to a freshman girl who almost choked to Death because Manny accidentally wired her jaws together trying to straighten out her crooked canine incisors by a System he named Oral Restraint.

My jaw ached but not too much to ask him how my Canine Incisors looked to him.

"Fine. Open up again for me. Wide. Wider."

Manny did not tell Aunt Sophie or Uncle Jake about the Fact of his Dishonorable Discharge from Cornell instead he let them think he was still up in Ithaca but in fact he was finishing off his studies at Dewayne-Bobinck Vocational College in Yonkers also living it up besides. Dewayne-Bobinck was not famed as the Last Word in dental Science but it did have one thing going for it i.e. a Tuition fee of $25.00 per Semester.

"That doesn't mean Dewayne-Bobinck has low standards," Manny reassured me. "The Dean of the Dentistry Department came there right from Brigham Young. Right after he got dismissed. I was his star pupil."

"Wa wa he deh-ih hor?"

"What was he dismissed for?"

"Eh."

"Oh you know," Manny shrugged it off. "He wasn't really officially licensed to practice dentistry or teach it. Turned out he taught auto mechanics." I pushed Manny's hand away and tried to get a foot on the floor but that stupid stool blocked my leg. "It's O.K. He taught body work. Grills."

I had to stick to it I did not Plan to go away from that chair before at least I had a Clue about where I should look for Uncle Jake. I went that far I took it for 1 Hour & it was hard on my Nerves hard on my mouth but now I can say it was not Torture. I showed him I was Relaxed I crossed my ankles very Casual.

Manny zizzed his drill he leaned down over me. "What do you want to know about Pop?"

"Ah-hh-hh!"

I am sure he could not hear my Worry over the zizz of that drill he was using to tunnel the rest of the way to China. *I will not flinch not a iota* that was my inner thought when Manny & his twelve fingers Manny with his zizzing drill & boiling eyes was trying to climb into my mouth . . . I did not have any Good reason I should panic O.K. so maybe Manny is looking out for Uncle Jake's safety O.K. maybe it is part of his deal.

It was O.K. all right. While he was shoveling some kind of gunk into my molar Manny tossed me some tasty tidbits namely—

"The last few letters from Pop *whew*. I don't think he's 100% in his right mind."

"How hum?"

"Look at this. I got his last one here."

He held the one-page Letter open for me to read. It looked Normal to my eyes full of Fatherly advice about saving money plus how hard Life was in Russia compared to New Jersey and reminding Manny to build a huppa in the backyard for Succoth.

"What's wrong with it?" I asked I added I did not know Uncle Jake was so religious.

"Pop hasn't put one foot inside a synagogue since he went through Ellis Island. You don't build a huppa for Succoth! Look at the signature. Look how he signed it."

I looked. Uncle Jake signed his letter to Manny this way:

Yours in Christ,
Rabbi Leo Nussbaum (Mrs.)

"Maybe it's just a precaution."

Manny opened a drawer in the cabinet under his Instruments he grabbed up half a dozen Letters & fanned them over his head. "In the last year and a half here's how I heard from him. Every one from a different place. One from Montreal, Canada . . . one from Philadelphia and here's one from Baltimore . . . This one isn't even in his own handwriting."

"Oh," I said. "I was hoping Uncle Jake could give me some good advice about my income tax. With personal matters like tax and oral hygiene I think it's a good policy to use family. You can trust family."

He undid the rubber bib from under my chin. "If you can find them."

"I found you." I tried to make it Sound like I went Searching for him high & low.

"I'm easy to find. I'm in the book."

Vicky handed a paper cup to Manny & he handed it to me. It was full of something Iodine Red i.e. I had to wash my mouth out with it. Then Manny crunched the empty cup in his hand & threw it down on the floor and let go of a Weary sigh. "I worry but what am I supposed to do Roove? I got Ma. She wants me to go bring him home. I tell her who does she think I am? The Green Ray?"

I swallowed my iodine fizz I felt it fizz out my nose.

"You're not supposed to swallow that by the way."

"Can I—" said I squeezing the stuff through my nostrils, "can I write to Uncle Jake?"

Manny passed me over the little manilla envelope. "It's a couple of weeks old. I don't know if Pop's anywhere near there now. Maybe he's in Timbuktoo."

If I had to go to Timbuktoo I was ready if that was where the Trail led me but by the return address stamped on the back I saw I did not need to Travel so far:

Ah-ha—P.O. Box 1138 Pikesville, New York. Ah-hh-ha!

Pikesville it is my guess looks the same today as it did when I went there in 1939 and in that time it is my guess it looked the same as it did before World War I. Now maybe they have a Ronald McDonald's there and a Coca-Cola machine stuck on the porch outside the hardware store or somewhere else but mainly it is The Land Time Forgot. This Fact is True about many of the upstate FISHvilles i.e. family stores bait & tackle shops and little bungalows all huddled in close down a Main Street a hole in the bristly woods. Troutville Pikesville Perchtown and there is one named Bass to my direct Knowledge just whispering pine places where a fellow can let his fly loose and doze off with his rod in his hand.

The Post Office boxes in Pikesville are set into the wall on the whitewashed wood porch outside the Post Office so it made my stake-out across the street a very easy job. Last thing before I left his office Manny gave me a letter from his Ma to mail to Uncle Jake it was a pink envelope I guess a Love Letter begging him to come home. There it was in Box 1138 so all I had to do now was keep my eye on it and sooner or later he was going to come and pick it up and that was going to be the Paydirt of my stake-out.

There was a coffee shop right across the street so I sat at the table in front of the window I did not have to leave the Comfort Zone I was going to stay warm and well fed (where does it say a person has to suffer for a Good cause?). I started off drinking a cup of coffee etc. and watching who went in and out of the Post Office (nobody). It was about 2 dozen cups of coffee & 16 pieces of cherry pie later I saw what I came to Pikesville to see. I wrote down very Accurate notes of my Observations but of course I did not keep the napkin—the times I show here are not the Actual ones but similar & Realistic about the order of Events—

7:30 A.M.   Post Office opens. Nobody goes to P.O.B. 1138.
7:31 A.M.   No change.
7:35 A.M.   I order breakfast—a cup of coffee scrambled eggs hash browns & a piece of cherry pie.
8:03 A.M.   No change but I am still hungry even after that pie.
8:12 A.M.   I decide to order another piece of pie & 1 more cup of coffee.
            Etc.

UNTIL—

5:25 P.M.   No change. No change from my $10 bill since I had to pay for all of that pie & coffee.
5:32 P.M.   A woman I did not see enter the P.O. exits the

P.O. & opens Box 1138—She looks like a Floozy
with dyed red hair high heels & a raccoon
coat . . . She takes out the pink letter & strolls
down the street. My head is zizzing from all that
black coffee! I am ready I tail Madam "X"

I tailed her to the Drugstore & from there to the Grocery store
& from there to the Hardware store she was the Last Customer
in each place. She did not Notice me I was as good at this as
Peter Tremayne all righty & I followed her up a hill I saw her go
in the bottom door of a woodframe Duplex set back off the street
at the end of a buckled & cracked Concrete driveway.

My feet hardly made a noise I was walking on catfeet when I
felt my way down the side of the house if I made a Racket the jig
was up before the curtain came down. I had to Learn the lay of
the land i.e. did he have Gunsels in there besides his Moll?

Through the kitchen window I Observed her Madam "X" the
"redhead" she poured some soup out of a can & stirred it in a
pot on the stove. So far it all looked Normal. *Too* Normal. Where
was Uncle Jake? Was this the Life of a gangland V.I.P. on the
lam—canned soup? I backed up slowly I followed the lights
switching on in each room—the bathroom—up I backed then—I
tripped over the Gas Meter & all of a sudden I was in the middle
of trembling stillness Inside & Out. I froze I listened until it felt
like it was all back to Normal I was not in Danger I stood up
under the back bedroom window & I saw slow Puffs of cigar
smoke roll up over the top of the mahogany headboard. The creak
of sprung bedsprings when a Weight shifted off of the mattress
his hand on the headboard a gold & ruby pinky ring—the slick
dome of Uncle Jake's head—

And that was all before the curtain of the world came down
right on my poor head and I fell through a Hole in the dark down
into the bottomless orchestra pit pulling the xylophones harps
cymbals & kettle drums down on top of me . . .

The only thing I know for sure when I come to is I am holding
a pain in my hand sharp hard & heavy as a drill bit it feels like
somebody is hammering a Spike into my palm. I look up. I see

the Floozy & she has her arm cocked with a mallet in her Grip. I look down. I see her high heel Drilling into the middle of my hand my palm is bluey white my fingers are purple cocktail sausages.

"Try anything tricky and I'll conk you another one," she drawled. "Tell Mr. Lipsky I don't know *where* he is *or* his goddamn books."

"Wait—" I tried to sit up but a snarling beast a living hunk of the horsehair sofa I was pinned up against landed on my chest. The stinking thing dug its back paws into my Groin and its front paws into my Ribs it pushed its crusty dribbling huffing yap into my face.

"One word from me and she'll chew your face off."

The pigmy warthog flicked its tongue around its teeth. My face was no oil painting but I was very Attached to it. "Let me up. I'm Jake's nephew!"

She drills her heel into my hand ouch OUCH there must only be a quarter of a inch of my Flesh left between her shoe and the carpet. Any minute she will strike oil.

"Jack hasn't got any nephew. Jack's in Canada."

"See that? Hear that? You call him Jack. How do I know I call him Jake if I'm not his nephew? Uncle Jake not Uncle Jack."

"You copied his name down wrong when you got the contract from Lipsky you dumb wop." She leaned on her heel.

"My name is Reuven Agranovsky! Where do you think I'm from? The Jewish part of Sicily?" The beast Growled on my chest & I started to lose Hope that human Decency was going to triumph over animal Instinct (It never does).

She Snapped her fingers. "Be sweet Blossom," she commanded the mutt & it skulked off of my chest it sat next to the redhead's feet Nuzzled her knee jerked its head up moony eyed and Adored her. "O.K. prove it you didn't come from Lipsky."

The heel came off my hand. I sat up Rubbing it trying to get the Circulation back in before it turned to gangrene. Past the pain I tuned in the problem *what did she want me to prove?* "How can I prove where I didn't come from? I didn't come from China either. Should I prove that while I'm at it?"

She came back quick as the snap of a whip. "I happen to know who Lipsky hires when he does his dirty business. Ginnies not Jews. Show it to me." She stroked Blossom's sleek head. "Lemme see it."

Well I did not Crave this kind of Adventure in my Life. From all I Observed about womanly behavior in this Area it is a mystery to me nor it is not full of joy & singing from my direct Experience only embarrassment. (Today I will say I have been around the block once so I Feel other things about this business but in that minute with the Floozy she was pushing on me to Expose my weakest point so I did not want to Experiment with her desires I was not even curious.) Besides that Blossom mutt was giving me the eye flicking its tongue in & out of its teeth.

"Not with that in here." I pointed at Blossom. Blossom answered me with a long mean low growl.

"It's a *she*," the Redhead spat out. She spoke to that dog in the same tone of Voice a teacher uses on her teacher's pet. "Blossom go wait in the hall now. Go wait for Mama O.K.?"

Blossom took in every word she did not need to hear Mama's Cue again she sank down on her belly & crawled out of the room to show What A Good Dog Am I.

When it was just the 2 of us human beings in the room I got up off the floor I held my hand over my fly.

"No tricks mister," she warned me.

"What am I going to do?" I piped up then. "Hit you over the head with it?" My Crippled right hand still had her red footprint in the palm which gave me a Good Excuse to fumble. Very slow I held it up to show her the Damage she did with her high heel also a Sign of no tricks up my sleeve. "Hey!" I jumped back for there I saw Blossom's damp snout peek around the corner of the door.

"Naughty Blossom! Naughty!" Madam told her off. The snout pulled back with a Feeble little whimper behind it & Madam got back to business with me. "Lemme see it you ginnie!"

I put my hand over my Heart & pledged, "You can take my word as—" I did not get another Honest word out she tackled me

106

down on the sofa she broke 2 of her long nails pulling on my pants!

With me Fighting her off on the sofa with her grunting into my crotch this was the Scene my own Uncle Jake stood staring at when he Entered. I Believe he could not see my face only his Floozy's big behind up in the Air & legs & arms flapping & kicking all around. I saw him just standing in the door there at the point in the Action when I rolled his Redhead off of me & she landed on her rear end flat on the floor in front of him.

He stood there sleepy & Confused he blinked his eyes slow so he could clear them. This did not Help him very much he turned away like he was going to walk out of the room & walk in again to Start Over but he stayed—my Papa's brother Jacob . . . Daddy of Manny, D.D.S. . . . the Floozy's sugardaddy . . . Jack the Clap . . . there he was in a brown plaid robe hanging open over his BVD's & worn out carpet slippers on the wrong foot each.

I hope my Voice is true to the joy I feel since I found him there & I wave my swollen hand at him "Uncle Jake! Hiya!"

His eyes look like 2 milky blue Marbles his lips hang open they hang slack. His Girlfriend wants to see if he will Recognize me so she does not Prompt him. His nephew or his Assassin she searches his face for a Clue. Finally he throws me a big grin & sticks out his hand & Ignores the Floozy altogether. "Moe! Hey!" He pats my back with both of his stubby hands. "I missed ya Moe . . . "

Moe? This shakes me up a little of course. O.K. so I was maybe 9 years old the last time he saw me but he calls me Moe? "No Uncle Jake. *Reuven*—"

The redhead chimes in, "Don't put any words in his mouth."

"I'm Paul's son—Reuven. Who's Moe?"

Uncle Jake steps back a step & Squints at me. Madam X nudges him in a Different direction. "No Jack. Moe's dead. Remember?"

Uncle Jake sighs & flaps his arms against his sides. He does it again. "What's wrong with me? I must need glasses Fannie."

Ah-ha. Fannie.

"Who is he Jack?" She looked at me over his shoulder very Suspicious. "Who's Reuben?"

"Reuven," I corrected her. "With a V."

This got Uncle Jake pondering he rubbed the back of his head. "Reuven. Unusual. I had a nephew by that same name."

What was I supposed to do what was I supposed to say? I just had to stand in front of him & watch him try to tune me in but when it looked like he was Receiving me O.K. my signal got lost in the crackling ether it drifted away over the rooftops so all he could hear was Static on the Brain. Uncle Jake dragged himself out of the room we heard him opening & closing drawers in the kitchen.

Fannie sat stiff-necked on the sofa she stared up at the ceiling to wait for Uncle Jake's mainspring to wind down or snap whichever Came First. At least she Accepted the fact I was not one of Lipsky's ginnies I did not come on a mission to murder. "He'll come back in a minute," she said. Underneath I believe she was saying, "I don't know who you are but I wish you'd take him off my hands for a hour."

Uncle Jake came back in & he had a fork in his right hand & a wooden spoon in the other. "Look what I found in the kitchen Fannie." Then he eyed me up. He Offered me the hand with the fork. "How are ya?"

"Better," I told him.

"Glad to hear it."

"He says he's your nephew," Fannie said to the ceiling.

Uncle Jake pumped my hand harder he Gripped it tighter. "How are ya? Manny! Been a while . . . been a while . . . " He spun around & asked Fannie, "You get him some tea with lemon?" and to me he said, "You like that. Don't I remember it right Manny?"

I was going to jump in here & put him on the Right Track but Fannie beat me to the Punch. "No Jack. Manny's your son."

He leaned back & squinted at me. "This isn't my son!"

Progress.

"I'd enjoy a glass of tea with lemon," I said but as soon as my words hit the Air I saw them whirling around his head just Confusing him some more.

Uncle Jake sat down next to Fannie on the sofa. All of a sudder

I felt like a hatstand standing in the middle of the room. "I know that! I know that," he said to her. "Don't get sore."

"I'm not Manny Uncle Jake." I crouched down to him. "Manny's the dentist. I just saw him. I just came from there. That's how I found out where you are."

He went bug eyed. "You found out where I am?" He curled up in a fit of fear. His lip was trembling at me. "Y-you go b-back and and and you tell—" he straightened up his back to tell me who I should tell, "you tell that sonofabitch Lipsky I got his books in a very safe place. S-A-F-E from him so it won't do him any goddamned good to shoot me in the back of the head . . . " Fannie did not have the power to halt him working himself up into a Froth. "So you can just run your skinny ginny ass outa here! This is my house!" A purple vein started bulging out of the side of his head what if he had a Brain Hemorrhage right there on the carpet & it was all My Fault?

Fannie stroked his forehead she pulled him back down to the sofa from the arm of it where he was partly perched. "Jack ssh . . . ssh . . . Jack . . . It's O.K. honeybunch. He's not from Lipsky. That's not why he's here . . . ssh . . . "

Uncle Jake was practically Whimpering on her lap about 1 second away from shoving his thumb into his mouth but he did not Reach that pathetic point it was pathetic enough already.

"What's the matter Uncle Jake?" He glanced up at the talking hatstand. So I asked Fannie, "What's wrong with him?"

"Strain," she said stroking him still. "He'll be better in a minute."

Yes he bobbed up then this time he almost sounded Normal. "Hello . . . " He waited for me to fill in the blank.

"Reuven."

"I remember now. I remember you. Reuven."

"That's it."

I was coming in Loud & Clear now he was just tweaking the Knobs to fine tune me in. "Paul's & Miriam's son. Reuven."

"Hiya Uncle Jake."

He folded his hands in his lap & said to me, "I want to talk to you about income tax." Funny thing I did want to talk to a

Financial Expert about my taxes etc. but the sad shake of Fannie's head told me it was not the right time. "You can't dodge it Reuven. Don't try it. Uncle Sam's got his eyes & ears everywhere. You can't hide out from the Treasury Department. The F.B.I. work with them on their hard cases." He lowered his Voice down to a whisper. "You married?"

I nodded. "Her name's Annie." (Why the hell not? If the Topic came up Further I could gain knowledge about the Tax Situation of a married couple and so forth.)

Question & Answer—Question & Answer—about dependants & bank accounts etc. and it did not make any difference if the Facts I told him about me at that minute were False ones they went in 1 ear and out the other he was just using my Voice to zero in on my face—so there I was Guiding him in & Appearing before his eyes even if he was talking to himself more than he was talking to me.

"Are your parents still alive?"

"Oh yes." I did not have the Nerve to tell him anything else about that. The Conversation calmed him down Sufficient even Blossom was calm on the carpet under his feet Snoring. Then Uncle Jake said a Remarkable thing:

"Sometimes these days lately I notice I make a mistake over remembering faces." He licked his cracked lips he Darted his eyes away. "I forget. The way I forgot you Rachel."

"Reuven."

"Reuven," he Repeated & clenched his eyelids around that Fact to hold it & seal it inside his Mind.

Fannie shook his arm. "Is Jack home now?"

He turned toward her very quick for a second he was Sore at her. "Sure Jack's home." Then he offered sweet words to make up, "I'm O.K. Sugar Baby."

"Who's that?" She pointed at me. Blossom looked over at me too.

"Miriam's boy. My brother's boy Reuven." He knew it but he was worn out Remembering. He stood up he smoothed out his Robe he nodded at me. "The dentist."

"Honey," Fannie tugged his sleeve. "Why don't you go bring

in dinner? It's all ready. It's in the kitchen Jack just put it on some plates. I made mashed potatoes and soup and—"

"O.K. O.K.," he said going out. "You two talk. Get to know each other." He stopped in the doorway and he read my Mind. "How did I get into this mess? Reuven. Reuven. It's good to see you. I don't remember did I tell you how I got into this mess?"

"No Uncle Jake. I just got here."

He pulled his flapping robe together and tied it up tight and Decent. "Four years ago I'm working for that S.O.B. Sol Lipsky just scrubbing his books and doing his tax. Very small stuff. Very small potatoes Reuven ya know insurance fires—bupkis. I met the guy back in Ellis Island that's how good we know each other 37 years. Suddenly he gets the brilliant God-given idea I'm skimming cash."

"You *were* skimming," Fannie reminded him.

"I was skimming sure," Uncle Jake confirmed it, "but Lipsky had no idea . . . " He shoved his hands into his pockets. "At first. Anyway it isn't anything like Sol thinks it is—in his insane mind he's got it 10 times worse. So one fine morning I'm driving my nice car down the road there's a red light and ba-boom my nice car does not stop. Are you with me?"

"No brakes."

"No brakes. Correct. Now I know the gloves are off. So I figure I need a insurance policy and I take Lipsky's books. I got 'em in a safe deposit box downtown with a letter telling if anything happens to me . . . " His Voice went cold.

"Don't talk crazy sweetheart."

"I may be crazy but I'm not stupid." He touched the vein that he felt Throbbing on the side of his head. "But I am tired of it. I tell you Reuven it would be a blessing in the skies if some big mick cop came in here and hauled me off. Locked me up and threw away the key."

"Jack don't talk like a loser."

"All right. Not throw away the key but put me someplace secret where Lipsky didn't know where I was. So. What was I doing . . . I was going to do something important wasn't I?"

"Fix dinner," Fannie nudged him along.

"Sure. Any mail?"

"A letter from your wife. I left it in the kitchen."

"Oh fine. Reuven . . . does your father ever mention my name anymore?"

"Sometimes."

"Don't tell me what he says. I just want to know if he remembers me. Maybe this thing with my memory runs in the family."

(I wish I had Uncle Jake in front of me this minute I could answer him NO. If it was his Mental Illness to Forget the faces and the places in his Life I can say I have got the Opposite disease.)

Fannie unwrapped a piece of cream colored salt water taffy and chewed it up and between chews she told me all about my Uncle's main problem besides the Vengeance of Sol Lipsky S.O.B.

"He walks down the street and he can't pass by a fire hydrant without patting it on the head and giving it a stick of gum. For a minute he thinks it's a child sitting on the kerb. Mailboxes he thinks are waiting to cross the street. It gets worse day in day out."

"How do you know anybody's really trying to get him then?"

"He says so."

"But—"

"I know it but it started before he started losing his memory. *Lipsky's ginnies are after me* he told me. *You're imagining it. Where did you get that idea?* I asked him. *From the voices in the wall.*"

"But if he wasn't in his right mind then Fannie . . . "

"No Reuben. *I* heard the voices too. They were from the radio playing nextdoor. The very next day he had his accident with the car."

I held back my Natural Urge to ask which Radio show the Voices came from and instead I asked Fannie how Uncle Jake treated her.

"If they got him in court he was supposed to say *I don't remember.* Looks like your uncle took it to the extreme," she said.

She stopped talking when the Sound of Uncle Jake's shuffling slippers reached the hallway behind us and he pushed into the room then he had 2 Dinner Plates with him Balanced on the lid of a pot roast pan.

"Dinner," he said.

I saw his dull eyes then all he had facing out of him were dead Sockets staring at Fannie and the furniture around her. Each plate had on it 3 brand new Spark Plugs next to a little pile of shredded cotton balls and another little pile of Q-Tips.

"Sausages. Mashed potatoes. String beans," he announced & he Pointed at each pile on her plate.

"You forgot the soup," I kidded him.

He glared at me. "Who the hell are you?"

I did not have a very easy job with Fannie trying to talk her into the Idea of allowing Uncle Jake to get rescued from his Predicament by the long arm of the Law. I saw I had a Delicate job on my hands when I saw her Flinch when I told her in my Opinion the pros and cons of it i.e. the Police are pros who will not con Uncle Jake into any False Confession or out of his Constitutional Rights if he be bound for the Big House the Bug House or both.

Uncle Jake snored on the sofa between us & Blossom snored by Fannie's feet while I pleaded with her she should consider his Mental condition . . . consider his Physical condition . . . consider his Personal Safety . . . consider his Legal Problems . . . consider your Legal problems i.e. aiding and abetting plus harboring a criminal over State lines . . . consider his Family . . . consider his Mental Condition . . . consider your mental condition . . . consider the Future . . . consider his Mental Condition etc. & so on until the wee wee hours. I saw how she was Stuck on him and she said she wanted what was best for him but she did not know for sure what it was—to go along with my plan or hijack a truck & drive Uncle Jake to the Yukon. So it was a ticklish moment I had to handle her with Care—all I had to do was rub Fannie the wrong way & she would flare up with a rash Reaction that was going to be rough on both of us before it was all over.

"For double insurance nothing will go wrong," I pledged, "I am going to tip off the newspapers."

She bit her bottom lip & thought about that one. I almost did not catch her words over Uncle Jake's snores when she sank back sort of all her breath knocked out of her she said, "I don't want to be here when they take him away."

"O.K."

"I'll go in a taxi right before."

"O.K."

"Which paper you going to tell?"

I did not have to think about that for one single second. "The Philadelphia Inquirer." It was the first thing my Family saw on the breakfast table before the lemon tea and it was read and Respected at many leading breakfast tables in New York City too from the Liberty Building to Gracie Mansion.

"O.K. Reuben." Her Voice was low she leaned forward over her knees & twisted her head to face me. "I'm going to read all about it," she said with no mistake of the hush of a threat.

The closest Police Department was not in Pikesville it was in the friendly town of Bass. I found the Station nextdoor to the Courthouse which they built with a front of gray granite & a square back of red bricks. The Ordinary bricks did not deduct from the picture of the presence of Justice it was there in the curtain of Snow it was rock solid in front of my eyes: cut granite for the pillars of the Law of the Land holding up the regular bricks of the Common People. As I looked upon the Bass Courthouse the hard core of the soft town the hub of a wheel with broken spokes as the streets changed Direction when the snow drifted that Branch Office of Liberty standing out pure & clean as a block of ice on the steps of that cement pedestal I felt like I was one of the Pilgrim Fathers viewing his vision of the American Civilization yet to be yet sure to be.

To be or not to be was going to be the Question if I did not get out of the falling snow in a big hurry it was piled up to my knees by now and if I stood there for 10 More Minutes I was going to turn into Frosty the Snowman doomed to be the Helpless Victim of the next playful child to come along with a carrot and a few lumps of coal. So frosty wet and my legs stiff as stilts I

Staggered into the Bass police station I teetered in like the ghost of Frankenstein.

The Sergeant on duty at the desk had the name of Burrows which sticks in my mind very distinctive Because it was the Name of our Engineer on the show Mr. Burrows who never stirred from the shadows of the Control Room only sat in his chair like a Toad on a Lily Pad. Sergeant Burrows was not like Mr. Burrows in body only in Name. In body he was lean and leathery he was living Evidence of the hunting shooting fishing kind of outdoor Life that is all in all the very Opposite of Life in a Radio studio. But I had a High Hope that when he heard my Story he was going to Recognize I was a regular joe and we were a pair of aces 2 of a kind just 2 Good men on the right side of the Law.

"Tell it to me again. Tell me your name."

A bare lightbulb was scorching my eyeballs and this was the THIRD time I told him my name. "Reuven Agranovsky."

"You're not from around here."

"No. New York. Like I said."

"Before that?"

"Philadelphia," I said, "the one in Pennsylvania."

He jotted this Fact down. "Before that?"

"I wasn't born before that & I don't remember where I was."

"Yep," Sgt. Burrows said to the notepad he was studying behind the scorching bulb.

Why was he Interrogating me? Did I Sound crazy to him because I was het up to get to Uncle Jake before he Changed his Mind? Was it he plain did not Believe my story? Was he thinking like my Mama and Papa i.e. did he suspect I was a suspect in some Unsolved Crime . . . or was it the Worst I was in his eyes was a freeloader looking for a warm cozy jail cell to spend the night inside at the taxpayers' expense? He was using his wiles to Extract the Facts to get my Story straight but it was just regular interrogation it was not torture.

"I want to get this part right," his Voice all deep and crisp and even, "You say Julius Feigenbaum is your uncle?"

"Jacob Feigenbaum. Yes. He's my uncle. But listen to me that is *not* the most important thing here!"

"I bet it is to him."

"He *wants* to give himself up. He's looking forward to it. He's been on the lam for so long he doesn't remember who he is! And that S.O.B. Sol Lipsky . . . Oh God. Are you listening to me?"

"I got that down here uh-huh. Insurance fires. Jack the Clap. Well." He slapped the desk light out of my face and leaned back in his chair and Shouted into the hallway. "Pat? Call up Eugene Brown over to Albany at the F.B.I." Sgt. Burrows tossed me a glance. "Ask him if he's got a wanted out on Jacob Feigenbaum alias Jack the Clap Feigenbaum." He did not Laugh when he said it to show me *I am taking this as a serious matter.* Then he showed me that stiff smile and said, "We can check this in a few minutes or two."

We sat there in each other's Silence for a few minutes or two then I heard the Irish voice of Officer O'Riordan come off of the telephone. (I thought Hooray a mick cop so Uncle Jake will have his Dream Come True!) He stood in the doorway and advised Sgt. Burrows "Agent Brown wants to talk to you personal."

Sgt. Burrows let the front legs of his chair hit the floor. "O.K. Pat. Can you stay in here and babysit this young man?"

The second he sat in the Sgt.'s chair and pulled it up to the table his hand on the seat between his legs I felt like I was going to babysit *him*. He had a wad of Juicyfruit in his mouth that was the size of a Ping Pong ball and he chewed it with a happy clown smile plastered on his kisser. His skin was all buttery it was pale yellow and slippery on his high round cheeks also blotched like cranberry stains.

"Want to play hangman?"

Before I needed to answer him Sgt. Burrows came back into the room and told us what I already knew i.e. it was true all True and now they had a job to do so they better step on it. The first place O'Riordan stepped was over to the Gun case where he took out a 12 gauge shotgun and weighed it in his arms.

"This is fun!" he said.

While the 2 of them did their Posse business I called up the Philadelphia Inquirer & I got to talk straight to the night Editor and no Trouble at all since I guess it was a slow news day but it was not going to stay that way.

ME: I have a scoop for you.
EDITOR: Aren't I a lucky ducky.
ME: A wanted criminal—a fugitive from Justice and the
           F.B.I. is going to get captured tonight in one hour
           in Pikesville, New York. Two miles West of Bass.
EDITOR: Who is it?
ME: Forget about who I am. The wanted man is Jacob
           Feigenbaum alias Jack the Clap.

He held the phone away from his mouth and I did hear him let out a Laugh maybe because of the Early Hour. First I had the Fear he was going to hang up on me but when I heard him Breathing on the line I felt I got his newshound nose twitching.

EDITOR: Sorry. I had to sneeze. Tell me again. Who?
ME: Remember all those insurance fires in the garment
           district a few years ago?
EDITOR: Yeah. I do. I reported on 'em. Lasky . . . Lansky—
ME: Lipsky.
EDITOR: That's right. Lipsky. Who am I speaking to?

All of a sudden I had to make a Decision I got the Feeling it was going to make a difference to the Result of my whole Plan. Do I *lie*? Do I tell the *Truth* about who I am i.e. do I tell him one of my Real Names? Or is it better if this is a famous anonymous tip? I wrestled with the Truth I wrestled with the lie I let him have them both.

ME: This is—The Green Ray!

And I hung up on him but I had a Hope he was going to play his Hunch—and a minute later I heard the phone ring on Sgt. Burrow's desk. Lucky ducky for the Philadelphia Inquirer & all of its readers & lucky ducky for me.

A ½ hour later I found Fannie & Uncle Jake where I left them sitting together on the horsehair sofa Holding Hands. Only now her two Straw Colored suitcases were stacked by her feet she knew I brought them to the crossroad of their Life together on the lam which as of now was No More.

"Do you want to hear what's going to happen?" Silence. "In a few minutes Sgt. Burrows and Officer O'Riordan are coming in a police car from Bass. I found a mick cop for you Uncle Jake . . . Uncle Jake?" I was sitting in that room like the Invisible Man.

"Did you hear a voice?" Uncle Jake turned Sarcastic.

"This is the right move Jack. Don't take it out on Reuven." I told him what move now it was Fannie's turn to Remind him Why. "You don't want to go on going this way do you?"

"No." he confessed. "What way?"

"In a big circle. Going away from your family."

"You're my family Sugar Baby." Uncle Jake scratched his stomach.

"No. You and me—" she stopped herself and started over. "I love you and you love me like a regular Romeo and Juliet."

"Romeo and Juliet," he repeated.

"Let's quit before the suicide scene O.K.?" Fannie this Floozy knew from William Shakespeare? "You need to be with Sophie now."

A tear rolled down my uncle's cheek his eyebrows Pressed Together he forced back the Memory of her. "Who's Sophie?"

"Aunt Sophie."

"Your wife Jack. Sophie is your wife."

"The short woman is that her? With black hair and make-up?"

"Sophie."

"Sophie," he remembered now.

Fannie squeezed his hands hard she made a Noise I thought came out of Blossom at first but then she said, "I'm gonna get outa here before the fireworks start."

"Will you bring back a Hershey bar?"

"I'm not *coming* back." She reached for her Raccoon coat & she asked me, "Remind him Honey."

We all heard the Sound of tires crunching the snow & pebbles in the driveway but Fannie was the only one who did not get Excited by it. When the car horn Beeped she said, "That's my taxi cab Sweetums. Give me a kiss." She puckered up & planted one on Uncle Jake's mouth & he Reached up & held her arms he Squeezed her with his hands.

Fannie broke loose and came over & kissed my forehead. She told me how she knew it was all Borrowed Time with him anyway and she was glad she was bowing out on a High Note she did not hold a Grudge against me. I started to pick up her suitcases but she stopped me.

"Stay here with your Uncle Jake," those were Fannie's last words to me before her pooch & her bags Followed her out the front door.

We could hear her taxi all the way down Main Street the only car alive out there then there was no Sound at all only the Sound of snowflakes on frozen window panes. I Wondered how Leon Kern could make a Sound Effect like that the Sound Effect of peach colored daylight cracking around the rolled up edges of snowclouds the weather stopped in the Sky over us this room on the tongue of the spring of a mousetrap as big as a house.

"I hope she remembers to get me a Hershey bar," said Uncle Jake & he twisted his neck all the way around to look out the window behind him. "Here she comes."

A knock on the front door. "THIS IS OFFICER PAT O'RIOR-DAN OUT HERE . . . WITH SGT. BURROWS OF THE BASS P.D. AND AGENT EUGENE BROWN OF THE FEDERAL BUREAU OF INVESTIGATION . . . "

"That's not Fannie's voice."

"No Uncle Jake it's a big mick cop. O.K.?"

"IS JACOB FEIGENBAUM IN THERE?"

"Tell him yes he is Uncle Jake. Think about Aunt Sophie."

"I'm O.K.," but he was panting now. "I'm O.K."

I shouted for him. "Yes! He's in here! Yes!"

"MR. FEIGENBAUM PLEASE COME OUTSIDE NOW . . . WITH YOUR HANDS ABOVE YOUR HEAD SIR . . . YOU WILL NOT BE HARMED . . . THROW YOUR

GUN OR GUNS OUT NOW AND COME OUT WITH YOUR HANDS ABOVE YOUR HEAD . . . YOU WILL NOT BE HARMED . . . HONEST . . . "

I walked him up to the front door and when I opened it Officer O'Riordan jumped back off the Porch. "Put your hands up O.K.?" I reminded Uncle Jake.

"Like a real criminal." He was smiling through his eyes so I Knew he was in his Right Mind.

We stood on the Porch & there was Sgt. Burrows on the lawn Crouched Behind the open back door of his sedan there was Officer O'Riordan with his shotgun Aimed at us from behind the front bumper there was Agent Brown behind him smoking a pipe and behind him was a little man hefting a big Camera. My Uncle had his arms down but his hands up like he was Eddie Cantor going to sing "Ma He's Makin' Eyes At Me". I nudged his elbow just to tell him *I am with you* but he did not take it that way he took it I Meant he should raise his hands Higher so he raised them way up over his head—his robe opened up like a Vaudeville curtain showing everybody his baggy Underpants—*Is Everybody Happy?!*

The flashbulb popped the snap of silver light the slap of frosty Air hit his legs he moved quick he moved too quick he pulled his robe down tight around him without a Warning—

"Down!" somebody shouted—both barrels of O'Riordan's shotgun boomed—the front door behind us Blew off its hinges—

"Down!"—we were down in the frozen mud under the rose bushes—"Cease fire! Cease fire!"

Uncle Jake was sobbing. "That S.O.B. Lipsky! He bought off the cops!" Now it was Dead Quiet around us & now I heard him he was not Sobbing he was Laughing. "Takes out a POLICE contract on me! Stupid bastard! Non-deductable expense and I'm still alive!"

Those 4 men stood in a circle around us. "Are you hurt?" It was Sgt. Burrows' voice asking us. When I hit the frozen mud I bit my tongue so I did not try to talk but Uncle Jake was giggling like a tickly 6 year old. (As soon as he saw both of us were O.K. Sgt. Burrows belted O'Riordan over the head with his hat.)

The Newark reporter got a Question in when Agent Brown Hauled my Uncle up on his feet & slapped a pair of Cuffs on him. "What's the joke Jack? What's so funny?"

Uncle Jake could hardly see past the Veil of Tears in his eyes. "I'm just happy to be alive."

The bulldog Edition of the Philadelphia Inquirer went out with that Front Page photo of the two of us on the Porch i.e. Uncle Jake with his hands up in the Air like he just heard he was elected President in his underpants and me behind him with my hand Clamped around his arm real Front Page Celebrities . . .

The afternoon Edition of the New York Times and many other leading Newspapers back East ran with that photo & the story about The Family That Repents Together Cements Together. The true Story was more like jail in haste regret in leisure . . .

Under the Front Page photo it said my Uncle Jack "The Clap" Feigenbaum was the gangland money monarch banking on the Feds to withdraw their charges against him on capital offences in exchange for depositing his mob secrets in F.B.I. files to finance the balance of his debt to society . . . They identified me as his *son* Reuben *Feigenbaum* (!) a *ordinary* New York City *dentist* (!) so after I saw that in Black & White I half expected to walk into the Radio Studio the next day & see my cousin Manny there behind the microphone wowing the gallery and wooing my Girl.

Every silver lining has a cloud maybe that was the Lesson of Life I had to learn in that time. If I took that saying for my Words To Live By I believe my happy days might number more or my unhappy ones less which Amounts to the same thing by The End which is where I am.

I saw the Silver Lining of my cloudy days shining around the diningroom table of my family home out of the Voices out of the faces of my Mama & Papa. This is the only time in my Life I can remember one Experience that came into the World in the same shape I saw it before in my hopes from the split pea soup to the cinnamon sour cream cake. Papa said: "You're a good boy. Excuse me. Young man. There is love for you in this house so much you don't know you can't count it. What you did—and I don't need to know particulars you understand what . . . so . . . I recognize you had to do certain things with certain people so you could find out for yourself where you're going in your life. All right. That's finished. You saw the bad direction Jake was heading you in so you stood up on your own 2 legs & did something about it. Good. My only worry besides God forbid you got hurt was God forbid you went in too deep with his business and you spoiled the rest of your life. Who knows where it could've wound up. God forbid. You think a father wants to watch his boy turn his Life into a dead loss? Well. You recognized in time. You corrected. You corrected your life. To cap it all you get your picture in the papers! So now we can look back on this time & see a permanent record of the highpoint of our lives! Now I can retire! I know you'll use all your brain power & devote it to a normal living. I have all my confidence to you . . . " He tapped his fork on his wineglass clear as a bell. "I dedicate this meal to you Reuven. My No. 1 Son— the best success of my life!"

By my Papa I had my feet on the straight lines he Recognized the trolley lines I was following Straight from the way he remembered me—his baby boy & his blue bear then his Innocent boy going away then after his Bar Mitzvah by Fire a young man of Experience coming back. He did not know half of the true Story and half of what he did know was not True and the rest he blacked out of his Mind but so what he let me Feel I was acceptable in his sight.

By the others I was not such a Prince.

Mr. Silverstein e.g. I can see his face from the clouds nose first pointed down like it has a knuckle in it. His voice of Authority cracking down on me: "I'll quote it to you Ray— here . . . listen . . . ' . . . tipped off by a man's voice on the telephone . . . ' la dee dah dee dah ' . . . he identified himself HE IDENTIFIED HIMSELF AS THE GREEN RAY comma a popular radio serial crime buster on the Liberty Radio Network . . . ' unquote. Miss Least has had the newspapers calling up all morning. Guess what they want—a quote from *you* a *comment* if you please on the case by Mr. Ray Green the *real* voice of The

Green Ray!" I suggested here it was the Perfect Time to Reveal my true Identity to the public i.e. on top of me really Performing this act of public Decency ... "I don't believe what I'm hearing from you! Don't you understand how ordinary people feel about this kind of thing? If you march out and announce who you are and what you did the papers and everybody else I *promise* will start shouting PUBLICITY STUNT! To tell you the truth I'm not altogether satisfied about your motive with this either." I vowed to Mr. Silverstein that when I talked to the editor in Jersey I *disguised* my Green Ray voice i.e. I used my Real Voice which kept me anonymous. "It was a risk Ray. A dumb goddamned risk & not just for you. It's lucky for all of us they got your name wrong. If any of this got out well I don't want to think about the kind of publicity. Act of public decency? No. Forget it. *Stinking brat!* That's what you'd hear. Stinking brat *who turned in his own uncle to the police!* The Green Ray can't go around inspiring the youth of the nation to haul Grandma down to the precinct for pocketing the extra nickel in her change from the Five & Dime!" Did that mean I was finished as the voice of The Green Ray? "Let's just thank God nobody knows who the hell you really are."

So that saved my Bacon and Mr. Silverstein let me go on doing unrewarded anonymous Good on the Airwaves but in his Judgement I was personally a bad Example for the children of America.

David Arcash made up his Mind about me in the chilly hallway outside his Apartment. It felt like he could not wait to tell me his Opinion of what I did. "You don't respect any rules at all do you Ray?! All along you got me thinking *this guy is strictly amateur* & all the time—boy! you had those greasy little wheels going." He tapped his finger on the front of my forehead. "I took a call from some cub reporter today. Did he want to talk to me no he did not! He wanted to get *me* to get *you* to talk to him. You want his telephone number? Here. Here it is. I wrote it down ... " He stuffed a scrap of paper down my shirt. "I think he's from one of the big upstate rags. The Troutville High School Gazette I think. Listen—Good notice in that and *presto* Ray—hello Broadway!" David opened up his front door and said the rest of what he had to say to me over his shoulder. "So here's the news you sonofa-bitch. You're not going to use *me* to further your stinking career! Not after this cheap selfish Go To Hell publicity stunt! And I'll tell you another thing. *This* time you *really* put the kibosh on any plans you *ever* had about Annie. I got it from the horse's own mouth she feels identical about it. I put your laundry in the Green Room. Goodbye Ray."

I missed our Manly lunch counter lunches at the Automat which came to a End after that but one Good Consequence also came from this bust up: from then on we had real Emotions spilling over the Airwaves every time arch-enemies Lionel Horvath and The Green Ray faced each other behind the microphones.

David was Correct about the Effect my newspaper caper had with Annie which of course was the Opposite of the Effect I Craved. I got the Cold Shoulder Treatment from her for a couple of weeks straight but she still acted out those Romantic scenes between Rosalind Bentley & Peter Tremayne with so much Romantic Feeling at first it kept up my Hopes that all was not lost between us. Until she said out loud what was on her Mind about me then I Realized what a strong actress she was.

Her Voice hit me like sleet in the face. "What makes you think you deserve more attention than us? What makes you so special? You get more lines?! Who do you think you are? John Barrymore? Or Errol Flynn? A big radio star? You're not!" This all spewed out at me in one breath in the Green Room all the poison that was backed up maybe going back to the kiss in the street. "I feel sorry for you Ray I pity you. Going so low for some attention. Sheesh! That phony photo might make you look like a he-man to a fruit salad like Leon Kern but I'll tell you what it shows me darling—it shows up how much you're out for iddy biddy you!" How was I going to tell her anything different so I did not try to try I just stood back & took it from her. "You aren't anybody special. Me me me! I I I! That's you all over. What do you know about putting anybody else first?"

All along I thought that was the one thing I *was* doing!

I did not have very much to do with Womankind after that I subscribed to the Magazines instead to enjoy in the Privacy of my own home so maybe afterall Annie is Correct in her Judgement on my character. But in my Opinion that is not the Final Verdict since out of all of them I am the only one alive who saw all the Evidence I know the Invisible Facts. 70 Years almost my Character does Not Change so who on Earth knows it better how it led me into these Actions?

They all saw the Front Page Photo of me & Uncle Jake what did they see? My hand holding his arm like that like what?

"Going so low just for some attention," Annie stated.

What did she know from the Pressure I put in my fingers around his arm? What did she know it did not mean *Aha! Got you! Don't try any false moves!* No he knew what I said: *Remember I'm with you. Our worries are over . . . Smile!*

And they all saw the Expression that was on my face for about $\frac{1}{10}$ of a second in the flash of that newshound's flashbulb.

"You're not using *me* after that cheap lousy goddamned publicity stunt!" David stated.

What did he know from the Expression I had on my face the second before it or the second after when I was down with my nose in the mud under the rose bushes with him with both of us Laughing & Crying maybe all the way to the Morgue! With my hand still around his arm yet! For Comfort & Protection! There! There! There!

"You had those greasy little wheels going in your head all along."

Sheesh!

"I'm not 100% satisfied about your motives in this business," Mr. Silverstein informed me.

In respect Your Honor what did he know from my Family Feelings or from 4 years on the lam or from Fannie with the fight knocked out of her the way she said—"I don't want to see it when they take Jake away." Or Especially from the new Feelings toward the pair of them that surprised me & took me over by the end. I want to know how anybody can see 100% of his Motives from the very Beginning?

Exhibit A to Exhibit Z examine this photo the yellow newspaper of it now it is crispy flakes in my hand applause applause now look how it Winds Up it is a pile of dirt on the carpet.

"God forbid you got hurt. Who knows where it all was going to wind up God forbid," Papa stated.

But what did he know from my Romantic Purpose toward Annie how I started out to Fight for her to do anything to hold her Attention & win her Affection. How was I going to tell him I did not *care* where else God forbid my Actions led me?

"You strive to do good for the sake of a beautiful tomorrow," Mayor Deasy stated.

He knew how I was in those days inside out in the beginning Believe It Or Not I was young & Innocent the Fight was still in me I was truly the defender of the defenseless in those days I Rescued Uncle Jake and I brought Hope to the hopeless too I Rewarded Fannie's charity. My Good character Preserved me in the Beginning which now I know was the Beginning of the End.

If my Life ended by itself in the Desert then and if Annie LaSalle was there by my side I Believe with my last Breath I could defend my Actions of 66 years and keep my Good Name. But before it could Wind Up that way my past Experiences came back to me under my skin suckered the Good nature of my character and led me to people places & actions that God did not forbid. It peeled off my Innocent skin but underneath it was not Experience it was Guilty.

I can see by the Dawn's Early Light also by the clock on the clubhouse wall now it is the next A.M. so in my Opinion I am Safe here for 12 more hours—Newberry will not come near at this Time I know from direct personal Experience he is a Creature of the night. He can do what he wants but not when he wants to he needs the dark to Disguise his deeds from the eyes of the World but I will not let him Disguise his Signature on them any further this I am going to turn the light on him.

I can hear all the normal Sounds outside starting up i.e. the traffic on Ortega also the Mail came downstairs—boys & girls on the sidewalk gangs of them barking & mewing into School—I just heard a bird chirp he must be right out by the kitchen window—a screen door just banged shut downstairs—all the normal Sounds the Relief made me think for a second it is all back the way it was. My Mind is wandering figure I have to figure & Concentrate on it before it all gets away from me before I get away from it. think think think—

John Newberry. He is not going to use me to Further his career in Law enforcement! I can do what I want now too & when I want this worm has turned over a new leaf HE IS YOUR EQUAL! HE HAS A GUN! So what the hell I am going to eat a bowl of Dry Cereal it is Breakfast Time. O.K. All I have in the kitchen is that box of Uncle Sam laxative cereal that Tonto delivered from the Convenience Wagon 6 months ago SO WHAT it tastes the same fresh or stale. I was saving it for some Emergency only I figured the Emergency might come on the bowel level not on the level of my Last Meal on Earth but I say NUTS to that—a Emergency is a Emergency do we agree? I am hungry so I eat! You live until you die do we Agree? and as long as I am in Control in my own Apartment in my Final Hours and if I want my last supper to be a bowl of Uncle Sam laxative dry cereal so I go out on a full stomach THEN THAT IS HOW IT IS GOING TO BE!! I am not going to let John Newberry with his polite manners & his cut-throat Razor ruin my Healthy Appetite. NUTS TO THAT.

Maybe this was the Act that opened the door that led me into my present Predicament maybe this was when I took the Fatal Step & Gravity took over from there . . . I put my Ad in the Classifieds of the Mason Examiner—

> Is the Hour of Darkness upon you? Is all
> Hope gone? No! I will blz/shds to df/dfl—
> F/C. P. Tremayne, P.O.B. 127 Mason, N.M.

The clerk on the Classified desk suggested the Abbreviations

(F/C = Free of Charge for instance) he Vowed everybody who read those ads knew all of the Abbreviations so what was the point of paying for a whole word when there was a low rate for 25 Words Or Less? I had to Agree with him on that & I figured it was a Good reason to Accept a case if a hopeless person understood the code of my Ad.

I got Mrs. Roderiguez to check my P.O.B. & see if any mail was there for me and guess what there was. Right off I received 6 Cries of Help. I read each one of them with care each one of them was a heartache wrapped in a envelope. If I was going to be any Good at all I had to use the Powers of my Mind first & my Heart second so I Decided to act on all of them but strictly in Alphabetical Order.

My 1st Case was a runaway teenage girl her name is Charmagne Abercorn. Her Father (Mr. Al Abercorn of Lot 8, Deauville Trailer Court, Mason) wrote to me & told me of his 14 Year old Daughter who got Involved with bad types in the old business district of Mason and he has not seen hide or hair of her in 7 weeks.

I wrote a few Fine Words on a post card to Mr. Abercorn so maybe the Fatal Act was when I pushed my Reply down in the mailbox. All I told him was Dear Mr. Abercorn I am on the Case & I signed it Sincerely, Peter Tremayne. I walked across the street to the bus stop where a Number 37 rode me all the way down to those broken buildings that start on Flower Ave. & line up like Rotten Teeth on a crooked jawbone just a gulp away from the East 8th.

I had no Worry I did not Care if I had to go back that way this time I had my Purpose to light my way plus it was broad daylight & all I was going to do was flatfoot it up & down the sidewalks to get the Feel of the lay of the land. Before that morning I never rode the 37 so far down I always got off at the Rexall Drugstore by the Ortega Mall maybe 10 stops away. It might as well be the Grand Canyon between the places.

Down there with the Garbage of beer cans and Hostess Twinkie wrappers etc. which I stepped into right off the Bus I looked up at the sky just to check on it—how could it be the same dry blue clean blue sky that stretched over the Ortega Mall it must be a

Different one here hung over that greasy asphalt & those corrugated shutters. Not that open light it was one more wall above like in the Bus Station yes it is the Bus Station all over . . . A place just Bleeds into people as much as people bleed into a place so I was starting to get the picture of what I was Up Against.

You know on the licence plates it says NEW MEXICO LAND OF ENCHANTMENT—If that is a Fact then the people down where I went must be the trolls & gnomes all right the Little People of the enchanted land with a Curse on them to live in the beer cans & Twinkie Wrappers. Or at least I do not think the losers live in the same Country as the rest of us.

Many Juveniles WHO SHOULD BE IN SCHOOL float in & out of a liquor store called The Lucky Dime I believe it is on the corner of 8th & Adams. Check down there or at Travis & 8th. On 8th anyway on the East side of Main. I ordered a Boloney Sandwich across from there in a coffee shop I ate it very slow & staked them out. (I.e. this is a Good plan tried & true also my ankles got hot & puffy so a little rest could help them.)

Which is a Tactic that paid off after 10 Minutes Because then I eyeballed my Suspect. She is a short girl very plump & I will say with a face too soft & young to be sucking on a can of Schlitz. The Pink Hair on her also I never saw such a Color walking around before maybe on a Munchkin in the movies maybe in Munchkinland not in the Real World! Therefore I followed my Hunch likewise I followed her around the corner.

The further you go the Worse it looks down in that Area I recall it is on East Main where the empty Warehouse is. All the windows Smashed out etc. but a Castle to a runaway Child. In the back is a Ravine full of old refrigerators shopping carts Plastic bags the Garbage Of The Ages piled up & beyond that is a hole in the wall. The Anus of the building with garbage stuffed up in it such a Pathetic Sight that is where she Led Me.

When she started to search inside every greasy pizza box & Twinkie wrapper I stopped her by a big Hello plus I handed her the other $\frac{1}{2}$ of my boloney & cheese wrapped in a napkin.

"I can't talk to you," she said.

Like a vending machine I am still holding out the wrapped up sandwich. "It's fresh boloney & cheese. You should eat something fresh. On me."

"You better get out of here. I don't want a sandwich. If you want something go talk to Carlos."

"Who's Carlos? Who's that?"

"If you want something go ask at the Dime. I can't talk to you."

"You don't have to talk to me."

"Damn straight I don't. If you want a date you gotta talk to Carlos."

"Can Carlos tell me where Charmagne is?"

"You want Charmagne?"

"I've got some money to give her." And I saw a jumpy twitch in her eye for a second it looked like she was going to break the Rules & tell me more but some boy's Voice broke in very quick from behind.

"Let's party!" He came he saw he conked me.

I woke up face down in the Heat Waves of that Dump I had to spit something sticky out of my mouth it was a Baby Ruth wrapper. From a bird's eye View I was just 1 more piece of garbage shoveled up on the stinking heap. But in my Heart where it counted I knew I was 100% Different from the pizza pie crusts melon rinds beer cans & assorted trash I had a memory of Events! I moved a little I felt around I just sank in deeper right where I was lying like a Limp Salami with my empty wallet stuffed into my open pants.

This Pain creased up my skull it felt like he was trying to scalp me with a broken bottle. Did I yell!

"Don't be a baby," Dr. Godfrey ordered me.

"You said this wasn't going to hurt."

"No I didn't."

"Yes you did. You *quack*."

He dropped his Tweezers back into the metal tray he took a step away from me & folded his arms on his chest. "Finish it yourself."

I fingered around my wound which was still halfway open. He Slapped my hand off it.

"Now I've got to disinfect it all over again." He swabbed & dabbed me. "They can hear you out there in the waiting room Ray."

"Will you tell me what the hell I said so I'll apologize so you can finish what you started here so I can go home for God's sake?" He handed me a Tissue so I wiped off my wet neck with it then he Grabbed it out of my hands before I even *thought* about wiping off my open Wound.

"You called me a—" he dropped his Voice he whispered the word to me, "—*quack*. Let me tell you Ray if I was a—*quack*—I just would've stuck 2¢ worth of gauze on there covered it up with a piece of masking tape charge you $25 for it & then the last word you'd hear from me would be NEXT!"

The examination room door opened enough for Miss Petersen to Poke her head in. "Do you want the next patient now Doctor?"

"No. I'm not finished with Mr. Green's major operation yet." By the little downward bend on the corner of her mouth Dr. Godfrey Recognized he used a gruff manner on her without meaning it so his next words to her he made Polite & Soft. "In 10 minutes. Give me 10 more minutes." He nodded and so she gave back a tight little smile & shut the door behind her.

"I'm sorry I opened my mouth," I made Peace.

"I'm putting in 11 stitches around a cut the size of a nickel. It's practically micro-surgery." He sniffed and picked up his Tools again. "I just want you to appreciate it that's all."

"I do appreciate it. But is it all right if I sound off when I'm in pain?"

"A big boy like you."

"You said it wasn't going to hurt."

"I always say that. If I didn't nobody'd hold still for treatment." I swallowed my Yelp but it Snorted out of my nose when he pulled another Stitch tight. "Think. What would be the result if every time I treated somebody I said hold still now this is going to hurt—? Panic in the streets. I'd be out of business. A stampede

131

of patients out my door. They'd all die of septicemia and gangrene and I'd die of starvation."

"There's a price tag on total honesty," I said in General but I was thinking in Particular. I heard the snip of his scissors.

"There," he said. "Want to see?"

I sat up I was facing the mirror over his washbasin and he held up another mirror behind my head like I was in a Barbershop. I saw a black circle it looked like thin Barbed Wire there in the shape of a Nickel up on the top of my head. Maybe it was a ballpeen hammer that bastard kid Conked me with. Also I saw I was in Strong Need of a haircut or at least a trim my hair growing like steelwool tumbleweeds out over my ears. I looked like Larry from the 3 Stooges.

"Did this really happen to you playing shuffleboard?" The Doubts in his Voice jingled like sleigh bells.

"In the quarter finals. The shufflecock ricocheted."

"Shuttlecock," he put me right.

"Shuttlecock."

"A shuttlecock is badminton."

"Aha."

"Somebody belted you one. Don't be embarrassed about it Ray." A timid Knock eeked through the door. "Just a minute!" he called over and came back to me with a Stare like a Searchlight.

"You know what a humiliation it is," I started off, "to go down from a shuffleboard injury."

Dr. Godfrey took the Cue but he did not back off all of the way. "It must've been terrible at the time."

"It was. It was terrible."

"I just hope it won't scare you into staying home alone in your apartment. You know what I mean. I mean I hope it won't keep you off the shuffleboard courts. Life can be like a game of shuffleboard sometimes."

"I'm not up to tournament shuffleboard."

"Whether you like it or not Ray your body wants to recover. And you want to waste all this marvelous molecular activity by sitting on your keister all day in front of the TV."

"Muscle cells don't replace am I right? I think there's a basic disagreement between me and my cells."

"Pick up your stick. Get back into the game," he said when he finished sewing. "Win one for Flipper."

I let myself down off the table. "O.K. Coach."

"How far back are you?"

"I'm running a soft second to a fella half my age. A pisher."

"There's no substitute for experience.'

To the Children you give a lollipop. To me you give a Pep Talk! I will say when I left your Office my cells chimed into Agreement with you Dr. Godfrey you were Correct about this I had Strategy on my side. Maybe you would not give me the same kind of Medical advice if you knew I was not going back to the Shuffleboard I was going back to the sick streets of the East 8th.

Before I made my Exit he clapped me on my back & cheered me on. "Boola boola," he said.

The Raymobile is my 1963 Ford Country Squire Station Wagon which was my coach & Chariot which now lies in a Dozen Pieces at the bottom of a canyon in Los Angeles, California. Rest In Peace My Dear Friend. That Accident was not your Fault you got driven to it. I fear the Raymobile will not run again as such this time it is beyond Redemption and maybe already what parts are not Destroyed by crushing or fire or breakage are Removed by the beach bums down that way to use for household items. The steering wheel for a flowerpot etc. they do that kind of thing in California I saw & other things on the Same Line. The Raymobile hubcaps are now a set of dinner plates very likely.

I am greatly sad Folks over the loss of this car as now I am thinking of it I think it would make a Fond Remembrance of me to my other friend Dr. Godfrey. If I am Honest I force myself to say mainly I am sad about the Absence of the Raymobile from the roads because I Remember it was my sturdy Companion over the years very Reliable except when wet for Some Reason.

I left it sitting in the Garage behind my Apartment maybe it was parked there 6 Months at that time since I did not have any Business during then that Beckoned me Farther than a Good walk only to the Rexall and baby aspirins I can carry in my pocket I do not Need the cargo space of the Raymobile. It did not need many attempts to fire her up & after some whining some Complaint by her she ran very Big Titted indeed.

Now the car is on my Mind again I must put it on the Record the Fact I was Especially very fond of the side panels which were pretend wood & they made a Contrast pleasant to the eye against the pale yellow color of the Bodywork. Even better than actual wood since it Dented it did not Splinter when hit so on the Occasions when Necessary it only needed spooning & hammering it did not Require any trees to be chopped down Live & Let Live used to be my Motto.

On the night in question I had to jump start the Raymobile off the Jap job which belongs to the couple in Number 2 (which if you ask me Number 2 is my Opinion of that Jap job: all the Trunk Space of a shopping cart under the Hood a motor in it that Squeaks plus bumpers & doors etc. made out of Plastic or some such thin Material!) Imagine this our 2 arch-enemies from World War II yet now they are selling us cars radios cameras & all kinds of luxury items! Is this the fair wind-up of such a War fought for our Freedom? We won the Right to lead the way with all kinds of advanced Luxury Items and look at how far we fell. Maybe next year at the Rexall you will buy electric toothbrushes from Cuba because nobody around here has any Idea about E Pluribus Unum anymore it is just every stinker for himself. No wonder the U.S.A. is going down down down nobody stands by the Pledge of Alligience nobody lives by it. This is not a place I Recognize anymore.

After the Jap jump start I went around the block a couple of Times to get back used to the Feel of driving also to Remind the Raymobile how it Feels with me back in the Driver's Seat. Headlights CHECK—Oil CHECK—Gas tank FULL—Brakes CHECK—Adjust seat COMFORTABLE—Ignition ON—So after a Bout of sputtering stalling and 1 or 2 False Starts we went rolling on our way with everything under Control. In 1963 the Raymobile rolled off the Assembly Line in Detroit over 25 Years ago which makes it by Human Terms equal to 175 years old. The

2 of us put together we had over 249 Years of Experience so my Confidence was to the utmost.

I left the familiar landmarks of Pecan St. behind me & the Landscape looked very Different it made me glad I was Viewing it from a moving car. Very dark shadows of the sides of low buildings cut across parking lots & loading areas it looked like I was driving past the backyards of all of these places with what was going on going on on the other side out of my Sight. The dark side of the Moon it felt like also what with the potholes like Craters in the street & the sidewalk cracking away into dirt.

A red light Stopped me for a minute Good thing too because a souped up pick-up truck full of screaming Teenagers came around the corner in front of me practically tilted up & over on 2 wheels so close when they came around a couple of them in the back of it Banged their fists on the Hood of my car! I will not say this Event shook me up at all but I did wait to catch my Breath for a second or two after my light turned green. I hit the gas and another crowd of the little monsters Waltzes out into the street so I hit the brakes hard and just miss the Butts of their bluejeans by a $\frac{1}{2}''$. What was it down there that night a Juvenile Delinquent Convention? At least 1 Good thing did come out of that Accident besides the Fact that I did not run them over I saw how my Reflexes were pretty sharp all right.

Before I blinked twice I was back driving down East Main where streets and sidestreets stayed busy with people in the doorways of stores open for Business late. The Ortega Mall I will say had nothing on the old business district regarding business. I did not find a Parking place on the street near the Lucky Dime Liquor Store even after I putt-putted around the block there a few times so against my best Judgement I parked the Raymobile in the sandlot right behind it. I picked up a strong Suspicion about the Safety of that place but like the saying says If Not Now—When? If Not Here—Where? If Not Who—Me? so I locked it & left it.

I did not go right in I Observed first I Cased. Under the streetlights the Stucco of it was the color of sulphur just a 1 storey cube of it Connected to a telephone pole on the corner. The windows in the back shined with lights inside I thought *hmm very bright & shiny for a storage room.* The back door opened up while I was just standing there Casing and a woman wrapped in a blanket came outside & Squatted down there & from across the sandlot I heard the zizzing of her pissing. It did not look like she saw me & I hoofed it into the street very quick.

Nor I was not Worried about the Chance I was going to get Identified as a outsider when I Returned to the streets of the East 8th. Let them leer & jeer & mock me THAT IS EXACTLY HOW I WANT THEM TO THINK! How I am not so Dangerous is the best part of my Disguise.

But 5 minutes on the sidewalk & what I saw was my Disguise was not complete. For I was not going to walk into The Lucky Dime like Mr. John Wayne (who had the actual name of MARION MORRISON so I was not the 1st person in History to change my name for Professional Reasons!) i.e. Slam my fist down on the counter & demand Satisfaction. Nor I am not Mexican so down where they are swarming I had to make a Effort and fit in—

To wit my Bermuda Shorts were the main item which Attracted the Curious glances from the Senors & Senoritas so the question in my Mind was how do I locate Charmagne & not Stir Up the locals?

The Answer jumped out at me from the Salvation Army Surplus Store i.e. a junk shop of Garments. What the Customers had on while they were browsing looked Identical to what was on the racks & in the big cardboard boxes in there I Believe the population around Main Street just passes all the same Garments around with no new ones ever coming into it. Nor I do not mean serapes & sombreros either I mean I saw a emerald green Safari Suit which was probably on its 3rd time around.

Which was a Garment appealing to me at 1st Sight it appeared to be a very well cut one with Sharp Creases in the pants diamond shaped lapels a belt in the back plus pockets all over in Different sizes I Imagined how they could come in handy. Also it looked Comfortable for any tricky Situation I could encounter but most important it was dry cleaned. On the way in I saw a few other Senors with similar suits on but none of them had this pleasing shade of Emerald Green. The whole thing only cost me $4.50 plus I did not have to turn in my Bermuda Shorts which I Expected. So I walked out of there wearing it with my Bermudas in a paper bag & 3 steps down the sidewalk I Recognized I was attracting the Glances but I believe they were not of the Curious Variety: from the Senors I received silent Respect from the way they pretended to Ignore my Presence & from the Senoritas I received silent sighs when they did not look into my eyes.

I am not kidding myself nor I do not want to pay Compliments on my own Behalf which I do not Deserve I have to be Honest here & admit that it was not the Unleashed Power of my Personality which challenged them into Silence it also was the color of my Safari Suit. Emerald Green is not a typical color in that Mexican part of Mason for why I do not have a Clue as safari suits are Plentiful. I Noticed this Fact while I took my time walking toward the Lucky Dime Liquor Store and in my Entire walk of 4 Blocks I did not see a green leaf growing in a pot or out of a crack in the sidewalk not the Bloom of green that changes the Rays of the Sun into a Breath of fresh Air e.g. This came into my Mind while I was noticing the Smell of boiled fat just holding still in the Air no matter which way I turned. It looked like all the greenery in Mason ended on the other side of Main right at the Borders of the East 8th like the ground on this side was full of Poison.

Missing was any Grass Green i.e. of wet lawns which I Remember calms the Nerves instead they had skid marks in their View in the dust & tar & grease of their streets. Also Jungle Green was absent not even a potted fern on a peon's porch to Remind them of the Wild Forces of Nature which can swallow a city faster than a peon can build one. Or soft Moss Green nothing was Moss Green either which spreads out in Peace & Quiet. Or did any of them Appreciate the Fact that Blue Green was the first Living Color of all Time the color of the Bug who was their real Adam & Eve? I feel a little Gratitude from them might be the tune to play on their marimbas if they saw Evidence to remind them of the color they owe their whole lives to that Blue Green speck of bupkis swimming in a Sea Green sea!

This time when I approached the screen door of the Lucky Dime I was ready to hear the Locals start beating their marimbas & shaking their maracas with Joy to see that shade of green flashing by to remind them when all Hope is Gone how help can leap from the shadows to shine by their side—¡No Senor! It no eez Emerald Green! ¡Si Senorita! Eeeez Ray Green!

El Rayo Verde to you Carlos El Rayo Verde to you.

The neon Dime on top of the roof kept on going through its Motions flipping over Red White & Blue both sides Heads. Maybe it was just a sign Flashing the message Heads I Win—Tails You Lose that was the Attitude of that place. This is the Time we live in.

While I had to keep my Peepers Peeled for sight or Sound of any hide or hair of Charmagne Abercorn I also had to cover my cover by hiding behind some kind of Innocent business. In the Lucky Dime that meant browsing up & down the 2 aisles to pick up 6 packs of beer twinkies frozen pizzas etc. & browsing over Magazines in the Magazine Rack I saw far in the back. I was making up my mind standing in the door about what order was most Realistic to do these Actions in i.e. magazines first then food after or food first then the magazines when it was a crush of shoulders around me like a Breaker pushed me inside. For the first 6 or 7 Feet of it I was not moving under my own Power I was Concentrating on keeping my Balance (I did & I wound up leaning over the frozen food so the Pizza was my 1st ploy).

The last thing I Felt like doing was Purchasing any food since as soon as I was in my nostrils stuffed up from the smells of sweaty armpits & chili peppers or some kind of Spicy thing. That herd of dirty T-shirts sweat shiny jowls & rolling shoulders & gassy bellies pushed up my Aisle & down the other one so this was Life in a termite nest! This tunnel leads to another one & the other tunnels down below. The workers dig out the dirt & carry the food and somewhere in this Colony is the Royal Chamber of the biggest Termite of them all the one they all circle around the one who feeds on their money.

In the front next to the door a little Mex girl maybe 8 years old worked the Cash Register she Played it like a toy Piano. What with all the Senors packed in there it looked easy to slip a Twinkie into a pocket or so but nobody was going to cross that Tina she had eyes on her like nailheads. Also I do not Believe there was higher than the National Average of Honesty amid the Lucky Dime customers only I Observed a Feeling pressing down upon every brow in there i.e. the Weight of feeling her eyes like a painting following them around the room. Not 1 Twinkie got lifted not 1 nose got picked.

By way of casing the placing I picked up a Few Bargains. Besides the ½ price Donettes I did not see very much to Interest my Taste Buds but I Pretended I was stocking up—a quart of milk a few Baby Ruth bars some chedder cheese—I picked out these Items while I Observed a pair of young boys hanging around the Magazines Drooling over the girlies. I did not understand their Precise words since they spoke to each other in their Native Tongue of Mexican but I Imagine I am not very far off the Target if I Report they had a Conversation about what they could do with those bosoms etc. if they got such a Chance.

While my eyes & ears stayed on them some other Mexicans maybe ranch hands e.g. squeezed past me without any Excuse Me or Excuso. They went through a door next to the Magazine rack it was a place the 2 muchachos wanted to see into. Before the door shut in their faces they Waved & Called Out a name— Carlos.

Ah-ha. Carlos was 1 word of Mexican I could Recognize. They moved over when I swallowed my Embarrassment & stepped in next to them. I saw Carlos stocked many enticing books. They showed more uses & Positions of the Female figure I could image from my Personal Experience but I did not think the same over the titles—CUM! or BUNCH O' BOOBS or LESBOS IN RUBBER.

Up that close I could hear what was going on behind the rack there i.e. manly Chuckling etc. which only Calmed Down a little bit when the men came out again shaking their heads & grinning Back & Forth. They held on to the little brown paper packages like Prayerbooks between their hands.

So I fit in I followed the Leader I grabbed a few of those girlie magazines to cover my True Intention and I took them over with

139

my Baby Ruths etc. to naileyed Tina at the Cash Register. So What? She sees more of those spicy covers in a day than I saw in my entire Life but she did look me over a little when the total price came out to $67.00.

I did not carry so much Cash on me so I asked her if my personal check was going to Satisfy her. I can not take the Credit for what Happened next it was not part of my Plan I was not even Improvising here I was just out of cash which in Ordinary Circumstances can be embarrassing & a Misfortune but not this time. She pushed a button under the Counter & I heard a buzzer Sound very fuzzy in the back.

A sturdy peasant Blocked the doorway next to the Magazines he just hung there for a second then came over to us. He looked like somebody all thumbs carved him out of a tree trunk he was all arms & legs very short & thick. Maybe he used Curlers on his hair it rolled out under a tight scarf & maybe his little Gold Earrings made him think he was Long John Silver. But his Personality was not sturdy he was a bag of Nerves like a hophead. How old was he 30 or 40 or 50 how can you tell? Cut him open & count the rings.

I Observed all of these Details while she Explained the situation to him & she called him Carlos and meanwhile he Nodded at her & checked me over by little twitches of eyework & he called her Tina. He put his square hand square on top of my Pile of magazines & approved of my Taste in literature by a little sidewise smile.

CARLOS   You show me a credit card?
ME: You mean I can charge this?
CARLOS: No man. For I.D.
ME: What—is there a age limit? You think I'm too young to see this spicy stuff? Or I'm too old for it . . . ?

I tapped my Ticker & Carlos gave me half a Laugh so now we are on Terms the pair of us. I fished around in the nooks & crannies of my paper bag to locate the Correct pocket in my

Bermudas & came up with my Mastercharge & Slapped it down on the counter for both of them to Admire it.

Carlos made up his Mind pretty quick he showed me a shrug with a bent little Frown which told me *My friend just ask me how much I care if this check bounces.* He squeezed Tina's shoulder he shook it very gentle.

CARLOS: He looks kosher. Ring heem up.

Was he trying to get to me or what? Tina was not so sure about me she had to Rake me over by a final naileyed Stare she Memorized my mug. Carlos had to Nudge her to make with the ringing up already. But I had to fish around some more before I Located my checkbook & she pushed a pen toward me so I could write it.

TINA: Put your address on the back.

I wrote down Mrs. Calusco's address then I Signed the check with the name Peter Tremayne so what so it bounces on him I was going to dump those magazines in the nearest Garbage Can! Carlos tapped the top girlie book on the pile CUM!

CARLOS: That's a good one man. I got it in my collection.
ME: I never saw it before.
CARLOS: Cherry. No lie. You like different stuff?

Good. If I went on with him Talking I had a Chance I was going to hear some juicy Clues regarding a particular Teenage runaway girl first name of Charmagne last name of Abercorn.

ME: Variety is the spice of Life.
CARLOS: No lie man. You into water & power?

Tina handed me back my Mastercharge with no Smile from her or any show of any Feeling True or False. I tried out my Gracias

on her to Win her Over but mainly I wanted Carlos to hear it
when I raised my eyebrows I Smacked my lips.

ME: Water & power? Are you kidding? Sure. I'm the
             original water & power man.

What the hell did he mean Water & Power? Welp I was going
to find out if I Liked it or Not. Carlos tilted his head to Invite me
to follow him This Way so for sure he did not so far stumble on
the Actual Fact I was the pure hearted Defender of the Defenseless
etc. who was there buying his girlie books & showing my Interest
in Water & Power for 1 purpose & 1 secret Purpose only i.e. to
Rescue a little girl from him who should better be home with her
Mother cooking dinner instead of using herself to further this
mutt's Immoral ends. For this Reason I went with him.
     Before we stepped into the back he Introduced himself like a
Gentleman by the magazine rack.

CARLOS: I'm Carlos.
ME: I'm Peter.
CARLOS: Pedro. All right man. This way. You like flicks?

Flicks. Ah-ha.
     About 1 foot past the door a Little Room is on the side there
which maybe 2 broom closets can fit Inside if you leave out all of
the Brooms. Carlos laid his finger on his lips to Show me to shush
and I heard the Sounds of moans & groans coming from in there.
When I looked in I saw a fat man like a load of wet Cement
poured into a beat up Easy Chair. He was in front of a T.V. Set
with a movie on it of naked girls Touching each other and that
was the Source of all the Moans but the source of all the Groans
was this old man who was playing knick-knack paddy-whack on
his own bone rubbing & twisting it back & forth in his Pants.
     Carlos got creased up holding in a big Laugh that was building
up in his gut but that fat old man did not Hear it. He did not See
us either I saw his eyes they were just 2 balls of cold chicken fat

in his head. Carlos pulled me Closer he gave me a Better View of him.

CARLOS: Sssh . . . He think he eez all alone.
FATTY: Mmmmnnnggg . . . MmmmnnnGGG . . . MmmNNNnnnGGG!

He rocked back & forth in his squealing chair all of the Screws squealing to get out from under him the chair Squealing to get out from under him . . . then Carlos pounced on him slap happy slaps on his hunched over shoulders.

CARLOS: Finito Baba?
FATTY: MMMMNNNNGGGGNNNNMMMM!!

He batted around with his Fists Batted at the air but Carlos Ducked him for fun then grabbed his wrists nor he did not shake them very gentle.

CARLOS: Finito Baba?

Fatty handed over a $5.00 bill then he pushed out right past me I do not think that he Sensed my Presence there but I sure Sensed his—the Air he pulled behind him pulled in warm smells of sweat & bleach.

CARLOS: Relatives they are always embarrassing no?
ME: I'm not interested in that kind of thing Carlos.
CARLOS: Ay no! I know! That's just especial for my Baba. Especial favor for heem! Eez my huncle.

Carlos pressed his wrists together maybe to show me how his hands are Tied when it comes to Family. Maybe he was Telling me that his fat old Uncle went Blind in jail & this Special Favor is his Good Deed of the Day. Or maybe he meant if he did not Deliver this cheap favor the alter cocker was going to blow the gaff on him say For Instance to the Border Patrol and Family or no Family back across the Mexican border Carlos was going to go with Uncle Sam's footprint on his behind. A Gesture you can Interpret in many ways.

Carlos made a Motion with his open arms & open hands showing me the way into the easy chair. I did not want to sit on the Steamy Cushion were Baba just Released himself but also I did not wish to supply Carlos with any Reason he could Doubt me. So I sat on the edge of the chair real Eager Beaver to see his line of Specialities.

CARLOS: Water & power right?
ME: Right.
CARLOS: Right on.

He was making like a Gopher digging into a cardboard box flush with Magazines which had some order maybe by Alphabet maybe by Type some on their sides some standing up. When Carlos turned around he handed me a Stack of the Dirty Books I was waiting for.

CARLOS: Ones on the bottom cost more. Ones on top—
              that one . . . that one . . . & that one—those
              cost 20.

I did not Believe the Proof before my eyes of such a thing going on in a Magazine! What did I talk myself into? *I'm the original water & power man*—vey is mir! This is the kind of character Carlos thinks I am?

On one page you got a Woman bent over a chair naked with her face in Ecstasy because . . . because . . . because a naked man (her Husband?) is standing behind her with a ENEMA BAG in one hand & with his other one he is pushing the HOSE up her I do not know where! His face is in Ecstasy too!

On the next page is a true Story about her it is titled "Linda's Sperm Diet" which I did not stop my Observations & read further I turned the page over & what did I see? More Photos of naked noodniks in Ecstasy because they have ENEMA HOSES rammed up their Keisters!

I guess I did not hear Carlos leave the room but he did so I was in there by myself to Sample his Merchandise further. I put that top magazine on the floor and flipped the pages of the next one down. It did not have any Articles it was all Pictures very similar to a Comic Book i.e. Photos telling a simple Story of jealousy & revenge amid a big orgy of ENEMA PEOPLE. How did they hold still for those pictures already tell me that!?! I did not have to read their lines to get the drift of the Episode which was in Mexican anyway and so far I only knew 2 words in Mexican: "Gracias" & "Carlos" which words I did not feel the Urge to use. In the first Photo was a nice looking couple saying Hello to another nice looking couple at the front door of their Apartment. Both of the Wives they are Dressed Up in hot pants and a frog hops up into my Throat when I see what the husbands have on of course Safari Suits . . . but it does not matter what they have on because halfway down the page all of the Hot Pants & Safari Suits they get cast Aside & instead of a Fondue Set out comes the hostess with a ENEMA BAG for one & all! I believe I got to see every room in that nice Apartment at least twice with his husband in enema Ecstasy with that other wife & visa versa this wife & that wife Together on the sofa one of them with her naked fanny Hoisted Up holding it wide open so her girlfriend can grease up & slide in with a solid foot of pink rubber hose & nozzle—she who holds the Water also holds the Power!

I dropped that one down on the floor & I pulled out one from the bottom of the Pile I Thought how much Worse does this get how low does it go? Now I wish I was Blind like that Baba I wish I had chicken fat instead of my eyes because I can not get those Photos out of my Memory. They did not have a Rhyme or a Reason with them they did not tell any Story which led from the first one to the last one they just went one after the other. But behind the Scenes I saw a Story i.e. the Who What Where & Why of it of those photos which did not show funloving couples bent over naked in Ecstasy under their Rubber Bags this time they were little children and they were not in Ecstasy they were in torture. On a tile bathroom floor somewhere & half in half out of a shower. On some kitchen table tied up like a Thanksgiving turkey. On Mama's naked lap.

If anybody could tell me where I could get a High Colonic in the area I am sure Carlos was the man to ask but when he came back to me all of a sudden my Constipation was a Blessing.

> CARLOS: You see anything you want? Hey that's a good book man. Very hard to get it. Very hot. That's 75 but if you like 3 books I can make a discount.

At that moment I was glad I Invested in that Milk which I drank a little because in the meantime my throat closed up.

> ME: Where did you get these books?
> CARLOS: You want a glass for that man?
> ME: No. I'm perfectly fine.
> CARLOS: I get new ones all the time. You check with me Pedro. I get you cherry books man. The bess. Mexican. Whenever man. All the time my mule get them across.

Carlos did not want to stay on that Topic of Conversation and I did not Feel very chatty myself I was just sitting there trying to clear my Mind from those Pictures but I did not Succeed that way. It was practically a Relief to my Entire System when my silence encouraged Carlos to plug in a "flick" on his T.V. so I may Sample it.

The title of it was called "Rubber Maids" and the setting was a bathroom decorated with Mirrors on the walls & Mirrors on the ceiling. I did not have any Idea before that day from looking over the pages of my Usual reading matter that any girl holds still for this kind of business. I was looking at those magazines come to Life with a dusky girl in a suit of Rubber but not something you see on The Undersea World Of Jaques Cousteau! I do not Believe that even a Frenchman with their crazy Fashions over there would put this suit on for the flap between her legs was open

146

to the world . . . which she kindly did the splits to show the camera then about 1 second later in comes her girlfriend in a Rubber Dress & she knows just what to do she knows what Miss Bathroom Ballerina wants & she gives it to her i.e. she squeezes a coke bottle into the flap & further! This I get to see from many Artistic angles at the same time due to the many Mirrors in there but I did not have the Stomach left in me to watch anymore.

I Scared myself from the terrible Idea that maybe one of those Rubber Maids was Charmagne when I heard a bump on the other side of the thin wall behind my head & the Sound of a very angry Curse. Carlos leaned out of the doorway he was hanging on the frame to face the back room. He yelled to make it quiet then he pulled himself back to explain it all to me.

CARLOS: I don't like swearing man. It's no nice for my little
           girl to hear words like that.

He nodded in the Direction of the store where Tina was. Now it was quiet & it was back to Business with me.

CARLOS: Look man I got this rubber flick for 50. I got some
           water & power ones for 70 but we can deal on 2
           up O.K.? You ready to make up your mind?
ME: Actually I've been looking for a film by the title
           of Hotsy Totsy Girls In Their Underpants.

Maybe you can tell I said the first spicy words that came into my Mind but it made Carlos scratch his head & try to Remember if he ever had that particular blockbuster in his Stock so my Confidence regarding my cover came back to me in a strong manner.

CARLOS: I don't theenk I ever seen that one. What hap-
           pens?
ME: That's all right skip it. How about Hoity Toity
           Goity The Goil From South Foity?

147

CARLOS: Never heard of that one my man. You know a lot
          of flicks Pedro.

A couple of Contrary Ideas sat on a teeter-totter in his Mind:
maybe I was a Vice Cop in plain clothes (my safari suit) going
to break up his Business or lean on him for a piece of the
Action . . . or on the other side maybe I was what I looked like
on the Surface i.e. a very Dedicated fan of his Merchandise who
was ready to be soaked for a few Extra pesos. Behind his eyes I
saw it teeter & I saw it totter then one side came down hard &
held still.

CARLOS: You want to watch us make one?
ME: Which?
CARLOS: I made that rubber one.
ME: Get away.
CARLOS: Swear to God man I did.
ME: Go on. Get away.
CARLOS: I still got some of those mirrors!
ME: Welp I'd enjoy seeing that Carlos seeing how you
          get the camera in and so on behind the scenes . . .
CARLOS: O.K. 10 minutes for $25.
ME: With all the rest of the things I bought? Don't you
          think I'm entitled to a discount?
CARLOS: $25 is a discount. O.K. let's call it 50 for the books
          an' I geeve you $17 credit on any 2 flicks you
          want.

He must have a Brain on him like a Chinese Abacus.

ME: Can I make up my mind after I watch a little?
          Maybe I'll put my order in for this one you're
          making now.
CARLOS: Maybe you want to star in theese one when you
          see my girl . . .

148

Carlos led me into the back of the Lucky Dime & here I will describe the Situation I saw going on—

2 floodlights poured their hearts out into the middle of that square room hot Light was spilling down into a round pool amid shadows all around. With a box spring Mattress on a metal Double Bed. I stayed back in the Shadows out of the way & my back up against a stack of boxes & crates—liquor boxes beer boxes & crates of Twinkies I guess which was my Advantage point to see all yet be Unseen.

Charmagne wriggled around on the Bed by herself with her thumb in her mouth & her other one somewhere up under her terrycloth robe. Pretty as a picture in fact pretty as the picture of her I had Rolled Up in the back of my Bermudas Good Thing I remembered it was in there or blooey good-bye to my Innocent cover of Pedro the Pervert.

Carlos got busy turning the Focus etc. on his camera (a very Expensive job it looked like too Japanese with Lights on & dials) & futzing with the height of the stand so he was in a Position to get a very Artistic angle of Charmagne's fanny.

CARLOS: Action time. Party time Charmagne!
CHARMAGNE: It's Miller time!

When she Rolled Over I saw she was Sucking on a bottle of Beer which had a Baby Bottle Nipple stuck on the end of it. Carlos pried it away from her and Tugged on her robe but all Charmagne did was give him a little moan like he was her Mama waking her up in the morning to get dressed for School only it was Undressed he wanted her—so he grabbed a piece of the robe & he rolled her out of it a game which gave her a Laugh. After I only saw her in her photo in her School Dress now I was seeing all of her hide & hair I had to take this Calm & be Careful I did not make my Move too soon or else blooey.

She had a very giggly laugh on her Pure from the little girl which was still inside her. Also I Observed she did not have any front teeth maybe in the Dental Regard she was a slow Developer or maybe they got Knocked Out what was the Difference the

Effect on me was here was this teenage girl with a big titted woman's body & the face of a 8 year old it was very Confusing to my Feelings . . . Until Carlos got the Scene going by calling out "Action!" & I Concentrated on the true Story behind the Scenes.

Charmagne let her thumb stray back into her mouth while she just forgot about her other hand she left it flat on the Bed her fingers spread out with no Life in them. She was staring at the Ceiling or up into the light lying back waiting for the next thing to Happen.

The next thing which happened was that a naked boy stepped out of the Shadows on the other side of the bed he was holding a rope in his hands he let it hang down Loose next to his dingus & he climbed up on the bed. He dangled his rope he Dangled his dingus over Charmagne's mouth.

CARLOS: Tease her man. Swing your dick down. Yeah . . . yeah man . . . Do it with the rope . . . Up & down it on her . . .

He was on his kees on top of her now he Twisted around and dragged the rope down her legs & I saw who he was he was Tony. He upped it & he downed it he Stroked his rope up over her Bosoms & around her Bosoms but she did not push him away or pull him on she just rolled her eyes & Sucked her thumb

CARLOS: Move your thumb girl! Ay caramba! How's Tony gonna get his dick in?

She dropped her thumb & opened wide here comes a big Surprise.

CARLOS: Yeah beautiful . . . You want it babe. You want it . . . Go on down man! Ay caramba . . . beautiful . . .

Now Tony starts pushing his skinny hips up & down I see he has a Ferocious Tiger Tattoo on his fanny very manly except he

150

Reminds me of Gypsy Rose Lee with those hips bumping & grinding. He ties Charmagne's hands with his rope on the bedpost it was Terrible to watch this it is Terrible to Remember but it was worse to watch him sink down & push his dingus very hard into her mouth between her lips he pulls it halfway out again & down in again with her head up with her neck all stiff & joining him.

TONY: Baby . . . Baby . . . Baby . . . Aaoh . . . Suck
              it . . . Suck me . . . Mmm-nnn . . .
CHARMAGNE: Mmm-mmm-mmm-ah-mmm-ah-mmm . . .
              (Etc.)

I have seen Oil Paintings which portray Young Love in Different poses and a few of them I will say can be very spicy yet beautiful but Tony & Charmagne did not Remind me of 2 naked Cupids they reminded me of dogs in the Street. Maybe the Sounds of theirs came from real feelings & Emotions but I doubt it I Believe they had to act up in front of Carlos in front of his Camera. So I can not tell you the True source of their Moaning & Groaning but I can tell you how it Sounded to me it Sounded like dirty animals.

I Remember all the Details of the Events coming now Because this blockbuster is now appearing in slow motion in my Mind I can not help it. I Believe the Effects of panic are very well known i.e. the Effects on a person's Nervous System & Muscles—you do not know your own Strength under Panic which is the reason a frail Female will be Blessed with the muscle power of 10 Males when a car pins her tiny tot under a wheel she has the Strength to Rescue him. This kind of Panic boiled my Blood at this moment it Blessed Me with muscles of steel & fists of iron—

I made my Move I landed on the bed behind Tony I pulled his arms backwards I almost Broke them out of their Sockets.

TONY: Aargk!

CARLOS: You loco man?! You Bastard!

Before Carlos was on top of me I pulled Charmagne's hands out of the loops of rope but her only Reaction was curling up on the bed with her thumb stuck back in her mouth—Carlos & Tony are after me now around the bed over the bed like the Keystone Kops but Tony grabs my collar he Chokes me back and now both of them are Punching me around my face my arms my back—to Punish me this horny old man who wants to join in the spicy fun! But enough was not enough when Tony recognized me as who I was. He pushed me by my chest he held me off him by the length of his arm

TONY: Hey. You!

But my arm's length was longer & I Slugged him hard enough to sprain my wrist—

TONY: Aargk! Roll him Carlos! Cut him!

It was too late to roll me etc. I was the eye of the white Tornado I slugged Carlos a slug in his guts I knocked him back I fought off Tony I whipped him with his own rope—*I was not pretending anymore!* While I was busy punishing Tony Carlos got the Chance to sneak up Behind me he landed a flying kick on my spine so thank God I landed on the bed which fell to pieces under me . . . All this time Charmagne is pacing back & forth shaking her head sucking her thumb drinking tequila & talking to herself she was no Help but at least she did not help Carlos either who knocked his own Breath out when he hit the floor after his Flying Kick.

I wrapped Charmagne's robe around her Shoulders I wanted to lead her out of there.

ME: All right doll? Come on. Let's go home. I'm taking
        you home.

But she did not Appreciate altogether I was doing this business for her sake and she hauled off & smacked me on my schnozola & I went over backwards. All of a sudden I have got Tony sitting on my chest the same way I saw him before sitting on Charmagne his skinny hips his naked dingus & everything.

I was in a very Humiliating position but I was not Helpless I still had my hands free. Tony pinned me down right between the wrecked bed & Carlos's camera I had 2 Choices in my Reach—1.) a brass ball that broke off the top of the bedpost or 2.) that Camera up on a metal stand. My only Problem was I had to make up my Mind fast which was more Offensive weaponwise.

Carlos was busy on the other side of the room punching Charmagne & yelling his head off in 2 languages at her with his drift being I am a peeg & she squealed to me & now I am Causing all of this Aggravation is that a fair way to treat him her Protector the best friend a runaway girl ever had etc.

I grabbed the Leg of that camera stand it was very Sturdy I rolled out from under Tony & I pulled myself up . . . when I came back around I had that thing in my hands I cracked Tony under his chin but I was not going to stop there! What was I going to let him think I am some kind of a Cream Puff? My next Move I had it up over my head like a sledgehammer I brought it down like that too *hard* I was Aiming for his head but I think I broke his nose with it. He Crumpled Over with little bubbles of blood blowing out of a sticky hole in the middle of his face. I did that to him.

Since Carlos did not stop with tormenting Charmagne already he backed her into a corner & since that Camera was still in 1 piece (I guess those Japs know how to build a camera that can take it) & I went up behind his back but I did not Crack him over his head then that is not fair that is not Kosher . . .

ME: Carlos?

He twisted around he saw me O.K. *then* I cracked him over the head with his Fancy Camera & I heard both of them crack open

153

both of them hit the floor at the same time so how is that for a smidgeon of poetic Justice?

There was not a Sound in the room which I Heard only the quiet of nothing & no one Moving after so much Action. I stood still in the empty space between the End of one thing & the Start of something else before Events turn around & Come Back. Life in the back of the Lucky Dime was not going to be the same way it was Before I entered the scene now Carlos was going to Remember this exciting Episode he was going to think about it the next time he cranked up his Camera he was going to think *Uh-oh is that meshuggeneh kop going to return* he was going to think twice.

By some Miracle the big lights on their poles did not get knocked by 1 Inch they still blazed down hot & white in the middle of the room which was a Total Wreck: the bed turned into a pile of scrap metal under the broken box spring Mattress . . . the camera was beheaded from its stand . . . Tony was lying flat on his back moaning . . . Carlos was lying flat on his face groaning . . . I wish I had a Polaroid of it those lights showed up a Perfect Picture of how harm leads to harm. I did not feel sorry about what I did to them for if a person has the Opinion he is doing Good he does not require his Conscience to accompany him further.

A crowd of Mexican faces Floated into the doorway like a bunch of brown balloons so I read it it was my Cue to vamoose. I picked up my paper bag I put my arm around Charmagne's shoulders I hugged her tight.

ME: Do you know what's going on?
CHARMAGNE: You won.

I Hugged her again I walked her toward the front door for this Reason: I was not acting Brave nor I did not feel Proud of my handiwork I wanted to show the local congregation a Sign of how the defenseless shall be Defended & the helpless shall be Helped & the hopeless have got a Reason from now on for some Hope in this world as long as I am around . . . but the Mexican murmurings started to sound to my ears more like growlings and what with the Fact that my fight was completely knocked out of me for

154

one night no matter *how* I felt about it at the Moment on 2nd thoughts I decided a Sign for them can wait.

Good Thing too because I got to the back door with Charmagne at about the same time little Tina got to Carlos. She went down on her knees by his side she held his hand & shook it he was coming around. I felt her nailhead eyes follow me outside so when the screen door smacked shut Behind me I pushed Charmagne in a bee-line toward the Raymobile which thank God was waiting for us where I parked it in the middle of the sandlot locked up very Safe.

The arrangement of pockets all over my Safari Suit which Before I admired now I Regretted strongly since I had to go into all of them to locate my car keys. Also now Charmagne was wandering away in the Direction of the street and the Mexican Gang was leaking out of the back of the Lucky Dime oozing in my Direction with Tina in front it is surprising how sudden Danger can Stimulate a person's Memory:

IN MY BERMUDAS!

I Reached in blind I shook the paper bag Upsidedown & oh I heard my Keys jingling around in there! I made a Grab for them it was like trying to catch baby eels in a bucket! I shook my Bermudas out of the bag I saw my shiny Keys hit the Dirt—the View from under my car was not a joy To Behold it was the Exact Opposite—it was the Sight of angry feet kicking up a cloud of dust on the march coming in my Direction.

A handful of dirt I picked up with my car keys in it maybe I made a Olympic Record getting the door open! I slide in—I slide out again I circle Charmagne into the front seat and pull the door shut while that Dustcloud comes kicking up all around us . . . Only arms & fists are poking out of it Pounding on the roof on the hood on the windows rat-a-tat RAT-a-tat-TAT . . . also the Sound of shoes kicking my sidepanels—the Raymobile shakes back & forth from all the blows maybe the mob wants to turn us over like a Helpless Turtle but does the mighty Raymobile motor refuse to turn over? Does it hell! A flick of my wrist is all it takes and BLOOEY: she *backfires*! I lean on her gas pedal & oh yes she fires up roars her heart out when I throw her into Drive and did I drive! I skid out of there on a Fishtail that shakes the whole mob off us & I lose them in a spray of sand a ball of Exhaust—we spin out of the dust heading straight into the dark—I hit my headlights pull half a turn and catch Tina holding her ground like a Ghost her arms raised up high in my high beams so she pitches a rock at my windshield & I swerve—hit the sidewalk—bounce off the kerb—skid across the street—I feel my arm I think I broke it but I can still steer straight so I keep On Course I roar away into traffic up Main across Plains down Ortega toward Bea's Bakery toward Pecan St. returning with my Foes in flight & Confusion behind me—

"You *kidnapped* me." She sat up straight in the seat full of Nerve now. "That'th a felony."

"Charmagne—"

"How come you know my name?"

"Your papa honey. He mailed me a picture so I could locate you. *Kidnap*," I said it very Disgusted out of the corner of my mouth, "my God. Look at you. Your arms are like stringbeans! What do you survive on?"

No Answer.

"What about vitamins? Or milk. You drink milk regular? Maybe if you took in more calcium you wouldn't get any problems with your teeth."

"My dad knocked 'em out with a frying pan." She defied me by that Remark & she pushed it a ugly step further. "Better for blow jobth."

I Forgive her since I Believe she was still a little bit in Shock from the power of being Rescued so I did not chastise on top of it. I kept my eyes Peeled for the turnoff of the Deauville Trailer Court which appeared on the next sharp turn so I swung the car around which move did not Settle my stomach where I had Cramps expanding in me like a bunch of balloons. The gravel Crackled under the tires I slowed it down when I Heard the pebbles snapping up hitting the bodywork.

"But Charmagne I mean what kind of problems between you & your papa can be worse than that business I saw downtown?"

She pulled her robe tight around her and she tied up the belt. "They're my friendth."

"Carlos."

"Yeth."

"And that other lover boy."

"Yeth. Not anymore." She looked away from me. "Now they think I'm with you."

I put on the Brakes I leaned over a little I shook her shoulder very gentle. "Your friends make you do those things on the camera? Carlos hit you around. I saw how he hit you."

"My dad hith me but I don't get paid for it."

"He's just worried for you how your life is going to come out. Fathers can't stand it if they see a waste of a life it kills them when they see that. Charmagne that's a biological fact I'm telling you. Does your papa know anything what you did away from home?"

She shrugged. "It's jutht thex! Not a thnuff movie! Carloth won't even *thell* thnuff flickth!"

Snuff movie? I did not even want to Ask. I saw what they did down there with Enemas I did not want to hear what they did with Snuff!

I pulled in through the chainlink gate of the Trailer Court and followed the Numbers toward Lot 8 but I stopped between 6 and 7 I was not going to Intrude I was going to follow my Formula of doing Anonymous Unrewarded Good.

Lot 8 had a long brown shoebox Trailer parked on it. No light was on inside Except a blue one Flickering on the curtains in the back window. By the Evidence I will say it was from a T.V. Set.

"See that? He can't sleep he's so worried over you." I cut the Motor but Charmagne was not in any Hurry to get out she was not in a Hurry to go in.

"He'll jutht yell at me." She hugged herself around her middle she bent over forward. "He'll lock me in hith bedroom."

"You feel O.K. doll?"

She pulled herself up & tried to Aim toward the window which she Accomplished but the window was Rolled Up. When she Heaved Up it splashed all over the door but Good Luck was with

157

me for the 2nd time in the same night since not even a Drop went on the carpet. I wiped around her mouth with a fresh Tissue.

"No he won't. He'll want to kiss you and hug you. That's what.'
She barely took a Breath I know how she Felt she had polio of the Feelings. "Why do you think your papa sent me to find you then?"

She shrugged I-don't-know & made a Guess. "To show off he can do what he wanth."

"I'll wait her till you're inside." I opened the door for her.

She made her little Barefoot walk up to the door in the side of the Trailer which she Banged on very Loud. When the door Opened a square of Light fell on Charmagne from inside she Appeared there like a foreign Refugee at the gates of Liberty so I turned the Raymobile around & drove away on tip-toes.

In the Rearview I see Charmagne running after me calling out but I do not stop—so far I am a Success with Anonymous so now I must skip the Curtain Call and bow out Unrewarded.

So far so Good.

A surprise I did not Expect I Discovered when I got home on the edge of my bed. It is a Medical Fact that a soldier who has a Mortal Wound on the battlefield can go on with $\frac{1}{2}$ of his Blood gone & he does not Notice maybe he Feels a little faint until he Keels Over. Well I did not Know it until I sat down on the side of my bed I had a Wet Stain the size of a dinner plate on the Front of my safari suit. I did not even Feel it in the Excitement I pissed in my pants. I can see the headlines now—Soggy Seat Crimps Hero Holdover: Low B.O. Hoses Comeback. So I did not have Visions of sugar plums Dancing in my head after I put my Safari Suit in to soak to leave it for Mrs. Roderiguez to finish off Washing it for me & iron it like new on Thursday.

I did go to Sleep in spite as soon as I lay down my weary head and I do Remember what I had a Dream of: a room full of man-eating slot machines surrounding me. I am not Sigmund Freud I can not tell you what it means I only know one thing—when I woke up in the morning my Pillow was all covered over with Blood Stains.

"I'm a little worried about how this looks. Your stitches opened up." Dr. Godfrey dabbed at the back of my Head with a cold wet Sponge.

"Can you fix them?"

"This time. If they open up again I'll need to call in a brain surgeon." He shined a Light down. "Tch. Not too bad. How did you do it Ray?"

"Thinking too hard." I turned around to see if that Line got a Laugh but mainly I Hoped that joke was going to Satisfy him so I did not have to dodge any more Questions. More than my Health even it was a matter of Life & Death I had to protect my secret Identity if Peter Tremayne was going to have a Future.

"I want to know," Dr. Godfrey pushed me.

I took a breath. "Horseback riding."

He was not ready to Swallow it. "You told me before you hate horses."

"Sure I do. That's why I ride on them. It's a superior position to be in with a horse."

Dr. Godfrey was in the Mood for a Conversation while he did his needlework on my Scalp but I did not have the Energy to come up with a whole Story correct in Every Detail for him to swallow whole so I fobbed him with a Fib. (I did not enjoy doing this I did not Plan to mislead him nor I did not want to corner myself into a Tight Spot first thing in the Morning. Every day of my Life I met a dozen Moral choices like this do I do something for my Good or for somebody else's Good and now in my Final Hour I Recognize it did not make a Difference how I Decided either way it was for my own Good.)

So I said, "I fell off."

"Uh-huh. That's when you hurt your arm too?"

"My arm. Yeah. Is it broken?"

"It isn't even fractured." I heard the snip of his scissors and the Pressure of his palm Peeled away from the back of my Head. I saw in the mirror he slid back a step to Admire his Work. "I could have been one of the greats in custom tailoring."

"How do you know my arm is O.K.? You didn't take a X-Ray. I've got a constant pain in my tibia."

"I don't need to take any X-Rays my eye is trained. Show me where it hurts." He stood in front of me he Bent Over a little ready to Examine.

I held out my right arm to him which he Squeezed up & down like he was Frisking it for a Concealed Weapon.

"Aarrggkk!" I yelped.

"Does that hurt with a small sharp pain or a wide dull ache?"

"Both!" I pulled it back out of his hand but not out of his Reach.

Dr. Godfrey held my Arm in both of his hands Weighing it up it was a Delicious sausage to his eye. "You sprained it. I'll give you a bandage and a prescription for some pain killers. Call me Monday if there's no change. No. Call me Monday if there is a change." He wrote it out very slow on his Prescription pad so Beautiful every word was Clear. Maybe he was only Buying Time dragging it out to keep me there because something for sure was tickling his Imagination or sparking his Intuition. He handed me the Prescription & he asked me, "You fell off this horse forwards or over on your side or what?"

"On my arm." He was boxing me in but I did not let him put me on the ropes. "Hey you were the wiseguy who advised me get back in the game!"

He yelled back in my face, "You didn't hurt yourself on a horse or playing shuffleboard or any other goddamned thing like that!" Maybe he was Angry over how I misled him how I Insulted his Intelligence which we both knew but he frowned at himself for raising his Voice. We heard a child all of a sudden start Crying in the waiting room on the other side of the door & the same Idea entered our Minds in the same second: that poor little pisher must be Scared Stiff he is going to meet Mad Dr. Frankenstein in here. But Dr. Godfrey's voice was calm & Gentle when he asked me, "Where did all the bruises come from?"

"What bruises?"

He frowned again and he Rolled Up the back of my shirt all the way to my shoulders then he pushed me Toward the Mirror. You could knock me over with a wet noodle but what did I see? My back looked like the Map of Africa—where it was not Blue it was Purple where it was not Purple it was Red where it was not Red it was not my back.

"Maybe I did fall over backwards," I said pie-eyed surprised.

He was Examining me & he was Cross-Examining me. "You live near Hoover High School don't you?"

"A few blocks."

Dr. Godfrey stood in front of me he locked his eyes on mine and both of us held still & shaky in Perfect Balance on our teeter-totter which had to tip over in the Next Breath. He wanted the true Story out of me and I was almost ready to give in—Kindness is like Torture to me I can only stand up to it up to a Point.

He Reached out Toward me I thought he was going to hold my hands but he only made a weak helpless Motion with his fingers. "You don't have to be ashamed about it," he said, "if kids gang up on you. Is that what's going on? Look I'm 20 years younger than you are and I don't think I could fight off a gang of teenagers. You don't have to feel humiliated about it."

I let my cheeks Sag I let my mouth Sink I looked away from him then when I saw his face in the Mirror looking after me I shut my eyes very Humiliated. Inside I was grinning from inner ear to inner ear! The punch that came from nowhere the Horseshoe in my glove! The home run in the bottom of the 9th the hole in one on the 18th green! Dr. Godfrey handed me a Perfect cover story Correct in every detail which 1.) Explained my Bruises and 2.) Explained my Behavior and 3.) Explained any Future bruises & future Behavior of mine which he happens to Observe.

You may have the Opinion it was a Rotten Trick to deceive him but on my side I say it is a Judgement Call. I am not the first person in the History of the World to Deceive for the sake of High Ideals after all people deceive for the sake of Romance which is a low Ideal in my book. The High Ideal I had in mind was Protection i.e. the less anybody knew about my whereabouts & whatabouts the safer I was going to be. (Like every other High Ideal in the History of the World this one was also Doomed from the Beginning.)

"It's unbelievable," I sighed, "the dirt you find on the street these days. What you come in with stuck on your shoes." Still I

161

was not looking at him Direct which I felt was how to play it full of Sorrow over losing my Manly Dignity etc. not to mention my Social Security check which I did not Mention I let him bring it up.

"How much did they take off you?"

"Exactly?"

"What you remember."

"$114.67. Plus a little change I had loose."

"Your Social Security?"

I nodded I opened my eyes and put on a flat smile. "I'll get by. It was only $114.00 and some change." I pulled my shirt down & I buttoned it up. Very slow. Very Humiliated.

"Did you report it to the police Ray?"

"No!" The word Exploded from my mouth before the Idea occurred to my Mind: *that was all I needed!* Alert the local Flatfoot Brigade and attract attention to myself! Not to mention there goes out the window all my power & freedom from remaining Anonymous also if word goes around how I associate with the police I can also ask them to bring a can of paint when they come to my Apartment so they can color a big bull's eye on my back!

None of this particular vein of Worry opened up to Dr. Godfrey who gave my outburst a different Interpretation i.e. it was a yelp of my former manly Pride. "If you act like a victim you'll be a victim. Report it to the police Ray. They know what action to take."

"I do too."

"You're not Joe Louis."

"So—what? You're Louie Pasteur? No you're not but you give out penicillin shots am I right? You do what you can do am I right?"

He was scrappy he was going to Fight for my Hide. "Maybe next time it won't be just a shove into some trash cans on the sidewalk. How are you going to live? I mean if they start making a habit of hitting you for your Social Security check?"

"I'll get by." I saw he was not Satisfied by that Answer. "I'll go around them. I see them coming I'll cross over the street."

"I want you to tell the police you're being victimized! Let them do the job they're paid for that's all!"

"Doc this town is crawling with packs of human vermin."

"You're not Joe Louis," he Reminded me but his Voice was not so strong this time also he was Staring for ½ a second like he wanted to throw a Net over me. "Ray—promise me you're going to do something positive for Pete's sake."

"I promise," I said nor I did not break my Pledge.

I went walking down the Sunny Side of the street feeling very Good about the prospects of my Life while I Remembered the action-packed Finale of the night before (2 nights before??) and it was still the Beginning again with so much Work Ahead. I was going to Treat myself to a spruce-up from Sal my barber then check in my P.O. Box for any further Developments.

My barber shop was next door to Bea's Bakery & it had a smell in there I can smell at night when I close my eyes with my head on my pillow—the hot bread & cookies the butter in the air mixed up with hair tonic & talcum powder. I also Enjoyed my visits to Sal because he always had his Radio on tuned in to a Ball Game if a game was on the air or the 24 Hour News both of us being very Anxious to stay informed of world Events.

I did not have to wait for a chair it was 2 Chairs No Waiting. Sal dusted off the red throne & snapped the loose hairs off the big sheet before he tucked it around my chin & clipped it behind my neck.

"Wow. What happened here?" Sal swung my chair half a turn to display my stitches to his brother Vern who was busy with the customer in the other chair.

"Wow. What happened Ray?"

"I had a accident playing shuffleboard if you want to know the truth," I told them.

Sal swung me back around and Vern swung his man around the Opposite way we did a little Square Dance sitting down.

"I never knew shuffleboard was a contact sport," Sal said.

"It is the way I play it."

"How'd the other guy look?" Vern inquired.

163

"The other guy was Mrs. Calusco. She did this to me on purpose Sal behind the ref's back. She'll do anything to beat me at shuffleboard."

The info clicked in Sal's mind. "Wait you mean Mrs. Calusco *92 year old* Mrs. Calusco? She did that to you in shuffleboard?" He let out a little Teapot whistle.

"There was a lot riding on the game," I explained. "It was a tournament."

Sal settled down to chopping through the poodle hair Hedge around my ears and Vern turned up the Radio and it was the 12 O'clock News on. Sal stopped clipping. "Wait a sec," he said. "Hey. You hear about this stuff Ray?"

"Tilt your head down Diego," Vern said to his crewcut Mexican regular and he started to buzz the Shaver up the back of his neck.

"Wait on't," Sal asked him he patted the Air meaning Vern's shaver.

Vern Obliged & switched it off and Diego looked up from his magazine to listen to the Radio too he stared straight ahead into the air & his ears twitched while he paid Attention.

NEWSMAN: Two more bodies have been found in the desert this time 40 miles from the Mexican border. It brings to 6 the total of illegal Mexican immigrants found murdered in the last 2 weeks. The bodies of the victims had been mutilated but the County Coroner says this probably took place after death as the result of scavenging by wild dogs. The cause of death in each case has been determined as a single execution style gunshot wound to the head.

Sal let a Hard Breath out through his teeth I felt it hit me on the back of my neck & I saw Vern drop a Friendly paw onto Diego's shoulder.

NEWSMAN: As yet police have no clear lead to follow. These murders coincide with the recent upsurge in public activity by the Ku Klux Klan who since January 1st have organized so-called "citizens patrols" along the Mexican border "assisting" the overstretched Border Patrol. Spokesman for the Klan—El Paso attorney Owen Meacham— issued a statement today which described the citizens patrols as lawful democratic activities undertaken for the benefit of the comunity and he dismissed any alleged KKK involvement in premeditated acts of border violence as "far fetched and laughable."

"You got your Green Card don'tcha Diego?" Vern patted the Mexican's back. "Tilt your head down."

Before Diego went back to looking at his Magazine he gave Vern a Glance over his shoulder & he said, "That better be a shaver in your hand."

That joke of his broke the ice of the Moment and while Sal and Vern and Diego laughed over it I sank down into my Inner Thoughts I started Wondering if I could solve The Case of the Mutilated Mexicans. So there was another Seed of my Doom sprouting a root while I Wondered how it Felt with them the poor Mexicans who had Hunger for breakfast and Starvation for lunch and for supper they had Hope maybe a better Life was waiting for them over the Border across the desert. So they follow over with The Virgin Mary or whatnot Cheering them all the way so they stand the hot sun etc. and the first American they meet says *Tilt your head down* and shoots them dead. What business can be Worse for them what kind of Life what kind of Death?

And then I started to Wonder how it Felt with the man with the gun *Tilt your head down* BANG! but I resisted I did not know where it was that Emotion in my Experience I am happy to Report.

I only Drifted back to Earth in the barber shop at the end of Sal's treatment which for my Enjoyment he dragged out by Applying lavender hair tonic & talcum powder & brushing me off very nice. But I did not rise up out of Sal's red barber chair when he was all done with me I was stuck to it like the hand of Goliath was Pressing Down on my chest squeezing my lungs holding me there it was the Voices I was hearing on the Radio—

Let me tell you what happened in the days of The Green Ray when Lamont Carruthers had to let some character in on the plot & keep him going forward—what he did was he created a Coincidence. Maybe it is a report on the Radio News which Peter Tremayne happens to turn on by Coincidence & it alerts him about the Criminal Doings of Lionel Horvath or maybe it is a Front Page news Story or a photo of some V.I.P. which just hits the stands by Coincidence at the Exact Time that Rosalind Bentley steps out of her taxi in front of the theater to Recognize him and this new Info makes her change Direction so she steps into Danger or out of its clutches depending where she is in the Episode the beginning the middle or the end. In the Green Room I made a point out of it I mocked & scoffed at a Coincidence like this since it can only Occur on the whim of Lamont Carruthers for 1 purpose & 1 purpose only i.e. for a Motivation so his Story can hurry up and keep going to the Finale. My Opinion was these Events do not occur in Life and for 66 years that was my experience until the day of my Haircut.

The Man Behind the Mike is called Joe Hayes hard nose hard head & hard heart and maybe hard of hearing but they let him have his own Show after the 12 O'clock News. His show is for Listeners to call him up on the telephone & Complain about this & that or criticize Joe's rough Opinions on the Topics of the day etc. Always he is very Tough on his Audience but they keep calling him up he is very Popular also very unpopular at the same time go figure that out. Being his Shows are action-packed with Insults flying back & forth (but mainly forth from Joe) this one was not different:

The Voice was a man's Voice trying to break into Joe's heckling.

JOE: Albert! C'mon my man! Get a grip on yourself! You can't prove any of this happened I mean if you've got any Polaroids I'd like to see 'em!

AL: Joe can I say one thing? Can I say one thing please?

JOE: Especially of your daughter. Yeah go ahead Albert I'm

listening if nobody else is.

AL: Peter Tremayne did it. He did it.

JOE: He's the guy you say saved your daughter from the clutches of those demented perverts?

AL: They forced their filth on her.

JOE: These sleazeballs aren't going to come out & support your story are they?

AL: It's not a story Joe he gave me my little girl back & I just want to say in public thank you Mr. Peter Tremayne. I love my little girl.

The Sound of newspaper pages opening up behind the Microphone did not Disguise another rude Remark from Joe.

JOE: In other words it's the same unbelievable story you fed to the papers. I see you've got your picture on the inside page of today's Examiner Albert. Why don't you come right out & confess to all my *honest* listeners that this is just your way of grabbing a little bit of attention? Hey— what made her run away from home Al?

AL: I love my girl. I'm good to her.

JOE: You want some more attention? I'll call my friend Mike Malone at Channel 5 and maybe he'll put you on T.V. Huh? You want to see your face on Live At 5?

So Al and everybody else who was tuned in heard the Sound of Joe Hayes dialling his Telephone or maybe it was just a Recording it did not make a Difference if it was Real or Fake it had the same Effect. Albert forced his last line out in a hurry.

AL: Somebody in this world respects a father's rights over his child.

JOE: Is that the moral of your little private soap opera story Al?

Now the Sound of a ringing tone on a telephone very Tense now.

AL: Forgive and forget and start over. Thank you very much.

And so Al hung up at the same time Joe's phone call Connected and it was not Mike Malone's voice it was only the Time lady he called up. After he heard what Time it was at the tone exactly he hung up on the Time Lady too.

JOE: Terrific story Albert but next time why don't you come
       up with one we can *believe?*

"Whew," Sal agreed. "He's a mean old so-and-so but hell if he don't get right to the truth."

I got a big Disappointment from seeing my P.O. Box did not have any further Letters in it by the time I walked over to Check on it. Since it was a new business to me this P.O. Box business I Wondered out loud to the clerk there (the bony girl with the boy's voice on her) I wondered if my Letters got put by some Dumb Mistake into a different number.
   "No way." She shook her head. "Uh-uh."
   Then she Reminded me how everybody at the Post Office works very hard delivering Mail pinpoint Accurate through wind & rain & dark of night la-dee-doo-dah across Mountains & over Seas etc. so if I got a letter in Mason that Arrived from the North Pole cross her heart & hope to die it was going to be Safe travelling over the last 25 feet from the back of the building where it came in up to the front of the building where my P.O. Box is.
   Wiseguy. She should go marry Joe Hayes.
   She pointed out a plastic chair which was Vacant also lopsided against the wall under the glass cabinet with the Wanted posters pinned up inside I believe she was telling me here is a Comfortable place where I can wait 20 minutes for the 2nd delivery to come in but I said nuts to that. In 20 minutes I was going to be home so I Decided better Mrs. Roderiguez can walk down here and Check there is more mail for me sealed with Tears & stamped with Hope.
   Let them arrive! Let those cards & letters come pouring in!

From far & wide! Let them Arrive from the North Pole I will dress up warm and go there! I will help helpless Eskimos!

If I get a letter from a little child in a Orphanage in Chicago who is Suffering because she found out how she is not really a Orphan she is in there so her mother can spend the Trust Fund which her kindly grandfather saved for the little girl so she never has to suffer *I will go to Chicago!*

If I get a letter from a widow in a fancy shmancy mansion in Florida who is sick from Fear since her no-goodnik son-in-law stole her Diamond Tiara which was in the Family for 200 years for quick Cash to pay off his gambling Debts and now he is part of a gang who kidnapped her daughter & he is holding her for a Million Dollars in Ransom *I will go to Florida!*

If I get a letter from a man in Trouble who worked hard his whole Life to build up a Respectable business so he can Provide for his family and now some big company wants to buy him out Cheap so he will not sell so now the big boys are trying to push him out of business out of his own Neighborhood and he wants me to help him push the big boys back *I will do it!*

Even if Mrs. Calusco writes to me to help her get her dog out who is stuck under the house *I will do it!*

Because I saved a little girl from Harm already I led her back home to her papa's loving Embrace where she should be where she was Happy now—I DID THAT! So I went out of the Post Office whistling a Happy Tune & I had it in my mind I wanted to buy a copy of the Examiner to see the photo and the story which Joe Hayes mocked on the Air. What is the next thing I see? A pick-up truck pulls up to the kerb loaded down in the back by bundles of Mason Examiners—the delivery boy wallops a bundle into the paper machine on the Sidewalk he snaps the lid down he drives off. The one on top is folded funny so the lid is not shut and I can pull it out. (I did plan to put in the Quarter for it after but I fished in my pockets & I found out I did not have the Correct change so at the time I took it as a Good sign. There is a little dish looks like a glass hotel ashtray on the end table next to my bed with some Change in. Mrs. Roderiguez please take 25 cents out of that & Deposit it in the newspaper machine outside the Post Office. You can keep anything you find in there over a Quarter.)

On the Inside Page there I saw their smiling faces Mr. Al Abercorn and Charmagne outside the long brown trailer. They hugged each other hard for the Camera but also for Each Other I believe. So it was my Proof all right how I changed their Life I DID THAT. So What so I am the only one Alive who knows who I am?! Look who has a headline:

NO CLUE TO TRUE IDENTITY OF MYSTERY HERO

I am in the News again!

While Mrs. Roderiguez was down at the Post Office I sat down with a nice boloney sandwich with my 5 other Letters on my T.V. tray. I went over them in Alphabetical Order but I did not feel very Attracted to these cases after all the Excitement with Charmagne & Carlos & the dirty magazines.

The next letter on the top of the Pile came from a 55 yr. old man called Hector Carillo who was hoping Peter Tremayne would give him $200.00 for the Downpayment on a pick-up truck.

The one after that came from a Greek man who used to make Circus Tents by hand but he wanted Peter Tremayne to know that the Modern World does not have a use for his skills anymore what was he going to do. I wrote a post card back with my Suggestion on it he could use his fine Skills for a different Purpose for instance the sewing of custom tailored Garments for very fat men & women. I did not feel energetic enough to go out & find him some wealthy Opera singer to start him off with so I drank a glass of milk and went onto the sofa to take a little Nap.

Maybe the best plan was just Wait & See if Mrs. Roderiguez comes back with any hard-up Hardluck Cases which pull at my Heartstrings and start with a "B". Maybe a better plan was take a day off and gather my Strength maybe take a High Colonic before I jump into another Arousing Adventure.

The front door was open only the screen was shut but she leaned on the doorbell to announce to me she was coming in. Besides the hot & curly Aroma of the take-out tacos she ate for lunch Mrs. Roderiguez Returned to me with a full deck of fresh Cases.

"How many you got there?" I sat right up on the sofa and she Dealt me the letters 1 by 1 on my T.V. tray. She counted in Mexican I counted under my breath I counted out 9 of them this time.

"Y nueve," Mrs. Roderiguez sighed over me she was Exhausted in advance on my Behalf since now I had to *read* them all.

"Gracias," I blabbed, "gracias."

This handed her a little Thrill. "Oh Senor Ray! Now you elearn Espanish?"

I was already opening my letters and Alphabetizing so I did not look up. "Si," I answered her. "Gracias."

"Muy bueno," she congratulated me and went into the kitchen.

I figured her Lunch Break was over and I did not Relish the Idea I had to read my Mail while she ate more beans. "No more buenos Mrs. Roderiguez. No more beans. Did you clean out the car yet?"

With her hands on her hips she came out of the kitchen to Answer me so all of a sudden this was a very Touchy Subject which I thought we Settled before she walked to the Post Office.

"No carwash Senor Ray. I clean in here."

"I want to sit in here. Do the inside of the car instead O.K.?"

"No O.K."

"Tell me how you say PLEASE in Mexican. *Please* Mrs. Roderiguez." About this she was silent & stubborn with her lips curled in & pressed so tight together her mouth Disappeared into a liver colored crease across the middle of her face. Ugh. "Don't make that face at me."

"Theez room eez filth."

"What filth? Some crinkled papers on the floor." I picked up the TV Guide cover and a few loose Coupons and I do not know what else maybe a label I soaked off some applesauce jar. "There. Clean. Inside the car is filth you can really get your teeth into."

"I clean *rooms* Senor Ray. In jour *house*. I ang no carwash!"

Was simple Human Logic going to help me? "Inside the car *is*

171

a room Mrs. Roderiguez. It just has wheels under it." And I added, "You don't have to clean the wheels."

I got the face again.

Was Yankee know-how going to help me? "I pay you $17.50 don't I?"

"Si."

"To clean for me."

"Si. Rooms! No cars! 1—2—3—4—*rooms!*"

Livingroom. Kitchen. Bedroom. Bathroom. Now we had a Basis. "O.K.! So that's $17.50 for 4 rooms so what I'm saying is—don't clean in here today. Clean inside the car instead. It's the same thing! If I pay you $17.50 don't you think it's fair if I tell you which 4 rooms of mine I want you to clean?"

Was this appeal to The American Way going to get Mrs. Roderiguez moving in the Direction I wanted her to go?

"Extra."

"What extra?"

"Cleaning jour car. Extra $3.00."

"Mrs. Roderiguez," I put a sob in my Voice, "don't work against me."

While we are going Back & Forth like that in the breath before she is about to Accuse me of treating her like my personal slave I am Saved by the Doorbell. I do not get up from my T.V. tray & Mrs. Roderiguez is planted in front of me like a potted palm so I do not see who is waiting by my door.

"Excuso," I said & I waved her Torso out of my view. On the other side of my screen door—

"Is Peter Tremayne inside here?" A woman's Voice.

"Open the door for me Mrs. Roderiguez." My Open Sesame words which led me on into new Experiences which I Regret unto this very minute with all my Heart with all my Soul & with all my Might.

"Por favor," she Complained at me on her way to the door also she dropped a few Remarks in Espanol under her Breath. Next thing she is holding a Conversation with my Mystery Guest & I hear enough to get the drift that in this house lives no Peter Tremang only Senor Green etc.

I stand up to say, "Who wants to locate Mr. Tremayne?"
She was not how I Remembered her she was Softer all around.
Same compact size as Mrs. Roderiguez & if she put on another
25 years also 40 lbs. spread here & there they could be Twin
Sisters. In the raw sunshine crashing down on the concrete Bal-
cony outside my front door her skin showed up Darker almost like
a Indian. From the other side of the room & through the screen
I thought her eyes looked much Younger than her skin like they
Belonged to a little girl but got trapped in the wrinkles to come.
This is what I Recognized about her.

"You!" I pointed her way & puffed out a smile of Surprise.

"Peter?" she Squinted at me she was not sure she got my name
100% Correct.

All of a sudden there she was standing in the Privacy of my
own home & there I am standing like a Sears & Roebuck ad in
my new Bermudas to welcome Amelia into my Apartment also
back into my Life.

"The blackout—" I opened up to say but what my follow-up
was going to be I had no idea.

"I wan' to clean in here," Mrs. Roderiguez announced to me.

"The car! The car!" I flapped my arms. "Go clean inside the
car Mrs. Roderiguez!"

"Ay-yi!" she Wailed & went into the kitchen banged open the
cupboard under the sink banged the bucket under the tap & let
the hot water Explode. The racket covered over the Further
Remarks she was making to me in Espanol.

Amelia stepped over to tell me in her low voice, "She's no very
happy cleaning out your car."

"Is that a direct translation?"

"No. You want to know what she say about your mother?"

"She should meet my mother." I rolled my eyes up to Heaven.
Mrs. Roderiguez sloshed between us with her soapy water.
"After inside jour car I go home Senor Ray." Then the screen
door bounced shut Behind her.

I gave my Attention back to Amelia. "How did you find me?"

She tilted her head in the Direction of Mrs. Roderiguez's exit.
"I write you a letter. I wait for you when you come get it from

the Post Office but she come there instead. So—" She tippy-toed
2 fingers down her arm & waited for a second to Witness my
Reaction upon that piece of News. All I did was I let out the
Breath I was holding in and it came out like a deep sigh of
Disappointment. Amelia picked this up very quick. "It's no her
fault O.K.? I hear about you on the radio so . . . You mad at me?"

I did not answer her Direct for what I was going to tell her? I
am not Interested in what she wants from me? Nor I do not care
what Happened to her after she Escaped over that backyard fence
like Bambi out of the forest fire nor I do not want to ask her who
was Nilo who was Perry how do such Types enter her Life what
did she do to Deserve such Treatment what is doing etc.? And I
am Sorry but it is 1 rescue to a customer so go on *beat it? Amscray?*
Look at my T.V. tray! More poor souls with Trouble riding them
like a hump on their back much poorer souls than you are—Greek
men who do not have your soft eyes & local welfare cases who do
not have a pick-up truck to call their own nor your Voice either
Tickling my inner ear? Others are hoping for my Attention too &
unless you fit in Alphabetical I must stick to the Rules I must put
them before you? You could be Dangling Helpless by your false
fingernails over the edge of Niagara Falls but I am sorry Senorita
NO CAN DO because I am busy at the Moment I have to
introduce the Fat Lady from the Opera to a Greek geek who sews
Circus tents for a living?

Well phooey to that! It is not a Feature of my character to avoid
evade or play hide & seek with Human Suffering on my doorstep!

"Can I make you a boloney sandwich?" I made a move toward
the kitchen.

She shook her head. "I'm scared you mad at me."

"What. Where you come from people get mad & they make
you eat a boloney sandwich?"

"What're you say Peter?" She only had a soft Mexican accent
around the Edges of her words.

"I'm not mad at you. You want it in writing?" She cocked her
head over to the side she weighed up the Truth & consequences.
"You want a nice glass of ice tea?"

Very delicate Amelia let her fingers do the walking through the

174

pile of letters on my T.V. tray & she pulled out her Envelope from there. She tore it up & stuffed the little Pieces down inside her straw bag.

"I'm going alphabetical," I explained to her.

"My name is Amelia O.K.?"

"Amelia. I remember." This put a little smile on her lips for I saw her Remember in a flash the obnoxious Experience which put us on Familiar Terms.

"Peter," she smiled back.

Well Folks my smile faded down & a Different one faded up which was holding some Embarrassment in. "Not Peter," I said, "not really Peter." I saw her calm smile Flicker but before she had a Chance to ask me I Volunteered, "I have to stay anonymous for maximum effect see?" I stuck out my hand. "Ray Green. How are ya?"

She squeezed my fingers which she did not let go. "I have trouble."

"Yes," I said very Understanding. "You want to tell me the whole story?" She started to talk then she stopped herself short. So I tried with a different Question. "Where did you go after?"

She clicked her tongue. "I stay in a motel & I don't come out for a while. Only now hm? Now I don't stay no more. Somethings might happen when I'm there."

"Something?"

"Accidents." She made the Sound of a bomb going off & showed me the Blast with her hands spread apart her cheeks puffed out her eyes all fiery.

"Those men," I fished back in my Memory, "Nilo and that Perry guy. Who're they to you?"

"Dirt on my shoes." Her Voice had steel needles in it. She sucked in her cheeks & turned her face away from me which was very Psychological i.e. she did not Believe her own words nor she did not want me to Doubt her if I caught her eye. "They don't matter. They're just—" she waved her hand & shook her head.

I did not want to come out & tell her Confess All or Else. As Peter Tremayne always did I used a little smidge of mild Psychology on her. I told her I did not Understand what she meant

175

by waving her hand around like that also looking like she was going to spit on my carpet when I said their Names.

Amelia was looking at me now—my Psychology worked. "They do jobs for a big man. What he tells them to. Anything."

"What did he tell them to do that night?"

"What they did."

"Who is this big man?" Silence. "You know him personal?" Dead silence. Now it felt like I was taking a Long Ride in a small Elevator with the Boss's daughter. So it was back to polite Conversation before I could probe & prod. "Blackouts can effect the behavior of some people. You know certain conditions can stimulate certain types to lose all their inhibitions. A guy doesn't have to be a screwball to start off with. They did tests with rats on this. Maybe those guys—"

"He told them to!"

"I'm not saying he didn't. I'm not saying that. I'm saying maybe he told them to go do *this* and they took it too far and they did *that*. Because of the blackout effect."

She stopped me short. "He probably made the blackout."

I sat down behind my T.V. tray. Another minute of this Direction and the whole Conversation was going to wind up out of Control & I was going to get Complaints from the Neighbors. A fine image for a big deal Crime Stopper! I tried to Calm her down with a dose of common sense. Sense is like money in the bank: you put sense in you get sense out with Interest. (Those wise words my Uncle Jake left me in *his* last will & testament. I pass them on F/C.)

"No really Amelia I think you're exaggerating. I read all the newspaper articles on it and nobody came out with any Evidence of any monkey business. It was those high school boys with the hamburgers. Reheating."

"Maybe."

"Nobody else was involved!" I clapped my hands together meaning Case Closed. In the Lull there I nibbled at the crust which I left on my plate before from my Boloney & Mayo. I gave her a look over my knuckles.

When she Answered me back her Voice was very Serious.

176

"Maybe it was *his* hamburger O.K.? And he Paid them some money to go and heat it up for him." She was talking herself into this Nonsense but the way she sounded so Serious on the subject so calm & cold she started a serious worry Bubbling in my Mind: "Who would do such a thing?"

Mrs. Roderiguez came in & she ignored Amelia altogether. She gave me a Smart Look on her way into the kitchen where she Emptied the bucket in the sink. I left her the Usual $17.50 on the kitchen counter & I Heard her sweep it into her handbag. Nor she did not give any polite Adios on her way out either.

"Jou put in $3.00 extra next week O.K.?" Then she was gone.

My apartment turned very Quiet after that. Some different Mood sat on us some Suspicious Mood. Was Amelia going to Trust in me? Was I going to Believe in her? The frame of my Mind was twisted around these Questions but also I Pondered if I did not make a Move in some positive direction in the next 10 seconds then when Mrs. Roderiguez came in a week from Thursday she was going to find us sitting there covered over in Spiderwebs.

"I was going to make some tea," I said. "You want some ice tea with a little lemon?"

She sipped in a tiny Breath & her shoulders did a little Shimmy when she turned her face back around she hummed, "Mm-mm," to Answer me. I think my Voice called her back to the Land of the Living.

We stood in the kitchen & I made ice tea which is a dish I make very Tasty not only with lemon but with fresh Mint too. Also a few tsps. sugar for a whole pitcher maybe 2 quarts. And no ice cubes until the Last Minute but put the glasses in the Freezer for a ½ Hour and it comes out very sharp & Refreshing.

When I had to squeeze in next to her to take down the glasses I smelled her skin which smelled Salty in the hot Weather but not sweaty very Unusual. I almost made a Comment on it I was going to pay her a Compliment but I did not come up with a way to put it which did not Sound indecent so I dropped it. (When I got to be on closer terms with Amelia I learned her secret: in hot weather she used to rub on a mishmash of Baby Powder & Baking

Soda 50–50. So there is another Handy Tip you can Remember besides the ice tea Advice.)

While we waited around for the tea to ice down etc. we Enjoyed a Friendly chat. It was cool in the kitchen with the window shade pulled so the light in there was pale. Puffs of breeze brought in that tangy odor of rust on the screen from the kitchen window you can Taste it on your tongue. We did not Discuss her Case only this & that e.g. the Mexican village of Tres Osos where she came from and I told her about Philadelphia. She wanted to know the exact Statistics of my Birth i.e. the place hour minute regular time or Daylight Savings all that she was going to use to draw up my Personal Astrology. I think maybe this was the ploy she used to find out my Age but I can tell you if she asked me Direct I was ready to tell her the Honest Truth within a Decade give or take.

I am a Sagittarius I found out which now I can add to American Jewish Senior Citizen Wanted Man La-Dee-Doo-Dah etc. et al I do not believe this Sagittarius business is all complete Bunk since I Believe that all beings are Connected to the Stars but I am just not sure about what some mop-top woman named Fidelia with her regular column in the Mason Examiner knows from my Personal daily business.

Amelia told me I look very strong & healthy for a gentleman of 66 and by this line of Conversation I learned that she was a woman of 37 which Fact surprised me something Drastic. Other people might miss this Point but my ear was tuned in to this kind of give-away: if she was ready to admit her right age with no Flinching then I was going to hear the Truth from her about the rest.

I was pouring out the ice tea & she was telling me about her Father she said he was a simple shoemaker who took his Family up from Tres Osos to Juarez and then to Texas when she was still a little girl. But this was not a Truthful Fact. She showed me a Photo of him holding her on his lap on the steps of the bungalow he bought from the Profits of his made-to-measure Cowboy Boot Business another American Dream Come True.

"When I was in high school," Amelia sipped & said, "he told

178

me you have to love a country that has John F. Kennedy for President."

We talked back & forth about J.F.K. like it was a J.F.K. Fan Club reunion! I Remember how that time Felt to me how the whole Country felt very Young. The Country had a Purpose & some verve with him like it was with F.D.R. at the Helm. All of us going Forward to a beautiful day. How he made us feel how we could do something big in the world. With the Peace Corps e.g. so young! So much vim & vigor! All the time in the world we had & with all the Power in the world to Achieve great things — all we had to do was we had to think it up & it was done! Go to the Moon — be a Shining Light to all the Nations of the World — cure hatred & inequality etc. All of those High Ideals are tarnished now I Regret to say.

By mentioning that time Amelia also made me Remember Exactly how I felt on the day J.F.K. got it in the neck when he died I Felt like I put on 25 years in 24 hours and we talked about that Black Day. The whole Country turned inside-out & upsidedown overnight. Or maybe it already was upsidedown from the day he moved into the White House and on Nov. 22 '63 it just turned back to the way it always was. A young man — a good-looking man like he just walked in off the Silver Screen — the Highest Ideals he was going to make the Law of the Land. I found out that is not the True Nature of the World we live in it was not the True Picture. That time was like a freak of the Atmosphere when your Radio for a few minutes can pick up a station on the other side of the World but nothing holds still very long the Static has to roll in again.

I told her my Inner Feelings about J.F.K. I told her my Sympathies but I did not guess it was her craft it was her Desire to turn it all back against me. I will say Amelia was a Sensitive actress all right she spotted her Cues before I knew I gave them. From my words yes also from tone of Voice & expression of face she found the Clues very fast she followed the trail Direct to the Heart of my Mind & the Mind of my Heart. The only thing she did not do was hang a sign on my back that said KICK ME. And the pin KICK ME hung upon was all that talk about J.F.K.

179

"I was so jealous of Jackie," she gushed out, "I always just hoped she'd get in some car accident. Or some plane crash. But he'd be all right and I'd be with him when he woke up."

It did not really Shock me I knew it was a Remembrance of her fantasy Romance. "Ugh! That's terrible Amelia! What about the children—whatsis—Caroline and little John-John?"

"They went with Jackie." I shook my head very Disapproving but she kept going, "So I marry J.F.K. and we start a new family."

"Ugh!"

"I was a crazy teenager O.K." She pulled her fingers through the thick waves of hair pouring over her ears. "I admit it."

We got Chatting so much & so easy I did not Notice that the sunlight was Going Going Gone and my apartment was holding in the gray haze of evening. The chill of it Rippled through me when I got up to shut the window but it was not a Change of Temperature or the Change of Day over into Night it was it felt like the end of one thing between Amelia & me and the start of something else. Maybe here is where I passed over the Point Of No Return i.e. the exact place hour second latitude longitude & Time Zone. On that side is Before—On this side is After.

I switched on the lights in the livingroom & then Amelia came in she sat on the sofa. She was Ready to tell me the tale of her Woe & I was ready to listen for she softened me up so I Desired to help her already if it was in my Power.

She started in, "When I heard on the news J.F.K. is coming to Dallas I went there you know on the bus very early. I camped out so I get a good place to see him drive by there. But I don't sit still I'm just too excited so I walk around you know? I drink coffee all morning."

I nod very wise.

She pulled this Story out piece by piece. *Piece by piece out of her Memory* I thought but it was piece by piece out of thin Air.

"Since I was outside so long I drink a lot of coffee and by the time the people fill up the grass I need a pee-pee real bad." She stopped to check the Effect on my face. "I think O.K. if I move then for sure I miss him. If I don't—" she Wrinkled her flat nose so she did not have to Paint me a Picture of the Dire Consequences.

"I didn't have time to go and find a powder room somewhere so I went behind a fence in some bushes."

I did not Think there was anything wrong with this Action and I gave her a Grin to show her so but she took it all Wrong.

"I said I was a crazy teenager," she Fluttered her hands to Emphasize. "Nobody is there so I do it quick. Cars started coming. I hear all the crowds you know cheering cheering for him so I get up on my toes and look over the fence." She Shut her eyes she held her hand out in front of her. "Wait," she said—a very good act of trying to Picture it—but Amelia did not know how to put her Story next. She went on slow & careful. "I can see everything from there so I didn't go back to the grass. All the people crowding down there." She opened up her big round dark brown eyes at me. "On the other side of the bushes on my same side of the fence there is a man with a rifle."

Amelia waited again this time for me. She wanted to see if I was Still with her. "You mean a guard? A Secret Service guard?" I was still with her all right.

"No." She rolled her lips in she made her mouth very Small.

"Who was he? Did you ask him?"

"I am *shaking* you know? Then bang! bang! bang-bang! Shots like that. Terrible. I screamed. I cried. I—and he—this man this killer—he looked at me. Backing up. He pointed his gun in my face. Backing up. He was backing up. This car is behind him and some men got out. Men in suits. Shouting all around going F.B.I.! F.B.I.! I'm F.B.I.! & so this man gives his rifle. The men put it in the back of the car. They put him in the back. They drove away."

"My God," I said. "Did you testify?"

In a very Soft Voice she said, "No."

"You're a witness! But you're a eye witness!"

She looked up her eyes all Pleading. "Yes. Understand?"

Lamont Carruthers could take a Lesson in Storytelling from this woman this woman was a Genius at it. I was on the edge of my seat the whole time all caught up in the Mystery and the Drama of it. I say this to my Shame how my Trained Eye did not Observe her false moves or false Emotions. She saw the Sympathy in my eyes I will say and with another person that might make them go Soft it only made my Amelia go for broke:

A tear Dripped down to her chin. "I woke up on the grass. How did I get there? I remember the man behind the fence. His face. I told my father. He was very scared for me. He sent me back to Tres Osos. Back to Mexico. Safe."

"How old were you with all that?"

"Fifteen years."

"That's a little girl."

"No," she shook off my Remark. "He died you know so I come back to Texas hm?"

"When?"

"Mm," she had to concentrate. "Two years ago. I don't worry you know it was 20 years. I'm not a crazy teenager anymore. But I don't forget. I know dangerous things. I know this man is still alive. I know who he is. He didn't forget my face either." She made the shape of a gun with her hand and held it up to the side of her head. "Now me. Now he comes for me." Then Amelia sat very still. I did not say a word so she felt the urge to fill up the gap. "Do you believe me?"

I am a patsy I Believed her. But Your Honor let me say a few words in my own Defence:

So much Happens in this World we live in so much goes on you can not Believe it. Events you can not Imagine until you read about it in a Magazine. I do not mean e.g. the Idea that alien Life Forms i.e. superior so-called Beings from Outer Space came down in their spaceships & carved something that looks like a Spider on a big rock in Peru somewhere and never came back to Explain No I do not mean I Compare such to the idea of mysterious Events which occur in Human Life as we know it. We put people on the moon & if you handed that piece of News to some tribe of Pygmies in the middle of the jungle would they Believe it?

So much goes on behind the Scenes. So what do we need alien visits from Outer Space to explain things? There is enough of Mystery in regular Life to go around as far as I can see. Like the Case of L. Ron Hubbard who invents a Religion makes a Fortune

182

by it lives the rest of his Life on a boat & communicates via tape recordings.

Or take the case of Howard Hughes. For Instance the Business with his Last Will & Testament. Also he invented the Support Bra.

Take that Watergate business with the 18 minute gap. Until that sad Episode I used to Believe whole-hearted in the Government but I recognize by that phony-boloney monkey business the Government goes to the toilet too. Deep Throat and whatnot.

Or take very recent that Religious Nut who told his Flock drink this bucket of cyanide flavor Kool-Ade even little children so Trusting. Unbelievable.

Or wrestling on the T.V. That is a Fix.

Now I come to the Opinion it is Human Nature to deceive & to tell the truth is Unnatural and very hard for people. Maybe this is Evolution for you. Human Beings can not go on Living if we admit to anybody what we do so we go on living. To protect etc. How we are Proud to murder & destroy. How we like to push others around. How we get what we want. We act this way & say it is something else it is this Reason or that Reason but it all comes down to human Desires. It all goes on all the time I believe in high places & low so what is news when a person tells me she saw who pulled the trigger on John F. Kennedy? He died that way which is a Fact but it was something unbelievable when it Happened.

Anything goes. My big mistake was how I used to Believe if anything went then anything which is Good goes just as far. So I since then Observed it has a limit there is a limit to Good.

On the other side bad does not have any limit it goes further down than Good goes up. It feels like I live in a room under a concrete ceiling and inch by inch the floor is moving Down Down Down Down.

I read this article in Life Magazine about the many witnesses in Dallas, Texas on that day on Nov. 22 '63 there are maybe 110–112 or some Figure of that order & all of them died by 1970 or so in peculiar Circumstances. (I believe the odds against this the Insurance people worked out at about 1 million to 1.) Heart attacks. Car accidents. Falling off bridges. Fires. Suicides. All of them & this is today a Well-Known Fact.

So the Story which Amelia fed me I did not React to it being far-fetched or phony-boloney.

"So those gunsels from the blackout—you're positive who they were?" I wanted to Probe just to be 100% on her side.

"You saw him hm? Dirty they—" she choked up on a word she could not find. "How can I say it? What else should I do? Tell me what you want. What do I do so you believe me. So you help me. Por favor O.K.?"

The Look in her eyes made me want to Believe the Moon was made out of gefilte fish. "You have to tell me what you want me to do. I have to figure how I can help. So far I—" I opened my hands to her, "I don't have a gun."

Look at the Emotional side—I knew from my direct personal Experience how men are really chasing her also I Remembered— yes they did make a Phone Call to some V.I.P. in their lives i.e. somebody else who wanted to get his mitts on Amelia. Also I saw how she was not acting for my Benefit she was truly scared for her Life.

"Who'd they call up that night? Him?"

"Who did?"

"The Blackout Boys. They called some joe on the phone. Remember?" I watched her close her eyes to think back.

"I don't remember. If you say so."

"Who is it? Who's their boss?"

This was going to be the 1st time maybe she spoke this Name out loud in 20 years but she was going to say it to me out of Trust. I did not have any big idea on what I was going to do with the dynamite of this Information but deep down 1.) I figured it might come in handy from a Defence Point of View and 2.) I was very Curious about it.

She looked out the window into her Reflection in the dark and her lips parted a little. "John Newberry."

"John Newberry." I repeated to get it right, "John Newberry?"

She did not say it Again.

"He was the guy with the gun? Or the boss of the guy with the gun?"

For this she did not have any Answer ready so she dodged it by Confiding in me, "He's in the F.B.I. He's high up in it."

Of course I was very Surprised to hear this at the time. But the Question did not come to me in that minute how did she Find Out the name of somebody who is the Missing Key to the biggest crime of the Century with all of the Government officials after him? Earl Warren and so on. What did he do? Write her Poison Pen Letters? No this Question did not come up in my Mind until this minute.

Live & Learn.

If you told me today that Abraham Lincoln was a woman I am ready to Believe it but before I recognized how crooked things can be in the world I had to gasp at the idea! A man who makes it his Sworn Duty to uphold the Law of the Land and protect citizens etc. is Involved in such terrible business? I pondered what would J. Edgar Hoover say about this rotten apple!

"My God," I said. "He can do anything masquerading under the cloak of Law & Order."

"You understand? He's very strong. I can't fight him. What can you do Mr. Green?"

"Call me Ray."

I was at Peace in my Mind when I considered the shape of the Raymobile how strong it Performed in the East 8th 500 past the checkered flag and no Damage to any of its working parts (or mine either) so if it is a safe ride to the Mexican Border she needs—

"Where can I drop you?"

"How much do you charge me?"

"Charge? I don't charge." I walked around the room very Insulted. "Didn't you read the big print in the ad? Defend the defenseless—*that's* what I do! Free of charge. For free I do it! Charge? I do Good for no glory! I face Evil with no fear! Charge? Who would charge for that? Is that *modern* to charge for giving hope to the hopeless when the Hour of Darkness is upon them?

What do you think—I blaze from the shadows with my blinding Light of Right in one hand and a receipt book in the other?"

"N-no . . . *What* do you say? You mad at me now?"

"You insult me with that question. I mean—the one before."

"I don't know what you say."

"I mean two before. Two questions before. About charging."

"No charge."

"No. Right. No charge. Just tell me what you want me to do for you. To help you."

"Will you take me to Mexico? Where it's safe for me?"

"I'll take you to Mexico."

She relaxed she had her Fish on the Hook. "To Dallas first."

Did I hear her right? "Did I hear you right? Back to Dallas?"

"Dallas then Ojinaga. Ojinaga before Sunday."

Certain Questions I could save up for later but after the tale of her trouble in Texas this one formed direct in my mouth: "But—Dallas?"

"My family is there. I want to see them. You understand?" She made it sound very Final very tear-jerking.

I had to Focus all of my mental Powers on recalling my Pledge TO HEED THE CRY OF THE HELPLESS & HOUNDED—TO DO GOOD FOR NO GLORY—TO FACE EVIL WITH NO FEAR—(AND ALL THE OTHER THINGS)—in Other Words just do the necessary & shut up about it & when I am finished just Disappear into the Mystery from whence I came from without looking back and without any Personal Involvement AT ALL no matter *what* kind of circumstances. I did such with all concerned in The Case of Little Girl Lost (Charmagne and so on) and I knew it was my Obligation I should consider the Case 1st & last the case the case and nothing but the Case!

But since I knew her from before already she knew who I was so that was that as far as Anonymous was concerned. So already it was a personal Case. The question kept nagging in the back of my Mind in my own little Voice there I pondered what I was Personal to her what part I am playing in Amelia's Life—

Over Christmas in 1941 the Government beseeched all Radio
Stars and such to do their duty in the War Effort. They took the
green out of the Lucky Strike packs to go toward Army fatigues
(or put it in to look like them I forget which) so Believe me if
everything down to cigarettes was going to War I was raring to
go too as far as my Asthma was going to allow. Of course if there
was anything I could do to pay back double those wily Orientals
who delivered a Day of Infamy on top of Pearl Harbor with their
Sneak Attack my mouth was at the service of the War Department.
(Also by extreme coincidence Dec. 7 happens to be my birthday
my Day of Infancy so to say which gave me a personal Feeling
about fighting the Japanese Empire besides being a proud
American.)

Mr Silverstein had all of us in his office to hear F.D.R.'s speech
and when it was over he read us a very Stirring telegram from
our Sponsor Mr. P.K. Spiller who shared all of our President's
sentiments especially how we must all pull together now & Prepare
for all the hard times ahead la-dee-do-dah not Republicans and
Democrats not employers and employees anymore just 1 common
people United by 1 common Good against 1 common Evil. It all
Sounded a little bit bolshevik to me until the very end when he
Promised he was going to be with us as soon as his yacht can
carry him from Havana to Miami where he was stocking up his
requirements for the Duration. I did not see him at all until the
Party they threw in the Studio on the night of our special Broad-
cast to honor him & some under-secretary mucky-muck from the
War Department.

Mr. Silverstein hatched the Idea of a special Christmas Episode
of The Adventures Of The Green Ray which could comfort &
Inspire our Nation in those dark early hours of the War. Our
show could give America hope & do some Good for real. It was
the only time I ever heard him go Emotional about us but it made
me question in my mind why he thought this was the 1st time
such Good was being done by The Green Ray I thought we were

187

doing that all the time. It was a bump to my Feelings which I did not shake off in a hurry.

He put his head together with Lamont Carruthers and 24 hours later they had a Show on paper that was a Radio Spectacular. I Believe the Theme of it was mainly Inspired by F.D.R.'s Earth shattering words to wit: RENDEZVOUS WITH DESTINY. I begged them to make it the title of this Episode but they stuck by The Birth Of The Green Ray which I had to agree was simpler to Understand.

The most Exciting feature of this broadcast over the wartime Airwaves: my own normal Voice rang out across the Land! I will admit it was surrounded by Leon's echo device cranked up to the Maximum so it came across with all of the Cosmic Authority required by the part but it was my Voice all right portraying the Voice of the Ancient Narrator. Only a few lines at the end I did in my usual Radio Character The Green Ray & in between I portrayed the Young Peter Tremayne. (Now I can come clean & Confess I borrowed that one from Freddie Bartholomew the way he was in Captains Courageous.)

Out of the Sound of the Cosmic Wind blowing through the black cavern of empty Space i.e. the Sound of the Universe before the big light switched on out I came with the Voice of the Narrator.

NARRATOR: Before time before the Seed of Life was sown the Universe was void . . . All was dark and hollow—yet mysterious forces beyond mortal comprehension were at work behind the scenes . . . And in a single moment long—long ago—long before memory—there sounded this Almighty Bang—

Leon provided the Sound of this mighty Force going off by exploding a fat firecracker inside one of his 5 Gal. water bottles also he cranked up the Echo on it something fierce. He made a very believable version of the Sound of the Creation of all Atoms in Existence all Matter & Energy all the ideas feelings beings places & experiences ever to be fanning out from the Center of the Universe.

NARRATOR: After this great moment the stage was set for stars to come forth—clouds of cosmic dust swirled and circled into the far reaches of the infinite void—atomic particles streamed this way and that. They Collided! They Exploded! They Combined! Thus the heat and light of stars which flew into galaxies illuminated the dawn of time!

While the echo of the Explosion roared & rumbled away Leon used a variety of Sound Effects to put these Dramatic ideas across: the heavy ticking of a big clock (woodblock & mallet) spooky music (mainly violins screeching) & pieces of glass from the water bottle dropped all over the strings of a broken autoharp.

NARRATOR: The fiery furnaces of new stars boiled and fumed and spewed out cosmic rays which pierced the deepest darkness . . . Like molten bowling balls the stars in their hearts held alike the first spark of the first day and one by one the star we call the Sun gave birth to its 9 children Pluto—Uranus—Neptune—Jupiter—Saturn—Mars—Venus—the Earth and Mercury . . . all held in Sol's benevolent embrace!

The Birth Torment of the Universe was calming down here so we could hear the gentle music of the Spheres—the mellow Ringing which was the Sound of bells humming. This feat was beyond the Talent of Leon Kern so Mr. Burrows brought in his niece Pat who had a special Skill. By rubbing her fingertip over the rim of a glass she could pull a beautiful Tone out of it it was beautiful to watch so Delicate. A different note singing out of each glass her fingers circling off one rim & onto the other with the fat

note spinning in the Air over the Glass. Leon did have the Talent
& timing to play a Sound Effect of waves breaking on a shore.

NARRATOR: But of all the planets circling all of the suns in
all of the galaxies the Seed of Life came forth
upon the face of the Earth. The warm light of
the sun shone upon the green seas and the
green land upon the teeming Life of Eden!

That last Line almost stuck in my throat since even in those
days I put my Faith in the Discoveries of Science and by pure
Instinct by the feeling in my bones I knew that this Adam & Eve
Garden of Eden business with a wily talking snake with the apple
is all complete hooey. A Good story full of symbols maybe but it
is not Reality. I am not saying I disbelieve in the Spiritual side
of everything—in this Idea I believe very serious. All I want to
say is the ones who wrote down the Bible had more Imagination
on them than any of the people who believe it word by word.
Today it is the Scientists with the Imagination. Look at relativity.
Look at DNA. I believe this is True today the same way I believed
it in 1941 but Mr. Silverstein did not want our Version to offend
the Religious Beliefs of any member of our audience so Eden was
in and Einstein was out.

Out of the fading away ocean Sounds came bird calls—more
music—some animal calls—more music—then the noisy crowd of
human Voices the hum of Humanity. Now the music from a
calliope playing Take Me Out To The Ball Game then it was a
crowd of American voices the voices of New Yorkers out for a
good time having fun all over Coney Island.

VOICES: Hey! Popcorn here! Hey! Popcorn!
Extree! Extree! Lusitania sunk by Germany!
Read all about it!
Get yer red hots here! Hey! Red hots!

NARRATOR: In the great city of New York—as it did in
cities the world over—Life marched on into
the 20th Century. Men and women met fell in

	love married and had children showing hope in the face of despair. For it is the nature of love to conceive a future where it may dwell!
VOICES:	America goes to war against the Kaiser! Extree! Extree! Here boy! I'll take one!
NARRATOR:	Wars killed . . . Disease killed . . . Crime and anarchy reared their ugly heads . . . Yet men and women still met and fell in love.

The Voices of Coney Island faded away then the calliope that was playing Take Me Out To The Ball Game slipped into a soft version of Here Comes The Bride to announce the Wedding ceremony of Raymond Tremayne who was being portrayed by David Arcash and Estelle Wainwright his Bride portrayed by Annie LaSalle. I will say they played their parts with plenty of feeling. Bernhardt of course played the minister with his Irish accent which Mr. Silverstein did not Approve. (He requested something closer to the Episcopalian side but when Bernhardt tried anything except Irish he Sounded like a Rabbi which for sure was not going to work.) To my ears & to many regular Listeners of the show it did not Sound any different from his Captain O'Shaughnessy character which brought a very strange picture to my Mind but the scene did not last very long I am happy to Report.

MINISTER:	Do you Raymond Tremayne take this woman to be your lawful wedded wife to cherish before all others to have and to hold in sickness and in health till death do ye part?
RAYMOND:	I do.
MINISTER:	And do you Estelle Wainwright take this man to be your lawful wedded husband to have and to hold to love honor and obey in sickness and in health till death do ye part?
ESTELLE:	I do.
MINISTER:	I now pronounce you man & wife. You may kiss the bride.

RAYMOND: I will! Oh! I will!

The bells came back in again and with a Purpose this time the
Wedding Bells ringing out. And David gave a lot of Reality to the
tender moment he planted a kiss smack on Annie's lips & I will
not say I was very surprised by this move although she did Resist
it and left him with a red scratch on his face.

The Sounds of the wedding party came very easy since it was
mainly the warm up to the party after with all in the Studio
clinking Champagne glasses & making merry.

RAYMOND: I love you very much Estelle.
ESTELLE: And I love you! Oh Raymond! I do!

Again the 2 of them kiss but now we hear the Sound of soft
Explosions in the background—perhaps it is the inner feeling of
Raymond & Estelle the Sound of the Love between them but also
it is more.

ESTELLE: Look darling. Fireworks!
RAYMOND: Say! Looks like they're over Coney Island!
ESTELLE: Oh nearer than that! Ooh! That one was
             closer!

More explosions. Louder. Closer.

RAYMOND: Oh-whee! Look at that! It's so bright!
ESTELLE: It's so beautiful!
RAYMOND: It's our wedding night.

Again with the kissing and Leon is not helping heaping on the
Explosions. This scene feels like it is going to go on Forever.

NARRATOR: Safe in their lovers' embrace Estelle and Ray-
             mond were not witnessing a display of fire-
             works over Coney Island but the shower of a
             strange light—cosmic rays exploding from the

very center of the sun which fell on them
. . . on their wedding night . . .

A gigantic Explosion rocks the sky! Finally no more Kissing
since this is coming down over their heads and shakes them up
something terrible.

ESTELLE: Oh! What is it Raymond? It's like summer
            lightning!
RAYMOND: We better . . . go inside.

But Estelle seems Hypnotized by the mysterious Effect.

ESTELLE: It's so beautiful.

BA-BANG! Estelle Tremayne is covered by a shower of Light
or Flakes of the Sun!

ESTELLE: Aah!
RAYMOND: Darling!
ESTELLE: It's green! It's emeralds falling! Aah! It feels
            so warm!

And then she Faints.

RAYMOND: Estelle!
NARRATOR: As he takes her up in his arms the emerald
            green flakes of light fall on lover and beloved
            together and then disappear from the world in
            a final flare and flash!

Leon was very on the ball with the Sound Effect he used to
portray the Final Flare & Flash it was the same Sound only
Amplified higher of The Green Ray Hand Beam well known to
our Audience. So there was a hint for them about the source of
my Hand Beam's true Power. He also handed us a chuckle when

he did the next Sound of a baby gurgling & googling the way his lips went flapping & bubbling was a Sight to behold.

RAYMOND: He looks normal. I don't understand it. Why doesn't little Peter ever cry?

ESTELLE: Maybe he knows something we don't.

RAYMOND: Honestly.

ESTELLE: Oh let's just thank our lucky stars he's so healthy. And we'll make sure he's happy. Won't we dear?

RAYMOND: Just as happy as we make each other.

Back to the Smooching here but nothing Passionate I am glad to say in front of baby Leon who was anyway playing again amid his Devices. Raymond & Estelle settle down very nice into their family Life making a happy home for me in Tremayne Manor—

NARRATOR: Surrounded by the love of his parents little Peter Tremayne grew into boyhood happy and strong but very different from the other boys.

The clomping Sound of running feet & the Excited squeaky Voices of little boys in a big hurry. This kibbitzing comes down to 1 boy in particular Peter's friend Timmy portrayed by Pat the water glass lady. She was a woman of many parts and in this Episode we saw both of them—she whipped herself up to such a high Excitement to say her big Line ("He's goin' up!") that her Bosoms jumped out of her dress. David saw me looking & the way I was looking & he passed me a note it said "I think you've got a chance with her!" but I did not let the idea take my mind off my Scene.

TIMMY: Hurry up Peter! C'mon! Billy's got a cat trapped up a tree! He's got his dad's shotgun & he's gonna—

PETER: You can't get a cat to come down by shooting off a gun!

194

TIMMY: Can if you blast him!
PETER: No!

In a big hurry little Peter & Timmy run back to the tree where
Billy is trying to hold the big gun steady.

PETER: Billy! Stop! Stop! Billy!
BILLY: Aw quiet! I'm aimin'!

We hear a sad meow (Leon) which sounds like "oh-no".

PETER: Don't hurt him Billy! He's just an innocent
             animal! It's not right!
BILLY: G'wan!
TIMMY: Watch out! You're pointin' it!
BILLY: Let go I tell ya!
PETER: O.K.! I bet you I can climb that tree and
             rescue him.
BILLY: You? Sissy pants? It's tall as a house up there.
             I dare you.
PETER: I'm going. Give me a boost.

The leaves rustle & the branches creak & I grunt from the
climb up 5 feet—10 feet—"Meow! Oh-no!"—15 feet—

TIMMY: He's goin' up!

Pat's 2 Bosoms jump out at me but it is a Tricky part here
tingling from Suspense so I can not lose my Nerve—20 feet—
"Meow!"—higher still higher—

PETER: Got you!

Very mushy organ Music played out to portray all of the
Emotions this Act aroused in Peter's breast and he had a Message
for his pals as soon as he got back down to Earth.

PETER:	Animals are innocent Billy.
BILLY:	Huh? You're dopey!
TIMMY:	Did you see how high up they were? Peter did you look down?
PETER:	(*very modest*) N-naw.
NARRATOR:	Courage was a virtue that young Peter Tremayne would soon need to summon again. For him still in his tender years happiness was merely the camouflage of tragedy.

The heavy oaken door of the library in Tremayne Manor sighs open as the faithful Tremayne family butler Jessop serves Young Peter his soup.

PETER:	Thank you ever so much Jessop. Please tell Cook this soup is delicious.
JESSOP:	I will young sir. Cook will be so pleased you enjoyed it.

Estelle & Raymond enter the cozy scene now.

JESSOP:	Oh! Ahem. Good evening Mrs Tremayne. Mr. Tremayne.
RAYMOND:	Hello Jessop. Hello Sport.
ESTELLE:	I know you'll be **good** while we're away won't you darling?
PETER:	Yes Mother.
RAYMOND:	Of course he will. He's my son isn't he?
PETER:	I don't want you to worry about me. Just enjoy your week-end with Uncle Jack and Auntie Kate.
RAYMOND:	Jessop we should be in Boston by 9 o'clock.
JESSOP:	Very good Sir.
ESTELLE:	Give Mummy a kiss good-bye Peter darling.

A kiss. I pecked the back of my hand but I did not Complain afterall it was Wartime.

196

| PETER: | Father? |
| RAYMOND: | What is it old Sport? |

A strange & hollow Feeling took Young Peter over it was a Sensation of Dread. All of a sudden he had 1,000 things he had on his mind to tell his father & 1,000 Questions to ask him. He had a Desire to bring up some childhood memory maybe a memory from his baby years—the accident with the little red wagon out of control down the driveway or the flood in the bathroom—something they both went through together so remembering it will hold them together now. Young Peter wanted to ask his Father to explain algebra to him again and look at the drawing of the Solar System he did in School he wanted to listen to his father read out loud to him 1 more chapter out of The Time Machine or he wanted to read 1 more to his Father anything like that except not this heavy hearted Good-bye.

| PETER: | N-nothing. Good-bye Father. |

Rain pours down on a slippery road & the tires of the Tremayne Dusenberg squeal on the turns. If Raymond Tremayne was not a World Champion racing car driver this might sound like Danger.

ESTELLE:	Don't you think we better slow down a little Raymond?
RAYMOND:	We want to get in by 9 don't we?
ESTELLE:	Yes. I suppose. You know best.

More squealing.

ESTELLE:	I hope nothing is wrong with Peter. Didn't he seem queer tonight?
RAYMOND:	He's the queerest dearest boy in the whole world. You know—he did seem to want to tell me something before we left.
ESTELLE:	Tell you what?
RAYMOND:	He never got around to it. Turn on the radio darling.

But the first few notes of rooftop danceband Music all of a sudden get Buried under the Sounds of screaming tires! crumpling metal! wailing brakes! glass cracking apart! & piercing the terrible noise 2 Voices screaming their last words into the air—

ESTELLE: Raaayyymond!
RAYMOND: Esteeeeeellll!

And the heaving hulk of the dying Auto plows to rest steaming in a heap in a muddy ditch beside a rainy road somewhere between Long Island and Boston. Quiet closes in. But not for very long.

NARRATOR: Perhaps in the hour before the tragedy—in the minutes before the awful accident which orphaned Peter Tremayne—he sensed a door closing behind him & another door opening before him. In the solitary moment of darkness between the two in the lonely moment when his heart cried out "WHY?" another voice inside him spoke the answer. It was the voice of his courage saying *This is the world you live in & it is full of pain—struggle against it!* It was the voice of his wisdom saying *Accept the acts of Providence & fight against the malice of men!* It was the voice of his conscience saying *With this knowledge do what you might for the sake of the innocents who suffer!* It was the voice of—The Green Ray!

A beautiful Fanfare by the entire Studio Orchestra rose up then it sounded like a Big door opening upon a blaze of blinding Green Light which was Inspiring to me also useful because then I had the time to shake off the Voice of the Narrator and summon up the character of The Green Ray.

GREEN RAY: I pledge my Life to this purpose: to heed the cry of the helpless & hounded—To do Good for no glory—To face Evil with no fear—To give hope to the hopeless when the Hour of Darkness is upon them! I will blaze from the shadows to defend the defenseless and punish the criminal—To purge wrong to keep America strong!

What with the Orchestra playing proud music behind me so loud & so beautiful I had a picture in my mind of 1,000 flags flying—busting out of the kettledrums—blowing out of the trumpets—Stars & Stripes unfurling all over the Studio—ceiling & floor & walls & doors decked out in our streaming Red White & Blue!

I was very Choked Up by the moment of my final line & when I heard the chimes come in I felt my Voice start cracking. But Leon let me have plenty of Echo so it sounded like I was coming direct from the Center of the Universe.

NARRATOR: *Ye shall be a lamp unto all the nations of the world.*

So roll out the barrel! Bring out the dancing girls! Make a big party! Happy New Year! Bon Voyage! You are on your way Up Up Up! Here it is the end of the beginning! Mazel Tov! Success! Only in my personal Experience I am sad to say the dancing girls can not find the stage from the wings with a road map & the barrel is full of rotten apples. All of it is a Optical Illusion. The mind will play its Tricks to make the body go on. It has to look like the end of the beginning after the climax of many episodes but here it is the beginning of The End.

I curled up in bed with Amelia curled up in my Mind. All I wanted to do was just Forget about it for a few hours so I could Consider the Case point by point when I woke up fresh when my mental Powers would be at the Maximum but it was no use. In the dark there & even with my eyes shut tight I saw her face Whichever way I turned.

So I turned on my reading light & I picked up my current reading which happened to be a book full of Encouragement called Spell Your Way to Success by A.J. Lyedecker. (He started out as a phys. ed. coach and rose from that to make himself into a Best Seller Author so maybe he knows what he is talking about.) I also planned to read his next 2 Volumes with my eye on self-improvement Punctuate Your Way To Success and Grammar Your Way To Success but it does not look like I am ever going to get to those now.

I turned the pages I looked at the Words I saw the Sentences but I was not reading in fact nothing was going in. I gave up on that. I made a mug of Ovaltine then I tried again with the lights out.

My mind went back to Amelia like a boomerang.

My Ovaltine made me a little bit Drowsy so I felt dull & void but I did not slip off into sleep. The room remained baking hot even with the window wide open it felt like Bea's Bakery oven inside. My bed was by this time covered over with hot spots & the same with my pillow with no cool Patch anywhere where I could Relax. I rolled this way that way $\frac{1}{2}$ on the bed $\frac{1}{2}$ off it $\frac{1}{2}$ asleep $\frac{1}{2}$ awake with my p.j.'s wrapped around me like Cellophane.

When I peeled my eyelids open my head was on my night table I was looking right at the clock so I saw the Exact time—4:16 A.M. a time too early & too late to try anything Except Sleep. I wanted to let go from Thinking & slip down into the depths that is the picture I used to portray Sleep & it started working. Any Sound I heard was dim & round not sharp & clear and I sank down deeper into the warm water so the Dark finally closed in around me— which I Noticed and started floating up all over again up into my bedroom up to the Surface—I rolled over like a Whale & plunged downwards I pulled the dark behind me (I think I had the sheet over my head here)—half-way down and I floated up through it all over—I wanted lead weights around my feet to pull me back down I pictured them there & yes down I went. I let go from everything so the current could sweep me away & it did it swept me deeper down into a steamy cave where the dark was almost Solid. I bumped it I pushed away from it & where it was open before it was a wall now. I turned over this way to get out I turned over the other way to get out to get back up to the Air! In the middle of the cloudy water I saw a dim speck of light & I kicked for it but what with those weights on my feet it was very slow it was heavy work. I had to take a Breath of Air but the dark held me down! Kick! Swim! Up! Up! Up!

I only saw my clock first looking up at it from the floor where I was with my pillow bunched up under my stomach & my sheet wrapped around my ankles. The exact time was 4:19 A.M. but there was light in my room like Sunlight aglow in my window. *This is very early for morning* I recognized then I recognized another Important Fact: the Sun does not come into my bedroom window in the A.M.! So what is this Light all of a sudden? And that rotten little dog yapping across the street.

The Sight I viewed from my window came over me like a splash of ice cold water. I saw Mrs. Calusco's house Ablaze as big as a bonfire—flames jumping out of her windows smoke curling over the Shingles all over her roof.

I was the only Good neighbor over there in such a hurry & I felt the heat come off the house all the way from the sidewalk. I hollered "Mrs. Calusco!" but I did not hear her Answer (if she did). I heard the crack of the wood inside like Bones Breaking. I got up close enough to see the paint bubble off little puffs of smoke under each bubble like a last gasp. In one place already the burning frame was Scorching through in 1 Glance I saw the whole Skeleton of her house on fire under the stucco skin of it. This fire was going to slit the roof open & whip the backs of the walls it was foretelling my Punishment.

Sparks flew off the Shingles they flew up in the wind yellow stars floating in the Air but it was not beautiful. The hot halo over Mrs. Calusco's roof was not beautiful it was the heat of Vengeance.

I heard the Sirens but they were very hard to tell apart from Mrs. Calusco crying. By this time the smoke was very dark &

Pouring Out wrapping around the house but I could see down to the end of the driveway & that was where she was walking out of it like a Zombie. Her eyes stared straight ahead of her & her hands hung down stiff by her sides. She was forcing Words out but I could not hear one of any sense maybe she was only making cries of Pain & Fear.

By now Pecan St. was blocked off at both ends by Fire Engines & Police Cars. Somebody came out of the Ambulance and he led Mrs. Calusco away to shield her from the Disaster. When she saw all the firemen open up their hoses full blast in raging streams drenching the fire in the windows I think she snapped out of her Zombie Trance. She twisted her head around to look back & yelled out "Princess!" i.e. the Name of her little dog.

I tell you I had no Idea how a woman of 92 years can have so much Strength in her arms! She pushed that poor ambulance guy off her & went screaming back into her house Dodging around the busy firemen like a Quarterback in a 4th Down end-run so she was back inside before anybody Recognized what was what.

Something else was what—I saw them under the rose bushes in front of the house a little pile of Magazines the pages peeling back from the heat not burning just curling back. Maybe after her squirrelly Behavior running into a fiery Deathtrap etc. the firemen may Believe Mrs. Calusco is squirrelly enough to be reading Water & Power magazines or LESBOS IN RUBBER.

A minute later I saw her dragged out of there on a Stretcher. Her hair was burned off right down to her scalp & her arms all blisters & some scorched black patches peeled off. They had the oxygen mask strapped on her face but I believe Mrs. Calusco was dead from that moment on.

The noise of the creaking & squeaking I thought was the wheels on the stretcher but underneath it there was Princess coughing up little arf-arf's trying to keep up with her. I guess that pup was outside the whole time & Mrs. Calusco did not look in the right place.

The fire went on & tore her house apart. More sparks sprayed out when ½ the roof caved in & I felt them sting on my scalp. To remind me how disaster missed me THIS TIME. This gave me the heebie-jeebies something terrible when the full force of this message hit me. Down the block on the corner I saw a car parked there & for sure it is not a car I ever saw around Pecan St. before. On the hood 2 men (Mexican hair) leaned up looking at the fire. If I had to swear on any book you name I would say I Recognized 1 of them & he was Carlos gloating over his Revenge against me. It was not going to be very long until he got the news that it was not my house he firebombed it was Mrs. Calusco's so where was I?

A flatfoot came over to clear me off of the sidewalk out of harm's way. He asked me who was this old woman & if anybody else lived in her house. It was hard for me to Talk about it but I told him.

"Where do you live?" he asked me. "Which is your house?"

Which got me thinking clear again. If Carlos sees me go into my Apartment he will know what place to firebomb next. So I was very Disturbed by this. I shook off the eager beaver officer of the Law and ducked into my garage the back way around the yard of the duplex nextdoor. Mrs. Roderiguez left my Safari Suit hanging on the line which I put on over my p.j.'s.

Sitting in the Raymobile out there I faced up to the Obvious Conclusion—namely it was too hot for me to hang around in Mason. It was much too hot for me to lie low wishing for a cool breeze to come blow over Pecan St. Better I should bow out while I still had my bowels to bow with. Better I should take my High Colonic in Dallas.

Dr. Barbara the Radio Psychologist Extraordinaire (she does not broadcast her last name which is a smart move if you ask me) gave out to the whole Tri-City Area with her in-depth Psychoanalysis of Guess Who. After this Episode she expanded her Remarks into a whole page article in the Examiner a fact which my arch-foe shoved under my nose a very unkind Gesture.

I was her Subject of the moment because Albert Abercorn was her Guest of the day since he turned himself into something like a local Celebrity by shooting his big mouth off to any 2 Bit newshound he could buttonhole with the story of his brush with Mystery. I did not know what a shifty & shiftless character he was or how he was in the middle of pleading with the Courts to let him hang on to his daughter Charmagne. His wife (ex) lived (or not) in Parts Unknown his 2 sons lived in Foster Homes all he had left was the girl to show the world *What a good papa am I.*

I am glad to say the glee of this Skunk did not last long!

DR. BARBARA:

1.) The urge to do Good—or what he thinks is Good—might just be the *public face* of Peter Tremayne. It is possible and I'd say it's *likely* that he has one almighty superiority complex. He sees himself as some kind of Superman.

Hardy Har Har!

2.) Good deeds can have dark sides to them. Once he's out there in his own moral universe everything goes. I can't say for sure what it would take to push his actions over the line. He might step over himself before he realizes what he's doing.

I can say! It took a lot! The weight of the world!

3.) I'll stick my neck out and say maybe his urges are already a kind of perversion. Perversions of the selfish desires we all have. Maybe in this man they are abnormally strong. I'd say he is probably a loner. When we live with other people sooner or later we find out that if we want to be accepted and acceptable we have to suppress or disguise our *animal* nature. We use deodorant. We wait in lines. On some level maybe Peter Tremayne knows he is capable of uncontrolled behaviour. This might be *frightening* him into doing what's "right".

Bingo!

4.) I doubt if he can form any long-lasting relationship—with women *or* men. So his

204

Now I'm a classic
example yet!

moral crusade could be a replacement for passionate love. He's the classic example of the Outsider—somebody who's only accountable to himself, but his standards are very high. Unreachable. This knowledge gives him a reason to keep going.

5.)
My best side is my
right side!

The individual we're considering here is a profile of denial. If Peter Tremayne was with us in the studio I'm sure he'd deny that he has any desire to gain attention for what he's doing, or approval or recognition or love. Or that he wants to prove he has power over events. If you let me have 1 wild guess I'd say he might be suffering from impotence or some other sexual dysfunction. Priapus.

Close! But no cigar!
6.)

Or on the other hand premature ejaculation. So that's my diagnosis in a nutshell based on all the evidence we've got about our mystery man. Maybe if you're listening Peter Tremayne you can give me a call on 639–4122

Sorry! I lost my last
dime!

so you can give us your personal views on the topics we've been discussing.

Point by point my Personal view is she came to the correct Conclusions.

Unroll the wide open spaces! The minute our magic carpet (Raymobile) carried us away from Mason the land spread out like a Picnic Blanket all around but I did not Feel like a ant on it. This far from my Apartment on Pecan St. I did not travel in 30 years. Longer even. I could see so far ahead of my hood I saw the Highway did not cut the flat land no it was just laid on top. Painted on. A skinny brushstroke across the dusty crust of the Earth.

For a hour Amelia sat back silent against the car door or

squirmy in the seat. She was a Nervous Passenger a backseat driver in the front but her jitterbug Nerves did not jump & jive because I missed the El Paso signs both times around the block or because on the 2nd time through I forgot about the Stop Sign there & bounced us around a parked school bus at Top Speed. I Believe her real Nerves came from trying to picture the whereabouts of John Newberry at the moment & what he was plotting for her. Or trying to black out this Grimy picture. Maybe she did not need to use her Imagination very much for she knew already Fact By Fact & that was the Worry that crushed her down to Silence.

My only Worry was she did not have her seatbelt on nor the door was not locked but these risks Amelia did not count very High or she did not even notice. Other Dangers distracted her Mind from proper automobile Safety habits. Yes the same way other Ideas distracted my Mind from driving namely I pondered how she got shaped by the personal experiences of her Life. I Observed her round shoulders very female but curved by muscles underneath. Compared to the figure of a swimmer it struck me the same so she plunges in she strokes hard she pulls herself through. Every time she spoke up with a little burst of words I pictured her the same way lifting her face up out of the water for a Breath. "You want the radio on?" for instance or "Look at this clouds Ray. Fline saucers."

"You believe in flying saucers?"

"I believe in somethings," she said. "Some aliens come down here sometimes. I think so." Amelia shrugged & squirmed around sideways again.

"I read a documented article in the Enquirer that said supposedly there's a Air Force base in Arizona where a team of government scientists are studying a preserved alien. Also they've got the wreck of his flying saucer in a hangar."

"You don't believe it hm?"

"Aliens in Arizona?" I thought this over while I changed lanes & slowed down and let a pick-up truck pass us. "I try to keep a open mind about outer space but so far the scientists don't have any concrete evidence to go on."

She had a firm Opinion on this. "They don't tell you every-things. How do you know the evidence they hide someplace?"

"Secret files! They have to leak out sooner or later. Because of human conscience." For Proof I reminded her, "That article in the Enquirer. Or what about Watergate?"

"No," she snapped at me. "If they don't want to tell somethings then—" Amelia made her Point she was not going to Repeat it.

"Aliens among us I'm sure we'd hear about," I said & just paid Attention to my driving. She clammed up & I clammed up back so I was guessing this busy silence was going to be it all the way to Dallas. But 5 minutes later she poked me in the ribs. "Cut it out. I could have a accident."

When I looked her way she had a smile on her like a drunk nun. "I tell you Ray," she said & she held her 2 fingers on her forehead pointing out like horns. "I'm one of those."

"Of who?"

She wiggled her fingers. "Of aliens."

What a Kidder! I had to laugh then & I have to laugh at it the same now I have to wipe my eyes.

When I picked her up at her Motel hideout I saw right away Amelia was planning for the Worst Trouble i.e. she was going in Disguise. She handed me the sports page of the Mason Examiner from the day before & switched the radio on to Dr. Barbara since the T.V. did not work in any way. Amelia went into the bathroom with her black hair brushed down then she came out with a blonde wig on instead. All puffed out on the sides & folded back like pigeon wings. Instead of her Mexican shirt with the parrots she put on a female Safari Suit of beige but she could not cover up her Figure which was strictly Hourglass as we used to say. Mae West the Second. My inner thought was I Doubted if this Disguise was going to make it easier on us sneaking out of there as anony-mous citizens but I did not dare to linger around that Motel & Discuss it.

In case Carlos was the kind of hoodlum who had his Peepers

all over Town I parked the car around the corner from Amelia's
& we got back to it by the Feat of climbing over the swimming
pool fence & beating it down the alley. Mae West the Second with
her Senior Citizen Hero eloping!

Except for the bunches of root beer stands gas stations motels
& telephone poles we were driving in the Land of the Bible.
Maybe if there is The Second Coming (i.e. the whole thing starting
up all over again) it will be in New Mexico it is the Perfect place
for it. There is the Empty Desert below with the Empty Sky above.
This time it will be the Mexicans in Bondage until the Mexican
Moses leads them all up unto the Promised Land after they wander
around Texas for 40 years before they cross over the Rio Bravo
into The Land of Enchantment. Maybe in modern times they can
do it in campers & RVs.

I am off the track here let me stick to the Facts.

Our Conversation about Outer Space etc. led very natural into
Amelia's personal Interest of astrology. From my birthday she
worked out I did not have a choice in certain matters in fact she
Foretold I was going to help her I could not Resist the urge of
the Stars.

"Sagittarius love exciting challenges," she explained to me.
"Good planets for you this month."

"I made up my own mind," I told her. "Where I find wrong
I trample it. Where I find goodness I raise it. It's in my nature."

"Sure sure," she agreed fast, "Sagittarius has high ideals." &
she turned ½ way around away from me & she let out a little sniff
as if I just Proved her point for her. "Somebody can make crimes
for high reasons sometimes."

"Selfish reasons."

"Selfish to make it fair."

"What fair?"

"All this powers!"

I will say Amelia took to Arguments very eager. But I tell you
if I got a 2nd chance at this Conversation with her this minute I
would give true Sympathy to all of her points it does not sound
like Anarchy to my ears anymore.

I Desired to keep our Conversation going for more than just

208

the Entertainment value. My true Motive was I had to Explore her Character so I would know what to Expect if we got into a tight spot etc. From the other tight spot I was in with her I knew she was no kind of limp noodle in a squeeze i.e. she was not going to fall apart when the Pressure was on. On the Fact side that was all I had to count on the rest of her was a Guess & strictly on Trust. So I was going to use this Innocent Talk to uncover her past Motives & tangled up Affairs which lay at the end of our road in Dallas. Any shade of light she could shine on her Personal Story for me was going to Reveal the shape of dark Events ahead. I had to make my Move & take the 1st step down into the secret chambers of Amelia's heart.

"So what sign are you?"

Her eyes went narrow & out of a tight smile she said, "Sagittarius."

"Ah-ha," I nodded. "Just so you know—the planets didn't influence me to help you O.K.? I've got better reasons."

"Planets influence planets so I think they can influence you Ray." She made it her final word on the Subject and yes I will agree how the big will always Influence the small.

We sat very silent after that until we got to the other side of El Paso. The Sun slipped in back of a flock of clouds & the next minute it burned a hole right through it the streams of silvery white light shooting down. The Gates of Heaven opening up to accept the Rising Souls. I felt very Peaceful since I had somebody next to me there seeing this Sight even if we saw it from a different point of view. I know we both felt charmed to be with somebody else who could truly appreciate natural Beauty.

We pulled in to eat lunch in a roadside diner that called itself The Chuck Wagon Coffee Shoppe. While we read over the menu (*Specialty of the House*: Upsidedown Pineapple Upsidedown Cake— I will Explain about that) we talked over the Game Plan.

As far as I understood it it was a Blitz up the middle to her uncle's house in Dallas where Amelia was going to say her Fond Farewells la-dee-doo-dah etc.

2nd Down was a End Run to the bank so she could pass to me

the shiny key of her Safe Deposit Box & add my Name to it. In there was money & precious belongings etc. which she was going to take out also more Important she had in there certain Documents she was holding over John Newberry. Which said Documents were staying in for a guarantee of her Safety all the way to the Mexican border. (I asked her if these certain papers related to The Case Of The Martyred Prexy but she Denied it she told me they only relate to John Newberry very personal and they are Strong enough to keep him off her back.)

3rd Down was a hand-off to a half-back i.e. Amelia had to buttonhole Newberry's boss a man very high up on the F.B.I. ladder of affairs and Inform him of her plan of Return to Mexico & never show her face North of the Border at all ever again & the Fact that I will be the Guardian of the Documents after she is home safe & sound.

4th Down was going to be a punt through the goal posts a field-goal over the Rio Bravo and a victory party in the End Zone.

I had other plays to add in there if we made up the yardage between Downs but I did not bespeak them at the time. I still wanted to get my High Colonic for one thing but just as Important I wanted to Convince Amelia how the Truth would shield her and Justice will triumph and the Conscience of the Nation will find peace if she will tell her Story to the Press the Public & the Government.

Fat Chance!

Leave out the Fact that her entire story was a shaggy dog with Rabies from end to end I was not going to enjoy any Success in the driving seat with her as long as Amelia sniffed the scent of Danger in the air. I was the one on the leash all the time all the time I was plotting this Persuasion in my Mind while I waited for our waitress (Evie the bent-over spinstery one with the banana colored hair pulled straight back & a Voice on her like a Marine Corps drill sergeant) to come back with my Tuna Melt.

Very absent minded I was rubbing my finger around the top of my ice water glass. By Accident I made it squeak out a feeble little Note a little churp that Amelia nailed to the table with a squinty stare.

"Which reminds me," I said which is a Saying of mine that I say when I can not think of anything else to fill in the Blank.

"What?"

I drummed my fingers rat-a-tat-tat on the corner of the table.

"What what?"

"What it reminds you?" She cupped her chin in her hands her round face like a Bouncing Ball she caught there.

"Oh," I said & I did not know what. Until Amelia unbuttoned the top of her safari suit & Fanned herself with her napkin & I saw the loose skin of the slopes of her Bosoms do the Shimmy.

My mind did go back to the Musical Glasses Girl the niece of Mr. Burrows. Pat. It was a Innocent Memory to dig out I did not Reveal any Intimate secrets about my Past especially I did not tell Amelia how I was The Green Ray. I did not Reveal all of the Circumstances all I told Amelia about it was once upon a time I witnessed a beautiful girl making this kind of music in a nightclub. I told her what a talent that Pat Burrows had to show people the Beauties locked inside ordinary Household Objects.

"Then you fall in love with her?"

"That's a personal question."

"Sure!" Amelia was not going to let go of this Topic she just stretched out down the table & waited for me to Open Up she was all ears.

I will Admit it felt very warm to hear somebody besides Dr. Godfrey or Dr. Barbara show something like Interest in my Life so I slipped off guard a little i.e. I was doing all of the Answering. But before I went too far I decided my Story could be my Bait: if I reveal then Amelia will reveal likewise. No Oath is stronger than the mutual TRUST between people who trade Personal secrets of their lives: the soft spots to Protect the INTIMATE places you show & you are not Afraid that somebody close Knows of them. And then I thought *Naked truth attracts like a naked body.*

So I spiced up my Story somewhat—

"I was just a lonely guy in the front row," I said very coy.

Amelia doubted this right off. "That's why you remember her all this years." She laughed out loud. "I don't think so!"

"Call me Mr. Memory."

She put her hand on her mouth to stop her Laugh right there. "You meet her after the show hm? I know this one."

I.e. my Cue to come clean & I hit it on the Money. "I did. You betcha. What can I say? She made a pass at me. I'm red blooded hey I'm a red blooded American boy but I held my nut— pardon my French. I didn't—"

"You didn't do the dirty deed."

"I didn't want to think of her like that."

A stab at the Truth. "Because your wife."

"No wife."

"A girl."

I let her Guess hang in the Air a second. "Sure." I let it go very Casual but I did not hold her eyes which Move told her a very different story.

"What was her name?" she asked me not gentle but careful.

"Annie." (Why not? I was Improvising a mile a minute!)

"You know something? I tell you hm? Annie—it's my favourite. My favourite name for anglo girls. Annie. Miss America."

"She was a little like that."

"Blonde hair."

I nodded.

"Curls." Amelia spun a finger near each side of her head. "And whatchamacallit—so many—dots. So many—freckles."

"You're very good at this," I said & I felt my Voice get shaky. Which I covered this over by a Gulp of ice water. "Let's talk about you now."

"No. I'm no very good. You are you know you stay faithful to her. You marry her?"

More ice water. "Somebody else did." I swirled the stack of ice cubes around in my glass and I Followed them around the Rim with my finger like before but I could not even make a Little Squeak. "Now I regret I didn't make a pass at the glasses girl when I had the chance."

I heard a little hum ring across the table & when I looked over I saw Amelia circling her finger around the rim of her water glass. "My husband taught me how." She stopped the circling & the ringing note Dissolved in the Air.

This new Information regarding her married status egged me on to ask a Friendly follow-up. "What's your husband's name?"

She turned her face away & gave herself a Private smile. "Julio. It's Julio."

"Julio. I see. What's it in English?" I took a guess. "Julius?"

"I'm not married to him now." She frowned she shrugged it off & she was staring out into the Parking Lot. Very down-to-Earth she stated, "He died."

"I'm sorry to hear that." But the words from my lips were not the words from my Heart. Yes I was sorry for the Sad Effect of her hubby's Demise on Amelia but some Feeling I felt from the bottom of my spine from the back of my ribs was Pushing me toward her across the table. I felt a Desire to sit on the other side of the booth with her & squeeze her hands in that moment but I Resisted the Urge.

She blinked the sun out of her eyes. "*You* remind *me* now."

"What—?"

"You don't want to hear?"

"I don't mind," I said Gentle Enough to let her out of it if she did not strictly want to go into it any Further.

"Don't worry," she said. "It's no real sad. I like to remember him."

THAT WAS EXACTLY WHAT I WANTED HER TO DO!

She sipped a sip of ice water then she said it again, "I like to remember him."

"Where'd you kids meet?"

"Our work. When I'm a teenager you know?"

"What kind of place?"

"You think it's naughty," she warned me.

I shook my head. "Don't I look like I've been around the block a couple of times? Go on. Surprise me."

"O.K.," she Prepared me for it. "A nightclub." Amelia threw her hand across her mouth & opened up her eyes very wide acting full of Shame & Shock.

I showed her I was no Slouch at ham Acting either. I let my mouth hang open. I gave her a little gasp. I Clutched my Heart. "Shame on you!" I said. "What kind of job does a young girl do in a nightclub?" For a second I was not Ham Acting my stomach went a little fizzy with Recalling my moments with Charmagne et al.

I got that sly smile again from the corner of her mouth and the corner of her eye. "I took the nice coats from the nice sirs & nice ladies. I put them on hangers. They go inside and see the show. I stay with the coats for them & I go into all the nice pockets. Sirs & ladies come out again. I smile very nice very pretty. I get a nice tip."

"Some racket." (And I meant this Remark! I always Wondered if hatcheck girls in fancy shmancy nightspots go through the pockets of the Unwary while they are Unwatched. So anyway that is one big mystery in my Life solved! Me I always keep a Tight Grip on my personal belongings in Public places because of the 5 truest words in the English Language: THE MANAGEMENT IS NOT RESPONSIBLE.) Now back to the Action—

"Julio met the customers from the door. He bow to the sirs and he touch ladies' hands on his lips. Then he give me their nice fur coats."

"He was the maitre d'."

"Very elegant. Very distinguish."

"That's a very snazzy occupation for a teenager," I said & I tried to make it sound like a sincere compliment.

"Teenager? Julio you mean?"

"You said when you were a teenager."

"I was 16 years Julio was 47 years. He was a man hm?"

I did some quick Math. The Difference between them was 31 years which by a strange Coincidence was exactly the Difference Between Amelia and me. I did a good job of Disguising my double surprise in a carefree Remark. "You fell for his tuxedo—am I close?"

She shook her head. "No. His hands. When I saw him play. He play so pretty songs you know I have to love him."

"Julio was a *musical* maitre d'. I see." I pictured him with his Perfect posture his wavy pompadour going silver gray on his Temples his sharp nose pointing down his square chin Thrusting out a Spanish smoothie with all the Angles standing in a hot spotlight Centre Stage behind his tray of musical glasses. Three notes into the 1st verse of "Lady of Spain" and he Captured her tender teenage heart. Or the popular favorite "More." One of those Songs I bet or "Volare". Amelia started Playing her ice water glass again & she had a Dreamy Look in her eyes on top of it. "What song did he play?" I asked her.

She was humming it. She was humming Chattanooga Choo-Choo. "Chatanooga Choo-Choo!" she snapped back with the Answer like it was the winning title in Name That Tune.

"Nice choice."

"I don't know I look at his fingers. Very gentle. Very soft. Maybe if I don't hear that music I can still fall in love with him. Sure. I think so. I fall in love from his touches."

My hands were lying there Flat on the table like a couple of Flounders. I picked up my Napkin I Opened it on my lap & I folded my hands down there too.

"I look at his fingers and I think *mm-mm* what does it feel like if he touches me? How he touches his glasses. With his fingers on my skin will I ring like little bells too? Very naughty for 16 hm? You think so?"

I am not a Swami I did not have the Powers to look into my ice water glass & see Julio the nightclub his musical glasses the fur Coats her Romance etc. it was all a colorful Fairytale made up on the spot by Amelia for my Entertainment. Also to Entice me. I will say it did the job all right this Story pushed me Further toward her it gave Amelia a very Strong Allure. And this new Allure was much stronger than the other allure of her Urgent Need it Lulled me I will Admit. I let my questions about the True Nature of her trouble slip down the back of my Mind which was my Fatal Mistake. I was going against the Number 1 Rule of a Crime Stopper:

DO NOT GET INVOLVED PERSONAL!

I had to think ½ a second if I wanted to hear Further from this touching exploit of hers. "So you married Julio then?"

"After 1 week."

"Was he—was it—was he—" (Why did I get choked up over this?)

"Very naughty. Very beautiful."

"So," I sipped a mouthful of ice water, "Did you two have any children?"

Her face went tight & her Voice Collapsed down to 1 dense point very Distant, "No."

"Hot stuff comin' through!" Evie shoved our ice water glasses out of her way with her forearms & set down our Platters. "Tuna melt slaw cottage cheese & onion rings for the gentleman. Cheese burger slaw & fries for the lady." She ripped our bill off her little pad and left it facedown on the table next to my plate. "Folks enjoy your meal now."

Once her Food was in front of her Amelia did not say much she just Concentrated on eating which was a very Serious Affair to her. I believe you do not need a Trained eye to Observe how a person's character can leak out in a Simple Act like chewing. By the Eager way she bit into her burger & rolled the mouthful around on her tongue & gave out with "mm-mm" every so often I saw in a Flash how she was a woman very Motivated by her Senses. She bit into that double-decker bun that $\frac{3}{4}$ lb. of charcoal broiled beef like a wild dog who learned the Party Trick of eating at a table. I practically Forgot about my Tuna Melt by the time she was on her last bite I felt my stomach filling up just by Watching her she ate so Vivid!

"If you're not going to eat yours can I have it?" she asked me.

I gave her half of my tuna melt just so I could Watch Again. I still had room after my slaw so I rounded things off with a mile-high slice of Upsidedown Pineapple Upsidedown Cake.

"While you're here the Management hope that you will take time out for a visit to our famous Texas Upsidedown House." Evie stood by my elbow with a fresh pot of coffee tilted over my Empty cup she came around the tables like Clockwork. Also like Clockwork she switched her Spiel on again which poured out of her mouth like the hot coffee poured out of her pot. "The building is the authentic replica of the actual ranch house built by Otis

Peachtree in 1881 & it preserves the mystery of the Cedar Room just as it appeared to the Peachtree family over 100 years ago."

"What's the mystery of the Cedar Room?" I asked her and I put my hand over my coffee cup which was Brim full. "No more coffee," I smiled up.

"Magnetism." Evie poured Amelia a fresh cup. "It's amazing. It truly is. I can't explain to you. Nobody can. If I try to I know I'll just get it wrong." She slid back into her sing-song. "Tickets are $1.50 for adults 75¢ for children under 10 which you can obtain in the Gift Shoppe at the entrance to the Upsidedown House. You'll also find a selection of unique souvenirs of your visit."

She stopped Reciting & stopped pouring she smiled all the way around from Amelia back to me (not a real smile it was a Authentic Replica of one) and shuffled off to bus the table across the Aisle. My Curiosity was Aroused very much by Evie's talk of the mystery of the Cedar Room. I just had my mouth open to ask Amelia if she would care to case said Premises when Evie is there again like the Genii out of Aladin's lamp.

"Did I forget to tell you you get a 10% discount off your bill if you choose to visit the Upsidedown House?" I informed her of that Feature being News to us. "Dearie me," she said, "I must be going senile. I left out Otis Peachtree to a customer yesterday."

"Who?" Amelia asked Evie very puzzled.

"Oh Lord. Did I leave him out of it again?" Her two eyebrows nosedived.

By the Glee that Fluttered across Amelia's face I saw right away she was Teasing Evie with it. In my book not a Good Natured thing to do but I let her Enjoy her joke a couple of seconds before I jumped down on it & Squashed it Dead.

"Now who's going senile?" I said to her very There There There & reached over & shook Amelia very gentle on her arm. Which she Answered me by pursed lips & she Shook her head a little. I gave back my Attention to Evie. "Does the Peachtree family still own the house?"

"Naw. Company. Company owns it. Maybe there's a Peachtree up in the company. Probably is—it's in Atlanta." Her joke this time but Evie was the only one of us who was laughing. "I can tell you one thing for sure. If I find out from a doctor my memory's affected on account of that magnetism well I know I'm only a lowly waitress but I'm gonna find a lawyer and sue somebody for compensation." Then she added on, "If I can find somebody up in the company who'd take responsibility."

I am a Sucker for this certain kind of Attraction I am Stimulated by any Scientific mystery which baffles the Experts. Amelia did not share my high level of Curiosity about the mystery of the Upsidedown House so I had to Compromise on how long our Investigation of it was going to last. We made a Deal I would not tarry inside over 15–20 mins. but Amelia was going to stick with me from Entrance to Exit and make sure I stuck to my Side of the Bargain.

The Theory which Amelia lived by was A Moving Target Is Hard To Hit. She got Nervous staying in 1 place longer than she strictly had to which is a Fear I did not Feel myself at the time but I do now. So now I Understand so now I feel it from the Inside it is too late to do any Good.

From the outside my Argument was the chances of John Newberry knowing she was on the Road with me I Calculated being Zero or lower & if I did not go see what was what about this Upsidedown House I was going to live to Regret it & what I missed will be on my Mind the whole time I am driving in Other Words a Distraction so the chances of driving off the road go up 100%. So what is the Worst that can Happen? We get to Dallas 15–20 mins. later but we have seen with out own eyes a Natural Phenomenon we did not even *know of* when we got out of bed this morning. Is that so bad? To Learn about 1 more of the 1,001 Mysteries of the Earth going on around us 1 more jewel from the treasure chest of Knowledge? Is this such a waste of time? For a person to spend 15–20 mins. Investigating & discovering a new fact in existence collecting it to add to the other pieces of Info in front of him to Contemplate it & try & understand how this one fits with that one how they Fit Together how it all makes Sense? I want to know what Goes On in this World! I want to know what I do not know! Is that a Crime? (Ah-ha. Maybe THIS is where all my trouble begins.) How can a Human Being arrive at any Conclusions if he only knows part of the whole big picture? Only the Ignoramus turns his back on a Wonder of the Modern World. A Double Ignoramus if he does not pick up such a Rare Trophy when it is placed before him.

I bought the 16oz. Upsidedown House Thermos Bottle in the Trading Post Gift Shoppe the 8oz. version looking too small to Satisfy 2 thirsty people for the hours of Highway miles ahead. To go along with the Theme of the place the real cup was in the Bottom of the thermos which unscrewed instead of the usual screwtop cup on top which did not. (Amelia chided me at first for Flushing $16.95 down the Toilet on buying this Item but she was happy to Receive her hot cup of Coffee later on in the Motel room at least she was after her safari suit soaked in the sink & the coffee stain came out in the Cold Rinse.)

The Entrance to the Upsidedown House is a regular wood porch the wood slats very dusty & gray. Inside it is what Evie said a ranch house Parlour of the 1880's—pot belly stove furniture carved out of sticks cattle horns on the wall etc. the whole place put together from it looks like giant popsicle sticks. A lace doily on a table with Kerosene lamp on it & a little glass bowl Decorated with purple berries was the only Female touch.

Amelia was the only other person in there with me so I was not Distracted it was easy for me to Breathe In the dusty smell and Focus on a Detail in the room (the glass berry bowl) and Imagine I am back in 1880. The way the light slanted in the front windows was the same way it slanted in 100 years ago. The Peachtrees saw days like this the Sky the same powder blue the sunrays smacking into the Parlour wall in that same square of gold light maybe while they ate their biscuits & black-eyed peas & gravy or whatever kind of Frontier food they had for Dinner. It Stimulated me when I Imagined the real people in that room they are only Tombstones now but they talked over Problems laughed over Jokes etc. they had Arguments over little things ("It ain't my chore to fill up the lamps!" e.g.) flesh & blood people walked around and talked around that place was full of the Voices of Yore.

"Looks the way it looks on the post cards," Amelia observed a drop Sarcastic.

"You don't have the taste for adventure," I aimed it right back at her. "Like I do." I let my own Suspense build up approaching the Mystery Room. A Warning Sign up on the wall of the hall had a big black arrow pointing the way. "You want to wait here for me?" I gave Amelia back her drop of the sarcastic.

The warning sign said:

WARNING! DO NOT ENTER THE MYSTERY ROOM
IF YOU—
—Suffer from a Heart Condition
—Suffer from Vertigo
—Suffer from a Nervous Condition
—Suffer from Claustrophobia
—Wear a Pacemaker
—Wear a Steel Plate in your head
THE MANAGEMENT IS NOT RESPONSIBLE FOR
INJURIES

La-dee-doo-dah etc.

I did not Suffer or wear any of the above so that warning sign was like a Special Invitation to me which might show up something about my Personality. I went in the Direction of the arrow down the square hall to the door of the Mystery Room.

Which is 2 rooms I saw—the major part of the Mystery Effect covers a Circular Area that cuts $\frac{1}{2}$ into the bedroom and $\frac{1}{2}$ into the Cedar Room which is Col. Peachtree's office behind. I stood on the threshold of the bedroom and from that point of view I see the Entire place is upsidedown—the ceiling is on the floor & the kerosene lamp hangs UP on its chain Floating in the middle of the room like a Sea flower. The bed is on the Ceiling all made up with sheets blankets & pillows all tidy all in place. Facing DOWN. On the little table next to the bed the hairbrushes perfume bottles chatchkas & whatnot all looking down from the ceiling! The clothes in the closet full of suits all hanging UP from the floor—

Around the middle of the room very Faint to the eye is a glassy

Shimmer like Heat Waves coming in through one wall going out the other.

This is enough of a Mystery already but the big jolt hit me when I took a step inside I will say it felt like I stepped through the Curtain of a Invisible waterfall. I stood in the middle of the bedroom & took a look around. It made my stomach feel Dizzy to see what I saw—the floor below & the ceiling above as per Normal but behind me Amelia is standing in the doorway completely Upsidedown!

"I want to go," she said very sharp. "I want to go now."

"Come in here first. You should see this! You won't believe it in here!" I waved both my arms over my head thinking how I look to her like a Fly on the Ceiling. "It's once in a Lifetime Amelia!"

"No. I don't like it." She sounded angry. "You come out O.K.?" She had her arms wrapped around herself when she headed for the Exit so I saw she was angry because she was Scared. Not just Scared on account of holding still for 15–20 mins. I believe she was Scared by the place with its topsy-turvy Effect.

"It's a natural phenomenon!" I called out to her I tried to Lure Amelia back but all I got for my Answer was the Sound of her hard shoes click-clacking away down the hard floor outside.

I agree with Dr. Gabriel Camisa, Ph.D. the Professor of Physics at Texas A. & M. University who offers his Opinion on the Reason for the Mysterious Effect of the Mystery Room on the back of the brochure. To wit: It is a possibility that the crust of the Earth is a little thin under the Peachtree house so this spot acts like a Funnel for the Earth's inner magnetism. I believe in the work of the late Albert Einstein scientists received a pointer towards the Discovery of how the magnetic field of a planet or star has the Power to bend light Rays. It could be this is such a case with the Upsidedown House i.e. the Light Rays coming into the Mystery Room being bent around in front of our very eyes by a Fountain of Magnetic Force. From the outside everything inside looks Upsidedown. On this side is Sense on that side is Nonsense. But there is a Reason behind both sides that ties them together so they both make sense at the same time. I believe here is another Lesson of Life through Science.

Over on the opposite side of the Cedar Room which Connected to the bedroom I was in—outside of the curtain of Shimmery Air—the flag of Texas hung on a pole upsidedown. (Like everything else from my point of view including Amelia who went pacing to & fro past the Exit door.) I saw what I wanted to see I had my Memories so I did not spend any more time looking over Col. Peachtree's office. I offered my salute to the Stars & Stripes which was draped on the wall over the rolltop desk. It was the Genuine Article the old model of 36 stars in Perfect Condition. In front of that Flag my Mama & Papa got granted United States of America citizenship so I could be born in Philadelphia. It was the first Flag that flew over the Panama Canal another great American achievement.

"I think you get lost inside," Amelia greeted me full of Relief now we could get going again.

"You should've come inside," I told her while I was still thinking back on my Experience. "It's really something to see."

I felt her take my arm & start Pulling me toward the car. "I don't need to. I can stand on my head for free," still with the sarcastic Voice on her.

For her Sake I did not want to Linger but for my Sake I did not enjoy the tugging & the pulling the way she wanted to bum's rush me out of the Vicinity of the most Terrific Display I ever saw outside of the Natural History Museum! I stopped on the spot on the Excuse I had to fish my car keys out of my shirt pocket but also so I could take 1 last look over my shoulder. There I saw a Sight which turned my stomach & broke my peace of Mind—

I saw Old Glory hanging Upsidedown. That Vision gave me a pain. So what so it was the Optical Illusion etc. but also it was a sight full of Disrespect for our Flag to see it Stripes above & Stars below. It is a symbol of Anarchy in that form.

"Wait a minute," I said to Amelia. "I'll be right back."

She had her hands on her hips now ready to tell me off. "Back from where?"

"I'm going back in there."

"That's not right. That's not fair."

"I'll be half a sec." I turned around in the Exit.

"Selfish," she judged me. "Selfish with my time."

I was through into the door but I came out again I explained, "I'm not doing this for myself Amelia. I'm doing it for all the visitors who come after me."

She made her mouth very small at me but what was she going to do? Wrap herself around my ankles? Still I would drag her in to do my Duty my Feeling about it was so Strong. I heard a Higher Calling I wanted her to understand.

If I had a lower calling I believe Amelia would not kick up such a Stink if I had to go take a leak for instance. The urgent Feeling in my bladder she would understand but not my urgent Feeling of Patriotism. In my earlier Life (3 weeks ago) if you asked me I would tell you on my part peeing & Patriotism have 1 thing in common: both of them are Natural Urges pure & simple. I do not Believe this anymore. Patriotism is much more complicated. It is not just a case of unzipping your fly & pointing in the Right Direction.

In a flash I was back inside the Cedar Room face to face with the Flag but also in some Confusion on the subject. Because in there Old Glory was rightside up. I had to Weigh it in my own Mind the pros & cons of the Situation—

Should I climb up there and hang it the other way around on the wall?

PRO: The world outside will look in to see Old Glory correct & proper.

CON: To accomplish this I will have to turn it Upsidedown in here.

PRO: This room is in the middle of a Special Condition (mystery effect) which cancels out Normal Rules.

CON: It is private property perhaps my act is Vandalism.

PRO: The view from the other side of the Exit is vandalism against all our Flag stands for.

CON: After I leave I am sure Evie or some body else is just going to put it back the way it was before.

PRO: So what. I am here now so I must do what I feel is right or I will live to Regret it.

CON: If I get caught doing this I will have to Explain things to the Manager and that will keep us on the premises & stall our Departure.

PRO: I can do it Fast.

CON: Not if I keep going Back & Forth weighing up the pros & cons!

PRO: I have to make sure I am doing the Right thing.

CON: If I have to think about it maybe it is *not* the Right thing.

PRO: Where there is *wrong* I trample it. Where there is *right* I raise it up.

Like a mountain goat I Climbed on top of the rolltop desk so I could Reach the top hooks on the upper corners of the Flag. They came off very easy only a flick of the wrist & in 10 Seconds flat I flipped the Flag around and went over to the Exit to Admire the new view. I saw the Rightside Up Stars & Stripes in the upsidedown room from outside in the Rightside Up world and I felt almost very Satisfied about it.

"Naughty boy," Amelia scolded me with a smile. "That's a crime. That's whatchamacallit."

"Vandalism."

"Vandalism. Naughty naughty."

"It's not vandalism," I pointed out while we kicked through the red dust in the parking lot. "I didn't hurt the furniture. I didn't hurt anything."

"You hurt the decoration."

"It's a relative thing."

"I saw you. I'm the eye witness."

"Stop talking like that."

"How?"

"You know how. You know how you're talking. Accusing."

Amelia stopped me a yard short of the Raymobile. "Hey. Who put a chilli pepper up *your* butt?"

"Don't try to charm me," I said then she said something to the sky in Mexican. "What did you say? Excuse me can you repeat it please in a language I understand?"

"You're loco." Another judgement from her. This time with her head shaking very slow. She tried to open the car door but it was Locked Up so she had to look over in my Direction. "Do you have your keys?"

I felt Crabby I felt like a steel belt was Squeezing my skull together. I felt the Pressure build up from poison fog rolling into my Mind very heavy very dark. Vandalism was not my crime my crime was worse—

CON: In relationship to the surface of the Earth the flag is hanging upsidedown.

By my own Hand I did that. It does not make a Difference how it looks from the parking lot either! The plain Fact is Old Glory is upsidedown on a wall in a room and I hung it that way: The End! That was the True Physical Fact: The End! A person had to be Albert Einstein on the moon to see it from any Other Angle.

"I'll be right back." I turned right around I marched across the parking lot toward the Upsidedown House Exit with Amelia dogging me.

She tugged on my sleeve. "I want the keys," she snapped. "Please I want the car keys."

"Let me do this first."

"Please I want the car keys."

"Please let me do this first."

Back & Forth like that all the way back into the Cedar Room. Amelia finally let go of me when I went through the Magnetic Effect but I was not alone in the room. A little boy was standing next to the rolltop desk staring at the Flag trying to figure out what was Wrong with it. I touched his shoulder to move him out of my way.

"Excuse me sonny." I climbed up on the desk.

"Daddy!"

I had both of the top hooks unhooked when I heard Footsteps enter the room behind me.

"What's he doing Daddy?"

His Voice up so I could hear him Daddy said, "Maybe the man works here. Did you ask him?"

The pipsqueak squeaks up to me, "Do you work here?"

"No," I told him & I was turning the Flag around.

Daddy steps in. "If you don't work here you mind if I ask you what you think yore doin'?"

I did not have to think about it anymore. I was hanging the flag Rightside Up. "I'm hanging the flag rightside up."

He stepped up to me this son of a sodbuster this Daddy who was built like a blond-haired tractor and maybe 21 years old. "You shouldn't do that."

"Yes I should. It was upsidedown."

"It's the Upsidedown House," Gomer spelled it out for me. "So it's supposed to be upsidedown. Now put it back the way it was."

"Daddy," Gomer, Jr. was hanging on his Daddy's back pocket. "Are you going to fight him?"

"Quiet son," he said but he was looking at me. "C'mon mister. You're just spoilin' the fun for the kids."

"It's not supposed to be upsidedown in any way." I was up on the desk again Stretching Up to hook the last corner. I missed & the flag hit the floor.

The pipsqueak squealed & clapped his little hands. "Fight him!"

My guess is Daddy used to be a high school basketball star he had a Reach on him like a Cargo Crane. He spread Old Glory by the corners & felt for the hooks on the wall to hang it back up Upsidedown—I made it very Difficult for him to do that because I was pulling on the bottom corners at the Same Time.

"Hot damn man. I toad you let go!"

I yank it hard & we both hear some Stiches on it somewhere Tear Open. We stop tugging. We stop yelling. We freeze solid.

"Fight him Daddy!"

And I feel the heel of Junior's junior cowboy boot Crunch Down hard on my toes. His Daddy takes Advantage while I am off-balance—giving out a little whimper & grabbing the Flag out of my hands he holds it up against the wall—he has his big flat hand planted in the middle so I am trying to pull it around by the bottom corner with one hand and trying to swat Junior off me with the other—now I am getting the pointy toe Treatment from his little boot in my shin *peck—peck—peck—peck—peck—pe*—all of a sudden it stops dead—

By the Salty Odor on the Air I know Amelia is there—but Junior is not anymore since now he is walking backwards with his arms pinned back until she turns the tike loose. Of course like a Genuine Coward he runs over to Daddy & hides behind him & Clamps himself to Gomer's stilty leg—

"She fighted me Daddy!"

This takes Gomer's mind off the Flag Situation. "Huh? Who did son?"

"Now we got a fair fight!" I lunged for Old Glory—& I missed it by ½ a hair all because Amelia had a Grip on my wrist at the same time & by it she Jerked me hard in the Opposite Direction. I raised my Voice, "Who's side are you on here?"

"You take too long!"

"I'm not finished yet!"

"I want the keys. I want to go."

"Yore s'posed t'set a good example for little kids," Gomer snorted at us.

"By putting the American flag upsidedown like that?" I made 1 more Grab at it.

"Fight him Daddy! Fight the lady!" Junior is kicking his Papa now & howling like a half-pint Cab Calloway.

"I'm puttin' it back the way it was before you came in here and messed it up Grandad." He did not look down from his Work he said, "Now quit."

Junior quit boo-hooing but he pointed his finger in my Direction. "Bad man. Bad man. Bad man."

The Flag was hanging Upsidedown with Gomer on guard in front of it with his red arms Crossed on his chest. Junior did what his Daddy said & he followed what his Daddy did—he stopped the pointing he tried to Cross his arms against us just like Gomer was doing.

Good Intentions + Will Power = Complications. By this I

227

made my Worst Mistakes. Also by this Formula a Mr. and a Mrs. lie down in the Marriage bed and this is how little children come into the world in a Vicious Circle. I am happy to say up to the very end that is *one* Mistake I never made.

In my rearview I saw the Romantic sight of the sun going down behind the tail-lights of the Raymobile and out the windshield I saw the long Indian rubber shadow stretch in front. With the Acceleration it felt like I was Riding on a Slingshot shooting into the dark of night which loomed before me.

I will not say I was in a Happy Mood at that minute & the main Reason for my temporary Misery was sitting nextdoor to me in the front seat. Amelia Decided to punish me on Account of my tardy departure from the premises of the Upsidedown House which she did by the Silent Treatment. By no means it was not silent in the car since she wanted to keep all of the windows wide open for the Air which I agreed about since it was so dry & hot my Air Conditioning being on the fritz since 1975.

Maybe we go 20 or 30 miles in this loud & silent Condition before Amelia loosens up & relaxes a inch so she feels the urge to converse with me again.

"Look at those trees," she pointed into the Landscape on her side of the car.

Those trees she meant were curly cactus things crooked Silhouettes propped up between the orange earth & the orange sky. Bent over branches hooks branching into hooks a nest of Question Marks hanging in the Air. But I did not Observe them Correctly so I did not see how they stood there for warning signs for me Personal.

"Nice," I grunted. (I had to warm up to being Pleasant Company again after those long lonely Miles.)

"You want coffee?"

I told her No Thank You very much not at the moment but she should help herself the Thermos was on the backseat. Here is another Example of how Consequences of certain Actions can sneak up i.e. how my past Invades me. And this idea applies to Objects the same.

I was Concentrating on the road in particular I was wrestling the Question around in my mind should I turn on my headlights. Only by Chance I took a glance sidewise when Amelia had the Thermos in her lap. "Remember—" I started to Remind her it was a Upsidedown Thermos with the plug on the bottom & the plug fits very Loose.

Of course she unscrewed it from the bottom which is the Correct move with a Upsidedown Thermos but she was holding it rightside up i.e. upsidedown from the point of view of the Bottle Inside. Hot coffee leaked out all over her hands all over the Safari Suit Pants too. Oh did Amelia screech! Out of surprise & out of pain she threw my Thermos on the floor she gave it a kick with her heel! All the coffee poured out and the smell of it mixed with the rubber mat & rubber coffee steam Plastered her side of the windshield.

I did not pull over it did not look like such a big Emergency. Her fury was a real Surprise Attack but I am proud to say I stayed very calm in the Circumstances.

"There's a kleenex in the glove compartment," I said.

She was still in a Panic. "Where?"

"The glove compartment. Just push the button."

She pushed but the lid stayed shut. "It's locked."

"The lid sticks. Push the button and pull the edge."

She pulled the edge. She pushed the Button. She screeched at it. I leaned over to push the button for her but she beat me to it with a Screech & a kick she hit the dashboard with one heel and the Glove Compartment with the other. The lid just dropped open then & the kleenex Amelia pulled out of the glove compartment was its white Flag of Surrender.

I will not say she was Unpredictable but I will say Amelia had a Explosive Temperament. In that minute I saw a glimpse into her True Character—all of her Reactions came very instant. When she got what she wanted when her reaction Satisfied her she sank back & waited for the next thing.

It is a Tradition to compare a Beloved woman to a flower of some Variety which captures her Nature. Annie LaSalle I will always Compare with a Rose thorns & pink petals. Amelia I will

Compare with a Venus Fly Trap. Sitting still until a bug lands on her—tickle tickle—then she springs into action DEVOURS then sinks back & waits for the next bug.

"What's that noise?" Amelia rolled up the window to hear better.

A rough rattle like Metal Maracas was knocking around somewhere Under the car.

"You probably kicked the motor off its hinges." I rolled my window up too & the Sound muffled down. "It's probably nothing."

So right on cue my steering wheel starts Vibrating in my hands and 1 second later out Grinds this loud sharp CRACK!—my Motor VAROOMS out of Control but my Acceleration is completely KAPUT! All along I only put in High Octane and I did not Detect any problem of a Mechanical Nature after the caper on the streets of the East 8th so even a car can Disguise its inner Injuries I found out!

Amelia had a instant Reaction to this Emergency: she sank down in the seat & she stared straight Ahead like she was facing a Firing Squad.

"Don't panic," I told her.

She was murmuring a Mexican singsong that was all & her 2 dull eyes staring Straight Ahead into the Valley of the Shadow of Death. This Behavior made my Nerves stand on end.

"Don't panic." I said it to Myself this time.

About ½ a mile further down at the end of a long Slope in the road I saw the friendly lights of a Gas Station flicker on. I was going 60 mph and I bet we had enough Momentum on us to coast all the way to the pumps.

"Look," I tried the cheerful Approach, "I bet we can coast all the way down."

She snapped out of her singsong. "No more car no more time."

"Sez you!"

My tires kick up rocks & dust I barrel down the hill & I must look like a Hot Rod from behind with a Rocket under the hood! Good thing my steering & my brakes were still in business so as

Planned I coast into the station and stop on a Dime right next to the pumps. The Raymobile shivered when I shut off the key.

I did not see him but the kid on duty saw my Entire Landing and he was right on the spot with his mouth full of half chewed tuna fish sandwich. His overalls were clean & perfect so I Figured he was at the start of his shift & he was going to be happy to help a Customer with a problem that was more of a Challenge than a empty gas tank. He had that Boy Scout look on him—straight blond hair with the part on the side very Neat.

He stuffed the rest of his sandwich into his mouth and got down on all fours for a look under the car. "Whatsa matter with it?" he asked me from down there.

"It won't go," I said. "I coasted in."

"Lemme hear the engine." I fired it up and Revved. He waved his sandwich in my window. "Whoa! O.K. that's enough."

"I step on the gas—I get nothing. I think maybe it's the fuel pump. Or a rod." I wanted to show him I am not a Stranger to Auto Parts. "One of those or the cam."

"Welp," he said, "You got a problem somewheres in your drive train. Maybe your transmission."

"Can you put a new one in? We have to get to Dallas tonight."

"New transmission," he gave out a shy chuckle. "Right."

"Also fill 'er up."

"Right. Wanna drive over to the bay over there?" He pointed to the Garage Area next to the office.

I started the motor & put it into Drive but the Raymobile did not drive. Amelia looked at me deadpan.

"Yep," said the kid. "Transmission."

I got out to push. And another car pulls in the Station it Swings all the way around & pulls up on the other side of the pumps. Very Ordinary for a car it was powder blue or powder beige it was a Ford or a Chevy. Either that or a Buick. The unusual Feature I did Observe was instead of a mirror on the door it had a Searchlight screwed on there.

Also the 4 men inside it gave us the Once Over which made Amelia turn away from the Heat of their Gazes. Only 1 of them stands out in my Memory in living color a hefty man with wispy red hair like feathers on his head & very hairy hands. I saw him in Broad Daylight when he Leaned out of his window to get the kid's Attention. His cheeks both very apple red too I thought from cramming his heavy neck into a shirt collar that was too Tight. Nice 3-piece suit though which Matched his car but dirty fingernails on him. Those dirty fingernails I Remember most of all.

"Hold it a minute," the kid said to me. "Lemme do this first." He stepped between the pumps & unhooked the Unleaded. "Fill 'er up?"

"You bet," the redhead said and he Climbed out of his car for a Stretch. He nodded to me. "Evening."

"Hiya." I did not want to get Distracted by small talk I had my transmission on my Mind.

He leaned over a little he looked right past me & he Peered in to catch Amelia's eye. "Senorita," he Greeted her before he came back to me with a Wink. "Or is it Senora?"

We nodded & grinned at each other very Manly. "My transmission," I Volunteered.

"Oh." He was Neutral about it. "What is that? A '65?"

" '63."

"How many miles you put on that thing?"

"Not as many as I've got on me."

"Right," he Agreed in a friendly manner. "Ford don't tell you how many they put in it at the factory. Never know when they're goin' to run out on you."

"It's probably just the transmission."

He laughed very easy at my Remark. I was starting to wonder what was the big joke about a little Mechanical Problem like a worn out Transmission! So what so I am stuck in a gas station ½ a hour for the kid to Open a Box take out a new one & put it in! Big joke!

"Got far to go?" he asked me.

"How far is Dallas from here?"

He put his head into his car. "How far's Dallas?"

Somebody inside Cracked Back, "From where?" and somebody else told him, " 'Bout 200."

"About 200 miles," he told me. "If your transmission's busted I don't expect you'll get inta Dallas till tomorrow night."

The kid hung up his pump and asked the guy, "Cash or charge?" and he got handed a Credit Card.

'Say son? You think I can get you to put up one of our posters in the office there?" He handed out a little Flyer which the kid took just being Polite.

"I hafta ask Mr. Pepper. It's his station."

"That's Choley Pepper iddn't it?"

"Yeah he's priddy pertic'lar 'bout advertisin' on the premises." The kid Finished with the Card & gave it back.

"Can I get that receipt?"

"Oh sorry. That's yours." He tore it off the Carbon he passed it over with a thin smile.

"Mr. Pepper'll be all right about it," he told the kid. "Tell him Wayne brung it over."

"Wayne. Yes sir."

"Wayne Feather."

"O.K.," said the kid but he did not look up from the Poster in his hands.

Before he Climbed back in the car Wayne Feather passed me over one of his Posters too. "Maybe you can find someplace for this."

I was Reading it over when he Drove out of the Station. It was printed like a Wanted Poster and where the Photo of the Fugitive is usually there was a Drawing of a drunk lazy Mexican stretched out on a whole row of chairs in a Welfare Office & all around him was a crowd of clean cut Americans fretting & fuming. Up over the drawing it said in big letters: WANTED! And under it it said: FOR ROBBERY AND MURDER.

According to the Information on the poster the ROBBERY was of food out of American mouths & money out of American pockets & jobs out of American towns. The helpless MURDER victim was the American Family. Innocent Americans had to Suffer from these terrible crimes Performed by the mobs of Wetbacks gate-crashing the U.S. border. They ruin the Economy. They breed they fester they Infest. They walk on the grass la-dee-doo-dah.

233

The Poster wanted to Arouse all Decent American to join up with their local Citizens Patrol to help keep out Mexican pests & parasites and keep America safe for Americans. This was a Community Service of the Knights of the Ku Klux Klan.

I Crumpled mine up I threw it Direct in the Trash but the kid left his Poster on top of a pump. "Let's get your car over to the service bay."

I was going to tell Amelia she will have to get out we are going to push but when I looked in she was gone. "You see where my friend went?"

"Uh-uh," the kid said from the Rear End of the car. He Suggested, "Prob'ly in the powder room."

I am not huffing or puffing at all while we push. "What do those guys do with this Citizens Patrol business?"

"Depends I guess," the kid said. "They say they don't do nothin' 'cept drive up & down the border around Juarez an' stuff. An' when they catch a wetback they hold him for the Border patrol."

"Can they do that?"

"If they can or not I guess they do."

He got the car up on the Elevator thing & he gave underneath a Professional Examination—he unscrewed screws he sniffed & tapped. He made his overalls very dirty on my Behalf it looked like a thorough job he was doing.

"I've got some bad news for you," he Concluded.

I saved him the trouble. "My transmission right?"

" 'Fraid so."

"Don't you have one in stock?"

That shy chuckle again. "No I don't. What is it now? A '63 Ford?"

"Country Squire Station Wagon."

"You be lucky to find a transmission for it around here. Maybe in El Paso."

"Can't you pick one up and bring it back?"

"I'm talkin' 'bout your whole transmission. You need a whole new transmission." He made it sound like my car needed a Heart Transplant.

"Well how long does it take to fix?"

He folded his arms he looked up at the dripping crankcase & concentrated. "3 days."

"Is that right?"

"Or 4. Depends when they can fit 'er in."

"Who?"

"Transmission place."

"No. I want you to do it. Right here. Where we are already."

"I can't even haul it over till tomorrow."

"What can I do?" I walked up & down under the Fan Belt Display. Under the tires. Behind the batteries. "All these new parts here! Are you sure there isn't a transmission somewhere? In a box? Maybe it'll fit my car."

"Best thing I can suggest is you get a room over to the Bluebird Motel. I'll ast Mr. Pepper when he gets here. Maybe he knows how to get it done quicker but I doubt it."

"Which way to the ladies room?"

I followed the kid's Directions step by step out through the garage into the office & around the side of the Coke Machine to the restroom door which I knocked *shave-and-a-haircut*. No *two bits* answered me back no luck no Amelia. I walked all the way around the station but all I ran into was a stack of Radial Retreads. On my 2nd lap past the Raymobile I saw the kid was outside pumping gas into a pick-up truck—and Amelia was Squeezing herself into the Shadows in back of the Coke Machine.

"Hey," I called over to her.

"Ssh!"

"Where did you go?" I whispered back.

"Drink a coke."

"I don't want a coke. It's bad for my digestion."

Her harsh whisper, "Make believe!"

I put a Dime in the machine I Pretended to futz with it for a Coke. "I've been all over the place looking."

"Those men."

I put in another Dime. "Those men—" I Invited her to finish the Sentence in her own words or less.

"They gone?"

"You mean those guys from before?"

"Yes."

"Sure. 15 minutes ago." I put in a Quarter I was out of Dimes. "This is getting expensive. Will you come out now?"

"No. Who is there now?"

I glanced over my shoulder. "A couple of guys in a pick-up truck."

"This is no safe Ray. No safe for me here."

"So come out of there. It's dangerous back there. It's electric."

We both kept quiet when we Heard the pick-up truck rev outside nor we did not start Talking again until whoever it was out there drove away.

"I think those men . . . " Her Voice faded before her Thought did so I caught Exactly what she meant.

"Nah!" I took a hold of her elbow I tried to pull her Towards Me but she went Stiff. "What—from your friend? You think they're from John Newberry?" It was not kind to do but I had to let out a Laugh over this Notion. "You think they're from the F.B.I.?"

"The way they look at me."

I punched the Coin Return Lever but only 1 of my thin dimes shook out. "If you stuck yourself behind a coke machine in Timbuktoo you couldn't be further from the truth of the matter." I jiggled the lever some more & got Zero back for my Work. "You know who that party was I was talking to?"

"He try to look right in my face Ray!"

"It was the Ku Klux Klan in that car!" I was steamed up now I shook the front of the machine so it rocked Back & Forth but *still* it did not Cough Up my change.

"I think one of them took my picture you know?"

"I think this machine just took my 35 cents."

Amelia came halfway out from behind with her eyes damp & her lips pulled back tight over her teeth. "I'm telling you something!"

I put the Coin Return out of my Mind I gave Amelia all my Attention. "Why do you think he did that?"

"Where I am," she shrugged. "He saw me. Sure."

"So what."

"He can recognize me."

"From where?"

This stopped her short. "From here. I don't know what he can do."

"That hamburger couldn't recognize you from Carmen Miranda." I think Amelia started to Defrost—either Defrost or it was getting too Chilly for her back there. She inched out into the office. "The kid told me. He told me what those guys do with their penny-ante patrols. They drive back & forth around Juarez and when they see a stray Mexican try a break-out over the border they . . . they . . . " I did not know *what* they did. I could Guess but I did not say. I Remembered what was on the Poster. "They really hate Mexicans."

"That's what I am!" Amelia hissed at me. "I'm Mexican."

"Sure but you aren't a *stray* Mexican," I reasoned out. "You're with me." I got back into the Fight with the Coin Return some more punching & jiggling and the machine did everything Except burp and say Thanks A Lot for the snack of my Dime & Quarter.

Amelia pulled us apart she Wedged herself between me and my metal mortal Enemy. "You said you protect me Ray. Your car is broke you make a lot of trouble and waste time in that place you talk to those men is no fair! It's no safe for me stopping hm? You know? It's no safe now because of you & your bad car & how you get me stuck in here!"

She kicked the side of the Coke Machine then I heard my Coins jingle out of the slot and hit the Floor. I did not give in to the Urge to pick them up or even look at where they went I just put my hand on Amelia's shoulder & gave her my full Attention. "As long as I am in the world Amelia as long as I live & breathe no innocent heart will suffer harm from the horny hands of the wicked."

She shook my hand off. "Pen-dey-ho," she said & for a second she Narrowed her eyes at me.

I took her Challenge. "Yes," I nodded, "pen-dey-ho."

Her head hung down her shoulders shook. I Heard her sobs. I

237

lifted her chin with my finger I Turned her face up towards mine—and I saw how she was not Sobbing she was Gulping Air killing herself Laughing.

"Pen-dey-ho," she cried through Gulps & Teary Eyes.

"Sure. I promise. Pen-dey-ho."

She was holding her Ribs Together now bent over Double from her laff riot. I had to laugh from Joy too and I will Admit my eyes went a little damp from the Idea my word of Comfort & my word of Honor set her light-hearted Feelings free. Such is the Power of the Bold word in the Tender moment. I felt a watery wave roll over me very warm it was the Feeling for the 1st time with Amelia I had the Power to shine a Light into her Dark Corner.

I found out later in my 1st and last Lesson in the beautiful Latin tongue of Espanol PEN-DEY-HO means STUPID IDIOT. It is the name they call morons who stick their fingers into live lamp plugs to find out how a 100 Watt lightbulb Feels.

PEN-DEY-HO! PEN-DEY-HO! PEN-DEY-HO! PEN-DEY-HO! PEN-DEY-HO!

I took Advantage of her Happy Spirits and I broke the news to her about the Transmission and the Motel in that order. Which said bad news brought her down to Earth so fast I almost heard her Heart go Splat on the floor. I tried to Comfort her by the Idea she was not Alone she had me to turn to but Amelia stayed in her Gloomy mood from that moment on.

We checked into the Bluebird Motel as Mr. & Mrs. so at least we looked the Part.

If I leave out the part about the Color T.V. in there that only picked up Electric Confetti on every Channel and I do not Mention the part about the stack of magazines on the coffee table being all last year's supply of Arizona Highway and I Forget about the part that there was only 1 bed 1 blanket & 1 chair I can say the room was not very bad.

Amelia stretched out on the bed on her back but she did not Rest she did not Sleep. She stared up at the Ceiling & I stared at the pictures of asphalt & cactus in Arizona Highway. I Decided already No Matter What I was going to fall asleep in the chair next to the window even after Amelia got up again & sat on the floor with her Books.

"You go on the bed," she offered me. " I don't want to sleep."

"I'm O.K. here," I nodded at her so the bed stayed Empty. I turned the lamps on since the Gloom Outside was pushing in to meet the Gloom Inside.

"The curtains." Amelia snapped her head around but her Voice was not rough.

To keep the Peace & Quiet I closed the curtains without any Remark about her Manners. I smelled the drizzle it did not make a Sound only the breeze bumped on the window and Shook it in the frame. Also that breeze stirred up a whiff of sweaty armpits so that was my Cue to hit the showers.

I had to step over Amelia & her books & papers which fanned out on the floor all around her. "Sorry," I said when I stepped on her Pencil & snapped it. "It's like a obstacle course here."

She sharpened up a new pencil. "Mm."

"What's that?" I pointed in General at the Books.

"I can make your chart."

"I don't want to know from that hocus-pocus."

"It's no for you."

The Meaning of that last Remark did not hit me until I came out of my shower so I just Mumbled something to her about my immediate Plans and shut the bathroom door. I peeled my clothes off & made the shower warm not hot.

I am of Mixed Feelings about showers. On one side it is a Good feeling with the clean water washing away the sweaty dirt & dirty sweat dead skin cells etc. with that Fresh Feeling after & the joy from seeing the Clean towel. On the other side it always Reminds me how many times in my Life so far I did this with the End Result being this is as Clean as I will get it is downhill from here Dirtwise. I will be looking forward to the next shower but ½ way through I will think *What's the point?*

This time also I have something else to Think About. I am thinking *Outside the bathroom door in this below average motel room in the Texas Panhandle there is a Mexican woman who has to pry into the*

239

Zodiac so she can decide how much of a false hope I am! I am Stunned by this. What is in my Future? Ask me & I will tell you what! A motel chair (the hell with it anyway I do not Sleep very Easy on a strange bed she is welcome to it EVEN if I was here by myself which I am Feeling I am) in front of a T.V. with live Confetti to watch & for this I am shelling out $27.50 Per Night. Forget it. I will feel much better when I put on Clean Underwear it always Helps.

When I make my Entrance Amelia is still sitting up with her pencil in her mouth Perusing the map of my Personal Zodiac. She does not look completely gloomy now I believe her Hobby is taking her Mind off her Worries. Twinkle Twinkle.

"If you talk to me maybe you'll find out the facts," I said.

"No this ones." She flipped a page she wrote down the Numbers of my Angles etc. the lats & longs of my entire Life. "This is not good times to start new projects."

"Is that a fact." I sat in the chair with the Arizona Highway where I left off. I tried to Concentrate on the only half-way interesting Story in all of the magazines up to August which was regarding the birthday party of a woman in Globe, Ariz. who just turned 110 Years of Age. Her secret was fresh water 1 tsp. of peanut butter every morning & no Sexual Intercourse. If she was right about this Formula all I had to do was stock up on bottles of Sparklets & jars of Skippy and I was going to live to 132!

Amelia was starting to Irritate me with her *mm-mm* her *mm-mm?* and her *mm-mm!* Furthermore I admit I was Curious regarding her Investigations in specific how did it Effect her Opinion of me? So the Next Time she went *mm-mm* I went, "What *mm-mm?*"

"For your rising sign. Aries."

"In English please," I showed some Interest. "Is that good?"

"Good or bad. Good or bad. How you use it." She leaned forward on her elbows. "This tell me how you look for exciting challenges hm?" Amelia pointed to some Chicken Scratches on her paper. "But other things. Some other things . . . " She Concentrated on the Correct words, "You have trouble to end some things. You know? To finish. Mm—" she thought then Laid It

240

Out for me Again. "Up to the last minute is fine—then—" she buzzed her lips.

The gap she left I filled in a Hurry. "Yeah? What *then?*"

"You change directions. You go someplace. You do something different so you don't—mm—" She started over to get it straight in her Mind so it came out Straight. "You stop early then you can say you don't really fail. But you don't succeed. You don't do both."

"Is that a fact." I folded my magazine on my lap and I Scowled down on her. "You think you know it all about me? Now you know what's up huh?" If her Case was going to get closed at the Bluebird Motel if this was as far as it was going to go that was O.K. with me IF she gave me a good reason BASED ON THE FACTS! Facts are not hocus pocus dominocus from a person's Zodiac!

"I'm no sure I want to stay with you Ray."

"You can't rely on *that* to advise!"

"You yell at me see? Explosion. Two fire signs." She stabbed at my chart with her pencil & Broke the Point off.

"Temper temper."

"Temper temper," she Mocked me she sliced my diagram across the floor. "I don't need to look any more hm?"

"Oh I see. Madam Walnetto has spoken!"

Amelia was Cramming her Books back into her canvas bag. "I want to go," she said & she started for the door.

I jumped up I Blocked her path. "All right. Just don't tell me you're deciding on the facts because you don't know all the facts. That's not how things happen. Planets do not enter into it. Or stars or constellations either! I decide. Sagittarius isn't deciding. I'm deciding. What if I decide I'm not going to let you go away from here by yourself?"

She ground her molars she planted her feet & I was not sure if she wanted to Smack me one or not. She was not sure about it either. She dropped her bag she let her hands Dangle Down. Her fingers went Plucking at the seams of her trousers then very slow they balled up into plump fists.

"I'll follow you," I warned her, "I'll follow you all over and make sure nothing terrible happens. I decided so I'll do that." I felt my smile Twitch on my lips.

Amelia picked up the piece of paper she threw before across the room i.e. the Zodiac Diagram with my Vital Statistics on it. "Now I know what it means for sure. Today you meet some big kind of challenge and—" She studied some scribbly corner of the page then she held it toward me so I should get the Message. "Today you succeed." She locked her eyes on mine.

I should have been completely Satisfied with this Victory but I was not I was completely Aggravated. I am not the Expert of all Experts on this topic but I will say I read every word of Astronomy For The Millions from cover to cover so I am not exactly a stranger to the majestic Truth about Cosmic Orbs.

I had a hard time arguing from Constellations Stars & Planets with Amelia she had firm Views about the Cosmos and things of this Nature so my facts went skidding off the surface of her Beliefs like flat rocks on a lake. And they sank under the same too.

Her view was:

Stars & Planets all hum and each one hums a Different Note. So they circle around each other & so every minute is a new Combo. Sweet notes by Venus sour notes by Saturn they beam down on Earthlings. In the certain minute a person is born the Orbs are Singing his tune the sky is Humming certain Notes around him. This Vibrates his bones his whole body is a Fingerprint of the hum of his 1st minute Alive. From now on the Pattern of the Planets will play him the way the Moon Plays on the tides of the World. So a person acts a certain way he can not help in certain Phases.

It is a Beautiful tale the way Amelia Explained it but this was her false Impression in regards to my Motives in this Episode with her.

"Sagittarius did not influence me!"

"You don't know."

"I know why I got out of bed this morning. I know *that* don't I? Not because of the stars."

"Because of the sun."

"Correct."

242

"O.K. this sun *this star* he tell you *Wake up now!*"

"Suggested Amelia. *Suggested.* I *decided* I had something important to do today so I got up out of bed & came over to pick you up. The sun did not influence me either."

"Why you didn't come yesterday hm?"

"Because I wasn't ready to then. I made my mind up this morning."

"I know. I can read in your stars. You don't like it because I find out somethings about you now. How you are."

"All you had to do was ask me. Did you ask me to find out what's on my mind? No. You go sneaking behind my back. Sneaking into my personal zodiac. And what: you come up with the kind of answers you get from a sideshow fortune teller." I Thought I finished it off there but I shook my head & Out Came: "On *this* you make a judgement of me!"

"You just make a joke. Or some big speech. You don't tell me something how you are. I don't think so Ray."

"I suppose in the last 18 hours you've told me everything about how you are. You hardly said *anything* to me between El Paso and the gas station."

"I'm Sagittarius like you. I don't tell private things. Except if it makes a difference hm?" She unfolded the other Complimentary bath towel & hung it over her arm. "O.K.? Now you know one thing how I am."

How she was in my eyes then I can Describe in 1 Word: Tender. My Voice softened up. "So what big challenge did you succeed at today?"

"When I decide I stay with you." She opened one of her books to show me some Diagram that looked like the Blueprint of a Swiss cuckoo clock. She sketched it with her finger. "You're almost a twin for a famous person from history."

"Let me guess," I leaned over to look. "Wrong Way Corrigan."

"Mm?"

"Nobody."

"Her."

Amelia turned over the page & I was looking at a full length oil painting of Joan of Arc. JOAN OF ARC! What did I have in common with a French Female fruitcake who heard Voices talking to her out of the Thin Air? Who did what they *told* her yet! SAVE FRANCE! That meshugganeh shikse! The girl gets toasted like a Marshmallow on a Gourmet campfire! Did I have to point out to Amelia the fact that the closest I am going to get to a burning stake is on my Hibachi Bar-B-Q?

"Don't constellation me anymore constellations Amelia or you'll give me a heart attack. They aren't really there!" I waved my arm toward the sky.

"You say stars are no in the sky? Ay-yi-yi yi-yi!"

"*Maybe* I'm saying. *Maybe* they're not."

"You can see them. Don't you believe it when you see something?"

"Not when it comes to cosmic orbs."

"Ay-yi-yi."

This was getting to be a Joke with her Already so I had to Pounce before she stopped listening to me altogether. "You know what it's like in outer space?" I said. "You know what it's like for you if you're a beam of light? It's a jungle. Curves in space like a roller coaster. And other things. The only way you know a star's up there is you see the light from it. Twinkle twinkle."

I was holding a glass Ashtray up in the air with my left hand directly in back of my right hand. The Ashtray was the Star. I wiggled the fingers on my right hand to Portray the light going Twinkle Twinkle.

"A beam of light from one of those stars—one of those Sagittarius stars—it has to come millions of miles and it takes millions of years to get here." I stopped for a Breath. All Amelia did was Blink at me. "You look up in the sky out there at night it's not the stars it's just the light coming from them from a million years ago. Maybe those certain stars exploded already & there're just holes in the sky where Sagittarius used to be. But we don't know because we can't see it from here yet. Understand?"

"Sure," said Mrs. Alberta Einstein. "Light is how the humming looks like."

She stepped into the bathroom but before she shut the door all the way I said, "I'm staying with you because I care what happens." I do not Know if she Heard what I said the shower was running very hard for her water to Heat Up.

I lay down on the bed & the minute my head hit the pillow the Phone rang. On the other end was the Motel Manager. The Message he gave me was my car was outside the Office the boy from the gas station Delivered it. What did I care it was the middle of the night? Did I question? I did not. I just Admired the jiffy service I just thought this must be the Swell Way they treat tourists in Texas.

Pen-dey-ho. Double Pen-dey-ho.

I crunched the 100 feet of gravel over to the Motel Office where they parked the Raymobile it looked as Good as New. Better even. They washed it & waxed it Inside & Out. The carpet they Shampooed even the coffee stain from around the rubber mat they combed it with a fine tooth comb so it came out Perfect. And the steering wheel they polished also the dashboard also the lid of the glove compartment. And in the glove compartment they made it tidy with a roadmap of Texas and a new pack of travel size HandiWipes. I Vowed myself I was going to tip that nice kid $2.00 first thing in the Morning.

I dinged the bell on the desk inside but the Manager was not around or anybody else. My car keys I saw hanging on the peg of my Room Number so I put them in my pocket & I cased the place for a pad & pencil so I could leave a Note but I did not even get to Dear Sir. I heard heavy tires grinding the gravel where I just walked over & I had to Focus my eyes to the dark before I saw what was there. I saw a pick-up truck it was rolling down the driveway with no Headlights on. It pulled up in front of our Room then the Air around there Exploded—

How many Guns went off I do not know but all the barrels (shotguns?) fanned out from the back from behind some Bales of Hay. A Blast blew into the siding punched holes in the door. A Blast blew the windows to Pieces. A Blast blew splinters back across the driveway. Still the Guns did not stop Blasting into our Room.

"What goes on?" I said & then I shouted it, "WHAT GOES ON?" I ran Toward them even when they Hit their Headlights I ran toward them faster I did not stop until I stood in front of the Bullets. Maybe I was standing *between* all the Bullets because nothing hit me not a Bullet not a ball of buckshot not even a Ricochet nothing not a Scratch. "Stop this!" I yelled at them louder than the Guns I yelled, "Stop this now! Stop this!" So they stopped Blasting then I yelled some more. "Get out of here!" Thanks to my Strong Voice they got out of there in a Big Hurry. Tires tearing up the gravel swerving out of the driveway skidding in the road they Punched a hole in the rain & Pulled the dark through it.

All of the Sound in the room went with them it got sucked out of the Smashed Windows & the only thing moving inside there was smoke & dust a Cloudy curtain of it from the Plaster they just Blasted off the walls. The Air all blurry with it. I caught one foot in a lampshade it lay on the floor like a Bear Trap & I tripped over the wire of the other one. Also under my feet I felt all the glass from the mirror and the Pieces of it even too small to Break Up anymore.

By the dim light my eyes got used to I saw all of the Furniture was Shot Up I do not know how many Bullets it took to leave the bed slanting on 1 leg & the chair blown to shreds & the door of the clothes closet hanging like a piece of Swiss Cheese by 1 hinge & all over the floor fingers of raw wood torn off from everywhere. When I saw where the light was shining in from a Dozen Holes in the bathroom wall the Silence stopped all around me I heard how the shower was still running.

I called Amelia's name I pushed the bathroom door open but I did not Rush in there.

If she got hurt in any way I was going to Reach by myself the Truth of the whole Situation. How I am a 66 years of age Pathetic Nobody. I am not the man who I was Before & even Before I was not him either. I am only somebody in my own Mind. I am a liar to myself and others I am useless on this Earth. I do not Deserve Love or kindness Affection or Respect. If Amelia has on her a Scratch even or a cut with Blood I will see I am not a Hero I am less than dirt, I will say out loud I am Good for nothing Good for nobody only Good to Forget About.

I found her in the stall shower she was Sitting Down on the drain with the plastic curtain Open Wide. Her back was facing the bathroom door. Cold water was Soaking her hair it went dripping down her back. Maybe she was just going to turn the hot on when all the shooting started. I crawled over to her on my hands & knees I had a towel to cover her up with. I leaned in to shut the water off then I heard her Breathing only little Hisses of Air. Amelia was trying to force one word through her teeth—

"Nada . . . nada . . . " she said & her Voice Echoed very sharp off the wet tiles. *Nada* which means *nothing* in her Language but now I see I am writing this word down I think I got it Wrong at the time. Now I think she was saying this: "Ojinaga."

She did not have a spot of Blood on her. She did not have a Cut or Scratch. I wrapped her in the Towel very Tender I held her in my arms I rubbed her to warm her up. Her stiff arms I rubbed I rocked her Back & Forth then she did not try to talk anymore I felt her Cuddle Up to me. She went so Weak in my arms but I felt very Strong for her to hold on to.

"I got rid of them . . . ssh . . . they didn't hurt you . . . they didn't hurt me," I told her. "You're safe now." She put her fingers on my lips & looked like she wanted to See the Words come out of my mouth. "They didn't hurt us," I said, "and here's why. I'll tell you a secret nobody else knows about me my sweetheart. I'm the Green Ray." There I said it Out Loud for the 1st time in 40 years. "Those weasels don't know who they're up against. I'm the Green Ray," I Revealed to her, "I'm the Green Ray."

The only Sound was the rumble of the Raymobile's radials and now & then the Hiss of rainwater spraying up underneath when we drove through Puddles. The slap of the windshield wipers kept time with the Beat of my Heart very slow & calm. The rain was not pouring down now it was just Spitting and I could see where the Raincloud ended a few Miles ahead. The Sun was rising underneath it & pried the edge up like the cloud was a Vacuum Seal Lid. The clear Air that came rushing in was the color of Ripe Peaches.

I did not wake Amelia up to see this Hopeful Sight I was Glad she fell asleep to rest & recover after the drama of the Shooting episode. I drove along and I pondered over the Conversation I had with her after we put 100 miles between us & the Bluebird Motel.

AMELIA: I don't know who did it. He did it. I don't know who else.
ME: Those creeps from the gas station. Those Ku Klux Klan creeps.
AMELIA: Still is him.
ME: The responsible party will pay.
AMELIA: Is him. For sure.
ME: Is Newberry going to be in Dallas? Waiting for us?
AMELIA: You have to be very smart for him.

This I Promised her I would. On that Note I added—

ME: I'll straighten him out for good.

I licked my lips I hit the Gas & put on some Speed when I saw the daybreak behind the Dallas skyline. We made the trip in 6 hrs. 10 mins. from Door to Door we had a tail wind pushing us from Abilene & in the city we caught all of the Green Lights.

Let me quote Lamont Carruthers here: "A clue is never a secret but a secret is always a clue."

I did not have any Idea what he Meant by that Statement when he Wrote it in his own handwriting on top of the Script of the Final Episode of the Green Ray. Nor I did not Connect it to the Conversation we enjoyed together that night with him sitting on 1 toilet seat in the Mahogony cubicle of the 39th Floor Executive Washroom & I was Occupying the one nextdoor. Both of us with the dizzy stomach from the Cheez Skweez & Powder Puf marshmallows also the Grief & Parting. Except for the words "This machine kills Fascists!" it was his last unscrutable Saying because 3 seconds later he Jumped out of the window of the 38th Floor Executive Dining Room in front of P.K. Spiller and

Howard Silverstein et al while they choked down their Jello-O cubes & Meat Spread sandwiches. Lamont's dramatic Exit lowered the boom on the Black Tie Cocktail Party that Mr. Spiller laid on to mark the Final Broadcast of The Adventures Of The Green Ray. I want to go back to tell Lamont Carruthers how I understand the Wisdom of his Words today but I do not want to go back to that sad day. Why do I Worry about it now since a person can not go back not even 1 minute no matter how much he Yearns.

This I Observe in this Case in particular: A Clue will stare you smack in the kisser deadeye like a rattlesnake if you pay Attention & Watch your step. It will bite you the same if you Ignore it it will sneak behind your back & bite you the same if you try to walk around.

I believe I am in step with the late Dr. Sigmund Freud the great Psychological Investigator when I state that it is NORMAL for a person to Guide himself by High Ideals & take his eyes off the True Clues & Evidence. It is NORMAL for a person to head for certain Conclusions and wander down the Wrong Track especially when it involves a woman! This is the NORMAL way a thinking man *behaves!*

I know a person can not Guide himself from the door of his Apartment down to the Drugstore on the Corner steering by the Stars Above. Like that he will get lost all right his eye being on the wrong thing at the wrong time. The Stars being the right thing at the right time for a Captain to Navigate a boat in the middle of the Ocean. I mean by this the Deeds a person does alone when nobody is watching him or when his Loved One is. His Deeds of Honor. His matters of Life & Death. Nor yet the Stars are not a handy guide to steer around a buried iceberg. And furthermore if F.D.R. or J.F.K. or Sigmund Freud was a passenger on the Titanic he would just go down with the ship like everybody else O.K. so High Ideals do not *protect.* So—

Forget it. The hell with Philosophy. I just want to make a Point how I at least Recognize 1 Reason for what Happened with Amelia for what I did & what I did not do. So here are some Clues coming up which I did not Recognize at the time my Mind's Eye being on higher things e.g. Justice and Love.

Let me go back to Dallas.

I parked the Raymobile across the street from a gray clapboard 2-storey in the middle of a Neighborhood full of clapboard 2-Storeys & bungalows walnut trees front yards full of dry grass & toys dusty air grinning down on the Cracked Sidewalks.

Amelia led me inside by the back door at the top of a Porch up half a dozen tarpaper steps. A Perfect Breeding Ground for black widow spiders I noticed & I was hoping that the Residents of the house bolted the Linoleum to the floor very snug.

The door Opened Up into the kitchen. The Radio on the table had the Baseball on from back East The Dodgers vs. The Phillies. Somewhere else in the house another Radio was playing Mariachi music. I saw the beefy back of a dark red man he was standing at the stove Listening to the Game & humming along to the Mariachi music also whipping some thick yellow Batter around a plastic bowl he Gripped in the curl of his flabby arm.

Amelia grabbed his gut from Behind. "Tio!" She could not Stretch both of her arms all the way around him.

The ladle full of batter Splashed into the frying pan & sizzled very quick into the shape of a Catcher's Mitt. "Lastima!" he shook his head over it and crossed himself then he Flipped the raw pancake out of the pan across the kitchen & into the sink. He hugged Amelia a Tender bearhug but he did not take his eyes off me.

Abba-zabba-zabba they chattered back & forth like monkeys in the zoo and all the time the Expression on Tio's face is changing from happy surprise to shock & confusion it stretches out to Anger and I mean something *furious* then it snaps back Dumbstruck into Misery. But Amelia is Calm she is in Control of her Emotions so she soothes & Explains until she gets Control over his. His big hand in both of hers that is how she Comforts him with a Squeeze on his arm & a steady look. In a minute Tio lifts his head up & to show her how her News has sunk in he gives Amelia a stiff nod before he slumps back over to the stove.

"He's my Tio." Amelia pulled me into the Conversation.

"Did you tell him who I am? Did you tell him about the motel? I mean what happened with those guys with the guns and everything?"

Tio answered me over his shoulder. "I don't 'spect the POlice showed up t'hep owt huh?" He had a perfect Texas panhandle Accent on him. What th-?!

"We got outa there right away," I said & I Heard how thin my Voice went from Surprise. I hoped it sounded more like I was just tired which was also a Fact. "Is there a bathroom I can use?"

"Top of the stairs," Tio craned his neck in that Direction.

Amelia stood up next to the door. "I show you the bathroom," she said and for ½ a second the way she stood there waiting for me to Catch Up Reminded me of Jackie Kennedy showing her Tour of the White House. She led me over to the flight of stairs that went up the middle of the house and she stopped at the bottom which I Figured meant she wanted to Tell Me something about Tio on the q.t. She opened her mouth & took a Breath enough for a Whisper but she did not whisper a word she let me go with ½ a smile.

I supplied the other ½ of that Smile so between the 2 of us there was some kind of a happy understanding. "I'll find it," I said.

Halfway up the stairs all of a sudden I Noticed the dead silence there. The Mariachi Music stopped playing and the only human Sounds came from Amelia & Tio speaking very low & Solemn in the kitchen. Every step I went up on Creaked which made me feel like a cat burglar on the Premises. But I was not Sneaking Around I was only searching for the bathroom & nobody told me which door so take a look at my Problem:

All of the doors Upstairs are shut just a Choice of 4 all of them the same all painted turquoise a nice Contrast next to the gray panels in the hallway. Nevermind about the Interior Decorating for a minute which way was the bathroom? O.K. this does not look like it is a very Important Decision in the course of Human events but look where it led me it led me face to face with a Clue I did not Recognize.

My ideas about washing my face & hands etc. got pushed to the side of my Mind when I sniffed a smell standing there it was

251

the scent of the East 8th. A cooking smell—hot oil—tortillas—refried beans—& salty sweat. A Voice Whispered to me it was the Voice of Peter Tremayne he Encouraged me SNOOP AROUND. If I walked in on anybody by Accident I could always say I am looking for the bathroom and I was Truly so I did not have to Compromise my Morals and lie about it. I opened the door in front of me it was not the bathroom it was a bedroom but it looked more like Army Barracks.

Maybe 30 faces stared at me all silent all Mexican all Blank just wondering what my Next Move was going to be. The cooking was on a Hotplate in the middle of the room and all around it they had blankets & sleeping bags with rolled up clothes for pillows. A few bunkbeds they Squeezed Up against the walls even in front of the window. The shade behind was pulled down Tight & I Observed it was nailed to the wall to stay that way Period.

"Howdy fellas,' I Greeted them I held my hand up & waved. "I'm looking for the bathroom."

Nobody answered me. They just Decided I did not come up to tell them off or tell them to can the Noise etc. and a few at a time they went back to what they were doing before I Interrupted. Combing hair playing cards stretching out reading magazines etc. (I think I recognized one of these with the Photos & the Comic Book captions very similar to the Literature which Carlos supplied for his Customers.)

Good thing the next door down was the bathroom. Also Good thing I did not go in there to take a bath because the bathtub was Overflowing from dirty clothes soaking in cold water. It was just a Foamy Scum of dirt & dead suds on top. The sink was not better but at least nothing was Floating in it. I washed all the hairs & whiskers down the Drain & filled up the clean sink with very hot water. I caught a look at my face in the Mirror on my way up from the sink dripping wet. I looked Exactly how I Felt i.e. dog tired: a bloodhound stared back at me from the other side of the mirror. I let my tongue hang out & I saw it was not just coated it was Whitewashed. Before any other Development in the Case I was going to find someplace in Dallas to take my High Colonic.

I waltzed back into the kitchen in the middle of some very urgent Business between Amelia & Tio abba-zabba-zabba over their empty pancake plates and the 2 of them Huddled Up over the corner of the table. Tio saw me first and I believe it was out of Good Manners not Secrecy he stopped talking grinned up and lifted the lid on a stack of Pancakes he was keeping warm for me.

"You hungry nuff for somma my flapjacks Ray?"

I Thanked him for saving those they sure look Delicious la-dee-doo-dah etc. and I sat down at the place he Set for me.

"Maple syrup?" Tio offered me some from a gravy boat. "Say when." He even Poured it out for me & from his other hand out of a fresh pot I got a cup of black Coffee.

"I come right back," Amelia scooted her chair out. "I can call my friend now," she said to herself out loud & left the room.

"Whoa!" I passed my hand over the Pancakes when Tio put enough Syrup on to coat the top and shiny strings dangling down the sides just like in the Log Cabin Syrup commercial on T.V. pretty as a picture. But I could not be the Hungry Lumberjack I could not swallow 1 forkful it stuck in my Throat like a little Fist. I gulped a splash of hot coffee down after it then I Gulped some Air.

"Take 'er easy Ray! You O.K. now? You O.K.?"

I nudged my plate away very Polite by my fingertips. "Delicious Tio. I just can't eat another mouthful." I hiccupped.

"Whoopsidaisy. Hold your breath."

"It's my digestion. If I eat certain foods I give myself the cramps."

"Mean flapjacks? Shoulda said Ray. I can fix you some bacon & eggs or—"

"No bacon. Thanks Tio. Coffee."

"So what's wrong with your digestion? If you don't mind me askin'." Tio pulled my plate in front of him & he picked at the damp Stack of hotcakes. "I got a simular complaint too."

I did not mind if he asked it did not sound Weak of me to talk about this Area. For in my High Ideals & Deeds etc. I am The Green Ray but my Earthly body is a different thing altogether bulletproof or no I am Ray Green to my 66 years old bowels.

Digestion problems do not Disqualify me from Glory nor vice versa.

"Blockage," I told him.

"You mean you cain't go?"

"Sometimes 3–4 days I'm cement in there."

"You eat nuffa that fiber stuff? Branflakes and whatever?" Tio leaned toward me very Interested in this man to man Discussion. I rolled my eyes from Remembering my kitchen cabinet full of every food & every Constipation Remedy known to Modern Science. "Bran muffins. Bran covered pretzels. Bran sprinkle. Tio did you ever hear of a product by the name Uncle Sam Laxative Cereal?"

"Naw. Whatsat?"

"No damn good," I said. "Pardon my French. I need the heavy duty treatment. I need to find someplace in town for a high colonic. You know anywhere you can recommend?"

"High what Ray?"

"Colonic. A high colonic. It's the only thing that does the job. You don't know what that is a high colonic?" Tio shook his head and Chewed Up the last scrap of hotcake from my plate. "It's with a little rubber hose. They put it up your—the doctor inserts this hose & pumps the water in and—" I was not Embarrassed by Explaining the Mechanics of it to Tio I just slowed down on the Details when I saw the picture form in his Mind & he started giving me a look like he smelled Gas Escaping. "Also it's called Colonic Irrigation. The doctor does it."

"That fixes you up huh?"

"For a week. Sometimes a couple of weeks. It feels great." Then I added in, "when it's over."

"It's like a enema," he said to make sure he had the right Idea.

"Something like that. Something like a enema I guess."

"I don't think that colonic thing'd hep me Ray," he said & he Slapped both his hands down on the edge of the table. "I got the opposite problem. I cain't *stop* goin'. All day long."

"Tio that could turn into something serious. I'd go take a check up. We could go down together."

"Naw." He cleared the table & Scrubbed my plate in the sink.

"Now that you jig my mem'ry I think I saw some pitchurs about colonics in a magazine. I don't wanta get *that* friendly with any doctor."

Amelia was smiles all over when she came back to us. "I go see my friend tomorrow." She let out the Sigh she was holding in since she went to make the phone call and she did a little Twirl for us in the middle of the kitchen.

"You sound like a different person," I piped up.

"Now I can be tired hm? Now we can sleep." The last part she said to her uncle.

Tio wiped his hands on a paper towel before he Reached Over to hold Amelia's hand. "I knowed it weren't as bad as you thought it was. Be awright."

"Hot dog," I chimed in.

Amelia said a few Serious words to Tio in Espanol and he Answered her sober & low, "Si . . . Si . . . Lo comprendo todo." He tipped me a Wink on his way out & I Heard his Footsteps all the way up to the top of the stairs.

"You can sleep in Tio's bedroom O.K.? Come on. Help me put on new sheets."

"Where are you going to be?"

She jerked her chin in the Direction of the stairs. "My bedroom. Tio is making for me."

Right on cue we Heard a noise upstairs of doors opening and feet scuffling and things Moving Around. "Who are they all up in that room?"

"All my cousins," Amelia told me & Led me by my elbow into Tio's big bedroom.

As soon as I saw the Kingsize Bed I felt a wave of Exhaustion Heave all the way through me from my feet up from my head down from my bones out. Since I was so Sleepy maybe any room with a bed in it was going to feel Comfy Cozy to me but Tio's room was Special that way. It was exactly a little boy's idea of a Cowboy Bunkhouse with cattle horns on the wall a heavy mirror on the wall Navajo rugs on the floor Navajo blankets on the walls. I got into my clean p.j.'s I crawled into the clean bed and I was All Ready to hit the Happy Trail down to Sleepytime Corral.

Amelia sat with me on the edge of the bed also she held my hand in her lap.

"Welp," I said. "We got here in one piece."

She squeezed my fingers. "Muchas gracias. Muchas gracias to you."

"Muchas gracias," I repaid her.

"No—you say de nada."

"De nada. What's de nada mean?"

"Means you're welcome."

"Thank you."

"Gracias."

"Gracias," I said.

Amelia held her Ribs to keep the Laugh in. "No Ray! I say gracias. You say de nada."

"O.K. I understand. Start over."

"You remember how it goes?"

"Yeah sure. Go."

"O.K. Muchas muchas muchas muchas gracias Raymondo."

"De nada."

"Bueno! Muy bien!"

"I know what that means. Beans you said. More beans. What is that? Some kind of a saying? I heard Mrs. Roderiguez say it once."

I do not think she was Listening to me by that point she was Laughing too hard. Like she was at the gas station Doubled Over. Anyway she was a very easy Audience she was in a festive frame of mind. Tears filled up her eyes & one of them hit my cheek when she leaned over to Kiss me there.

A knock came on the door in that Tender moment and Tio poked his head in. No Hanky Panky so he squeezed into the room he had a empty suitcase in his hand. His hair was Combed Back & he had a snazzy suit on. I gave him a Wolf Whistle which I think handed him a slightly Nervous Moment & that handed me a Laugh. He put on a pair of Cowboy boots from the bottom of his closet also he scooped a few things up from his Bureau a set of silver hair brushes some cuff links etc. a couple plaid shirts.

"Real nice to've made your acquaintance Ray," he nodded at me.

"Sure Tio. Likewise."

"Right. Well. See ya around sometime."

"Bye," I waved.

Amelia hung on his neck for a Hug. "Via con Dios." He Kissed the top of her head and I thought she was going to Follow him out of the room but she sat down next to me again.

"Where's Tio going?"

She shrugged but not Because she did not know or Because she did not want to tell me only Because she had something else on her Mind. "You do all this things for me."

"Gracias," I said.

This brought out the little Bloom of a Smile on her lips. She started over. "You do all this things for me and you don't want something back." She left a Blank that she wanted me to Explain.

Instead of that I gave her the Chance to give me something back or maybe that was the way I wanted to Explain. "Those people upstairs. They aren't all your cousins are they?"

She still had a hold of my hand & she did not Let Go of it.

"How many? A few?" She Shook her head. "A couple?" She shook her head. "One?" She nodded—then she Shook her head.

"No cousins. That's all. O.K.?" She Tensed Up & tried to go.

I held her wrist to keep her Close. "Hold on! Don't get mad at me! I'm on your side Amelia! You did fine. You don't have to tell me anything else. That's fine. That's fine with me. There—see that? See what you did for me? You told me something out of trust. The way I told you before."

"*What* you told me before?"

I will say this Remark of hers sank in hard & hit me where it hurts. For on the floor of the bathroom in Room 12 at the Bluebird Motel of Van Horn, Texas in a Tender Moment after Danger passed us over I revealed a personal secret to her. Which it appears she altogether forgot about 6 Hrs. 10 Mins. later. *I reveal who I really am to her* and then this minor little Fact just slips her mind! Words I did not speak for 40 Years she heard me say! To her! To her alone! Amelia was who I Singled out to tell this to! Out of the entire population of the World she was the woman who I handed this live Ammunition for I Trusted her she was never going to use the Knowledge against me. I can not Believe how she can just Forget what I told her.

"*What* you told me before?"

"Try & remember," I was pressing & I think she Felt on her the instant pressure in the air around her.

Amelia put on the same Blank Expression when she had a Hunch she was going to hear bad news or sad news or if she had to Brace Herself for Trouble ahead. She did not Blink & her eyebrows came down very slow. She did not look at me nor she did not look away she just waited stiff & calm for the dumb-bell to land on her neck.

"I'll give you a hint," I said. "Who delivered you from danger? Who drove you to safety?"

"You."

"Absolutely. Who am I?" She squinted at me. "I'm not asking you a trick question. You want a little hint?"

"I don't know how you want me to say."

"Say who I am."

She shifted on the bed & said, "Ray."

"Sure. That's right. But I mean—" (I Defeat my own Purpose if I put the words in her mouth so I gave her another Clue.) "When people are in despair they want to believe there is somebody somewhere in the world who could care for them if he only knew about their terrible trouble & show up in person right on cue. You know? Somebody special who'll make a difference in their sorry circumstances." This did not jig her Memory so another clue I gave her. "You know how a desperate person hopes it's just not empty space out there around him? I *know* it isn't. That's a fact. You know what? I can hear all of the despair going on because it's my purpose on earth *to find* people in despair. I know what you're going to say," I said, "HOW CAN I GET AROUND TO EVERYBODY? My answer is: I CAN'T. I can't be in two places at the same time but so what Superman can't either. I have to single people out. Remember that's what I was doing when you came in? I was doing it alphabetical. Then I singled you out. I

258

found you so you don't have to wonder about is there somebody out there who cares what happens next. You know there is & you know who." Another hint she needed. "I'm here today & I won't be gone tomorrow. The Green Ray is with you all the way."

Maybe I made this Hint too Strong I saw how wide Amelia's eyes went and she just sank away like a sea anemone at my Touch. When she came out again she came out with: "O.K. I know. I know you are. Mr. Green Ray. For sure. I know. For sure."

"You can call me Ray." I left a quiet gap (or Amelia did).

Then she said, "Tomorrow is all finish. I see my friend so maybe you don't take me to Mexico. Is no important anymore you go with me." Her Voice flashed bright from the Idea: "You can go *home*."

This I did not wish to Discuss. "Is your friend going to advise you what to do about what you know?"

"I don't know anything." Quick panic pushed her words out.

I guessed she did not want to Talk about this Matter out loud in Tio's house. I tried to make it Easier for her to tell me what was in her mind. "About K."

"Que?"

"Yes."

I waited for her to say something. She waited for me. So both of us just Waited. Amelia finally shrugged & blew a Breath through her lips.

I lowered my Voice & spelled it out for her. "J.—F.—K." Her flat deadpan deadeye look filled her face again and for $\frac{1}{2}$ a second I wondered if the guns etc. maybe gave her a Case of Temporary Amnesia. "You know what I'm saying? There's a whole department of the Government completely *dedicated* to Justice. The Justice Department all right? You know what I'm talking about Amelia?"

All of a sudden she did Know & she Slapped her forehead. "Ay! Si-si! I know what you are saying. Si-si. Don't worry. My friend he tells me what I better do."

"You trust him all the way?"

"He knows somethings like I do. They don't believe my word anyway."

"Sure they will. Who won't?"

"They don't believe a dirty greaser hm? I want to go home."

"You can still do that. Right after."

"No. I don't want this strings on me here. They don't let me go then."

"Strings? What're you talking? Justice isn't strings. The whole country would show its gratitude. You'd be a V.I.P. You'd be the toast of the town."

"I don't want somebody else to know things about me." Amelia stood up then she leaned over me. "Only you." She Kissed me on my cheek.

Which Reminds me—

"You're the missing piece of the puzzle of my Life."

"You're not going to tell her *that*!"

"Soon as I can get her alone."

"In those exact words?"

"Why not?"

"You'll get a laugh."

"No I won't. You don't know her."

"I don't want to argue about it. It just sounds like the gooey kind of a line Lamont Carruthers'd think up."

"We belong together. We go together like peaches and cream."

"Like pickles and milk."

"Why do you have to be so negative about romance anyhow?"

"Just tell me why you have to put it in such definite final words like that.

"It's true. That's why. Isn't that enough of a reason?"

This Conversation between David Arcash & me went on while we waited for the Elevator in the Liberty Building maybe a month or so after the Episode with Uncle Jake etc. Actors I think can be over-emotional under the heat of a moment *pleasure* or *pain* more like little Children than other Civilians. Emotion Flares up very hot and it passes through in a Hurry to make room for the next one so David did not hold a Grudge about my Photo in the papers et al. we got back on Speaking Terms afterall.

A Blessing in the Skies that came from our bust-up was I moved into my own Apartment where I Enjoyed myself living alone but I did endure several long nights of Torment. In the wee wee hours ideas about Annie Returned to my Mind they caused me Insomnia something frantic. I shut my eyes & I saw snapshots of how my Life could be with her in a Sweet Moment on a summer lawn or fresh coffee & Sunday newspapers in the kitchen. Etc.

Nor this was not a Fairytale to tickle me back to Dreamland I had a reason to believe in my Chance of Success: Annie was not apt to be giving me the Cold Shoulder these days she even eyed me up sometimes by the drinking fountain e.g. or just a Curious glance up off the page of her Script she granted me some soft kind of Interest. I know it is a easy matter to mix up pity & tenderness also how a wishful person will read into Events but I Felt some other Emotion underneath those glances of hers. Which line of Thinking led me back on the track of reckless Romance.

For 2 or 3 days I did not run into David so I figure this is a Good sign he must be working on Annie for me like a True Pal but no I am about to walk into a big Surprise. The only thing I thought I was walking into was the Green Room to be by myself for a hour & Calm my Nerves as Usual but the Sight I saw in there fired a jolt of Electricity into me that curled my toes & straightened my hair—

DAVID AND ANNIE mouth to mouth they could pose perfect for the famous statue entitled The Kiss by Auguste Rodin.

Annie saw me first. "Oops," she said & she only Smoothed Down her skirt she only picked up her Script. She had to walk past me to go out of the room to get away from that Shameful Scene but when she was right next to me I saw how all of her Blushing was not out of Embarrassment. She stopped by my side for a second to plant a Kiss on my hot cheek. "You're sweet Ray."

"How do you know?" The words came out of my mouth so fast that it sounded like Somebody Else in the room said them.

"I know a thing or two," Annie clicked her tongue cocked her head and left the smell of her Perfume laced in the Air.

261

David did not stand up but he answered my Question before I even asked. "We didn't start last week." He dragged a chair toward him with his toe. "You want to sit down & hear the whole ugly story?"

I Listened to him talk just to keep out the loud Hiss of some Ocean breaking over & over in my ears. When I saw his lips stop moving I cut in. "Why didn't you just tell me what's what?"

"Because I consider I'm your friend."

"That's sick David. You need a doctor if you believe that. It's just *sick*."

"For your information both of us like you. Nobody wanted anybody to get hurt over it. Especially not you."

"Especially not me," I did not Mock him but I had a Different Meaning to my Mind while I walked around in a little circle & my eyes glued to the floor. "You're worse than Lionel Horvath."

"Don't get hysterical." David dropped his hands on my shoulders to Stop me in my Path. He kicked the chair around for me to sit but I stood there stiff & Frantic. "I'm your friend!" he shouted at me, "Don't you know that?"

"I do now!" I said very Sarcastic. "Thanks for letting me in on the secret."

"Boy you really don't get it do you?" I started back & forth across the room again so every time David spoke to me he got the back of my head. "You want to know the truth? I've been protecting your pink little fanny you pisher you! Will you stand still and listen to what I'm saying? I was protecting you."

I Obliged very Polite I stopped to say, "Who from?"

"Annie."

"You liar."

"Annie *wanted* to go out with you Ray! She couldn't wait."

"This gets worse and worse."

"It's worse than you think. She was going to—I don't know what—do something terrible in public."

"What for instance? Enjoy herself with me maybe?"

"Fill in the blank. Dance on top of the table in her underwear. Or tell everybody who you are & what you do. Don't ask me. She didn't get very far with the idea."

"Sounds like fun to me."

"Because you don't know how low she can go. I do. You don't know how Annie's mind works. You don't know her at all Sport."

David wanted me to guess from his Statement he was the guy who DID know her very Intimate but I did not Rise to bite. I Acted Dumb I let him take all the rope he needed to Hang himself on the Hook of the Truth. Let him Confess to me. Let him Confess how he was all the time Wooing her behind my back in front of everybody on the Show. All the time I had my High Hopes for her. Let him Confess how he betrayed i.e. how he offered Help & stabbed me in the back.

"You talked her out of going on a date with me?"

"Right."

"Because you're my friend."

"That's right."

"Ah-ha." I said and the Big Idea entered my mind. "You *would* blame it all on Annie."

"Hey I was the guy who stopped her in her tracks pally! She was ready to wipe the ballroom floor with you. I mean what am I feeling guilty for? You owe me Ray. You owe me one."

"Is that a fact?"

"Annie was going to treat you so bad you'd drop her like a hot brick and *that's* a fact."

"Which would've been fine with you. Fine and dandy with you."

"I just told you I was trying to figure out a way to let you down easy. You don't believe me that's your business."

"Tell it to the mirror when you shave tomorrow morning. Tell it to Annie. I'm not dumb David. You just revealed yourself. You couldn't face me like a man so you figured you'd wait for me to come in here by accident. I find you & Annie going at it. I scream & run away. I'm such a pisher I drop her like a hot brick so I don't bother Annie or you ever again. Isn't that how you had it figured?"

"Of course I didn't. I didn't figure anything. That's how things happen. Life's a lot more complicated than you think it is."

"I don't expect you to be honest to me but for crissakes David you should try and be honest to yourself! You want to let your own conscience down easy. That's who you want to let down easy. You want off the hook. So easy me no easies Mr. Scruples! You gangster! You thief! You cheap con artist!"

"This *is not* how I wanted you to find out about me & Annie O.K.? Believe it or not you dumb little pisher!"

"I'm a dumb little pisher! O.K.! So spell it out for me because I don't believe my eyes what I saw. You and Annie? It doesn't make sense to me."

"Use your imagination. You think she's a angel or something? She's my kind of girl. And vice versa. You think she came down from heaven? You think Annie's a virgin or something for crissakes?"

Lamont Carruthers for one knew everything about their Romantic Escapade so it Tickled him silly to write up tricky Scenes on purpose for David & Annie to do on the Show. Between Lionel Horvath and Rosalind Bentley for instance Rosalind falling for his oily charms and Horvath cheating on her etc. in other words Emotions raw & tender which they had to act out on the Airwaves for all to hear. I am guessing here but in my Opinion this Mischief planted certain doubts about each other deep inside their Subconscious Minds therefore from then on I believe part of the blame for everything that Happened between David & Annie belongs to Lamont Carruthers.

By the time of The Kiss Of 1939 Annie was already pregnant with child but David had to go on his bended knees to Convince her to throw in the towel & Marry him. This they did but it did not stick. About 1 year of Marriage Bliss was the high score for Annie & she took her little girl to go live with her sister's family in Far Rockaway. Which proved my Point about her Desires in that Direction but I never opened my mouth about it to David for Revenge was not in my Blood until Very Recent.

But on the night of our famous Episode The Birth Of The Green Ray downstairs in the lobby of the Liberty Building Annie's mouthpiece served her Divorce Papers to David's mouthpiece. This ripe moment was a gift horse on a silver platter to Lamont Carruthers for upstairs in the Studio meanwhile David & Annie

are busy portraying the Voices of those chirpy lovebirds Raymond
& Estelle Tremayne.

RAYMOND: I love you very much Estelle.
ESTELLE: And I love you! Oh Raymond! I do!

Ha Ha.

You can not find a Limite on Desire not high or low. Also you
will not find a Limit on how a person will Behave to get Satisfaction. For Satisfaction a person will insult he will start rumors
plant Doubts twist Facts a person will conceal he will double-
cross to Satisfy his Desire he will betray to be Superior so he can
look down on one & all. But every Desire & Satisfaction turns
into dirt I believe.

In the course of Human Events I will tell what Happened after I
woke up in Tio's house now. I did not hear a Sound anywhere
around not outside my bedroom door not in the kitchen nor not
a Voice in the Thin Air. I thought maybe I slept right through
all the early morning Excitement of breakfast etc. but when I went
on the Grand Tour of the downstairs area I started to feel like a
marble rolling around a Empty Shoebox.

I called Amelia's name up the stairs I did not get my Answer
so I decided it was the correct Procedure I should Investigate.
First off in the room where those 30 Mexican boys used to be now
all there was left of their Presence was the smell in the Air from
stale tortillas. Empty as a packing crate in there besides a little
pile of dust all Swept Up in the middle of the floor.

I tippy-toed down the hall over to Amelia's door I was the
lonely ghost floating upstairs amid that Vacant Place. I knocked
shave-and-a-haircut but the door was not shut all the way it
Squeaked open at my Touch. Amelia was not in Residence. Her
bed was made up Perfect with the sheet folded back as per a hotel
her Safari Suit was hanging up in the closet and the bottles &
tubes of her make-up were there on her table so if she fled in the
night she did not have time to pack her Belongings. Or she did
not need them where she went. Or she was Coming Back soon.

I am busy mulling the Above Thoughts back & forth in my Mind also I am looking through the window down into the street I can see the nose of my Raymobile. Also I see 2 little Negro boys leaning on the hood. One of them drops down & crawls under halfway behind the front tires. Maybe he is looking for a Baseball for Example but what else if maybe not? The kid leaning on top of the hood is futzing with the latch so I bang on the window & shout at him, "Hey! Hey sonny!" but they do not hear me or Heed my Cries.

In 10 Seconds I am out the front door & on my way across the street. "You want something with my car?" The boy twists his head around he slides his tushy off the hood & kicks his pal a little kick on the foot. They walk away a few steps then they sprint down the sidewalk all the time giving me the finger. "All right," I say "you can go now." If they Scratched my Paint Job for sure I was going to Investigate who they are & make sure they pay to fix it like new which is Fair you will Agree.

How much can you get for used Spark Plugs or a Distributor cap or a filthy dirty dipstick? Or maybe it was just boyish Mischief. While I am bent over giving my hood a close-up Examination a Voice pops up behind me.

"No respect for private property is there?" this high raspy Voice says. I picture it is a neighbor lady but when I turn around to agree with her Judgement I see it is not a lady it is Napoleon Bonaparte in a 3-Piece suit.

That Napoleon haircut all combed forward toward his round face which is maybe 5 Feet 6 Inches above Sea Level. I Observe the Female Details of smooth white cheeks & ruby red lips his mouth very small and puffed out. Also I took in his Physique since he was standing back from me a few feet I saw his entire form so I Noticed his tight muscles on his thighs which stretched the pockets on his pants. With a vest & tie & jacket in that hot weather but he was not Sweating a drop.

"I stopped them in time," I spoke up for small talk.

"That's what matters." He stood there on the spot like the soles of his shoes were Stuck to the Asphalt.

I have never felt Comfortable around door-to-door salesmen I always end up buying just to get them to shut up & go away so I did not want to Encourage him at all further. I walked back across the street back toward Tio's house but it turned out Napoleon was not Stuck into the Asphalt afterall nor he was not going to let me off the Hook so easy.

"Can I save you some time?" I said. "If you're from Fuller Brush—"

"Do I look like I'm trying to sell you something?"

I Remembered what my papa used to do at a moment like this. "My wife isn't home now. You want to talk to her for this."

"Your wife?"

"She handles all of this business."

"Yes I would like to talk to your wife. Is she going to be home soon?" We were on the sidewalk & the Pressure of his Spiel pushed me back onto the lawn where I dug in my heels. "I'm from Fuller Brush Incorporated," he said & he opened his Wallet he flashes me his I.D. and he was Chuckling the whole time. A shiny Badge flashed back sunlight in my eyes. "F.B.I."

I did not need to read the Buzzer I had the right Idea about who he was. On Tio's lawn I was standing face to face & toe to toe with John Newberry.

"Just a few minutes of your time Mr. Green."

A helpful Tactic I thought of in that moment was I had to Surround myself with Law Abiding citizens i.e. if I stayed in the Public Eye I was not going to be the victim of any freak Accident for instance when I am doing the dishes a Steak Knife slips out of my hands & into my Chest.

"I was just going for a walk in the park," I bluffed him.

"Is there a park around here?" He said it like he knew the Answer. "Mind if I walk with you?"

"I'm going for a high colonic right after."

We started strolling along. "You don't know Dallas. Do you? If you need the name of a doctor I can point you in the right direction."

"Thanks anyway."

"What's that for—a colonic? For some condition?"

"High colonic," I corrected him.

267

"High colonic. You look like you're in the pink to me. For a man your age."

A car a Ford or a Chevy one of those I think or a Buick came up & kept up with our slow steps. With a little Flick from his hand Newberry sent it down the Block I saw it slip around the corner.

He did not Know who he was Monkeying Around with. If he wanted to chit chat I could chit chat him into the Ground. "It gives me added pep. You should try it. You look like you need one."

"Pep!" Newberry laughed very Loose & Easy. I think that word Tickled him and he tried it out himself. "Pep. Right." We kept on walking. "Well Mr. Green I sure need something." He slipped a Photo out of his jacket pocket & inside I saw the Gun slung in his shoulder holster and then this Conversation & this stroll all of a sudden came down to Earth very hard. He held up the Photo right in front of my Face so I could not see where I was walking I had to Stop & Stare at a mug shot of Amelia.

I know the ABC of this Business so I knew I had to Deny. I did not want to put anything on the Record I did not want to load Ammunition into his Gun. So very deadpan I told him, "No. I don't recognize him."

"Her," he corrected me. He pulled out another Photo & on this one I will Admit he pinned me to the mat. I was in that Picture I was pumping gas into the Raymobile and Amelia was sitting in the front seat.

"Let's cut to the chase huh?" Another swing of his hand a Flick from his fingers and that car was back. It pulled in & parked right near the kerb 10 Feet in front of us.

I was not going to run I did not feel up to Dodging Bullets at the moment. I was not going to beat him in that moment by Brawn I was going to beat him by Brains. "Where're we going?"

When Newberry held the back door of the car open & I saw who was in the driver's seat I Felt a Flush of needles & pins up & down my arms all the Sharp points pushing up through my skin. The big redhead from the gas station the gunsel from the

K.K.K. I Remember he said his name was Wayne Feather. My Brain said to my Brawn do not budge any Further.

"Get in the car Mr. Green," Newberry Urged me.

I spread my arms & legs out I curled my fingers around the edge of the Roof I Locked my knees & my elbows.

Newberry pushed on my back but I did not Bend. "This is stupid behavior. Get in. Please. Oh Christ," he sighed.

A housewife came walking by with her 2 little kids & her bags of groceries I Memorized her face for Future reference. I caused a scene that she was not going to Forget about in a big hurry. From the top of my lungs I cried, "Oh God! Oh Lord! Please mister! Don't hurt me! Where're you taking me? Oh God! I'm a old man! Why are you doing this to me? Oh Lord!" Etc.

When she witnessed me Mrs. Housewife was passing by the front bumper of Newberry's car and I made sure that she got a long look at my sad face so full of confusion & fear before I was going to let Newberry shove me in. She did not cross Over the street until she went by him by the rear end and her arms around her Dear little ones.

"It's all right," Newberry flipped his wallet open to show her his badge, "F.B.I. We're assisting this gentleman downtown." Then I felt his Gun barrel nudge me on my Spine. "Don't be unruly Mr. Green. Show me what a Good Citizen you are & get in back there."

When he Squeezed in next to me the very first thing he said was Sorry about the Gun. He asked me was I Comfortable do I want the air conditioning higher or lower la-dee-doo-dah etc. but I did not give him the Courtesy of Conversation. On the freeway he made a promise he was going to Explain all of his Reasons (ha ha) as soon as he had me Safe & Sound in his office. Also I should not be alarmed because of the Presence of Mr Feather he was going to explain about him & the Ku Klux Klan.

"They want to make him a Grand Kleagle," Newberry said nor I do not Exaggerate I heard him announce this Honor with Pride.

"No kidding." That was all he got out of me until the off ramp when he Offered me a Lifesaver (Peppermint) which I Accepted by saying, "Mm." I rolled it all around my mouth I found the hole with the tip of my tongue I did everything a person can do with a Lifesaver while I Pondered the Question Is Newberry Going To Explain All About The Shooting With The Shotguns Into The Motel Room? which pondering lasted until the hole was the only part left of my Candy.

Besides being the twin brother of Napoleon Bonaparte maybe the F.B.I. hired Newberry because he was a A-1 Mind Reader. He passed over the last one in the pack & he said, "It's nothing you should worry about. We're all on the same side." But even with the peppermint lifesaver I doubted it.

All the time Newberry is telling me how his Trusted friend & fearless collegue Wayne Feather is Involved in deeds of derring-do & derring-do-not Undercover amid the Ku Klux Klan I am Observing the decor of his office. I can bet that 9/10ths (maybe even 10/10ths) of what I am hearing is all lies from him so I do not give him my whole Attention I use my Powers to search for Clues about his true character which he can not hide in the Decorative Items he loves & Displays on his desk & on his wall.

From his mouth I hear his Friar's Club Testimonial on Special Agent Feather how he is breaking the K.K.K. from inside but so they go on trusting him and Respecting him as a White man of Honor he must go in with them on a few foul Deeds. The latest one he was Sorry to report was the surprise Attack on us with Shotguns. Even if it was risky for him he took the Trouble to try & save our lives by that Phone Call so now we are in the air-conditioned comfort & safety of Newberry's office together we can Shake Hands & be Friends.

I did not altogether take that cue and I am sure they both took it the wrong way i.e. Bad Manners from me or bad Temper. To tell the Truth my Concentration was wandering over other things. (But I do not think I felt Forgiveness toward Feather so soon after & I do not Forgive him now.) In particular photos all over the wall behind Newberry's desk with him shaking hands with Famous faces. With President Ronald Reagan in one. With J. Edgar Hoover in another one. With the Governor of Texas and the Gov. of Arizona and the Gov. of New Mexico. (A lot of Hand Shaking

I wondered what they had to Forgive Newberry for?! Or maybe HE was forgiving THEM!) Also in a Special black frame was a photo of John Fitzgerald Kennedy with a signed Autograph under. Such a obvious Camouflage!

But this did not touch my Heart so deep as all of his personal snapshots in plastic frames on his desk his Family all before him. The little boys had Newberry's flat dark hair & thin eyebrows and I saw from the picture of his Bride in a silver frame where his little girls got their wavy Blonde Tresses. All the people who love him no matter what there they are to Remind him all the time. The Innocence he put into the World will balance out his Guilty Deeds or shrink them away he thinks.

"Which is how you got a new transmission in your car so fast. You didn't want to hang around there and I bet Amelia didn't want to waste any more time than she strictly had to. So why didn't she come out to the car when you did?"

Silence snapped me back into the Conversation. Newberry had to ask me the Question all over again and this time he made the point to mention he Expected BOTH of us were going to be in the Raymobile a mile away by the time the Klaners showed up.

"She was in the shower," I told him flat. "Let me ask you a goddamned question. How about that?"

Newberry rocked Back & Forth very gentle on the springs of his padded chair. "You can ask any kind of question you want to."

"Why didn't Mr. Feather over there just stop it? That's all. Stop those demented maniacs before they got a chance to use a public motel for a shooting gallery. Answer me that one." I was Halfway out of my seat my throat muscles tight & Pulling me up.

Wayne Feather put on the Cool he put on the Calm. "I'll tell you why. My butt's been on the line for 3 years Mr. Green. Now Mr. Newberry tried to explain how I have to protect my rear on that. I gotta act like I'm a good ole boy just the same as them. That means sometimes I do things I'm not too proud of. Things 'at go against my nature."

I did not want to let him off the Hook so Easy. "If this is some kind of apology," I said, "it's just pathetic. Pathetic."

271

"I mean *I breed guppies* at home! Holy smoke Mr. Green. I help my kids with their science projects. I *live* with them. I only go to a Klan meeting a couple times a month!" He was standing up leaning against the door now. He kicked away from it & sat down again when Newberry aimed him a tight flat smile. "Anything I do it's for the good of the country. Including you," he dropped those words out of the side of his mouth.

"I'll remember that," I said, "when you're burning a cross on my lawn."

"O.K." Newberry's Voice cut through the Atmosphere between us. "Thanks Wayne. Thanks for bearing witness." He nodded and Feather stood up again since he got the Hint he was not Required around there for anything else. "Ask Shelly to come in. Thanks."

Feather put a pally hand on my shoulder on his way out & so I should not feel Excluded Newberry said, "We'll keep it very informal at this stage."

Those words had the Opposite Effect on me. What informal? What Stage? Stage of what?

Shelly came in from the outer office she sat down in the chair Feather used next to Newberry's desk. "It's so hot & sweaty," she complained and I thought she meant the chair but no. "Air conditioner's on the blink all over the floor."

"Cool in here," Newberry chit chatted.

"You don't get the sun on this side. All of us are sweating like pigs in heat out there." She settled in with her Notepad but she did not even say "Hello" to me for I was just the job she had to type out before Lunch.

"Old business." Newberry stretched across his desk to hand me a Flimsy pink piece of Paper.

"What's this?" I read it over I saw it was a bill for $658.85 and I have it on the table in front of my eyes in this Minute.

"For your transmission. You can pay it off in installments if you want to." I did not do a very good job of hiding my Surprise I did not Expect to see such a High Figure. I did not Expect to see a Bill at all. "I can't let the taxpayers cover your expenses can I?"

I was reading over the Items on the paper. "Do I get a guarantee with this?"

"Parts," he snickered. "Labor you have to pay for." He watched me stuff it into my Wallet he waited until I did that then he said to Shelly, "Let's get a few vital statistics down on paper. Your full name. Last name first."

"You know it already."

"You tell me. Of your own free will. That's the way we do it in the big city," Newberry said pretty breezy.

"Green." Shelly scribbled this down. "Ray," I said, "Green." Newberry ignored my Clue. "Residing at?"

"You mean now?"

"Where do you get your mail delivered Mr. Green?" For informal Newberry was sounding very Formal all of a sudden.

"What is this a intelligence test?"

"Only if you fail."

"My address—" It was not on the tip of my tongue it was not on the back of my tongue. "I don't remember the Zip Code."

"Not important. We've got a book. We can look it up." He made a joke out of Pleading with me. "Don't play hard to get Mr. Green."

The numbers came to me out of the Fog of the back of my Mind. "My address is—Apt. 6, 12055 Pecan St., Mason, New Mexico. I don't remember the Zip."

"Not important. Hair. I'd call it gray."

"Silver." I pointed this plain Fact out very Firm and 1 other plain Fact: "You can get all this off my driver's license." Which I took out of my wallet I handed it Direct to Shelly. She did not even glance at it she passed it over straight to Newberry.

He eyed it up. "This expired 2 years ago. You know that?" I shrugged. A real hardboiled criminal. "I can get you a brand new one. You don't even have to take a test. Any state in the Union." He held onto it for a second & waited for a Answer which he did not get out of me. Then he Passed it back to Shelly. "You can take the rest off this."

She took it from his hand she gave him back a heavy Sigh and

Hauled herself out of the chair. Before she opened the door back into the hot & sweaty Air she braced herself for the Blast.

Newberry Encouraged her. "I bet they fix it before you can say Grand Kleagle."

"Grand Kleagle," Shelly said & when she pulled the glass door open it was Cool Air that Blew in on us.

Newberry flipped his palms up for her to see he Knew it was going to be all right all along. Then he picked up with me where he left off Before. "I'll do you a favor. You'll do me a favor. Back & forth like that. You know. Give & take. Then we'll get somewhere."

"I want to get out of here."

"We need to talk first." His Voice dipped low. "Seriously."

"You start."

"How did you meet Amelia Defuentes?" Ah-ha. Beans and more beans Newberry invited me I should Spill about Amelia so this Question was going to be his can opener. "What can you tell me about that?"

This Innocent Question will lead to that Innocent Question and before I know what end is up I Reveal already certain pieces of her Personal puzzle. Which Newberry will fit together into the Big Picture he will see Amelia's survival plan so my Duty appeared like a Guiding Light before me.

There is a Time to attack & a Time to defend also there is the Time when you have to make one of them look like the other one. I did not forget that a sworn duty of The Green Ray is I must be the shining example of Truth & Honesty if I am in the company of a cop or a criminal or neither or both. But in the company of Newberry a True answer from me could wind up worse for Amelia than a lie was going to Smudge the character of The Green Ray so while I figured out how to play this for laughter or tears I improvised something Unbelievable—

I turned my face down very shy I Buried my smile in my chin. "It's embarrassing."

This act tickled his Sympathies also his Interest to follow the rabbit down the hole. "You can't say anything wrong in here."

"Promise it won't go out of this office."

"Your secrets are safe with me."

I let out all my Air in a long sigh to show him O.K. he wore out my Defences. "I don't want to say revealing things Mr. Newberry. I mean it shouldn't hurt your opinion of her." He waved his hand in front of him to tell me his Personal Opinion did not add up to a hill of beans. So I confessed. "In the newspapers. In a Lonely Heart ad."

"Whose ad? Hers?"

"No. I put the ad in." I lowered my face from him again I did not want to look him in his eyes for this part Coming Up. "See— I don't think you can understand about me with my different experience of life." I picked up one of the photos of his kids I was trying hard to squeeze a Tear out to land on it. "You have a beautiful family."

"Thanks. That's Michelle and Alison in that picture."

"They're both so pretty!" I Gushed Out then I tilted the big silver frame so I could see it. "This is their Mother?"

"Last time I looked. Her name's Chantal."

"French name."

"I guess. I'll take your word for it."

"Where did you meet her?"

Newbery let a beat go by to let me know that he did not mind this Line of chit chat but also he was not going to let me go very far in this Direction. "Met her in Washington. When I just started with the Bureau. First week in fact. She was a clerk in records."

"Imagine that. She's in the F.B.I. too. So I guess it's twice as hard if you think about two-timing. I don't mean disrespect by that I just mean in theory." That pinchy smile on him gave me the Message loud & clear I should Quit while I am Ahead.

"Chantal quit her job when we got married. Anyway. So explain away. What wouldn't I understand?"

"Oh. Sorry I got off the track. I was just saying see—you get to my age—" now I looked up at him with my Puppy Dog eyes, "My entire life I lived alone so far. It hasn't been so bad. All along I thought that's how I like it but one day I woke up & recognized something." Another big Sigh here. "I recognized I've just been tolerating. So what the hell I figured. I put the ad in."

"You shouldn't be ashamed of being lonely," Newberry consoled me.

"Who said I was lonely? Did I say that?"

"I was interpreting."

"Don't interpret me please," I told him off very touchy. I did not plan what I was going to say next which that is the True Secret if a person will improvise something believable under Pressure. Also he must go Forward and save himself the Woe of going around in the same sad circle. "I would like to get off of the subject now."

"Right," he said but he did not Let Go of it all the way. "So you met Amelia. She answered your ad. Then what happened?"

"We went on a date." I tried hard to Remember what people did together when they went on a Date. This is what Entered my Mind: "We went bowling. We drank a few milkshakes."

This Description dragged a raggedy Laugh out of him. "Amelia Defuentes & milkshakes! They go together like hot fudge sauce & pepperoni pizza."

While he was Chuckling away there I slipped in the main Question which was buzzing around my Mind since I came in. "You know her very well Mr. Newberry?"

He cleared his throat. "We've met," he said. "I know for sure a milkshake isn't her favorite drink."

For sure it was not the raw Info of his Remark that made me want to catch my Breath only it was the raw Emotion inside it. He Knew things about her & he was Telling me so. So what was he Pestering me for if he knew Details down to the milkshake level?

I looked over the Plaques on his wall with the Certificates and so on the Honors of his work for the F.B.I. and I got the idea maybe both of us Obey the same Code. If I am plain & true he will be plain & true to me out of Respect. He will Recognize my purpose he will Respect it like a Gentleman.

I looked right between his eyes I asked him straight: "Why do you want to find out such personal things?"

"I just want to understand what kind of relationship you've got

with her. I want to know how you're involved in her life." He
said this all Courtesy but no Respect came after.

So I did not lie but I did not Reveal. "I'm involved."

"Tell me more." He leaned forward he sucked on his upper lip
for ½ a second.

"I don't know what you want me to admit Mr. Newberry. I
don't understand what's happening here now." I dropped down
in my chair I sank back in my Old Age.

My Appearance I believe softened him up a little but he was
ready to close in on me. "What did you & Amelia come to Dallas
for? C'mon Ray. This is one of the easy ones."

I let my answer out a few words at a time. "We came to
Dallas—so she could introduce me—to her uncle—who is her only
living relative. Amelia wanted me to meet him—before—" All of
a sudden this was not a easy one it was a Blank one. Think Think
Think! All I came up with in a Hurry was this: "—before we get
married."

"You don't mind if I say right out I doubt it?"

"I said you wouldn't understand."

"Are you a millionaire Ray?"

"Me? No. I'm not a millionaire. I'm not a thousandaire."

"You have a big dick?" This I did not Dignify. "So what does
a woman like Amelia want from a man like—" He stopped himself
right there I Believe Truly he did not want to Insult me below
the belt.

"How do you know what she wants out of life?" I asked him
Sincere.

He held his thumb & fingers a little apart like he was holding
up a Invisible sandwich. "I've got a file on her this thick." He let
his hand drop down on the desk. "You're not her fiance. I don't
think you're anything like that. Not a chance. What are you doing
with her? You her new partner in crime?"

I turned myself into one of those alien heads of Easter Island—
I was not going to help him Guess the Truth but I was not going
to Deny anymore.

"Or maybe you're just a patsy."

"No."

"Then what? You pick the right word."

"Her protector." I stared him out I stared him down until he got my Message i.e. I was going to Protect Amelia from *him*. I had to Admit this Fact to him because the chimes inside me told it was the Time for Truth & Honesty. "Let's talk turkey."

"That's all I want Ray," Newberry said like he just closed a deal on a Used car. He left himself wide open for the whammy I was all ready to throw.

"I know about you." I planted my Dukes on his desk & I stood up to face him to shame him by my bold Disgust. "I know things. You Jekyll & Hyde."

For a second he screwed his eyes up at me like I am saying this to him in Hungarian. "What do you think you know?"

I looked down on him & said, "I won't let you touch her. You did enough harm already."

His Confidence shook his Confidence cracked. He did not put up his dukes he was all of a sudden a defenseless boy sitting in front of me. A hole opened up like the iris of a eye & I saw into the dark place of his very Personal Emotions. "What did she say about me?"

I did not pull my Punch even if I did see him Wounded by my words. He did not shake from Anger something else shook him up now I believe this was Fear for he knew Amelia Revealed his secret Identity to me. I pointed at the photo of our late President J.F.K. & I said, "With him there looking over your shoulder all the time you should hide your head from shame."

"Speak English." He was Recovering very fast & the hole started closing up again. "I thought you wanted to talk turkey."

"Gobble gobble."

"Say again?"

"You can't kill everybody."

I could Feel the hot Blush on his cheeks heat up the Air around us. He stood up very steady but if he had the idea he was going to Slug me it boiled off in a hurry. Newberry smoothed down his hair instead. "I don't care what kind of twisted crap Amelia Defuentes gave you. I'm going to do you a big favor now and

278

forget what I just heard you say. I advise you to sit down in that chair. You and I are going to reason together."

"Give up," I said & I meant the General Idea also the Specific. "Turn yourself in Newberry. You can't kill everybody who knows."

"Sit down!" he Hollered at me he came around the desk & he grabbed my wrist to Force me.

But he did not Daunt me with his Indian Burn I stood up to him. "I know all about your dirty business—" (while we are arm wrestling I am saying this!) "What're you going to do? Murder me too? Or just break my arm for a warning?"

"Man!" he spat out when he let go of me. To calm down he went over to his window & took a couple of deep Breaths & dabbed his Forehead with a tissue. "This is not funny," he said to himself then to make it Clear he said to me, "this is not a joke. Why do you take her word for anything? I mean—why should you trust Amelia Defuentes and not me?"

"I met her first." I was not trying to be a Weisenheimer this was the Honest Truth besides—"I don't have to take her word. I saw things with my own eyes."

"Saw things. What things?"

This way Newberry Challenged me to give out with the goods & put him wise to my angle. This I Decided to do & show him I am not Afraid of playing hardball. "Those dumb gunsels of yours back in Mason. How they punched her—"

"Name names."

"—how they threw her in their car—"

"Name me some names!"

"—how they locked her up in a rat trap in the East 8th & had her helpless and how they called you up on the phone so you could come down & take her away like a portion of sweet & sour pork!"

"Who did? C'mon Ray. You know a name? Or is this more b.s.?"

"I remember both names! Nilo. You like that one? Perry. You like that one better?"

With his finger in Thinking Position on his sealed lips Newberry

279

backed off very Casual. Then a laugh like a Chihuahua bark escaped out from his mouth. "I don't know anybody called Nilo," he said oh so careful. He Concentrated on a Question he tried to trap before it went out of his head. "What did you call them? My what? My dumb what?"

The word Jumped to my lips. "Gunsels."

This tickled him harder than pep did before. "Gunsels." He smiled over at me my fond friend now. "All right. Ray if you want to stay out of serious legal trouble I want you to tell me something. And tell me true."

"Why should I lie to you?"

"Right. Exactly right. Good. Satisfy me with a good answer and you can walk out of here ricky-tick."

My turn to get tickled. "Ricky-tick?"

"Ricky-ticky-tavi." (This did not clear it up for me strictly at all but I Decided I could look it up later when I had time.) Newberry sat on the edge of his desk about 6 inches away from me. "I want you to tell me how you & Miss Defuentes ended up in the same house in Mason. Was this before you went bowling or after?"

"It was all after."

He sucked in a Breath and leaned back. "What I want to know is what brought you & Amelia together somewhere both of you'd be threatened with violence?"

"Fate." It was the Correct Answer but it was not the good answer Newberry wanted to hear from me.

"Zero out of 100. Ray believe it—you're going to tell me true or you're not going to walk out of here." Then he added on, "Not today Jose."

My Conscience must live in the back of my Mind because that is where I felt the pressure Building Up. Just like the Pressure in my stomach when I do not eat all day or the Pressure on my eyes when I do not sleep. That kind of thing or like the pressure on my groin when I can not Relieve it on a long bus ride or the pressure in my head when I do not know the right Answer or a Fact. I can eat a boloney sandwich & Satisfy my stomach I can take a snooze & ease my eyes or I can find a men's room etc. I can look up the Answer in a book & ease my mind. If I want to satisfy my Conscience I must Defy. Newberry is a Pervert of the Law he uses the F.B.I. for camouflage so he Disguises his rotten intentions to take Revenge and silence all witnesses. Yes but John F. Kennedy was not on his Mind in that minute I believe he made Amelia a personal Item on his list so my duty was the pressure on my Conscience to Defy & Defend and this forced out of me the Voice of The Green Ray—

ME: You can't scare me with threats Newberry! I've been threatened by big leaguers! I'm still here. If I took the heat from Lionel Horvath I can take it from you.

NEWBERRY: I'm about one inch away from arresting you Ray. Who's Lionel Horvath?

ME: You can't arrest me. J. Edgar Hoover gave me the key to the city!

NEWBERRY: Sit down. This business isn't concluded yet.

ME: I said what I had to say. I've had too much of you for one day Newberry Now I'm going.

I had my hand on the doorknob but the next cold Blast out of his mouth froze me on the Spot. This Insult from him I was not going to pass over.

NEWBERRY: Are you aware of the immigration laws of this country?

ME: I may not be from around here but I'll bet I'm more of a American than you are!

NEWBERRY: Did I touch a nerve?

ME: I'm still here.

NEWBERRY: And before you go you're going to tell me every little thing about what you're doing with Amelia Defuentes.

ME: I'll stand up to you and to a dozen like you Newberry! Justice makes all men equal and you're going to be around to see criminals who cower behind the false fronts of law-abiding lives bow down to cleanse the soiled garments of their victims!

I was shaking my finger at him when I said those Words I felt the Blood shaking my ribs loose. Newberry did not come up with any Answer I think I surprised him by my Fury. He shook his head only & Punched the button on his phone to call his Secretary. He kept his eye on me the whole time he was waiting for Shelly to answer his call.

NEWBERRY: We're going to talk a lot more.

On the other side of the glass door I saw Shelly pick up her Phone & sit up straight when she Heard her Boss's Voice.

NEWBERRY: Conference Room. Take him down!

In the Readers Digest I saw a Artist's Impression of a Conference Room it had a walnut table in it with Individual lamps for each chair maybe a dozen chairs—in the picture window behind was the skyline of Manhattan roofs of skyscrapers Near & Far since this was a illustration next to a Story about the Reality of High Finance. But the Conference Room I was in did not Measure Up to the name I will say the word Bunker is a closer Description.

At least the cement walls had a coat of Whitewash but that did not Cheer the place up. For furniture a square table & 2 bridge chairs and no individual lamps just the fluorescent one up on the Ceiling. I folded my hands on the table & the table teetered it tottered so to kill some time I got Underneath with a folded up business card and made the short leg Even. While I was down there I saw in the middle of the floor a Drain then I pondered what is the Routine after a conference in this Conference Room? Does the janitor come in & hose the place down?

For Escape it was a worse Predicament than the notorious Chinese Box Room where they Imprisoned me with water coming in up to my neck in The Adventure of Emperor Zero when I fought against a nest of Japanese spies & suicide saboteurs in Santa Monica, California during the dark hours of World War 2. So the Drain in the floor calmed me down since no water could Flood In there even up to my ankles.

But my Safety was not the 1st item on my Mind I pondered why I obeyed Newberry's command I should wait for him nor I did not put up any Fight. I know I did not want to Discuss with him or hear from his Opinion of Amelia I did not want to study his Motives the only thing I wanted for sure was a nice nap so I could Think about things fresh. Between the stiff chair & the fluorescent light I did not rest and I Confess it did Steam Me i.e. the Bare Fact I was at his Mercy and how I let Newberry box me into this dark corner. What am I doing in the power of this nickle & dime Napoleon who besmirches his Badge with every breath this rotten apple who does not even come up to my knee-caps with his crooked Morals & sneaky behavior what am I doing waiting on his hand & foot? No I did not need a Nap to think about it fresh I let my own Free Will lead me over to the door yes I yanked it open all ready to walk out of there then there I was cheek to cheek with Newberry again!

A cardboard tray got Crushed between us and he Juggled it back & forth so he could keep the 2 sandwiches 2 cups of coffee etc. in his arms. "Careful," he said, "you'll miss out on a free lunch." Mr. Cheerful he was all of a sudden Smiles All Over while he pushed in and I backed up to the table. "Break bread with me Ray. Boloney & cheese or chicken salad."

So it was not the right moment to try & Escape also I figured Food = Strength so I pretended I gave in in case the moment came when I had to slug it out with him. "I'll break boloney."

"Luncheon is served," Newberry made a Big Production out of handing over my sandwich & my cup of coffee. "Sit," he Invited me and very Polite he waited for me to pull in my chair before he sat down.

Maybe this Occurs to you Likewise it did to me—So What is it going to hurt if I stick around for a bite & by sly Conversation I find out why Newberry wants to treat me with such fond Affection—

The plastic wrapper on my sandwich had its own ideas about its Purpose in the world it wanted to keep this particular boloney & cheese from being Touched by Human Hands. My only Accomplishment with it was I tore the top piece of bread in $\frac{1}{2}$ but I did not even put a Scratch in the plastic.

Newberry reached his open hand across the table. "Here. Let me help you with that." In a Flash he flipped open that silver cut-throat Razor of his & he sliced the plastic wide open down the Middle. So smooth & sharp he did not Disturb even the boloney. I did not take my eyes off of the mirror of that Blade which he Observed so he tilted it so I could get a long look. "Heirloom," he said & showed me the picture of a Racehorse running down the handle. "My grandfather gave it to my dad. My dad gave it me. When I graduated from the Academy." After my eyeful he folded it up & slipped it back into his pocket.

Maybe Newberry wondered about my Manners when I peeled back my damp white bread & picked out both of the floppy rubber orange triangles of so-called cheddar so-called cheese and I Concentrated on the boloney which was not bad but not Oscar Meyer either. I did not want to start the ball rolling so this I Showed him by the way I stared into my coffee cup with my sad eyes. I broke up the Monotony by stirring in my sugar but I stared down the same.

"I found out something about you," Newberry informed me maybe this is what Cheered him up so much. He slid a Xerox page over to me he Nudged my fingertips with it. I Recognized it was a page out of the Classified Section of the Mason Examiner with a big red circle around the ad I put in. "How come 'Peter Tremayne'?"

What point did I have to Deny who I am? So what so now he will know the true Force of the Enemy he faces he will see who is standing between him & Amelia he will start to show some decent Respect.

"We don't have to talk about this," he suggested & he tugged the page out of my fingers. "I just want you to know what I know so we don't waste our time together. You know—" he acted out

284

2 kids in a Tug of War— *"Is too!*—Is not!—*Is too!* See what I mean? Agree about that?"

I stopped Chewing my boloney but with a mouthful of it I told him, "O.K."

"You've got a piece of boloney stuck in your teeth Ray." He handed me a toothpick. While I poked around my Canines he spoke to me very Sincere. "I think I understand how you got mixed up with Amelia. It looks like it's all very innocent on your part. Which is the way I was hoping things were."

I pulled my lips back tight to show him my Pearly Whites. "Did I get it?"

"No. It's still there."

"You have to guide me in." I aimed my toothpick between my front teeth.

"Over to the left," he said very soft he was not going to blow his top because I Distracted him from his Purpose. "No—your left. Got it."

I speared the little ball of boloney I Examined it like a Specimen. "Look at that," I observed. "What's the yellow in it? Fat?"

Newberry pulled me back to the Topic of the Day. "Ray I want to begin at the beginning here. You don't lie to me & I promise I won't lie to you. Now tell me what she told you about the kind of trouble she's in. I'm sure I can help."

"You don't want to help her," I tested his word.

"No sir I don't." His voice was steady when he Confessed this to me. "I want to help *you*." He took a silent sip of coffee and he frowned maybe it was cold maybe it was bitter. "You're going to have to tell me how I can get you to trust me on this. Amelia is a dangerous woman. She can be vicious. I've been able to keep you from getting hurt so far but my hands are tied now if I don't know what she's planning to do next."

"I don't know," I answered him and Truly I did not.

Newberry leaned toward me on his elbows to drive in his point. "If she goes to Mexico—well—there's a limit to what I can do in a hurry. You'll be on your own with her. I can see she's got your defenses down." He leaned back & he broke open a pack of

285

Dentine gum. He chewed a stick very slow before he lowered his Voice & asked me, "Did she go to bed with you?"

I did not move a muscle & my Voice I made as low as his when I delivered Newberry my Reply. "A gentleman does not ask. A gentleman does not answer."

"I'm sorry," he nodded. "I guess there's only one gentleman in the room." He Repeated how he was Sorry very Sincere then he softsoaped me with his further Apologies. "It's the selfish side of me coming out. Gung Ho. I want to *solve* this thing Ray! What I was thinking—I was thinking pillow talk. I worry Amelia could use a tender moment to drop some poison in your ear. She's a smart woman. Very intelligent. With sharp instincts. She thinks ahead."

This was not exactly Perfume he was pouring in my ear either but I did not mind the Earache for this was a Chance opening up.

If I listened between his lines I could hear the Echo of his Inner Thoughts I could find out how he was Plotting against us.

"What poison?"

"Lies about the kind of trouble she's in. Lies about me. See I think she'd cover herself. Every possibility she could think of." He twirled his fingers by his head to show me he can pull a good Example out of the Air. "In case I got to you she'd do a little character assassination. Make it very hard for me to unconvince you."

"I try to keep a open mind about people."

"Including Amelia?"

"To me it looks like Amelia needs my help more than you."

"You worry me Ray."

"I hope so."

"What did she tell you about me? Play fair. Give me a chance to defend myself. I know what it's like. When you're lying naked with a woman. She can say anything to you and it's hard to believe she'd tell you anything that isn't true. That she'd hide anything from you since you're lying there with her & you can see every mole on her. Every hair. Man! You know how she *smells*. She doesn't try to hide any part of her so it doesn't occur to you that she'd want to hide any part of her life!" Newberry clammed up his lips pinched tight. I believe he did not want to Reveal how much Emotion he felt over Amelia but before he calmed down all the way a few Honest words leaked out. "Everything she touches turns rotten."

"You won't convince me," I told him off. I pushed my chair out but Newberry Grabbed my wrist his hand Caught Me very fast the way a frog's tongue catches a fly. For soft pudgy hands he had a strong Grip also his pinky ring bit down into my skin & I think he Knew this because he Squeezed hard on that spot before he let go.

"Believe me. I know what I'm talking about." Like he heard my Silent Voice or a Voice from the ceiling ask him Newberry glanced up blinking & settled back to tell me how. "I might as well be married to her Ray. I know more about Amelia Defuentes than I know about my wife. Every night for the last 6 years— every night since I've been on her case—she's the last thing I think about before I fall asleep. When I wake up the first thing I see is my file on her. I'm sick of looking at it. I'm surprised my wife hasn't sued me for a divorce by now. I'm this far away—" he showed me the same measurement with his finger & thumb he showed me before "—from snapping the lid on this case. I don't want to start getting sick of looking at a file on you."

My Hope was finally here it was the right moment I should try & Reach for his Reasonable side. "Can I have a stick of Dentine?" He tore the tight wrapper back & flicked a piece out by the tip of his thumb. He chewed. I chewed. We sat there man to man Chewing over all the things which had to Come Out in the open. "I don't know Amelia the way you do Mr. Newberry but I know something for sure. She won't talk. She only wants to go home to Mexico. She doesn't want to talk to anybody about what happened in the past." He looked up at me & his eyes all soft around the edges but hard on the Surface. I had his whole Attention now which gave me Encouragement. "It's all over now. Stop this stupid nonsense."

"If she told you anything *like* the truth then—"

"I'm the only person she told so I could help her get home.

You don't have to worry about it anymore. Close the lid on this now. How about it?"

Newberry pinched his chewed up Gum out of his mouth he folded it into a paper napkin he put the napkin back in the cardboard tray. While he talked to me he Collected the garbage on the table—the empty coffee cups the sandwich wrappers the plastic stirring sticks etc. he made it all Tidy. "I've been with the Bureau for 10 years and every month I take home $958.17. I have a wife who can't work because she has to take care of four kids. You said something about Justice before up in my office. In *my office* you yelled your head off about it and I'll tell you the truth Ray that *really* pissed me off. For your information I didn't graduate the Academy & join the Bureau because I had a hope in hell of pulling down some terrific salary. What do you think the big reward is? Not the money. You understand? I had the idea in my head that our country is the best place to live in the world. And of all the opportunities on the shelf I went for this one—" Newberry slapped his badge down on the table in the place he cleared in front of me. "And now I'm somebody who protects your right to make a million dollars from fried chicken or porno movies or whatever. From Cabbage Patch dolls! Any opportunity you can name I'm protecting it for $958 a month. I'm not complaining Ray. I get a reward. Satisfaction is my big reward when I cut out a hustler like Amelia. Somebody who turns every decent opportunity up-sidedown and shakes it to see what falls out of its pockets." To Demonstrate this deed Newberry shook his own pockets which Move I think triggered the idea of his Heirloom in his Subconscious Mind. He scooped out his silver Razor he rolled it over & over in his palm. "Amelia Defuentes only knows how to take *out* that's all. She doesn't want to put anything in. Oh man. I'll tell you—" He shook his head very stiff or maybe it was a Twitch. "My reward is see I know when I put Amelia away I've done something for the good *of the country*. For my kids' generation understand? I've kept things in the right hands so a little corner of the future is secure for the benefit of my children. I can hand opportunities down to them safe & sound. The same way my dad handed opportunities down to me."

For a 4th of July speech he did not Rehearse this was not bad
Material but I did miss the chorus singing America The Beautiful
in the background which in my Professional Opinion that would
add the right note of Emotion to the Grand Finale. But who did
he think he was kidding with his Shmaltz? Did he think my eye
nor my ear can not tell the difference between T-bone and ham?!
 "Your father is he still alive?"
 "Very." Newberry looked Glad I asked. "He's in Washington."
 "Retired?"
 "He's only 63."
 "Oh," I Remarked so casual just Conversation like I was not
leading up to anything particular, "Where does he work?"
 "He's with the Bureau. 41 years now. Last year the President
gave him a crystal punch bowl." He twitched his neck again. "I'm
very proud of my dad."
 "And he's very proud of you?"
 "I'm sure he is."
Now I let him have it I let him have both barrels this Loving
Father this Patriot this crying *shame*! With his chutzpah how he
could talk about FOR THE GOOD OF THE COUNTRY when
all the time he is hunting down the last Living Witness who saw
who pulled the other trigger on our young President John F.
Kennedy! What kind of a crazy Conscience does he have he thinks
he can get away with it because he tells me OUR COUNTRY IS
THE BEST and MY PAPA IS PROUD OF ME is that right? is
that True? Maybe his Papa does not know what his darling sonny
boy is doing today with all of his Opportunities!
 This was the hot frame my mind was in in that minute against
Newberry I could not hold back the Fire & the Flood which roared
up from my Guts. "Shame on you! Shame on you! I hope your
father never finds out what you're doing with your life. How he
made such a low animal come into the world." My Voice shook
out of my mouth.
 "Now wait—"
 I did not wait. "How can you drink one cup from his punch
bowl the President of the United States gave to him yet? 40 years
he's in the F.B.I. guarding and protecting for what? So his own

son can go behind his back & wreck all his decent values. How can you face him with such dirt on your conscience? Such dirt and blood—"

"Shut up now."

"—the blood of the best President we ever had since Franklin D. Roosevelt! Shame on you!"

This stopped him blank. "Huh?"

He was going to Hear what he wanted to Hear all righty! He did not know what I Knew! "Amelia saw you on the grassy knoll she saw your face didn't she—"

"*What* did she say?" Newberry's eyes opened up wide.

"You can cut the comedy because I know what's what you bastard. November 22, 1963 she came up here to see J.F.K. but she saw somebody else too. Amelia saw who shot him from behind the fence and—"

He cut in on me. "Hold on. I was 13 years old in 1963!" He Forced out a Laugh that sounded like a dry cough. "My God. Hold it there." He flipped a notepad onto the table & Wrote Out what I said so far. He wrote very fast in Shorthand. "All this is news to me." The tip of his tongue peeped out of his lips like it wanted to see what he was writing down so Important. Newberry hunched over his pad & pencil he put all of his Energy into it all of a sudden in a burst he turns into a Cub Reporter with a real Scoop on his hands. "*Then* what did she say?"

"It's what I say," I said to put a Fine Point on it, "I'll say it too how you have to silence her because she saw who it was. She saw who pulled the trigger. She saw who helped him get away!"

"She said *that?*" he smiled down on the page he filled up with my Testimony. "Oh man."

The same way my Professional eye showed me before how Newberry was ham acting now I saw he was not acting for my Benefit anymore. I already Observed how he did not have the Talent to Convince me of his other Emotions so this surprise on him I believe truly was because he never heard before the J.F.K. story according to Amelia. According to me I will say Newberry did not look like a Marked man on the hot spot under my Gaze.

I tried very hard but I could not erase out of my Mind the picture John Newberry: Cub Reporter and this led me to figure yes he probably was a 13 yr. old pisher over 20 Years ago. And the harder I tried to shame him down by the Details of Amelia's eyewitness Story the more he took the whole thing as a big Relief.

He did not look at me at all he just wrote down all I said. On some occasions he spoke up with, "Oh man!" or "That's priceless!" in particular I Remember when I came to the Fact of her father Silvio how he was a humble shoemaker. "This gets better & better," he chuckled over that one.

All the time I am Talking I Ponder a big Question from the back of my mind i.e. If Newberry Was A Pisher Then Who Was The Mystery Man In Dallas? When I got to the part about the men in the suits the men Amelia said she saw drive the car up the Answer fell down from my Mind to my stomach and for a minute I did not say a Word.

Which halt gave Newberry time to read over & catch up. In that shaky kind of silence I Heard every noise in the room I heard his pencil Scratching on the paper I heard the buzz from the white light in the ceiling I heard the screechy creak from the seat of my chair when I sat down Heavy in it.

My Feeling was I only said the next words to myself but I know I said them Out Loud. "Your father. It was him. This is all about your father."

Now Newberry looked over at me & the smile that was always tickling around his mouth sank back under his skin. "What did Amelia say about him?"

"I just figured the whole thing out," I said to the Air.

"Well. If you're doing any figuring from *this* incredible garbage you're so far out in left field you're—you're—" he tried to point out someplace farther than Left Field, "you're over the fence. You're out in the parking lot."

Starting then I did not feel like the shining Avenger anymore I felt like I was Underwater with all of my Breath Gone. I did not know what was going to Happen next this made me very Shaky. Did I have to Slug it out with him now? But no his happy Mood was filling his face again 1 muscle at a time & I saw how he was trying to bring down a serious Expression over it but this defeated him it was just a Slippery rubber mask which did not stay put.

For a long time he stared at his notepad he read it over Frontwards & Backwards. Finally he stood up he said, "O.K." and he walked all around the table. "You're not making it very easy for me to help you Ray." (To tell the truth I did not care all I wanted was my afternoon nap now I needed it more than before.) "I mean—" Newberry tapped the stack of Notes with his fingertips "you know that most of this is a vicious lie and the rest of it is a loonytoon. For your sake and mine I'm going to try and comb out this plate of spaghetti. I'm going to straighten this mess out right now." He Paced very slow & full of Thoughts like a Professor in front of a blackboard. "Listen to me—"

I believe I had a Decent Excuse for why I did not get up & make a run for it which was I did not feel Spry. I had a Cramp in my stomach also a Cramp in my head so I was not in the Perfect Condition to start up a slug-out and anyway then what? Then Newberry used a old trick right out of the Bible he grabbed my Attention with a socko opener:

"I'm going to tell you something only half a dozen people in the world know. I'm going to tell you how President Kennedy was assassinated. And why. I'm going to tell you how Amelia was involved and how my father was and how I am. Because now I think it's fair for you to know what the sides are and which one you're on. I've got the feeling you want to do the right thing so I'm prepared to tell you everything you need to know to help you make up your mind." He pulled out Every Word almost he was catching his Breath after each one.

We both knew the Question I was going to ask him next & I had to ask him to end the Suspense. "Help me make up my mind about what?"

"Who you want to help. Amelia or me." He flipped the pages of his notepad back to the Beginning & ran his eyes over the Page. "After you hear all the facts what happens next is up to you."

"Go ahead," I said. "Tell me what I need to know."

"Thanks." Newberry showed me his smile of Good Will before he sat down to tell me, "Amelia told you the truth about something anyway. Her father's name was Silvio. But he wasn't a humble Mexican shoemaker. He wasn't a shoemaker he wasn't Mexican and he was about as humble as Henry Kissinger. Until '59 he owned a big casino in Havana. Silvio's ideas about free enterprise and private property weren't very popular with Fidel Castro & his merry men so about 10 minutes before his casino was turned into the Palace of Culture or whatever Silvio shipped his family & his money out of Cuba and into Miami."

This I tried to picture & the picture which I saw was the Nightclub the way Amelia Painted it for me. Mink coats full of Dollar bills and Rudolf Valentino the Maitre d' whatsisname Julio. Playing the musical glasses.

"He fit right into American life. He had friends who made it easy for him. He bought a beach house. Sent Amelia to a private school. The works. And Silvio's American friends were really in very high places. These are men he knew from the casino days. Going back years. Now their sons are congressmen and senators. His friends ran banks. They owned shopping malls. Silvio invested too. In businesses but never in property. Because he was sentimental and homesick. His heart was back in Havana and there were a few thousand other Cuban refugees who felt the same way and told him so.

"So Silvio got his congressman to lobby his senator to lobby J.F.K. Maybe you remember what happened then. The C.I.A. and the N.S.A. and the F.B.I. everybody down to the White House gate guard persuaded Kennedy what a spectacular idea it would be if we gave guns to Silvio and his people. And L.S.T.s. And air cover. And the whole D-Day enchilada. My father met Silvio then. And Amelia and her mother. He was there to make sure nothing happened to any of them before Silvio landed his troops in the Bay of Pigs." Newberry stopped a Minute there & he asked me if he was Going Too Fast did I want him to Repeat any of it but no I told him I was Following Fine.

"Did you meet Amelia then too?" I asked him before he picked up where he left off. I do not think he was Expecting a personal question since he was Concentrating on the Historical part of the Story so far.

293

His eyes stayed down on his Notepad. He read something that made him Click his tongue & Shake his head & his Head was still Shaking when he looked up at me. "Say again?" So I said again then Newberry nodded, "After. Right after that. Uh-huh. Let me get to it. Her father went missing in action. Maybe he got killed on the beach. Probably they captured him. If they did they tortured him. Maybe to death. Maybe not. Silvio might be alive in some prison in Cuba. Who knows?" Then he said & he Meant it, "It's a crazy world."

Oh very crazy! Did they hang him from a pipe like a cow in a Slaughterhouse? Did they Force him to swallow things? Did they cut him open with a Knife? Did they Throw him in the dirt?

"My father had to break the bad news to his wife and Amelia. He said he didn't have to say a word to them. They knew. Amelia's mother said she saw it in the stars. Bad stars for any counter-revolution that month I guess. But the real reason was at the last minute Kennedy called off the planes. He might as well have sent Silvio in there armed with a squirt gun.

"A week later Amelia's mother had a stroke and she died. So Amelia didn't have any family left and my father sort of adopted her. She's a couple of years older than me and we got along all right. But she stayed angry about what happened to her father and she stayed in touch with her father's friends. I don't want to identify anybody—for your sake believe me not for theirs," he said very Confidential. "These people have very strong feelings about honor. Not to mention about friends and family. They trusted Kennedy and he pulled the rug out from under them. Certain people in Washington felt the same way." He Waved this away it was not the Point.

"The Point is—Amelia locked this big pain inside her. She was only 14 when all of this hapened. It hurt her very hard. She lived with us for most of the time she was in junior high but she spent vacations with a Cuban family in Miami. All summer in '62 and '63. She didn't go back to school that fall. My dad just got a letter from her with the address where he should send all of her things." Newberry Measured his next words out very Careful. "The next time he saw Amelia was on the grassy knoll in Dealey Plaza on the 22nd of November." Newberry licked his dry lips.

When I heard the news J.F.K. is coming to Dallas I went there on the bus very early—I remembered Amelia's Exact Words about it & further words besides—*if I move then for sure I miss him*—maybe Dr. Sigmund Freud would have a Revealing Explanation for why she used those Particular Words when she told me her Version—*I said I was a crazy teenager*—yes this time I pictured Newberry's Version I saw back 20 years when Amelia was 16 yrs. old in her white dress with the flowers & birds across the top walking up from the grass then she was Squatting down behind the Fence until she Heard the crowds cheering cheering for him then she stood up this time she had a Rifle in her hands BA-BOOM!

"No," I said, "you better spell it out for me."

He breathed in a breath & held it there then he said, "Amelia was the trigger Ray. She was the 2nd gun everybody was looking for."

"Ooohf!" If Newberry Punched me in my Stomach he would have got the same Sound out of me. "I have a headache." I rubbed both Sides of my Head I had to stare down at the top of the Table.

"Do you want me to stop?"

"Is there more?"

"Only a lot." He reached into his pocket & came out with a few Tin Foil packages. "I think one of these is aspirin. This one is Alka-Seltzer."

"Can I have that too?" I held my palm out for it. "I'll use my coffee. It's cold now."

"You sure?"

"Yeah." Plop Plop Fizz Fizz they went into my Coffee which I did not even Taste going down. Newberry waited very Patient for me to Feel Better & Recover & ask him all of the Questions I had to Satisfy my Doubts. "If this is the real truth," I started out slow, "why didn't the F.B.I. or anybody pick her up?"

"Somebody did. I told you who. My father got to her. Dad was the senior agent on the ground and he threw her into the backseat of his car and drove her down to Mexico." I only had to ask by the hard look in my eyes and Newberry answered my Doubt *What about your father's sworn duty?* "He cared more about Amelia's life than he did about John Kennedy's in that instant. My father isn't a sentimental man he's a moral man and I think he decided the U.S. government scrambled her life up well & truly and what happened was poetic Justice. He couldn't give her Silvio or her mother but he could give Amelia her *own* life back. Either that or shoot her in the head. He didn't want to see the government chew her up all over again."

I tried to see some Clue of Feeling from his eyes when I asked him, "Do you take after your father?" But he Blinked this away.

"I don't think I would've felt the same way about it. But I was only 13 then. The world is a different place for grown-ups."

"I didn't take after my father either," I said & those Words felt heavy in my Mouth.

"There's nothing personal about this business. It doesn't have anything to do with the Kennedy thing anymore." Professor Newberry kept going with his History Lesson. "The Warren Commission came & went. Jim Garrison. And 20 years down the line the Senate sub-committee opened it all up again and they pretty much left it the way they found it. So." He Spread his hands open Dangling at his sides. "Are things starting to look different to you Ray?"

"I don't follow how it affects Amelia now. If it doesn't have anything to do with President Kennedy I don't understand what it does have to do with." I bit off the end of this Thought before I started Talking it into a Circle. "Will you tell me where you're leading me with this?"

"I hope it doesn't sound like I'm taking the long way around. I'm telling you all of this for your benefit," Newberry said all of a sudden Touchy with me. "You should know what kind of person you're dealing with."

"Who?"

"Who are we talking about?" he said through his tight teeth.

"I thought we got up to the part where you come into it."

"Did Amelia tell you how she makes a living?" I did not think of such a thing until Newberry made me. He Bowed a little

Towards me & said, "There aren't very many careers in Mexico a woman can go into and make the kind of money Amelia makes." He looked at me the Same Way a bird looks at a Bug on a branch. "You mean you don't have any idea?"

I had a Idea & I tried it out on him. "I believe she's in the nightclub business."

Newberry balanced on his heels & he leaned right back against the wall but his Voice was not Cool & Casual he said this full of Force, "Amelia runs wetbacks into the U.S. Ray. Illegal Mexican immigrants understand? They pay her money and she gets them across the border. The house you're staying in that's her safe house for the muchachos she brings into Texas. Did you meet a man there she calls Tio? On the fat side. Looks like the Frito Bandito but he talks like John Wayne."

I do not know why my Instinct told me to Deny maybe I made a fast Judgement from the way Tio made me my breakfast & the kind way I saw him treat Amelia. "No," I said, "I didn't meet anybody of that description."

"It doesn't matter," he said & pushed away from the wall. "She started out as a mule. Just the Girl Scout who led them across the border in 2s and 3s. By 1980 or so she was doing business from dozens of places in Mexico. Running them across in Texas up & down the Rio Bravo. In New Mexico between Deming and Mason. Places in Arizona. She turned into what we call a sponsor. Half of the mules in Mexico work for Amelia Defuentes. I wish I could tell you it was my brilliant investigating work but when I got this assignment my dad sat me on his knee and told me he never took his eye off her all this time. Her foster father. Trying to keep her out of too much trouble."

My Mind worked on this too. "And out of the country."

"All right," Newberry gave in. "For their mutual benefit. Then I got the job of busting up the wetback business. So for old time's sake we made a deal. Amelia isn't the only sponsor down there. She's got plenty of competition. Whenever I wanted to put any of the other guys out of business she'd set him up for me. She knows how to do that—convince men to trust her. And she's stayed alive all this time so you can guess how smart she is."

"What's her trick?"

For a answer Newberry just Frowned at me Man to Man. "Anyway it's all different now. Things've changed and we can't go on like before." This idea sat on him very hard I will say Newberry was sad to say it. Out of curiosity also sympathy I asked him how his father felt about this. "He's leaving things to me. I hope you can understand my problem."

"I don't know," I said. "The only time I had to make up my mind between my papa and my conscience I decided the wrong way." We both started Talking at the Same Time then I said, "I regret it so much."

But my words did not Rise over Newberry laughing out, "That's not my problem!" Which Misunderstanding made me very Embarrassed I Revealed a Personal thought. At least he did not Hear it or at least he did not Care he just went on telling me, "It's the bastard Ku Klux Klan! Maybe you know about the dead wetbacks turning up in the desert. Well they aren't just ordinary wetbacks. They're mules. Mr. Feather informs me that the K.K.K. has people in Mexico and they're working their way through the families. They'll get to the sponsors. They'll get to Amelia and if you're with her when they catch up she'll toss you over like a sandbag out of a hot-air balloon. The best thing I'm hoping for is if you can make it look like we got to the right place at the right time. I can bring her in myself before she crosses the border. Otherwise like I told you—there's a limit to what I can do for you. I don't want to have to choose between saving your ass pardon me and exposing Agent Feather. I like you Ray and I respect you but there's no contest. I can close down the Klan in the Southwest and that's a little more important to me."

The Big Idea sank in. "But I promised Amelia I was going to protect her."

"Good. You own a gun?"

I pointed at him. "Protect her from you."

"Tell me how you plan to do that," he said very Firm but it was a Plea.

"I don't know about any of this. I have to think about it." He

298

Accomplished what he wanted to i.e. he planted a Doubt about Amelia in my Mind. "I want to see proof," I said.

"What kind of proof?"

"Evidence."

Newberry sucked his lips in & he Pondered this. "All right. Give me 24 hours. I've got to get a courier out here from Washington. I'll let you browse through Amelia's file."

"Do I have to come back here?"

He Pondered again. "Didn't you say you wanted to see a doctor about something?"

"Yes a high colonic."

"O.K. We use a medical center a couple of blocks from here." He scratched the Address down on a scrap of paper & held this out to me beween 2 fingers. "Can you read my writing?"

"Arroyo Seco Medical," I read out. "Are you sure I can get a high colonic here? Only certain doctors do them."

"They do everything there."

"I'll take your word," I allowed him. "It's a good test."

"Right. I'll make the appointment for you. It'll be with Dr. Epps. This time tomorrow." Newberry checked his watch. "It's 2:15."

"Dr. Epps. 2:15," I double checked.

"Yes. Now when you get into the examining room one of the nurses will bring you the file. Lie back. Enjoy your high colonic—"

"You lie on the side."

"Whatever you do you can do it in there with the file until 4 o'clock. Read over anything you want to but don't take the file out of that room. Just give it back to the same nurse when you leave."

I heard my Voice come into the room from far away. "She only wants to go back to Mexico and live a quiet life."

"That isn't possible anymore," Newberry said his Final Words on the Subject & he held the door open for me. "You convince her."

I Sat still I did not Jump to his Invitation. "Is it O.K. if I sit here by myself for a minute?"

299

He checked his watch he had Business on his Mind. "For a minute."

"Will you switch the light off please?" When the dark hit the room and Newberry let the door hush shut behind him the silence Rushed In on me it fell in from the 4 walls. The same Sound of my Radio when it blew a tube. I know the Show is still going on but I do not Hear it I can not Hear what is coming on the Airwaves. So this kind of Quiet all of a sudden made me very Jumpy & I did not sit & stew there anymore I made a Move I opened the door.

Pipes & boilers motors & vents & plumbing filled up this basement I did not Remember Exactly which way to the Exit. I followed the pipes they led me over to the boilers & I followed the vents they led me back to the pipes. I made a Circle between the boilers & the motors so I Followed the vents from there back to the pipes back to the Conference Room what did I have to do to get myself out of this? Did I have to sit down Helpless in there until he came back to get me? I did not wait I have to Admit this is my only way out so I called him but not very loud—

"Newberry?"

By the time I got back to Tio's I did not have a Cramp in my head anymore no it was a ball of snakes there which Hatched Out where my Calm Mind used to be. I did not know heads or tails with them hissing & slinking in & out of each other I did not know Truth or Consequences with Amelia—if she is Innocent & Mexican and she did not Come Back to meet me yet because her big man in the F.B.I. helped her outsmart Newberry and now she is on her way Safe & Sound South of the Border—or if she is Guilty & Cuban and she just wanted me to be a Decoy for her so she could shake Newberry and get to the Bank and get what she Wanted and get back to her Hideaway in the hills.

All of my Doubts curled around this Idea *Am I her Champ or am I her Chump?* Even when I put on my clean Pyjamas it did not help Lower the Pressure my eyes ached hard even from the weak light that came through the windowshade. I shut my eyes but it was not dark it was not a Relief. So I covered my face in my hands but it was not Enough Because through my fingers I saw Tio's bedroom expanding—and I was in the middle of the Big Bang with everything Flying Away from me. The floor dropped down Under my feet—the closet took off Backwards—the steer horns went Spinning Up to dark space—the dark space came spinning down around me it faded out all the Light in the room. Then I could not Feel any Breath in my chest nor not any Bodily Feeling either. I did doubt my Senses but I saw the edges of the ceiling Crack & show the Starlight Beyond and that was my last View before I blacked Out on Tio's bed.

Some nap I took some little snooze! I can not tell you how long I was Knocked Out but I woke up in the Dark. For a minute I did not Recognize my whereabouts I had the idea I was in My Own Apartment on Pecan Street. And from the head resting upon my shoulder I had the idea further that Mrs. Roderiguez— tuckered out from vacuuming my car—just crawled into Bed with me to Rest Up before she started cleaning the bathroom.

From the smell I figured this is not the case this is Amelia asleep in bed next to me. She kept her hand on my arm like she was sizing up my muscle and her cheek she Dug In right above it. When I sat up I by Accident shook her out of her Dream but she brought back some of it with her I believe because her head came up to look around but both of her eyes stayed shut.

"Que es?" her Voice came out Jumpy. "Ray?"

I shook her shoulder to wake her up all the way. "What's going on?" I said down my arm.

She fluttered her eyes open she Let Go of my arm. "Oh Ray," this time she groaned my Name out and pulled her pillow down to her stomach & Doubled Over it. She spoke Espanol into the mattress just a Mumble of it then she hauled herself back on her knees. This Move pulled the blanket off me which I Pulled Back over me pronto. "I scare you in your bed," she said, "I'm sorry O.K.?" I did not hear any Sorry Note in her Voice only her Polite Apology.

"You didn't scare me. You surprised me," I said. "Being here."

"I'll go away O.K.?" She unwrapped from the blanket now I

saw what she was Wearing to sleep in only a T-shirt on top of my Bermuda Shorts.

She twisted around on the end of the bed but before her feet hit the floor I said her Name & Stopped Her. "What's going on? I thought—I don't know what I thought. I thought you weren't going to come back here."

"Why?" Amelia asked back very sharp. "Where did you think I went to?"

"I don't know. How should I?" I took a stab at it. "Mexico," but I said it Soft & I gave it a Shrug. Just a Wild Guess I may say.

She cocked her head back. "Where did you go all day?"

"I was looking for a doctor. For my high colonic." I did not Look Her in the Eye when I said this but in the dark it did not make a difference.

So this made her Relax a little bit and she gave out with some News. "I came here in the afternoon but you didn't come too for a long time."

"It's hard to find a doctor who'll do it. Then I got lost on the way back."

"Oh. Si."

"Did you talk to your friend?"

I saw her head shake Sad & Slow. "He went to Washington today." She looked back to give me her Opinion face to face. "I don't think he want to help me anymore." Amelia rocked herself off of the bed she stood up Almost Bent Over like a very old woman. "Thirsty," she said on her way out of the door.

I did not Wish to Grill Her with any 3rd Degree for what was that going to Accomplish except I get the 3rd Degree from her right back? I Believe if that happened Amelia was going to hear the Truth about my Exciting day before I was going to hear any of the same from her. I told the True Story to Newberry I did not Resist so how was I going to Resist Amelia how could my Conscience Conceal any part from her?

She came back in 5 minutes with 2 glasses of pink lemonade (canned i.e. the Concentrate) and she Handed me mine at the same time she Drank Hers all the way down. "Not so good like yours," she frowned when she Finished.

I sipped a Few Sips and I Agreed with her. The pink sugar just Disguised the pink acid so it did not Refresh it passed down my throat like a Bottlebrush. "You can always tell the canned."

"Mm." Amelia rolled her cold glass Over her Forehead. "Now is only you," she told me, "My only friend now."

"Oh? Yes?" I tried to smile but I did not Keep It Up. "Where's Tio?"

She bent down she hugged me. "In the morning we go to the bank hm? Then Ojinaga."

I wanted to look Amelia in her face at this Moment so I pushed her shoulders away from me. "My doctor's appointment. Remember I told you?"

"When it is?" She waited for this Information the same way a Adding Machine waits for a Number.

"About 2 o'clock," I said, "A little after."

"I can go with you O.K.?"

"You don't want to do that," I said in a Hurry. "We'll go to the bank in the morning. Like you said."

Amelia let her hands drop down On Top of Mine. I did not Notice before how round & plump her hands were how much they looked like they Belonged on a little girl. Maybe she knew what I was Thinking because she Squeezed my index finger and she held on to it. I Believe this is a Reflex Action for a small baby for it Arouses the Desire to Protect in the heart of the Adult on the receiving end.

"I don't want to wait for you here. After the bank is easy for him to find me."

I did not Resist the automatic Desire I had to Squeeze Back & give Confidence. From sitting next to me on the side of the bed now she had the Confidence to Hug me again to lay her head on my chest. "You know the big supermarket a few blocks from here?" I felt her nod Yes. "How about if you wait in back of it. Where they pick up the trash." She nodded Yes again. "At about 3:30 all right?"

This plan came to me by Natural Instinct it was a Safety Net

no matter how Tough things turned out after my High Colonic—
if Amelia was the Innocent Victim of a dishonest Fed then I could
Save her because I knew where she was but Newberry for sure
did not—if she was the Guilty party then likewise but I could lead
the G-men straight to her gate.

"When I came back I see you lying down in bed," she told me.
"I try to go sleep upstairs but—" Amelia brushed the hair out of
her face & she kept her hand over her eyes. "Up there I got scared
by myself."

"I wish you woke me up when you came down here."

"I scared you hm?" I heard some Mischief in her Voice this
time.

"It was a surprise that's all."

"Bad surprise?"

"A surprise is a surprise," I said very final. "Anyway when did
you get back?"

"I stay away all day. I think maybe John Newberry watches
this house." And she was Watching Me the same.

I looked at her face and on the outside I saw it was as Strong
as the face on a cigar store Indian but a Tremble went across it
Underneath. Then it came across to me so I did not Refuse what
she was asking. "You can stay in here with me if you're nervous
upstairs."

She pressed in very close she Snuggled up the same way I found
her when I woke up before her head on my shoulder & her hand
on my arm but this time she did not Hold Still. Her leg came
over my legs so I did not hold still either I gave her a pat-pat on
her back.

"Ray?" she said up to me then I held my Breath I did not
move a muscle in Any Direction. Not even when she Stretched
Up to Kiss me on my cheek & she held the side of my face in her
hand.

"Amelia?"

I kept my Calm I did not try any move. What Move do I try?
If this is Amelia the Innocent One who is only after some Comfort
from me should I Deny her? What did it mean with her climbing
all over me that way so Desperate? Or if this is Amelia the Sly

One wrapping me up in her Plot who wants to Trick me into sticking with her by finding my Weakness to use it against me to make me putty in the palm of her hand *then* what is my Next Move?

Speaking of putty in her hands now the pair of them started wandering under my p.j.'s around my stomach. She lowered herself then I felt her Bosoms press down flat on my chest and her legs spread open now like a Bow & my stiff legs for her Arrow. "Mm," she went rocking with her hips but I did not know did I bring this on her or did she do this By Herself?

Her mouth traveled up to my ear and little Kisses she planted across my face across my mouth still I did not Pucker Up for her but this did not Discourage her. She went Lower with her Kisses down my neck down my chest she Unbuttoned my p.j.'s with her lips & teeth a button at a time Lower & Lower she shimmied down me. Then she Nibbled around the top of my p.j. bottoms—

Can a person be Naked & still Deceive? All Naked can a person still Hide what they want? I thought I was going to stop her where she was & just say *What led up to this?* or *What is this leading to?* but I started Choking on my words I could not Force them out of my throat.

"Ooh-hoo," I only said.

"Mm-mm."

Her Bare Bosoms I felt on my Bare stomach dragging across me there out of the bottom of the T-Shirt they fell & with one of her hands she Pulled Her Shirt all the way off & with her other hand Amelia untied my pants. I will say this Scared Me Stiff for I was almost in her Power. Her fingers around my p.j.'s she pulled them down & then I wanted to Fold Up under the blanket under the bed under the floor under the ground but I did not stop her then but something did when she Reached down between my legs.

"Where are you?" she breathed out.

I was there & there I was only waiting for her to Find Me. Not a weakling not a softling either a little soldier! *Stand up tall Little Soldier!* But he was not standing up Tall he was standing up small hiding behind her little finger.

Amelia did not say one word but she Kissed me there. I saw

the copper desert of her back roll side to side I tried to keep my eyes on that but I watched her lips close Around Me so now I know how she looks when she puts on her Lipstick I know how the Lipstick Feels.

"No. Amelia. Please don't do that. Por favor," I said to the top of her head. I pushed very hard on her shoulders which Encouraged her going "mm-mm" until I pushed again & her face came up like the Full Moon over a desert valley.

"No more," I winced at her.

She knew why I did not want this Attention. "He's cute," she tried to Ease me & Kissed me there again.

"Don't."

"Why you say don't?"

"It's obvious." To myself I added, "I mean it isn't." I did not have to hide it anymore my dingle ducked back under my hairy hide the way a Turtle ducks back in its Shell.

Amelia sobbed out a soft little laugh. "I like him," she coo-cooed & Tickled me a little around down there.

I yanked my pyjamas back up I Pulled them Shut. "No more I said. Show's over."

But Amelia was not going to give up before she saw a Encore. "Come out Poquitito!" Big Joke she cupped her hand around her mouth to help her call down to my fly, "Little chilli pepper! Yoohoo!" Well I tied up my p.j. cord into a Double Knot but this did not Deliver my Message to her for she had some more words for my Crotch. "Like a little boy,' she said then she sounded like her Breath was almost gone.

I started feeling sick in my stomach since I did not know what it was going to be now with the ball in Amelia's hands. Is she going to make a Joke or put in a Newspaper Ad if I do not do what she calls for? She is going to use this against me I will be in her Power because I can not be Manly with her and my stomach Churned Over from this Idea.

For a second her next move was a Mystery to me. She put her face forward & her fanny up in the Air until I heard the snap on her Bermudas pop open. She wiggled out of them & when she pulled them down all the way & sat up on her knees I was on

306

eye-level in front of her Mossy Nest. When she Spread Out on top of me she pulled the sheet back & it blew a whiff of Peat Moss to me under the Salty Smell of her arms.

Her body did not Remind me of any of the girls they print in Playboy Magazine especially in the fold-out section she Reminded me of a plump grape. Tight skin but Soft Wet Fruit underneath. On this Idea I did not have time to Linger because Amelia pulled my hands down around her sides & She Led Me to her hips. She bent she swayed with her hair tossing she could be a Palm Tree in the Wild Wind and the next thing I know my p.j.'s are all open with her sitting on me still Bending & Swaying.

My little chilli pepper did not stay where she Guided It I did not fill her up I was not a big man for her but she went Pushing down on top of my hips with her legs wide apart her Skin Stretched so tight I thought something was pulling on it from the inside up from her Soft Bone—so she Grabbed my fingers she led them up & led them in she Showed Me where I should Touch her how soft & how hard there—"Mm-mm," she made this beautiful Sound when I Touched her: she was humming from the Touch of my fingers!

"Si si," she said, "*that* way," then her eyes shut.

I kept my eyes open the whole time I did not want to miss these Sights—every private place on her Amelia showed me so I could be as close as her skin and no Mystery between us anymore—she was going to hold me there until she Convinced me until I gave— She Gripped Me all around by her legs—she made her legs like a belt around me & her hips for the buckle Amelia buckled me down tight—

I did not move it was only her who was Shaking her hips on top of me so hard it wore me down to the Bone but she could not help it anymore she did not have the Power to Stop in her–I will not say I Attracted her down like a Magnet I will say the heavy weight of something else pushed her down on my chest & pressed her mouth close with her arms around my neck—then it came out of her—the cry I heard her make when I saw her running in the street the night this started—the Voice of Innocence crying in terror—

"Raaaaaaaaaay!"

For a minute I lay Calm & I felt the world holding still and furthermore nothing else was going to Happen. Nothing was outside nor nothing was Before or After nothing led up to this nor it did not point in any Direction this Episode was a bubble floating in the Air. In that minute my Feeling about it was *Now this is never going to change* but this Feeling was the 1st thing that went. It all boils down to the Physical not the Feeling this is my View.

It is the Truth you can not Deny i.e. the Physical is what has all of the Power only the Physical will change the world around. The feelings are just the Consequences that announce the Deed and lead a person on to the next one but it is always the Deed that counts. It can be a Gun or my little chilli pepper it is the same thing it is the Deed I do with it that changes what is what.

For instance John F. Kennedy. Bad feelings by a certain party did not Blast Him out of this World they did not have the Power only Bullets did. That is the Truth you can not Deny that is how the whole shmeer Changed when the Bullet parted his handsome hair. Then came all the Consequences i.e. our Country full of disbelievers. I did not Believe I was living the same after that Deed I did not Recognize the place anymore like somebody moved it in the Night. Everything changed around Permanent no Power can put it back like it was Before.

Also with Amelia. The Physical changes right in front of my eyes. I felt her oil on my fingers from between her legs I Noticed it poured out during. What do you call it? Her grease from there or whatever. I rolled it around my fingers I admit I never Knew of this part of a woman. I would like to know the Chemicals in it for instance is it the same as Tears only thicker or is it some kind of sweat down there? I am not a Expert on Romance or Biology but from my Experience I deduce it is the glue that glues us down & the gum that gums us up.

Nor I do not claim I am a Expert on Life in Foreign Lands (leave out Mexico I did not Observe enough down there for a all around

Opinion) but I know how it stacks up in the U.S.A. in our Times. Forget about a Baseball Game where you will see the better win by Honest Sweat. Forget about a Museum with the fossils of the Past on display which point out all the Progress we made so far since our days of Pondlife. Forget about Washington, D.C. with Democracy in action i.e. the debates of Congress or the Supreme Court making up the law of the Land. These places do not broadcast our American Way of Life today for your information! Go over to the Johnson-Peabody Bank in Dallas, Texas and ask for Mr. Jim Lovebird who is the guard of the Safety Deposit Boxes there. (You can not miss who he is: the 6' 6" + 300 lb. shtarker with the Johnny Unitas crewcut on him carrying the Gun.) Let *him* show you the modern American Way on parade!

Besides for the Sentimental I never Treasured my Belongings so much. My Philosophy on Belongings is WHY ACCUMU-LATE? You can not take them with you like the Saying goes and if you want to take them it just means before you know it you are up to your rear end with Cardboard Boxes & Plastic Bags. So a Safety Deposit Box I could live without until this late point of my Life but now I have a Valuable to my name. This resides in Box No. 3310 in the Johnson-Peabody Bank. Hereby I grant you my Permission to go take it out with my Blessing!

My bet is you will think it is Valuable for all the Wrong Reasons.

This kind of a Argument you can leave outside on the sidewalk because inside nobody is Confused about what is worth more or worth less. This Fact hit me smack in the kisser as soon as I saw the place it looks like the Ancient Egyptians built it. Red stone polished very high Slanting up to the Green Marble & Gold Letters over the glass doors. They open up by Electric Eye nor they do not make a Sound so they do not disturb the Valuable Business going on. Cool Air comes up from the pink stone floor also down from the marble walls mossy green up to the Ceiling. But of all the Features built in to Impress I think the carved columns up to the skylights have the most Influence on everybody to keep their Voice Down led by the Pretty tellers. All in a row in white blouses ready & waiting to serve like Maidens in a painting from the Pharaoh's tomb. Flat & stiff & smiling the same the identical Appearance minus the Naked Bosoms & the sheep fat on their hair. If a Atom Bomb does not land on top of it the Dallas branch of the Johnson-Peabody Bank will stand for 5,000 years like the Pyramids in my Opinion it is a National Monument dedicated to our Valuables.

"Good morning ma'am. Nice to see you again," Lovebird said when he saw Amelia walking over he made it sound like he really missed her. She pressed out a Smile for him Mild & Polite and he caught it in his teeth then he Tossed it over to me. "Morning sir. How're you today?"

"Don't ask," I answered him deadpan with my eye on the key in Amelia's hand & my Mind on the Mystery of what is really doing with her Motivewise. Now I am Sorry by my short Reply I gave Lovebird the idea I think of him Below Me. I did not try to act Superior but I saw how he took it with a smile as if "None of your business" is the correct Reply which he always Expects.

"My gentleman friend is coming in with me," she instructed him and no smile this time only the Little Key she gave him. "3310."

Lovebird ducked his chin. "Yes ma'am."

It is a Known Fact that the Ancient Egyptian Pharaohs deposited all of their bodily Organs in clay pots for Eternity to keep them fresh and so I Pondered this over while we walked in the Inner Sanctum down the rows of Safety Deposit Boxes. Kidneys in 2150. Lungs in 3807. O.K. so Mr. Lovebird dresses like a flatfoot and not like the Jackalhead God Anubis in a loin cloth the Vault of Safe Deposit Boxes still Resembled the treasure rooms of old to my Mind. I could picture the sand dunes piling up outside with us Buried amid all the Treasure.

"Sorry. I'm in your way here." Lovebird was trying to make 2 moves at the same time in & out. In to the corner of the wall where 3310 was and out of there so Amelia could carry the box herself. He slid it out of place & he Handled it like it was a Fragile Urn from the Wall of Remembrance. When he swang back around he Squashed me into the corner too since both of us were trying to get behind Amelia as soon as the metal Box was Safe in her arms. "I'm very sorry sir" he said to me & by his Sincere Apology he tried to make his 300 lbs turn Invisible. He was showing us how he knew where he fit in with his $125 per week job & his uniform which was not on the same level as people who owned so many Valuables they had to keep them in a Safety Deposit Box & hire him to Guard them yes Private Property is King. It has certain Powers it can change the world around it is the owners in the end they will Influence the Future. Honesty does not come into it or raising up Good & trampling down Evil no not any idea like that only who owns more. Only Property has the weight these days.

In the National Geographic I read a article about a Tribe somewhere in Africa with cattle. You want to know who gets all of the Respect & Honor of the village? It is the man who has the biggest pile of Cow Manure in front of his house! This Rule applies in our Country today the same I believe. By my Observations here is the difference between a Somebody and a Nobody. I say it is all Piles of Manure.

In a little room all decked out with a marble ledge & lamps for our Convenience Mr. Lovebird left us alone. "Now I show you somethings. They keep us safe in Mexico." Amelia dug down to the bottom of the box down to her elbow & she came up with Treasure Galore.

1. Pearl Necklace— very nice it can go with a cocktail dress or other form of eveningwear
2. Gold Rings— about 1 dozen mostly for a man all with jewels in I will say very crude & vulgar lumps
3. Diamond Tiara— for a fairytale princess but at the moment I figured it could be true to Julio & the nightclub etc.
4. Stocks & Bonds— judging by Newberry's version now I felt turmoil on my mind for these smelled of dirty dealings—payola from the F.B.I. or heirlooms from Cuba
5. Bank Books— so many she could use a good set of bookends!

"My God," I poured out over them, "Is this all real?"

"As real as anythings." So Amelia spread out her Valuables to show me them all also how I won her Trust. I flipped through the pages of one of the Bank Books and it hit me the True Meaning of the wise old Saying "Safety In Numbers"! Food (caviar) Clothing (mink underwear) & Shelter (Taj Mahal) she could Pay For by this Wealth in advance until the Second Coming.

But Amelia's treasure trove did not land in her lap by a Magic Lantern it did not drop out of the Sky. *So where did it come from* that was the main Question on my Mind & out of my mouth. I Decided she better give me a Decent Answer & Satisfy all of my Doubts or I will give her over to Newberry no muss no fuss.

"Different places," she said & she wrapped up her Jewels etc. in Newspaper she shoved the rich packs down in a shopping bag she tucked them under the Cottage Cheese & Tortilla Chips.

"What places?" my Voice rose up.

"From business," she said, "doing business."

This Answer did not Satisfy so I grabbed back her Attention I grabbed her wrist I froze her solid by the Cold Look of my eye. "I'm not going to Mexico," I spelled out, "until you tell me what's doing with this stuff."

She pulled her arm free but she did not go back to wrapping up her Belongings. "I'm no in this business anymore."

"Fine. I'm glad. I'm very happy about that," I Congratulated & I picked up her tiara. "Did they give you this at your retirement party?" Amelia watched me fidget with it she watched it like it was her Baby in the arms of a Gorilla.

Instead of asking me calm & gentle *Please put that down* she said, "I don't do this things now. Por favor Ray."

I Obliged her I obliged her Worry but it did not go out from her eyes when I held the tiara out for her she should take it. "What's Newberry got on you Amelia?"

She just Answered me by a word, "Strings."

"From the Kennedy thing? What about it?" She bit her lips tight together then she Shook her Head very sharp. So I held her shoulders & I Forced her to Face Up. "Don't clam up on me Amelia. Believe me it's the worst thing you can do now."

She held still & I held still like a couple of dancers waiting & waiting for the Music to Start Up. She shrugged a shoulder to shake me off and I let go of her Because I saw how the band was not on the bandstand anymore this Waltz was over. I Recognized this sad Fact & the Consequences in this moment I felt downcast by it now it was my turn to clam up. She picked up her wrapping where she left off at the gold rings & at the same time I pictured the Scene behind the supermarket that was going to be in a couple of Hours with her waiting there and instead of the Friendly Sight of the Raymobile coming for her she will see Squad Cars close in & Newberry with his arms wide open. Furthermore it choked me up after how close we got to each other a couple of Hours before i.e. just our Skins between us in this last minute she wants the dark Secret of her Past to push me away. I know I know! The Green Ray must be Immune but in my form of Ray Green I can get hurt by Human Behavior so I did SO WHAT. What if it was Because of something else she clammed up For Instance she did not want to tell me something to lower my Opinion of her nor she did not want to tell me any more tales?

Ah-ha.

"I don't want you to hate me," she whispered out, "for somethings I do before." By my Silence I let her talk onward. "I don't bring wetbacks over here anymore. O.K.?"

I did not notice how I was holding my Breath until I blew out my long sigh & my backbone turned into rubber for this Confession tied up Very Neat to the Story Newberry told me. But by Amelia's Interpretation of my sighing & bending I showed her how I truly did not hold Faith in her enough. How I am too weak to take this Honesty of hers.

"You want me to tell you hm? My business—" She had to catch her breath before she could tell me, "Ten years for this good money."

"That's your opinion. I want to hear about the other," I said. "About President Kennedy." My Voice was very quiet but not very Calm.

"You hate me," she said & she Meant I was going to hate her

as soon as I found out this Answer. She looked away & covered her mouth with her hand.

"I can help you."

"Help me in Mexico." She Reached over for my hand but I pushed it into my pocket instead. "I tell you in Mexico hm? I promise Ray. All the truth. About this things."

"It can't wait," I said flat then I saw how hard she took my words & I said them over softer."It can't wait."

She nodded. She Reached up to Touch my face. "Ray?"

Out of Sympathy I Touched her hand I held it so I could make the next part Easy for her. "So tell me."

"I make it up in your house. All the story about him."

I faded out I faded in. In a hurry I had to call upon my Superior Powers of Concentration and examine this Possibility! So what is it going to be if John F. Kennedy does not come into it? What led to what in this case? Consider! If Amelia can make up a juicy story to lead me on—then so can Newberry with his Cuban kooks & his icebox Conference Room in the basement! What kind of Impression is a place like *that* supposed to make? With his Threats & Promises yet. Also I was considering the Sincere Tears splashing down Amelia's face. If I could Believe her Before when she told me she was the eyewitness of that evil Deed also I could Believe how she only made it up to win my Protection. I Believed she could do the former & I Believed she could do the latter. So I Considered Again and I came up with a Definite Feeling face to face I Recognized this certain Fact of her character—Amelia could tell a lie or Amelia could sneak poor Mexicans over the Border illegal yes against the Law of our Land but *murder* a person? *Kill* a human being? Even worse a President of the U.S.A.? In cold blood or in hot blood this I could not Believe and by my X-Ray Sight I saw it was True. Let John Newberry accuse! What kind of Evidence could he pull out of his hat?

"What's that bastard got hanging over you?"

She did not wipe her eyes she just let them pour. "I'm a dirty wetback! Illegal here see? Anytime he want he can catch me in jail. Do what he want to."

"He hasn't done it so far," I observed to her.

Amelia dug down to the bottom of the Safety Deposit Box. She pulled out a thick Document double folded over. She held it open right in front of my face. "See? I have this."

I am not a Expert on reading Legal Documents but right off I recognized what it was it was a Land Deed. I will spare you the Details of small print (anyway I skipped over most) and give you the bare Facts. It said 10,000 acres of New Mexico are owned by Dolores Defuentes also the same is held in Trust by John Newberry.

Before this minute if you asked me the question *What is love?* I could not answer unless I could say *The Feeling that goes from a Mother to her Baby.* If this Reply Satisfied I would feel Sorry for now I Know better. Ask me *What is love?* the way they ask it in the Love Songs and now I will tell you a new Answer—between a man & a woman it is this: Curiosity + Sympathy.

It is a sad joy it is a monster of Emotions. And this monster Stood Up under my skin. Amelia maybe saw the hairs on the back of my neck stand up or the hairs on my arms because she leaned close to me then she put her arms around my middle. My monster made me drop the papers & pull her closer.

"Mi vida," she called me, "Querido. I show you everything in Mexico." Then she buried her head under my chin I felt her little Kisses on my throat.

Between John Newberry's picture of Amelia and the Version I got by the Evidence from my own Senses I will say the Truth about her was somewhat between the Opposite Extremes. So hence out of FAIRNESS I force my Mind to stay open to both Persuasions.

Nurse Dubovey—Nurse Dubovey—NURSE DUBOVEY! In this Very Minute I am thinking of *you!* In case you Forgot about me already let me make with the Intro's all over again:

"Green," I said, "Ray. I'm here for the—"

"Yes Mr. Green. You're here for something special aren't you." You Greeted me like I was a V.I.P. in your eyes and this Treatment came with special Privileges. (What I want to know is did you mean my special High Colonic or my special looksee over

Amelia's secret File? This I did not Clear Up at the time so I am asking now.)

Did you Notice how I could hardly take my eyes off your figure? I Observed right off the smooth way your Bosoms stretched the top of your tunic. Satin it should be! Silk they should give you!

By my word of Honor my Voice is not so weak in normal Circumstances—it was from Nerves Attacking my throat & strangling me from inside I sounded like Mr. Peepers. "What do you want me to do first?"

"Pardon me?"

I backed up to the Beginning. "Should I sit down & read first or the other first?" I was talking to your hands then I was Following the freckles up your arms while you Filled Out my card. Do they go up to your shoulders those Freckles of yours? I Believe a good set of Freckles is perfect for a Redhead. Your shoulders are like the Colors of leaves turning in the Fall. I am just guessing here.

"We're ready for you," you smiled up & Buzzed the door Open. I did not move fast because I did not stop at your freckles Nurse Dubovey with your dove gray Eyes! When you took me down the hall to my Examination Room & you said, "You can get undressed in here," I stood & watched you through my open door now I can tell you—how I Admired the round part of your thighs when you Bent Down over the bottom drawer of your desk to find Amelia's File. I entertained myself by the Idea of you saying the same words to me in your Apartment some night then I could be in the Position to hear all of the Sounds you make when you Kiss a man and the smell of your hair from the back of your neck. *My Cookie* I would call you by that Affectionate Name if I was in that Situation. This is what I was thinking when you handed me that handful of bad news.

"Dr. Epps will be in right away. If you need anything just shout."

Oh Nurse Dubovey! I need something all right! What I need is I want you should know I am not the Dumb Schlemiel who let Certain Persons lead him around by his nose & who got Deceived so easy by these Parties! Nor I am not the Constipated Alter

Cocker who you met by Brief Acquaintance i.e. who has to Depend on a regular High Colonic to keep his Bowels juicy so they do not turn into concrete vermicelli!

My Cookie I am The Green Ray and I was here to lift up Good & face down Evil but lo & behold I did the Opposite. While I was bent over in that Position they kicked me from Behind for I did not expect Good & Evil coming in disguise.

Dr. Epps knocked very polite & Entered then all fingers he appeared. Long fingers dangling & his thin legs & his long chin so sharp he stood there like a big index finger Pointing at the Ceiling. "Ah-ha," he barked out, "our referral."

I was still sitting down on the chair next to the big Scale in my Underpants I had Amelia's secret File on my lap but I did not try and Hide anything. "I'm here for the high colonic."

"I know." Dr. Epps snapped a Rubber Glove on his hand. "Any serious blockage?"

"Enough."

He pat-patted the table and I climbed on. When he wheeled the bag over he tapped me on my Rear End so I Obliged & lifted up. "O.K. Ray," he whistled & he tugged my jockeys down, "Here he comes." Dr. Epps did not have a Gentle Touch he was more wam-bam I will say. Since I was looking Upward anyway I searched the ceiling for the hidden Camera. He slipped the tube inside in a slow move so all ideas about you & the night & the music Disappeared from my Mind I had to Concentrate on the warm water Dribbling in. I did not want you to see me in such a Position holding my water etc. if you came in by accident e.g. or doing your duty Nurse Dubovey any idea in that Direction made me twitch. I can Imagine if I end up in one of Carlos's dirty books!

Dr. Epps broke into my Worries. "How does that feel? Nice and comfortable?"

"If it did I'd need my head examined," I said. Which Remark of mine handed him a Chuckle but maybe you can tell me if he chuckled over my funny gag or my Discomfort. To tell you the Truth what felt nice & comfortable to me was the big Relief when he went out & left me alone to pursue my Purpose.

317

You may Love to know a few particulars of the Evidence which you kindly handled between John Newberry and I. Especially since it led me from one thing to another it changed the Direction of Events I hope you will be Interested to hear of these Items which influenced what Happened Next. (I do not place any Responsibility on you!) In case you are Curious about what became of me after I gave the file back to you I plead with you DO NOT believe the Report of your boss Newberry! I Inform you this way because of your personal fingerprints being all over the File who knows what kind of Trouble he can stir up against you.

I do not Remember word by word but I Remember a few Examples. To wit:

REPORTS about Amelia from 1962 etc. this little teenager girl they name her "Subject A"—Subject A confirmed in Soviet Embassy, Mexico City. In the company of ▇▇▇▇▇ and ▇▇▇. Received small Package which Subject carried onto bus. Remained onboard the bus for several blocks. Disembarked near Main Entrance of the Banco Nacional. Entered appox. 11 a.m. Individuals ▇▇▇, ▇▇▇▇▇, and ▇▇▇ (foreign nationals) Diplomatic Corps. so must be considered

Etc.

Mixed in I saw PHOTOS (off a smudgy Xerox like all of the rest) of Amelia in the company of Tio but they did not I.D. him by that Name. According to the label he was Julio Figueroa from Cardenas, Cuba. In another photo there he was again younger with his arm around a chorusgirl & his other arm around a handsome Gentleman with a Serious round face. The Weight of the World pressing on him. The Name of the chorusgirl they did not mention but the Gentleman the label said was Amelia's papa Silvio A. Defuentes. The photo was from his casino from Christmas, 1959.

Also PHONE BILLS from that time concentrating on '61–'62

when Casa Defuentes was in Miami Beach. Many calls to Washington, D.C. and New Orleans, Louisiana and Fort Worth, Texas. Stuffed in these pages I saw HOTEL BILLS from Mexico, City. And CANCELLED CHECKS from there also Juarez, Mexico & Dallas, Texas then more from Miami. Some to Amelia and some to her Papa. Some of them from 20 years ago & many from Recent days.

And a Pamphlet entitled FAIR PLAY FOR CUBA put out by The Fair Play For Cuba Committee from their H.Q. in New Orleans. But the Main Point about it was a telephone number somebody wrote on the back & Circled. I think it was Important in the Past but it is probably Disconnected now.

Nor that was not the final mention of that Tropical island. The next page I turned over was the BIRTH CERTIFICATE of Amelia Elena Defuentes and this Info I Remember so clear it stated she was Born on October 25, 1948 in Havana, Cuba. How do you argue with a Fact in front of you like that in Black & White?

I do not Regret to tell you I stole this Document so I could rub her nose in it & teach her a Lesson of Life i.e. how lies lead liars to Defeat la-dee-doo-dah how Guilt leads to Punishment. And that was the way this Case was going to turn out if I had anything to say about it & I had Plenty to say about it all right! In my Mind I started Rehearsing my words of Anger & Mercy when I flipped her File facedown and I saw my Surprises for the day did not finish yet.

A little white envelope Newberry stuck on the back there. Inside it he put a coupon from a magazine the usual pitch i.e. THIS FREE GIFT IS YOURS TO KEEP EVEN IF YOU SAY NO! Underneath where it had the Toll Free Number to call & say YES! Newberry wrote in a local number instead. Also his instruction—4 O'CLOCK.

This was my Free Gift from him: a brand new Driver's License. This one will not expire for 10 years already! Maybe he did not want me to Worry about traffic Court or a driving test at my Age or he wanted to Encourage me on my travels but now I Believe his True Desire was to lure me by this favor.

I have a Free Gift for you Nurse Dubovey since this is my Last Will & Testimony. I want you to have the Contents of my manure box in the Johnson-Peabody Bank. I hereby grant you all the Permission you need so you can open it just ask Mr. Lovebird to direct you to No. 3310 in the name of Reuven Agranovsky. What is in there is the Land Deed that belongs to John Newberry so you can see how far he went outside the Code of the F.B.I. for the sake of his private Property. Since I lost the Raymobile the only Property I have left is the money in the ashtray on my night table but that is not the only Difference between him & me. Now you can see where High Ideals get a person.

I doubled up Amelia's File I crunched it down I used it for a pillow though I did not rest my aching head on a pile of Answers it was a pile of Questions. Namely & Foremost I pondered how certain parties Deceive out of selfish Motives & certain parties Deceive out of Fear.

"Ooh-hoo," you heard me cry then the Pressure doubled me over too I felt like I was holding the Pacific Ocean inside. "Ooh-hoo!" I was crying so that was when you walked in on me.

You could call me The Human Sponge the way I dragged my heavy carcass out of there but by this Idea I do not Refer to a Side Effect of my High Colonic I Refer to the soggy condition of my Emotions. A soft squeeze on me a tiny tap for instance some shmuck leaning on his horn to make me put on some Speed & all was going to gush out of me the Waves of wild Ideas sloshing around under my skin. I say 15 miles per hour is a High Enough Speed for a person to drive when he is Upset.

If!

My Uncle Jake had a Saying on the subject of If: "If A Rabbi Had A Square Tuchas He'd Poop Matzohs!" To my dizzy Mind let me tell you such a notion made more Sense that any Fact I knew for sure about Amelia Elena Defuentes —

If the authentic reproduction of her Havana Birth Certificate in my safari suit pocket was for real *then* what? Then this: Amelia made up a False Story about the affair of her Birth & if a person will lie about the 1st day of her Life she will lie about the 2nd day. So when the 1st lie falls it will knock over the next like a Domino then her next steamy Story the same until they all fall down in a crooked line the Dominoes that led up to this minute. With this piece of paper I will knock down the sad story of her poor Papa the shoemaker then Julio her sweetheart the False Facts then the False Reasons 1 by 1—why she hustled wetback Mexicans—why she is scared of John Newberry—why she Followed Mrs. Roderiguez back to my Apartment & hooked me on her hooey about Dallas—why she pulled me so Close & made me want to hold her there—why she wants my Companionship all the way back to Mexico—1 by 1 her Falsehoods will fall in front of me until the only Story standing up will be the Truth!

Far away in the distance the Sound of a siren squeals up & down which causes Amelia a sudden case of Nerves. She folds the top of the shopping bag over a few times & hangs on to it Tight with both hands. The siren fades away already so now the only Sound is her quick & jumpy Breathing. But this Stops Short when she hears the throaty purr of the Raymobile motor turn around the corner of the Supermarket & pull up behind the dumpster. Amelia runs to meet me.

AMELIA: (gasps) Ray!
ME: Here I am.

The car door clicks open & slams shut then the Raymobile growls out of the Parking Lot into the street & away. After we are out on the open road Amelia starts to Relax & she lets the warm wind from the window blow her hair around. She Settles Back in the blast of Air like it is a warm bath.

AMELIA: Mmm . . . Feels nice. Feels good.

I do not Reply for my Mind is on my Duty not on small talk.

AMELIA: Why you no talking Ray? You mad at me I theenk.
ME: I'm always this way after I get bad news at the doctor.

AMELIA: What bad? You no sick Ray! You beeg healthy man
          last night!
ME: Yeah. If I keep doing my exercises and eat up all
          my vegetables I'm going to live for a hundred years.
AMELIA: (*giggles*) *What* you say?
ME: The bad news wasn't about me Doll. It was about
          you.

I pull the Raymobile off the Main Road & the raw dirt crunches
under the tires.

AMELIA: What you doing? Eez crazy Ray!

I cut the Motor I throw it into Park & now Amelia shifts in her
seat closer to the door. I see her hand Reach for the handle but
before she can pull it I make my Move—1 hand Reaches around
her & slaps the lock so I close off her Escape and my other hand
forces her Birth Certificate in front of her eyes.

ME: The party's over.
AMELIA: Who give theez to you?
ME: J. Edgar Hoover.
AMELIA: (*spits*) Newberry. Leetle Juanito.
ME: Tell me about Havana.
AMELIA: I was going to tell you about all this things—een
          Mehico.
ME: You can tell me now. This birth certificate—
AMELIA: Si. Eez—how you say it?—the real McCoy. My
          past—it catches up finalmente. O.K. I tell you now.
          Everythings.
ME: Start with your father. The humble shoemaker.

This unfair Description makes her eyes glow red! She finds
Strength in her hot heart. She sits up insulted & Proud—

AMELIA: No! He was a big man! No humble! No like some
          other man!

ME:	Only just like every other tinpot casino boss who gets rich on the measly paychecks he cons off ordinary working stiffs!
AMELIA:	Men are so weak. This lesson I learn when my father die. When he leave me alone.
ME:	Cut the softsoap. I don't believe a word.
AMELIA:	Sure you believe me. You are a man. A weak man. You believe me when I tell you I see who shoot your President Kennedy! (*laughs like a maniac*) I have a million dollars in the bank from weak men! They theenk they are so strong this big bosses in Mehico! Yes! I go in bed with them & after I finish they do anythings I want! (*more laughing etc.*)
ME:	So you hustled the competition. A regular black widow spider! They never had a chance. You loved them & left them—to Newberry.
AMELIA:	Si. They deserve it. Pen-dey-hos. Estupid men! I take all the business.
ME:	How many poor souls do you hustle over the border in a month? How much living breathing humanity does it take to pay for your diamonds & pearls?
AMELIA:	Si si Raymondo. Gringo! You understand everything now no?
ME:	No. I don't understand why you had to deceive me so Amelia. How you could feed me 1 lie after the other from the very beginning.
AMELIA:	Easy. Too easy.

Maybe this is the only Answer I am going to Hear—or maybe I do not want to Hear Further from her. So I fire up the mighty motor of the Raymobile & drive very slow now down the dusty bumpy road and turn back onto the smooth asphalt of the Interstate.

AMELIA:	Wh-where we go now? Ray you take me to Mehico?
ME:	Not that far.

AMELIA: You are taking me back to the city! No! Por favor! Not there! Not back to heem!

ME: You broke the Law—and there's a price tag on that. I'm just escorting you to the cash register.

AMELIA: No! I tell you everythings! I use you yes! I pretend I love you and fool you in bed yes! But now I see I was wrong and I love you Ray! You theenk I can not love. You theenk I only love money. No! I love you! What is a woman without love? Por favor Ray! Believe me! (*lots of sobbing*)

ME: That's one thing I can't do. Not anymore.

I know of her Crimes & her Lies so now I am a giant in her mind & her Voice is trembling from desperate Panic . . .

AMELIA: W-we can go live in Mehico for good Ray! You & me. Together. I can show you how I love you . . . how much I love you . . . querido . . . mi vida . . . mi corazon . . .

I slam on the Brakes & pull the car over. I cut the Motor. The only Sound is the dry desert wind blowing across the empty Highway.

ME: You're dreaming Doll. It's too late. They're coming. I called them before I picked you up. The only thing we're going to do together now is wait here for Newberry.

The Sound of a Police Siren wails high & low it pierces through the gusty wind it drowns out Amelia's final Plea—

AMELIA: Save me from heem! Ray! (*she sobs truly sorry*)

No Dice. The Siren screams down on us. The Police cars pull up in front & in back. Half a dozen doors open. Voices sputter out of the Radio from Police Headquarters. And footsteps clomp toward each other straight & slow in the soft dirt.

324

NEWBERRY: Good work Ray. Couldn't have caught her if it wasn't for you. On behalf of—

But I walk right past him & do not say a Word I am too Choked Up. I see her standing there in her Uniform with her clean white Nurse's hat on her pretty head. She clutches a First Aid Kit against her Bosom.

NURSE DUBOVEY: I thought maybe—maybe you might need a Band-Aid.
ME: Just a bottle of iodine. And a shot glass.
NURSE DUBOVEY: Ray I—I was worried about you. Are you all right?
ME: Yeah sure. I feel like a million dollars.

Meanwhile back in the Real World with my foot on the gas I missed the Entrance of the Supermarket Parking Lot by a few feet & I drove up on the kerb which big bump shook me out of this Daydream. To stay on the safe side so as I do not Alarm any Bystanders with any suspicious moves I Pretended I was searching for a Choice Parking Place by going up & down every row checking this way & that. So by the time I drove around the back of the building a Bystander would Figure I just did not see any place I liked and I was going to circle back for another Reconnoitre.

I saw her as soon as I came around the corner. Amelia was all by herself back there nor she did not see me for a second so I got the Privilege of a peek at her Genuine Character. She was sitting in the shade dangling her feet over the side of the Loading Zone where trucks deliver vegetables etc. she was kicking her heels against the concrete wall carefree like a Tomboy. By this same token I got a big smile & a little wave from her when I pulled up.

"You come early," she slid in & said.

"Nothing's wrong," my Reply came out too hasty it did not nip the bud of her Fears it Fertilized them. So likewise in a hell of a hurry I said, "Here we go!" & I stepped on it with the High Hope I left that tricky moment Behind.

325

I let her Enjoy the cowboy music on the Radio until I saw the City in my rearview & up ahead the open spaces closing in on Mexico. The Air around there was hot as a oven it felt so heavy in my chest I had a little trouble catching my Breath from time to time. Every other one dragged out of me the same as a sigh. "Thirsty," I said & licked around my lips.

Amelia used the Excuse of fine tuning the Radio to lean over & study my face for the telltale signs of some Worry which I was hiding from her but I Concentrated both of my eyes on the road. The best way to treat Human Worries is 1 at a time and Number 1 then & there was I had to find a good location to pull over before 4 O'clock. After that I could Worry about forcing out the Truth behind her dishonest Deeds and what I was going to say when Amelia started Begging me not to hand her over & begging me to Forgive etc.

"I want to pull over here," I said as soon as I saw a Diner set back off the side of the road. They built it out of a Authentic railroad car boosted up on a train platform in the middle of a raw dirt lot. Also very Important in my Scheme of Things I saw a phone booth behind the other side of the Diner so I parked where Amelia could not see it from the car. I sighed again & I did not stir.

Amelia twisted around in her seat she twisted back with the Thermos in her hands. "Maybe they got some ice tea here hm?"

"Wait." I dug into my pocket to pull out the Proof of her True Past to watch her trip up on her own Fancy Footwork but I had to get some other Items out of the way first in this case some loose change a gas-station Receipt & my pack of Certs."Wait," I told her again.

"I have money," she offered very cheery.

"Wait a minute." I found the Birth Certificate in my other pocket. "What's this?" I Challenged her I flapped it open in front of her. My Driver's License fell out in her lap.

She peered down at it. "You no look so handsome on here."

I rattled the paper I was holding up practically in her face. "This. Tell me what this is. I want to know about this."

She picked up my License she handed it back very slow &

gentle but I did not take it because when she turned her face in my Direction I saw the Tears Rising. Just a Blink & they could spill out so she did not Blink. I Believe Amelia knew how it was all going wrong for her it was all falling to pieces at the Final Minute.

I pushed the Birth Certificate toward her but her hands were full of the Thermos & her purse & my Driver's License so I took the thermos & at the same time my License but I dropped the Certificate on the floor. We bumped our heads together when we both bent over to pick it up which Move also opened up her purse so we stayed down there playing tiddly-winks with her Nickels Dimes & Quarters.

When we sat up straight again I had ahold of my License & the Thermos. Amelia was holding the Birth Certificate in front of her. I watched her eyes cover the whole Page she read it over & over.

"Please explain this to me," I Urged her cool & calm.

"Sure sure."

"Just explain it O.K.!"

"Don't shout at me!" she showed me her Teeth. "I'm scared you know? I'm scared how you get this."

"What's the difference how I got it? I got it. Now please explain about it before we go one step further."

"You tell me one thing too."

"O.K.," I agreed. "What thing?"

"How you get this."

I tried to keep my calm tone of Voice so I did not Spook her but also I wanted to let her know I am the Master of this tricky Situation. "I got it from John Newberry."

She Screamed at me like a wild animal & Kicked the dashboard she was going to kick my windshield out! "You meet him? You cheat!" She yanked on the door handle very Furious she butted her shoulder into the door.

"Wait a minute!"

"You cheater! You stink Ray!" And on this tug she pushed the door open & Grabbed her Basket she ran out in the Road.

I was out of Breath when I caught up with her. "I said wait a minute." She booted me in my leg & kept walking. She called me a Stink & a Cheat a few more times also other names in Mexican which must be Equal or Worse.

We got about 100 yards away from the Diner when she stopped all of a sudden & I flinched when she grabbed my arm. "You tell him I'm going to Ojinaga?"

"Uh-uh."

"What do you tell him?"

"Come back in the car Amelia. Let's talk in the car."

She stuck her thumb out for a ride. "Go away from here," she ordered me, "go away from me."

"Not until you tell me what's doing with this file of yours Amelia. Your official F.B.I. file! Will you get back in the car before somebody stops?"

She did not stop with that thumb of hers nor she did not stop walking. "It's no mine," she spat out.

"Oh sure. It wasn't Mother Teresa I was reading all about."

"You say explain so I explain."

"Come back to the car with me. Please."

She shook her head. "John Newberry give you that paper so you believe him. You believe *him* about my life! How?"

"Why can't you just give me a straight answer for crissake?"

Out of the side of her mouth I got Disgust from her & she turned on a Reckless smile for the cars going by. Except the next car did not go by it pulled in ahead of us & the driver waited.

"You can't get in a stranger's car," I told her. "You don't know what kind of person he is."

The car idled. He beeped his horn & waved out of his window for her to Hurry Up. Amelia waved back but she did not go ahead & I Believe we were already walking back to the Raymobile when he ran out of Patience & drove away.

"I told you. It's no mine."

Except I could not leave this with her thinking I was a Sucker of some sort. "You say. All I know is somebody's leading me around by my nose. I've been doing things for you."

"Sure. This things make you feel like a big good man. So . . . ."

"I know what I am so don't tell me. You don't tell me. You can't open your mouth & say one true word. You lied to me in my own apartment."

"Big lies!"

"You don't think so? May I mention President Kennedy? All that business in my own home when all I wanted to do was help you out. Wonderful gratitude."

"This is big lies too." She poked the Document so hard it creased up. "From *him.* So you hate me. So you cheat me."

"What do you think Amelia? It just came from him? It's evidence. It's proof in black & white. It's something official from the F.B.I.!"

"F.B.I.! F.B.I.!" She waved her hands over her head. "He can make this things up! Just fake! Anythings he want. Any papers. *Any.*"

My brand spanking new Driver's License glared back at me from the dashboard & this Thought pinged in my Mind: GOOD POINT. I was the guy doing the Begging now. "What do you want from me? It's very confusing business Amelia! *Tell me what's really doing.* Please I'm asking you. Tell me so the next move I make I won't regret."

Amelia did not even need a second to think it over she just said this to me, "I'm safe with you. I think so."

"Then you can give me the real story right? Let's go honeybunch. How about all the truthful facts now . . . "

So Amelia gave out with the Following which according to her own personal Knowledge & practically in most of her Own Words is

THE STORY OF WHAT WAS REALLY DOING

Not in Havana, Cuba or Tokyo, Japan or Nome, Alaska the Story is Amelia Defuentes was born in Tres Osos, Mexico on October 25, 1948 which by a Coincidence also happens to be the birthday of the famous Modern painter Pablo Picasso so maybe something in the Stars on that date makes a person grow up with a cockeyed view.

329

Her Family was a poor one in a poor place because her Papa did not rise higher than a lowly Bartender. Her Mama did not mind eating Corn Tortillas for breakfast lunch & dinner she had more Important things on her Mind namely the secrets of the Zodiac. The Knowledge of the push & pull of the Planets & Constellations did not help her foretell how Senor Defuentes was going to get squashed to Death by a runaway bus nor it did not foretell Amelia how her Mama was going to go crazy from Loneliness and get lost in the Desert and die of a rattlesnake bite.

When this load of Misfortunes befell upon her Amelia was just 16 years old but she did not drag out the Weeping & Wailing instead she went direct into the Garment Business up in Juarez. Her authentic Serapes & Sombreros the American tourists lapped up by the trunkload but by the end of the Tax Year the number of jumping beans in Amelia's Cash Register was very low. Every single time she helped some Gringo load a pile of her pretty Serapes in the back of his shiny Cadillac and she watched it hump Away over the Border like a sleepy cockroach she Imagined how cozy it feels to be a tiny Flea Hiding inside those Serapes plus how her Life would turn into something Better after she jumped out of the Trunk in the Land of Opportunity.

This Idea ate her brain away until it took up all the Room in her head it did not Stop there it burst out into Action. She took a bag of Food with her & a spare Serape & all of her jumping beans which came out to about $500 American. The night Amelia went she did not tarry on the bank of the River to wait & see if the coast was Clear she did not bid any sad Good-Bye to Mexico she just waded in the water up to her Hips across the Rio Bravo and over to the Lone Star State.

When her Heart stopped Pounding around her ribcage she Heard Whispering Voices in a ditch a few feet away. "Ssst! Aqui! Sssst!" When she crawled over half a dozen Hands pulled her down with them in the Ditch they covered her mouth. One of these Muchachos peeked up at the Road & then he ducked down fast when the rumbling Sound of heavy tires came at him out of nowhere. A Spotlight scraped the ground in front of the Ditch & the Patrol Car parked there.

The very first American Words that Amelia heard in the U.S.A. came out of the Beam of a flashlight pointed straight at her Face. "Lookit here. Fresh fish." And the next thing she Heard in Espanol was that Border Patrol Guard asking her what was her Name.

And next this—in a sweaty little Hut inside a wire Fence it was John Newberry asking her the same Question but in a Gentle tone of Voice. This Tactic of Persuasion worked on her the same way she waded right across the Rio Bravo she Revealed her Plans & Hopes. This Personal info he wrote down on the Official F.B.I. Report but he did not put Amelia's on the pile with the rest of them he Folded it up & Hid it in his pocket.

When the Sun came up she was sitting on a bus going back across the Mexican Border but she was not Alone. A chubby man with dimples on his Smooth Cheeks & sweat stains on his Cowboy Shirt was caring for her on their free ride back to the Land of Hot Tamales. His name was Julio Figueroa but on account of the Sympathy & Respect he gave her then she called him Tio. It is a kind Endearment it means Uncle.

Tio was not any Ordinary Wetback he had the Honor of being a Mule. Now this Pet may not have much Endearment attached to it but it lifted him above the Common herd since Tio was the Trailblazer who guided the Muchachos & Muchachas who were yearning to Breathe Free over the river & through the woods. Yes he had a kind Heart on him but No he did not do it for Charity.

Tio was a working stiff for Senor Aguilar who did this low manner of travel business for a Living. For a small Fortune in jumping beans he could Guarantee delivery in California/Arizona/New Mexico/Texas but on the other side a Muchacho was on his own. "You Pays Your Pesos & You Takes Your Chances!" that was the Business Motto of that Senor Aguilar a rotten Attitude which Tio ignored so to him it was a job with a Silver Lining it was a Service to the Needy.

It was a Spark he Recognized flaring up inside Amelia also & before they pulled in to the Parking Lot in Juarez he Offered her the same kind of Well Paying job. He Appealed very hard to her sensitive Nature he pointed out how such was a Perfect Way for her to do a Good Deed for the poor huddled Muchachos yearning to Breathe Free la-dee-doo-dah etc. plus at the same time Boost Up her supply of Tax Free jumping beans.

So this is exactly what Happened.

Maybe out of his Curiosity or likewise maybe from seeing her Success take off so fast John Newberry felt a Urge tingle him to write a Letter to Amelia. He wrote to her of his Private Feelings about the unfair & unsquare shares of Wealth in this World. How he felt sincerely this cockeyed Arrangement was nobody's Fault it was just a mess by Nature & by Accident. For Instance which side of a Border a person is Born on or if such a person is a Woman or a Man. Or a Criminal or a F.B.I. Agent. Newberry Wrote to her how he Felt Sick in the pit of his stomach when he saw his own Dear Father toil so hard over his F.B.I. desk for the miserable payment of a few Dollars when crooked Union bosses or Casino bosses etc. from poor backgrounds got to live the Life of Riley. Such are the Opportunities in the U.S.A. At least it did not take his Best Years to Learn that this is the way of the World & it is up to every free Individual to even out the Odds a little. By this he tried to tell her how he understood her Motivations & how he Sympathized with her utterly & truly.

Curiosity pulled on Amelia harder than her Suspicion pushed her back. The day after she read Newberry's Letter she Wrote a post card back to him with only 7 Words on it: "How can you be unhappy in America?"

She got her Reply back in a taxi cab from Juarez. In this Letter he Described how they can Help each other make Improvements in their lives. To Wit: it would be a pretty feather in his F.B.I. Homburg if Newberry could put Amelia's boss Senor Aguilar out of Business. If she will Help him set the old gorilla up (he Advised her) Amelia will see what a Good career move Betrayal can be.

Could she attract Senor Aguilar to a motel in El Paso? Before he can get his socks off Newberry will Burst In on them with a Warrant in one hand & Criminal Evidence in the other. All she had to do was Trust him and she will see how much Happiness the Future can bring.

So in the Bluebird Motel 8 years ago it was the End of one

thing with Aguilar & the Beginning of something else with John Newberry.

Amelia & Tio did all of the Business on the Mexican side. They hired new Mules. They offered a money-back Guarantee to any Muchacho or Muchacha who could pay for it. They put the Competition Out Of Business 1 by 1 the old gorillas Fell. Because John Newberry was doing the Dirty Work on the U.S. side. By his Influence & inside Information certain Muchachos & Muchachas could bust through the Border and Disappear into the Sun Belt & have better Lives as busboys or migrant fruit pickers. And not Newberry nor Tio nor Amelia ever heard a Complaint from any Dissatisfied Customer.

The secret Life going on between them pulled Newberry close to Amelia. Or the rest of the World around him who did not Know or Care pushed them Together kisser to kisser. So he felt Romance at last! Not inside the walls of his family home—not where his Wife is safe inside—not with his healthy pink Children—not with the skin & bones of his Life. He could hear Amelia's Heart Beating on the other side of the Border so close to him.

Mother Nature knows a Opportunity when she sees one. During the Full Moon he visited her South of the Border where he left Amelia pregnant with Child.

When he Heard the news his new Romance rushed out of him like Air out of a broken balloon. Newberry gave her some Advice in a stern tone & strong terms, "Do not let this baby of yours live!" Amelia did not Agree with his selfish Advice and this Caused a Strain & a Crack between then. Business started going Downhill and the Tidy Sums stopped rolling in. After a couple of months of this Newberry was the one who Threw in the Towel. He Wrote her a Letter & told her he Thought it over & Deep Down he does Revere the great American institutions of Motherhood and Free Enterprise. It was the sudden Shock etc. that Threw him but now the Gringo Cockroach will forget if the Mexican Flea will forgive.

So that is what Happened next of all.

And after the Usual 9 months besides their Agreement they had a Baby Girl between them. Newberry Adored this package from the minute he saw her since she Inherited her Father's round

Brown Eyes. From his Heart he Promised Amelia this: No Matter What may Happen in the coming Years little Dolores will have all the same Benefits of Life which he Bestows upon his pair of pink kids in Santa Fe.

Time goes by and things Change. Some things change *this* way & some things change *that* way—*this* way the Smuggling Business can not be Better with more Muchachos than they can handle & Muchachas lining up as far as Mexico City. This is at the same time that Newberry & Amelia put away some very Desperate Characters who used to be in their line. So Amelia got to be the top banana South of the Border Down Mexico Way and Newberry got promoted to a big office in Dallas. But he was not as Happy as he could be. *That* was Another Story—

By now he had 2 More healthy pink Kids. He was smoking more & Enjoying it less. He did not find Happiness anymore in his Work for the F.B.I. even if this ploy did Protect his own Behind. Newberry was ready to Retire before the strain broke his back & before he was his Father's age with a crystal punch bowl for the Neighbors to ooh & aah at. Newberry made fast Plans to get out of Law Enforcement and into Property Development.

But for this Vocation he needed a lot more Money than the steady stream of Tidy Sums he was Collecting by way of his Business with Amelia. So he did not Tell her a Word when he called up certain slippery types far away over the Isthmus of Panama and he made a Deal to buy a planeload of Drugs for this Item is in short Supply but in big Demand. Not really like Muchachos & Muchachas at all.

With this valuable Merchandise in his hands he was not Clicking his Heels in the Air. Newberry had to face up to plenty of new Problems. For One How was he going to move his Precious Bags of Powder Over the U.S. Border? For Another One How was he going to keep his sneaky Business a trade secret from Tio & Amelia? And between these what was more Important?

He did not need to sit Alone in the Barren Desert for 40 days & 40 nights he did not need to read the Guts of a Goat. He only Required 10 Minutes with a cup of black coffee before his Conscience spoke up & told him: "I'm leaving. From now on

334

you're doing this by yourself." All of a sudden everything was clear. Amelia & Tio will Learn what is up sooner or later so why should he waste his Vital Energy wrestling with that Hairy Ape before it was On Top of him? So now Newberry could go out & find the Lucky Monkeys he was plotting to swing over the Border with his Powder in their pockets. He went to Tempt them out of Juarez with a brand new deal & Once In A Lifetime Offer—*Tonight you may be a empty handed muchacho shivering in your cardboard shack in a garbage dump on the wrong side of the Border but tomorrow morning you can be a free citizen in Deming, New Mexico! Yes! A real live nephew of your Uncle Sam with all of the necessary official papers in your possession to prove it!*

He had them lining up around the Block.

Months & months went by before Amelia & Tio felt the pinch of this anonymous Competition. Then a empty handed Muchacho begged Tio for a little information over a beer in a bar in Juarez & by Accident he Revealed What was Up & Who was Who & Why Tio was losing his Mules just as fast as he found them. He Drank many more Beers Before he was ready to pass on the bad news to Amelia. Then he Drank many more & passed out on her hard floor in Tres Osos. So Amelia was the Hairy Ape who paid a Surprise Visit on Newberry that night in Deming.

That night Amelia's personal Stars moved to a new Arrangement. The Picture in the Sky over her head Showed her now it is a time of Topsy-Turvy Upheaval & sudden Encounters with friends Departing & strangers Arriving. She felt this in her Bones but it did not daunt her it Undaunted her.

Newberry was leaning over a hot TV Dinner all by himself at his kitchen table when Amelia let herself in by the Back Door. He put on a friendly Manner & pulled out a Chair for her to sit down but she just Stiffened Up where she stood. "Do I get 3 guesses?" he asked her. By her tight mouth & narrow eyes he got the Message that Amelia did not come over to play cutsie-pie Games with him so from his own tight mouth he said, "Do I get to eat my last meal?"

Such a Sour Joke only meant Newberry was not going to Dodge her or lie to her further since he Figured from the start this

335

moment was coming. So he told her all & he told her how he was Thinking of her all along yes & thinking of Dolores too. He was thinking how much Amelia hated all to do with Drugs etc. so for her Sake he did not want to scare her or turn her Away from him. And Besides with this & that—that is with the Ku Klux Klan do-gooders intercepting his Muchachos—and with his new Wealth in the bank Newberry was going to be all Finished with this monkeybusiness any day. "I've got a nice surprise for you," he turned around & told her.

He had to claw back a corner of the Lino behind the refrigerator to get at the heavy Envelope. Inside Amelia found the Deed of Land made out to Dolores and held in Trust by Newberry. "You keep it," he said, "keep it in a safe place."

"What it is?" asked Amelia.

"Houses," Newberry replied. Then he Corrected his Answer. "Or soon. Now it's just 10,000 ugly acres of desert lying there waiting for a concrete facelift."

"I want to tell you—" she dug in, "what you did to me."

"No baby no. What I did *for* you. For Dolores. C'mon. I want to show it to you. I'll take you out there. Sure. We can talk on the way.

They did not talk on the way since Amelia kept Silent to save her Strength to Defend herself from Newberry's Charms. He smiled half a smile & cocked his head when they drove past the big Billboard with the happy kids painted on it under the shelter of the Name of their pretty neighborhood beneath the Frontier Slogan of New Plains.

Newberry walked Amelia across the soft sandy dirt of a vacant lot in the middle of a Hundred vacant lots. Little plastic flags on the ends of sawed-off stakes Fluttered a few inches off the Ground. Straight Lines of them stretched out of the shadowy Desert into the setting sun. "Streets," Newberry pointed very Proud at all the little Flags. Amelia only Glanced Over them for a second before she pinned Newberry on the end of a Sharp Stare. He took in her Disrespect for the place & for him. "Aren't you impressed? Amelia?"

"For this big secret Juanito? Now you want me to say muchas

336

gracias! For this big place. You want me to kiss you. You want me to go home & tell Dolores how much her daddy love her!"

"Hey baby—"

"I know what kind of dirt you do for this. Now you want me to say muchas gracias you are so generous!"

"Hold on a minute—"

"I hold on too long Juanito." She took a sudden step Toward him. "Behind my back you been doing dirty things. You been doing anythings you want."

He did not give her any more Room. "Since when do you own all the marbles? You're on my side of the fence. Over here we play by my rules."

"No more."

"Sez you."

"No more you don't cheat me. No more you don't lie in my face."

"I did it for the kid." His Voice was not calm it was cold.

"No more dirty business Juanito. No more of this drugs. This . . ."

"Say it. Say the word. Dirty Juanito's dirty business." And he Crowded In on her so she had to Step Back or Fall Over. "Say the naughty wordy."

"No. Stop doing this."

"Say it. I'll give you some help."

"Stop it John. Stop—"

They danced some kind of a sloppy Tango back toward his car until Newberry had Amelia bent Backwards over the Hood. "You can say it! Go on! You want to say it! What's stopping you Angel?"

"I'll—make—you—stop—" she choked out.

"Stop what? Stop doing what? You just can't stand the idea that your little girl is set up sweet for the rest of her life & I'm the guy who tied the pretty pink bow. Her gringo Daddy with his dirty white powder. You know what else you can't stand Amelia?" Newberry hung over her Nose to Nose. "How much you still love me." He Smeared his pouchy mouth over her lips he Slithered his tongue between them.

"Mmpf!" Amelia twisted her face away then she twisted back

& Spat at him. "I no love you!" She Kicked him hard so he Doubled Up & rolled off her but he did not let go he Dragged her down on top of him.

Newberry coughed out a hard little Laugh. "Sure," he said, "O.K. What's the plot? Going to complain to the F.B.I.?"

She yanked her wrist out of his grip. "No," Amelia said. "Your father."

Newberry's smile Twitched & fell. "What're you going to do for evidence?" He stood up. He Opened the car door. "Anything you can do I can do better. Now get back in before you get hysterical."

She let him Help her up to her feet but she did not make any Move Farther. She stared into the car & she did not see a front seat she saw a Bottomless Pit. Newberry pushed her a helpful push in the right Direction and all of a sudden her legs went Stiff.

"Evidence? Si—I have evidence!" she let loose at him. "Plenty of evidence my querido!"

Of course Newberry had a Decent Answer ready for any piece of Evidence Amelia could name. *A wise investment—a dummy company—a phony charity—*all of the Legal Arrangements he Arranged. He did not worry about his Fingerprints on the Deed of Land nor his Footprints upon the New Plains Neighborhood.

On & on he bragged about his Smart Arrangements and the more he told her the Safer he Felt. Because he was Reminding himself how Perfect he tied up every Loose String how he covered his Tracks so clever & cunning from Start to Finish. By the time he stopped to take a Breath he was not Worried anymore about the Threat Amelia made of telling all to his Father. Newberry puffed his chest over her very Proud of his Fancy Footwork. He was sure that he was big & Amelia was a small bug Beneath Him.

She did not know the Law of the Land frontwards & backwards the way he did nor she did not know if her last Piece of Evidence could stand up in Court. All she wanted to do to him was pull the rug out from under his feet and make him Feel Sorry. "Your letters," she said. "I keep your letters."

"You didn't keep any letters," he Dared her but now he was not so Sure.

"*All* them," Amelia answered back. "Love letters."

Newberry did not have a decent Answer or a clever Reply to this he just shouted her name in her face & Socked her in the stomach. He never raised a hand to her Before and so in the middle of the wave of Pain & shock that tossed her down Amelia knew she Possessed some Power over him. He Cursed her for it for Love Letters she turned into Hate Letters. She cursed him for his Greedy Cheating ways. Their curses went off like Firecrackers in the night. And the wind-up was she did not get back in the car with him then his Anger drove him on.

"Mexico's that way!" Newberry Jerked his Thumb over his shoulder & gunned his motor & tore into the Dark across the Desert.

When the plume of Dust settled down when she did not see his tail lights Blinking anymore Amelia started walking. She let the Lights of Mason guide her steps since she knew of the Bus Station there & of the 9:25 to Juarez. The soft dirt Slowed her down her High Heels sank in but she kept her eyes Dead Ahead on the hazy yellow Glow. She was not Close Enough to see the Bus Station Sign but she Knew somewhere underneath that nest of Light was the End of her Troubles for the night.

If the Dark can Flash then in a Flash of Dark it was Gone. All the Lights of Mason went out in the puff of a Breath & a Hole in the Night hung there instead. Amelia shivered from the Idea of Newberry's Reach and the Force of it so powerful he can Black Out a town & crush out her Hope.

So she sneaked down the Dead Streets of the West side of Mason she roamed toward the broken Sidewalks of the East 8th. And by this late Hour what was doing in that neighborhood was not soothing to a Living Soul. Sounds of Footsteps starting & stopping. Laughs inside a closed up shop. Some car slowing down next to her & Wolf Whistles shooting out from the back window but Before Amelia can turn around & Curse in their faces the Cowards step on the gas they squeal away around the corner.

So she keeps her head down and keeps Walking toward the Bus Station likewise she is thinking *Maybe the blackout delayed all departures & maybe the Juarez bus is still waiting*—this Hope hurried her up so she cursed Out Loud when her High Heel snapped off on a crack in the Sidewalk. When she Heard the car slow down next to her she was Ready to throw her shoe at those joyriders but it was not the same car this time. This time it was a white Cadillac with 2 men in Front.

Perry did not Wolf Whistle he just leaned his chalky bony face & arms a little way out of the window & Enquired, "Amelia?"

He Kicked the car door open but Amelia was already Running the other way down the Street. And the broken shoe she clutched in her hand was her only Weapon so she was Helpless when Nilo swerved his car around her she was Defenseless when Perry ran her down & let her see how he just had Harm on his Mind.

Now who came Busting Out of the shadows to Defend her? Who came out of the thin Air to Comfort her in such Danger? Who came Busting Out of the Blackout now?

"He try and protect me! No afraid of them *ever*," Amelia told Tio. "He crashes the door for me to get out of there!" She Described this to him in her safe motel room she told him how this Stranger Conquered her Captors. How he Acted so Brave for her Sake.

Tio nodded his head very slow & he Listened very Careful to every Word. When she finished her Story he begged Amelia to keep her feet on the ground because he did not Know of any man who ever did Something for Nothing. Besides this they had to face up to the thunder cloud of Trouble on them so what Good did it do for Amelia to Expect more Help out of the thin Air? "Keep your feet on the ground," he warned her, "and let's be practical."

He Counseled Amelia with Wise Words & a smart Plan of his own:

While she hides out in the Motel he will take the Deed of Land to Dallas for safe keeping & to keep little Dolores safe he will send his Sister to watch over her. And after All That is done he will try to talk to Newberry & find out all that is Doing & make a safe Arrangement for Amelia so she can come out again.

Altogether this did not happen at all.

When Tio left her there Amelia Felt her Hopes fade away. In the daytime she shut her eyes to fall asleep & push the ugly world away. But at night she was all Soggy from Sleep and she stayed awake under the inky Shadows in the Air over her bed. She stretched out Stiff or curled up Tight with her eyes Wide Open & for days & nights she had the Radio on just to have the Company of other Voices in the room.

Her own Voice nagged her from her Pillow. How can a man who Loved her so long ago Treat her like his Enemy now? And how can a man who she did not even Meet Before Comfort her like a long lost Love? Amelia did not Believe such a man can be in this World such a Good man in such a Rotten place.

Then a Voice woke her up in the middle of the Afternoon. It came bursting down the Airwaves & out of her Radio telling of a Dramatic Episode in Mason at a liquor store called The Lucky Dime. Amelia heard about the Innocent little runaway lost in the Dangerous Neighborhood of the East 8th where a tricky customer held her young Life & limbs in his Clutches. He made her his Prisoner & Playtoy until a mysterious Stranger broke in to Rescue her and Return her to the Loving arms of her Papa.

Many in Radioland did not Believe this Story and they Spoke Up to say so. They did not Believe in this Mystery Man who Appeared out of the thin Air all of a sudden in their local Newspaper spreading such Wild Claims no they did not Believe in a Hero who blazed from the shadows to Defend the Defenseless.

"Not these days!"

"Figment of your imagination!"

"What a phony stunt!"

"Liar!"

"You just want some attention!"

The Public Mocked that grateful Papa they Doubted his Words & wanted to Believe the world is a puny place. It can have tricky customers Living & Breathing in it also liars & the weaklings who Believe them but not a Hero of flesh & blood who sees wrong and Tramples it & sees goodness and Lifts It Up.

Hooray for this happy minute because Amelia knew afterall he did Live & Breathe! She Knew he was the stranger who Helped her Before & she Knew he was in Mason very close by. A Wave of Calm rolled over her and after that a Wave of Courage since

341

she knew by Experience he was not a man like others. So that night she went to Sleep with the dark closed around her like a Giant Clam Shell just the way she Remembered how she used to Sleep when her old Papa Kissed her good-night. And the next morning Amelia did not mind the Danger she walked out of the Motel with a Plan to find him to beg him On Her Knees if she had to she was going to use all of her Wiles to make him Believe how desperate she Deserved his gallant Help again.

(THE END)

Personally I do not Believe all of the Stories in the Bible. The Garden of Eden etc. Joshua making the Sun stop in the sky etc. I was not there at the Time but to my ears it sounds Exaggerated. Not to mention The Greatest Story Ever Told i.e. Jesus Christ of Nazareth. I know many citizens of many Lands believe it word by word and live & die by it. O.K. that is their Choice. If a person is not a Eye Witness he has to Rely on Somebody's Word & make a choice of what he Believes. A person must put his Foot Down & Choose or else he will not know what to do or which way to go next.

Between Newberry's Story & Amelia's Story I will say I did not reason out & Analyze nor I did not flip a Coin to make up my Mind. A person can not find out what the Truth is by Logic he needs to Feel it in his Flesh & Bones I mean the Emotion of it. By this I am saying other things besides the Evidence I saw & the Pleadings I heard led me to my Conclusion.

I picked the Thermos up out of Amelia's lap. "I'll go get the ice tea," I said & I left her sitting by Herself.

"You want money?" she called Behind Me but I did not turn around in my tracks I Pretended I did not Hear her.

Inside the diner I Ordered the ice tea then I Sneaked out by the back door to get to the phone booth. When I heard Newberry's voice answer on the other end I came down with a case of Stage-fright like I never had it Before. Ripples in my stomach squeezing out my ribs & a gallon of pee ready to run down my leg.

"Hello?" But I did not speak up. "Ray?"

"It's me."

"Where are you?"

I looked around. "Phone booth."

"A phone booth where?" I swallowed back a retch. "Hello? Are you there?"

"I'm here."

"Where are you Ray?"

"Here."

"Right. O.K. Are you with her now?"

"Right," I said. "Yes I am."

"I understand."

"It's very difficult for me. Doing this now."

"I understand. If you just keep talking to me we don't have a problem about that. You understand me Ray?"

"Yes."

"You're in good shape my man."

"If you say so."

"Tell you what. I wasn't 100% positive you'd make this call."

"No." I caught my breath. "Same here."

"That whore can talk you into anything."

I let the phone dangle down in the torn up Yellow Pages to disguise my Getaway for I did not have the Heart to face his Voice further.

Listen a minute! I had a scary time in the Bathroom just now! I can not Explain this according to Anatomy but Dr. Godfrey maybe you can make a new Medical Discovery if you Analyze these exact Details—

I got up from my T.V. tray to go to the toilet. I stood in there as Usual the same way I did many times Before. So I start going but I CAN NOT FEEL MY OWN PEE COMING OUT! No it Feels like I am watching *somebody else* from the neck down doing this in my bathroom! I Concentrate all of my Will Power on my groin muscle & Stop Going because a cold fear rolls over me like a fog: No I am not truly standing there in my bathroom peeing into my toilet I am in the middle of a NAP on the SOFA & I am *dreaming* this Event & peeing in my pants like a Little Boy! By now I am seeing Sparkles of Light crackling around the edge of my eyes nor I can not Catch My Breath either I had to sit. I was gulping Air like a fish for the last 20 Minutes! What is wrong with me now? I am still a little Dizzy but I took some Aspirins for it. I will wait for this Sensation to end before I tell what

All quiet on the Western Front. All quiet on Pecan St. right now even more than Usual for this time of the night since there is no more arf-arfing from Mrs. Calusco's pup. I Peeked out of the bathroom window to check on Developments and I saw her house I mean the Remains of it. A burned up turkey in the Oven is how it looks only the cold black Bones left. I think I heard teenagers inside over there but I did not Shout at them they should get out. So What. Let them Learn about Danger. Is it my job watching over them?

I had to dig right down to the bottom of my Magazine Barricade to get out that particular Article I was looking for. When it came out in the Newspaper I only read down to the Diagram so when I was resting a minute ago I grabbed the Opportunity to finish it off. The Subject is very Absorbing to me being about the Scientific Discovery of what is behind all of the Black Holes in the Universe. I Congratulate all who made this Observation! I Nominate them to The Nobel Prize in Science also let me say Thank You because now I understand a new Fact of Life which I did not Imagine in my Dreams before. How a Star can burn down until it is a Cold Lump maybe the size of Africa with so much Gravity inside it pulls in everything in the Neighborhood. Atoms & Molecules also Cosmic Gas also Light Rays it will suck into a hole in Space so I learn!

If a Black Hole appeared in my Apartment this minute I would crawl in & crawl out of the Other Side to reach the other Worlds beyond. The other Dimensions & whatnot where Time will go backwards. I Hope I would Depart before John Newberry arrives

here with his heart set on paying me back for the Sorry Business
with his little girl because I coud not face the Matter two times
in a Row.

Such is not Appearing to Happen so I will go eat a boloney &
cheese sandwich with a glass of milk with it. A Square meal will
perk me up it will give me some Zip. Like the saying goes Calories
= Strength. Instead of the boloney & cheese I wish I had a
bowlful of Spiller's High-Energy Buckwheat Breakfast Flakes for
all the Calories I need to tell what I must tell next.

Here is the picture of Amelia coming into my Mind now:

Water up to her knees with her hands on her hips. I can see
her Shape bending over with her neck Stretched Out so she can
peer down in the River. Some plump kind of a wading bird in
Bermuda Shorts hunting for a nice fish there.

This Sight of her is Murky Because at the time she advised me
turn off the headlights for sake of Camouflage. Also the dust &
squashed bugs on my Windshield made another Veil then another
Veil on top of that was the shadow of the plump Clouds cramming
in under the Moon.

"Oh look at that!" This painful whine Leaked Out of me when
I saw the muddy Footprint Amelia put on the carpet when she
sat down inside the car again. "Pick your foot up. Pick it up
Amelia. Look at down there—it's got to dry out all the way now
before you can clean it. With a vacuum cleaner. And a brush a
stiff brush. You have such a thing at home I can use on it?"
Hereby I Quote my Words for Evidence showing how tired I was
how Exhausted from all that fast driving I did to get here etc.
how Short Tempered. I know from my Past 9 times out of 10
Patience is my middle name but now you see Proof of how the
Physical Condition will Exaggerate a person's Emotions.

And this particular Problem of a mess on the Raymobile carpet
Bothered me so much I did not Concentrate very hard on the
Indian Scout bulletin she kept trying to Deliver. Mud was not the
Number 1 Item to Amelia in that minute no her only Consider-

ation was how do we drive across the Rio Bravo this way In Secret.

"You said it was completely dry here," I Reminded her & waited for her Answer with my full Attention.

"Maybe it's raining last night," she pushed her palms toward the sky. This Explanation tormented her too it crumpled her forehead and she did not Speak Further. I Believe for a few seconds she was trying to figure how Newberry can even turn the Weather against her.

In my book I say it is a sorry Waste of Time to discuss the Weather & double to *argue* about it so I told her, "Let's drop it." I asked her if Please she could Repeat her Bulletin about the trail ahead and she told me there was no Danger if I steered around a certain rock in the middle where she was standing Before. The water only comes up 2 Feet all the way over to the other side which does not sound Extravagant for a River but this was almost to the top of the Raymobile's tires.

"I'm not driving a Patton tank in case you didn't notice. This is a Ford station wagon."

"You no driving anywheres now," Amelia poked back at me & very Sarcastic she added on, "Case you diddin notice hm?"

"How do I know it's safe going across? You only went out to the middle."

"So we stay safe here!" she chuckled bubbling over from Disbelief before her Patience boiled away. "Just go! Get me out of here Ray!"

"Not with my headlights off!" my Voice rose up to match hers. This was turning into a Evening With The Bickersons! I cleared my throat to Calm Down then I switched on the lights & dropped the gears very gentle into Low.

"Just—drive!" Her Words hit me in the side of my head like a spray of Hot Gas.

I switched the Motor off. "When you're in a hurry that's when you make mistakes. Mistakes you can prevent." I pointed down to the filthy floor under her feet. "For example."

She shook her head & blinked a couple times for Dramatic Effect. As if *I* was the one who was blowing it out of Proportion!

346

"I'm just saying you could be considerate. I don't care about the circumstances. It doesn't cost anything to show consideration for somebody's clean carpet."

I started the Motor up again & pushed the Raymobile further through the water with some coaxing words of Encouragement to the dashboard. From the Steering I could Feel how the current was pushing on the side of the car also what with the mud & rocks etc. very Uneven Underneath it was not a easy job driving in a Straight Line we swung this way & that. I Felt a little Relief as soon as the headlights landed on the white rock Amelia told me to aim for. It stuck out of the middle of the stream like a broken Knuckle. Boulders bounced us & water slapped the doors but the Raymobile did not Falter nor it did not spring a Leak. I do not wish to Compare Unduly but a person & his car can grow very Close by way of the same Experience so much like a Married Couple in some cases. The Highway of Life is not a cheap Expression it is a True Description I believe. So I did not blow it out of Proportion when I was speaking tender words down to the dashboard I will say with all my Might every step onward every foot Further that the Raymobile rolled it spoke the same back to me.

When we pulled around Knuckle Rock I saw my highbeams stretch out & scrape upon the foreign shore of Mexico. This I was looking Forward To I did not Sigh from Regret over recent Events which led me here. Though this Feeling is a Psychological Trick of the Mind i.e. the False Sense of Relief which always comes $\frac{1}{2}$ way through any human Endeavor. *If I have made it O.K. this far I will make it O.K. the rest*—which this self-trick could be a leftover from Caveman Days. Cro-Magnon or Neanderthal etc. Because a person will not Survive & Triumph if he does not Believe he will.

It was a beautiful view from inside the car in the middle of the river with this Country behind & that Country ahead so there we were in the Raymobile in our own Country between.

"Why you stop? Don't stop here," Amelia shook my shoulder. "Go."

I did not even Recognize I took my foot off the gas! I did not Hear how sharp her Voice was toward me! I just said, "I drove

347

through the Car Wash one time. In Mason they let me. I saw how all the brushes worked and the hot wax treatment too." Amelia just made her mouth small & tight and stared straight ahead through the Windshield. As if she could pull us the rest of the way with the Power of her eyes. "This is better," I let her know, "this is closer to Nature."

Certain Tender Words of this kind *Oh Amelia all which has happened to us so far is for the Good!* sprang up in my Mind in that minute but they Stuck in my Throat. When I looked over at her again she was blowing long hot breaths out of her nose & I did not need X-Ray Vision to read her Inner Thoughts. Amelia already had her Mind in Mexico and the pains crawled through her because her Body was far behind. When I Observed this I Remembered my Pledge to help her all the way & Fight for her behalf. I owed her all my Strength to help her Body catch up so I nodded to her, "Let's go," then I stepped on the gas—

The Raymobile rocked up then it rocked back. I revved in Neutral & popped her into Low and I heard the back tires hissing and this time we settled back at a Angle. I threw it into Reverse but this move only made the wheels Spin Around like broken paddles on a riverboat.

Amelia belted the dashboard with both of her hands and she Drilled a Look into me which honest to God made me feel like a heel as if I did this on Purpose.

I sat straight up to Defend myself. "What—I did it on Purpose?!" Amelia made a slow move to get Out of the car but I tugged her by her arm. "No. You sit here," I said & I opened my door. I slid over & I gave her room Behind the Wheel. 'I'll go out & push. When I signal you step on the gas. Just a little pressure understand? Just tap it a little. Nudge it."

"Sure sure. Slow." Still with the Death Rays shooting out of her eyes. By Amelia this Predicament wiped out the other Memories of my Triumphs from before so I did not wait around for any Thank You.

The water was cold it was ice cubes running around my ankles but it was not Deep on that side. Around the back I saw as soon as I bent down how the bottom ½ of Both Wheels was stuck in

348

the Mud & they Sank so far in they dragged the back bumper down Underwater. A bad Position yes but the Answer was not beyond my Mental Powers since I saw the bare bones of it scattered under the Raymobile Right There—a Ramp of Rocks will lead the wheels Up & Out for such are the Laws of Physics wet or dry.

From the rocking Back & Forth Motion both tires cut a slopesided hole in the Mud which the water already was Digging Deeper. I had to Work Fast I had to pack up the front end of the little ditch on the shallow side before that tire got Buried up to its neck the way the other one was. Flat rocks about as big as baked Potatoes I picked up from 10 Feet around they were lying in my easy reach & they fit together very Smooth. All the time the River was Fighting Me by its sticky mud it was Helping me since it filled in the gaps in my Ramp like wet Cement. The price tag on this Effect was the bucket of mud which also filled in Behind so it was not going to work trying to gain any Momentum by rocking back it could only rock Forth.

I got ready to push. "O.K. Amelia. Give it a little gas," I told her and I leaned all my Weight on the back of the car right over the tail-light. I heard the Motor catch & by my fingertips I Felt the skin of the car Vibrate I felt the Pressure of the gas pumping down the fuel line yes by my very hands I felt it Exploding in the pistons *then I pushed*—I was Pushing so hard I made the Veins pop out of my arms & maybe they already broke through the skin behind my knees the way my legs started Burning when I dug my toes in & my stomach also the same like I swallowed a sizzling ball of Electricity—I put in all my Power to this Feat of Strength. I was not up against this Automobile stuck in the Mud it was all our Trouble stacked against us—Newberry breathing down our necks with his phony Evidence . . . Amelia's sorry Past which led her into his net . . . His cruel Desire reaching out with his long arm to squash her like a Flea . . . My Desperate Times with her in the shower in the Motel & in the dark in Tio's bedroom . . . Can I pass this Test? Pushing against Newberry with his Greed to guide him . . . armor plated behind his F.B.I. Badge & his Legal Powers . . . and no Morality to slow him down . . . The Human

349

Being who lives by The Ten Commandments wilt not have any Protection in this unfair World . . .

All I can do for her is all I can do such was my Inner Thought when I started seeing Stars I almost fainted on my feet from the heavy Weight I was pushing—"Do it! Do it!" I screamed this to the Sky Above then Amelia heard my Plea & took it to her Heart she really poured on the Gas—

The back of the car Kicked Up fast the bumper Belted me in my knees. The wheels spun around whistling in the muddy holes in the water sucking Air in & spitting out all the Rocks of my Ramp. The mighty Raymobile bounced backwards and my ankles buckled Under Me so I fell flat on my can in the water up to my Armpits. From my front row seat I watched the car dig its Rear End down into the mud like a frog laying eggs.

Amelia shut off the Motor but she did not come out to see what was what but to Defend her I will say I do not think she knew about my crippled Condition. My ankle is the most Vulnerable Location of my whole Physique being the Weakest Point so I did not try and stand up on it for a minute. I wanted to get up on my knees but a Pain like a redhot pepper hit me in there that Forced me to fall over flat on my face. When I wiped the water out of my eyes Amelia was standing over me.

"You have to help me. My knee. I punched it on a rock," I said.

Did I see Sympathy on her face or was she Weary from standing up to all of our Trouble? Very slow she stretched her hand out for Support which I Grabbed. It was a shaky Effort all the way over to the car with me leaning on her shoulder etc. & Hopping by her side until I could sit down on the front seat. It was just the right height for my leg Dangling Down for the ice water made my ankle go Numb & the flow of it was a Massage all around.

"How bad it hurts?" Amelia questioned me.

"It feels like my calcaneus is still in 1 piece." I pressed on my foot to Examine it to the full. "I think the medial cuneiform feels O.K.," I could tell her, " and the cuboid is all right. I'm checking my navicular now," I said Step by Step & I Felt around it with my thumbs. "Fine. Good. It's fine," then OWEEE! I touched off a spark down there it shot a spray of Pain straight up my leg. "Yeah! O.K.! I knew it! My talus. It's my talus. Give me 5 minutes. I'll be good as gold in 5 minutes."

"How bad your leg hurts? Tell me." Amelia leaned her head into the car. The corners of her mouth Pulled Down hard & on top of this the corners of her eyes Drooped so Amelia showed me 3 Seconds of weary Sympathy & Worry. "TELL ME! WHAT YOU DID RAY?"

I leaned up to her so that put us nose to nose where I saw up close this was not Sympathy I was getting. "I twisted my ankle! Give me 5 minutes of peace & quiet *then* I can try *again*."

She looked back over her shoulder back Toward the U.S. shore. She was Expecting maybe Special Agent John Newberry standing there pointing at her with a nasty smile & dangling a pair of shiny Handcuffs on the hook of his finger. Amelia pulled at my arm. "Try!" she spoke very Rough to me.

"Let me rest my leg for 5 minutes. You can collect some more rocks. Forget the flat ones this time. Triangle ones. Like this." I curled up my fist & Demonstrated the Ideal rock she should gather. She Gripped on my hand so Strong she put a blue mark on it from her nails. "What? What do you want me to do? Lift the car out with my bare hands?"

"Try and walk. We have to walk. We have to get out of here now." Her Voice calmed down to me like she was teaching the Alphabet to a drooling Idiot.

"Back up," I said, "I'll test it." I slid off of the seat I hung on to the door I put my foot down. This Hurt me like I had a migraine headache in my ankle but I could Lower my Weight on it & let go of the door.

This move Satisfied Amelia so she squeezed my hand a gentle squeeze. "We can go slow over there. Get a taxi in Ojinaga."

I did not take 1 step in this Direction when I Recognized what Extreme Idea she had on her Mind. "You mean walk to Mexico?"

"Only 1 miles or 2 miles over there."

"I thought you meant try & walk to the back of the car."

"Leave this car."

"Abandon it? Abandon the Raymobile in the middle of a river? No!"

She let go of my hand. "You stay. Stay here. Sure," Amelia said & she almost pushed me back down by Reaching around to grab her big bag also she grabbed the Thermos.

"Wait a minute,' I said to her back, "I said I was going to get you home safe & sound. I pledged you. I pledged you I was going to do that."

"You *do* Ray. You make me safe & sound this way. From here O.K.? Wait for him. For when he comes here. When John comes here you can keep him away from me. Give me time to do things. Time to do this things I told you about. And get away from there safe & sound." She tried to make this Plan very Convincing by her calm Logic.

Under her words she did not sound Calm anymore only Quiet only Hushed Up like a Italian opera on the Radio with the volume turned down. I choked myself on my Surprise from this Suggestion! For my chosen Mission was not Accomplished stuck in the mud amid the Rio Bravo River nor my Duty was not done by leaving her go by herself nor this was not my Plan in the first place. This cowardly Behavior I never had in me and this was the saddest surprise how Amelia could think I will Fail Her at the moment of Need.

"Who do you think I am? I'm not Dagwood Bumstead! I'm not Fibber McGee! You think I can't take care of you anymore? My ankle's perfect now! Look!" I splashed my foot up & down a few times to show her. (I will say this Particular Move was not Smart if I judge by the Pain but by the Effect on Amelia i.e. did she stop & consider yes it was a big Success.) I had her Attention so I Proposed her this: "What if he goes some other way? Then what am I doing here? What do I do then? Sit down in the car & wait for the Auto Club to rescue me?"

"No I think he comes here. I think so. He follow me everyplace," she said like she was gazing into the Future. "You stop him Ray. Tell him I run away from you in Dallas. So you look for me here. So your car get stuck in the river and . . . " In a second she picked up again. "Talk to him like you talk to him before hm?"

I almost had to catch my Breath from the Punch of her harsh Remark. "I don't think he'll listen to me. I don't think we're friends anymore. So here's what . . . " She was waiting to hear my Big Plan & so was I waiting to hear my Next Words come out. My brave words! "You're not going to go over by yourself you're not going to walk in the dark over there all alone. I won't let such a thing happen. I'm going to walk you to Mexico right up to your front door. I'm going to watch over you from here to there." My voice did not shake nor I did not keep it low for my Confidence made it rise higher. "Stay here? Are you kidding? I'm staying with you all the way to the Grand Finale. I'm going to be there when you see your little girl again when she jumps up into your arms & hugs you around your neck. I want to hear you tell her it's all right now because her Mama's home. Who's he Mama? Who's that man? she's going to ask. You can say Someday when you're old enough to understand I'll tell you the whole story. I gave you my Pledge to the end Amelia and this is not the end yet . . . "

" . . . ssh! ssh-ssh!"

I did not Notice how Amelia was hissing like a boiling kettle trying to shush me up the Whole Time I was re-pledging but I did not take this being Disrespect. She just did not Recognize the Truth of the Situation. "I mean look! Who do you think got you this far already? The Getaway Fairy? *I* got you here . . . " Amelia lingered a long look over the Raymobile stuck in the Mud & she did not say the Obvious. "A *little* gas I told you put on. The key word here is *little*. A *nudge* I said."

"I don't know what you say sometime," she croaked. "Now Ray. I want to go now."

"Maybe *nudge* means something different in Mexico."

She groaned. "We're no *in* Mexico Ray! We're in the middle of the river!" She kicked out & splashed me with Ice Water head to toe.

For the sake of the Truth which is my Duty before I went further with her she had to Admit why we were in that Predicament was because with her 1 Track Mind her Hysterical Panic & her lead foot she put on too much gas—"It's your fault! You can't admit it can you!"

"You made us stuck!" she answered back. "You stop & look at the pretty view! *This pretty carwash . . .*" she Mocked me by a prissy Voice.

"For your information I said this was *better* than going through a carwash but now I truly doubt it!" I forgot all about my aching ankle I took a Giant Step toward her. "Listen Mrs. Vasco Da Gama—you told me this is the place you always cross over *because it's always dry here*! It was your idea to go this way. I trusted you."

"How do I know when the rain comes in Ojinaga? You crazy man. This rains come and you blame me!"

"If you tuned in the Weather report instead of that cowboy music we wouldn't be in this stinking mess."

"If you don't want somethings from me I think you never drive me down here. If I don't go in bed with you."

Her Insult bit very Sharp. "What kind of man do you think I am?"

"Sure. I think so," she said. "If I don't go in bed with you."

And Back & Back & Back. If I did not listen to Newberry. If he did not show me his Files. If he did not make a Fake License for me. If he did not Lure Me out of the Bluebird Motel. If Amelia did not come to my Apartment. If I did not put my Ad in the Newspaper. If I did not put my foot outside Pecan St. in the Blackout. Back & Back & Back. If I was never born. Then maybe all of this would be happening to Lamont Carruthers.

"If *you* didn't make lovey-dovey to *me*?" I started to Correct her Misnomer, "No. If *I* didn't make lovey-dovey to *you* . . ."

Her mouth puckered tight enough to Spit at me but Amelia bent it into a hard frown to say, "I hate you for a man. I have to show you how. I have to show you everythings in bed."

I Forgive Amelia for these Words I Forgive her for the miserable Emotion behind the Sound of them. I Believe she used to fight by Tooth & by Claw for all her needs since she was a little girl. In the dirty street she learned the Lesson of that poor kind of Life i.e. she had to hit before she got hit. Nor she did not waste her Energy on Regrets. She did not Regret her crude Behavior by her

354

it was all of the Past. A minute ago or 10 Years ago Amelia will say what is the Difference? In my Opinion this is the Reason why I never heard her Apologize for this or that so I Forgive her for speaking to me in this fashion. She obeyed the Law of the Jungle amen. I obey the Law of Relativity so I Forgive her amen. I will say she lost her Temper at the drop of a pin if she had 1 Weakness here it is. Also with Affection the same all of her Feelings flared up & sank back so fast. I know this by my Personal Experience & I think also by this open door John Newberry jumped in on her and took Advantage he played on the harp strings of Amelia's Emotions.

"Why do you want to make me feel like this?" I moped I acted Downcast by her cruel streak & I sat inside the car again. I mumbled a little about how can she throw me down like a Used Tissue. Very slow I rolled up the windows nor I did not let her see my face I Pretended I had to hide my Tears.

By the time I had the glove compartment open so I could Collect my Personal Effects out of there Amelia was standing in the water next to me. I did not look her in the eye until she Kneeled Down then I was going to let her off & tell her that is going too far she should save such a Gesture for the Queen of England but she was just crouching in to see what I was doing in the glove compartment.

I always put a flashlight in there a Tool I find comes in very handy in many assorted Situations as I say the Raymobile stuck in the middle of a muddy River in the middle of the night is the Perfect Situation which proves my Point. Except I did not change the batteries since last year when they went flat but I took it out on the Idea I could buy new ones in Mexico if they sell such a thing as batteries there. When I reached in to see what else was under the A.A.A. maps Amelia picked the flashlight up out of my lap. "It doesn't work," I said these words the same time she switched the Switch on it & the white beam lit up the whole dashboard.

She gave me a wiseguy smile & shined it into the glove compartment so I could see. Under the washcloth I use on the windows I saw something Metal & solid. By this I knew a definite Sign of

355

Newberry's inner thoughts. "I didn't put that there," I said & I was looking at a shiny nickel-plated Snubnose .38 Revolver. I felt the weight of it in my palm I never beheld such a Item before. Newberry's kind of Warning or his kind of Courtesy. It felt like I was shaking hands when I put my finger on the trigger.

My Lifetime Subscription to Popular Mechanics paid off and how! I figured out the angle on the Mechanism & quick emptied out all the Bullets I stored them in my pocket to save for later. We both felt Chilly at the same time & I saw Amelia's face shrink I will say for this minute The Dark Unknown made the Air cold there. Only one Question bloomed down & sat like frost—was Newberry still Behind us or Ahead?

Some Events overwhelm this is a Physical fact. Some Powers are too Fierce for a person to beat. A Flood is such or a Earthquake. A Knock Out punch from Joe Louis is also a fine Example. Some things a person can not Oppose. A Champion boxer is not immune from Physical Facts for all men reach their limits we are all Flesh & Blood. His muscle tissues clog up with Acid nor there is not enough Oxygen so a man's muscles Refuse him they do not Respond to his Wishes. THIS IS A PHYSICAL FACT HE CAN NOT PREVENT! If a Need strikes him in this time when he is Exhausted it is not his Fault if he can not get up & do the Required his own body Prevents him. A person can fight to his Limits but after that what can he do more? At the end of his Strength he can pass out Unconscious so do you expect a Unconscious person to put up a Fight? It is nobody's Fault it is the Normal way that the Human Body acts you can check this with Dr. Godfrey. It does not mean a person Fails if Events ambush him at his Low Point. A person can not hold back a Flood.

I do not blush if I admit I am no Olympic Athlete & I had to crawl up the muddy Mexican shore on my hands & knees. On top of this my aching ankle made me Rely on Amelia (I do not Flinch with Revealing this either) she pulled me Up & Over. I arrived in Mexico very pooped out & a sad vista met my eyes from there—the Raymobile my Old Paint I saw stranded & slanting out in the water which is not a Fortunate Position for a station wagon. I started picturing the worst—

Starting with the scraping squealing Sound of metal grinding over the Rocks as the rushing River turns the Raymobile around the way the needle on a Compass turns. Nosedown now pointing downstream with more water pushing from Behind—little waves going *slap—slap—slap* on the back window. The Mighty Raymobile teeters it totters & it Shoves Off—but it does not sink since I rolled up all the windows & locked the doors it Departs very Dignified it floats away like the Titanic—

My head was still buzzing from this Dizzy Trance when I heard Amelia's Voice telling me how her Amigos with their Jeep will come & tow my car out of the river 1st thing in the Morning. She patted me There There There on my shoulder. Before this minute I did not Believe she was Interested I did not expect Amelia to Sympathize but here it is the Proof how she truly cared to Investigate my Emotions & Ease them. The way I look at it this makes up for her Temper Tantrum from before. She did cheeer me up over the Raymobile but deep in my Mind I already bid my metal friend Bon Voyage.

"He's O.K. there," Amelia said & she tilted her face up to me then up to the sky. "If it no rains no more."

In the sparkly sunshine of Ojinaga all of Mexico is on sale from soup to nuts. From behind the row of wheelbarrows down the street little Muchachos Attract your eye by their jumpy arm motions so happy if you Notice their Display of Tropical Fruits— cantaloupes & papayas over here & over there that one is selling peeled mangoes served on a stick! Or maybe you need a new pair of Sandals—did I mention the Native Arts & Crafts? Tan leather sandals with the soles made out of Used Tires which still grip the road like new! Or go enjoy a relaxing stroll on the Promenade under the shady arches. Watch out for pesky street Urchins who tug on your sleeve begging can they Shine your Shoes even if you have Sandals on! Did I mention the charming shops? Under the awnings behind the bead curtains you can haggle with them oh! the Natives enjoy this Activity! You can haggle them over the price of a Hershey Bar! And around the corner you find more treats for the hot Weather. There is Paradise this stand where the little Muchacho sells fruit juice & soda pop you can stop there all day to taste the Different Flavors yes a cool drink in one hand & a Hankie in the other to mop off your Sweaty Brow.

I never saw this side of Ojinaga I had to Imagine it to myself while Amelia Described. She talked the whole time we walked I believe out of Mercy. She wanted to take my Mind off the Weather which was like this: another Thunderclap & another Dark cloud cracked open right over our heads. Rain did not sprinkle down by a Gentle Pitter-patter it fell out of the sky by Firebuckets. And the Firebuckets came down too. Every Raindrop was so big it made a new puddle when it hit the Sidewalk. By my Calculations of Velocity in Nautical Knots the Raymobile was on the last leg of its Viking funeral somewhere out in the Gulf of Mexico.

Do I need to Mention that we did not see a taxi anywhere? Like a couple of lost Orphans from a Nursery Rhyme with mud all over us & soggy down to our socks we kept walking around the Town i.e. taking a longcut to avoid Certain Parties who might be lurking.

A sewer rat would not lurk in Weather like this!

I was still limping a little bit mostly for the Disguise Value but who was I fooling? Nobody was outside where I could fool them! Every person in Ojinaga was inside staying warm & dry Except Us! I was hearing Whoops & Hollers via the windows we went by—yip-yip-yipping punched through the trumpets & maracas of Mariachi music playing on the Radio. The windowshades pulled down behind those windows looked like stretched yellow Skins hanging there.

Dirty water backed up from the gutters it curled up & coated the Sidewalk. The walls of the Buildings even did not look washed by the rain they looked sticky & dripping with Sweat. Sweating from worry. Now this place Reminded me of the East 8th.

"Are we in the bad part of town?" I asked over.

"Here's all like this. All the same," Amelia said. Then she ducked around the next Corner & she put on Some Steam here with her arms wrapped around her chest holding her sweater shut

& her face down out of the Force of the Rain. She was almost sniffing a Scent up from the Ground.

Amelia also Described all about the wonderful Welcome we were in for from her dear Friends since they will be Thankful she is with them Safe & Sound. They will put on a Mexican Thanksgiving for us with a banquet of Delicacies & Beer followed up by a hot bath followed up by clean sheets & a soft bed. After this Fiesta is over she can find out how far Newberry is Interfering with them for Mexican folk eat first & Ask Questions later. Considering my delicate Digestion etc. I Pondered if I would commit a Insult if I asked the chef a Question or so *before* any eating since I did Doubt if I could find a Doctor in the neighborhood who knew his way around a High Colonic. So before we got there I already Decided I was going to stick to the refried beans & plain tortillas.

We stopped outside a Hotel in the middle of a empty Block. This place is all Stucco with fake arches Painted On all dirty & cracked. A entire Corner of the Building got torn off somehow which by the Evidence I will say it was by a bus driver who Did Not Care if he turned 100% on the Street.

We went in around the side where a stairway was like a shadow sliced into the wall. I covered our Flank I let Amelia go up in front a couple of steps. Here I Remark a funny thing—she walked up & not a Sound but every step I tip-toed on Squealed out a Complaint. (This Phenomenon I can not figure but because of it I am sure we did lose our Element of Surprise.) The damp plaster & broken linoleum did not Invite & my shoulders could practically scrape both of the walls at the same time which also rang my inner Alarm Bell this could be a filthy trap. Beer or something like it trickled down into a Sticky Mess a few steps from the top. It only showed up under the bare Lightbulb which poured its little heart out at a cockeyed angle from a bent wire over the landing. Up there besides the thick damp of the Air the smell of cigarette smoke & sweaty dirt hit us in the face. If I Remember correct this place is called the Hotel Imperial.

Amelia pulled the door open and we made our Grand Entrance. This Lobby is a big square room & all the Lights hang down from

359

the ceiling so all the Shadows build up around the walls. All faces turned Toward us from there—from the padded bench built in around the edge of the room & from the Card Tables set up under the Lights. A couple of dozen blank & dark faces a couple dozen Hottentots in torn T-shirts & greasy trousers & torn sweaters the same Sunkdown Faces I saw Before in Tio's house. Whatever they were doing in that minute they stopped doing it then. Playing cards or talking low but the way it looked to me Waiting was their main Purpose. If they were not altogether waiting for us I Detected the Feeling that we would Satisfy Fine until the real thing came along. I Remembered very clear this is the Identical manner the Zombie Guardians of the Taboo Temple acted while deep in the secret Chambers their Masters prepared for their fiendish Fiesta. When they went back to playing cards & talking low this did not Trick me for it is a sure Sign something is up if all Appears Normal.

"Donde esta Benito?" Amelia spoke up. She Repeated this a couple of times & looked at each face in the room. So did I. Where is Benito she wanted to know. But they only Chattered to each other.

As soon as Amelia started walking across the Lobby they all Stopped Talking. As if their chattering was something Solid that tangled up the aisle so they made room for her to get through. To my ears this Quiet sounded more Solid than the Chattering. From my spot next to the door I could view the Entire Crowd in this Sensitive minute while Amelia waited in front of the Reception Desk.

This Desk is behind a wire cage and by my Experience this is not a Good Sign. She had to ring the buzzer & wait there so everybody was just waiting for the Next Thing to Happen. Well the Next Thing happening to me was I Felt somebody tug on my Sleeve. Not a pesky street Urchin it was a old man Tugging. He was sitting there since we came in the door but I did not Notice him until he started on me with the Tugging Business. The Army blanket he had on from his waist down did Blend Him into the Shadows so Forgive me if I missed him right off but I Remember him in every Respect. He is blind in 1 eye. He does not have any front teeth Upper or Lower. He has More Hair in his eyebrows than he has on his head.

Those eyebrows he Arched Up at me & he said, "Ho ho."

I smiled for him I nodded. I did not want to Offend on the outside chance he could be the Hotel Chef.

He tilted his head toward Amelia. "Ho ho," he said & this time he Pinched my leg.

My shout of Surprise made Amelia turn around. I gave her a wave & told her, "Fine," then I said the same to the Old Man. "I'm with her," I let down my guard, "I'm helping her."

Again with the Tugging. A little string of Spit Dribbled Out of the corner of his mouth. He wiped it by the back of his hand & wiped off his friendly smile too. Word by Word he said, "Amelia—is—Flower—" now he jutted his chin at the rest of the room but mainly in the Direction of the Desk, "—in—pigs!"

The door behind the wire cage cracked open & a chunky man stepped through. This Benito packed his fleshy torso into a shiny shirt at least 2 Sizes too Small for him. Chubby rolls of tight skin squeezed out under his arms & over his belt. He wears very thick round Glasses about as big as Soup Plates. His little beaky nose pokes out it is the only Hard Point on his Face since his loose cheeks sag around it. Benito does not look like he ever Laughed at a Joke in his Life or not out loud anyway. He opened the cage door & let Amelia inside & when she was in his Reach he moved fast. He grabbed her by her shoulders he pulled her close he Kissed her on the mouth so she had to Squirm away from him. She saw he did not Kiss her out of Love his Kiss tasted sour to her which was how he Meant it. She touched her lips and Benito held her there by a stiff necked stare I could see how much he Hated Himself for having any Feelings toward her at all.

Did I Rely on X-Ray eyes to see up Close? I did not Because by this time I was up against the wire cage I was pulling at the door with my Bare Hands. I could rattle it but it did not Budge. This Move did not worry Benito maybe that kind of thing Happens a lot in the Hotel Imperial. He beetled his brow at me. Abba-zabba-zabba Amelia told him enough about my Presence so he opened the cage door very slow to let me in & show me up. A few new faces Appeared in the rear doorway & Amelia Recognized them by Name. I did not need to know any Words of the Mexican Language to tell me this was not a Happy bunch.

Somebody pushed me in my back & I thought it was old Ho Ho again but instead it was 3 more Muchachos inviting me come on & follow Benito & Amelia & the rest of them through the door and Down the Steps. We went Down twice as many as the ones we Walked Up in front so in my Opinion the room at the bottom is Underground. Those guys crammed in ahead of me & I got pinned to the back wall so I only got a Glimpse of Amelia before they cleared a trail for her & sealed it up Behind. The Mumbling started up around her it Followed Her over the other side & faded away when she got there the way a wave curls back into the ocean. Also just like the next wave which comes Roaring Up over the edge of such a Silence I heard Amelia cry—

I pushed through them all I Knocked Down every Muchacho in my way—their arms sprang up around me but I Punched through to Defend Amelia before any harm befell upon her from Benito's horny hands—if he was Hurting Her then blow by blow he was Hurting Me—my ribs split when I heard her cry again— no it was not that Kind of Pain for her I saw Benito did not lay a finger on Amelia. It was Misery which Pierced her & came out the other side for I Felt it enter me when I stood Behind her.

Do not Flinch here because I did not flinch I Forced this Sight into my eyes & now I have to Force it out.

On a table stretched out against the wall it was Tio there. His mouth hanging open & dried Blood on his lips. A plug of Skin flapped out of a Hole in his jaw. A pond of crusty Blood sat on his chest. Splinters of his Ribs torn up out of his Skin. The raw meat of him scooped out for all to see. Down below on his pants 2 Stains wet & dirty joined up between his legs. Not because of Fear in his final minute I do not believe Tio was Afraid then. It is a Medical Fact when a person Dies he will Lose Control so his dirty business comes out he can not stop it this Last Act of his on Earth. I say it is a Wise Comment on Life from somebody who is leaving.

Furthermore this is Nature. By the noted scientist Dr. Wesley

Gumm I learned the Natural Process in his book The Wonders of Microbes. Organisms dig into the Dead Object they eat it from the outside in & the inside out. It is a Feast it is a Banquet to a colony of Microbes who digest our Human Anatomy. They eat a Body down to the Molecules down to our Chemicals and show up what a man is made of. Skin & Blood & Bones which is not higher than a hyena or a vulture no a man is Lower. Look at the Evidence. Look how a man starts out full of Hope when he is Alive now look at what he does when he is Dead. Full of pus & Microbes. He can not even hold his Bowels shut! Hereby I give you the end of his Hope. Cold fat soft bones dry hair sticky fluids limp muscles loose skin *a bag of fertilizer*—

OH THE HUMANITY!!!

The same I am in the Market holding on to my Papa's pocket. On his Weekly Errands he lets me carry his shirts all Clean from the Chinese Laundry & stand on line with him in the Kosher butcher. I hear him sniffing like a Bloodhound sniffing up the cold air with many Different Smells in it. The fruit on the Wagons. The fresh egg bread. The starch in his shirts. He does not look at me but he holds my hand & he Squeezes it. "Look at this variety," he Instructs me. I look up at him. "America is a wonderful place. They teach you in the First Grade what a beautiful place you live in Reuven? I'm telling you here is my dream come true," he says when we Arrive in the line for the butcher. I can see the tops of the wooden cages where the Chickens are Squawking & Fretting. I watch the butcher with his short arms reach down & drag out a fresh Bird for his next Customer while my Papa tells me, "Do something what you want in your Life. You decide what you want to be when you grow up. Just tell me early. Promise Papa?"

"Promise Papa," I say for him.

"I'll help you get going on the right track." He squeezes my hand again. "I'm not going to live forever." Then he lets go of it so he can point out the Chicken he wants.

Now I can see the butcher's arms up close he is shaped like a Woman in this way. His Skin is so smooth & pale it looks like Soap nor he does not have a hair on him. He darts his hands into the cage & pulls out the Exact chicken my Papa wants which he shows him Before he takes it out back. I go around the corner of the counter so I can see how that Feathery thing turns into the plump pink dinner my Mama stuffs into the Oven. I hear Papa's Voice over my head. "Don't go back there Reuven. That doesn't make Papa happy." I Pretend I do not hear him & I just keep my eyes on that butcher's White Arms I watch him pull his Knife across that bird's throat & hang it upside down so all its Blood sputters out. But it still Kicks with Life this Chicken! It flutters & it flies off the hook! It sprays Blood all over me in my mouth in my hair all over my face in my eyes—so I Spit I Retch I cry in a circle, "Tell me what to do Papa! Tell me what to do!"

When I Blinked my eyes open again when I unstuck them from the Sight of Tio I saw I was standing all by myself in that room. The shockwave from this Surprise rippled over me but I did not Fear for my neck then I only Feared what Benito & his rough boys already did to Amelia. If he did this much to Tio could a Woman's Body stop him from doing more? I Forced my Inner Thoughts away from this Idea & I switched on my Concentration I listened to the walls. In case they had her trapped in some room nextdoor I tapped by my Knuckles the Ancient Signal SHAVE AND A HAIRCUT which your average Mexican does not Recognize.

I did not get back TWO BITS then I heard tap-tap-tapping behind me from the Direction of the steps. No it was not Amelia's Morse Code but the Cuban Heels of a couple Muchachos coming for me. Benito sent down boys to cover me little pishers up to my chest. "Where is Amelia?" I made my Question sound like a Threat. This they did not take very Serious they only cooed to me I should stay calm & the bony one with the Joe E. Brown mouth shoved my shoulder & called me "Senor Coco" to my face. His jittery Partner just put his finger up to his lips he was Advising me Keep Quiet Or Else. *So get ready to show me Or Else What* I thought I was ready to make my Move—until many footsteps full of Purpose tramped down the Stairs & saved them from my Fury.

Benito was the 1st one down. He was smoking a little Cigar now in a tortoise-shell holder which he sucked on & blew the

Smoke out fast around it. His forehead was still ploughed up by Worry.

"*Amelia*. Where?" I Urged him for this Information. I think he wanted me to work for it so I had to go fish for the Magic Words. "Don-day es-ta Amelia?" By Accident my fingers found the Bullets in my pocket so I Remembered the Gun I had inside my jacket. What did he know. Those Bullets could be extra. So I said his Name I Repeated my Question & this time I was pointing a Revolver at his chest.

Did it work? Abracadabra. As good as the blinding Green Flash of my Hand Beam. The Cigar dropped out of Benito's loose mouth & he Ordered his Muchachos to stand still. Me he tried to Quiet Down by pushing his open hands in front of him & pressing them up against the pillow of space Between us. "No Senor. No Senor. O.K.," he Guaranteed me. "O.K. Senor O.K."

I heard her Voice outside the room I will say I was not Prepared to see her again so Beautiful. Amelia was all dressed up in local Garments a flowery dress & a scarf over her head she stood in the doorway it was a frame around her. In the dim light & soft shadows clasping her she Appeared to my eye like a young bride who Rembrandt would paint.

"Take off your clothes." She did not give me a Choice either. "Trade clothes now." She pointed over to a Muchacho next to Benito who was about my size. If this big idea came out of her pow-wow & it was part of some new Plan I was going to hear the Good Reason for it Before I unbuttoned 1 button on my Safari Suit.

"What for?"

"We go to Tres Osos now. We go in the bus."

"Wait a minute. Who are these people? Tell me who these people are. What do they know about—" I waved my arm behind me over the Remains of Tio.

"Some men leave Tio on the stairs. Benito he told me."

"Is changing clothes his idea?" I nodded toward Benito. The Suspicions in my Voice pulled Amelia over to me.

"Before they think I did this to him," Amelia shook her head & said. "Benito heard stories in Ojinaga."

"What stories? True stories?"

"Crazy stories about me. About John. Other things."

"What kind of a story could make them think you'd do something so crazy? To somebody you love. To Tio. What the hell on Earth do they think could possibly entice you to do such a crazy thing?"

The poor Muchacho was already standing in his Underpants & holding out his bluejeans & flowery shirt & Cowboy hat for me to put on. So in front of everybody I took off my Safari Suit & I shook the Bullets out of the front pocket. "They're my extra ones," I informed Benito.

I gave over my clothes so here is another Unmarked Crossroad I can name going back. If I did not dress up like a real Mexican if I did not act like a Mexican hither or yon then probably this Episode would not end so sad. His pretty shirt would not be ruined by my Bloodstains nor my Doom would not Approach me so Fast. If you ask me I think he got a better Deal even if you take in Consideration the Mud all over my pants because Mud you can get out after it dries by mild Brushing. Then a little bit of Soap & Water and it comes out like new.

On the night bus to Tres Osos Amelia connected the dots for my Benefit: Benito etc. et al. in the Hotel Imperial were her Mule Pool i.e. the trusted ones who Guided her Customers all the way North over the U.S. Border. If they all resembled Zombie Guards of the Taboo Temple at the moment then there was a Earthly Reason i.e. all Mules were held in the Grip of Fear they were all Stalked by shadows because a very high Percent of them lately only made a 1 Way Trip. Different Stories came back instead Dark Tales spread through the streets of Ojinaga like a wave of poison gas—

    1.) New Sponsers from Chihuahua want to run Amelia & Newberry out of business by making their precious Mules disappear.

    2.) The Authorities know all about Newberry & Amelia

now so they made a deal for their own Protection. Tio did not go along with them & now nobody is Safe.

3.) The Ku Klux Klan is going on a Torture & Murder Spree. Newberry can not stop them. Tio was on their Death List & Amelia is next then anybody she knows. (Also a version said John Newberry was in this filthy business too just to cover his Own Behind.)

4.) Drug Smugglers made these lucky Mules a sweet deal so now Amelia's Muchachos will Double-X her for the Money.

5.) Newberry is Double-Xing Amelia. Also he killed Tio & anybody Loyal to her he is going to do the same.

Amelia could add up 2 + 2 she did not need a IBM Computer to solve this Problem & Reveal the Truth. She told me very Certain her Life was not in any Peril she Remembered how Newberry has a Sentimental streak to his Behavior which he can not Resist. He did not want to Harm her he did not want to Bury her in the Ground he only wanted her to go to Jail for him. She Figured this out by her mathematical Mind this Answer which Revealed how the World is. Nor she did not Flinch to tell me in the brave way of Copernicus or Galileo. All she did not tell me was what she could not say Out Loud i.e. she could not say how far Newberry was going to go to make her yearn to Surrender.

I can add up 2 + 2 all righty I can add up FRACTIONS. Here is the Reason why Amelia sent Tio to Tres Osos before Ojinaga — so he could hide Dolores from the clutches of her Sentimental Papa! EUREKA but here comes the $64,000 Question: Did Tio meet his Doom before he got to Tres Osos or after?

"Do you think Dolores understands your business?"

"Dolores is a smart girl. No like me sometimes." Amelia turned over on the Seat she hunched up her back. I did not take this Gesture Personal she just Desired some Privacy I think she had enough of the World for 1 night. She let her head rest down against her bag instead of my shoulder but I watched over her the same & Amelia fell asleep in a minute which her little Snorts & Snores told me.

All of the other Passengers slept very sound too which was a Impossible Feat for me. Not from the bouncy ride nor not the clatter of the bus Motor nor not the tight squeeze cramped up on the slats of that seat. You know by Appearance we fit into that clump of Mexicans so Alike we could be Family all with our paper bundles all snoozing our cares away. This was not Difficult for Amelia being a Mexican to begin with etc. but my Inner Thought was our Secret Story made us the Foreigners & black sheep. Why we had to Hide amid them etc. why I wore a shabby Disguise. And mainly my Personal Responsibility towards Amelia & my Personal Conflict towards the Papa of her little girl.

I sat up Awake & I was the only one who did. All the way to Tres Osos my Mind did not settle down. A merry-go-round out of Control I had inside my skull & this Idea riding up & down on it—JOHN NEWBERRY endows himself with certain POWERS *a la* he can BEND THE LAW around him & RUN US OVER with it. *This is the size of the trouble I must face while the rest of the World sleeps!* From my years of Experience plus my Observations combined I could Predict his Plan very Precise I could deduce the Details. To wit:

A.) Newberry truly does not want a trace of his Trail of Crime to Remain so he will change the Evidence of the Past. He will rub out anybody who Remembers what he did (Tio etc.)

B.) Until only Amelia is left & certain Feelings toward her which he can not rub out. He will make up a new File on her & Convict her of his Crimes.

C.) He has to Lure her in & he will not use Money or Promises or Auld Lang Syne he will use little Dolores he will use his own daughter for Bait. He will use her for a Bribe to make sure Amelia does whatever he wants. He will twist her love into handcuffs.

Is this the way a loving Papa behaves to his Daughter? He uses his dear darling Flesh & Blood to forward his own Selfish Purposes? He should try & bring out the Female Traits of Mercy &

Tenderness but instead he teaches her how to be greedy & heartless. A father is supposed to PROTECT his little girl from such vices PROTECT her from all the Harm that comes with them! He is supposed to EDUCATE her in his Care so she can tell the genuine article from a phony boloney not to mention he should point out the many Wonders of the World. He is supposed to be a fine Example of a man she wants to marry someday.

Do not Believe a word John Newberry says on the Subject. He does not follow in this decent Tradition he twists it around his little finger. I Accuse him he is a pervert of Family values! I Reveal him he is my Arch Foe! *Protect* Dolores? Because of him she saw the stupid acts the Berserk Acts the bloody acts Desperate men do! *Educate* her? He shut her out of his Sight in a Private School like a prison camp he sent her away to learn her P's & Q's in a cave of Ignorance!

WHAT IS GOING ON WITH FATHERS & DAUGHTERS THESE DAYS?

I Remember the land of Mexico before we came to Tres Osos. The red ground spread out so empty & untrampled. Shadows from rocks & plants streak it below the cold Sun. No people anywhere only plants & dirt & the Creatures who belong there. And us coming by with our Trouble in our belching bus. People foul up every Beautiful Place with their Behavior they ruin every place on Earth with their selfish Deeds. I ask you this: Tell me why did Evolution end up with Human Beings? Information Please! I want to Know! What do Human Beings ADD to a Landscape?!

By me Tres Osos is a sorry place to Live also a sorry place to Visit. Go look for yourself I do not say this from Cheap Spite I do not hold this View from my angry Memories. Powdery brown dust sticks to every Surface there a crust of it cakes on the walls & steps. A dry puff of Air and it sprinkles off the corners of the roofs like sand inside a Hourglass. Plus there is a Constant Supply of that Dust it is always curling up off the low slopes behind the houses. If a Astronaut by accident looks down on Tres Osos the view will Remind Him of a tiny handful of mushrooms sprinkled on a crinkled Paper Bag. I say it looks the same from Ground Level.

Besides the Dust etc. I Observed a few children when we came up the dirt road. They scampered all over & watched us go by their front yards. Now I know how Macy's Thanksgiving Day Parade feels. A little boy who was only wearing droopy Jockey Shorts glued his eyes on us & forgot he was holding a dripping hose in his hand which was making thick Mud under his feet. His sister pushed the nozzle into a bucket and the 2 of them carried the sloshing Load into their house. The same as the nextdoor house & the house after that perched up on its very own mound of Bare Dirt. The whitewashed walls all the same also the wood shutters & no glass in the Windows. Little faces popped up & looked out as soon as they heard the Sound of our crunching footsteps. We were the biggest Excitement they had there in days.

The only red brick house there belonged to Amelia. The only one with glass windows & a heavy front door. A new Affair with shingles instead of red tiles on the Roof this place maybe was hauled down from my Neigborhood of Pecan St. or Amelia ordered it out of the Sears Catalogue! Her American house stood out very Proud at the end of the dirt road where it was a cul-de-sac it portrayed her Financial Achievements. I Believe her neighbors did not Resent this Dream House for somebody watered the shrubs even the sprinkler was still going on the Lawn when we got there.

Amelia hurried up a few steps ahead of me when we came close enough to see how her front door was not shut it was Hanging Open & the edge of it all split & splintered to Pieces. "What happened here?" was the simple part of the Question on my lips when I stepped inside. This is what Happened—

Maybe a Bulldozer drove through her house. Or at least a bull. All the furniture was turned over on the floor & Ripped Up besides. Stuffing from the sofa & cushions & broken armchairs was lying all around Amelia's feet that room was a Slaughterhouse of Furniture. She just stood still a minute I heard her try & catch her Breath she made little gulping noises. I do not Blame her being so affected by this violent Sight. Even the carpets were ripped up & the floor torn up Underneath & holes hammered in the plaster walls. In other words the exact Wounds I saw on Tio's battered body therefore I saw what Happened in a Flash—Tio got in the way of this violent Force it punched right through him & ploughed through the house I say Tio was not Strong enough to stop it. To Fight Off so much Hate a person needs to have the Equal hate inside him and Tio went there on account of Love. The Remains of his Love I saw in Ojinaga but the Remains of the Hate that beat him I Felt still buzzing in the mid air.

This is the kind of Behavior you Expect from persons of Low I.Q. with backgrounds to match i.e. parties who let Emotions run away on them Because they do not know how to take Disappointment. To Wit from here I can picture that hamhead Nilo throwing his weight around—bouncing in Fury from wall to wall & wall to floor like a TV wrestler. Nilo the One Man Tag Team! So what gives him the Right? What gives him the Right to muscle in & lose his Self Control? That Monster who Dr. Frankenstein made only threw the little peasant girl in the lake beause he wanted to see her Float like a pretty Flower! Even with such a Monster *it was a accident!* But with Nilo it is Anarchy—Tio is not enough for him he has to break the back of any piece of Furniture that Stands in his Way! He has to boot the lampshade across the room and the big Gorilla has to tear all the doors off the kitchen cabinets & knock holes in the wall he can not Stop until the Entire House is his Helpless Victim because Amelia is not where he wants her! Vey is mir! If I owned a *goldfish* this crazy I would beg my Vet on my knees to give it the needle!

Amelia was not there either when I turned around to tell her of my Theory. I had to play it by ear & follow the Sound of her raspy growls into the big bedroom. The bed was still in 1 piece & rightside up but the boxspring Mattress did not Survive the Chainsaw Attack which cut it in $\frac{1}{2}$ very neat like a slab of Cheese. Forget it. *Minor redecoration* compared to the job Nilo did on Dolores's frilly bedroom. Where she used to Play & Sleep tucked in bed safe & sound it was a Nasty Wreck with no Respect for the delicate Belongings of a 8 year old girl—

Her chest of Toys he toppled over & trampled on the Contents. Beautiful dolls smashed open under his heel he ripped the covers off her Storybooks & when he was done with that he broke into her pink plastic lunchbox with the Portrait of Princess Di on it— I mean for Godsake! For Amelia's Sake I stood very firm I was a Pillar of Strength for her to lean on. Therefore I choked down my Worry & Disgust when I saw what Newberry's dumb gunsel did to Dolores's bed. He did not care if it is the Innocent place a child sleeps & feels Safe he flipped it over on the side & the Bugs Bunny sheets strewn down with his Grimy Shoeprints all over! Where her soft pillow was before Nilo smashed a hole in the wall as big as a Basketball. Now I preserve my full Disgust for this Nasty Act.

"You see?" Amelia nodded me her I-told-you-so. "You see him now?" I took another look at her daughter's besmirched bed & Agreed about the Meaning of the whole Depraved Mess. Oh yes Newberry was Behind it but by my Analysis of the Scene of the Crime he was a long way behind it by then. At least I hoped Fervent that he took Dolores away from there when Tio was still Alive & when her bedroom was still the way she liked it for 8 Years old is too soon to know any bad Memories. Amelia put the Toy Chest up again very Tender she brushed her hand across the pieces of Dolores's toys. "She's no here Ray. Her favorite one. Her special toy I gave her." Amelia started Crawling around the floor picking up a dolly's leg then a scrap of Plastic & she turned these over in her fingers.

"Maybe Dolores took it with her. If it was her favorite." This did not cheer her up at all. "What do you think? If it was her special toy I don't think she'd leave it behind her. What do you think?"

She dropped the broken pieces back in the Toy Chest she Crawled in front of the open Closet not even steady on her hands & knees. So what did she have to Answer Me in Words? I know she Felt a hard kick in her stomach when she saw the messy pile of Dolores's clothes yanked down off the hangers. I heard her sharp growls when she pulled them out so they heaped up in her lap until it was the Empty floor there nothing else. Amelia hugged the Loose Skirts & Sleeves she Sighed into them.

"Can I do anything?" I said.

Amelia ignored me. She crawled inside the Closet. I heard a Sob from in there. Maybe it is better you should leave a person Alone in their Grief but you should not leave them Alone in their Closet. In about 5 Seconds I Decided on this being the right Idea even if I did not know what to say to coax her out but Amelia saved me the Trouble. She spoke up very Calm. "Get me a hammer."

"What did you say Amelia?"

"Go look in the kitchen somewheres. Under my sink. A hammer O.K.?"

"What for?"

She squeezed Halfway Out of the jammed closet door. "O.K.?"

Nilo probably used it to knock his Holes in the Wall Because I found the household hammer on top of a pile of plaster chips in the hallway. Outside the front door a few Scrawny kids played in the sprinklers Tag or whatever in & out of the Water. I did not have the Heart to tell them Scram I did not have the Energy to Worry about a soggy lawn.

"You find my hammer?" Amelia was sitting Indian style on the bathroom floor. In the cradle of her 2 hands she held on to a pink Burro all of paper mache. Like everything else in there Dolores's toy Donkey got cracked in Half kicked in the Guts his poor stomach crushed & open. "Dolores love him," she said & laid it down. Amelia smiled up at me with her eyes so Tranquil now with the shock Cleared Out of them. I handed the ballpeen to her. What did I know? She pounded that donkey to a pulp!

"No! Cut it out!" I grabbed her arm the next time she Raised it up. "Stop it! Calm down!" I figured she was going Delirious she was caught in temporary Hysteria from Grief & Woe.

Some kind of Emotion made her grip very Strong! Amelia beat the hammer down over & over until it was a worse day for pink burros than it was for her. She only Stopped when she mashed it flat as a dry Tortilla.

I let go of the handful of shower curtain I Clutched in the height of the moment but I am not a Daredevil so I did not say another Word. Also what Paralyzed me for a second was the fierce smile frozen on her lips. Nor it did not Melt either when she tossed the ballpeen down in front of my feet.

I picked it up quick. "How do you feel now?" I probed her. "You feel a little better after that?"

"Sure. Sure," Amelia said, "Better." Her smile left her mouth & Moved Up into her eyes. She Reached past me to drop the plug in the drain & turn the hot water on in the bathtub.

"That's a good idea," I told her. "Take a hot bath. A hot bath is a surefire relaxer. Amelia? You take it with bubbles?" I poked around in the cabinet to find some for her. "Is any bubblebath in here?" But she did not pay any Attention to me she just sat on the side of the tub flicking her fingers in the slow dribble of water which coughed out of the faucet.

Water pressure is not a Cosmic Mystery it all boils down to Plumbing pure & simple. All of the pipes are Connected below so the Solution was: Shut Off The Sprinklers. I heard the Desired Result behind me at once I Heard the hot water gush into Amelia's bathtub. Satisfaction for her Satisfaction for me too.

When I lifted my eyes what did I see? Nothing but Blue Skies Above & Sunshine soaking up the shadows of Tres Osos. This moment truly felt like the Perfect Ending to me. The Perfect time I should Disappear very mysterious what do I need a Symphony Orchestra for a Cue? The Story is over when it winds up on such a Happy Note—*how else?* Clear weather ahead of me & Satisfaction behind me! I leave a woman safe & sound who learned the valuable Moral that *The more you have the more you have to lose*—

Amelia I must Depart now it is time to say Good Bye! Remember how I answered when you called upon me to bring you home & here you are! So you may stand up on your own 2 Feet & build your Life upon the foundations of Truth & Honesty from now on! Good Bye! There is a time to Meet and a time to Part and now I must Return to Pecan St. where I will always keep you Safe in my Heart!

Or similar Sentiments I went back into the bathroom to say to her. I did not find her soaking I only found her in up to her arms. The steaming water was Dyed Pink going pinkest where she swilled her hands under the faucet. Something is cockeyed here! What is such a Dreamy Smile doing on her what is that Sticky Mess bubbling in the foam? With soggy little bits of it little curds of Pink Cottage Cheese floating up to the Surface! Good Move I did not Panic because in 5 Seconds I saw Amelia was not Bleeding by her wrists she was rubbing something under the water rubbing this thing very tough with her thumbs. She raised it out & swished off more of the Pink Curds then I made out she had the Carcass of Dolores's toy Donkey in the tub rub-a-dub-dubbing all the skin off its spread-out Flanks. "Look," she said.

Very slow the way a Photo Develops in the Lab something else came up before my eyes. Yellow paper wrapped up in Glad Wrap I counted 6 Strips Amelia pulled out. And she hugged them on her shirt to dry them also to Adore them. I could Guess What & I could Guess Why by how she leaned back on her elbows & let her head fall back & her eyes shut with her mouth open for a minute. All of her Energy escaped or dragged out of her Body by the hiss of a long slow Breath. She lay still & Rested. So she let her Thoughts of Dolores flood in & fill her up until they leaked out of her eyes drop by drop. I did not Intrude on Amelia for this was not the right moment for words of Farewell. Or a few seconds later when she sucked in a fresh Breath & sat up & came back to Life that was not the Right Moment either—

All of his Love Letters in his Handwriting is what those were Amelia put Newberry's personal Love Letters in my hands. What moxie in this Woman! "Now we make him bring Dolores back." She curled my fingers closed around that incriminating Evidence. "You can beat John now. With this power against him."

Let John Newberry tell you this is a Figment in my warped Mind then let him show you the Proof. Let him tell you what he wants I say he has his Reasons. He will pull out Expert Testimonies on me which he wrote out very neat on a typewriter the same as the rest of the lies in his Files. I DID NOT STAY BY HER SIDE BECAUSE OF WISHFUL THINKING NOR SHE DID NOT LURE ME INTO IT. I am the one who Knows the Motive of her words for the simple Reason *I was there*! I am the person with the flesh & blood Memory of it so MR. NEWBERRY DO NOT DO ME ANY FAVORS! I know what Amelia was saying when she Trusted Me Alone with your tender Love Letters the Lady was saying how she Yearned for my Fight against crime to be Continued. *This is not a thing of my Mind!* Even you can see she finally Meant to say how deep she Believed in me. So you can choke on it!

I want to tell you I am not a man who is against doing Manual Housework. I Admit on Pecan St. I did slip into a rut with Mrs. Roderiguez but what is the Point of basking in the dry Air if dusting is going to Irritate my Sinuses? Also vacuuming Interferes with my Reading which I do not count as a Medical Excuse but I put it up on the same Level. Under different Circumstances I did this work & I did not suffer so my Attitude toward it is different today i.e. if I was not going to Shoot Myself in the head in a few minutes I would start on the Dusting & Vacuuming in my own Apartment & save Mrs. Roderiguez the Trouble not to mention save myself $17.50 a week. A Lesson of Life coming too late to do me any Good!

I did not Consider it Housework the Dusting & Vacuuming I did in Amelia's house by me this was Fine Tuning. After the Masculine work of fixing her Furniture etc. pushing the vacuum cleaner over the carpet was Relaxation. Her King Size bed I put back together with a couple of Bricks under it I made it Solid as the Rock of Gibraltar. With the sheets & blankets back on your Naked Eye would not Believe this is the same bed a crazy lunkhead cut up with a Chainsaw I made it Perfect Again. No creases etc. The sofa was altogether another drawn-out Story! I tried it 9 Different Ways but I could not Compress that foam stuffing down to the Nth Degree required to make it all fit back Inside the cushions. The Extra I stuffed into a trash bag. With a beach towel wrapped around it turned into a Kingsize pillow which came in very handy later. Until night I worked on this job all the time Amelia was out Buying Food. And when she was in the kitchen cooking Dinner I already finished with the vacuum on the carpet

& I was in the middle of Dusting the coffee table then I Noticed here we are the Masculine & the Femuline Tradition side by side. Our house spic & span plus all the warm smells of Dinner such Satisfaction I never felt so Strong before!

Nor I never Felt so Contented compared to when we settled down on the livingroom floor to eat like a couple of Newlyweds who just moved in. Candles we had going & no other Light in there. (Not out of Worry either—for the Enjoyment! What was to worry about? Nilo was not going to come back in the door! The Light from the Candles Pushed everything else away into the Dark around us very Safe.)

Eating is a wonderful Event for 2 people to do Together—eat a meal with somebody Near & Dear and see it is a Tested fact the Enjoyment is Double. You can Experiment and Prove it. Eat your meal on a T.V. tray by yourself in front of your T.V. & you can even switch the T.V. set on then eat the same meal across from a person you Care For then you will see what a Difference! I liked it Better with her. I tasted every bite TWICE Because I knew Amelia had the same Morsels in her mouth at the same time—the Sparkle of Hot Chilli on our tongues e.g. —"Mm-mm" as she says & I know for sure how she Feels.

"You like frijoles hm?"

"I like these," I said with a mouthful. "I know a poem about beans."

"About refry beans?"

"It can apply."

"I know some poems by your Walt Whitman."

"That kind of thing. Only not on such a high level." I scooped up another Forkload & closed my lips around it. "Mm-mm," the stuff went down as smooth as Peanut Butter. And a Tangy Taste stays behind. I could eat a dish of them right now No Kidding. "I don't know if I should recite it to you." When she asked me why not I told her it was a Indecent poem which only made Amelia open her eyes & ears very Eager to hear my Recital. So I did not hold anything back I gave it to her with a real Announcer's Voice—"Beans! Beans! The musical fruit! The more you eat them

377

the more you toot! The more you toot the better you feel! So let's eat beans at every meal!"

"Too fast!" She waved her hands at me Smiling Hard with her lips pressed tight Trying to swallow & Trying to say, "You did it too fast! Tell me again . . . "

She made me Repeat it over plus Explain every word in Detail. I tried to go Delicate when I came to the *toot* part but this Effort was a big waste of Energy since the whole idea of tooting handed her the most Enormous Laugh I ever Heard! She has Tears in her eyes & she is rolling around on her side gasping for Air! And the whole time what am I doing? I am shoveling more refrieds into my mouth so now I must be on my 3rd Portion so when she sees me filling up on those beans she starts Laughing even harder! Imagining the Consequences so to say.

Now I Notice this meal was practically the only time with her when both of us Forgot about our Worries. For a minute the World Beyond left us alone together no Regret from the Past or Fear from the Future broke in on us. So now I Discover the Secret of Happiness! A person can not Recognize it until After!

When she caught her Breath Amelia invited me, "Try this salsa." She showed me how & ate some herself. "Mm-mm."

I dipped the lucky Tortilla in & let it suck up the Sauce. To the Naked Eye tomatoes & onions. To the Naked Tongue a red hot Blowtorch! A Rocket Exhaust! A Branding Iron! "Argh! Ptui! Ptui! Argh!" & that was all the Sense I made for the time being which hit Amelia very Comic & generally creased her up. A few minutes + a entire bottle of Beer later I was flat on my back on the floor & I only had enough Strength in my limp Muscles to lift my head up & Sneeze. I lay there breathing through my mouth & Amelia looked over at me across the carpet a little worried.

"My salsa made you sick?"

"That's something," I said, "we probably won't know for years. Who knows what the longterm effects are?" I sneezed again.

She reached her hand over & stroked the Side of my Head. "Oh pobrecito . . . "

"It's probably just the dust in my nose. From dusting in here before. I think the fumes from that sauce just stirred it up."

"All my fault," she whined out a Mockery of Misery. "I'm sorry forever."

"Forget about it. I feel better now." I wiped my nose on a paper napkin & Expected to see a Streak of Blood there. "Dr. Godfrey advised me to lay off of spicy foods."

"I didn't have to make it," she Apologized.

"I didn't have to eat it."

"No. I didn't have to make it so hot," she said & a Gentle smile followed her Words out.

"You fixed it how you like it. You didn't know." I was only looking into her eyes then this Question came up so fast in my Empty Mind it Escaped out of my mouth before I could do anything: "Did you mean it what you said to me back at the car? About being in bed with me?"

Her smile sank back but what stayed on the Surface was Brave & Tender. Amelia let such a silent look keep me Occupied then I could tell how the Answer had to come to her from a long Distance away.

I Believe that silence was booming in our ears Because neither of us Heard the front door Open. Therefore I do not Know exactly how long Dolores was standing there Watching Us from the hallway. She held still like a Wild Bird we coaxed out of the trees with breadcrumbs she kept her eye on us very Careful. To see what was what in the dim Light before she made a Further Move.

"Dolores?" Amelia sat up to say. Her shaky tone of Voice did not mean *Are you really here?* it meant *Are you really here alone?*

Dolores turned her head a quick ½ inch she shifted her look Toward Me. I Felt it rake me over from behind the Veil of her short hair all Messed Forward across her face. Then the only Move she made was she raised her hand up to her mouth & pressed out a spritz from her Asthma Inhaler.

This sore sight yanked Amelia's arms up like they were on wires and Dolores ran right into her Máma's bear hug. She ran by me so Fast I could be a Shadow Hanging in the middle of the room. They hugged each other Very Close & I Heard Amelia's sobs of Joy it was such a beautiful scene to Behold. By my eyes as fine as a famous Painting with Amelia on her knees & Dolores standing

379

up tall in her arms. Nor Dolores did not sob a Tear she stroked her Mama's hair she Comforted her she patted Amelia's shaking back. What was the Story here? behind her dirty bare feet & both of her knees scraped raw—how Dolores held up the Emotional bundle of her Mama in her tiny arms & down below she crossed her foot behind her leg & Scratched Around very casual. Let me tell you this little girl had a lot of her Papa in her.

"He is Senor Ray." Amelia brushed the tangled hairs out of Dolores's face & turned her around to Greet me.

"Hello dollface," I said very soft. Except Dolores was not in the mood to take in anything new so no Reply. She drooped her head she stared down at the carpet & her Hair Flopped over her eyes again. Amelia clung on to Dolores's limp hand & wagged it to get her to say Hello to me but I told her, "She doesn't have to now. Not if she doesn't want."

Better they should pow-wow Alone in their own Language & no Interference from 3rd Parties so I washed the dishes in the kitchen. I heard the sad Details of what Happened from the pony's own mouth later & if such Events happened to me when I was a little child maybe I would Forget all of my Nice Manners too. From the Sound of it I do not Believe they Expected to run into Tio there nor they did not come for a Fight. Nilo plus a pair of local Muchachos knocked on the door very polite with a sledge-hammer while Meanwhile in the back Tio was pushing Dolores out of her bedroom window. Nobody saw her run up on top of the hill behind her house so she squatted down & Watched them from Afar—in the frame of her window she saw Nilo smash up her bedroom then she saw those Muchachos push Tio into a car & drive him away. Of all the things in this World a baby girl should Eye Witness!

"Maybe you should tuck her in," I said when I saw Dolores curled up in the crook of her Mama's arm. "I did a perfect job on her room. Clean sheets on her bed too. Rabbit ones. It's like new in there."

Amelia pressed a chain of Kisses & Soft Words over Dolores's forehead which woke her up. "Hm?" she jerked her head up and you know she said this Expression exactly like her Mama does. She was only ½ awake & here is the thing of Children how they Trust Us when they are in a Daze how they look toward us to Guide them. Dolores let Amelia pull her off of the sofa & go past me hand in hand.

So what was it then that all of a sudden turned a groggy little Munchkin into a Screeching Wild animal? "Nuh! Nuh! Nuh! Nuh!" this Alarm made me drop my dirty dishes & run to her Side. I almost cursed Out Loud from Amazement I did not Predict Nilo could pull the oldest cheapest trick a Hood can pull—JUST SNEAK IN BEHIND MY BACK & HIDE IN THE CLOSET!

Dolores's raspy Cries stuck in the back of her throat with the Sound of a whistling top Winding Down. As soon as she saw me standing there she stopped Kicking at Amelia instead she dug her heels into the carpet & locked her knees—she dug her fingers into the door jamb & Locked her arms Stiff—this Angry baby donkey belting out "N-nuh! No! N-nuh!"

Acting Up like this was a scary Surprise this Wild Behavior put a jolt of Fear through Amelia. She backed up & gave Dolores a Breathing space so she did not over-excite her into a Asthma Attack. Nobody was jumping out of any closet around there so I stayed out of the Argument until Amelia illuminated me: "She's scared of her bed." Dolores wrapped her arms around Amelia's waist for Protection as if I was the Bogeyman From Hell coming to Force Her. "Senor Ray made your room so pretty for you," her Mama tried Persuading her.

"That's blackmail," I said under a smile. Which Dolores did not see but she Heard whose Side I was on by this. For she grabbed all of my Sympathy since I saw what was up with her it was the rotten Memory of Nilo in her room still in there like a Rotten Smell. Some Invisible mark he left Behind some Disturbance in the Atmosphere. Memory is the 6th Sense I believe.

"She want to sleep in the big bed," Amelia said, "with her Mama."

This Bulletin did not need a Reply but I Agreed what a Good Idea and I bent down to say to Dolores, "I don't want to sleep in there either." My Confession did not Impress her (smart kid!)

& she just nuzzled deeper into Amelia's dress. So Dolores did not see her Kiss me on the cheek for Good-Night.

"You can go sleep in her bed," she offered me.

"I don't think she'd like that. I'll sleep out here. I'm fine on the sofa."

The girls turned their backs on me very Weary. Amelia let the bedroom door sway open but Dolores came back and Banged it Shut. I do not Blame her for this Move. I know from my personal Life there is a time to be Public and a time to be Private & privacy is worth its Weight in Gold. I just never slammed a door in anybody's face like a Barbarian who does not Care how it can make a person Feel Left Out. I Excuse Dolores. Look at it from her Angle. Inside the big bedroom was her own dear Mama. Outside was the Grinning Idiot who cleaned the house & washed the dishes.

Dolores being there Changed everything. So Newberry did not get away with her afterall she was home & this was a Big Relief. I did not Dare & bask in it since this did not Mean the end of all our Trouble it Meant here we go again. He was going to make a Move oh yes! he Knew it & so did I. Only I did not Know what his Move was going to be. At least Experience informed me he would wait for us to catch our Breath and strike when we started Breathing Easy. The power of a Crime Stopper is Equal to his Power of Thinking the way a criminal Thinks. Be he a Criminal Genius like Newberry or a Criminal Dunce like Nilo. Every crook has got his own M.O. and if I was going to outsmart John Newberry I had to crawl under his Skin. So with all of this to Think about after 5 Minutes I did not mind it out on the sofa by myself it was a better Arrangement since I was 100% Awake & full of beans.

My usual Routine is reading before I close my eyes for the Night. My Advice is go to sleep with a new Idea in your Mind & while you snooze it plants itself & sends out roots you might say. The Reading Matter of the Night in question practically sat up & begged for my Attention. All the Clues of Newberry's Character & the pattern of his Past Behavior stared at me from the pages of his Love Letters. Believe me I cherish the American

Ideal which stands up against the invasion of Privacy but I Plead with you do not Judge Me by this devious Act. It was a *necessity* I broke into them on account of special Circumstances as anybody will Admit!

He was a different man in Word & Deed in the Beginning. He wrote to Amelia full of Compassion & Understanding he showed how much he could Sympathize with her. Newberry told her it was greatly Unfair she should Suffer & be poor her whole Life because of where she was Born. And by the way how she is a Beautiful Woman with brains to match—

! QUOTE → "You are a *beautiful* woman. Why don't you put your beautiful brains to good *use*? I know I can help you somehow."

! QUOTE → "The rewards from the system are only *part* of the score. The nabobs pay us off for punching in and not asking any questions. I've been asking a few g.d. impertinent questions. I know how to squeeze out the really big rewards now. The ones you have to ask for at the back door."

He Wrote to her about his Wife & Family for instance when his baby girl Michelle was born—

! QUOTE → "I held my daughter in my arms today. It felt like my whole life made perfect sense at that moment. I'm a father! Wow! I'm a family man! When Michelle's pink little fingers grabbed my thumb I felt so *responsible*."

Also at the bottom of this same letter he does not hold back his Further Feelings—

! QUOTE → "In the hospital I sat next to her bed. My one and only thought should have been about my wife and baby daughter. I love them both dearly. I can't imagine living without them. But

383

another thought came out of nowhere and went through me like a knife. How different my life could have been if I met you first. Amelia. Amelia. Amelia. I'm sure I'd be thinking at a time like this how beautiful life is with you."

Now he will Deny his Words but these flattering Remarks & kind Offers he made to her came Direct from his Heart I believe. Newberry did not start out having sneaky Motives toward Amelia he only had wholesome Intentions at first. In my opinion Curiosity + Sympathy led him on to Romance the Romance led him on to Desire then Desire led him on to Greed. This is my personal Theory. If you Measure them for 1,000 Years you will not find 2 Human Beings with Identical size arms to each other i.e. Individuals do not all carry around a Equal amount of this World. A person is going to find out his Personal Limit on the day he asks for too much.

Newberry had his arms full already with his Regular Job & his Regular Family. He should have stuck to this but he Desired Amelia too. And more & more etc. I ask you is a Man like a Starfish? Can a Human Being grow his arms longer? Can he Fight Nature no! he will bow to Nature! Leave it to the World to teach him a Lesson! It always takes the Extra away. (Some other person e.g. one day could Desire a Family of his own nothing Fancy only the Benefits of the basic model i.e. someplace he knows he Belongs nor I do not mean a Apartment or just a area of household Geography I mean a place with intimate Voices in residence & familiar faces who Miss Him when he is Apart or Welcome him when he comes in the door—persons who Recognize him from a Distance you might say so he is not just somebody in the Crowd. So then he finds out his arms are too short to carry this size of Happiness and the World has to obey the Laws of Nature & grabs it back out of his hands. The World tells him, "Desire is not enough! Your arms have to be the right size!")

I will tell you what else about Desire it is not the same as Hope. I tell you Hope means you Wait & See. Desire is a bug that makes you force Events. Therefore a person can Desire a wholesome thing that turns Inside Out as soon as he pulls it Close.

This is the Idea I contemplated after I stuffed his Letters under the towel of my pillow to sleep on them. Step by step that way I traced Newberry's inner thoughts from the very Beginning. How he used to Feel for Amelia & Dolores etc. I found out the Facts. But the only sure-fire manner I Knew of to tune in his particular M.O. was Step In Where He Stepped Out. So I let my Contemplation wander over to the other side of the bedroom wall. Meanwhile I lay down & kept still then I could Hear them murmur so Intimate Together back where they Belong lying in each other's arms in their Family Home. I.e. the perfect time Amelia should tell Dolores I am not the cleaning man per se I am the man who Answered her Prayers & reunited them tonight. And was I finished with my beneficial Deeds yet? No Dolores! Rest in peace!

The Green Ray never sleeps!

I Scrounged around the kitchen drawers & dug out some glue & nails & string and for the rest of the Night I worked on a few of Dolores's toy puppets which did not end up in Tiny Pieces. A skinny man in a top hat & tails. A fat woman with a bowl of Tropical Fruit on her head. A chalk white Donkey with a Sombrero. All of the cracked edges had Splinters on them which took the glue & held together perfect so her wooden Friends were ready & waiting to say Hello when Dolores woke up in the morning.

I tell you this. Until Dolores I never was very much around Children of any Description so I was a ignorant Amateur at comprehending childish Behavior. I *do not* claim I am a Expert at it now on my Experience from last week! I Regret I never got around to the works of Dr. Spock in my Readings since I would like to Compare my Findings. If I had the time left I could go into this Subject deeper & work on the Fine Print of my Theory which I call The Theory Of Babyish Behavior. By my Study I Observe when you look at Children truly you are peeking at the hidden Behavior of the World. Furthermore the younger they are the better which you can see this Phenomenon in Action. I Claim a Human Being does not outgrow his Babyhood he just learns mature monkey business to cover it up & I Claim you strive for the same Comforts from the Beginning to the middle to the end. A Baby in his diapers Desires the same as the Chairman of the Stock Market.

Unless this magic key I Discovered only applies to Dolores Defuentes then in such a Case I am still a Ignoramous! Ha Ha Ha. Some surprise *that* would be! I ask you Dr. Spock did I do what you Advise i.e. 1st I treated Dolores like a Person and 2nd I treated her like a Child I tried to Educate & Protect. Let me Inform you for your Statistics this approach made her open her Heart up to me & no sourness came between us over our Entire Acquaintance.

I say Further what I learned by knowing Dolores. It is the real Wonder of Life how a certain pair can meet & they Recognize lifelong understanding is Staring Them in their Eyes. In a Flash this occurs it is Mutual in a blink. This is my Belief. If somebody will let it Appear this is where a person's Soul floats up. I will state it on the Record I never saw Amelia's Soul float up to me in her eyes instead it was always a Shadow in there.

The Joke is on me! Out of both of them what does it turn out? It turns out the particular pair like what I describe is *Dolores* & me! THERE MUST BE A SCIENTIFIC EXPLANATION OF THIS EFFECT! E.g. maybe beams of Electricity are in motion when Souls recognize each other or is it Gravity? in a small form it can be the same mechanicals that make Planets attract & circle i.e. the Physical Attraction of Personal Atoms? I know this can be between a Husband & Wife pair when they fall in Love or between a Mother & her Baby at her Breast this is easy for me to Comprehend. Tell me how come this Happens between a 66 Year old man (Retired) & a 8 Year old baby girl!

By my Calculations we could count on staying safe in Tres Osos for 24 Hours further. This temporary Vacation from our Dark World of Worry was a boon to the front lawn at least I am happy to say. Gardening is not a favorite Hobby of mine by any Extension of the Facts but as of now I can see the Appeal. All the time my hands were busy planting back the divots those kids dug out of the grass I looked over my Repair Job & got a kick of Satisfaction

I put that torn up lawn back in Order. Then Nature takes over from the Roots up & finishes the work voila.

Out on the lawn I did not even stew for a single minute on the fact Dolores Ignored her puppets which I put up in Lifelike poses on the easy chair. Instead she stayed in the kitchen & helped her Mama cook breakfast which was all American (Sunny Side Up Eggs) in my Honor. Besides I could see into her Serious Character which I Observed this Sample: Amelia being Frisky with her for a joke she dropped a towel over Dolores's head. Dolores did not say Boo she did not laugh or whine either she just tugged it off & folded it & Laid It Down on the Counter. By this slow Gesture she gave off her Message "Stop it now. Enough of this horsing around."

Listen to this:

I push down a flap of wet grass & the next time I look up I see Dolores in front of me with a bottle of Beer in her hand. Her eyes are glued on me like she just caught me in the Act of stealing her lawn instead of Fixing It. She takes a long pull from the bottle & fills up her mouth until her cheeks puff out before she Swallows.

"Does your mama allow you beer?"

Dolores wipes her mouth on her wrist & looks Behind her. Then she holds the bottle out to me. "She said give this to you," she answers me.

I Tease her by a mild kind of Sarcasm. "Sure you're finished with it?"

"My arm's tired." Dolores is still holding the bottle out in front of her with the Idea any second this Offer is going to Expire.

"Gracias." I wipe off the Rim before I drink out of it which is a Natural Reflex all over the Animal Kingdom but she takes it personal & puckers her mouth to show me.

"I don't have germs," she says.

"Everybody has germs."

"I don't have."

"Movie stars have germs. Even the ones who sell toothpaste. They have germs in the mouth."

All of a sudden she is more Interested in Gardening. "What are you doing that for?"

I tuck in the edges of another lump of brown-green Grass. "See the roots? Those are still good. So they'll grow back. A week from now you can look at this lawn & it'll be like new." I kidded her, "We should put up a Keep Off The Grass sign so your friends don't run around all over it again."

"They're not my friends," Dolores warns me I got it all wrong, "those Mexican kids."

If I say any Further on this Topic I am asking for Trouble so all I do is Remark how those boys & girls are not the best Friends a front lawn ever had either. By now Dolores wants me to think she can take or leave a Conversation with me no sweat & very Nonchalant she digs into the front pocket of her bluejeans. When she pulls her hand out she comes up with a Walnut which is about ½ the size of her fist. This she pushes all the way into her mouth & closes her lips around it & Chomps Down. The CRACK I hear is not her Molars or her jaw—Dolores spits out the sharp chunks of brown shell & the rest of that Walnut into her hand. "Want some?"

I shake my head. "Doesn't that hurt your teeth?"

"Nuh-uh." She chews on it by Quick Bites like a squirrel sitting on a safe branch. Out of nowhere she asks me, "What's your favorite food?"

Honesty is the best Policy especially when it comes to Questions of this nature since 9 Times Out Of 10 your answer is out of your mouth before you Ponder it. "Prune Whip," I say. "What's yours?"

"Walnuts." And she crunches another one in her teeth. The crack is so Sharp I hear it through my Gums!

Dolores crunches & munches and I plug in a couple more divots then lo & behold—what is Underneath this patch of mud I dig up? like the Free Surprise in a box of Crackerjacks look what I find.

"Let me see," Dolores pulls my arm over to look at the tiny Treasure I am rubbing the dirt off with my thumbs.

"It's a fossil. Look at that. A fossil of a fern plant or—"

"*What* is?" she whines to see & whines to Understand.

I pour some Beer over it & clean off the rest of the dirt & Show It to her in the Light. "For a minute I thought we had a toeprint. It's a fern all right. A fossil fern."

She touches it. "It's a rock."

"Sure it's a rock. It's a fossil fern." I put it in her hand.

"It looks like a leaf."

"That's what it is."

This Idea pickles her & she hands it back to me. "It's a rock," is her firm Opinion.

"You never saw a fossil before?" Dolores gives me some silence & her Serious Attention i.e. she is going to listen to me as long as I am not Teasing her with this. And so for the 1st time in her Life she hears all about The Story Of Fossils. "How old are you Dolores?"

"I'm 8."

"A big girl already." She shrugs away my Compliment. "Now I'm 8 times as old as you. Plus 2 years. I'm 66 years old. You think it was a long time ago when I was born?"

"Yes."

"You bet. Compared to you it's a long time ago. The world was a different kind of place then. Before T.V. was invented. Or washing machines. But compared to this fossil 66 years is nothing. It's a flash in the pan. Add up your age plus my age then multiply it by a million and that's how long ago for this fossil. You wouldn't even recognize this area back that far. All over here was covered by a swamp. Look. Where the hills are now? You know what?" Dolores squints the Sun out of her eyes & looks up at the brown hill behind her house. "Underwater," I tell her. "And palm trees growing in the sand. With fern plants soaking up the free moisture. Sure. All around here it was quicksand & dragonflies like a regular garden of Eden."

"Where did they go?"

"Everything died."

"Why did it?"

"The experts don't all agree on the reason but . . . " and I tell her all the main Points which I Remember from a Article I read in the Reader's Digest fairly recent about the Prehistoric Climate but it does not Satisfy her.

"You're making it up," she decides.

"Honest Dolores I'm not either." I present her the genuine

Evidence which is the Fossil. "You've got a piece of the history of the Earth there. It's proof of what lived here before. It's a marvelous thing. A permanent record of what happened then."

She shakes the hair out of her eyes & quizzes me, "What happened to it?"

And I describe how the Ancient fern plant died & sank down into the layer of mud also I Demonstrate by way of a couple of mud pies to help Dolores picture the whole Process. "A new layer of mud lands on top & sandwiches down so heavy it turns the mud into this sandstone with the fern leaf in the middle. A little thing that was alive such a long time ago left its mark. From then until now & now we find it. Such a marvelous thing." When I say those Words the Idea sends a cold shiver through me as if I am hearing the echo of my own Voice & I Notice how Dolores is in her Rights if she thinks I am drifting off & talking to myself! She hands the Fossil back to me but I fold her fingers over it. "For you," I say.

"Hold it for me," Dolores pushes it back so she can reach into her pocket for another Walnut which she pops straight into her mouth. CR-CRACK then she shows me how this time she split it down the middle right on the Money. "I get 10 points," she declares. I Observe her Voice is rough & sticking in the back of her throat.

"Careful of the shells." She nods & chews up her Walnut. Since we are on friendly terms a Personal question occurs to me so I ask her, "Didn't you notice something different in the livingroom when you woke up?"

"Nuh-uh."

"On the easy chair."

Dolores pushes a few loose Walnut crumbs from her bottom lip back into her mouth. "What?" she says & looks away from me.

"Didn't you see I fixed your puppets?"

"I don't play with them anymore."

"No? Why not?"

"I outgrew them."

"Well that really surprises me Dolores. I mean it. When I was 8 I only dreamed about having puppets like those to play with."

390

She lets her head dip forward & hides her face under her dangling hair. Dolores avoids the Subject of her puppets by this snappy Move so I play it her way Because I am not fishing for Gratitude. Also I Observe I did not lose her Attention for nothing—she has her eyes on a fly which is crawling very happy-go-lucky up her arm. Her Papa will not Contradict me if I Remark this about Dolores: Noah did not handle animals better. Noah & Clyde Beatty put together! She let that fly think he landed in the middle of a deserted beach on the French Riviera! With waiter service! She lets him Relax on her arm & soak up the Sunshine—then Whips her hand down on him so fast he goes out cold! "I'll tame it," she tells me & lifts him up by his Wings. Except she is not speaking of this fly which is coming back to Consciousness now—she means a sandy brown Lizard perched about a foot away. Dolores moves so slow & Delicate she does not scare him off not with the shadow of her arm or the buzzing fly pinched in her fingers. She stops with it a Inch in front of the Lizard's mouth. "Come on boy," her Voice squeeks at him, "Come on. Jump up. Jump up boy. Jump . . . Jump . . . " Like a trained dog it jumps up! Grabs the fly & sits comfy cozy in the palm of her hand for Dolores to pet him on his head.

This gag of hers deserves Investigation! "Can I pet him?"

"He won't let you."

"You know this reptile from before?" I reach my fingertips over at the same time she lets him drop out of her hand. He hits the ground & springs back into the Wilds. "You could take that act on the road."

Dolores does not Know what I mean by this but she Knows I just handed her a Compliment and she Returns me a smile before she rewards herself with another Walnut.

CR-CR-ACK!

I did not hear Amelia's footsteps stop Behind Me until I saw Dolores jerk her head up & stop chewing. The Walnut pieces pushed her cheeks out so even with the Innocent look that went with holding her Breath she did not shame Amelia out of her hot Temper. If the Virgin of Guadalupe appeared out of the sky & bestowed a Halo over Dolores's head & named her Child Of The

Year all she would hear from Amelia is the Mexican version of "Sez you!" and "Butt out!" Which message she Flashed Me in her eyes when all I said very Calm was, "Hey-hey . . . " at the point Amelia shook Dolores's jaw very rough.

Her own jaw clenched tight then she said to me, "It make her sick!"

Bits of Walnut sprayed out of Dolores's mouth & she bent over sucking back the Air—her raspy rough wheezing was Terrible!—in a second she went gulping for Breath & a second later her face was puffy almost the color of a Red Cabbage—

"Jesus! Does this happen all the time?"

Amelia was helping Dolores up to her feet but she turned around to scold me, "She's no allow walnuts!" And she slapped me with a dirty look that also Flared Up with Panic.

So now I Know how that stunned fly felt! But I shook off this slap in a hurry & followed them into the house. I ask you what *goes on* with certain Individuals sometimes? With their Emotions mixed up like Acrobats inside them all tumbling over & under to be the one on top. All of that Frenzy holding still!

Dolores was Doubled Over on her knees in front of the sofa and now I did not hear her exhaling only inhaling hard Breaths. By the Sound it could not be harder for her if she was trying to inhale a brick. Her pink pillbox handbag laid open & all of her choice Belongings she spilled out of it very Desperate she was scrabbling in them but Amelia just stood still by the door *watching Dolores suffer!*

"Help her—" I said very Astonished nor I did not move in. And why? Such a sight is beyond Belief & it Paralyzed me where I stood also I do not butt in where a Mother is Best. "Aren't you going to help her?"

Amelia told me off, "Let her do it! She can. I want *her* to!"

By no Stretch will I let anybody tell me a suffering Child deserves a Punishment! This is Opposite to my Creed. And before you open your mouth I state this Issue goes beyond Walnuts. "What's wrong with you?" I cursed Amelia & I kneeled down next to Dolores on the floor. "O.K. dear . . . O.K. dear . . . " some Help I was to her with this feeble Expression meanwhile she is stretched out on her stomach clawing at the pile of her Valuables. And kicking my arms away when I try to hold her & Comfort her.

Amelia's Voice went quiet & weak she almost cried to herself, "So she can do it Ray . . . When she is alone anytimes . . ." I only Heard every other Word of this then I caught the Meaning when she said it over again.

Now I saw what Dolores was clutching at when she pulled her arms against her chest & her hands over her mouth it was the plastic tube of her Asthma Medicine nor she did not need anybody's help to use it she gave herself a Good hard spritz. In a second a Breath squeezed out of her as rough as sandpaper & the Breath right after came smoother then she was Breathing Regular but this big Effort wore her out. You could see more Energy in a limp lettuce leaf. But those hot red patches Evaporated on her cheeks & some pale putty color came back which looked like a big Improvement to me. I lifted her head very Gentle & I let it stay on my lap where I could stroke her hair until I Heard her Breathe Easy again. This is what I was Thinking then: *A bad Memory is forming like a bubble in her Mind—this bad Memory of the dizzy moment she was suffering & her Mama did not Help her.* My inner Powers melted down here so I could not look Amelia in her face I did not want to see her Regret so absent there.

Dolores came around about a minute later & broke the ice of the Silence by her groggy Moans. She woke up talking Mexican. I kept my eyes on her & I said, "What'd she say? What's she want?"

"She want her purse," Amelia answered me.

"I can't reach it from here."

So Amelia bent down & gathered Dolores's items & put them all back together then a few more Quiet Words of Espanol rolled past me. Now these sounded tender between Mother & Child.

"Is she all right?" I looked up this time. "Amelia?" And I saw by her eyes how I misthought her Motives I saw how I sold her short. Or maybe I am looking back on her this way for I see how Amelia did try and Protect her little girl. She was trying to Prevent Dolores from Depending which is a Wise Move I believe. To keep her from the harm of Expecting anybody to help her in a Emergency.

"She says about you Ray."

"What's that?"

Amelia translated: *Mama. I like him. He no shouts at you.*

"Why should I shout?" I heard my Voice going shaky. I said to Dolores, "What's going on I should shout about it?" I opened up the lid of her Purse so she could put her Medicine in.

She held her purse open when I tried to close it. "I want to show you," Dolores said.

I recognized the Privilege of this. "Sure. Show me. What've you got in there doll?"

"Old things." She took out a Wristwatch on a brown leather strap. Most of the stitches were split nor it did not Tick. "It's my antique."

"What time's it say on there?"

"Not a time."

"It doesn't run at all?" She shook her head. "It's exactly right twice a day then."

Dolores dropped it back in & pulled out a bunch of rusty Keys. She twisted the oldest one out of the rest then she just barely opened her mouth to tell me something about it when a raw Shriek tore out of her Throat. Out of Nowhere I mean it broke through like a Oil Gusher with a stream of giggles gurgling up after it! You will be Surprised like I was: Dolores was Laughing at my dumb watch Joke! Back went the keys & out came the watch again and she was looking at it like she never saw it that way Before. Listen to this Question she asks me — "How many watches do I need for a whole day?"

Her other prized Article was a shiny Silver Dollar which she rubbed on her shirt before she Displayed it to me on the palm of her hand. "It's lucky."

"Is a genie going to come out of it now?"

"Nuh-uh." Then she all of a sudden realized she did not understand about a Genie & she jerked her head up smiling, "What?"

"With wishes. A big guy in a puff of smoke with a towel on his head & shoes that look like bananas." That smile of hers unsettled

& Quivered on Dolores's lips while she tried to Figure why kindly Uncle Ray was about to pull the rug out from under her. So I jumped in quick. "How lucky's it been so far?"

"Lucky," she shrugged.

"Tell me something lucky that's happened with it."

She sat up & Remembered, "The fossil we found!"

I hugged her. "You're my lucky charm." I laughed out her Name & she stayed in my arms this time Laughing & Hugging as hard as I did. I dug the Fossil out of my pocket for her I was very Proud it rated so High next to her lucky Silver Dollar. Then a sour Idea rose in my Mind. "Your papa gave it to you?" She nodded Yes. "Just this one? This special one?"

Dolores went on nodding. "So I always have a dollar."

"From now on you'll always have a fossil too," I said. "A lucky fossil."

My true Role in her Life started from this Episode. As far as Dolores went I was there for Loco Parentis and as far as I went I took this Responsibility very Serious. I do not Regret it if it looks like I Forced things this way & took over from her Legal Guardians so what look at the unbiased Evidence. How all of the memories I brought to her Mind are happy ones (except 1 single Catastrophe). I will dare & say Further also I added something Beautiful in the World. i.e. I added a Child to the population with enough Hope & Education & Good Memories inside her they balance out all the Rotten.

Before her nap before Dinner while she sat & Recovered from her Asthma Attack I entertained Dolores with her Puppets. I acted out a special version of the True Story Of The Blackout. The Donkey portrayed my part & the Fat Lady with the bowl of fruit on her head I cast her in the part of Amelia. I Censored out all of the violent parts of the Story i.e. Nilo & Perry i.e. the hitting etc. but I left in the barking Voice of Princess The Dog to give it a hint of Danger.

I told Dolores this way:

When all the Lights went out the Fat Lady was going to town to sell her exotic fruits. She always made a tidy Profit by this Business which was a Well Known Fact in the Area. But in the

Dark by herself all of a sudden the Invisible footsteps all over the streets made her very Nervous & she lost her way which made her nervous Double. The Donkey did not mind the Blackout since it was a Opportunity for a quiet stroll around his Neighborhood & when he ran into the Fat Lady she was running around in circles going Ay-yi-yi. In spite of the sad Fact in his early Life this Donkey was a man who got Mocked & misthought of by his own Family so many times he fell under a Spell that made him this way he was still usually a Help.

Therefore he Helped her out of her Jam and by & by the pair of them ended up as best Friends. Which was a lucky twist in this Case since they landed in a adventure where they got chased over hill & dale by The Skinny Guy with the Sombrero. This led up to the Grand Finale when they faced a Showdown but when things looked pretty Bleak for the Donkey in a surprise Move he turned around & kicked that guy out of the ballpark. For the Happy Ending the Fat Lady planted a wet Kisseroo right on the Donkey's nose and then guess what—*presto change-o* he Disappears behind the sofa & comes back up in his True form of a Real Man. (For this Effect I had to use The Skinny Guy with the Sombrero again but for this double Role I brought him back minus the Sombrero.)

Dolores got such a big kick out of my Performance she right after took her Puppets in bed with her. She did not want to be away from those dear Characters for a minute. Even when I tucked her in she begged me I should talk to her in my Donkey Voice & no other! Up close & face to face when I told her "Close your eyes now" & Dolores tried to hold them open I saw how I was Looming There. This is how I have such a Confidence to say on the Record no doubt about it I Endeared very strong to Dolores that day & Dolores Endeared likewise to me. Nor I do not Rely on a imaginary Appearance in her eye for the Facts were all around her the way she gathered her Puppets around her pillow she looked Toward them with so much Affection especially the Donkey I got the Definite Idea she was only going to get separated from them again by extreme Force. I Reunited a little girl & her toys I Reunited her & her Mama so what is that something I should be Sorry For? How I let a Child go to sleepy-bye with my

Story circling around in her Memory with my Voices keeping her company so she could Feel Safe & Sound with no Troubles hounding her? I just made sure Dolores could take her Innocent nap like every tired out tike Deserves I made sure she did not have any Worries. Or Fears either about anything Unpredictable happening to her so she can rest Secure in her bed.

The ground is solid underneath & the sky is clear above the World is not upsidedown the Law Of Gravity still Applies here! And it will always be this way as long as there is Gravity in the Universe there will be Justice! Innocent Motives protect the Good at Heart & selfish Motives will bring the criminals crashing down in Punishment so nap in Peace my dear one! All Because of me she went to sleep very glad since I convinced her Tomorrow is going to be even brighter than Today—

THAT'S ENTERTAINMENT!

"You always want somethings different. You run around and catch somethings then you want it different."

"Who?"

"You." Amelia pointed a dripping spoon at my chest. "Men."

"That's some opinion," I said. "Are you including pygmies & Eskimos?"

"All of you men. Sure. The same way."

"It's a ridiculous statement you're making," I said & I tried to keep this Conversation on a Academic level. "Concentrate for a second & see if you can think of 1 exception. Out of the entire masculine population of the World a single specimen."

She stopped stirring the refrieds & showed me she was fishing in her Memory to come up with the Name & the Face of some man she knew who Said what he Meant & Meant what he Said to her start to finish. After a few quiet seconds she gave up and did not give me Another Word she just went back to her Cooking.

"Excuse me," I said, "I'm not like those men you mean." She buzzed her lips & belittled my Remark which this only egged me on to put it Stronger, "I'm not like other men."

"Normal men act like that. The normal way for them hm?"

"I'm not a normal man!"

"You run around this way sure. You chase somethings like a normal man. You catch it then you see this other things over there so you run & catch them too. I think men don't want to get satisfy ever. Afraid you stop. You stop then you can no get this other things all the other men can go catch." Then she said down to the frying pan, "Waste of love. Waste of women."

"I'm not saying you don't have a right to think about John Newberry that way. And forget about me for a minute. What about Tio? You include him the same?"

"I tell you a thing you're no going to believe it. You think Tio is Santa Claus?"

I did not Judge the Illegal Business he was in with her. Next to the horrible way he ended up I Believe I am on safe ground if I say the Wetback Trade compared to Human Murder is small potatoes morality-wise. "Maybe that's exactly what he was those boys he helped get over—"

Amelia cut me off. "No those *boys*." The beans bubbled like a pool of hot mud & a Splotch landed on her sleeve she raised it to her lips & nibbled it off. "He try & catch me too. Touch me you know?" She whined out Tio's Voice—"*Oh darling . . . I love you so much . . . I'm just a normal man . . . Oh darling . . . I want to feel a woman again . . . I want to touch your skin . . . Bla bla bla bla . . .*"

"When we were in Dallas this happened?"

"Before," Amelia let her Voice go soft. But she did not want me to get the wrong Idea of her Weakness so she looked me square in my eyes for a Emphasis. "I no let him."

"Poor Tio." Which words I did not mean the way they sounded since I was only thinking of his final Fate. "I mean what happened."

The lid Amelia was holding slipped out of her hand & slammed down on the frying pan. I Recognized this was a Freudian Slip so I Interpreted she wanted to end this Useless Talk about Tio. Which was fine by me since Dolores was still asleep in the other room so here it was the Perfect time to bring up the Obvious i.e. the $64,000 Question—What are we going to do after dinner?

I worked out on a piece of paper by pure Logic all of our possible Choices which I narrowed down to the Grand Total of

398

2. And both of them ended up with the same Logical Conclusion. By Plan A we stay in Mexico but not in Tres Osos. Amelia & Dolores can change their Identity etc. but no matter where I take them we are only going to be a jump or so ahead of Newberry. By Plan A we are running all over just Waiting for him to Catch Up & the Odds are when he does it will not be him anyway. Nor it will not be Nilo it will be some other flunky Amelia never saw Before . . . By Plan B we go back to the U.S.A. together & ruin John Newberry with his tender Love Letters. Let him try & drag me into it if he summons my Testimony for the Prosecution all roads lead to the Obvious Conclusion—

"Marry me."

Amelia stood back very Astonished. "You crazy Ray. Crazy man."

"You think so?"

"Si si. Crazy." She clicked her tongue. "Pen-dey-ho."

"I think you should consider it. Believe me Amelia I went over this 100 times already. Let's settle this business. We can get it all under control now."

"You go fight him," she Suggested very Sharp & pushed Newberry's Letters over to me across the kitchen counter. "You go back."

"I won't do that."

"Why? This is my good plan."

"It isn't logical."

"Tell me. Why my plan is no logical?"

"Because it doesn't make sense." I shuffled the loose Letters in front of me. Meanwhile Amelia kept quiet to let it sink in how dumb this Answer of mine was & how it Insulted her. "What do you think? I can just go back to my apartment after this? I can sit comfy cozy on my sofa and I don't even know where you are? It isn't logical. Say I get back home with these—" I stabbed at the pile of yellow paper, "only I can't get in touch with our mutual friend so he doesn't know I've got them. He still thinks *you've* got them. So while I'm trying to get Newberry to answer his phone some anonymous meathead with a sledgehammer & the morality of a trash compactor is banging on your door to finish the job

Nilo started. In my Opinion Dolores has been in & out of enough bedroom windows for a 8 year old already."

Amelia jutted her chin out but this was only her Instinct Defying my Argument. When she answered me back this time it sounded more like Pleading. "He want to put me in jail. Finish. Blame everythings on me. No . . . "

"He has to prove it in Court. In *Court* Amelia. You know what that means? He can't condemn you in public. He's involved. And you can prove it. With the letters. With Dolores. With me. I'm a witness for the Defense get it?" She was not 100% Sure yet. "In Court is perfect for us. We can dominate the situation. It's where we can bring this to the wonderful ending everybody deserves. Listen to me. I'm an United States Citizen. This what I'm telling you is in the Constitution. Nobody can make a husband testify against his wife. Or vice versa. If you marry me it's your protection for life."

"Is crazy," she said but she started to Doubt her own Words.

"No. It's logical. Look—" I shoved the scrap of paper with my Plans on it under her nose. This is it:

PLAN A	PLAN B
1. Stay in Mexico	1. Go back to U.S.A.
2. N. wants the Letters + Dolores	2. N. wants the Letters + Dolores
3. Must run & hide from him until D. is 18 (10 yrs)	3. Meet N. face to face & ruin him in Court
4. Must have protection of new Identity	4. Must have protection of the Law
5. AMELIA MARRIES RAY	5. AMELIA MARRIES RAY

"I'm not going to disappear." Whatever we have to do we will do I told her. Furthermore I Admit I was already caught amid this Chain Reaction of the Emotions which I misthought was pure Logic on my part. I ask you what is Logic compared to the Emotions of a man when he sees his chance to prove how he is Loyal & Strong how he will be glad to Fight & earn a woman's

Love how he found her out of the millions of millions. This Glory with the Physical side for a crown.

"Marry me and your whole life is going to change."

"For more trouble in my life hm?"

"It's going to be the *end* of all your trouble." Furthermore I am a bully I learn. Amelia shied Away from me like it Hurt her ears to hear my Proposal & she bowed her head. I asked if I Offended her by this Rash Plan and she looked up then telling me No or maybe it was her Disbelief how Events could swerve by such a Sharp Turn.

A Relief arrived in the shape of Dolores who Appeared by my side with her puppets flopped over her arm & the strings all tangled. "Will you help me do this?"

I bent over & said, "Only if you marry me."

"I can't. I'm only 8." She kissed my face. "You're too old."

"I forgot for a minute."

I do not look at Variety anymore I can not get up the Interest. Ever since I Departed from that Glamorous Field the appeal Disappeared for me. I learn via the grapevine (Sal my barber) about Modern Acts who rise very high in the Public eye but by his Description (a girl who sings in her Brassiere! they pay her millions of $$$!) this Talent would not make it to the Airwaves when I was in the business. If there is such a thing as Progress in Entertainment by me this is not it. Shirley Temple rising up to the height of Ambassador to Ghana that is what I call Progress. Besides this kind of Exception the realm of Stage & Screen is a shallow place and Variety is the Seal Of Approval.

I Discovered right off the bat I can get a better picture of what is going on in our World from the pages of The Mason Examiner. Here is another Difference between Variety and The Mason Examiner—the Examiner does not lure the Hopeless or tempt the Defenseless to leave home & lose his Personality. By the corny way Variety entered my Life I should have known it had to end up in Tears! Look at me:

I am sitting Forlorn on the streetcorner. Why am I Forlorn? Because I just Failed my entire Freshman year of College. Why am I sitting? Because I am loaded so heavy under Guilt & Shame I do not have the Strength to go home & face my Family. So I sit on the streetcorner dangling my feet in the gutter which is a place I think I have to get used to. A puff of warm Breeze pushes the ripe smell of the mud & moss in my face—and it sweeps a open page of Variety up against my legs. Between my soda pop in my hand plus the next gust of Wind which wraps that flapping sheet around me I can not Get Rid of it! It sticks like fly-paper & while I am trying to wrestle it off a Classified Ad circled in red jumps out at me—

> Liberty Broadcasting Co. Offers You
> The Opportunity Of A Lifetime!
> Could You Be The Unknown Talent
> We Are Searching For?

Etc. la-dee-doo-dah so instead of taking the bus home I take it all the way up to New York City right to the door of Mr. Howard Silverstein. Etc.

Now I Contemplate the natural Acting Talent of Dolores & it knocks me out. Such a ideal Actress! And I am a ex-professional talking so my Standards are of the highest you can Trust my Word when I tell you Dolores sure made me believe in Future Happiness. By her sincere Performance she Convinced me how Love will conquer the way it always does & Innocence in the World is the living Proof. But I would Protect her from such a business which pimps this Talent—all the time you Perform for your Sponsor he Reminds you how much you owe him for the Opportunity. And all the time you swallow your Inner Thoughts & your real Personality leaks away into the Air. So at the end of the Broadcast day when you are not Required Further what you are is Mr. Nobody you are The Little Man Who Is Not There and just a scraped-out Shell of who you think you are walks into a room. If I had the Power to turn back the hands of Time to 1938 I would by no way be a party who encourages such a Talent like Dolores. Even if they gave me a Guarantee she was going to grow up & be United States Ambassador to Venus.

The puppet show we put on for Amelia was all Dolores's idea in honor of our Engagement Party. For this happy Memory I thank her for the rest of my Life and Beyond. She made up the whole Story which picked up from where the Blackout Episode left off. With a minor change in the Cast namely the Skinny Guy In The Sombrero was not our Foe this time he was the Justice Of The Peace. Dolores portrayed his Voice meanwhile I portrayed the other Voices namely The Donkey & The Fat Lady & this Arrangement made fine Sense since the beautiful Scene we presented Amelia was of our Wedding to be.

Therefore I entitled it—

"HAPPINESS BOUND!"

The Donkey & his fiancee The Fat Lady are both practically out of Breath since they have been walking all over Mexico looking for the ideal Chapel for their Wedding. If The Donkey liked this one for the big oak tree outside the door then The Fat Lady hated it Because it was too dark Inside. If The Fat Lady liked this one for the pretty windows The Donkey hated it Because the walls were too square. The only thing they both Agreed on was the simple Idea they both had to Agree on the Chapel or the Wedding was off. So far they saw 192 of them & when they climbed to the peak of the next hill (sofa) their Hope was starting to fade.

DONKEY: This is hopeless! There just can't be any more chapels in Mexico!

FAT LADY: The last one we saw it was perfecto.

DONKEY: Don't be ridiculous. Perfect? The one with pigeons congregating in the rafters?

FAT LADY: No pigeons. Doves.

DONKEY: They made pigeon noises.

FAT LADY: Doves of Peace. They flock over our head Donkey just to bless us.

DONKEY: What they were aiming at us were *not* blessings. I know the difference between a blessing and a—

FAT LADY:	(*screams*) Look!
DONKEY:	Don't do that! Where? What?
FAT LADY:	Down there in the valley! A chapel! Look how beautiful!
DONKEY:	Yeah. From here.

Down the hill they Hiked until they got to the Chapel which was even more Beautiful Close Up than it looked from on top of the Sofa. And almost as if he knew they were coming the jaunty Justice Of The Peace had his Wedding table all Arranged. The only Light was from a pair of candles & the only Sound was happy accordion music he special put on his Record Player.

J. OF THE P.:	Buenos Dias!
DONKEY:	Likewise Your Honor.
J. OF THE P.:	May I help you?
FAT LADY:	We want you to perform our Wedding if you have a minute.
J. OF THE P.:	I have a minute.
DONKEY:	(*whispers*) I *told* you everything was going to end up hunky-donkey. Hunky-dokey. I mean dory.
FAT LADY:	Ssh!
J. OF THE P.:	Be quiet please. The Wedding shall begin now. Hold hands.

I defy anybody to be a Expert at controlling 2 Puppets at the same time after 15 minutes of Rehearsal! When Dolores gave me the Cue HOLD HANDS the strings I pulled by Accident made The Fat Lady bend over & The Donkey lift his leg up so from where Amelia was sitting this looked like I was Kicking her in the Rear End! And all I wanted to tell her was the Opposite! Even if Amelia already Accepted my Proposal I was full of further words on the Subject i.e. I could say them by those Harmless Puppets. Therefore no Embarrassment for anybody in the room.

I hope I do not Flatter myself if I figure she accepted me 49% from personal Affection + 51% Desire for those Legal Benefits of being my Wife. I do not make up these figures from the thin Air I base my Mathematics on the later Events of the evening. You can Argue and you can Remind Me how animals fornicate. I will answer you a Human Being is above the animals when he figures out the Meaning of his Events. You can Answer Back how the other trick a Human Being can do is he just Imagines the Meaning that is not there so he Feels Settled. Let me answer you this Reply—SO WHAT! Answer back *that*!

J. OF THE P.: I have to ask you some questions for the ceremony.
DONKEY: Fire away.
FAT LADY: Si si! Ask me!
J. OF THE P.: First Donkey. Do you love her?
DONKEY: From the bottoms of my hooves to the tops of my ears. From the tip of my tongue to the tip of my tail. From here to eternity. From New York to New Mexico. From sickness to health. From rags to riches. From—
J. OF THE P.: Say I DO!
FAT LADY: He does.
DONKEY: I do too. I do!
J. OF THE P.: Senorita do you love him?
FAT LADY: I love him from my heart & Soul!
J. OF THE P.: Say—
FAT LADY: I love him because he defends me from wrong & he protects me from harm.
J. OF THE P.: Just say—
FAT LADY: I'm not finished. I love him most of all because he no is like any other man in the world.
J. OF THE P.: He's a Donkey.
FAT LADY: I know who he is & I'm the only one who knows him. I'm the only Senorita he adores.

For the sake of the Mood here I admit I *exaggerated* The Fat Lady's Emotions a little bit. I got caught up in the Story. Amelia did not Object & from this surface Evidence I believe I can say my Fat

Lady lines resembled Amelia's true Feelings at least as much as The Fat Lady puppet resembled Amelia in the flesh i.e. the bare Minimum i.e. a Female in a flowery dress leading her faithful Donkey.

J. OF THE P.:   Now say I DO!
FAT LADY: He is so brave! I do!
J. OF THE P.:   Donkey—do you love children?
DONKEY: Where would a family be without them?
J. OF THE P.:   Huh?
DONKEY: There's a certain little girl who I adore.
J. OF THE P.:   Do you promise you won't go away on business?
DONKEY: My business is being with the ones who I adore.

I did not Exaggerate my own Honest Emotions here I let them loose. Now I looked direct at Amelia when I spoke this Tenderness. Her Reply was she blew me a Kiss & Dolores had to kick my ankle to get my Attention back.

J. OF THE P.:   And you promise you won't go away either?
FAT LADY: No even ever Senor.
J. OF THE P.:   Not until all of us are old.
FAT LADY: Till death us do part!
DONKEY: Till we're all old.
J. OF THE P.:   I now pronounce you Husband & Wife. You can kiss.

My string Control was not too bad on this Maneuver I got The Donkey & The Fat Lady to seal it with a Kiss all right but got into Trouble trying to break them out of it. About 10 Seconds after Amelia jumped in with her help we had a tangled mess on our hands so for Act II all 3 of them went on a Honeymoon in a stringy Clump. For this part Dolores spread out a pretty Green scarf very Luminous in the candlelight. She pulled it tight & lay down on the floor by it then she blew across it so it Rippled.

I let my Donkey Voice slip & in my Stage Whisper I asked her, "Where are we?"

"The ocean," Dolores said. "For a picnic on the beach."

Like she was letting me in on a Family secret Amelia whispered out, "Acapulco." Then she leaned over the back of the sofa & Kissed me & Hugged my neck.

Dolores Pretended she did not Hear what was going on Behind her back & very brazen she spoke up she Informed me herself, "It's Acapulco."

"We go there soon. Sure." Amelia nudged in between us on the floor & grabbed Dolores up in her arms. "We can go there. In Acapulco. If you want . . . " And she passed me a empty shotglass & a full bottle for our Wedding Toast.

A Liquor I never drank before is Tequila & I am happy to tell you I will never know the Taste of it again. It is like swallowing Novocaine. I repeat I am not a boozehound by any Description so I can not Analyze it next to Whiskey e.g. or Mogan David but the Effect of Tequila is very sneaky being this: it makes a grown man Unconscious when he is still walking & talking right up to when it pulls the plug on him & Blacks Him Out for the Count.

I Remember the next time I looked over at Dolores her head was down on the Green Scarf where she fell asleep. We left her alone there with a pillow from her bed & a fluffy blanket over her for the night then Amelia pulled me into her bedroom. On her big bed she laid her finger over my lips she did not want me to Ruin the Night by making a Speech. Good for her. She taught me a Lesson how the blossom of Romance will droop under too much talk. So I only held her hand & Quoted her this:

"In the immortal words of Mr. William Shakespeare . . . If music be the food of love—let's eat!"

Lest I am not Sounding Off like a foghorn on my favorite Topic here I present you with a Bona Fide Quote by "Artie" McGovern a old master on the study of Physical Fitness. "AMERICA IS THE MOST CONSTIPATED COUNTRY IN THE

WORLD"—! His work entitled The Secret Of Keeping Fit is my Bible on the Subject today the same way it was since 1936. "Artie" McGovern espouses further on "The Great American Plague" of Constipation he digs down & gets inside the Reasons behind it. Reason Number 1 is the American habit of hurry. "WE SIMPLY DO NOT TAKE TIME AT A REGULAR HOUR OF THE DAY FOR THE COMPLETE EVACUATION WHICH IS THE *SINE QUA NON* OF GOOD HEALTH"—! Except this is not The End of the Story.

I Respect his Teachings but I must Proclaim "Artie" McGovern was a prisoner of his Times. Going back to the date in question his Expert advice prompted millions of well-behaving livers abdomens arms & legs in all walks of Life therefore it behooves Us we should sit up & pay Attention when he speaks out on Constipation but I say he never knew all the Facts. In particular he never knew of the sinister Party responsible for America being Constipated from Coast to Coast who I Unmask now none other than the Revered Industrialist—P.K. SPILLER.

I Judge him on the Variety of sticky foods he Foisted on the American population which he also foisted very Generous on the Banquet table of the Farewell Party he threw us. On the night of the Final Episode of The Adventures Of The Green Ray that putty joweled stiff necked corset wearing Pillar of Society got away with Blue Murder—he was playing God with my entire Purpose in Life—he was shooting craps with my bowels—*and he wanted me to enjoy it!* Try & tell me everybody has a Conscience try & tell me P.K. Spiller did. Bring up the Fact he manufactured Spiller's High Energy Buckwheat Breakfast Flakes *with their gentle laxative effect.* From his Good Conscience he did this? Because his food Experts advised him, "Look P.K. all the rest of the snacks you make clog people up like cement so you better put something on the market that loosens them up again!"—? Go call it Good Conscience GO & WHISTLE DIXIE! Better you should whistle Heigh-Ho Heigh-Ho because P.K. Spiller just calls it Good Business. I am not Surprised if they put up a Monument to him next to Fort Knox.

In the Dark Ages those people knew what they were doing when

408

they built Cathedrals so huge & towering with stained glass lining the walls they knew of the Message those Sights bring forth. How God is so big & a person is so small. How something Beautiful is in Power. In my opinion Cathedrals are the Skyscrapers of those times. Maybe the Dark Ages are not over yet anyway not by March 5, 1946 because I got the same Message from the Executive Dining Room in the Liberty Building. No stained glass in the windows but they are 20 Feet tall & set back over Dark Green marble benches which they positively Invite you to peer down 38 Floors and scoff at the Human tide below. Between the windows dark oak panels stretch up which the Founders took off the planks of The Mayflower or some other Pilgrim Vessel. So there is American History staring you flat in the face everyplace you look. Outside the windows all you see is the sparkling Lights of Manhattan they are flung at your feet like a box of junk jewelry spilled out there. And the Human ant colony digging around in it Ignorant of the Drama Ordained to Unfold high above their heads.

The Buffet courtesy of P.K. Spiller appeared very Elegant from across the room. Up close was a Different Story. Besides the crystal bowl full of rum punch & the matching ones with the pyramid of Wax Fruit the rest of the food was a Smorgasbord of Spiller Products. A special treat that night was he Offered Us the 1st Taste of a new line he was not bringing out until 1947. This was the famous Cheez Skweez and you can find Descendants of it in the Supermarket today being a fat tube which squirts a orange worm of Cheddar Cheese Spread out of the nozzle on Request. Progress in eating! And here is the rest of the menu— Orange Jell-O Cubes with Spiller's Powder Puf Marshmallows floating in them. Tiny Tot Pretzels next to a bowl of Onion Dip. Potato Salad coated very thick by Spiller's "Mr. Whitey" Mayonnaise Dressing. White Bread sandwich squares with the crust cut off & a layer of Monsieur Meat Spread inside. And for Dessert at the end of the table a party mix of Powder Puf Junior Marshmallows which they colored special in our honour Pistachio Green.

"Help yourself to the refreshments!" Mr. Spiller clapped his puffy hand on Leon's back & Beamed him a Hearty grin. Like a Zoo keeper who just tossed a Pound of Raw Meat to a snarling

Beast then Realizes he still has the Scent of sirloin on his clothes he stepped back & gave Leon enough room to move in on the Buffet. Leon loaded up a paper plate & started to say a word of Thanks but Mr. Spiller already had his Back Turned on him. He was very deep in some manly Conversation with Howard Silverstein & a tight knot of Liberty V.I.P.s who all dressed up in Tuxedos for the Occasion. Spiller squeezed his hands together in front of his chest he leaned Forward on the balls of his feet & Bounced into the joy of selling his point of view.

The Deflated look on Leon's face said the same for Us All. P.K. Spiller's refreshments could not Refresh our worn-out Emotions. And I would say the person worn-out the Worst if you go by Appearance had to be David Arcash who did not even put on a clean shirt for the Occasion. He turned up in a camel color Sweater it had buttons Missing & the rest hanging on by a Thread. Nor he did not take a shave that morning either I will Guess it was Because he could not stand to see his miserable face in the mirror. If he even owned a mirror that is for 1945 was the Year that Knocked him Down and 1946 was the one that Knocked him Out. Back in August his Golden Glove Gym went bankrupt so he had to sell off his Apartment just to keep up with Alimony to Annie. A week after he moved out he heard the Reason he could not Visit his little daughter Amy as usual was because she was in Havana, Cuba for the weekend. Why Havana, Cuba? Because Annie was there. Why was Annie there? Only to say "I Do" to Mr. Rand Comyngore II. When Spiller & Co. pulled the plug on our Radio show it was a Death Blow to his Living so for David being "down in the Dumps" was not just a Figure of Speech anymore. He stayed away from us mainly he Occupied a corner of the dining-room chain-smoking & staring at the carpet. His eyes Flashed Up whenever he Heard somebody Arrive then he locked his gaze on the door very Jittery. David wanted to be the 1st to Know when Annie & her new Hubby came in so he could Cold Shoulder them also the 1st one to greet the Great Heavyweight Champ Jack Dempsey who was a personal Invited Guest of the Spillers. ("Hello kid!" was about all the dialogue he got out of the Champ all evening but the crush of the crowd Forced him into a ugly Scene with Annie right in front of our hors d'oeuvres.)

Amy was toddling on her way back from the Buffet like a big girl with her paper cup of lemonade & she wound up in the corner with David. She Waited there knee-high & slurping her Drink very Patient until he was going to Notice her. Except Annie noticed him first. "Say hi to Daddy," she pushed Amy on.

David ignored Annie & kneeled down to give his girl a Hug. "Hiya pipsqueak." When he lifted her up in his arms she started Kicking & Whining he should put her Down. "Yeah," David said, "great to see you too."

"Really David. She's just a baby."

"She gets that from you."

Rand's voice broke over David like the shuddery boom of a Temple Gong. 'I'll look after Amy for a while. I'm sure there's a small private room where you can express your feelings more freely to each other."

"For that I'd need a whip & a chair," David told him.

Rand sighed he gave his head a Wise old shake. "Don't you really want to look forward to when you and Annie can bury all these bad feelings? When you can enjoy a drink together. You know. Socialize. Treat each other like friends."

"Confidentially?" David pretended he was trying to be Friendly. "Personally? I'd rather gargle with razor blades." And Jack Dempsey picked that second to brush by behind Rand. David grabbed ahold of Amy's hand & pushed Rand out of the way he dragged his little girl in the Champ's wake. Her heels made wavy lines where they Ploughed through the carpet. "You never met my daughter I don't think." So Dempsey swiveled around to see who was Talking. "This is Amy. Amy say hello to Mr. Dempsey."

As soon as he turned her loose she swung around & punched David in the leg. "Cute kid," the Champ chucked him & then he Sidestepped into the huddle of Tuxedos around P.K. Spiller. Brushed off by the Best! I could almost hear David's shoes squeak as his toes curled up inside them while he stood there with his Feet nailed to the floor waiting for Bozo The Clown to run in with Fire Bells Ringing & smack him in the face with a Custard Pie.

Instead Howard Silverstein went over to him & showed him the way to the punch-bowl.

This other Sight wrenched me—Bernhardt Grym sinking to the Tricks of the Stage to cover over his Upset Emotions. The more Cheer he poured on the less I could Believe it so there is a Lesson of Acting and a Lesson of Life rolled into One. Nor he did not want anybody in there to miss his Command Performance. A person would have to be Blind in both eyes & Deaf in both ears! Even with his slumped shoulders Bernhardt was still the tallest man in the room also the one with the Loudest Voice. Like a Hebrew Patriarch stepping out of the pages of Genesis he was there to let people know he was Coming Back with a Vengeance!

His only prop was a copy of Variety he did so much flapping of those pages it sounded like Pigeons Flying around the room. And Bernhardt had a stooge too by the name of Vaughan Cherry the day rate Actor who Mr. Argyll hired to portray our Narrator for the last time. Bernhardt quoted out from every page some Big name of his Acquaintance who was producing a Big Show now all he had to do was walk in the Stage Door & walk back into his real Life in the Theater—

"Oh my dear! Arthur Beaumont is in the Old Vaudeville for 12 weeks with—" Bernhardt forced out a chuckle, "with a musical by Raul Raskob & Nat Firelli— Oh no . . . " he dropped his Voice down very Serious he read the page very close, "Oh he's not waltzing *that* prehistoric behemoth out in front of the public again! Madman!"

"What's that Mr. Grym?" Vaughan was on his tip-toes to read the news over Bernhardt's arm but caught the Full Force of the page in his face when Bernhardt flicked it over.

"Ah!"

"What?" Vaughan begged to hear. "What?"

"DeKalb!"

"Where's that again? In Indiana isn't it?"

"Not *Indiana*," Bernhardt Winced to show off how Vaughan's Ignorance gave him a Pain. "Morris! *Morris* DeKalb of Happy Pappy! Of Sing To Me In Springtime! Of Jazz Baby Serenade!

412

You know—" And he Crooned a Verse of the Hit Tune from that show, "There's no tax to pay on apple blo-oo-ssoms . . . there's no rent due on the dew . . . Nobody can cha-aa-rge you for falling in love . . . So I'm free to fall in love with you-oo-oo . . . " Bernhardt did not Notice only Vaughan Cherry did how heads were starting to turn Namely Mrs. Spiller's. He did not know what kind of Trouble could come from Offending the Wife of the Sponsor but he did not want to Stick Around & find out either. A mincing step or so did not get Vaughan very far anyway Bernhardt Reached Out & nabbed him before he could Sneak Off. "Moe DeKalb! My God don't you attend the theater Mr. Cherry? You should know his name if you want to get any further in this business. He produced all the early classics on Broadway. And look! Look what he's auditioning!" His big stiff finger stabbed the middle of the open page. "A revival of Belvedere Boy! I wonder if Moe even knows I'm in town. My God. The part of cunning old Major Van Loon the flowergirl's father. Not her *real* father. That comes out in the Second Act. I was too young for it in 1922. I tell you I'm ripe for it now. Manna from heaven! I'll bring you along to meet Moe. I'm sure if I ask him pretty please with a cherry on top he'll give you a crack at one of the smaller parts. You don't want to stay in *ra-di-o*," Bernhard sneered, "any longer than you have to . . . "

Here you are I hand you a night when Theater History was made for this was the Occasion when David Arcash dubbed Bernhardt Grym with his famous Nickname which dogged him all over Broadway & some will say it Hounded him into his Grave. You could hear it drip from the greasy lips of any pickle sucking wiseguy who rented a Theater & called himself a Producer. On the 1st day of any Audition going in New York City, "Here he comes," some weary Voice had to groan, "the Kosher Ham."

Exactly the way a Pinball rolls around a Pinball Machine that was how Leon came across the room. He circled around each bunch of Guests in his path he caroomed off the walls & back into the crowd until he zigzagged over to Mr. Burrows & me. "You want some cheese & crackers?" Leon pointed at his Almost Empty plate. "I can go get some more," he said.

413

Mr. Burrows glanced at the shiny smear of Cheddar in front of him then over at P.K. Spiller. "I wouldn't touch that stuff with a 10 foot Polack."

"No appetite," I said. Now all 3 of us had our eyes glued on Mr. Spiller & his Intimate Party who Included Walter Winchell & Arthur Murray & Arthur Godfrey of course nobody took the plunge and Introduced us to these High Flyers. "I wonder what they're talking about."

"Business." Leon sprayed my shirt with cracker crumbs when he chirped this out.

"I've been over it 1,000 times in my mind," Mr. Burrows shook his head, "and I can't come up with why. How can he pull the plug on us like this?"

"I didn't think Howard would just throw in the sponge like that," I said.

Mr. Burrows put me Straight. "Silverstein's got a dozen other shows he has to worry about." He gave me a Sarcastic shrug. "What's so extra-special about The Green Ray?"

"The Sound Effects," Leon said behind a mouthful of onion dip. He swallowed. "Mr. Silverstein was saying something about television."

The mention of the Word made Mr. Burrows want to spit. "Oh hell Leon. Spare me."

"Hey what did I say?" Leon appealed to my Judgement. "I didn't say anything."

"You said a mouthful," Mr. Burrows informed him. "Those geniuses can't comprehend the fact Radio's still in short pants. Gimmicks we haven't tried yet. Ideas you can't improve on by adding pictures. If I want to see pictures I'll go to the Art Museum."

"You go to the movies," Leon said.

"That's different."

"What's different about it?"

"You don't think it's different from the big treat of taking your wife or your girl downtown in a cab and eating a delicious dinner out and going into Radio City Music Hall and sitting in a plush seat with a box of popcorn for a couple of enjoyable hours and maybe stopping off for a nightcap to round the evening off? And you come back home with the satisfying feeling you've been out on the town—you don't think that's any different from straining your eyes looking at a little box in the corner of your livingroom *where your Radio used to be?*"

Right here Mr. Burrows ran out of Breath & I jumped in to take some of the heat off of Leon. "Maybe that's what they call Progress."

"Malarkey. It's just business to them. Silverstein doesn't care what he puts on the air. To him it's all *numbers*. You think he sits around with P.K. Spiller & they congratulate each other on broadcasting something wonderful like The Green Ray? Not a chance. He only cares about how many more boxes of Spiller's dry cereal got sold last week. Or how many less. Go on. Tell me I'm wrong." Zingo right on Cue a blast of Laughter roared out of the guts of Spiller's crowd. Mr. Burrows forced up a bitter smile & said to us, "And now a message from our Sponsor."

I am not a Sentimental type except in this Particular For Instance I was not going to let dat ole debbil Regret creep into the Studio with us & sabotage our Final Episode. Nor we should not dwell in this heartsick Emotion as if we Enjoy it otherwise our Performance will fall flat & why should we give our Enemy the Satisfaction? Let P.K. Spiller & Co. have all the Regret while they watch us come in swinging & go out in a blaze of Glory! While we hark back to our heydays & fire up our fighting Spirit!

"We can all be proud of what we did," I said, "from begining to end. Every minute on the air. For 8 years remember?"

Mr. Burrows nodded very sure. "I remember. Indeedy I do."

"When you got trapped in the cargo hold of Horvath's gambling boat," Leon poked me in the ribs to remind me, "and sank to the bottom."

I dug my fists into my hips I pushed my chest out & Showed him I still Knew my Stuff. "And I lived to fight another day."

"You floated up in that sealed oil drum."

"You rose to the occasion!" Mr. Burrows grabbed my arm & shook a Chuckle out of me. "Wait a minute," he stopped right there & said, "the sealed oil drum was how you got out of that Jap submarine in San Francisco Bay."

"No Mr. Burrows," Leon said, "Ray got shot out of the torpedo tube on that one. Remember how I used the bicycle pump with the echo on it?" Leon encored his famous Sound Effect by a sharp hiss between his teeth & skidding one of his palms off the other to portray my underwater launch.

"I'm sorry you're wrong," Mr. Burrows told him flat. "You used the bicycle pump for the Sound of the air decompressing when the lid came off the oil drum *after* the Jap sub blew up. That was the whole thing of it. Remember? That was the suspense. Nobody knew if Ray got out in time. Until right up to the end."

Leon stood there shaking his head No! No! No! just waiting for a Gap so he could put his 2¢ Back In. "I'm sorry I'm *not* wrong. The oil drum was on the gambling boat. The torpedo tube was on the Jap sub. And . . . " Leon perked up with a new idea to prove his point. "If it *was* the oil drum on the submarine how did he get out of the sunken gambling boat? By way of the *torpedo tube*?" He made this sound like the Dumbest Idea he ever Heard.

Mr. Burrows was not in the mood for this particular Challenge. "I'm not sure about it Leon," he waved a limp hand under his words, "but some smart way."

"Let's not fight between ourselves," I said here. "If I'm so smart how come I let Horvath lock me in his bullion vault?"

"Ask Lamont Carruthers,' Mr. Burrows tickled himself by this Notion. "How does he think that stuff up? Traps you in a lead vault so Horvath can suck the air out of it! You have to have some kind of sadistic imagination to come up with a gag like that."

"Gag is right," I said. "I think I did my best work of all time in that Scene. Got suffocating down to a fine art."

"If I hear of any vacancies . . . " Mr. Burrows said.

"Remember the phone calls? The whole city wanted to make sure I was all right."

"I used a balloon for the air escaping," Leon bounced back

416

into the Conversation. "For the realism. I had to pinch it just right."

"It was fine all the way," Mr. Burrows patted Leon's back, "All the way up to the mouse fart at the end."

"C'mon Mr. Burrows. Nobody remembers that."

"Nobody remembers that? Leon are you kidding me? They named a sandwich downstairs in the coffee shop after it. Great Moments in the History of Radio—The Leon Kern Mouse Fart."

"Oh yeah?" Leon dared him & floated out a Little Boy smile. "What's in it?"

"It's delicious. That's what I order every time I go down there for lunch. Openface thing. For $1.25 you get a slice of whitebread with a teeny tiny skid mark of mustard on it," he said. "And a beet salad."

Now Leon decided the joke Was Over. "Nobody remembers it. That ain't what The Green Ray means to the public."

We both knew he struck our Sentiments exactly. "They don't know what they're killing off," I said when I Noticed how Leon was gazing at P.K. Spiller again. Almost Hypnotized by that Snake Charmer across the room who was busy glazing the brains of those Network hotshots. Oh they just rolled over & let him drip Poison into their ears i.e. his Personal Suggestions about how they can Replace The Green Ray so easy by a soggy Soap Opera or a Quiz Show they can fix & keep the fix in for just as long as the Nation swallows it! Who are the Bosses afterall whose show is it? Nor I was not Downcast in the face of this mortal Insult—for reminiscing over The Green Ray's past Triumphs uplifted me. "We are too Good to lose," I said Calm & Firm.

Mr. Burrows said, "Amen to that. You know we got about a thousand fan letters last week? Lucy Least told me."

"I swear," I swore, "I can rescue this situation."

"You can't Ray. It's hopeless." Mr. Burrows summed it up, "It's a hopeless situation."

"I'll persuade him," I said.

Leon snapped his head around. "Who? Him?" He jabbed the Air he pointed hard at P.K. Spiller—who happened to be waving both of his arms over his head for some Reason except in that Moment to me it looked like a Sign of Surrender. When Leon started to Picture what I was going to try his cheeks Bloomed Pink.

"I'm just going to bring certain facts to his attention," I told him. "I'll persuade him with the facts."

"Here's a fact my boy. At 8 o'clock on the button the final episode of this show goes on the air & at 8:30 it goes off the air. Look in the dictionary—final means *final*. Finished. The End. And that's a fact." Mr. Burrows squinted at me. "You read the script. You know how they made Lamont end it."

"I read it forwards & backwards and all I know is there's a lot that happens before we get to the last Scene."

"What the hell do you think you're going to change?" Mr. Burrows pulled me Closer by my lapel. "Don't make a monkey out of yourself. You can't just switch endings on everybody! What're you going to do? Invent something new on the spot? I'm telling you for your own good—don't make enemies Ray. Some of these people around here you're going to need after tonight."

"Where's the law that says this episode had to end the way Lamont wrote it last week? All he needs is the green light from Howard Silverstein and he can write me a miraculous escape."

"Don't get your hopes up."

"It isn't 8 o'clock yet. And 8:30 sounds like a year from now. I'm going to talk to Mr. Spiller."

Mr. Burrows held me back. "Pardon my ignorance but tell me why should P.K. Spiller or your friend Howard Silverstein or any of those other mucky-mucks over there—why should they listen to you?"

"I'll show them I know what I'm talking about. It's my responsibility."

"Argyll should go. He's the producer. It's his responsibility."

"No. I'm the main character." And I let them hear a Chorus of the National Anthem I was about to warble to our dear Sponsor which this Rehearsal let me loosen up my vocal cords & I hit all the high notes with ease—Oh! Say! Can you see how The Green Ray is Above & Beyond the call of Business—When he is gone who will Remain on the Air to give Hope to the Hopeless week after week?—Who will stand up for what is Fair?—Who else is the Living Proof of our healthy drives which guaranteed American Triumph in the War?—What kind of a Ideal does the younger Generation have to look up to now? I will tell you Sir! Boston Blackie. A crummy Ideal! lurking around back alleys & locked office buildings with a Gun!—This is not Progress! This rash Act of pulling the plug on The Green Ray does not serve any Higher Purpose! Do not kid yourself Sir! For as sure as water is wet you will Plunge our Shining Spot on every Radio dial into total Darkness & hereby henceforth your name will be emblazoned in Letters of Fire at the bottom of the notorious Roll Call that schoolkids learn By Heart in their 1st History Lesson—those lightning rods of National Shame & Disaster: step forward Benedict Arnold . . . John Wilkes Boothe . . . Typhoid Mary . . . *and now* . . . P.K. SPILLER—

"Go piss up a rope. You'll get a bigger feeling of accomplishment." Mr. Burrows squeezed my shoulder very Affectionate & I walked away from him. I turned around & saw him drop his pipe out of his mouth & raise a weak smile to me in place of it. Then he called over, "Hey!" & he put up his Dukes. "Sugar Ray!"

"Lotsa luck," Leon cheered me on. "I'll inform your next of kin."

A man must do etc. except a Gentleman must watch his Manners in the company of Gentlemen so I did not butt in full steam ahead into their Conversations. I stood behind Howard Silverstein & waited for him to Notice Me. *Wait for him to bring me in & introduce me around* I figured out of all of them he Recognized my Position. His chummy chums there are V.I.P.s but Howard understands it is only a few $ makes us Different (to be precise a few Million $) but on all the Important points I am a Equal—in Brainpower I can match the Best! nor I am not a Lowly Employee I am up to the VIP level in Achievement (anonymous it may be!) I am not any Ordinary Joe who walked in off the street & sneaked up by the service elevator I AM A INVITED GUEST AT THIS SPECIAL PARTY—*Howard will vouch for me* he will show them how he Enjoys my Company & pays Attention to my Views so they know it was not a Act of Charity which brought me to the Executive Dining Room on this fine night! Let them Welcome Me where I Belong in the Serious Circle of men I expect Howard to open up a door for me a gap in the pride of men there a welcome place amid all those monkey suits with markings of Success on them & the Wealth of them & the Weight of them that pushes up the Air Pressure all over the room—let me in I can keep up! I am fit to join into your lofty conversation—

"Rooty-Toot."

"Rooty-Toot-Toot!"

"Sambo!"

"Goody Chew."

"Goody-2-Chews!"

"Fungo!"

"You're all missing the point." Mr. Spiller clasped his porky hands behind his back & stopped the baa-baaing around him. "A 9 year-old boy winds up at the candy store after his Saturday sandlot baseball game. Let's say he made the catch in deep center field for the final out and now he wants to cap the day off with a soda pop & a candy bar. He wants to talk about the game with his pals. Argue about who made the best play and so forth. I remember what that felt like. Late afternoon in the summer. Your hands smell of dirt. Your neck is all sweaty. Close your eyes and you see a high pop fly dropping out of the sun heading straight for the pocket of your mitt. Open your eyes and this wonderful Saturday is still going on. And it doesn't have anything in the world to do with your Mom or even your Pop. It's your time. You and your team. Think back now. You must remember Saturdays like that." By the way some of those manly eyes started to mist up I guess they did Remember dusty sandlots & high Pop Flies just the way P.K. Spiller painted it for them but the way he told it I Believe if he wanted to he could make them Remember days of Whale Hunting & blubber burgers with their Eskimo pals in the Land Of The Midnight Sun. "You plunk your nickel & dime down on the counter and you ask for a Coca-Cola and a —"

"Baby Ruth." Howard Silverstein had enough Importance he could break in with a Joke like that. All it got was a soft chuckle out of a couple of tight mouths since everybody was waiting to see how P.K. Spiller took it.

The corners of his eyes smiled. "No Howard."

Which gentle Reply boosted the Courage in general & other Voices piped up with, "Hershey's," and "Tootsie Roll!" and more chuckles all round.

Before everybody beat the Gag into the ground Howard cleared his throat & asked, "What *are* you going to call it P.K.?"

Mr. Spiller opened his arms to his patient flock. "Cubby Bar," he announced. "And it's going to beat the pants off Tootsie Roll."

"All I know," Annie said to him at the same time she was manhandling Amy away from the platter of Green marshmallows, "is candy rots children's teeth."

"Rand," Spiller said very amused, "will you talk to your wife?" Then he talked to her himself. "You know over 63 million Hershey Bars were sold in this country last year? That's 1 bar for every other freedom loving man woman & child in these United States. There will always be candy. And thank the Lord," he patted Amy's head, "there will always be children. The only question is who is going to make the one for the other."

I will have to say the great Howard Silverstein was a major letdown in the Door Opening Department. Once the rumble of locker room belly laughs started rolling out at Spiller's double play on words my dear Friend did not turn around & bring me into the Fun. I just stood Aside there like a Dumb Bystander at the Scene of a car crash looking at the crowd break up & start diving for fresh drinks etc. until I got Elbowed out of the way. The elbow in question had a point on it as sharp as a fencepost & it was connected to Lamont Carruthers. He jabbed me hard to make sure I got the big Idea that I was the last Solid Obstacle between his empty glass & the punchbowl.

Likewise here is what Hit Me—Lamont was not 1-legged at this time. In special Circumstances he strapped on his Wooden Leg so his 3-Piece navy pinstripe hung on him very Dapper. He stopped wasting time on Polite & Dainty dips with the ladle about a Dozen glassfuls ago & this was a shock to my System to witness

Lamont teeter-totter that way like a old featherless blue jay pecking down into a bird-bath.

"How d'you like the party?" He twitched his mustache (i.e. that tweezered pencil line riding his pale lip) in case I Missed the Sarcastic drift of his Small Talk. "Tasted the punch?" I looked down & shook my head. "Then Sonny why the stinking hell are you loitering in front of my punch-bowl?"

"I'm just waiting to get a chance of a word with Mr. Spiller over there."

"What word?"

"I'm going to say—"

"What word are you going to have with him? This is something I want to hear. A word of your very own with The Lord High Grand Foobah Woobah. You don't say!" He swung his glass down into the punch & came up with a sludge of Orange Peels he just splashed them back into the bowl by a nasty flick of his wrist. "Fruit salad!" he cursed it & about as Disgusted as he would be if he just scooped up a juicy wad of chewed cigar butts.

"What I'm going to say to him is—"

"I'm all ears Son! Don't keep me in suspense . . . "

"About the end of the show." I held it right there & gave Lamont time to get in his next Sarcastic Crack but it did not come. So I kept going, "I want him to let us change it."

He bit his bottom lip & made a grab for the edge of the table like he was going to Faint from this News. "Gosh. Is—" he gulped, 'is there s-something y-you don't like about the ending I wrote?"

"Not exactly. But I mean it seems so final."

"Why yes. I suppose it *is* final," he blinked & sounded Flabbergasted. "Since tonight it's the final episode I just naturally figured there was only one way to end it. But golly—" again with the fluttering eyes, "I see I was wrong. And now . . . it's . . . too late."

"You can mock me all you want," I spoke up to him, "but I'm serious about this. We aren't on the air yet. There's time for us to do something. Even when we start broadcasting maybe we can *still* do something. You could come up with a new ending. How about it Mr. Carruthers?"

He answered me very sober. "You mean one so you can come back next week."

"You know it."

"The Return Of The Green Ray."

"Something like that."

"Son Of The Green Ray."

"Why not?" I said. "How long do I have to be gone before I have a comeback?"

Lamont swallowed another glass of punch & pulled a Dangling Orange Peel out of his mouth. "Are you insane Green or just feeble minded?"

"I just want to save our show Mr. Carruthers. And by the looks of it I'm the only person who does."

"Jesus Christ on a bike! It never fails!" he barked at me. "Put a guy in a toga & let him playact Julius Caesar and the next morning he's giving the waitress Et Tu Brute because she burned his toast."

"I'm saying I'd appreciate your help."

Lamont whipped out his fountain pen & brandished it toward P.K. Spiller. "I'll just wave my magic wand and make it all come out different. There. I'm helping." Then he got tired of this Gag & moved in on me to Deliver his Message Direct in my Ear. "YOU IMBECILE THIS IS REAL LIFE!"

"If you want to be a defeatist go ahead," I jerked away & told him, "but if you ask me anything can happen before they broadcast that last Scene."

"Nobody's asking you." Lamont broke this news very Gentle. He laid his hand on my shoulder & leaned most of his Weight down on it. "Let's all just stick to the script."

"But why?"

"You're a professional actor. Correct me if I'm wrong."

"Which is another good reason I should stand up & fight for the show."

"You're a professional actor? Then you ought to know when to bow out."

I stiffened up & said, "That's the last thing I'm going to do."

Which Unbowed Stance irked Lamont so terrible he pinned me

against the edge of the Buffet Table & held me there nose to nose with sour Rum Fumes blowing hot off his tongue he tried to put me Straight about the ways of the World. "Listen to me Horatio Hornblower!" he bawled down my windpipe. "You do not make things happen around here. P.K. Spiller is something that's happened *to you!* He's the cause and you're the effect! Haven't you figured that out yet? Let me describe the situation to you in another way. By means of a parable. I ran into Rudolph Valentino one time. In a fancy Italian restaurant don't you know! Saw him standing a couple of feet away from my table with his slicked back hair & his ruby red lips. His patent leather shoes. Thought he was the head waiter. I tugged his sleeve & told him to bring me a plate of linguini. *And that was Rudolph Valentino!* WHO THE DAMNED HELL DO YOU THINK *YOU* ARE?"

Howard Silverstein had to wade over & Pry him off me. "Corrupting the youth of America as usual Lamont?"

"As usual!" he hooted back happy to Agree.

"Let's get ready to go down to the Studio. All right gents?" Howard slid his wristwatch out of his sleeve & tapped it with his fingernail. "We've just got a few more minutes up here."

"I'm having too much fun at our pa-aa-arty Howard," Lamont said under big round (bloodshot) puppy dog eyes. "Do I *have* to go down to the Studio?"

He watched Lamont reach for a Refill of punch. "If you're having too much fun maybe it's time to call it quits."

"Absolutely,'" Lamont said & slugged down his drink.

"We'll just have to get along without you then."

"Howard?" I caught him before he drifted away. "I'd appreciate it if you could usher me over there to Mr. Spiller. I want to ask him something before we go on the air."

"You can ask me. What do you want to know?"

"I am asking you. To take me over to him for a personal word."

Howard let a careful Pause tick by then he said sure he was glad to & he walked me around the end of the buffet where P.K. Spiller was in the middle of Demonstrating a Golf Swing to his wife et al. "Excuse please," Howard cut in on them with a Charlie

424

Chan voice which he Dropped as soon as he got their Attention, "Ray Green wants a word with you P.K."

Mr. Spiller nodded me a Greeting, "Nice to see you." Then his wife Ethel repeated it by a Faint Nod & she mouthed the word Hello.

In the Speck of Time before I knew what I was about to say next a flashbulb went off inside my Skull. The Light burst out of my eyes & froze the Spillers just how they stood in that ½ second giving me their kind Attention. Plus in that White Flare or in the X-Ray Pulse of it I saw right through how I truly looked to blushing Mrs. Spiller: *her Husband is a giant in my Mind & I am a jittery midget of a man who toddled over to ask him a favor—she can afford to forget about who I am as soon as I depart—I am a blur in front of the background—*

Say a Landslide dragged me down of my wild Emotions which I could not stop & I went somersaulting—the only Sound in the whole room was the Sound of my own Voice & I heard it say very loud, "You make all of my favorite foods!" oh I was Cartwheeling Down Down Down now!—I grabbed up every single cracker on the table I stuffed them all into my big mouth until the dry Crumbs & damp pieces Spilled Out on the carpet nor I did not stop there either boy oh boy I squeezed a tube of Cheddar Cheese Spread on the back of my hand & licked it off telling her, "Can't get enough of this chewy gooey stuff!"—smacking my lips Hungry for MORE—

If I was only a goofy Clown to her eyes with my bow tie spinning & my Red Nose & floppy Shoes etc. to this day I would Remember I Goofed Up all righty but *in the Party Spirit*—I am Wincing all over now I Remember it was Worse to her I was a stinkbomb exploding in her lap! Already I was Reaching for the Jell-O with my bare hands & the Pistachio Marshmallows too—"Did you cook this?" I said to her face. "This Jell-O is better than my mom makes! No kidding! Can I have the recipe?" And those silky Financiers those Liberty V.I.P.s & Arthur Murray & Arthur Godfrey stood around me just as still as Boulders with painful smiles Balanced very Delicate on their lips.

And do not let me Forget the Effect of this Excitement on my

Benefactor Howard Silverstein since he was the Humiliated Figure who Introduced that pinhead song & dance of mine. The whole rotten business about Uncle Jake & the newspapers came back to him like a wet slap in the face he told me after & he was Sorry he ever Trusted me to behave myself in Public. I.e. those were the only Words & Sentiments we had together that night and none ever after.

It could be I was Infected all of my Life by a rare Disease. Based on many Articles in Print the Doctors agree such a thing can Happen & the person in question might not know about it until it is Too Late if they missed the correct Diagnosis at the time. So it just Escalates. You know I wrack through my Brain now I am searching for a Medical Explanation of my Behavior which makes Sense & by the obvious Symptoms the only thing I can come up with is I believe I suffer from Epilepsy of the Emotions. (Dr. Godfrey maybe when you Autopsy me you can Explore this Possibility. Hereby you have my permission to fractionate my Brain Tissue all you want. Maybe I am the First Recorded Case of this incurable Disorder!) Let me say when my Fit wore off I felt a hot brick drop in my stomach. I do not think I got Nauseous then (or Constipated later) strictly from the bout of E. of the E. I am sure $\frac{1}{2}$ of the Blame can go Beyond A Doubt to the mound of Spiller's Fine Foods I crammed down my esophagus.

To be 100% Fair about it P.K. Spiller treated me very kind considering the Pain & Strain of my obnoxious Routine. The surprise Fact is by this abrupt Experience he Revealed his pardoning Nature which still Affects me for I Remember how he did not try & understand my Nervous State nor he did not Condemn me either. I bet it struck him he just saw a specimen of the Human Condition he never came across Before & the glimpse of it tickled his Curiosity. While I excused myself out the door I overheard the only thing he said about me to Howard Silverstein — & his Remark followed me into the elevator it rode down to the Studio with me 30 Floors below it sat with me behind the Microphone where it did not stop ringing in my Inner Thoughts. Nevermore I did not have to wonder about our Sponsor's Esteem of me if I was a profit to this Radio Show or a loss I heard it in his own exact Words:

"What a character!"

DA DOO DA DA DUM! DA DOO DA DA DOO! DOOM DOOM DUT DUT DUT DOOM! WHEN THE HOUR OF DARKNESS IS UPON US—WHEN ALL HOPE IS GONE—HE BLAZES FROM THE SHADOWS TO DEFEND THE DEFENSELESS! TO PURGE WRONG TO KEEP AMERICA STRONG! SPILLER'S FINE FOODS—THE MAKERS OF SPILLER'S HIGH-ENERGY BUCKWHEAT BREAKFAST FLAKES—PROUDLY PRESENT . . . THE ADVENTURES OF THE GREEN RAY! TONIGHT—OUR FINAL EPISODE . . . OBLIVION BOUND!

The Nation heard the click of the switch on the Radio in Peter Tremayne's library. As my man Jessop hummed along to the Melody he tuned it from the light-hearted Dance Music to the somber tones of the nightly News.

TREMAYNE: Leave it there Jessop. I want to catch up on the events of the day.

JESSOP: As you wish Sir. Would you like your cocoa here in the library or—

TREMAYNE: Wait a second. Turn up the volume will you?

As usual Peter Tremayne's sharp ears Sift the News for the Story Behind the Story. He listens for the hidden Clues that tell him what is really going on—and what is going to Happen Next . . .

ANNOUNCER: . . . eminent gathering in the elegant ballroom of the Sherryland Hotel. The organization goes by the name G.L.O.B.O.S.—initials which according to founder Dr. Septimus Ogilvy—stand for Global Law & Order through the Brotherhood Of Science. Dr. Ogilvy—the world renowned Atom

427

Expert—is mounting the platform now to address members of the Press and the Scientific community. The next voice you hear will be that of Dr. Ogilvy. Now handing over.

And from the Remote Microphone all the way downtown Dr. Ogilvy's crisp Voice crackles through—

DR. OGILVY: Ladies and Gentlemen of the Press. My fellow Scientists. And all those listening at home via the miracle of Radio. Our organization is not Republican or Democrat. We belong to no single political party. We have but a single Purpose and that is to ensure that the peace most painfully won will be Eternal. Our aims are no more & no less than to redeem the hopes and justify the faith placed in Scientists the world over to bring about a prosperous day and a tranquil night. To give these precious gifts to all survivors of the past tragic conflict as well as for the generations yet unborn. I ask for your support—however you may give it—in behalf of the children of the Atomic Age. For in truth dear friends we are *all* these children. I thank you.

JESSOP: My. What fine ideals. Do you think they can ever succeed?

TREMAYNE: Well they cured Yellow Fever. Discovered penicillin. Who can say?

Tremayne rustled the pages of his Wall St. Journal (I shook the loose pages of my Script).

TREMAYNE: You can turn it off now. I want to read the Wall St. news—and no cocoa tonight thanks.

JESSOP:	Very good Sir.
TREMAYNE:	Hmm. Very intriguing.
JESSOP:	May I ask—?
TREMAYNE:	A surge in Brazilian Kikapoo Nuts.
JESSOP:	In Brazil Nuts Mister Peter?
TREMAYNE:	No no. Kikapoo Nuts. Grown in Brazil. By the looks of it a certain company in Maryland is buying up a controlling interest in the only other refinery in the world that produces Kikapoo Nut Oil.
JESSOP:	Oh. I say!
TREMAYNE:	Yes. It could be worth keeping my eye on this. Jessop—get Benjamin Armistead on the telephone.
JESSOP:	Your stockbroker Sir?
TREMAYNE:	He's at home. Here's his private number.
JESSOP:	Excuse me Mister Peter—but what exactly are Kikapoo Nuts?
TREMAYNE:	For a start Jessop they aren't nuts at all . . . Actually they're the tuber of a genus of spitweed—*Saramaxis raewallii*—which happens to be the sole source of a kind of super-refined oil used in every form of modern day manufacturing. From auto parts & nylon stockings to jars of mass produced mayonnaise. And so far no method exists to synthesize a substitute for it.
JESSOP:	They sound like a valuable commodity those Kikapoo Nuts. And a sound investment if I may say so Sir.
TREMAYNE:	Blue chip all right. They're known to thrive in only 2 areas—the Amazon region of Brazil and here in the United States on 50 acres of marsh just outside of Baltimore. Quite frankly Jessop without Kikapoo Nut Oil life as we live it would be impossible. If the world supply was threatened or cut off

all industry would be paralyzed in a matter of weeks . . . or even days.

Right away the Suspicion hit me I had to hurry up & figure out What to do & When to do it. Time was Marching On so if I sat on my behind & pondered for too long certain tragic Events could overwhelm me. Because meanwhile everything was going According To Plan at the headquarters of G.L.O.B.O.S. where the telephone is ringing off the hook—

LOUISE: GLOBOS may I help you? Why of course we're grateful for any contribution you can make. And 50 Cents is very generous Madam. As a matter of fact we haven't had anything over a dollar yet. Yes you're right—it all adds up. Good-bye and thank you so much!

The office door opens & slow heavy footsteps announce a Mysterious Arrival.

LOUISE: Ooh! I'm sorry—you . . . you startled me.
VENNEMA: I wish to speak with Dr. Ogilvy.

The thick European accent oozes from his mouth.

LOUISE: Is he expecting you?
VENNEMA: That depends. What is the date today please?
LOUISE: It . . . it's the 14th.
VENNEMA: No—then Dr. Ogilvy is not expecting me. Santa Claus does not usually arrive until December 25th! Ha ha ha ha ha ha ha!

Louise is upset when she knocks on Dr. Ogilvy's office door & walks inside. Her Voice quivers.

430

LOUISE:	Dr. Ogilvy? There's a gentleman who wants to see you. And he—
DR. OGILVY:	Who is he Louise? Did he tell you his name?
LOUISE:	Not exactly.
VENNEMA:	Vennema.
LOUISE:	Hey mister! You can't—

No rum punch fouled up Leon's timing he timed it on the button: the telephone started Ringing again in the Outer Office.

DR. OGILVY:	It's all right Louise. You better go answer the telephone.
LOUISE:	Yes Dr. Ogilvy.

And she shuts the door Behind her. Vennema's Voice sweats into the quiet room.

VENNEMA:	It's very warm in here.
DR. OGILVY:	What do you want to see me about Mr. Vennema?
VENNEMA:	You Americans like to—how do you say it?—get down to business. I apologize for my manners. They are the habits of a lifetime.
DR. OGILVY:	That's quite all right . . . I can't place your accent Mr. Vennema. Are you from—
VENNEMA:	You should know I do not represent myself in this matter. I act for a certain party who feels it is in his interest—and yours—if he remains anonymous.

The thud of a bulky Envelope hits the table in front of him.

VENNEMA:	He wants you to have this. It is 10 thousand dollars in cash. I am instructed to say— with his compliments to the worthy cause of GLOBOS—it is only a downpayment.

431

DR. OGILVY: But this is incredible. I can't accept such a large sum of money without knowing who it comes from.

VENNEMA: Principles can be such a hurdle sometimes.

DR. OGILVY: What does he mean—a downpayment. A downpayment on what?

VENNEMA: On a brighter day Dr. Ogilvy! On a happy future!

DR. OGILVY: I see.

VENNEMA: No I don't think you do! Forgive me. It's the heat. Please let me continue. Of course my employer was relying on you to be the same man of principle he heard on the Radio last night and he hoped you would prove your discretion by rejecting his suspicious gift. Congratulations. Would you consider coming with me to meet him?

DR. OGILVY: I might consider it.

VENNEMA: And he might consider increasing his contribution by another 90 thousand.

DR. OGILVY: You mean 100 thousand dollars all together?

VENNEMA: For this tax year.

DR. OGILVY: Oh. Now I understand.

VENNEMA: Come on now. Be practical. Are his motives really so important to you?

Dr. Ogilvy's footsteps cross the room—

DR. OGILVY: Don't forget your 10 thousand dollars Mr. Vennema.

—and he pulls the Door Open very sharp.

DR. OGILVY: Louise—I'm going out for some fresh air with our friend here. It's too hot to stay indoors.

LOUISE: Dr. Ogilvy! Wait a minute! Don't go yet! I just took in our highest pledge!

Dr. Ogilvy is already out the Door & halfway down the Hallway.

DR. OGILVY: Back in a hour or two.
LOÙISE: He pledged 5 dollars! Can you believe it?

But the only Answer she gets is the Fading Echo of Vennema's barking Laughs as they Ricochet around the empty staircase— until Organ Music buries them under a cloud of Suspense. The growl of a big car Motor punches through it & the whitewalls Mash the gravel on a deserted Backroad.

DR. OGILVY: Why do I have to wear this blindfold? I
                don't understand.
VENNEMA: You've been very patient so far. And very
                understanding. I promise just a minute
                longer and—yes. Here we are.
DR. OGILVY: In Heaven's name where?

As soon As Vennema shuts off the motor & opens the car door Dr. Ogilvy can tell where he is by the Sound of a diesel Locomotive tugging Passenger Cars down the Track & the Clanging Signal just a few feet away where the Caboose clacks to a Stop.

VENNEMA: The time has come for me to say "so long"
                Dr. Ogilvy. I leave you—with regret—but
                leave you I must.
DR. OGILVY: So now can I—
VENNEMA: Keep the blindfold on please for the
                moment. A private railroad car is waiting
                for you here. You will find Mr. Regis inside.
DR. OGILVY: Not with this thing on I won't! What am I
                supposed to do?Vennema! Mr. Vennema?
                Are you there? I'm not playing Blind Man's
                Bluff anymore—do you hear me?

NARRATOR: But what was this? A strange sight greeted
                 the good doctor's eyes. Yes strange even to
                 a man who has peered into the heart of the
                 Atom. A sleek black aerodynamic railroad
                 car proclaimed the end of the train the way
                 a stinger proclaims the end of a wasp. As
                 Dr. Ogilvy stepped inside and shut the door
                 the train lurched & started to move—

The Bump & Grind of the train Tracks shakes his bones for
now he is in the belly of this Shadowy Force hurtling him onward.
He can not stop it nor he can not slow it down or change the
Direction it is going with him.

NARRATOR: All of his senses warned him that he was not
                 alone—and yes: something else *was* in there
                 with him . . . Call it ice cold dread—and it was
                 clinging like fog to the dark corners of the long
                 room. It seemed to stretch out to him and seep
                 into his very mind where it formed the formula
                 of his fear: *What thing in the shadows is not of the
                 shadows . . . ?*
DR. OGILVY: Hello? Is somebody there?
MR. REGIS: Thank you for coming Dr. Ogilvy.
DR. OGILVY: I can't see you. It's so dark in here.
MR. REGIS: Yes.
DR. OGILVY: Your man—Mr. Vennema—
MR. REGIS: (*chuckles*) Ye-es . . .
DR. OGILVY: He told me you are interested in contributing
                 a large sum of money to GLOBOS. Or is this
                 your idea of some elaborate practical joke?
MR. REGIS: The scientific mind! How I admire it! How
                 you analyze suspicions and cut straight to the
                 core!
DR. OGILVY: Signal the engineer to stop this infernal
                 machine! I want to go back to the city.
MR. REGIS: Calm yourself Doctor. We're headed back to

	the city. Enjoy the ride. I brought you here for a purpose. A purpose which will advance the aims of GLOBOS. But before we go any further I must have your word that whether you agree to my terms or not—you will never speak to anyone of this meeting.
DR. OGILVY:	I am a man of honor Mr. Regis.
MR. REGIS:	I'm an idealist myself! Like you. Perhaps I'm a little more practical. I know you can't achieve your ambitions begging in the street with a tin cup.
DR. OGILVY:	Tell me about *your* ambitions.
MR. REGIS:	The same as yours. Global Law & Order through the Brotherhood Of Science.
DR. OGILVY:	You're not a scientist.
MR. REGIS:	That's right. I'm a businessman. But don't we both live in the same world?
DR. OGILVY:	I suppose so. Yes.
MR. REGIS:	Listen to me. In a secret vault in my office in Baltimore I have certain blueprints. And in my warehouse 50 miles away I have certain materials. With your expertise we can build a new Atomic Bomb.
DR. OGILVY:	This . . . this is staggering! How can you think such a thing can advance the aims of GLOBOS?
MR. REGIS:	It's simple. I propose that we give the secret of the Atom Bomb to the entire world. By building one ourselves we can show the Government bosses and the Generals & Admirals that only you Scientists can be trusted to control the terrible power you've discovered.
DR. OGILVY:	When you put it like that . . .
MR. REGIS:	The genie is out of the bottle Dr. Ogilvy! And the point is—who has the divine right to make 3 wishes? Who else besides a Scientist has the wisdom to know what to ask for?

435

DR. OGILVY: I won't do anything that can harm the work of my organization.

MR. REGIS: Heaven forbid! Are you forgetting my offer of 100 thousand dollars? I wish GLOBOS great success! As the founding father of that worthy body shouldn't you be interested in a plan that could be a shortcut to your highest goals? Think of it! You & I are going to build . . . the last Atomic Bomb.

Something maybe you Noticed i.e. I did not Appear in that important Scene nor I did not put in a surprise Appearance for it was too early in the plot for me to turn the Tide my way. Also Before I made my Move Before I threw the rest of the Cast a curve ball & made up my own Scene on the spot I had to know if I could count on David or Bernhardt to follow the leader & give me some Help. Judging by the Teacher's Pet performance Vaughan Cherry was turning in at least I was 100% Sure about what I could count on from *him*. Vaughan was going to do his Duty & keep the Episode on the right track just steering us Straight all the way down the line—

NARRATOR: When the urgent midnight conference with his stockbroker confirms his darkest suspicions Peter Tremayne sets up a secret meeting with Police Captain O'Shaughnessy. Extraordinary circumstances force the worried Crimestopper to reveal a Government Top Secret just to convince the Captain these are no mere phantoms he's chasing . . .

O'SHAUGHNESSY: Tell me again—what in St. Pat's name does the world supply of Kikapoo Nuts have to do with the price of tea in China?

TREMAYNE: Look—a little company in Maryland called Baltimore Brace & Bearing is

436

> buying up majority shares of every
> Kikapoo Nut farm in the Amazon.
> Here see for yourself—68% of this
> one—71% of this one—89% of this
> one—

I fan the pages of my Script under Bernhardt's nose.

O'SHAUGHNESSY:	Don't be wavin' your facts & figures in me face Peter! I still don't understand why this is a matter for the 89th Precinct.
TREMAYNE:	Baltimore Brace & Bearing has a total net value of less than 250 thousand dollars. But since last April it's managed to acquire shares in Brazilian Kikapoo Nuts worth over 35 million. What do you call that?
O'SHAUGHNESSY:	I call that none of my business.
TREMAYNE:	Concentrate on the date. April. What happened last April. Around the 15th.
O'SHAUGHNESSY:	I paid my Income Tax.
TREMAYNE:	What else?
O'SHAUGHNESSY:	Fort Diablo!
TREMAYNE:	Bingo. That was precisely when a truckload of Uranium-235 was stolen from the Army in New Mexico.
O'SHAUGHNESSY:	But—but the Green Ray helped the F.B.I. solve that case months ago. You—he—hauled in all that Uranium stuff—
TREMAYNE:	Not all of it.
O'SHAUGHNESSY:	What?
TREMAYNE:	I said—not all of it.
O'SHAUGHNESSY:	By all the Saints this is—
TREMAYNE:	Top Secret. Nobody wanted to cause a

437

needless panic. I'm telling you because *I need your help* . . .

I tried to signal Bernhardt with my eyes how I really *did* need his Help I beseeched him could I Rely on him later—but the Dramatic Pause turned into a cold gap which only made him Nervous & all he Signaled back was Panic since I still had another Line on the Page.

TREMAYNE:	. . . Dr. Septimus Ogilvy has disappeared.
O'SHAUGHNESSY:	That scientist fella you mean? The missus made me listen to his speech on the Radio. Him?
TREMAYNE:	The same. It doesn't make sense. He makes a public announcement about his own world-wide organization and next thing he ups & leaves his secretary in charge of it. It's unbelievable.
O'SHAUGHNESSY:	If it was anybody else tellin' me this Peter I'd say he had bats in his belfry. A crazy Scientist on the loose with radioactive Uranium! Don't worry. My boys'll bring him in before you can say Albert Einstein!
TREMAYNE:	No Captain. I'm going to find him. I know Dr. Ogilvy. I studied atomic physics under him at Harvard. Take it from me—he's no crazyman. He's a gentle hearted old soul with a brilliant mind & a sincere belief that he & his fellow Scientists can lead Humanity to peace & enlightenment.
O'SHAUGHNESSY:	I give up! A disappearing Scientist . . . Stolen Uranium . . . World peace . . . Kikapoo Nuts! Where's the connection?

438

TREMAYNE:	I can only think of one man deranged enough to use his financial muscle to warp the good intentions of a scientific genius *and* control the world supply of Kikapoo Nuts. A man who only worships power because he wants power to worship him.
O'SHAUGHNESSY:	Horvath.
TREMAYNE:	I'll be on the 3:47 to Baltimore.
O'SHAUGHNESSY:	Peter lad—
TREMAYNE:	Yes Captain?
O'SHAUGHNESSY:	Don't do anything . . . the Green Ray wouldn't do.
NARRATOR:	Posing as a wounded war vet out of work Tremayne finds the Manager of Baltimore Brace & Bearing Co. in a helpful mood.
MANAGER:	I'll tell ya bud—yer comin' in at a pretty good time. Never seen so much goin' on around here. Not since '43. You say you was at Guadalcanal?
TREMAYNE:	I saw some action against the Japs. Submarine Service.
MANAGER:	That how you busted up yer leg?
TREMAYNE:	I can still drive anything that's got a motor in it.
MANAGER:	I'll put you on that forklift O.K.? We're expandin' all over the place. New owner. Wants to build us up.
TREMAYNE:	That him? That oil painting on the wall?
MANAGER:	That's Mr. Regis all right. Queer fella. Nice though. Now look. I got a ton of scrap gotta git moved outa the warehouse and . . .

As he kibbitzed away Explaining about Scrap Metal etc. my Inner Thoughts echoed over the Airwaves—

439

TREMAYNE:	*Such a flattering portrait of you—Horvath! Did you pay the artist something extra to add all that hair to your scalp? To melt the yellow fat from your cheeks and shrink your sagging belly? Well the Artist's brush paints deep Professor. You can't disguise who you are. I recognize you! Vainglory in the cold glow of your smile . . . Contempt in the swagger of your pose . . . Catastrophe waiting at your fingertips.*

My time was Ticking Away for only 10 Minutes only 2 more Scenes stood between me and Oblivion. If anybody in Radioland expected I was going to sit on my keister & let them do away with me & not put up the Fight to end all Fights then I say he did not Comprehend how deep my character runs! For a Trouper the 11th Commandment is THE SHOW MUST GO ON and Ladies & Gentlemen if I was anything in this Life I was a red-blooded Trouper so watch what Happened—

When the Brace & Bearing Manager heard the boss's limousine whoosh into the Warehouse he jumped into Action and how!

MANAGER:	Pete! Git over here! Load that funny lookin' machine into Mr. Regis's airplane. And git a move on! He's gotta take off in 10 minutes.

Inside the Warehouse I Recognized what that funny Machine was waiting there next to the cargo bay of his war surplus DC-3—and I Recognized who was tinkering with it. Dr. Ogilvy was completing the Final Assembly of his homemade A-Bomb.

TREMAYNE: The big boss told me to load it onboard.
DR. OGILVY: Just one more bolt . . . there. If I steady it on this cradle . . .
TREMAYNE: Dr. Ogilvy? Do you remember me?
DR. OGILVY: Don't remember faces. Remember names.

TREMAYNE: I'm Peter Tremayne. Harvard '35.

DR. OGILVY: Ah yes! Plasma wasn't it? Are you working for
              Mr. Regis too?

TREMAYNE: Not exactly. Dr. Ogilvy I think you may be in
              great danger from him. He isn't at all the man
              he appears to be. You can't trust him with
              this!

DR. OGILVY: Pish-tosh young man. Oh yes! I thought like
              you did at first. But when you get to know him
              better you'll see he's a man of vision.

TREMAYNE: I know him all right. He's a vampire. He's
              using you for some secret purpose. Secret from
              you!

DR. OGILVY: The only secret is Mr. Regis & I are about to
              fly this up to Washington, D.C. don't you
              know! To show those smug so-and so's they
              aren't holding all the aces. It was his idea—
              Mr. Regis's—for the sake of GLOBOS don't
              you know!

HORVATH: Are we on schedule Doctor?

DR. OGILVY: On the dot. As soon as we load Fat Lady
              onboard—

HORVATH: Well well well! Tremayne . . .

DR. OGILVY: Wh-what's going on here?

TREMAYNE: Don't expect a straight answer from "Mr.
              Regis"—I suppose if you can lie to Dr. Ogilvy
              about who you are you can lie about your true
              purpose.

HORVATH: I don't mind telling him my real name now—
              why not? Ha ha ha ha ha!

DR. OGILVY: That voice! I recognize it . . . you're
              Vennema!

HORVATH: No—Vennema was me.

TREMAYNE: Try again.

HORVATH: Professor Lionel Horvath. At your service.

TREMAYNE: The most notorious criminal mastermind at
              large today.

441

HORVATH:	Is that your puny attempt to embarrass me with my past? It won't work. As usual Tremayne you're a day late and a dollar short. Haven't you heard the news? I've turned over a new leaf. I'm legitimate now. I'm in the Kikapoo Nut Oil business. I don't have to rely on outsmarting you & your pet police captain anymore.
TREMAYNE:	Careful Horvath. Your toupee twitches when you lie.
HORVATH:	Is that nasty habit of suspicion something you picked up from your friend The Green Ray?
DR. OGILVY:	Please! Please you two! Just listen to me. This man has donated 100 thousand dollars to promote the cause of my organization. In fact he's the most generous benefactor GLOBOS has got! Mr. Regis—or what do you call him—Horvath?—he isn't the first philanthropist in history who disguised his identity so he could do his good works.
TREMAYNE:	Good works! Spare me!
HORVATH:	Save your breath Doc. There are none so dumb as will not hear. Tell you what Tremayne—why don't you come along for the ride? We can keep an eye on each other.
TREMAYNE:	I've always wanted to see Brazil from the air.
HORVATH:	Brazil? Did I say anything about flying to Brazil?

The mighty Sound of its twin propellers spinning hauls the DC-3 up into the Wild Blue Yonder—with Horvath in the driver's seat & his Explosive Cargo loaded onboard!

HORVATH:	Here's a tip Tremayne. If you want to make some money in a hurry—invest in Brazilian Kikapoo Nuts. The price is going to go through the roof.

442

TREMAYNE:	Do you know something Wall Street doesn't know?
HORVATH:	Could be. Doctor—is Fat Lady locked in her cradle?

Dr. Ogilvy steps into the Cockpit from the rattling Cargo Hold.

DR. OGILVY:	Yes indeed. She's safe & sound. How long before we get to Washington?
HORVATH:	I think we'll do a little bit of sight-seeing first. Look down there. Those luscious green fields are where most of the world's Kikapoo Nuts grow . . .

I knew what was going to Happen next then what I had to do about it jumped out at me from the dark of my Inner Thoughts. *Who decides the Future? Who dares to do or die! Now the Nation expects me to fight back with all my Powers & give of my Best and STOP THAT BOMB FROM BLOWING UP!* Thus my Counterplot hatches out—If I do not feed David Arcash his cue i.e. if I do not say, "This will be a far better world without you in it!" then ipso facto Horvath can not Reply, "It'll be a simpler world without The Green Ray! Sing Fat Lady! Sing!" which line is Leon's cue to explode the A-Bomb in our faces. Therefore the Episode can end before I Disintegrate in a fountain of Radioactive Particles & voila we avoid the violent Conclusion which means it is possible I can Return next week—

HORVATH:	Take over the controls a minute Doc. I want to go check on Fat Lady.
DR. OGILVY:	I don't know how to fly this contraption!
HORVATH:	It's just like driving a car. Hold her steady.
TREMAYNE:	Don't do it Dr. Ogilvy.
DR. OGILVY:	Mr. Horvath! Sit down! I'm not a qualified pilot!
TREMAYNE:	*Does this gangster's greed know no decent limit? Does this maniac's madness know no bounds at all?*

Very quick I got my Answer: the Sound of the cargo door opening & Air whistling into the Fuselage—

DR. OGILVY: Wh-what's going on? What are you doing back there?

The motors whine! The plane dives out of control!

HORVATH: Get back to those controls! Keep her level!
DR. OGILVY: What are you doing? That switch arms the detonator!

And the tick-tick-tick starts ringing in our ears counting down the Last Minute to our Doom . . .

TREMAYNE: You can't do it Horvath! There are innocent people down there. American citizens!
HORVATH: Shut up and watch me. I want you to report it step by step to The Green Ray. He's the only man alive who'd appreciate my genius!
DR. OGILVY: I won't let you! Move back!
HORVATH: Drop that monkey wrench Doc. You can't stop this. It's too late.

Horvath takes a feeble Punch on the shoulder and they snort & grunt they Scuffle hard but Dr. Ogilvy is too Weak to Fight him off—

HORVATH: Get off me you old fool!
DR. OGILVY: Aah! Help me! Tremayne!
TREMAYNE: The door! Look out! Keep away from the door!
DR. OGILVY: Tremaaaaaaaaaaaaaaaaaaaaaayne!

I hear his Voice fade away with him Plunging out of the plane down to his messy Death far Below. Do you think Horvath cares?

444

By him Dr. Ogilvy performed his job so now So What he is out of his sight & out of his Mind—

HORVATH: Get us back on course! You—you're flying us out over the ocean!

TREMAYNE: That's right Horvath. You've just gone too far and this time I'm going to stop you for good—

The Music of my glorious Fanfare surrounded him—my Blaze of Green Light flared up & Blinded him—it Transformed me into his Arch Foe there I was as bright as a Star glowing indoors! I humbled him by the power of The Green Ray—

HORVATH: It's y-you! All this time! All along it's been you!

GREEN RAY: Yes. I invented Peter Tremayne in order to protect my true identity. I am The Green Ray Professor Horvath. And your sworn nemesis.

At the Sound of a bolt from my Hand Blaster the control panel goes flooey with Short Circuits fizzing & popping all over. But the plane keeps ploughing through the Air with both motors purring very steady.

HORVATH: Oh smart move! You just wiped out all the controls!

GREEN RAY: Yes they're locked solid. At least America's supply of Kikapoo Nut Oil is safe from your hands.

HORVATH: It ain't over till the Fat Lady sings. If you don't turn us around I swear I'll reveal your secret to the world! You'll be all washed up as a Crime Stopper.

GREEN RAY: I'm almost sorry you won't live to regret that threat. This is the end of the line.

Both of us hold our Breath for $\frac{1}{2}$ a Second & louder over the motors we hear the tick-tick-tick of the Timer—

HORVATH: Back off from that bomb!

He Knocks me back & pulls me into our Fight to the Finish— every Punch lands with the flat thud of a Baseball bat whacking a horsehair mattress & we hiss at each other in the Clinches—

GREEN RAY: You're the one who's all washed up!
HORVATH: If I'm finished (*grunt*) then so are you! Don't you understand? We're brothers you & me (*snort*)—both of us live outside the Law—! We act as we see fit in the world—to achieve our own ends!
GREEN RAY: The only thing (*grunt*) you peddle in this world is filth. The stink of selfish greed!
HORVATH: It's a free country! And what do you do? You just make life easy for weaklings! Crybabies who need you to get them out of their miserable jams. Pathetic peons who can't look out for themselves—they all have to count on you!
GREEN RAY: I fight against wrong (*grunt*) wherever I find it.
HORVATH: You keep them weak so they have to depend on you! You want things (*grunt*) that way! That's how you like it!

Right here David Arcash expected me to say my Line about this is going to be a much Better World without him in it etc. & stand by for him to Taunt me with his fine Line about the simple world to come when The Green Ray is no more—and KA-BLOOEY!—Leon can hit the button & the Bomb can blow us to Smithereens. Except my Mind reeled back from this Fatal Direction & instead I said something else—

GREEN RAY: My purpose on Earth is defending the defense-

446

less & helping the helpless! And you better believe I'll be here to give them hope day after day—week after week!

David's eyes rolled in his head and when they came back around he Aimed them at me very Fierce. He had a Personal Message for me too which I decoded in a Flash i.e. *you jerk what do you think you're doing here putting me on the spot? trying to make me look stupid? step on my famous last words? pay me back for the way I treated you before? for the way I treated Annie?* Except I could not get across my genuine Motives to him by eye signals & while David tried to wrestle me back to the Right Lines on the page Leon kept going with the Sound Effects of our struggle he had that Baseball bat up over his head now & my next Punch split the seams of his horsehair mattress!

HORVATH: (*oohf! grunt*) Are you blind? When that ticking stops you're going to follow me into Oblivion!

I saw how he was trying to box me in but I held him off by quick Thinking. All I can compare it by is a Strike of Lightning in my Mind then I knew how it Feels to be in Control of Events for once—

GREEN RAY: If I can (*grunt*) get my hand free I can neutralize the detonator (*grunt*) with my Hand Blaster . . .

HORVATH: Your Blaster fell out of the plane! I saw it with my own eyes! Say good-bye to the world Green Ray—nothing can get you out of this!

Tick-Tick-Tick-Tick-Tick . . .

GREEN RAY: Except . . . my Reserve Blaster! If I can just reach . . . the secret compartment (*grunt*) in my (*grunt*) belt . . .

447

Did he Despise me in this instant! Did he go sour! Oh he was not going to continue this game of Tic-Tac-Toe nor he was not going to let me ruin his big Exit either. We are still on the Air and David yanks me over by my shirt & he bawls me out by such Personal words!

DAVID: Enough already! This stupid stunt of yours is making it worse for everybody! It's just complicating all our lives! Why can't you act like a man?
ME: Yeah? Well this man is fighting for his Life! Is that simple enough for you?

All of his Worries melted away into the Air & the Hate that clotted up his grim Expression drained out of his face & he played out this moment in his Mind for his own Enjoyment before he played it on the Air. David was in control now for I fed it to him on a silver spoon—

HORVATH: It'll be a simpler world without The Green Ray!
ME: No! Don't—
HORVATH: Sing Fat Lady! Sing!

KA-BLOOEY! Leon triggered the sound of a Thunder Storm echoing 100 times over—plus a Earthquake destroying 100 cities—plus the molten Heart of the Earth cracking the surface & pouring out—it was a boiling cloud of noise that wiped every other Sound off the Air until it dropped down to a low rumble under Vaughan Cherry's gloomy undertaker Voice.

NARRATOR: The still of this empty dawn is broken by the roar of a thousand volcanoes—the dark is shattered by the light of a thousand suns. The ground trembles & recoils from a fantastic release of energy—as the demigod we knew by the name of The Green Ray disintegrates into the Atoms of his

448

being . . . And for a single instant a pure green sheet of light flashes across the surface of the ocean from the horizon to the shore . . . For his final message blazes from the shadows to give Hope to the hopeless just as he did before: The Green Ray lives on—yes—the memory of his heroic Deeds will remain on Earth as his Voice mingles among the Stars . . . And the green sea never shimmered so bright nor the night sky danced with so much light.

DA DOO DA DA DUM! DA DOO DA DA DOO! DOOM DOOM DUT DUT DUT DOOM! YOU HAVE JUST HEARD THE CONCLUDING EPISODE OF THE ADVENTURES OF THE GREEN RAY . . . YES LISTENERS HE MAY BE GONE BUT THE GREEN RAY LIVES ON IN TWELVE TOUGH WASHABLE PLASTIC STATUETTES AVAILABLE FOR A LIMITED TIME ONLY INSIDE SPECIALLY MARKED BOXES OF SPILLER'S HIGH-ENERGY BUCKWHEAT BREAKFAST FLAKES! ASK YOUR MOM TO BUY SOME TODAY!

"Are you going back to the party?"

"What?"

Annie had a fragile smile saved up for me. "We didn't get any chance to talk upstairs."

"No. Well. It looks like we'll have something to talk about now."

"I think it was brave of you. I do Ray."

A knot of Cramps twisted in my stomach therefore I handed her a dishonest Excuse about how I had to sit down by myself somewhere & collect my Thoughts before I said my fond Farewells to all concerned. Not 100% Dishonesty I hope for as soon as Annie was in the elevator I went up by the stairs to the Executive Bathroom. This place is not a Grandiose affair like you may Expect it is only 2 closed off Cubicles for maximum Privacy. Pilgrim woodwork & brass hinges on the doors close a person in like it is a sanitary Library. And this I never saw anything similar before: frosted glass Splash Guards down in front of the urinals so the Liberty VIP's do not also have to worry about pee splashing back all over their Alligator Loafers.

When I sat those Cramps came out with a Personality of their own & folded me over Double! Mutiny of my poisoned bowels! The fumes of rotten juices Inflated to a bubble in there so I massaged it like bread dough the way the Expert of Experts advises. "Artie" McGovern does not pull his Punches on counteracting "bodily swamp gas" he Instructs you should Expel it A.S.A.P. unless such Action will lead to Social embarrassment. I speak from my Personal Experiences it is not Healthy to flinch from this vital function of Relief. "PAIN IS THE ALARM OF HARM"—! So as per Expert Advice I rubbed my lower stomach & got all set to Expel then right on the edge of it I heard footsteps walk across the tile floor so I pulled my bubble back. I heard the door on the other cubicle swing open & bang shut then came his Voice cracking through the wall—

"Why shouldn't I? *Well why not?* Why the stinking hell—" I caught Lamont fighting a drunk Argument with himself and Losing.

By now since I stopped in the middle I felt like I was holding in a Concrete cube or a block of wood was trying to squeeze out of me the Pain was too sharp & I let off a loud one—P-P-P-THUUUT!

"Who's that? Who's there?" Lamont pounded on the partition.

"Me."

"Green?"

"Yes it's me."

"Oh. It's you." A slow hiss from him which turned into a breathy sigh Informed me he did not Care if I was there then he let one off louder than mine—H-H-HUUUUUUUUH-THUT-THUT! "Aah," he moaned, "that bastard's ruined my health."

"My stomach's churned up too."

"Yeah," Lamont said, "The end is nigh!" and one more Fart stabbed into the Toilet Bowl. "Gad. Hear that? He poisoned me. *I want to go but I can't.*" Then I think I heard him sob.

"Are you usually regular Mr. Carruthers?"

"What?" he sniffed. "Like clockwork. Twice a week."

"Well that's not very good. You should be moving your bowels every 24 hours. At least."

"Move 'em where?"

"Twice a week is unhealthy. So is taking pills for it. Do you—"

"Are you the world expert on bowel movements Green?" Another jet of Rotten Air breezed out of him. "Ooh! Bastard!"

I Believe all the Barriers fall down in the Men's Room & we can be men together Honest & Equal. Nor I did not hold anything back from here Onward since both of us were in the same boat Constipationwise. Except I was not slobbering drunk on top of it so I let him talk & he let me listen to all the Pain pouring off him like steam.

"I wrote my stinking heart out on this one Green. They think they paid me off. Spiller. And that jellyfish Silverstein." THU-UUUT! "Watched me type The End . . . and then . . . " PHUT-PHUT-PHUT! " . . . told me to empty out my desk! The End. Well . . . *bull!*"

My Cramps kicked & rolled over each other then I thought I must be spraying Blood already—PHTHTSSSSS-SSSSSS-SSSSSS-HHUUUUHSSSS!

"Hah! You said it! Nice one Green! Hah!" He Laughed so hard he started choking on it until he stopped himself by a phlegmy Cough. I Heard him spit. "I don't have to apologize to anybody . . . for anything. I'm a honest man Green. Don't lie to myself about the world & I won't lie to them about it. Some people you have to *rub their noses* in the truth for their own good. I can't bottle it up inside just because certain parties won't like the sound of it." He ground out a dry Fart that died away like the Groan of a small animal. "The truth's always a pain in the ass. Wouldn't you say?"

"I think you're right."

"You better believe it! The end is when all the truth comes out. That's how you know it's the end. And don't I know what I know."

451

"What don't you know?" I leaned all the way over. "*What* do you know?"

"Ooh! Aah! A blade . . . of fire . . . 's going up me!"

"Mr. Carruthers?"

"*What?*" he strained & he yelped.

I waited untill I Heard him Breathing Regular again then I asked him very Direct, "Do you know the reason . . . why they killed off The Green Ray?" He just answered me by a Moan. "Can you tell me why they—"

" . . . that Cheddar Cheese gissum."

"What about it? *What about* the Cheddar Cheese?"

"Sonofabitch fed it to us down there . . . his human guinea pigs . . . aah! ooh! aah!"—PHUUUTT-THUUUTTT—"Son! Of! A! Bitch!" Very slow & word by word I asked Lamont my Big Question again. This time I broke through the fog of rum punch this time he Answered very sober, "He's afraid," Lamont warned me. "He's afraid of The Green Ray. Every action has a equal & opposite reaction don't y'know."

"I don't understand. I don't understand what you're saying."

"Isaac Newton! Dem bones of the whole universe! Pick up a book on science if you want to know the reasons. Look at biology. You already have a healthy interest in other people's bowels . . ."

"But the *show* Mr. Carruthers. You said he's afraid of The Green Ray. Who is? You mean Spiller? Or why would Howard Silverstein—"

He sang to me or to himself, "Silverstein bone connected to de Spiller bone . . . de Spiller bone connected to de Liberty Broadcasting bone . . . Now hear de word of de Lord!"—PHUTTT-HHHUUUUUSS-THUTTT—"That's a gasser!"—THUT—"Better. I feel better." And he went into a heavy silence which he only shook off to Blurt Out strange Sayings like, "Gravity is my sweetheart . . . Ooh! she's my mortal enemy . . . " also, "I gave my typewriter to Mrs. Shapiro . . . " also, "Science is the King of Knowledge!"

I tapped my fingertips on the wood. "Are you all right?"

"Gad," Lamont said, "I feel bad. Have to clean myself out. Empty it all out before I fade into yesteryear. Green?"

"I'm still here."

"I'M GOING TO TELL YOU WHERE YOU CAME FROM! Truth is," he whispered, "got the idea out of National Geographic. Read about how when the sun sets in certain latitudes under certain conditions just at the exact second it sinks under the horizon—if you watch it then you can see the surface of the ocean *turn bright green.* Supposed to appear there like a sheet of green ice that melts as soon as you see it. How d'you like that—as if *looking at it* makes it melt."

"There really *is* such a thing?"

"They don't make things up in the National Geographic! I'm not *lying* to you Green. It's based on fact. Absolutely. Scientific *fact.* I base it all on the facts! That's what scares him. I told him if he wants somebody to help him put on a Comic Book of the Air he can just find himself another boy. I said those words to his face at the very beginning. I meant 'em then & I mean 'em now. *Don't threaten me!* he said. You think I can seal my integrity up in a jar? My *artistic* integrity I'm talking about. Seal it in a tin can and take it out for Christmas when it's convenient for everybody? Well I want to be stinking INconvenient! *Don't be difficult!* he says. Every time I want to interject a little intellectual *verve.* You know what I'm talking about?"

"Verve."

"Verve! That's it. Put in a few serious ideas. A little *gravity.*" Lamont let one go which sounded like his rear end sputtered out the word HOCKEY-PUCK but he just ignored this heckling. "I'll tell you a fact about William Shakespeare. He was a *popular entertainer* in his time just like I am now. Moneymaking playwright. Just the same. Look at Hamlet. What's that story about? I can tell you in 1 word—revenge. Hamlet's a thrilling revenge story with murder for a motive and a sword fight for the big finish. What about the gravity? What about the poetry? He sneaks it in while everybody's busy wondering when that bastard King is going to get it in the neck! I do the same thing! I'll tell you what Green—if William Shakespeare was alive today he'd be writing radio shows."

453

"You mean all this—he's taking us off the air because he doesn't like your scripts anymore?"

"P.K. Spiller couldn't tell a quality script from a manhole cover. What he doesn't like is the idea of The Green Ray dogging him. *What's he going to dig up next week? What other ghost from my past are you going to expose?* Answer: relax! I wouldn't let you go *that* far Green!"

"You let me get blown to smithereens. I disintegrated tonight. You let me go that far."

"Don't be a whiner. It's a beautiful way to go."

"I still don't know why I had to go *at all.*"

"Oh brother!" Lamont snapped. "His revenge! Revenge makes the world go round! It's the only motive there is. Ownership is the revenge of dependence! Science is the revenge of confusion! Love is the revenge of loneliness! And vice versa. Around and around. Since the earliest times Green it's recorded in the Bible. So what's the big mystery? A swift kick in the balls—that's the revenge for telling the truth!" He dropped his Voice down I Believe a Inner Thought slipped out & twanged his vocal cords when he pondered, "*And vice damn versa* . . . " He spoke up then very Exhausted & faint, "They still perform the works of William Shakespeare but mine just get flushed into outer space. Radio waves vibrating out there forever. For the mutants on Mars to tune in."

Out of Kind Consideration a person might say All Is Not Lost even if he does not Believe this for giving Comfort repays a person with Comfort the same. "I don't know how else to make a living," I confessed & gave Lamont the chance to comfort me but he did not reply. "I look into the future & I'm scared to death I'll end up living on Social Security in a run-down neighborhood somewhere. My apartment's going to be a lonely place. Where I just sit in my underwear all day in a chair in the middle of the livingroom and I cut out paper dolls & just do crossword puzzles for entertainment. I eat dinner out of tin cans. And tubes. I don't know my neighbors & they don't want to know me. I'll remember when the whole world turned its back I mean from tonight. I'll think back to tonight Mr. Carruthers to this exact conversation.

To the night I lost my purpose in life. What do I have to look forward to? Waking up in the morning and going back to sleep at night. Around & around like you said. But I won't be all there & conscious during the day or knocked out unconscious when I'm asleep. I'll be in two kinds of a trance because some part of me is going to be back here with you and Annie and Bernhardt & everybody else. Back when I was doing something with a point. Mr. Carruthers I'm starting to wonder if I'm living my life backwards—a big success in the beginning & I wind up in a heap at the end. Is there only one way to go from a pinnacle? Down down down and down? I'm scared of this feeling I'm getting a little bit that I don't really have a good reason to live anymore."

His Voice of Experience leaked in under the cubicle door. "I think . . . that's very . . . depressing. Yes. Very . . . bleak," he said. "And I think . . . you might be right. Yes. Yes. It can happen that way. What *is* the point of waking up tomorrow? That is the question . . . " Lamont sounded shaky but he Continued this way, "Nobody to tell my stories to . . . can't bring them to life now so . . . " Everybody decides on his own Personal Solution to his troubles and I Heard by the firm way he flushed the toilet then & there Lamont made his Mind up what he was going to do. "Good-bye Green. I'm sure I'll miss you."

"Good-bye Mr. Carruthers. I'll miss you too."

He went over to the sink he scrubbed his hands & started humming the Theme Song of The Green Ray. "I'm going down there & tell 'em all . . . "

"Are you talking to me?"

"Enough to give that fat bastard a heart attack!" He left the hot water running hard & over the foaming noise of it Lamont asked me if I was Planning to go back to the Party.

"Just to say good-bye to Annie," I said.

"I want to bid 'em all my fond farewell. Those S.O.B.'s who think they can just give me the air. I'll take the air when & where I want to! And not a stinking second before!" He pulled the towel down by such a yank I thought he pulled the roller off the wall— "I'll show 'em fear in a handful of dust la-dee-doo-dah. *ET cetera!* You hear me Green?"

"I do."

"Remember—he who doesn't remember the past is doomed to forget it." His footsteps clicked away with him mumbling about P.K. Spiller again, "Sonofabitch doesn't know who he's dealing with . . . " and Lamont's Voice of Authority boomed to me from the bathroom door it nailed me to my seat when he shouted back—"VENGEANCE IS MINE!"

You Know what I saw when I looked at my Face in the mirror over the sink? While I washed my hands there I Saw a Old Man looking back at me. The great artist Michelangelo I learn by my Readings could see the Complete Shape of a Statue in a piece of marble or in a tree trunk etc. & that was the way I saw the Old Man who was inside me i.e. the Alter Cocker I am Today. I just went into the bathroom here and guess who I saw in the medicine cabinet in my Reflection there I was the young man of yesteryear staring me in my face. The little pisher who made all the Wrong Moves and led me to a unescapable Conclusion.

Good-bye Green. I'm sure I'll miss you . . . What is the point of waking up tomorrow . . . I want to bid 'em all farewell . . . A Red Alarm bell started ringing in my ears—nor it was not only my downcast state of Mind which jumped to the Conclusion he was going to spite P.K. Spiller by a act of public Suicide—my Red Alarm was what if I was who pushed him into such a Drastic Idea by all my bleak talk about Social Security & *1 way to go from a pinnacle Down Down Down & Down* etc.—!

I ran down the stairs 2 at a time I sprinted into the Executive Dining Room and I was not Too Late to see Lamont climbing up on one of the marble window seats with a fresh glass of rum punch in his spidery hand. "And another thing Ladies & Gentlemen," Lamont uncoiled his finger & aimed it like a Death Ray straight at Spiller's heart, "He's a damn imposter! This man wears a damn corset!"

"Come down from there Lamont," Spiller urged him very no nonsense.

"It's not a corset anyway," Ethel Spiller let him & everybody else know, "it's a back brace."

"For my next trick," Lamont slurred, "I will reveal the truth about Professor Lionel Horvath. He's—"

"Enough Lamont!"

"Somebody get him down."

"Somebody shut him up."

"Shut up Lamont!"

Only nobody made any move toward him not even Howard Silverstein who stationed himself beside Mrs. Spiller. He kept his arms folded & hid his Inner Thoughts behind a patient smile & his eyes locked stiff on Lamont.

"He is . . . he's . . . that greedy backstabber . . . that plundering pirate . . . that Black Market profiteer . . . Meet his secret identity! Don't be shy P.K. step up here and take a bow!" Lamont clapped his hands very Limp & Feeble a few times and when it looked like he was going on with his Speech a few of the Liberty V.I.P.s started clapping louder to drown him out. "Did you know Ladies & Gents . . . did you know that is . . . are you aware of the fact . . ." Now the Liberty wives started joining in & giggling very silly at each other but Lamont raised his Voice over them all. "P.K. SPILLER DIDN'T MAKE HIS MONEY BY SELLING DRY CEREAL! I'LL TELL YOU WHERE HIS FORTUNE COMES FROM—"

The clapping dwindled down & Spiller's angry words Halted the rest. "That's *enough* Lamont!"

"More than enough," Ethel chimed in.

Lamont did not even soften his Voice for the quiet room. "NO—IT'S NOT ENOUGH OF ENOUGH! THIS DECENT MAN HERE USED TO BE THE BIGGEST BOOTLEGGER ON THE EAST COAST!" And now he spoke very polite to P.K. himself, "Why *did* all the girls at Masie's call you Screwdriver? Or maybe I should ask Ethel. Well Ethel?" He tottered Forward & spilled his drink.

"Make him stop it Poppy!"

By this heartfelt Plea she spurred her hubby into Action & Spiller made a grab for Lamont's sleeve—Lamont jerked back out of his Reach then he held on to the brass Window Latch whereby he straightened himself up. Howard tugged Spiller away from the

457

Excitement but he kept on barking at Lamont until his chubby face went dark red & his neck Inflated he was squealing at him like a stuck pig. "Tell everybody about *you* Lamont! Where'd I find you in '29? You square peg! You ingrate!"

"In the stinking gutter! Oh sure! I'm not ashamed of it either. Taught me a permanent lesson that fateful day. When I lost all my security in the Great Crash. Found out everything I needed to know about human nature," he sneered at the whole room & ended up looking right at Spiller.

"Who put you back on your feet? Tell them. Go on you miserable misfit! Who gave you a job?"

"Driving a truck! You took advantage of my circumstances and don't you know it. I'm college educated you crumb! By Jesuits! And folks he *lets* me drive his beer wagons back & forth between Toronto & Detroit for $35.50 a week."

"And a Christmas bonus," Spiller snarled very insulted.

"Oh yes. Right. I don't know how I would've made it to New Year's without those 12 extra bucks in my pocket. I learned a lot from you P.K."

"You never learned a blessed thing from me Lamont."

"Not as much as I did from Karl Marx." Every mouth in the room hushed up quiet as a Clam. "From Lenin . . . Uncle Joe Stalin . . . and Kropotkin!" Lamont bellowed this Name across the Dining Room & shocked the execs' wives practically to Tears. "Matushka Russia! V'period! How do you like *them* red apples Howard?"

"You're sick in the head," Howard diagnosed him, "and I pity you. I just pity you to death."

"Likewise. And here's a little tidbit left over especially for you. I put *oodles* of Commie propaganda in every episode I wrote. In every episode you approved. Something's there. Showing up the rotten foundations of this stinking society. My messages of hope!"

"Oodles," Howard frowned.

"Oodles and oodles. You think about it in bed tonight."

"I think we've heard all we want to from you Lamont."

Lamont mowed down the whole crowd with his sweeping arm. "Say good-bye to exploitation of the wage slave! The days of fat

458

cats hitching a free ride on the Gravy Train are coming to a goddamned fiery end!"

"We can rush him," Spiller said.

"AND ANOTHER THING . . . "

"Let the police handle this," advised Howard.

"Oh fine!" Lamont leaned back & gave out with a Daredevil Laugh. "Bring on the police—the blunt instrument of the oppressors of the masses . . . ! A river of blood is going to run in the streets . . . !" Then the Window Latch clicked & he thumped his chest—"This machine kills Fascists!"

I Know I cried his Name out I shrieked it from a few feet away & I Know I got a Grip on his ankle with both of my arms wrapped around there Before I felt Lamont teeter backward. I squeezed my eyes shut & held on for his dear Life when I Heard the window sigh open but I will not say I felt him fall out. My Memory of the moment AND I WAS THE CLOSEST PERSON TO HIM was Lamont pushed himself through it he *pushed* himself so I could not stop him. I clutched very hard & tight with the Wind Whistling in around my ears where I kneeled under the freezing window seat. I still had Lamont's wooden leg Standing in my arms and the window was slapping in & out like a loose sail. It was P.K. Spiller who stepped in & forced it shut then after he did that he pulled me free from the leg and all Pandemonia broke out.

"I hear you went a little crazy up there." Detective Gillespie jerked his thumb at the ceiling i.e. he meant the Executive Dining Room above & beyond.

"Is that what everybody thinks? Did they say that?"

"Not everybody," said a Smart Aleck Voice behind me, "Just everybody we talked to." This mean Remark from Det. Gillespie's sidekick Joey DiMarco blew right past me & hit his partner's weary face like a whiff of Sour Milk.

The 3 of us were sitting too close for any Comfort downstairs in Lamont's office since the Police decided it was a Convenient place to collect the Facts of their Investigation. I will Record in Black & White here a Fact about Det. Gillespie—he never used a Harsh Tone on me nor he was not Sarcastic like that pisher

459

DiMarco who was Harsh & Sarcastic for both of them from the word Go. By his eyes I could tell Gillespie just wanted to get to the whole Truth of the tragic Episode for now I Recall they were pale & blue but very warm a strange combination very womanly. Ditto his milky skin. On the manly side he did not preen his Appearance his feathery red hairs grew out wild on his scalp & his eyebrows likewise down to his knuckles the same. When he tapped the metal top of Lamont's desk click-click-click his Marine Corps ring stood out on his finger like a Doorbell.

"What do you want me to say?"

"Say what happened."

"In your own words," DiMarco did not even Pretend to show me any Consideration he had to twist it into a dumb joke, "In 25 words or less." He walked over special to stub out his cigarette on the corner of the desk right under my nose and I Resented this rude Gesture so I did not Flinch I told him so. Gillespie brushed the dead butt & flakes of ash by a quick sidewise sweep of his hand into the Trash Can.

He was tired of cleaning up after DiMarco. "Give Mr. Green a little room to breathe," he told him stiff & stern and DiMarco paced back to sit in the chair against the wall.

This Sympathetic display by Gillespie urged me on to talk to him Man to Man. "I tried to save him."

"I understand. Mr. Carruthers was a friend of yours—for how many years? It's 8 or 9 isn't it?"

"Not that long."

"Anyway Lamont was a friend of yours and you knew he was tipsy so when you came in and saw him horsing around the open window—"

"The window wasn't open," I corrected him, "I heard it open. I heard the latch click. Then I ran over & grabbed him."

"You tackled him so he wouldn't fall out of the window but you bumped him off instead."

"What?" I said & I held my Breath.

"You bumped him off balance by accident and down he went. Is that what you say happened?"

"Lamont pushed himself out. I couldn't hang on to him."

For reporting this Fact of the Matter I got a mocking snort out of DiMarco but Det. Gillespie just said to himself, "All right," & to me he said, "let's go over this again." He flipped through his little Notepad & squinted at the pages like what was on them was written in Hebrew. "Mr. Burrows," he said & glanced up at me, "he's a friend of yours too?"

"Did he say he wasn't?"

"I'd just like to hear it from you if he's got some axe to grind against you." I shrugged & shook my head. "Right. Mr. Burrows told me you were pretty upset about the show going off the air tonight." Gillespie tilted his head he Invited me to Reply.

"Almost everybody was."

"Who else besides you tried to talk Mr. Lamont—excuse me: Mr. Carruthers into changing his mind about the script?"

"Nobody else was going to talk to him. Nobody else wanted to."

"So you begged him on behalf of everybody else."

"I didn't beg him," I said & sat up. "Who said I begged him?"

Gillespie ignored my Sincere Question & flipped the next page over. "Howard Silverstein. Friend or foe?"

"I don't think he's one or the other. You know Howard hired me."

"I hired DiMarco over there and I hate his Eyetalian guts!" He smiled a little bit to show this was maybe a little bit true. In this gap I made a Point very Strenuous which I did not know & was in me until I opened my mouth & it came out how that Friendship between Howard & me got longer but not any deeper year after year it just went on Stretching like a Rubber Band. "He told me he had to pull you & Carruthers apart right before the show. It was getting ugly he said & he had to peel him off you like a piece of flypaper. True?"

"That happened. That's true."

"Well what were you fighting about?"

"It wasn't a fight. We weren't fighting about anything. Maybe it looked that way to Howard."

"And Burrows. And Leon Kern. And Arthur Godfrey," DiMarco added to the list.

461

"Maybe it looked that way from the outside," I said, "but it wasn't a fight. He was demonstrating a point about Rudolph Valentino."

"Kissy kissy," DiMarco smooched.

"O.K.," Gillespie brushed him off the same way he brushed the cigarette mess off the desk Before. "Was it before or after Rudolph Valentino when he told you he wasn't going to change the script the way you wanted it?" If the real Question on his Mind was What Happened When then the real answer was *during* but I did not Reply this for I detected a dozen other Questions behind it. My mouth felt Paralyzed when I tried to Answer all of them & I saw how it looked to the Police at the time it looked like I was clamming up. "C'mon Ray. Help me here. Help me figure out what happened tonight."

"I'm trying to help you."

"Try harder," DiMarco suggested. "Try explaining why you went berserk like that with the food. Throwing it at nice Mrs. Spiller—"

"Wait! What?"

"—throwing Jell-O and all that crap."

"Wait a minute! I didn't throw food at anybody!"

"Must be a case of mass hypnosis then. You think that's what it was? You didn't really go berserk with the cold buffet. It was only a crazy hallucination."

"Who told you I threw Jell-O at Ethel Spiller?" I stood up very Excited & spun around so I was toe to toe with DiMarco. "Whoever told you that is a filthy liar!"

DiMarco shouted back, "Oh yeah? Arthur Godfrey told us! Are you going to tell me *Arthur Godfrey* is a filthy liar?"

Gillespie smacked the desk hard. "Sit down! Both of you!"

"Arthur Godfrey," DiMarco had to get in the Last Word, "he's a big star for crissake."

"He didn't act hoity-toity with us at all," Gillespie clicked his tongue in wonderment. "Nice as pie. A big celebrity & he talked to Joey & me like we're up on his level."

"Imagine," I said.

"Y'know you don't expect it," Gillespie grinned like a bashful

462

boy. "A big star like Godfrey being such a regular guy up close. It's probably different for you. You must meet 'em all the time."

"I never met Arthur Godfrey before."

"I mean famous celebrities." Gillespie cut himself short he bounced his fingertips off his forehead. "What am I saying? Look who I'm talking to! Geez. I'm sorry Ray—you're a radio star yourself!"

All of a sudden very buddy-buddy DiMarco ups & asks me, "Hey—do you know Jack Benny?"

"No."

"Bugs Bunny?" I Ignored this. "Eddie Rochester?"

"Cut it out Joey," Gillespie moaned & he kept his eyes glued on me. "What's it like? Being a radio star and all?"

"What's it like?"

"You know. The treatment." I guess he was thinking of the Executive Dining Room & limousines to my hotel Suite & buckets of Champagne on ice & my own table at The Stork Club la-dee-doo-dah.

"It's different for me," I said. And I explained all about my Secret Identity etc. how it was against my Contract to Reveal the Fact I am The Green Ray. Instead of head waiters & bellhops jumping up with jiffy service and doormen bowing & whistling me up a taxi cab and instead of free beer at the bar & Cocktail Parties with starlets I was busy enjoying much more important Pleasures—for all this time I was a Model for Americans to look up to & be Proud of & all across the Nation I was one of the Family. I was their favorite Son. When they tuned in & heard the Voice of The Green Ray sometimes I thought I could hear them applauding from Maine to California. I stood for all of them I was the Statue of Liberty of the Air. Not to mention the Pleasure of being in the Studio week after week with Bernhardt and David et al. even when things did not go easy with us on the Personal side. As soon as the green light went on we all brought our characters to Life & for the whole time we were on the Air the world made sense mister! "What's the difference now? Maybe a tragic event releases a person from his legal Obligations."

"Funny," Gillespie said. "I just realized. My kids won't believe it when I tell 'em I was in the same room as The Green Ray."

"Don't tell them what I look like."

Det. Gillespie crossed his Heart. "Scout's Honor."

"Are you finished with me now? I should've been on a 10 o'clock train."

"Where to?"

"Philadelphia."

"What's there?"

"The Liberty Bell," DiMarco cracked.

"My father," I said, "he's in the hospital and I should visit him before—"

"Before he croaks."

"Before he gets out. I understand," Gillespie drowned out his junior partner's sick joke. "What time is it Joey?"

"2:32."

"You won't get a train to Philly until 5:40 Ray. Besides," he opened his hands & held them out to me he was practically Pleading now, "I think we're finally getting somewheres with this. All I want to do is collect all the facts I can while I'm here. You know what can happen later when you try & go back."

"No. Tell me what."

"Things change. Scrambled up. You understand me?" I nodded Yes but I did not mean it. "Emotions can scramble up the way you see things at the time. Sure they can. Earlier tonight for instance. By the time you got down to the Studio I'll bet you were in a pretty agitated condition."

"I was worried. Worried is the best description."

"Worried about what happened upstairs. Worried about your disagreement with Lamont. I know how it can get under your skin something like that. A few butterflies flying around your stomach before the show starts. I get that way when I'm at the scene of a crime."

"You got them now?" I asked Gillespie.

He shook his head just once very sharp. "They always go right away. Did Howard Silverstein think it was a good idea to make any last minute changes in the show?"

464

"We didn't talk about it."

"You have to remind me of this term . . . the term I want—what is it when the actor starts making things up? His dialogue & whatever. His lines. What's the correct term for that?"

"Ad libbing."

"That's it," Gillespie smiled back, "thank you. Ad libbing. You did a little last minute ad libbing tonight. How come?" I stared at my fingernails & let him go on without my help. "Leon Kern thinks you wanted to sabotage the show. So does Mr. Burrows. In a conversation with both of them about 45 minutes before you went on the air—"

"Hold it a minute—!"

"This is a firm opinion shared by David Arcash also."

"Sabotage?" *I did not believe what I was hearing!* "Did Leon say *sabotage?*"

"What would you call it? This surprise ad libbing. What would you say you were trying to do?"

"I was trying to—save—our—show!"

"The way you tried to save Carruthers," DiMarco heckled me.

Gillespie did not shush him up this time. So I challenged him, "Do you want me to answer that?"

"It's a free country," Gillespie said, "Say what you want. Don't say what you want. We don't live in Russia." He watched me close he was waiting for some Answer out of me & my Answer was I blew a rough Breath through my teeth. "Maybe you can appreciate the problem we've got with this so far. I've got a man pushed out of a 38th Floor window in front of a couple dozen people and from what I've been hearing in the last 6 hours I've got my own suspicions about how this terrible thing happened. What I don't want to do is chase my own tail around. I want to eat breakfast at home and you want to get to Philly and Joey wants to be there to beat up his girlfriend when she comes in so *please,*" Gillespie let me know what a Gigantic Strain I was putting on his Patience, "please help me Ray. I want to leave here with a story that fits the facts."

"You just told me you've got your own suspicions about it."

465

"I'm about *this* close." He opened a tiny gap between his thumb & index finger.

"I don't know what you don't know."

"Plenty. I'm not sure I understand all the connections," he said & he gave me a Humble look from under his furry eyebrows. "I don't know my way around here. It's all bluff with me. I just go on my instincts. On percentages."

"Tell me what you're sure about then maybe I can fill in some of the gaps."

"Smooth out the bumps," Gillespie pointed at me, "that's what you can do for me. Absolutely right." BOOM! he slapped the desk & glanced over at DiMarco I guess to see if he was paying Attention & then he jumped in with both feet kicking— "NUMBER ONE. After tonight The Green Ray is no more. O.K. I understand a few people aren't very happy about that. In particular you aren't very happy about it. Sure. Of course. Because from now you're a ordinary member of the Public. At 8 o'clock you're a National Hero and at 8:31 who are you? The Little Man Who Wasn't There. A very upsetting prospect. NUMBER TWO. What can you do about it at the last minute? Go to the guys who make all the decisions and talk them into changing their mind. You ask your friends to help you. They advise you to forget about it but you try this idea out on Carruthers anyway. This ends up in a fight that Howard Silverstein has to break up. NUMBER THREE. Right after that you go berserk with all kinds of food— you humiliate yourself and embarrass everybody else and then you go down to the Studio in a very agitated emotional condition. NUMBER FOUR. When the show is going out on the Air (& I think you did this out of spite) you pull that ad libbing stunt & try to sabotage the proceedings which just about ruins everybody's night. After that—NUMBER FIVE. Nobody remembers seeing you or Lamont Carruthers for at least 25 minutes which is when he staggers back into the Dining Room up there so drunk he can't walk in a straight line. He hops up on his soapbox & starts screaming the Blues and 10 minutes later guess who appears out of nowhere—you run into him like a snowplow & he ends up on the sidewalk as flat as a Swedish pancake. Then you tell Sgt.

466

DiMarco & myself *All I was trying to do was save our radio show . . .* I gotta tell you Ray— put it all together and it don't spell Mother."

My mouth was dry when I said, "It's not as complicated as that."

"Pardon me? I didn't hear what you said there." Gillespie leaned forward & I told him he was jumping to the wrong Conclusion.

"I'd say that's what Carruthers did," DiMarco could not Resist the gag. "You have to blame somebody if your career falls apart. It's not your fault. Is that where you guys were right after the show? Fighting it out over a few martinis?"

"Hold it Joey. Let's hear what Ray's gotta say about it." He tilted back in Lamont's chair & folded his arms across his belly.

"You have to try and understand," I said to both of them, "the Green Ray was his whole purpose in life. Lamont wrote every single script. He came up with every story. All our dialogue. Everything. I mean he created the character understand? I think Lamont just wanted me to stick to the script because that was how he wrote it. Every word of it was important every word of his that they broadcasted. Mrs. Shapiro told me how much he hated actors and now I know why. I proved it all right. His worst fears come true. I tried to ad lib my way out of the real ending. It ended anyway. When it was really over— I mean when Lamont actually heard the finale it must've felt like they were tearing his tongue out. Howard Silverstein & P.K. Spiller personally. I think there was a Personal reason why they took the show off the air. Something personal between Lamont & P.K. Spiller. Something so terrible he couldn't live with it anymore."

Gillespie let the chair rock him forward. He cupped his chin in his hands & stared me Dead in the Eye. "How do you know that?"

"How do I know what?"

"All of that stuff. Personal stuff. Is that what you talked about after the show?"

"He talked. I listened to him." Then I said, "He got suicidal."

DiMarco scooted his chair across the room & planted it & planted himself right next to me. "Now we're getting somewhere.

So you guys got together a little after 8:30 for a farewell chit-chat."

"We happened to be in the Bathroom at the same time."

"Oh ho!" This idea tickled DiMarco silly. "How much can a guy say to another guy about Rudolph Valentino?"

I answered him back the same way, "He was teaching me how to dance the Tango."

"Didn't mean to touch a sore spot."

"What *was* going on in there?" Gillespie wanted to know. "In the Bathroom for 25 minutes . . . "

"The usual business."

"Did he actually say to you—*Listen Ray I'm going to jump out of the window* or did you just get the wrong idea? Maybe he was upset about what you did on the radio. That ad libbing of yours upset him."

"If it did he didn't say so."

"C'mon Ray. You already said he didn't like it when anybody monkeyed around with what he wrote. The exact words were important. I wrote it down verbatim. Did I get that right?"

DiMarco did not let me Answer. He broke in with the Newsflash he knew a certain Secret about me. "Ray Green isn't your real name. You're Reuben Agranovsky."

"If you asked me in the 1st place I would've told you."

"Why didn't you tell us in the 1st place?"

"You didn't ask. Are you asking me now?" Which Wisecrack shut him up for a second. "Not Reuben," I said. "It's with a V."

"What kind of a name is that? Reuben with a V. And what's Agranovsky for Pete's sake? Not Russian by any chance . . . "

"It's American. It's a American name. What's DiMarco?"

"You still have family living in Russia?"

"Philadelphia. I gave you this secret information already. You didn't even have to torture me or anything."

"What's your father's Christian name?"

"General George Washington Abraham Lincoln—"

"All right Ray."

"—Douglas MacArthur Curtis LeMay Bing Crosby—"

"O.K. enough."

"—Bob Hope Uncle Sam Jesus Christ O'Agranovsky. Is that American enough for you?"

"Yeah. That's fine."

Gillespie stopped the Ping Pong Game between me & DiMarco. "Ray can you define what it means if a man's a patriotic American?"

What are you asking me?"

"Answer Detective Gillespie."

"I don't have to," I told him off. "It says I don't in the Constitution."

"Reuben Agranovsky. The All-American Boy," DiMarco slapped my back he gave me sarcastic Congratulations.

Gillespie ignored him & Concentrated on me. "I'll narrow it down a little. If a man found out that somebody he knows—somebody he works with say—is perpetrating some un-American activity you think he should inform the Authorities?"

"Oh yes," I stated beyond a Doubt. "Naturally."

"What's your opinion of Communism?"

"Communism?"

"You want me to spell it for you?" DiMarco said. "You know the thing Det. Gillespie means—Karl Marx Down With Wrigley Spearmint Gum Sieg Heil Hammer & Sickle All Workers Equal—"

"I know what Communism is," I stopped him there.

Gillespie came back, "Do you have any opinions about it? What do you think of Communism?"

"I think . . . the way I understand it . . . from what I read . . . I think it's a practical joke."

For a second DiMarco was not too sure if he should get Angry at my Reply so for the meantime all he said was, "Russia must be a pretty funny country to live in," then he handed me back to Gillespie for further Questioning.

"Ray," he said, "have you ever met a Communist?"

"I've never been to Russia. I told you. The farthest I've ever been from New York City is Philadelphia and vice versa."

"I mean any American Communist."

"That contradicts its own terms I think."

"Maybe it does maybe it doesn't. Try & imagine it. There you are—face to face with a Communist who's as American as you are. In the same room. A room you've been in before with him only this time he takes you into his confidence and he confesses to you. He confides in you. He tells you a deep dark secret about himself. About the work he's doing here. Sabotage maybe. What would you do?"

DiMarco had his hand on my shoulder & he turned me around to ask very Serious, "What would The Green Ray do?"

"Stop him!" I shook his hand off me. "Call in the F.B.I.! Call up J. Edgar Hoover!"

"I'm a little mixed up," Gillespie admitted. "You'd report this person to the Authorities. Is that what you say you'd do?"

"Yes!"

"Even if he had some kind of power over you?"

"Nobody has any power over The Green Ray." (I said this joking!)

DiMarco did not even crack a smile. "He means somebody who had power over your career. He means Lamont Carruthers."

This was to laugh. "Oh cut it out!"

"He's been a member of the C.P. of A. since the end of 1929."

"Oh boloney."

"Well either you didn't know about him before tonight," Gillespie flipped over the pages in his notepad, "or else you let him keep on doing what he was doing. Or . . . " he sighed very final, "you were helping him."

Now I got Serious too. "Lamont *created* The Green Ray. Don't you know what The Green Ray stands for? Defending the defenseless and helping the helpless. The Green Ray gives hope to the hopeless! Does that sound like Communism to you?" Gillespie & DiMarco slid each other a glance but I did not stop defending Lamont, "He purges wrong to keep America strong! Listen to me—I've been The Green Ray's voice for 7 years already! I know whatof I speak!"

"Practically his last words were—" and Gillespie quoted a few of them, "*I put Communist propaganda in everything I wrote . . . My messages of hope . . . Police oppressors of the masses . . . turn the street into a red river . . .* What is that? What do you call that kind of talk?"

"Don't you get it? He was just ad libbing a speech to needle Howard. To embarrass Mr. Spiller in front of everybody at the party. All the bosses and all of us. They broke that man's heart don't you understand that? Lamont was just getting back at them the best way he knew how. He was no Communist!"

"And neither are you," DiMarco grunted. "You're a joker."

"No!"

"You're all American."

"Yes!"

"You were the Voice of The Green Ray."

"Yes!"

"You *hate* Communism."

"I do!"

"So when you came in & heard Carruthers belching out his pinko spiel in front of the window you went a little crazy in the head for a minute. You didn't believe your ears! Your friend— a closet Red! Somebody you trusted—he used you for a Public mouthpiece. Then it hit you in a flash: all this wonderful work you thought you were doing for 7 years turns out it's just been the candy-coating on his subversive propaganda. You hated him so much in that flash you lost control of your own actions then you ran across the room & attacked him with your bare hands . . ."

"Listen to me fellas. This isn't funny. Lamont Carruthers isn't a Communist!"

DiMarco slapped a card down on the desk he turned it around so I could Read it. It had Lamont's name typed very Official above & he Signed it below. And the date on it I Remember to the Exact day i.e. November 1, 1929. I do not Remember his personal Number maybe you want to look it up maybe it is in some Records somewhere. Unless the Communist Party Of America destroys all traces after a paid-up member dies. Or maybe the F.B.I. put it in their Files.

"You're not collecting facts," I said to ashame them, "you're collecting ammunition! Is that what everybody says about me? That I could do such a terrible thing? Hurt somebody? Who do

471

you think I am? What kind of a person? Do I look like the kind of a crazy maniac who lifts his hand against a drunk old man? I couldn't do that . . . such behavior isn't in me . . . talk to Mr. Burrows . . . or Leon could tell you . . . ask Howard if I'm like that . . . he knows me . . . they all know me better than that . . . this is a mistake . . . there's some misunderstanding going on here . . . did David say it too? I went crazy & I pushed him out? This is wrong of you . . . ask Annie about me . . . she knows me . . . so does Bernhardt . . . they'll tell you I'm not a violent person . . ."

4:30 A.M. was when I walked out of the Liberty Building for the last time of my Life but worse I had to step over the smudges on the sidewalk where Lamont landed. Howard Silverstein got the Colored janitor out of bed to run the hose over it which he did for a Solid Hour & even after he scrubbed it by mop & brush the Stain was still there. I think they had to replace 9 Feet of Concrete to get rid of it once & for all.

Furthermore I honestly Regret I was the last person out of there since I never got the chance to say Good-Bye to the others no matter what of the Circumstances. To Bernhardt Grym & Annie. To Leon & Mr. Burrows. To David Arcash or Howard even i.e. to those persons who were near me in that time. You must say something when things finish between Friends the same as a Funeral i.e. words do not change the Sad Fact but they settle it permanent in your Mind.

Nor on the train down to Philadelphia I did not look back on my night full of one tragic Event after the other instead I imagined to myself the happy Reunion with Papa waiting ahead. And I knew In Advance what he was going to say when he laid his eyes on me —

PAPA: You promised your Mother you were coming down last night.
ME: Something happened. Something terrible happened at the last minute.
PAPA: Tell me what. Are you all right?
ME: I'm good. I'm fine. Papa listen to me. I want to tell you . . . I can tell you something now that I haven't been able to tell you before.

472

PAPA: First tell me how is it going to make me feel—better or worse?

ME: What would you say if I told you that I don't really sell used cars in Yonkers for a living . . .

PAPA: Here it comes.

ME: No—you don't understand. See they didn't let—

PAPA: Do me a favor Reuven. Show some respect for my intelligence and don't tell me any more fairy stories. You don't need to report me what you do with your Life anymore.

ME: But I want to! I want you to know I haven't been wasting it! I've been doing something very worthwhile Papa. Something that will make you proud. Do you still listen to the radio every night at 8 o'clock?

PAPA: As usual. What else?

ME: On Thursday you ever tune in that show The Adventures Of The Green Ray?

PAPA: Even here in the hospital I make sure I don't miss it. The nurses—it's their favorite program. They enjoy it even better than Arthur Godfrey!

ME: Brace yourself Papa—I'm him. I'm The Green Ray.

PAPA: Don't talk crazy.

ME: I don't have to keep it a secret anymore. I am The Green Ray.

PAPA: (shaky) N-no . . . Ray Green's The Green Ray. Everybody knows that.

ME: And *I'm* Ray Green. I changed my name on the train up from Philly that day in 1938. Before I ever met Howard Silverstein or Lamont Carruthers or anybody else at Liberty Broadcasting. I see now it was my Purpose in this Life to become The Green Ray.

PAPA: Slow down! Slow down! I may be a sick man in a hospital bed at the moment but I still have my wits thank God. You don't expect me to believe—

ME: I hoped my word would be enough . . . Listen Papa— close your eyes.

473

| PAPA: | You'll break my heart with your crazy behavior. |
| ME: | Please . . . you'll understand everything in a minute. |

Then Papa closes his eyes maybe not for my Sake then only so he can shut out the painful Sight of his own dear Son putting on a new Performance in public that does not make Sense to him. Maybe he shuts his eyes to hide his Embarrassment if the Nurse comes into the room but Papa does not shut his ears when I speak to him in the Voice of The Green Ray—

ME:	I pledge my Life to this Purpose: To heed the cry of the helpless & hounded—To do Good for no glory—To face Evil with no fear—
PAPA:	Reuven . . . ?
ME:	To give hope to the hopeless when the Hour of Darkness is upon them!
PAPA:	Ray . . . ?
ME:	I will blaze from the shadows to defend the defenseless and punish the criminal—To purge wrong to keep America strong!

His eyes flutter open & my Papa sees who I am for the 1st time since I was a Baby!

PAPA:	You mean you're really . . . ?
ME:	Yes Papa! That's who I am!
PAPA:	I'm flabbergasted! This is flabbergasting!

With all the shouting & crying etc. the Nurse comes running in very Worried she sees my Papa's arms wrapped around me nor she does not see it is a Bear Hug she thinks he just wants to jump out of his bed. Maybe he does!

| NURSE: | Calm down! Mr. Agranovsky! You'll give yourself another heart attack! |
| PAPA: | From joy Nurse? From too much joy? When I get out of here you know what I'm going to do? Retire! |

NURSE:	Who is this young man?
PAPA:	Reuven. Tell her.
ME:	I'm his son.
PAPA:	No . . . the other part! Nurse—be a good Nursie and shut your eyes a minute.
NURSE:	Only if you promise to calm down.
PAPA:	I promise. Reuven—show her.

And for him I show her.

ME:	I pledge my Life to this Purpose: To—
NURSE:	I recognize your voice . . . it's . . . you're . . .
PAPA:	Quick catch her Reuven! She's fainting!
NURSE:	Aah . . . ooh . . .
ME:	I've—got—her—!

I ease her into a cozy chair next to Papa's bed and while I am stroking her forehead to bring her around he winks at me & says:

PAPA:	She's very pretty . . . don't you think so?
ME:	Papa . . .

A unhappy Shock was all lined up & waiting for me on the news stands in the Station: the morning Edition of every East Coast newspaper & right on the front page of the Philadelphia Enquirer was guess what yes it was a photograph of Lamont lying face-down in a pond of blood as if he fell asleep & drowned in it. This picture was snapped by the great Weegee & it became very Famous by its own rights—more famous than Lamont Carruthers per se & more famous than The Green Ray. I even saw it in a Special Edition of Life Magazine they brought out 20 years ago i.e. 20 years after the Fact & if I look at it now it Affects me the same. I preserved that Issue around here somewhere I think it is in the pile inside the bathroom.

"You promised your Mother you were coming down last night," he says to me & his eyelids crack open a little.

I doubt Papa knew I was already there for a hour I sat next to the foot of his bed watching him sleep. And smelling in his old smell which really put a hook in my nose. A soft hook of Talcum powder & warm newspaper. Was it Friday A.M. in Room XXX of the Jewish Hospital?—no—by my nose it was Sunday A.M. at home with him coming in the front door so dependable back from the Delicatessen with a paper bag in each arm. Bagels & Kaiser rolls and a cinnamon coffee cake in the big bag—Lox & cream cheese and just for himself some smoked whitefish in the other one. At the same time my sisters drag the Wedding Album out of the Hutch & hog the sofa with it spread out between them. They turn over every one of the stiff black cardboard pages & ask about who is who in the Pictures who are all these people they knew before we were alive. Who is this with the mustache? He is Henry Stack who was driving the Chestnut St. trolley when Mama went out of control on her bicycle in front of it & bashed into Papa and that was the start of the love story which ended up with us. Maybe the Reason why I was born is somewhere amid those facts—because of the accident then from Love I came into the world. If he knows how it happened then out of Love maybe he can explain how everything else happened to me since.

"I had some trouble last night," is all I say.

He lifts his head up off the pillow. "What trouble?"

"We don't have to talk about it now."

"I didn't ask."

I help him avoid the touchy Subject. "Are they letting you out of here soon?"

He waves 3 fingers then 4 in the Air & frowns. "Always more trouble," he shrugs away from me. And he does not mean how long he has to stay in the Hospital either. "Serious trouble Reuven?"

"A lot less serious than yours. You look tired."

Papa grabs at the Relief of talking about something so simple. "That's the word in a nutshell. I'm exhausted beyond my belief. And what do these crazy nurses do? They give me sedations. To put me back to sleep. *I'm tired* I tell them until I'm blue in the face *I don't need any sedations.* They give me anyway. So I'm awake 4 o'clock in the morning & I don't know which way is up." Then his worry breaks loose from him he can not hold it under control

476

another minute. "You have some medical problems you're not telling me about?"

I spare him the grisly Details of my poor Digestion and I skip over the whole toilet side of last night's Events but I tell him all about who Lamont Carruthers is & how he fits into my Life. I show him the Front Page Story of Lamont's violent finale then I work backwards from there. The 6½ hours the Police had me under their Suspicion for manslaughter of a card-carrying Communist. My Humiliation with the food in front of those Very Important Persons including the Liberty Broadcasting crowd not to mention Arthur Godfrey et al. I tell him all about the Final Episode of The Green Ray and back to the Beginning that way I tell him about the strict Contract which Howard Silverstein practically made me sign in my own blood thereby the Legal reasons which sealed my lips silent for 8 years of my Life. AND FOR THE GOOD OF THE NATION! I tell him *listen Papa* every week since 1938 I was the secret Voice of The Green Ray which I can reveal now since I am not anymore & the only thing that matters to me is it is not too late we can start from here and treat each other like Father & like Son. Especially my dear Hope is he can Advise Me & guide me by his Wisdom what I am supposed to do when somebody takes away the only worthwhile part of my Existence the only Happiness that I know of.

He sighs heavy air from his lungs. "I look at you—you're my son Reuvie & I love you but I don't know you anymore. I mean it. I'm sorry I don't understand what you're trying to do with your life."

My lips close & open a couple of times but the Sound that comes out is not a clear word of my baffled Emotions it is only a click in the back of my dry throat.

"Tell me what then," Papa gives me another chance to explain from the Top, "I'm listening," he says & puts his Patience on a timer. He buttons up his rumpled pyjama shirt the maroon stripe ones.

"I told you everything," I say to him & now tears are pressing behind my eyes. "What don't you understand?"

"This version of what you're doing. What happened to the used

477

cars? Before it's used cars. Now it's selling radios. I'm not in the business Reuvie so how can I advise you?"

"Not *selling* radios Papa! I said I was in the radio business. On it! *On* the radio every week. Just like Arthur Godfrey!"

"I don't know. I never heard you on the Arthur Godfrey."

"Because I wasn't on his show Papa. I was on my own show. The Adventures Of The Green Ray. I told you."

"Well ask your mother. Whatever it was I never heard of it. But if you say so then I accept it." He lifts his hand halfway to a salute.

This pulls a light ungrateful laugh out of me.

"Reuvie this pressure isn't good for anything. What can I tell you?"

"Tell me what to do." I stare at my fidgety hands in my lap & I laugh so I do not cry like a baby.

"They fired you from your job." He counts this part he Understands So Far on his thumb.

"Not exactly."

"What then?" he asks me but he does not let go of his thumb or the basic Idea of my Unemployment.

I will tell you here is What then—I do not want you giving me a Lesson about how far I can go from my lucky Background what I want you to give me 1st is your Attention & 2nd is a little Comfort! A drop from the Supply of your Fatherly Love from the Kingsize case of it I did not use up yet from my Babyhood. Out of the amount I came with when you took me home from the Hospital when I was your little boy a drop must Remain somewhere—at the bottom of the box! under the lid of the jar! a crumb of Curiosity even a pinch of your Sympathy if it is dried up after such a long time I can still use it from you in this Unlucky Moment. Please give me it Papa the same kind of soothing Remedy that you used to bring me in Before—when you knew what I wanted & I was only screaming WAH WAH WAH in my playpen I did not have to say any Words. Help me out of this misery Papa! Apply the ointment!

"You don't have anything to say all of a sudden? All right." He starts again counting off my problems on his fingers. "You've

478

got to get a job. So you can afford food & shelter. And pay off all the rest of your bills."

"I've got savings."

He lets his hands flop back down on the bed. "How much?"

"Enough to live on," I say to the floor. "Enough for me."

"I don't want to be a wet blanket here but what happens when your savings runs out? I'm talking about the future Reuvie. I wish you'd think about what's going to happen then."

"I can't think about anything else! It's happening *now*. My problem is beyond savings if you want to know. My problem's beyond the future."

"What's that supposed to mean? That doesn't mean anything," he presents me a strained smile & goes on, '*My problem's beyond the future*—you're not making sense with a remark like that."

"Nothing makes sense to me right now."

"Because you're flying around in the clouds. If you want sense you have to come down to earth. That's your main problem *since you ask* and I've got a simple answer. You need money to pay your bills. You need a job to get money. Reuven you have to wake up & start living in the real world with the rest of us."

Well what else is this all about? Going back to see him in the Hospital & telling him everything which has Happened to me up to & including what is Happening to me Now just to hear his Views etc. the Good Judgment of the manly person who is the Reason why I am Alive. Tell me why this clear Desire is so soupy to him! "What do you think I've been doing since I moved away from home? It's the real world where I live too. For your information the real world doesn't stop at Chestnut Street!"

"I'm not in the radio business so what do I know about it? If things aren't working out for you," he smiles the best he can for my Sake and he reaches down to pat my knee, "try some other field. I don't have any other thoughts on it. You've got to live somehow."

"Why?"

The mere suggestions in the major Drama of this Question bring down the shutters behind his eyes & he pulls his hand away from me. "I wouldn't dignify that."

479

I will not let him get away so Easy. "I thought everything started from why," I say. "All the big ideas in science did. What goes up must come down. Why? And somebody finds out—gravity. That's how people advance—by asking big questions."

"What is gravity your business Reuven? You're not a scientist. It's your business to make a living. Then on the week-end you can ask why does everything fall down all you want."

"Science is just one *example*. Listen a minute—I mean," and I try again with a personal Big Question, "Why did you have a heart attack?"

"I know why. From worrying about my children."

And again, "All right then why didn't this one do you in?"

"For the same reason."

But I can not come up with any surefire Answer like that in my own Predicament so I try & keep it Simple. "Well I can't think of a good reason why I should even get out of bed tomorrow morning. Not now. I don't have—"

He does not give me a Chance to talk anymore about my Personal pain for I used up all his Patience. "Because you're not a poor sick invalid! That's why! You're not a weakling! You're a living breathing grown-up person who needs to go out & earn enough money to put food in his mouth or else you'll end up in the gutter! How's that for a reason?" This blow-up sucks all the wind out of his Lungs so while he bends over & catches his Breath it gives me room to jump in.

"The gutter doesn't scare me," I defy him. Very Brave as usual! "Living without some worthwhile reason behind doing what I do—*that* scares the pants off me. You have your children but who do I have to worry about? I don't have anybody. So when I'm in bed at night it's just me there—by myself—facing the monsters in the dark. Which is O.K. by me except now they know I'm not The Green Ray anymore!"

He lets my wild Words float by he is waiting for me to settle down & talk Sensible. Or he is just waiting for me to spit out the rest of my Nonsense & then he can jump back on my neck. I do not care which way it is. I want to say it out Loud so he can hear my Inner Thoughts I need to see the Effect of them face to face—

Now I count my ex-blessings on my fingers. "Papa when I was the Green Ray people believed in me. They heard me on the radio every week & I was the living proof of something else being in the world besides the forces of destruction. What I did showed everybody how a human life is worth something special because a human being can recognize the very highest principles and behave by them. Clean living. Fairness. Mutual respect regardless of race color or creed. Freedom of choice. Standing up to the bully & beating him at his own game. People *knew* me by those trademarks. Now there's no chance for me to do any of that anymore and what I'm afraid of is without The Green Ray I'm going to sink down to the level of a dumb animal who just eats to live & lives to eat. I don't know how I can forget about everything that's happened and give up and just do that. I need a better reason to go on living besides my appetite!"

"What are you going to do? Shoot yourself in the head?"

"I want to make people recognize there's something else going on around them."

"In that case Reuven you're going to be very disappointed from now on. Very dissatisfied in life." This Argument is Exhausting him. I am Exhausting him but from somewhere underneath it maybe from his deepest Worry over me he gets a boost of Energy that fires these words out of his mouth—"If you want to be Albert Schweitzer you have to move to Africa. And I'll tell you something son—you'll get there & you'll find out as soon as you unpack your suitcase that you have to eat regular meals there too. But if you want to live in New York or Philadelphia or anyplace else in the U.S.A. you have to do something besides carrying around other people's problems on your back. Leave the problems of society to President Truman & get used to the idea of doing a job somebody pays you for. And I mean something real—something serious not playing a quiz game on the radio."

I can hardly croak the necessary Reply, "The Green Ray *was not* a quiz show Papa. It's a—" but what is the Point by now? I interrupt myself for this important Message—"The Green Ray is just as real as anything that isn't on the radio! Or anything that is!"

Papa jerks on the plastic tube connected to his arm. "Like this isn't on the radio? I'm talking about real life! As real as this is?"

I say a automatic Yes.

"No Reuven. I don't believe that's so. You avoid the serious responsibilities of life up there in New York. That's what I think. You want the benefits of my thoughts on the matter? There they are."

The Nurse turns up here to give Papa his A.M. dose of Aspirin and all of the time they are talking Back & Forth very lighthearted e.g. "Is this young man annoying you Mr. Agranovsky?"—"My son came all the way down from New York City to check up on me."—"I can tell he's your son. I could tell from a mile away." Etc. & I am looking at his face from a Distance.

What I see is he is not just getting over a Heart Attack this time he is Fighting Back from a Beating. His damp hair is bunched up on the side of his Head a foamy breaker crashing up & over & Paralyzed there. Underneath the peppery stubble all over his cheeks I see the Bones of his Face trying to poke through & Underneath further I see the 16 Year old wrestler who he used to be on the boat coming over squeezing his very 1st Nickels & Dimes out of Irish boys twice his size. Plus I see my face of the Future there I see Time i.e. my rotten Enemy passing by between us meanwhile I am watching with my mouth shut & something ugly is Developing—

"I'm not talking to a infant here. You're almost 30 years of age. That's a grown man. You want some happiness out of this world? Of course. You have to work for it. You understand the meaning of that word? Open a new door in your life Reuven. All right. So you found out the radio business is very iffy. Find some work that gives you a regular paycheck. What happens is in your own two hands. Don't be afraid to get them a little bit dirty! Do anything what you've got to do Reuvie but don't sit like a lump on your keister. Jobs aren't dropping out of the trees."

You think it is in my own 2 Hands what Happens to me now? I can hear it rolling in Exactly what I tried to Avoid like hell— this muddy wave of Emotion it pulls me under & sinks him too so we swim around in it declaring our true Feelings about who owes what to who & what kind of Consideration we deserve & every other Feeling curdling inside us that we can finally put into Words & it all comes out as clear as if we are shouting at each other underwater—

"Your boss jumps out of a skyscraper window—I never heard of such a thing happening since the Crash in '29! Forgive me if I'm short on the details but I'd say something was going wrong somewhere along the line. You won't get very far if you can't recognize the position you're in is the result of your own mistakes."

"It just looks like mistakes to you. I know the reasons why I did certain things. And why other people did what they did."

"A mistake is a mistake Reuven. It isn't a crime. It just means something that ends up in a failure. So your experience in the radio business ended up that way. The best thing you should do now is go back over your steps & see how you antagonized these people. Learn from all of this & change your direction before it's too late & you can't correct yourself anymore."

I Repeat I used to follow the best Principles to my highest ability & the Result let me tell you was I was on top of the world— I WAS THE GREEN RAY UNDERSTAND? I was a Radio Star!—but the only Question my dear Papa wants me to answer him is What do you have to show for it? Now I know what the View is from the bottom of the world & that is mainly my crabby Answer.

"Oh yes—and the footprint on the seat of my pants that they save for any peon who's got the nerve to think he can do something special without permission."

And I say I am going to be a Radio Star again.

He pretends to hide his Doubt of this & leaves it this way, "In the meantime how do you plan to live?"

I praise Social Security & I say very cool I just have to face up to it & do whatever it takes. "Whatever has to be," I say.

"A bum in the street lives on Social Security! Is that the way you want it? I hope you enjoy yourself—eating your dinner out of a garbage can. And not even the same garbage can two nights in a row! A man without a country is where you're heading Reuven—"

Why do I let myself in for this Torture why am I his Helpless Victim? I hear his Voice & it acts like Hypnosis on me. His Voice of Authority the one I heard in my cradle that Voice who told me the Truth about the rest of the World I can Trust him to tell me about the Dangers there—hot radiators—slippery bathtubs—bee stings—never open the door to strangers—he always told me the Truth before so I am hearing the Truth from his lips now—I sit still & listen to him foretell the Tale Of My Downfall—

"You've got to make your own opportunities or else this economy kicks you where it hurts ... One wrong move & you're standing in line in front of a soup kitchen for your social life ... When you're my age you'll end up walking around Times Square for 25¢ a day with a sandwich board strapped to your back advertising vegetarianism and nudists ..." And so on more of the same about my Poverty to be etc.

I want to tell you something I did not get around to it in the Hospital. I learn by my own Personal experience that they are not so separate the Real World and Radioland. You can say I only think they are the Same & Equal in my own Mind but like always the True Facts come out in the End and I have seen the Proof. I Regret I walked out on you in the middle of our Reunion even if it was not a joyful Reunion anymore it fell into the sticks & stones of a low down Stink Fight. And I Regret Further how we did not live to enjoy another Reunion during the years after so your last living View of me was in my lowest moment of Heartache & Failure. Likewise my last living View of you was the Voice of Doom condemning me dressed in your pyjamas.

I do not hold you to Blame for misthinking who I am or the Reasons behind my confusing Deeds since I did not do much to help your Understanding. I walked out on you to your face and I walked out on you over & over & over in my Inner Thoughts nor I never Trusted you with my Sensitive Facts. I covered my Life up from you so you are Correct about how every person earns his Fortunes he builds them up every minute. Now I scrape off the scabby Crust so what should I be surprised it is a miserable mess Underneath! A person walks out in the middle of some Event it is the same thing as if he turns a Program off in the middle.

484

You spare yourself the Sight & Sound of it but it goes on broadcasting in spite. What is done is done NO what is done is still doing.

Too bad if this disappoints you Newberry but in Contrary of my Papa's dire Predictions I did not wind up tramping around Times Square like a nameless deadbeat advertising my Lifelong Mistakes to everybody in the street. I did not go that far. I stayed in the area. For a few minutes I wandered up & down the stairs until I went out through the basement Fire Exit nor I did not care where I went after the Hospital. I just followed my feet & they led me all over Downtown Philadelphia in a trance of Misery. From the outside I was a stumbling sleepwalker let loose on the Public sidewalks & from the Inside I was just a blank body without any Senses or Memories to Guide By. Come On Newberry! I Invite You—let your F.B.I. headshrinkers study my colorful Past here is my Permission in writing! I know how you are going to do it with your pet Doctors: 1—You hand them these pages & say "Get to work!" then 2—They come up with the Psychological interpretation i.e. this is extra Evidence against me. More examples of my deranged Behavior therefore 3—You can prove it in Court how I had a screw loose going back 40 Years! So 4—Very convenient you can Blame everything on me.

Let me save your Gov't. Doctors the trouble. I will Interpret for them to wit the Psychological Facts behind my Criminal Record. I did not hang my head in Shame then nor I do not hang my head now to repeat the Details. My chin is up! I do not Apologize for my Disturbing the Peace—sometimes a patriotic Citizen has to disturb etc. to get people's Attention & let them know something is rotten in Denmark. If they want to know about it or not. ALL IT TAKES FOR THE BASTARDS TO GET AWAY WITH IT IS IF A HONEST MAN KEEPS QUIET! For your information a person's Emotions can arouse him into strange Behavior but it does not mean he belongs in the Bug House—the Mental Reason I was shouting out loud in the street was for a minute I felt like I was floating out of my Skin & shrinking into little pieces in the air so I had to hear the familiar Sound of my own Voice to hold

485

on to it. I could Feel it in my throat & it pulled me back like a rope down to Earth—

"THAT'S RIGHT HORVATH. THIS TIME YOU'VE GONE TOO FAR—AND NOW I'M GOING TO STOP YOU FOR GOOD!"

It's you! For all these years! It was you from the beginning!

"YES! I ONLY INVENTED PETER TREMAYNE IN ORDER TO PROTECT MY TRUE IDENTITY. I AM THE GREEN RAY YOU BASTARD!"

It's been you all along . . .

"YOU BETTER BELIEVE IT!"

You're all washed up—you freak of Nature! Back off from that bomb . . .

"NUTS TO THAT! YOU'RE THE ONE WHO'S ALL WASHED UP! THE ONLY THING YOU PEDDLE IN THIS WORLD IS THE STINK OF GREED!" & likewise all the way back to 40th Street Station so let me Level with you it was NOT the mere Sight of the late Editions & that attractive photo of P.K. Spiller in his Tuxedo which triggered me off. I was not talking boloney either because those particular words of The Green Ray meant something to me they came back to my Mind from the guts of my rightful Grievance. I am sure this Background fact makes as much Difference to you as it did to the hunchback Newsboy whose foot at the time I was (by *accident!*) standing on.

"Offa me! Offa me you whacko!"

Until I felt the sharp Punch in the middle of my back I thought I was Hearing Things in some Foreign language. At least I was still seeing things in English. I yanked the paper out of his hands & read the headline out loud. "MILLIONAIRE INDUSTRIALIST MOURNS TRAGIC DEATH OF FRIEND—It's a lie!" I told him & then I told the next guy who flipped him a Dime and walked off Reading all about it.

"Will you get outa here? You're bad for business," that Newsboy turned around to tell me. "Are you gonna buy that paper or is this gonna get ugly?"

I held up the Front Page to his face I told him he was peddling Lies. "I know what really happened! I was there!"

"Go sleep it off somewhere fella." When he made a Grab for

486

the paper I hoisted it over my head to Expose it to the people passing by & between us it ripped apart. "O.K. fella. That's a dime. Gimme a dime for it. I want a dime for that paper!"

A few of his Customers stood around waiting for him to finish with me & serve them As Usual & a chubby little ticket clerk from the Station poked me. "You got a problem about something mister?" He backed up a step. "Does this guy have a problem Davey?"

"He won't pay me for a paper," he told his pal.

"Can you beat that?"

"Don't you want to know the real story?" I pointed at the bundle of newspapers Davey still had cradled in his arms. "You won't find out about it from this!"

"Pay Davey his dime and take a walk," he said to me & he made it sound like he was Letting Me Off light.

"There's something going on here!" I yelled at him & held up a fresh paper the same way Harry Truman did. "I was there at the time! I'm telling you this is a lie! P.K. Spiller couldn't give a crap about what happened to Lamont Carruthers!"

"You're up to 20¢ now fella," Davey advised me. "Keep goin' why don'tcha." Bubbles of spit broke out on his lips.

"Just pay him mister," the chubby guy coughed out & said out of the side of his mouth. "This guy's some nut. I'm going for a cop."

What did I care where he went or what he did? My Duty drove me on to set the Record straight. "You think the facts will come out? You think these are the facts of the story just because it's in the papers? Listen to me—"

The only Sound anybody heard out of me next was a squeaky croak which was the best I could do with Davey's fingers wrapped around my throat. We both danced Backwards into his stacks of Magazines while I tried to peel him off me & gasp in some Air.

"He's breakin' up my stand!" Davey started screaming. "Please somebody—help me!"

I Fought him back as far as I grabbed him by his wrists which felt as thin & weak as a little girl's. And I held him that way & he pumped his hands into scrawny fists he tried to twist loose.

487

There was a bigger Crowd around us now but nobody was there for a Paper—

"Can you believe this guy?" somebody said from the front row, "Beating up on a cripple!"

"I'm *not*." I said & I let go of the Newsboy who dropped down on a pile of papers. "I wouldn't *do* anything like that! Look—I was protecting myself. In self-defense see! I mean—close your eyes a minute. You hear my voice? Recognize me now? I—"

This time he Tackled me from behind & in a speedy blur all the faces Disappeared instead I saw the sidewalk coming up to kiss me. I could not see him but I would say all the time he had his foot planted on my back that Newsboy probably looked as proud as Christopher Columbus claiming America. I heard the people in the street give him a warm round of Applause.

"I got him! I'll hold him here. I'll hold him . . . "

All I had to do was buck my shoulders & I shook him off. I held on to his ankle to protect him from falling over & hitting his head God Forbid but his rubbery knees folded under him & he swayed into the side of the stand. The *crack* everybody heard was not his frail Bones it was the orange crate that broke his fall which all could see but it did not stop the ripple of Worry that whipped around the crowd. So picture this—the hunchback Newsboy is gasping for Breath on the ground with his Newspapers & Magazines & Magazine Covers torn up all over—if anybody breathes hard the crummy little News Stand is going to fall down on top of him—the Party who is Responsible for this Disaster is also gasping for his Breath & even if I am a Honest citizen in the Right by all the eye-witness Evidence I am a thief (2 newspapers) plus a bully plus a dangerous troublemaker who is making it Worse by sweating & trying to Explain—and the murmuring crowd in a solid doughnut around us. On a National Basis I am sorry to say I believe this is the usual Limit on people's Involvement when they Observe something is wrong. Maybe a shout maybe a yell. Only a 1 in a Million person will make a move. My dumb luck he was there too.

"Don't let him go! Did he get away?" The chubby clerk hurried back puffing short hot Breaths & he pushed through to get a look at Developments.

"Make a Citizen's arrest," somebody egged him on.

"Don't have to," he said, "I got the police." He ignored me & kneeled down next to the Newsboy & started slapping his hand to bring the poor guy around. He was already around & practically weeping into his sleeve he only looked up to take a sad look at all the Damage & then he Sank Down again.

"Here's the police Davey," the clerk told him but he was looking right at me. "Sit up and tell him what this nut did to you."

The Officer broke up the crowd on his way through nor it was not only his Uniform which they Respected it was his nightstick he already pulled it out. "What happened?"

"Can I say?" I stepped over & the Officer grabbed my arm. He had a grip on him like a All Star Bowler.

"Shut up." He tapped the tip of his nightstick on the tip of my nose. "Strike 1," he warned me & his jaw set like a marble ledge.

"He stood on my foot," the Newsboy said. "On purpose."

"I didn't," I said. "Not on purpose."

'*Ssh!*" I got from him & this time the stick touched my lips. "That's 2."

"He broke up my stand," he started out slow but from his chubby friend rubbing his shoulder Davey let out with the full Symphony Version.

"Tell him Davey. Say what happened."

"And he was screamin' I-don't-know-what at my customers. My regulars! And tearin' up my papers and steppin' on my foot. What'd I do to him?" Davey tilted his shiny face up to me. "What'd I do to you mister?"

"All right," the Officer soothed him. His grip got tighter on me the more he Heard. "A car's coming. Prowl car," he said Because he saw right away nobody needed a Ambulance since *there was no harm done.*

"I can't believe it," the clerk Complained so everybody could hear it. "Attacking a cripple."

"I didn't attack him!" I bent down to say it to his face. For this I almost got my arm broken.

A few Eye Witnesses joined in all the fresh Excitement. "You beat up on him! For no reason!"

"I saw the whole thing Officer!"

"He took a paper & he didn't pay for it—"

"What kind of a —"

"Creep!"

"Whacko!"

"Nut!"

"You nut!"

The Officer did not ssh them up either my guess is Because the siren of the Prowl Car was already homing in on us. I can stand up under Mocking you can not Taunt me it never has a Affect on me I can Defy it by my inner Knowledge. I know I am not a CREEP or a WHACKO I know I am not a NUT likewise I know I am not a CRIMINAL who turns against all the Laws of Decency & harms another person even to Defend Myself *I draw a line!* In this case my Duty was not done & the closer the Police car got the faster I felt my chances fading away which is why I went against all Odds & stood up to tell the Public what they deserved to Know —

"Certain parties in New York wouldn't let me reveal certain sensitive facts before! But since last night everything changed and now I think it's my duty to inform you why they took me off the air! I'm talking about corruption in high places here! I'm talking about the death of a man! I want to tell you why they killed off The Green Ray!"

Some reaction I got! A gasp of Shock? A hush of Dread? I got the names again! And some Clapping & Hooting so I raised my Voice louder then they could hear my Credentials & take me Serious.

"I'm the only one who knows what really happened! Listen to me! I'm—I'm The Green Ray!" I stood up on the orange crate so everybody could hear me all the way in the back. "Can I have your attention please! I am—The Green Ray."

"You're the Green Nut!"

The hilarious Laugh after that was the last Sound I heard before a wallop from that nightstick cracked across the back of my head.

I swear to God it was as big as a Baseball Bat & I went down like a sack of potatoes.

I do not fear the BULLET I fear the BOX! If you box me in where I do not belong I will go Nuts you might as well Confine Me in a hole in the ground & you can Achieve the same thing. A solid wall every way I turn. Cut off from the people who know me so what is the Difference between being Dead or Alive. You know what goes in that kind of a place you can trump up any kind of Unbelievable Charge against me & I can not get out of it. Which is where you want me where I Step in front of me it is Pitch Black. I will tell you on the level Newberry a Gun does not terrify me now as much as Jail which is a sensitive Personal fact about me I want you to Know so you can add it to the list. Any honest Doctor in the Land will testify how this is a Normal Mental Reaction in the extreme!

Furthermore I know from the inside I do not Speculate upon this. In Philadelphia they did not treat me like Public Enemy #1 nobody figured I was so Dangerous. So I did not deserve a Private Cell they put me in with the day's collection of tramps & deadbeats etc. the common losers who the Police Dept. had to clean up out of the alleys & railroad yards. The Human Dog Pound is where they put me with the stray Human mutts stretched out & yawning on the concrete floor or sitting on their Haunches & scratching fleas off their coats up against the wall. From the dirty windows we did not get much Daylight in there we got a pale fog that stopped dead in the Air about 10 Feet over our heads & the flat square shadow of the wall Underneath blocked off the Electric Light that was squeezing in through the Cell door.

I sat down in the corner of the Cell which had the most empty space around it where I could sit by myself & Comfortable even if the floor was a little bit Damp. At least I put some Breathing room between me & the yellow-eyed Stares I was getting & the Dirty Laughs & Remarks etc. about my snazzy white slacks. After 5 Minutes I forgot about the sharp stink that smelled like it was leaking out of the wall behind my head likewise the Revolting shock I got when I reached down & Felt my Palm skid through some slick wet patch next to my leg. I did not Flinch I did not give those bums the Satisfaction. I Reacted nonchalant I slipped my hand back in my pocket nor I did not show them a crack in my Expression and this Effect took some Nerve because I was sick in my stomach at the time. Never Again Mr. Newberry—this was no joy! I do not Believe I can survive such a place at my age I can not face it again. I KNOW A BULLET IS A BETTER ANSWER.

If your Weissenheimer Psychiatrists investigate behind all the National Statistics and go by the idea Normal Mental Health = How Most People Think then I predict you are going to find out my Exact Attitude toward Jail is shared by many. And I can give you a fine Example at random—

"Say friend. You're sitting in the terlit area."

By his gentle tone I knew right away this Message came to me in Sympathy—not for a cheap Punchline to a joke In Progress on the other side of the Cell. If I looked at him Before he said a Word to me I would think the other way around which Proves the old Saying about a book & its cover la-dee-doo-dah etc. I took him in from the scuffed points of his 2-tone wingtips (no socks) up his cream colored flannels to his flowery Hawaiian shirt. The pocket flapped down from the Seams being ripped halfway around & he fidgeted with the flap tugging the loose Threads off while he waited for some kind of Rise out of me. I watched him twitch his head back & forth a couple of times he tried to get me in Focus between his wall-eyes. He gave up on this very quick & Peered Down on me nosefirst pointing me out again by the sharp hook of his beak. Such a gentle Voice out of that rough face! Like hearing Harp music come out of a Cement Mixer.

Maybe he thought I did not speak the English Language or I was hard of Hearing because this time he made it very clear by a certain manly Gesture & as plain as he knew how to put it he said, "That's where everybody pees."

The Idea he was not Kidding Me sank in at the same time the clammy damp sank in through the seat of my Pants. I jumped up so fast I almost knocked my friend backward off his feet but the only thing in my Mind was the cold stain Spreading down the back of my leg. I Felt around for it but likewise I did not want to Touch It as if it was a Open Wound down there. "Why didn't somebody tell me before I sat down?" I clenched my teeth I had to stop a Retch coming up.

"You're O.K.," he said & looked it over. "It's not too bad. It's just a spot. A couple of spots is all. Sorry pal. I didn't see you till it was too late. You were already sitting in it."

"Thanks anyway."

"Sorry I didn't see you in time," he said. "It's almost dry. I bet it feels wetter than it is. Honest. It's nothin'." He put his hand on my arm for a further Apology also to calm me down. I saw the ugly row of his fingernails & each one of them was filthy also chipped or torn gnawed down or split. "I know," he said, "I ordered a manicure from Room Service but she never showed up." He pulled his hand back & I do not Know if it was that Sad Move or his lame joke that made me smile so easy. "Stand over here. The ventilation comes up over here." He swilled his dangling hand around by the corner of the Cell door & made room for me to stand there. Warm Air came puffing up out of a iron grate. "Stand with your back to it," he advised me which hit me as a Good Idea for other Reasons besides drying my pants.

"*This place,*" I said when my eyes Adjusted & I looked around & I was thinking how far I fell in 24 Hours. "I don't *belong* in this place."

"That makes a pair of us."

"Last night I was at a fancy cocktail party in New York. With my friends and everybody. Arthur Godfrey was there. And Jack Dempsey."

"No kidding? Dempsey?" he twisted out the Champ's name in a choirboy soprano.

"I'm not making it up! Walter Winchell too."

"Look—I know a gentleman when I see one. Why do you think I came over? Because you're a gentleman. You don't *look* right in here."

"I'm glad it shows."

"Sure it shows. Takes one to know one," he complimented me.

"Us Knickerbockers got to stick together. What part of New York?"

"Manhattan," I told him just to keep it simple.

"My old stomping grounds. Anywhere near Riverside Drive?"

"You know the Liberty Building?"

"Sounds grand. Really grand."

"It's grand all right." I compared the wood panels in the Executive Dining Room to the wet Concrete Walls I compared the Persian Carpets to the Concrete Floor I compared the Tuxedos to the greasy overcoats & my last Conversation with Lamont which was the last Conversation of my old Life to this Conversation the 1st one of my new Life with a convict in Jail.

"I'm just like you," he said. "This afternoon I'm eating a Bacon Lettuce & Tomato at a lunch counter and the next thing I know I got handcuffs on me. It was a couple of blocks from here! Can you beat that? Marched me down the middle of the sidewalk in front of the whole city. I think they get a kick out of causing humiliation. Or causing it to me anyway."

"What did they arrest you for?"

"Oh," he swished his hand in the air, "it's a dirty business."

"Let's change the subject then," I offered him.

"I don't mind talking about it. It's just I don't want to impose on you. On your time. You don't want to hear my sob story."

"Only if you don't want me to hear about it."

"I don't mind. We're friends huh?" And he told me his name Jimmy Ginkus plus his nickname Jinks — "Spelled K-S so it's not like I'm bad luck or anything. Don't worry!" — then on with his Tale Of Woe about the roadside diner he was running very happy with his sex bomb Wife until out of the Goodness of his Greek Heart 6 Months previous he hired a guy who was down on his luck as a dishwasher. Before Jinks knew what was up this seedy grifter put the moves on his Wife who for herself was not slow on the Uptake. Jinks ends up sleeping in the garage which is not enough for that Jezebel & her Loverboy and they try & fix Jinks's wagon by crying to the Police that he lightfingered the diner's funds which a year ago he put in his Wife's name for Tax Reasons.

"So he's diddling my wife behind my back and I'm in here on

false charges. What're you gonna do huh?" His bottom lip started shaking I think he could not put the brakes on he was so Upset by the Memory. "And those bastards took my nailfile away so look at me." Now he held up his paws & put 10 rotten fingernails on Display. "To keep me from sawing through the bars. I mean what are we in here for? Rehabilitation? Boy oh boy. I'd rather put a bullet right here," he pointed to the middle of his forehead. "I'd rather shoot myself than stay in jail. Even one more day. I'd shoot myself right now." Then he gulped a Breath & held it in which calmed him down or anyway slowed him down to Normal. He Touched my elbow just by his fingertips. "Let me see your pants." I turned around to show him. "They're dry," he said. "They feel O.K. now?"

"I can still smell it."

"Can't even see where it was. Besides everybody else in here smells worse."

"Jinks," I said & glanced up at the living piles of dirty laundry all around us, "why doesn't that make me feel any better?"

"Ain't it the truth." After a Pardon Me & a sharp little cough & a Excuse My Manners Jinks stuttered out, "Wh-what'd they get you for?"

Loud & clear I told him, "I disturbed the peace."

"Well you have to do that sometimes," Jinks nodded he Approved.

I nodded back, "Too true."

"Raise a little hell," he was still nodding and he looked me Up & Down again he clicked his tongue & shook his head. It still did not make Sense to him how a pair of Gentlemen like us deserve to get locked in a Jail Cell with such a Low Calibre of person. "They must have some kind of a quota or something they gotta fill up. You & me need to get outa here."

"Jinks!" somebody hollered at him from someplace in the Cell.

Jinks looked around & snapped back, "What?"

"Shut up is what!" the fella stepped over to say and show us what a Beauty he was—stringy blonde hair plastered flat on his pink scalp & he scraped a few Strands out of his eyes when he stood in front of Jinks toe to toe. His mouth bent down at the

495

corners & he let it hang a little ways open like the mouth on a Shark plus he had the row of crooked teeth to match. Gills in the white flesh of his scrawny neck would not be a Surprise. He planted himself very firm on the spot & leaned into Jinks & hocked a gob of spit in his face.

Jinks rolled his cheek into the collar of his shirt he wiped it off nor he did not say a word back except, "Leave it alone huh?" & then he looked over to me & let out a jumpy smile.

"Hit him Sandy!"

"Yeah Sandy! Pop him one!"

"Sonofabitches!"

I have a Theory about what is Happening here I entitle it The Theory of Entertainment. Boredom is the enemy of the People you can Quote me. In Jail it is a worse Condition the way regular Life holds still there so any Change is a big Improvement. Some exciting Event will Arouse a person & keep him interested in his Surroundings. It will wake up a person's Mind & keep him involved etc. which leads me to the Idea of every Human move comes from Entertainment being the revenge of Boredom as Lamont Carruthers would say. From Inventions (Wheel e.g.) to exploring uncharted Regions (Christopher Columbus) to Radio and Shakespeare up to the St. Valentine's Day Massacre and the World Series I believe every move in History boils down to some party or other doing something to Change what is what in the World for his own Entertainment. Mainly this goes on Unconscious i.e. it is a trick of the Mind a trick of Nature to keep Human Beings going. You want to keep going to see if something Different is going to Happen. Which is why a person pushes things to a Climax.

"Who's your boyfriend?" Sandy asked Jinks & tilted his head in my Direction.

Jinks did not Answer him instead he said to me, "They gang up on you if you're different."

"I didn't hear that Jinks," Sandy pulled Jinks by the front of his shirt & I saw how his pocket must have gotten itself Torn Off. "Who's your new boyfriend?"

"Nobody you have to worry about," I said.

496

Sandy zeroed in on me. "As long as I keep my butt to the wall you mean." A few dirty chuckles tumbled in behind him & he smiled back around at them. "I saw 2 nellies like you doin' the deed out behind a oil well. In Texas! I couldn't believe it. Worst thing I ever seen. Used the oil right out of the ground to grease up their butts with." Sandy stuck his tongue out. "Ugh! Made me sick watchin' 'em."

"If it made you sick then why'd you stand there looking at it?" I asked him.

He still had a Grip on Jinks's shirt & he twisted it Tighter. "I couldn't believe my eyes," he said. "Made me sick." He pulled his fist away & the shirt pocket with it. Very Jokey he blew his nose in it & dropped it on the Floor.

"Worst thing I ever saw," one of the chucklers said from where he sat, "was a bunch of sailors all butt naked together in a lifeboat. Slappin' each other and carryin' on. That was in Pearl before the war."

"I seen a guy floy-joy a dead corpse," somebody else said. "He pulled his pants down & stuck it in him in a boxcar."

A few Groans rolled around the Cell. Jinks said, "Maybe he didn't know the guy was dead." The groans turned into Belly Laughs even Sandy laughed a lot at this Remark and this big score in The Worst Thing I Ever Saw Contest prompted Jinks to go for the Daily Double. "I saw a Spic bellhop crap in a shoebox. A real log of a turd he laid in it & he delivered it to a Priest. Right in the hotel restaurant this was. The Priest was halfway through his meatloaf at the time." Jinks snorted a laugh out of his nose. "You shoulda seen his expression! I don't think he ate the rest of his meatloaf."

"If he was a Spic Priest he probably ate the turd."

"Spics will eat anything."

"They'll eat garbage & brag about it."

"I seen a Spic hold his little boy up & help him pee in the Holy Water right after Mass."

"Pee is what Spics put in the communion cup because they can't afford the wine."

"Jews is worse. I seen this old Jew once squat down & take a crap right outside a Christian church. With the Pastor watching him in the window the whole time. I went over & cleaned it up myself. I hadda use a whole newspaper on it it stunk so bad."

"That's because of the food they hafta eat. Fish heads and stuff. Jews hafta eat certain things or they can't get into Heaven."

"They can't get into Heaven anyway."

"Why can't they? As long as they eat the right food."

"Jews killed Jesus. God's not gonna let one of them in Heaven. Some people kill your son you're not gonna invite them into your house for all Eternity are you."

"Especially if they stink of fish heads."

"Jews stink of worse crap besides that," Sandy said & showed off how much he Knew. "On Easter they hafta drink a cup of some animal's blood. Could be a chicken or a sheep or anything like that except a pig. They ain't allowed to eat pigs."

"That's O.K.," Jinks chipped in, "means there's more for us."

"Sandy," the guy next to him spoke up, "you mean Jews can't eat bacon for breakfast?"

"That's right. Or pork chops for dinner."

"Jeez. That's a hell of a punishment on them. What's God say they can eat then?"

"Like Murphy said they can eat fish heads. Any part of a fish. The fins & the eyes. Yids eat the tails of course & make this thick kind of soup out of the fishguts. They pour sour cream all over it. And also they eat dogs."

"Jeez!" the guy snapped his head up shocked to his socks.

"That ain't nothing." Sandy had some more Horrors to tell him. "Up in Williamsberg I seen these yids one Easter grab a collie dog right off of somebody's stoop and take it down the alley around the corner & cut its throat with a silver knife. Then they hung it up on the fence by his hind legs & took turns catching the blood in a big silver goblet. They drank it out of there while it was still warm. Passed it around singing some kind of yid prayer. Blood all over their beards & everywhere else. That's another reason why they don't smell like a white man. It's a sin if they clean their beards off so the dried up blood just stays on permanent. But Eastertime is when Jews stink the absolute worst."

"I know something about yids," Jinks was proud to tell us.

"Yeah? What?" Sandy said.

"Yids put their babies up for sale. Usually. Devout Yids I'm talking about. It's in their Holy Bible they have to do that. But they only sell to each other so it doesn't leak out."

"Then how'd you find out about it?"

Jinks finished what he was saying, "They don't respect a child's life like we do," and then he caught Sandy's smart aleck Question. "Huh? Oh. On account of my nose I guess." He stroked his bumpy hooter. "I was doing a friend of mine a favor in North Philly and these Jews come up to me. I'm the only man on the street who's wearing a decent suit you know what I'm saying? So one of them says *Pardon me brother. You want to take a look at a beautiful baby boy?* Get outa here I tell those yids. Get straight outa here with that business! And I chase them halfway down the block. Then I see about a dozen more all standing around & half of them have got little papooses in their arms & half of them are counting out 100 dollar bills. When they saw me there & they figured out I wasn't one of them they all just blew away like leaves. You ever see anything like that Sandy? Bunch of cowards the yids. That's why you don't see them do anything big in sports."

"I'll tell you what I saw," I said & I left it quiet for a second until I got everybody's Attention. Enough of all this boloney I was going to tell them something For Real. "I saw a man fall 500 feet to the ground & die in misery. He was a honest man which is why he died so miserable. Certain people in high places cheated on him behind his back. Pushed him out. He was too honest for his own good & now he's dead. I saw that happen last night right in front of my own eyes."

Sandy just shook his head nor he did not take his gaze off me. "That's a goddamn lie."

"The hell it is," I said. "I was in the same room. It's been all over the papers since yesterday."

"We don't get the papers in here."

"Hey I read about that," Jinks backed me up.

"Shut up you geek," Sandy fired at him. "Who cares what you think?"

Jinks mumbled into his hands, "I saw the picture on the front page."

Sandy Ignored him this time since he was busy calling me a Liar. Of all the Insults I take this 1 the *foulest* it Offends me to My Core. And I try any way I can think of to put this across to him in the strongest Terms but we just end up going back & forth in a squabble that does not go above IT'S THE TRUTH I TELL YA and THAT'S WHAT YOU SAY variety. The 2 of us going around in a Vicious Circle that way with the mutts on the sidelines howling & barking at all the Excitement—

"Hit him Sandy!"

"Bull!"

"You're full of it!"

"Tell him he's full of crap Sandy!"

"He knows he is," Sandy answered back, "he knows he's full of crap."

I let him pull me into it I did not Resist the Temptation maybe this is the weak fault in my Personality which led me from Regret to Regret. I have to be Honest when I face Ignorance I have to correct it & when anybody calls the Truth a lie I do not have enough inner Power to leave it alone. Nor I did not hold myself back this time either. Let them Condemn me & call me a Fruit-cake! I can Condemn louder! I can not Resist this!

"Things are going on around you that you don't know anything about! Dishonest crooks masquerading as great pillars of society! You think it doesn't matter to you. What they do doesn't affect your life but you're making a mistake if you think that way. Because what they do changes the place we live in & because of them you end up living in the middle of a lie. Brave doesn't get you to the top. Honest doesn't get you there. These men get busy behind the scenes and turn everything upsidedown. In public they're V.I.P.'s who get respect for what they do but you never see it all. They hide what they do behind big ideas like Free Enterprise. Well listen a big idea *is not* the same thing as a high ideal! They say What's Good For Business Is Good For the U.S.A.

500

well that's just another lie they tell you. You can't imagine what these millionaires are willing to do to make everything turn out the way they want it. And the only thing they want to do is protect their own interest. Other people *don't matter* to them. Human beings are just their raw material! You think I'm afraid to name names? *I'm not afraid to.* LAMONT CARRUTHERS has been using The Green Ray on the radio almost every week for a *very* important purpose—to expose our boss's crooked past. *His* name is P.K. SPILLER & he came on like he was Lamont's only friend & protector in the whole world. How did things end up? A honest man gets forced into a horrible death and a selfish crooked coward drives home in a limousine. I'm telling you something invisible & very powerful is going on around you all the time and last night I saw the effects of it. I *saw* it." I singled Sandy out for my final Remark, "It happened right in front of me."

"I heard it on the radio," Jinks held his finger up in the Air when he Remembered, "I heard every word of it!"

"You're full of it," Sandy said & he was surer than he was before. "You're *both* full of it." He waved me away from him & he turned his back on me then all of a sudden he turned back around with a cocky smile. "What do you know about anything you stupid gink? How do you know what goes on with millionaires?" Sandy swung his arms around & stopped them stiff pointing in opposite Directions. "Lookit where you are! You're in jail you jerk!"

So I told him who I was I told him that I was The Green Ray. Before the catcalls & the stomping & whistling got too Noisy I did what I had to do to Prove it. I spoke out in the Voice of The Green Ray & quoted him this, "THE ONLY THING YOU PEDDLE IN THIS WORLD IS FILTH! THE STINK OF SELFISH GREED!" Between the concrete walls & the metal bars in Jail the acoustics are pretty snappy they added the perfect Echo in my Voice and it worked on that captive Audience like a magic spell.

"Oh man!" Jinks burst out. "Him!"

"Do it again," Sandy requested me. "Say something else."

"I FIGHT AGAINST WRONG WHEREVER I FIND IT!"

Sandy clapped his hands very Gleeful now & he shushed up everybody else he wanted to listen to me some more. So I gave him, "I INVENTED PETER TREMAYNE IN ORDER TO PROTECT MY TRUE IDENTITY. I AM THE GREEN RAY PROFESSOR HORVATH! I'M YOUR SWORN NEMESIS!"

I had that rough crowd Speechless not to mention Sandy in the front. In the Front Row you can say Because all dozen of them sat down cross-legged on the floor in a ½ Circle around me I was Entertaining them the way Bob Hope entertains the Troops!

"More! Keep going!" Sandy egged me on.

So this was a Opportunity which I could use & fill them in on the Story So Far i.e. what was going on & what was *really* going on. "We're in this plane see up over the ocean fighting for our lives because there's a bomb in the cargo hold which is going to blow up any minute. And if it goes off that's the end of everything."

"Tell how Horvath tricked the guy into making that bomb. That was something. That was incredible the way he did that," Jinks put in. He was lucky nobody brought in any rotten fruit in their pockets because in 3 Seconds they would bury Jinks under a pile of it to shut him up. Instead he just got a few shouts of Shut Up etc. & that was all since they wanted to Hear what I was going to tell them. Sandy stayed the quietest he did not even join in with shouting at Jinks he sat there showing me a big smile & Every Ounce of his Attention. That is the Power of Entertainment for you.

"What happened in the beginning," I said, "was Horvath waltzed into Dr. Ogilvy's office in disguise. He pretended he was a European gentleman called Vennema who was just the mouthpiece for a mysterious philanthropist by the name of Mr. Regis. Of course Regis is none other than Horvath all along. He lets the Doctor think he's building this bomb—this Atom bomb—for the good of humanity but the only good that Lionel Horvath is interested in is the benefit his homemade Atom Bomb is going to bestow on his stocks & bonds & bank account. And this isn't even *half* the story." I saw a glimpse of Jinks nodding how much he Knew what came Before & After & he bit his lips together by all his Might so he did not Interrupt me further & risk the verbal fruit. Then I broke the silent Suspense I told them, "From the very beginning Lamont was blowing the whistle on P.K. Spiller and he used Lionel Horvath to portray him all along. All of the crime he made his fortune on. What kept Spiller up at night what gave him *ulcers* was the idea of The Green Ray dogging him every week of his life. He was scared stiff of us. This I heard from Lamont's own lips 5 minutes before he dived out of that window."

"Get back to in the airplane," Sandy flashed his smile up at me nor he did not think anything about the Bombshell I just dropped he wanted to hear some more from The Green Ray maybe the Truth is not very Interesting unless you are Involved Personal. So What so I do not give up on it now the way I gave up on it then. In my own livingroom I do not get Defeated! "So you're in this airplane with this guy who's tryin' to murder you." Sandy clapped his hands truly eager.

Jinks made sure everybody knew what a Desperate Situation I was in. "And it's outa control. There's no controls on the plane because they got blasted right?"

"I shot out the controls with a ray from my Hand Blaster. Right," I said. If this was what they wanted instead of hearing the True Story of what is what & what is going on Behind their backs in their own country then I was not going to Force It anymore. All of a sudden I was Exhausted from Forcing. "And if I don't get the plane back on course Horvath says he's going to reveal my secret identity to the world."

"You're The Green Ray!" Sandy pointed his sharp finger at me he stabbed it in the Air.

"Right," I said. "I'M ALMOST SORRY YOU WON'T LIVE TO REGRET THAT THREAT. YOU'RE THE ONE WHO'S ALL WASHED UP!"

"Yow! Yeah!"

"Uh-*huh*!"

"Tell that bastard!"

"Horvath knocks me into the side of the plane—we trade a few punches—the bomb's ticking fast—the engines start to sputter—he's got me pinned down and he taunts me—Horvath says When the ticking stops you're going to follow me into oblivion!—*then*

503

I get a brainstorm. IF I CAN GET MY HAND FREE I CAN NEUTRALIZE THE DETONATOR WITH MY HAND BLAS-TER—Your Blaster fell out of the plane! Horvath says. Say good-bye to the world Green Ray! Nothing can get you out of this!—I've got to think of something quick and I come up with my Reserve Blaster—IF I CAN JUST REACH THE SECRET COMPARTMENT IN MY BELT . . . !"

Sandy sprang up on his feet & started joining in. "It won't work this time! You're pinned under a time bomb!" he snickered & took over for Horvath.

I know where he is going with this Ad Libbing afterall he is the Amateur & I am the Professional between us so I lead him along in the same Direction. "We both go together when it blows. And I'll die happy because I know when this world gets rid of you it gets rid of a contagious disease."

He took a step toward me & sneered, "Nobody'll cry when you're dead either!"

Which line is not bad Ad Libbing for a Amateur. Nor he did not break out of his Character either which meant I did not think about it I could Relax & React. "Then I don't care what happens to me—and that makes me dangerous."

"That makes you *nuts*." Sandy heard the Laughs he got from this Punchline & he turned them into a tight grin he aimed at me. "You're going down."

"No criminal as low as you are has a long enough reach to drag me down!"

"You're the slime in the gutter."

"You're the cess in the sewer."

"You're the lowest crud I know of."

Instead of thinking up on the spot some Answer that was lower than crud I moved in on Sandy & showed him who he was fooling around with. "I AM HERE TO HEED THE CRY OF THE HELPLESS & HOUNDED—TO DO GOOD FOR NO GLORY & FACE EVIL WITH NO FEAR—TO GIVE HOPE TO THE HOPELESS AND JUSTICE TO THE INNOCENT—I'LL BLAZE FROM THE SHADOWS TO DEFEND THE DEFEN-

SELESS AND PUNISH THE CRIMINAL—I'M HERE
TO—"

Sandy's face clouded over very Serious. "That makes you The
Green Ray right?" He grabbed the top of my shirt & bunched it
up under my throat. "You think we're all assholes in here? You
think I'm some dumb asshole?" I did not look him in his eye.
"I'm talkin' to you. You hear me?"

"Sure. I hear you," I said. "Let go of my shirt."

His grip wound it Tighter. "Any crud can make his voice sound
like him. Teach you a lesson you wiseass." Sandy pushed me up
against the bars of the door & then he pulled me by my shirt he
was dragging me back to the Toilet Area. "Try to make us look
stupid with all that crap. That *crapola*. You really think you're
something special. Huh? Hm?" He Slapped my face & pulled me
along some more. "Did you say something?" This time he Punched
me in my Cheek. "I don't want to hear boo out of you understand
me?" He dragged me over to the corner & pushed my nose into
the wall & I started to smell the pissy Stink dripping down there.
"Kiss it," Sandy ordered me & Forced the back of my head with
his hand. "Say who you are," he said & then I Felt a kick in the
back of my knee which folded me up so I was Kneeling on the
floor Kneeling in a puddle of pee. Sandy dug his knuckles in the
back of my neck he rolled up my collar in his fist. "Say who you
are."

I said all I could say. "I'm—The—Green—Ray." He aimed a
Punch at my ear but his fist skidded off my cheekbone & smashed
into the wall which Surprise pain twisted him into a Rage like a
wounded animal. He jerked my shoulders back & leaned all his
Weight on me & tried to make me sit in the pee again.

I can not Explain my Reactions here I will say I answered him
on the animal level since I did not Think about what I did it just
sprang up from my Gut Feelings. I spun around on my knees like
a Cossack dancer & belted him in the middle of his face. I felt his
nosebone crunch I hit him so Hard & Fast. He fell backwards as
stiff as a ironing board & his head knocked into the bars & he
rolled down into the damp corner where he wanted to put me so
there is a Lesson of Life in this Action & Reaction I believe. I am

not Proud of this Violence it is not in my Nature as a rule but other Vital Functions take over in a case of Self-Defense.

"You're kidding with that!" Jinks was over there by the time I was on my feet.

"I'm not kidding," I said then I sat down in the Place of Honor in front of the Ventilator. All eyes on me of course or going back & forth between me & Sandy who was still stretched out cold in the Toilet Area. Those men kept their Distance from me but not out of Fear I believe it was from silent Respect.

Not Jinks. He sat down right next to me. "I knew you wasn't lying," he said & got Comfortable by wiggling his skinny hips in. "I listen to The Green Ray show all the time. Every week practically."

I did not want a Conversation I wanted to dry the pee off of the front of my pants my knees were soaked so I Concentrated on them. Lifting the material into a little tent & flapping it in the breeze that was about the size of what I could do.

"Sandy's the one who's full of it. Nobody in the world can impersonate your voice. Not so perfect. I knew it was you the minute you opened your mouth Sir."

"Uh-huh."

"Mind if I ask you something?" Jinks did not wait to hear Yes or No from me he just kept going, "What happened after the bomb went off? Did you have some kind of a parachute or something?"

He snagged my Attention with this. "What do you mean?"

"Or a device or something?"

"Huh?"

"To get out of the plane." Jinks thought I was just being cagey but for a couple of seconds I did not know what to tell him. "O.K. just tell me did you land in the water or land on the land."

What was I going to tell this person? About P.K. Spiller again? About Howard Silverstein & the Liberty V.I.P.'s? About David Arcash's little girl? About Annie getting married in Cuba? About Lamont all over? About Gillespie & DiMarco? About my Father in the Hospital? So I made it easy on us both. "The water," I told him.

"So there's a boat or something picked you up."

"A submarine."

"That figures. Now you see it now you don't."

"It's the safest way for me to travel."

"What happened to Horvath? He was wearing some kind of a bomb-proof suit I bet." I nodded Yes. "And I bet as usual your friend O'Shaughnessy met you on the pier when you came in." I nodded him Yes again.

"I wish I saw his face then! So that was the celebration party you went to last night? Mind if I ask?"

"The party," I remembered it in Detail. "It was some party. All night. If I didn't go to the party maybe I wouldn't have wound up in here." I felt too low to wonder about Causes & Effects back further than 1 Night.

"Don't look so sorry!" Jinks cheered me up. "You shouldn't be sorry. It doesn't tarnish your reputation. It's better. It means you're just as human as the next fellow. Practically. Not so lofty."

"You think so?"

"Oh sure." A funny Idea skipped through his Mind. "It's one thing after another with you isn't it!" Jinks was looking at my wet knees but he Meant how I was stranded in Jail. "I suppose you hafta do something to get outa here before next week."

I saw his eyes shining so Hopeful at me I had a little Trouble coming out with the Words of bad news just waiting to Disappoint him.

"So can I ask you something?"

"Yes."

"Think you can spring me outa here too?"

Then I saw what he really Meant & the chill of it stabbed into my chest like a Ice Pick. "Pardon me?"

"What's the plan?" Jinks plunged in, "Can you blast a hole in the door with that Hand Ray thing?"

I Claim Amelia Defuentes Is My Dearly Beloved Wife! And I do not say so from the pretend Wedding Ceremony with Dolores's puppets either I base it on the Act of Love between us which

507

came right after. What do I need a Law from somewhere to make it Official? It all came very Natural this time on both parts (no nerves about it no jitters Before During or After) so this qualifies as Genuine I believe. If I ever have to choose between Genuine and Official then I will choose Genuine every time. I do not know if Amelia loved me up to the identical Degree but I will swear she acted like it. Anyway I can not tell the Difference I do not have the Experience in this area to compare. All I Know is she fell asleep in my arms & I saw a peaceful smile on her which made me want to prop my eyes open & watch over her & Shield Her from harm and by my Experience this is a Natural Reaction of Love. They do not hand out this Emotion at City Hall when you pay for your Marriage License! It comes from inside a person or it does not come at all. We slept in her bed side by side for the rest of the night.

This is 5 Days ago I am telling about now.

Usually I do not wake up very early in the Morning by my Nature I am a nightowl and anything before Noon is a mystery to me. Except this Morning in question I opened my eyes & looked at the Clock it was only 7 A.M. Maybe it was the knot in my stomach from the Undigested Tequila plus all the jumping around in the bedroom with Amelia in the middle of the night that changed my Sleeping Routine. My Mental Condition I will say was very calm & now I put it into Words for the 1st time— *because I belonged somewhere* right there with Amelia. Even if such a Feeling enters a person's Life toward the End instead of the Beginning it is just as strong it makes him contemplate the Future look Forward to new Experiences even the hard times ahead Because you will be there Side By Side to Embrace each other etc. or nudge each other in the ribs over some Joke.

At 7 A.M. Amelia was not there by my Side I was lying in our bed By Myself. When I dragged the pillow off of my head the Sounds of the World started to seep in & wake me up Further— I Heard the tea kettle wheezing a high note in the Kitchen & there was Mexican music playing on the Radio out there too. I smelled burnt toast. But I did not get out of bed then I lay there Contemplating for a few minutes. Being alone I learn can be a

508

very Endearing thing if a person Knows it is only temporary. If he Knows all he has to do is walk into the other room & there she is the Woman he knows so Intimate who knows him likewise. This is a Endearing Moment this is a rare Sensation & I am glad I encountered it at least once in my Life.

Here is what Happened after I got out of bed at 7:05 A.M. (give or take a Minute) now I will Account for my Actions between then & 7 A.M. the next Morning. I hope you will Agree how my Story conforms to every Physical Fact—

I did not loll around I turned Left out of the bedroom door & another Left into the Kitchen. First I thought *Amelia does not have the know-how or the knack of making breakfast!* You know the Old Joke about a Bride who can not boil a hardboiled egg etc. but that is what I saw on the stove: a dry pan with 2 Eggs in it & the eggshells Scorched Black on one side. The Boiling Water in the kettle whistling away at the top of its lungs & the burned toast Smoking in the toaster. Amelia did not come out from anywhere when I called her Name neither did Dolores and all of a sudden I saw the back door was open & this time I Knew I was Alone in the house. It was no picnic this moment a chill like a boa constrictor twisted around me Very Tight. 1 Minute your Life is going in This direction & something happens & a minute later you are facing some Other Way. Before it was THIS. Now it is THAT. And a person has to move or else he sinks in the Quick-sand of the Moment.

I did not Sink I went out of the back door. The Footprints all over in the dirt around the back porch looked like a Arthur Murry dancing lesson the Apache Dance or the Tango. In the middle of them I found Amelia's nightshirt & all the buttons ripped off & Torn around the Collar. Out of the mess of footprints a Trail of them led up the hill Behind her house up into the Shrubs & Bushes—I followed them like a Bloodhound.

The Sight I saw Punched a hole in my stomach the Shock of it choked the Breath out of me—Amelia lying on her back all Naked & her head propped up in the broken branches of the bush where they Threw Her. Her eyes were Open & she was staring out like she was in a Hypnotic Trance or trying to Remember where she was or what comes next. Or stunned open by her last Sight which was Nilo's fat face while he was dragging her by her pretty nightshirt around the backyard—Nilo's lardy arms & legs around her to pin her down with one hand over her mouth & the other one squeezing her throat in the bushes. Where she was Helpless in his Power. I hope she did not see Nilo's boys shove Dolores in their car I hope she did not Suffer at the End & take that painful Memory with her.

I do not know when Amelia Died I can not give you the Exact Time. By my Calculations it is between 6 A.M.–6:45 A.M. last Thursday. It was Nilo O'Connor who strangled her to Death but I accuse John Newberry it was his Invisible hand which Deprived Me of my Love.

"Ooh-hoo—ooh-hoo!" I cried over her I slumped down on my knees by her side. "Ooh-hoo!" I Kissed her face I patted her hand & I cradled her in my arms but it did not Change anything. You can not bring the Dead back by your Love nor you can not by Physical Methods when they are gone you need to let go of them not cling. I feel Death is something you can not affect by Mind over Matter so what is the point but I did think of that at the time I was too Emotional.

Automatic Behavior took over then I did not linger & Mourn I ran back into the house I was thinking of Dolores. What if she was a Eye Witness of this Crime? In my state of High Emotion I went all over the house in & out of every room to Search For Her. I was not ready to Believe the Obvious i.e. Dolores was gone too Because look how she walked in the front door all by herself that night we came in & found everything Upsidedown. But this time she did not get away to Safety & if I was going to make some move *to help her* I had to swallow this Repulsive Fact I forced myself to Accept the Worst.

Back in our bedroom I went into the closet to take out Amelia's favorite clothes her Flowery Shirt & her white dress with the Parrots on it to Bury Her in. When I pulled her shirt off the hanger I could smell her Fragrance in the Air around me a few Molecules of Amelia that still Remain on Earth. I Believe they contain the Memory of our Dear Moments or else where do they all go? Dissolved in a Vacuum? I do not know how long I stood in the bedroom closet rubbing my cheek on her dress & rubbing my nose on her shirt I tried to Breathe In all of her that was left for me. Let me call it 20–25 Minutes.

By the Evidence I believe Nilo only stayed there long enough to get Amelia out of the house & kidnap Dolores. He did not Ramsack the rooms he did not take her Jewels nor he did not look for John Newberry's Love Letters. I found those Valuable Belongings where I left them—the Tiara & rings & pearl necklace etc. in the straw bag I wedged behind the toilet & the Love Letters inside my pants folded up. And my Gun still in there too plus the Bullets in my back pocket.

Here is how I buried Amelia.

I dressed her & I brushed her hair. I dug a Grave next to the place she Died so I did not Disturb Her Further. You can find her & bury her correct by Christian Customs I did not say any Prayer at the time I was too upset & Exhausted from digging. She is still there as far as I know unless Newberry went back & dug her up again & planted her Dead Body in my garage for the Police to find it. Maybe he went further already & he shot a bullet in her head for more Evidence against me I do not put this kind of dishonest Behavior past him JOHN NEWBERRY IS NOT ABOVE THIS KIND OF FILTHY TRICK!

I was collecting rocks until 3 in the Afternoon or about 3:15 it took me Hours to carry over enough of them to mark Amelia's grave & build it into a Decent Tomb. You will find her Jewels in with her all of them except 1 Gold Ring which I am wearing for my Wedding Band. The rest is buried Treasure & I include my dear Amelia in this Description. Because here is how I thought of it—the same as if I Married her 50 Years ago & we lived as Man & Wife for 2 Weeks then she died of a disease. And I stayed Faithful to her from that day onward so 50 Years of happy Marriage packed into 2 Weeks. Here it comes around again somebody takes away my Purpose in Life! The whole time I sat there I was wiping Tears off my face. "I want The Green Ray to come back and find ME!" this time I was crying out. I Yearned to see him pop out of the thin Air & tell me what to do. Inspire me &

encourage me or show me the right Solution! And prove there is something else in the World besides the cold blooded Actions of greedy people something Higher & Beyond.

I am not a Candidate for the Loony Bin of course I did not expect The Green Ray to appear out of nowhere only this was my saddest Inner Thought I hope you Understand Me. But I will tell you what did turn up—a Scorpion crawled out of the middle of the pile of rocks over Amelia. It sat on the back of my hand it did not try & sting me it just sat. I know there is a Natural Explanation but I do not want to Hear it. Do not quote me Insect Behavior in a hot temperature la-dee-doo-dah etc. I Believe it is Beyond I Believe it is connected to something Higher. This little living Creature which means something in particular to Amelia came to me in the exact time I was Thinking of her so I say maybe the Zodiac is not altogether boloney. It could be the way a person is connected to the Stars so what so Dr. Nobel Prize did not discover the Scientific Terms for it yet. The smartest Caveman did not know about Electricity! Other wonderful things could be waiting for us.

As soon as the Scorpion crawled off me (3:45 P.M.) I went back inside to pick up my Weapons to pursue JUSTICE. I folded up Newberry's Love Letters & I loaded the Bullets into my Gun then I sealed my solemn Pledge—I aimed up over my head & fired off a Shot so that is how the Bullet Hole got into Amelia's kitchen ceiling. "Now I am dangerous!" I yelled out as if Newberry could hear my Voice wherever he was. Then I was Prepared since I heard exactly how Loud this Gun sounds when it goes off so I will not be Nervous about the noise I will not Hesitate when I have to Shoot Again. That test was the Shot that woke up the whole street from their Siesta it punctured the deserted quiet of the hot day. The Children calling to each other & their Mamas wailing back & forth & all the dogs in every front yard barking too. "Happy days are here again!" I shouted outside & I Meant the Opposite. At 4 P.M. I walked out of Amelia's house in Tres Osos. The only Plan I had clear in my Mind was I had to pursue John Newberry & then reap Havoc.

*

512

I have got my own Personal Theory of Relativity. In specific I put it like this: a Minute Late or Early in many Spheres will cause a different End Product entirely. The Sphere of Buses is a perfect Example of my P.T.O.R. in action. The bus going up to Juarez was waiting at the bottom of the hill when I came down Parked There like it was Waiting for me. My Waiting Chariot to drive me to my Rendezvous With Destiny i.e. this was not just a lucky piece of Good Timing the bus I saw was a Message saying *Seize Your Future!* A puff of wind kicked up the dust of the road & somewhere on the other side of the ragged red cloud Swirling in front of me I Heard the rattling motor of that old Bus choke & growl so I ran for it. Like the Old Saying goes: A BUS WAITS FOR NO MAN & it applies to Mexican buses the same. I was fast enough to be in time to get a Blast of Exhaust Smoke in my face so while I am coughing the Poison Fumes out of my lungs & wiping the soot out of my eyes what I am thinking is the Chariot of Destiny has just Farted on me what a perfect start of my day! This is my instant Interpretation when I am standing there watching it Disappear down the road. Sometimes it is a Smart Idea to turn it over in your Mind & look at the bright side of a Disappointment that is the way with many things not only buses.

I can hear the Big Question on your lips already i.e. WHAT IS THE BRIGHT SIDE OF MISSING A BUS? I will tell you in this case here is where Relativity comes in. If I rode on that bus I know by the time I got to Juarez Newberry's people would be on Red Alert looking for me. The shoeshine boy—the bus station barber—the little girl selling postcards of The Virgin Mary—it could be *anybody* he Employs they could spot me from a Photograph & let him know I Am Coming. If I caught the bus from Tres Osos all of this would turn out very Different in some ways I Believe. The beauty part of missing it by a Minute was that Juarez Bus turned into my temporary decoy & gave me time To Think.

What I was thinking was this: *I am going to make Newberry take me serious!* Etc. in this vein & by the time the dust blew away & all I was looking at was the long stretch of Empty Road in front of me I saw this long walk was a terrific Opportunity to iron out

the lumps of my new Plan. "Be Prepared!" is the Boy Scout motto
& So What I am not a Boy Scout by definition but I subscribe
to this Philosophy to the letter. Therefore I ironed out the fine
points of my Strategy on this line—

PLAN A-1

1. Sneak Across The Border (to end up near Azalea, N.M.)
2. Get back to my Apartment on Pecan St. in Mason by bus
   + take a shower + take a nap.
3. Put Newberry's Love Letters in a box in my Bank.
4. Track J.N. down & advise him I have his Valuable Pos-
   sessions & Force Him by this Knowledge to give up & turn
   himself in.

By 7 P.M. I was close enough to throw a rock across the U.S.
Border—also I was covered in dirt from head to toe & my Sweaty
Clothes did not help me look like a man who Means Business.
But even my Miserable Appearance was in my Advantage since
the rags & the grime Disguised my serious Purpose. I was Anonymous there because I blended in with the Mexican crowd like I
was a Native. So I ate like a Native (refried beans from a roadside
Cantina which DID NOT taste as Delicious as the ones Amelia
cooked for me) and I drank beer like a Native I finished 4 Beers
outside watching the Sunset. It set all the way across the Desert
& on the other side of the Border the same. The same color of
Light the same streaks in the sky over Both Places in the Same
Moment. The Sun sank down over Amelia's grave then also wherever Dolores was at that time. Wherever John Newberry was in
that Moment it was the same for him & it was a Moment in Nilo's
cheesy little Life too lighting up whatever he was doing—frying a
kidney or boiling some liver. Divide that Moment by a Million
for all the other people it is the same Moment passing except it
is Different at the same time. This boy is falling off his bicycle.
This girl is kissing her boyfriend on his lips. This man is dropping
Dead from a Heart Attack. A baby is being Born somewhere.
Babies. Multiply it by a Million & it is the same single Moment

514

also it is Millions of Millions. All the individual Moments put together. And the Moment after that & the one after that think of all the Moments mounting up think of the racket they make Combined!

I was still sitting on the porch 2 Hours later (9 P.M.) in the dark there until the cook came out & sat down next to me & lit up a cigarette. Very polite he Offered me one out of the pack but I am a 100% Non-Smoker so I Refused it with a smile. He pulled hard on his smoke then let it out slow & steady it was like breathing Fresh air to him. I smiled. He smiled & nodded then he said a few Words to me but I can not tell you Which Words exactly since they were in Mexican I smiled at what he was telling me & nodded I Agreed with him and he smiled back. So he kept the Conversation Ball rolling by asking me a Question. I could tell it was a Question by the way his Voice went up at the end of it and by the way he looked at me when he stopped talking I mean like a man at the front of a soup line waiting there with his Empty Bowl.

"Mm," I said & I nodded.

"Si si," he nodded back. "Claro . . . "

"Claro," I Agreed with him again.

And he looked around over his shoulder in through the screen door of the Cantina & I guess the coast in there was clear Because he pulled out a Bottle from under his Apron. Before he opened it he stubbed out his cigarette in the dirt with the heel of his cowboy boot & he made a Big Production out of it wiggling his fingers over the top of the bottle to Portray leaping Flames. You tell me which is more Dangerous—more of the 1 Sided Conversation which only had to go on maybe 2 More Minutes before it exposed the Fact I am not a Mexican so what am I doing acting like one OR taking a drink out of a bottle of Lighter Fluid.

He glanced Behind Us again then he held the bottle up so the Light from the Cantina window shined through it. He shook it & tapped the bottom to show me what was Inside. I will tell you what & you will not Believe me but my hand to God what he wanted me to see was a Dead Worm. A Dead Worm curled up on the bottom of the Bottle! So I am going to drink something that is a Fire Hazard plus it kills Insects Plus this one is on top of the 4 Beers & refried beans I had already.

So he wiped the top of the bottle with the cleanest corner of his Apron & passed it to me for a Honorary drink. Could I say No? I held it up in the Light. I smiled at it. I nodded at it. "Mm," I said and he was on the Verge of getting Frantic I should hurry up & drink so I did I swallowed a Mouthful. Anyway I swallowed the part that I could hold onto in my mouth it Burned my gums & tasted like carpet cleaner. I felt his hand patting me on my back since I was doubled over coughing and between gulps he was telling me, "Ssh! Ssh! Ssh!" So I hold my Breath which keeps us both quiet but makes me Dizzy.

He waves the open bottle under my nose & I grab his hand just so I do not fall off the porch and he does not Interpret this in the Correct Way he helps me take Another Drink. This time I did not lose so much down my chin & the whole inside of my mouth was Numb so I hardly felt the bug juice go down. I smile Gracias at him but if his smile of De Nada was anything to go by we just looked like 2 grinning Idiots there teeter-tottering on the edge of those steps.

"Muy bien," he grinned at me, "muy bien."

The only other part I Remember which is the only Benefit I got out of this Occasion was I learned how to sing all the Words of the song "Guantanamera" in the original Language. The Accent & everything now I can sing every Verse of it Perfect. Another secret unlocked!

On the last time through the Chorus I noticed how I was singing by myself in the dark outside the back door of the Cantina. The only Light I could see anywhere was coming from a yellow streetlight on the other side of the Building so I headed for that. The Cantina was shut tight for the Night so I believe it was after 1 or 2 A.M. when I left there. Since nobody was around to hamper me then this was the perfect time to sneak out of Mexico.

In that stretch the Border is just a Chainlink Fence that runs right through the middle of the Desert only loose rocks & low bushes scattered around the Area. It could be the surface of Mars (if you Ignore the bushes). A lucky thing from the point of view

516

of Camouflage was I only had to go about 100 Feet & it was pitch black in every Direction. Which was my Farewell Sight of Mexico when I turned my back on that place it was the streetlights of Juarez tearing a hole in the dark and then ahead of me was my Welcome Home—look how I returned to my own Native Land by crawling under a loose part of the nextdoor neighbor's fence! I trade in my Dignity for some Personal Safety so what I am in Good company with this (King Charles II of England—King Louis XIV of France—and in modern times Celebrities such as Greta Garbo go around in Wigs & Sunglasses to be on the safe side).

A Mathematical Fact is a man usually walks at the Speed of 4 M.P.H. even a man 66 Years old walking in the Desert at night a little bit woozy from beer & bug juice. As long as I steered in a straight line going away from Juarez I figured Boy Scout or no Boy Scout I could Navigate myself to Azalea, New Mexico which is 4 Miles from the Border ergo a 1 Hour walk. The lights of Juarez behind me will Guide me halfway and the lights of Azalea in front of me will guide me the rest so I checked my watch then I would know when a $\frac{1}{2}$ Hour was up & I should see the lights of Azalea. That is how I know with Confidence I went under the fence at 3:10 A.M. on the dot.

American soil was under my feet again & I was on my way home under the American sky. On this side of the Border American was the language everybody spoke & I could speak it Perfect. If anybody asked me to I could name all of the Baseball Teams in both Leagues. I know 10 Dimes make 1 Dollar & likewise 20 Nickels 100 Pennies or 4 Quarters. Ask me what is the Capital of any State and I can tell you in Alphabetical Order. The Pledge of Allegiance I could Recite backwards & forwards. But a strange Feeling got ahold of me & it set in Stronger every step I went it felt like I was going deeper into Enemy Territory. Any local Citizen could look me in my eye & they could tell how I do not belong there. The only Reason why I came back is JUSTICE the only string that connects me to this place now is my Personal Hate which sent me here to ruin John Newberry.

When a person has got such a strong Intention pushing him on his Body can stand up to all kinds of Torture. I did not Feel the blisters on my feet nor I did not feel my Wobbly Knees. You can go beyond your own Limits I learn it is a amazing thing how far. I went through the horrible business with finding Amelia in that Condition then digging a hole in the ground to Bury Her also carrying rocks. Then that walk all the way from Tres Osos to Juarez in the hot weather combined with beans & beer plus the Side Effects of that Mystery Drink. A few hours later I am walking 4 Miles further in the dark so by this time I can hardly pick my feet up a Inch off the ground and take another step but I Endure it Because my Mind is on my mission. And it will pay off any minute now for I can see the Glow of the Lights of Azalea up in the Sky. This Sight drives my Body on a few more yards until THERE IT IS—the edge of a empty street & the pool of Yellow Light spilling over it. By my watch I went 4 Miles in 2 Hours + a few Minutes so my Average Speed dropped down to 2 M.P.H. but I was on my knees from Relief since my Goal was so close!

What mighty Hand had a grip on me up to there let go of me then it left me crumpled on the ground. All of my Strength poured out of me & every Pain poured in—the bones in my legs splitting under my Skin & my poor arches aching—my Stomach had a bag of nails rolling around inside it—the Muscles in my back all frayed apart like rotten rope—and worst of all is the Sound I heard which was my own crying with my face down in the dirt crying for Amelia who I Lost—dry tears stuck in my throat I cried for her all of the tears I had. Even if your Mind forgets your Body remembers everything it will bring everything back to you.

If I fell asleep at that time I will say it was 4:25 A.M. so it was circa 6 A.M. when they woke me up by a kick in my ribs from the sharp toe of a cowboy boot.

"Habla Ingles?" This time a kick in my armpit. "Habla Ingles amigo?"

I Rubbed the Sand out of my eyes & I Rolled Over to look up. I saw a man in a neat baby blue suit standing by my head & his friend was by my feet I Believe he was wearing Brown.

The brown one said, "You speak English?"

The other one kicked me again. "He means you Pablo."

"Huh?"

"It made a noise Terry."

"Wha'?"

"It sounds like it's trying to talk."

"Kick it again."

His boot landed between my shoulder blades & the Shock not the Pain made me suck in a Breath and sit up. The Worst Move I could make was if I showed Newberry's gunsels I was some kind of a weakling so that is what I let them think.

"Get on your feet," Terry said down to me but I did not move fast enough for him. "Tell him to get up Curtis."

Curtis ducked his head out of the Sun & cleared his throat before he told me in Mexican what he wanted me to do. I shaded my eyes so I could look at him Direct & I saw he was a older gentleman with so many Lines in his face it looked like a Fingerprint. So what so Newberry did not think I was a big enough Danger & he sent in the 2nd String Reserves off the bench to stop me FINE he is going to get the Surprise of the Week! And likewise these cocky bastards. "You have to help me up," I said & lifted my arms a little.

They each grabbed one & yanked me up. "You been running greasers over the Border you sonofabitch?" Curtis shook me around.

"Is that what you've been doing?" Terry added as if it was a Personal insult. "Well you just walked into a world of trouble."

Curtis took over & shook me agin to get my Attention. "This is the last mistake of your career buddy. You been stopped for good this time."

"Not for good," I said. "I know what for."

"I bet you do," Terry answered back. "I bet you're part greaser."

"The part that don't work," Curtis chuckled at me.

Terry said, "No part of a greaser works. 'Cept his dick." They started to walk me over to their Jeep which was parked 30 Feet away. Almost like small talk Terry asked me, "Your dick work like a white man?" but he did not wait to hear any Answer he just said to Curtis, "Go get this on the radio O.K.? I think I can take care of him from here."

When he had me standing next to the Jeep I saw John Newberry's plot against me in every Detail—in the back there on the floor a Mexican boy was tied up also his hands they tied to the roll-bar by some Nylon Rope. And Curtis let somebody on the other end of his CB know that the Citizens Committee from Azalea just picked up another Offender & he gave my Description. Of course! Let the Ku Klux Klan do his Dirty Work & get rid of me the same way they got rid of those poor Mexicans before! And Newberry's hands end up spic & span! Terry dug a pair of handcuffs out of his pocket. "Let's go."

"Absolutely," I said & I Punched him in the Stomach as hard as I could I pushed him out of my way & I ran. Clumping around the bushes & over the rocks etc. I am no Gazelle but I got a big lead on him when I heard Terry puffing behind me. Then I heard the Jeep rev up & spin out & roar down on me like the Cavalry—

I cut a corner behind a rock a sharp turn that Jeep did not make so he circled around the other side & stopped for a second or so to let Terry get in and I took off the Other Way—I zigged & zagged out of their sight I was the Matador of New Mexico for about a minute for a few times I Outsmarted them—I doubled back & they whooshed past me maybe 18 Inches away on the other side of a bush then the Idea hit me Curtis was trying to run me over! I ran back this way—I ran around the other way—each time I heard them whooping it up & the Mexican boy cheering me on when he went by—his smiling face in the dust that the Jeep was spinning up into the Air all around—now I did not see them coming until they were on top of me bursting out of the dustcloud—they got me going back & forth like a fly in a bottle!

While the red dust was in between us I was safe for a second & I Heard the motor of that Jeep idling somewhere on the other side and I started Backing Up away from it—nor I did not have the Speed or the Breath to run around anymore then a Accident came to my Rescue! I took 1 more step & I dropped backward into a dry Ravine I dropped out of Sight down the soft slope of it. I did not move I doubt it if I breathed for a whole minute since I Heard them above—

"Where'd he go to man?"

"I don't see him. This is crazy."

"Try over down there."

The Jeep drove away a little bit & it stopped. Then it turned around & came back & this time it stopped right at the edge of my Ravine I saw the front bumper hanging over it. Terry jumped out of the car I heard his footsteps crunching in my Direction.

"He's down here somewheres Curtis. I can smell him." He slipped & slid down the loose slope about a Car Length from where I hid. "Here boy!" he was calling to me—"Here Greasy! Here Greasy!" and he whistled for me too. Wiseguy. What does he think? I am going to give up as a Reward because he is such a Genius he tracked me down?

He was stalking me he was walking on eggs I could hear him sniffing me out. I backed up behind a bend in the rock if I Reached my arm out I could Touch him but I let him find me instead. And when he did I had my Gun out pointing between his eyes. "Here I am," I said.

Terry let out a sudden little cry. "Woah!"

"You find him?"

"Yuh," Terry said. "He's got a gun Curtis."

"What kind?"

"The kind that's pointing at my head!" Terry yelled back.

"Tell him not to come down here. Tell him to say where he is," I said as calm as I could.

"I'm coming down!" Curtis warned us.

Terry only got 3 Words out of his mouth—"Don't do that!"—& the next Sound we heard was Curtis throwing himself down into the Ravine & hitting the bottom maybe a little faster than he wanted to.

"I'm all right Terry," he huffed out, "I'm O.K."

"Stay back there!" Terry told him. To me he said, "Now what?"

"I don't want anybody to get hurt," I said.

"What's the deal then man? You going to take me prisoner?" A jumpy smile tugged up the corners of his mouth.

"Just sit down on the ground there." He did. "Cross your legs. And put your hands in your pockets. Your pants pockets." And he did that too. "Tell your boss—no. Forget it. I'll tell him myself." The side of the ravine was a lot Steeper where we were & it took me a minute to find a toe-hold also I had to pull myself up practically by my Fingertips with the Gun in my other hand then all stretched out I was still 2 Feet from the top. "Uh-oh." I must have said this Out Loud because that was Terry's cue to Attack—

'Yaaaaaah!" he let loose his war cry. "I got him Curt!"

"Let go of me! Let go of my leg!" I shook him off & pointed the Gun toward my feet and he backed off a little but he crouched down all ready to tackle me again. It did not take a killer Instinct to notice I was Balancing up there by my toes & fingertips and all Terry had to do was wait for me to land in his lap. That was why he was crouching in Attack Position when Curtis sprang around the corner & jumped into the Action.

"Yaaaaaah!" Curtis came screaming in belly first & hit Terry at Full Speed which knocked him into the side of the Ravine right under my feet. I fell down on top of both of them so there we are in a pile with the Gun on the floor a few feet away.

"His gun's down! It's down Terry!"

"You see it?"

"Get the bastard! *Get it!*"

So out of this tangled mess rolling around on the ground 6 Arms & 6 Legs are wrestling grabbing kicking & pulling also reaching for the Gun which might as well be made out of Soap! Somebody's hand gets a grip on the handle—and it slips out just as fast! Somebody's hand grabs the barrel of it—and this foot kicks it out again! Arms legs hands & feet springing out in Every Direction with Grunts & Curses in the middle of them—we roll over again then I am in a sandwich between the Bodies of those men Terry's bony chest is pressing my head down into Curtis's pot belly but I stretch out my legs & very quick I trap the Gun by both of my Feet so Nobody can get it. Even in such a Desperate Fight I did not expect anybody was going to BITE me in the leg but when Terry sunk his teeth in my Natural Reflexes took over & my foot swang straight back up and hit him in the Face & he roared & rolled off me—so we are all on our knees now clawing at the filthy ground pushing & shoving spitting & scratching to get at my Gun! Look at us there! 3 Old Men fighting each other in the dirt like 3 little kids Fighting over a Prize Marble! over a Baseball Card! Only it is a Deadly Weapon and my Life is at stake when I see Terry scoop it up & Cock It with his thumb I go against my own Moral Rules I stoop down to his level & Fight Dirty—

"O.K.," Terry said & he was panting out of Breath & wiping his mouth with his fingers. "You're finished. You're *over* you bastard!"

I put my hands up over my head. "I surrender," I said & I kicked him with all my Might a swift hard kick between his legs. On his way down I twisted the Gun off him as easy as shaking hands & then I aimed it at Curtis nor I did not have to say a Word of Warning. He sat still where he was he did not make a False Move he just let me back up out of his Sight. Nor he did not dare & Curse me either.

"Ola! Amigo! Hey you! Hey you!" the Mexican boy started calling me as soon as he saw my head pop up out of the Ravine. He spread his fingers out as far as he could stretch them & he shook his ropes so Furious he made the Jeep bounce. "Hey you! Amigo!"

I am sorry to Report I was running away from there with his last Hey You! ringing in my ears but here is my Good Excuse: DIRE CONSEQUENCES IF I LOSE ANY TIME—if that stinking ravine did not come between us or if it was not so steep up the other side I could stop & Help him & set him Free but for my own Sake I needed a fair headstart so I did not wind up being another Victim. I beg you on my knees you do not think I turned my back on a needy cry of Help I hope you Agree it was the Desperate Circumstances that Prevented Me this time!

I did not Know how far I had to run through the blurry haze of heatwaves & reach the safe streets of Azalea but I heard the Jeep speeding down on me then & I did not turn around & Measure which was closer I just kept going. Until the Sight I saw in front of me stopped me cold and it still came rushing up to

greet me—a chainlink Fence was there between me & the street
Beyond only it was not Azalea on the other side—it was Juarez!
So it hit me what Happened last night when it felt like I was on
my way I was on my way 4 Hours going around in a stupid
Circle—THE STORY OF MY LIFE!

I sagged up against the fence there I hung onto it like a drowning man nor I did not look Behind me I heard the Jeep break
through the bushes & hit the flat ground out in the open—a few
more yards a few more Seconds & the front bumper was going to
crush me then what a pitiful Finish! My Inner Thoughts went to
Dolores how I Failed her so terrible also I Remembered Mrs.
Roderiguez did not clean my Apartment for the last 2 Weeks so
it is going to be dirty when the Authorities go in.

I Heard those heavy tires rumble the ground—I heard them
spin & skid then I heard the wheels squealing—I smelled hot
rubber I smelled the *friction*—I heard a PUNCH of glass breaking—I heard a CRUNCH of metal crumpling & I heard the motor
whine & rev high—*this is how my Death sounds this is how it feels*—
a spray of rocks & dirt fanned over me head to toe—and all of a
sudden it went so quiet around me the only Sound I heard was
my own Heartbeat & I heard my Last Breath whoosh out of me.
And I heard a pair of car doors crack open.

"Cover it!"

"I got it covered!"

"Cover it Nilo!"

One ugly thing on top of another. Which is a perfect Description
of what met my eyes when I turned around i.e. a shotgun pointing
at my face & that bullethead Nilo smiling up behind the trigger.

"Not at him!" Wayne Feather slapped the hood of his car &
aimed a finger over at Terry & Curtis. "Cover those geniuses in
the Jeep."

Nilo slid the gun over the top of the car door to where he had
them in his Sights. This did not stop Curtis from pushing &
pulling on his door to get it open but the big dent where Wayne
rammed into him froze it Solid. "You're not goin' anywhere so
just sit tight," Nilo told him & Curtis swore at him & belted the
steering wheel before he settled down.

On his way over to me Wayne bent down in front of his fender to take a look at the smashed headlight. He brushed the loose pieces of glass out of the squinted metal socket & he showed me the same Tender Care. "Are you all right Ray?" he said & put his hand on my shoulder.

"He's got a gun!" Terry shouted over.

Very polite Wayne said, "I'll have to take it now O.K.?"

I reached down into my pocket I started to pull the Gun out then I felt his fingers around my wrist & he pulled my hand out the rest of the way. He emptied all the bullets on the ground & he singled out the empty one. "I shot a hole in the ceiling," I told him right away, "that's what I did."

Wayne kicked the good ones under the fence & dropped the Used Bullet in his pocket. He patted my arm & in a warm way he said, "Tough guy."

While this is going on Curtis gives out with a priceless piece of Information about me. "He ain't a greaser we found out."

'Right," Nilo said, "he's a Jew bastard."

Wayne patted me again. "Ignore him," he tilted his head toward Nilo and walked back to his car. He rested his foot on the front bumper so his coat opened up I Believe he wanted Curtis to see the Gun in the holster on his belt. "We're just not going to tolerate much more of this. You hear me? Stunts like this are getting expensive. Albuquerque's about ready to set fire to my ass over you boys. You're getting to be more trouble than you're worth."

Terry spoke up then, "What about this? What do you call this?" He yanked that Mexican boy up by his Hair. "We're doin' your damn job!"

Wayne glanced at Nilo & Nilo shook his head. "I want you to wait here," Wayne told them, "and hand that illegal over to the custody of the Border Patrol."

"How long we got to wait?"

"As long as it takes for somebody to get here," Nilo joined in.

Wayne led me by my arm over to his car. "Let's get back to civilization huh Ray?" I was not going to be Alone on this ride Because I saw somebody else was sitting in the backseat. A Mexican gentleman very clean groomed in slacks & a red & white Cowboy Shirt. Not even a sweat stain on it! "Nilo," Wayne said, "why don't you sit in the back. Let Ray sit up front."

"With him?" Nilo pointed at the Mexican & frowned down on him to show how much of a Insult this was.

"Be a man about it," Wayne nodded.

Nilo swung the barrel of his Shotgun into the car when he climbed in & waved it in the Mexican's face. "Boom!" he laughed out loud. The Mexican laughed too & Wayne just rolled his eyes.

We drove back by the Border road & headed for the Highway. "Where are we going?" I asked.

"Where do you want to go?" Wayne answered me almost Cheerful about it.

"I want to go home."

"Oh," he said & stared straight ahead, "I thought you wanted to go someplace else first."

"Here's O.K." Nilo was looking out of the back window when he said this.

We peeled off the road and I Believe we stopped somewhere between Juarez and Azalea where there was no traffic besides us. Wayne reached back over the seat. "Gimme that thing Nilo."

Nilo said, "I'll do it."

"Right. You do it," Wayne said like he was talking to a spoiled Child. He turned back around & crossed his arms on his chest.

I will say I did not get teary I did not get scared I got Angry. How I let them drive me to my Doom before my time. I did not think of Dolores then nor I did not think of my Apartment. I did not think of How I got there nor I did not think of Why is he going to do this to me. Then I was not Angry anymore. This is what my Last Thought was going to be: *At least I know how The Story Of My Life ends up!* Not like a Heart Attack sneaking up on me & taking me by Surprise—AT THE MOST IMPORTANT TIME OF MY LIFE I AM NOT IN THE DARK. (Which was not my *absolute* Last Thought I have to be Honest about it. My Absolute Last Thought was I WONDER IF IT HURTS VERY TERRIBLE GETTING SHOT IN THE HEAD BY A SHOT-

GUN) so I was on the brink of Life & Death for the second time in the Same Day which I am sure is some kind of a Record.

And then I was in the Dark. "What's that? What're you doing?" A baby in his cradle would know what it was & what they were doing.

"We'll get back on the road in a minute Ray," Wayne said to calm me down.

"It's just a blindfold," Nilo cooed into my ear & pulled the knot hard against the back of my head. "It's for your own benefit."

"Sure it is."

"Orders from On High," Wayne said & hit the gas.

I will say we stuck to the Main Road maybe we went all the way on the Interstate we did not stop for Traffic Lights. We were in the car for about 1 Hour and all of us stayed silent for the Whole Ride. Except for Nilo at the Beginning he started singing a tune that went Why Don't You Love Me Like You Used To Do How Come You Treat Me Like A One-Eyed Jew which I believe he did to taunt me. Before he got to the Chorus again Wayne told him to shut up or get out & walk.

Look how it can be Normal & Decent to your eye and Perversion & Lies inside. Now my Sincere Hope is you can locate John Newberry's house by my Description I am sorry I did not learn the name of his Street or the closest Town because of the blindfold. You should draw a Circle around Azalea, N.M. and make it 50 Miles wide it will be in there by my Calculations from how long I was in the car with Nilo & Wayne.

His house has a kidney shape Asphalt Driveway in front & a concrete porch with 3 Steps going up to the front door & a white painted rail around it. Like the house across the Street also the houses nextdoor on both sides all of the bungalow type very boxy & square they put them up in the 50s I will say. His address is 4420 to my best Memory. I dearly ask you please try & go there & dig up any Evidence on him you can find. (He is so smart about Evidence I doubt it you will Discover a microscopic Hair but this is worth a try)

I stood at his door & I rang the doorbell like I was a Fuller

Brush salesman or the Avon Lady. Newberry answered me from inside I should come right in & I saw him in the Kitchen waiting for me. He had a frilly apron on & he was waving a spatula in his hand. "I'm making breakfast. You want some coffee & a doughnut? A couple of eggs?"

I stared at him & said, "I don't think so." Before I saw him in front of me I had a Speech in my Mind all ready to go about Amelia and Dolores and why did they have to Suffer by his hands & why did I have to Suffer on top of it. But it all came out in 4 Words. "I feel like hell."

"You *look* like hell!" he said very chipper.

"That's the way I feel."

"Well that's the way you look." He balanced a Egg in each hand as if he was going to juggle them for me. "Sunny side up? Scrambled?"

"One minute Amelia's alive then the next minute she's dead. You know that?" I raised my shaky Voice a little louder. "*You know that?*"

"Ssh!" his finger flew up to his lips. Besides this he Ignored the Topic of my Conversation but he did not Ignore me. "Look. You want to take a shower or something?" he invited me & set 2 plates & a bowl on the table. "Why don't you sit down before you fall on the floor Ray. Tell me what happened. What's your version? That's what I want to hear. Come on. Sit." He pulled out a chair for me.

Sometimes a person has to trust his Bodily Reactions & let them be his Guide when he has got too much on his Mind. Do the Simple thing & Rely on it & let your Basic Needs take over for a few minutes. It is not the easy way out it is the easy way in. So I sat down & I hid my dirty hands under the table not only dirt either there was dried Blood on my arms from the Scratches I got on that fence.

Newberry cracked 4 Eggs into a big copper frying pan. "I'll scramble them with a little butter. It'll be easier on your stomach." He looked over at me. "How are you feeling now?"

"I've had a terrible couple of days."

528

"I know." He stirred the eggs around with a fork. "Nobody touched you did they?"

"Your monkeys ran me into a wire fence." I held up my arms. "Does that count?"

He slid the frying pan off the stove & came over to me very concerned. "Hey you don't want to let that get infected," he said & turned my hand around to examine my Wounds. Also he Examined the gold ring on my finger and he smiled at it. "I've got some Bactine in the medicine cabinet."

"Nilo tied a blindfold on me too. He tied it so tight I got a headache from the knot."

"He did that? Nilo did?"

"You told him to. He does what you tell him to."

"I never told him to do that."

"Wayne said so."

"That's *outrageous* Ray. I apologize." He turned my head by a very gentle touch & ran his finger over the bump behind my ear. "But you're O.K. besides this?"

I shook his hand away. "It's nothing compared to the rest."

"I'm going to take care of you from now on," Newberry told me & forked the eggs onto my plate. He started to say something further but he stopped short when he Heard the water running in the Bathroom. "Just something we've got to get out of the way before we do anything else. What did you do with my letters?"

"I buried them. In the desert. In Mexico."

"No you didn't."

"How do you know that?"

"I know you. That's how. I think you brought them with you. Can I ask you to stand up a minute?" He patted my pockets by the Professional Method & he found them in 5 Seconds flat. "Thank you. You can sit down again. Eat your eggs." He unfolded the yellow paper. "Let me tell you what I like about you the most. You're a bad liar. I admire you for that. I'm counting on your honesty. You couldn't lie if your life depended on it. Am I right?"

"Honesty is the best policy," I threw at him.

"Sometimes." He was reading the Letter on top then he shuffled it to the back. "Sometimes," he said it Sadder this time.

Then Dolores was standing in the door next to us & we both choked up. She did not look at me but I saw the bags under her eyes which means either Crying or No Sleep bags are a dead giveaway of Disturbance. I think in front of her true Papa she was shy with me.

"Hi baby," Newberry said to her but she did not Answer him. "Say good morning honey," he prompted her. "Bring Daddy the Bactine from the big bathroom. And some tissues. Go on." She obeyed him Immediate. "I love that little girl," he told me.

"I do too," I said. "She deserves all the love she can get."

When she came back Newberry crouched down & coiled his arm around her waist & held her still. "Dolores do you recognize this man? Is he the man you saw with Mommy yesterday? Remember? In Mexico. You recognize him honey?"

Now she looked up at me. "Hello darling," I said. "You remember me don't you?" Dolores tried a smile.

Newberry stood up. "You can say hello to Uncle Ray. Look how he hurt his arms. Help him with the Bactine baby so his cuts don't get infected."

She squirted the stuff on a Kleenex she dabbed it very Gentle on my Scratches a real little Nurse taking care of me. Only I did not see any Emotion in her eyes or she did not want to Show any to me. I do not think Dolores knew what Happened to her dear Mama & I say this was a Mercy & a Benefit. All she knew was Before she was with Amelia in Tres Osos & now she was with Newberry in this house.

"Eat your Rice Krispies," her Papa said.

"I'll take over sweetie." I took the Kleenex out of her hand & like a perfect little girl she sat down & waited for her Breakfast.

Newberry poured out her cereal. "Tell Uncle Ray where you're going today."

"School," Dolores said to her bowl.

"Which school?" he wanted her to tell me.

"Holyoak."

"Mount Holyoak," he helped her with this important Detail.

"Mount Holyoak," she Repeated after him.

He Confirmed it by telling me the Name again. "Mount Holyoak. You know what that is Ray?"

"No. I never heard of it before."

"The best private school in the state. The Governor sends his kids there. It's just in Santa Fe so I can visit her every week." He covered her hand with his. "I'm coming from Dallas to see you every week O.K.?"

'Uh-huh." She chewed her Krispies & we both watched her.

"She's going to get a decent education," Newberry nodded. "Dolores it's almost 8 o'clock now honey. How long's it take for you to get dressed for school?"

"A minute," she said & ate another spoonful.

"The bus gets here at 10 after. I don't want you to be late O.K.?"

"I didn't finish my Rice Krispies."

"That's all right. Mrs. Murphy told me they make big lunches at school. Come on," he tugged the spoon out of her hand. "Show Uncle Ray how pretty you look in your uniform."

Dolores squeezed out of her chair & put her bowl in the kitchen sink & ran some water in it on her way out I tell you I thought she was going to stop & Curtsy to us before she left the room.

"Eat up," Newberry pointed at my cold eggs. "Now I've got something for you." He went into the Dining Room behind me & I Heard him open a drawer then he came back in with a Black Briefcase. He cleared my plate away & laid it on the table in front of me.

"What's it do? Explode when I open it?"

"Funny." Newberry snapped the latches open. "It's the best kind on the market. Made out of Samsonite or some sonofabitching thing like that. You can drop it off the Empire State Building & it won't break." He opened the lid & showed me what was inside. "This is your life," & he sounded proud to Announce it to me!

The manila F.B.I. File is the only thing that was in there it is a Inch Thick as of now & my Name is on the tag on the top— GREEN, RAY a.k.a. PETER TREMAYNE then right on Page 1 all of my Vital Statistics to wit my Physical Description i.e. my

Height & Weight also the color of my Eyes & Hair (ha ha) besides my Address & the license number on my Departed car!

"You don't have to read it all here. Keep it. I've got another one in my office." He untied the strings of his Apron & hung it on a hook on the back of the kitchen door & he Smoothed his tie down & sat next to me. "The gist of it is Ray see I put your name on the VICAP watchlist." He sipped at his black coffee & nibbled a buttermilk doughnut.

I do not think Newberry expected a crazy Reaction from me when I Heard this News anyway I only gave him ½ of my Attention since the contents of my Official File absorbed me. I turned the pages & I saw photos of Amelia including a few snapshots of us at that gas station. Also pictures of us at the Bluebird Motel I do not know how they took those. By a special Periscope or a Spyhole maybe. I skim over these pages and a few flakes of Newberry's Conversation drift through to me—

"Violent Criminal Apprehension Program ... your strange behavior in the East 8th in Mason ... old man who lives by himself ... a loner ... living on Social Security ... "

He has everything in there down to a Word By Word Copy of what that know-it-all Dr. Brenda the Sigmund Freud of the Radio said about me 3 Weeks ago—WHEN SHE WAS JUST ENTERTAINING HER AUDIENCE! I turned over another page nor I could not Believe my eyes *again*!

"That's a transcript of the chat I had with the Abercorns. Albert and his little girl Charmagne. He's strictly from the raincoat brigade."

"I never met him," I said. "Is she all right?"

"Yeah sure. She's fine. She's up in Oregon with her mom," he said. "The important thing is she isn't living with that slimeball in the trailer anymore."

"That's the important thing," I said & I flipped over a couple more pages. Newspaper clippings from the Mason Examiner. A Report on me by a different Psychiatrist which I will bet John Newberry wrote instead. Now if he can change my Deeds he can change my Words too he can make this Version come out the way he wants it too he can Exploit me when I am in my Grave. "You twisted all the facts!"

"Please—let us have no pissing and moaning at *this* late stage. What did I make up? Let's face what is and go from there. With me?"

I pointed to the middle of the page."What's this then?" and I read it out loud: "His perceptions conform to a pattern common in the elderly. To them the world *isn't as good as it used to be* and it *isn't the world I grew up in.*"

"Well," Newberry asked me, "is it?"

"No!"

"I told you I didn't make anything up."

"According to this I'm a crazy person. According to this I'm a danger to the community!"

"Don't get excited Ray." Newberry dunked his doughnut & grinned.

"This description isn't me! Look what it says—*suffers from the delusion that he is the only good man in a bad world.* What is that? I know the difference between good & bad! And right & wrong! I know what the facts are!"

"That's a matter of opinion. Let's just say your actions are all a little misguided. The tragic consequences of disordered thinking."

"Everybody's a critic."

"You don't understand. I respect you Ray. For what you did. Well what you tried to do. For instance with that little girl. Charmagne. Who else goes out of their way to help anybody these days? I don't see it. You did something. You remind me of my dad." Newberry stood up & put his hand on my shoulder. "It just backfired on you. That's all."

"That's enough."

"I'm glad to hear you say that. You don't know how relieved I am that you feel that way."

"I'm not taking all the blame for things."

"I don't blame you at all. Between you & me. Things went wrong when Amelia got crazy. No doubt about it. It's all on her."

I am disappointed by my Behavior in this Moment I did not act firmer with him. I only said, "I blame you."

533

"Take it easy there," he answered me very Grim.

"Who then? I have disordered thinking—Amelia acted unpredictable so everything went wrong—which makes you a living angel in the middle of all of this I suppose."

"Did I say I'm perfect?" For about a second Newberry was on the verge of some Humble Pie but he all of a sudden spat this out, "Hey do I owe apologies to anybody? To you? Who do you think *as a matter of fact* has been looking out for you from the minute you got messed up with her? Let me tell you something Ray it hasn't been easy! It hasn't been easy keeping you alive & well all this time." This Flare up came & went like a lick of gas out of a stove the quiet was sharp too. He poked his head out of the Kitchen door to check if Dolores was around (not yet) then he lowered his Voice at me. "You know how I spent most of last Thursday? Fishing your goddamn station wagon out of the Rio Bravo."

"My car?" I did not hide my Relief or joy. "You got my car?"

"I was standing in water up to my waist for 7 hours so I could supervise it personally." He bowed his head a little as if I hurt his Feelings I did not show enough Appreciation. "It was going to be a surprise."

"What hasn't been?"

"You can relax now. I want to conclude this business between us today. Listen. I'm sure this doesn't make any sense to you right now but believe me," he tapped my Official File, "this is going to protect you from now on. This is your insurance policy."

Was I in Wonderland now talking to the Mad Hatter? Words mean the exact Opposite on the other side of the Mirror! "You just told me how it's going to incriminate me! You didn't make this for my comfort Newberry. It's for yours. To use against me right to the end."

"I don't have to. I don't want to. All I want you to know is I can. If I want to. But I don't want to."

I stared up at him & my mouth was open. "This is beyond my belief."

"Just accept things the way they are. Forget about why-this & why-that. There are complications you don't know about. Other

534

dimensions of this you can't comprehend. By the way," Newberry put on his coat & asked me very casual, "do you still have the gun?"

"They took it away from me. Wayne did. He had to for his own safety."

"You shoot anybody?"

"He stopped me in a nick of time," I said as if that kind of thing happened to me every day.

"I'll make sure you get it back. And with a license this time. Make it official."

"Aren't you scared I'll use it on you?"

"Should I be?" I kept quiet & I let him wonder. "I want you to move out of the area. Out of the state. I want to watch you live to a ripe old age."

"I already am a ripe old age."

"Riper. Older. I'll tell you how that's going to happen. I want you to forget about Amelia and Tio. Forget about Dolores. Forget about me. We never came into your life."

"I can't," I said very weak in my Voice but very strong in Feeling. "When somebody comes into a person's life—maybe you're too young & you don't understand this—but they stay in no matter what you do. Or what they do. Even when they die. Maybe that's when they're with you more than before."

A slow smile came up on him. "Make us the exception."

"You know what I'm going to do?" I got my Voice back & said this to his face: "I'm going to fight you." And then my Strength came back as soon as the Words came out of my mouth & I spelled it out for him I did not care about the Risk. "I'm going to fight you for it. For which one of us is going to tell his story to a judge."

He chuckled out of Sympathy. "Honest to God Ray it isn't even a contest, I mean what've you got? What kind of *proof* have you got honey?" He tipped the lid of the briefcase shut. "I did my research. Believe me I did. I've got a statement testifying to your dubious behavior & strange ideas from a Mrs. Silvia Roderiguez who I believe you employ as a maid. Where do you get the money to pay for a maid if you're living on Social Security? Also a Dr.

535

Eugene Godfrey made a few enlightening observations about your general state. So did a Post Office clerk in Mason. Then there's the whole ugly business about abducting that teenager. For all I know you might make a habit of grabbing little girls off the street."

"Shut your rotten mouth," I ordered him. "Shame on you. *Shame.*"

"I'm just making a point. You see where it all can lead. How everything connects. And I'm not halfway finished yet. I'm going to keep on digging into your past Ray. All the way back. It'll be my hobby from now on. Who knows what I'll uncover." Newberry leaned in & let me in on a piece of Confidential Information, "I can prove you're capable of doing absolutely anything."

"That's *you* you're talking about. I didn't do anything wrong! I stay inside the human limits. Not like you! I'm not anything *like* you which is a fact certain Authorities can recognize when I tell them."

"You can try and tell any story you want to. Any story about me at all. I know what I'm responsible for. I know how I've behaved. So I don't want to hear how you're going to fight back now!" Newberry gave in to all his Frustration with me. "It's a stupid waste of our energy. I want you to give it up. You can't do anything else."

Oh yes! I am the Champion of Helpless Victims! "I feel a little funny. Can I get a glass of milk?"

He went right over to the refrigerator & poured me one. "What is it? Your stomach?"

"Yes."

"It's just from the tension. Emotion does that to you." he handed me my milk & watched me Drink it down. "I don't suffer from that at all. Funny thing."

Newberry did not bring me over a napkin so I had to wipe my mouth on the back of my hand a vulgar Gesture of low manners which I never use but I did not want to have a milk mustache when I said once & for all, "I'm going to fight you Newberry. What's the worst thing that can happen to me?"

If he was going to tell me the exact Details of what I could Expect he stopped himself short when he saw Dolores standing behind me. But he put a definite End on the Conversation so I did not have to guess about it. "What happens to the hole when you eat a doughnut?" He clapped his hands together & the next second Newberry turned into a proud Papa showing off his pretty little girl. "Look at her Ray. A real lady isn't she."

The black dress went down a few inches up above her ankles & she had to wear a black tie on her gray shirt. Dolores looked closed in by those dark clothes. At least he let her keep that Pink Purse of hers she had the plastic strap around her wrist.

"Say good-bye to Uncle Ray. You can kiss him on the cheek."

Dolores let her little plaid suitcase slip down to the floor & I leaned over so she could Kiss me. "You still have your lucky fossil?"

She showed me a secret smile. "Bye Uncle Ray," Dolores said & hugged me around my neck & only let go of me when the bus pulled up outside & beeped for her. Newberry walked her over to the front door & when I saw Dolores with him that way in her Uniform & silent & Obeying then I saw what he was doing to her it was a Perversion of her Nature.

Like a Normal daddy he stood & waved Dolores bye-bye and he said to me, "I'm sorry Ray. I don't think you've got time for that shower."

Here is why —

It is all Connected by him Deliberate this way Newberry was confusing me with Kindness. It was the next stage of his smart aleck Plan to get me where he wanted me & then watch me do what he Expected me to do. Oh Boy! When I look back over it I see it Step by Step so bright & Obvious it hurts my eyes & when I was in the middle of the Events it was like I had a blindfold on and now since I remember the Details of what I saw I wish I did.

"How come I don't have to put on a blindfold this time?" I asked him when we passed a sign that said it was 14 Miles to Deming. (Already we were in the car 45 maybe 50 Minutes going South and then a sharp turn East so you can plot the area by this Data + what I gave you before from Azalea —)

Newberry took my Question all wrong. "How many different ways can I say I'm sorry for that? Y'know Ray? I *apologize*. It wasn't my fault. I didn't think I had to specify No Blindfold like I didn't have to specify No Ball & Chain. No Punching In the Stomach . . . " As he ran out of Examples of other things he did not tell Wayne not to do to me Newberry saw by my Expression that I meant my question completely Serious. He did not say "sorry" for this rough Treatment either but his Voice was softer when he said, "You don't have to. You can see where we are."

Where we were was not where we were going i.e. after a stretch of red rocks and scrubland we only stopped in Deming for 10 Minutes for a tank of gas then back on the asphalt tongue of the Interstate: next stop Mason. He drove me in from the West Side of town and a lump swole in my throat when he turned up Aurelio Boulevard. The red light caught us 1 Block down from Bea's Bakery.

"I live around the corner here."

"I know it," he nodded & did not look at me but he beamed out a friendly smile.

"You can drop me off at the corner," I said, "I can walk to Pecan from here."

He shook his head & shook his smile loose. "I'm taking you to your car."

In spite of his funny Behavior I will say I Believe Newberry did Respect me & Regard me as high as he said he did. I Judge this by the Fact he only pulled 1 Rotten Stunt on me (I agree it is *very* rotten) plus 2 Dirty Tricks but he did not tell me Lies. I do not count the phony File on Amelia since her Story was a phony too so they cancel out. Nor I do not count the File on myself Because he did not play Hide & Seek with what he was doing he told me A to Z how he will twist the Truth. At least he did not Lie to me from here on.

Dangling my Apartment in front of me by driving around the back that was his Psychological Tactic. To Remind me how Safe & Sound I will be in my Nest how I do not want to be in the World of Trouble anymore & this worked on my Mind I will confess. When I saw the blue fiberglass roof over my empty garage & my Kitchen window when we went by I thought of my green leather chair how it is waiting in front of the T.V. and the 2

Weeks' worth of dust in the Livingroom etc. my home there without me in it.

I waited in the car while he unlocked the heavy chain wrapped around the Double Gate & I waited there the same when he locked it up again Behind us. Then it was just the empty acres stretching all around. Nothing growing on them Except a crop of little sticks with plastic flags fluttering on top they mark off where the Streets are going to be. And the Vacant Lots for the houses which Amelia told me about in every Detail. In the middle of this place we drove up to another fence which went all the way around a Quonset hut the only survivor of some Army base of Yesteryear. Wayne's car was parked out in front but I did not see my dear Raymobile.

I started to make a noise about this but Newberry jumped in & said, "It's supposed to be here by now. Let's go wait inside."

If I know John Newberry you should not waste your time searching the desert the Quonset is gone by now and I am 100% Sure he scraped the ground after so you will not find a nail or a hair or a speck of Blood. My Advice is look in a Junkyard in the area. Look for a metal sink about 3 Feet long x 2 Feet wide x 2 Feet deep. Also look for a metal table you can not miss it it is as big as a door. With the Extra Added Attraction of gutters down both sides & a drain sunk into the bottom end. If you find these pieces I hope you can Connect them & Newberry but he is very Smart about all types of Evidence so I will not hold my Breath.

When we came in Wayne was leaning against the metal table with his eye on the Mexican gentleman from his car who sat on a stack of cardboard boxes in the corner of the room. He stood up as soon as he saw Newberry.

"Where's Nilo?" he asked Wayne & at the same time he waved to the Mexican he should sit down.

"Bien Senor," he waved back & patted the tight skin of his pot belly & burped & sat.

By this time Newberry was Ignoring him and listening to Wayne complain about Nilo. "You know how he's been acting lately. He thinks he's his own boss."

Newberry smacked his lips to Confirm this was his exact Feeling

539

about Nilo too & he paced over to Wayne. "Who's got Ray's gun?"

"I got it here." Wayne lifted it out of his pocket.

"It have any bullets in it?"

Wayne shook his head & Newberry told him to load it & give it back to me. He held it out on his Handkerchief & I took it with my finger on the trigger. "Safety's off," he warned me.

I Psychoanalyze a big part of John Newberry's Character is he is a Addict of Risks. He will push everybody to their Personal Limit to see what will Happen. He will push Events as far as they will go to show off he has the Power over them. He shares this Trait with Richard Nixon also Casanova and Adolf Hitler I believe.

"Put the gun in your pocket Ray," he aimed his Voice very steady at me from across the metal table. "You don't have to shoot us to get your car back."

Somehow he made me Feel like I was doing him a Personal Favor if I dropped my hand so I did & I let the snubnose cartwheel off my finger down toward my front pocket. I only missed the corner of the seam by a fragment of a Inch & the Gun clattered on the floor so I was bent over double trying to get a grip on the handle which by Accident I kicked with my toe so it was spinning around like a Roulette Wheel in front of my foot. I was still down there trying to pick it up when I saw the back door open & 2 pairs of cowboy boots come stumbling in. And another pair stepped in behind them.

"Hey hey! The gang's all here!" Up above the dirty boots Nilo's face was mooning over at me.

"You bring Ray's car back in one piece?" Newberry did not waste his Breath on any Hello.

"Yeah," Nilo reported to him, "sure. All ready to go."

In Espanol Newberry told the 2 Mexican boys they should sit down on the cardboard boxes & from a shelf under the sink he pulled out a folded-up sheet of clear plastic. "You didn't say hello to Ray," he reminded Nilo. "Say hello to him for crissake."

Nilo nodded at me, "How ya doin'?" he said & wandered over to scrape the side of his boot on a corner of a cardboard box.

Newberry wanted something else out of him. "Nilo."

"Huh?"

"Tell him you're sorry about the blindfold."

"Sorry about what?" Nilo turned around to Newberry with a stiff grin that practically split his face in $\frac{1}{2}$ from the size of it & the Effort. He was not sure if the joke was on me or on him.

"What did I tell you about blindfolding him?"

Nilo rolled his eyes up into his head while he searched his Brain for a Answer & he finally came out with one. "Nothing."

"Right. Nothing." Newberry unrolled the plastic & it was not a sheet it was a pair of coveralls & he stepped into them. "So tell Ray you're sorry about it."

"I'm sorry about the blindfold," Nilo said it to Newberry not to me & his grin was gone. He said the Words as if they were in a Foreign Language he was just starting to learn.

Those coveralls must be from a Atomic Powerplant they must be for keeping out Radioactive Contamination with their built-in gloves & shoes with a hood to top it off. Newberry slid the long zipper up to his chin & gave me a look from in there. He flung his arm out in Nilo's direction & said, "Satisfied?"

It looks like he is being Polite it looks like Consideration but this is just the Camouflage of Newberry's true Purpose. Here is the next stage of his Plan he unfolded like those plastic coveralls here is the bait he used to trap me & turn me into a Criminal—

Newberry called over & snagged his Attention again.

NEWBERRY: Nilo.
NILO: Uh-huh?
NEWBERRY: Tell Ray what you did in Mexico.

Nilo wanted to go careful this time in case his next step led him into quicksand.

NILO: When?
NEWBERRY: Day before yesterday. With Amelia and everything.
NILO: Right. Right.

NEWBERRY:	Was I there?
NILO:	No you was not.
NEWBERRY:	Good. Did I help you? Or did you handle it all by yourself . . .
NILO:	It was my job all the way.

Newberry raised his arms to show me I Told You So. Nilo had a proud smile shining on his face & he was looking right at me since he Realized he was out of Danger & now the joke was on me.

NEWBERRY:	I wasn't in 100 miles of the place. Tell Ray what happened. Don't leave anything out.
NILO:	Jimmied the lock on the front door. Saw your little girl sleeping on the floor there—
NEWBERRY:	After that. Skip over that part.
NILO:	Right. Well—
ME:	I don't want to hear this thanks.
NEWBERRY:	Hey. Listen to every word Ray. I want you to listen to what Nilo did down there.
NILO:	What happened was Amelia was in the kitchen and she didn't hear me come in. Don't know why not. It was a miracle or something.
NEWBERRY:	What'd she have on? Don't leave out what she was wearing.
ME:	I know what she was wearing. I can remember.
NILO:	That nightie. That short nightie. It just came down to the top of her legs.

Newberry pushed Nilo over toward me almost toe to toe so I did not miss a sour Word.

NEWBERRY:	Tell him what you saw.
NILO:	Every hair.
NEWBERRY:	Every hair.
NILO:	Every hair on her. Up her legs & all. Saw

	everything when she lifted that fry pan over her head & tried to hit me! But I got on top of her Ray.
ME:	You deserve a medal.
NEWBERRY:	So you're on top of her in the kitchen while Ray's still in bed.
NILO:	On the floor in there. That's right. Got me kind of horny all the rolling around.
NEWBERRY:	Tell *him*! Tell *Ray*!

Look at what he is doing—this is the Rotten Kind of person Newberry is how he gets other people to Behave lower & lower. You can see how much I stood up against here I had to Bite my Lip to the point of Blood almost to stand Hearing the rest—

NILO:	She wouldn't let go of me she just kept on squirming around. It was a good time. It was a helluva lot of fun until she poinged her nails into my neck & scratched up my arms. Then I got angry at her for real.

I doubt it the Mexicans knew what Nilo was saying but they did get a kick out of all the Drama! Or maybe they were laughing at Newberry in his Radiation suit.

NEWBERRY:	Silencio! Go on Nilo. Then what did you do?
NILO:	I dragged her outside by her hair. By her nightie too. And the damn buttons tore right off!
ME:	Get away from me.
NILO:·	No you want to hear this. It's the most exciting part.
ME:	I don't want to hear it.
NEWBERRY:	Come on Nilo! He missed what happened. He slept right through it.

NILO:	My Lord—then he could of slept through a damn earthquake!
ME:	Nuts to that.
NILO:	Listen to me. Don't talk.
ME:	And nuts to you.
NILO:	You pissy little coward.
ME:	And to you. Double.
NEWBERRY:	Tell him everything.
NILO:	I pushed her down on the ground. And I put my hand over her mouth. This way.

Nilo put his salty hand over my Mouth & my Animal Instinct told me "Bite him!" but I was not going to give him the Satisfaction from lowering me. I bit my lip harder instead.

NEWBERRY:	What'd she have on then?
NILO:	Skin and hair. She was rubbing her hair pie up against me.

Newberry pretended he was Shocked about this—

NEWBERRY:	Amelia was *naked*?
NILO:	Naked as a little baby.
NEWBERRY:	She had a terrific ass on her. Didn't she Ray?

He pulled Nilo's hand off my mouth.

ME:	Peachy.
NILO:	Brown peach. A coffee bean ass. I had her down & she still wouldn't quit. I guess she liked what was goin' on so then I got her up in the bushes. You know the ones? Up the back of the house.

I turned my face away & by a shove I hardly felt Nilo danced me backwards he pinned me to the wall.

NILO:	She would *not* shut up Ray. She wouldn't just let go & accept how it was so what am I supposed to do with her? Didn't make a difference to me which way she wanted it. You see what I mean?

This was when I started Singing a song I believe it was Irving Berlin's cheerful Blue Skies I was singing to Block his Dirty Talk. I shut my eyes from his porky face. Nor I did not see Newberry behind me he jerked my head back around so I had to smell Nilo's cheesy Breath all over.

NILO:	So I got one hand up on her throat & my other one in her hair pie & I'm squeezing both ways.
NEWBERRY:	He had his hand on her private parts Ray! You hear that? Choking Amelia while he's got his hand on her pussy . . .
NILO:	Had my fingers up inside her too. Up her greasy crack. Then I heard how her breath sounded. Kinda like a leaky balloon & it wasn't so much fun after that.

So I Fought back with rotten Memories the same way—

ME:	What kind of a noise did Perry make?
NILO:	Say what?
ME:	Sort of like bacon sizzling? When the shock hit him—
NILO:	Perry *died* from it—you kikey kike!

Nilo threw a sloppy Punch at me his hammy fist clipped my jaw & landed on my ear—he grabbed the front of my jacket then I Twisted Out of his Grip & stood a few feet away from him to catch my Breath—a bad move I just turned into a Target for him—he ran into my chest headfirst & Knocked Me back into the wall—I felt Newberry's hands under my arms he hauled me

up on my feet and threw me right back at Nilo—he Caught Me
by my throat Nilo had my windpipe Squeezing between this thumb
& fingers I think it was the raw Idea of where his other hand
could be Reaching that pushed me so far I pulled out my Gun—

NEWBERRY: Nilo! He's got a gun!

Nor I was not Afraid to use it on him—I brought it down hard
I lowered the boom on him I conked Nilo a good one on his
forehead—Nilo grabbed my wrist he pinned it to the wall & my
Gun was pointing at the ceiling—

NILO: Grab it John! You got it?

He could not see it since he kept his head down Ramming into
my chest—Newberry pried the Gun out of my Sweaty Hand I felt
the rough seams on his Plastic Gloves scrape my palm I Heard
his plastic suit crackle when he moved & I thought *this is the last
thing I will ever feel* and *this is the last Sound I will ever hear*—then
another Sound exploded in my ear—BOOM!—only I did not Feel
any hole open up in me I only felt Nilo's flabby Weight peel away
& thud on the floor—his fingers scratching the Air over his head
until they landed on my ankles & he Grabbed Me tight trying to
pull himself up from his knees—Newberry stood next to him &
shot Nilo in the back of his head then his Blood came spraying
up the front of my pants up to my knees & splashed on my shoes
when Nilo hunched over on his face & Stopped Moving.
    Newberry flashed Wayne a look with Death Rays in his eyes &
that was the only Signal they needed for the wild circus to start—
the Mexican boys were both Enjoying the Show until Wayne
pressed his Gun against the back of the little one's head & when
he pulled the Trigger a Gold Tooth went spinning across the floor
in front of a burst of Blood & Spit—as fast as that tooth Newberry
had his knee bent into the other Muchacho's back & wrestled him
down on the Floor he shut his eyes & turned his face away before
Newberry put a Bullet into his neck nor he did not stop squirming

546

so Newberry put another one in & this time the top of his head Cracked Apart—

I took my eyes off of this sickening Sight just in time to see the cowboy shirt Mexicano rear up & block Wayne out of his way & push himself outside by the back door & he ran for the fence like Crazy Legs Hirsch—

NEWBERRY: Don't hit his stomach! Not in the stomach Wayne!

Wayne took off after the Cowboy Shirt and Newberry took off after Wayne very clumsy in his plastic suit I thought of a baby Elephant running behind his Mama. He shouted at Wayne again then 3 or 4 Shots in a row maybe from both Guns I did not Concentrate & count how many Bullets they shot at him nor I did not Witness who did what Because they chased him behind the other side of the Raymobile & I can only tell you what was the terrible Result. For a few seconds it was as quiet as a Vacuum all around me nor I did not move or Disturb it. It is a Medical fact when a person is asleep special Glands make his Muscles go Limp even if he is almost awake the Glands do not let go of him. In my afternoon naps I used to get such Dreams of being Paralysed on my sofa nor I could not wake up or suck in a deep enough Breath now I Know this can happen if I am Awake. I forced down a shivery Breath when I saw Newberry & Wayne carry the dead Mexican in by his arms & legs I saw his head was red & wet & seeping it was Split Open like a watermelon.

"Hold it," Wayne said & hooked his foot around the edge of the door & flipped it shut Behind him. He let Newberry lift the top part of the Body up onto the metal table then he came around & helped him slide it the rest of the way so it lay there Belly Up.

Newberry crouched down next to me & he checked me over he tilted my face into the Light. "All your color's gone," he Noticed then he slapped the Gun into my hand he pressed my fingers around the handle so I did not Drop It on the Floor. "Don't be afraid," he said & gave me a firm shake on my shoulder Before he stood up & turned his back on me.

What do you Expect a person to do if he has got Decent scruples about Life and Death? I will say I was not afraid of the Sight of those poor dead bodies or of the way Newberry Killed them so easy I was afraid of what I was supposed to do about it. What was he waiting for what did he Expect from me with that Gun? I am going to blow my Brains out for his Convenience? Or stand up to him with it so Wayne can shoot me completely Legal from behind my back? YOUR HONOR I *HAD* TO SHOOT HIM! THE CRAZY MANIAC PULLED HIS GUN ON MR. NEW-BERRY! (You know something I write down these Ideas now but I did not think of them Before I did not think of it on the spot. When I was on the spot something else took over—

I aimed the Gun at John Newberry and he turned around when he heard me cock the hammer back. The Sigh that huffed out of him made me think he was Exhausted from Waiting all day for this to Happen. "O.K. Ray," he said, "please!" But his shaky Voice did not have a Effect on me nor his weak smile did not touch my Heart. Very slow that smile curled up at the corners until he stood there in front of me like he was posing for a snapshot at a backyard Bar-B-Q. I say it was his kind of Mockery that put the sudden Strength in me. Or put in the sudden Human Weakness that curled my finger around the Trigger. Wayne did not make any kind of a Move toward me & I will tell you I Remember I Felt a sob swell up in my throat it was the last Particle of my Sympathy leaving me.

Newberry turned away from me & said, "Playtime's over."

"Yes it is," I choked back but I could not pull the Trigger like a man.

While Wayne & Newberry are splitting their sides from the High Hilarity of my unmanly cowardice I can Feel the hot mud bubbling in my stomach & I can taste the sour salt of it before it hits my back teeth & splashes out of my mouth.

"For crissakes Ray! You have to do that in here?" Wayne pinched his nose between his finger & thumb.

"C'mon Ray," Newberry stopped laughing to tell me, "you're right next to the door. Stick your head outside if you hafta do that again." He caught Wayne's eye & said, "Some guys don't have any consideration." Which wisecrack sparked off another round of private laughs between them. But it was Newberry who came over & sloshed a bucket of Water across the floor where I Threw Up.

"So . . . so . . . " I dragged it out very bitter, "so sorry," I said but he Ignored Me.

Newberry got busy with Nilo's body he picked up both legs under the knee & dragged him out of the way. Wayne grabbed one of the limp hands and he steered him around so Nilo ended up Side By Side to the Mexican boys he Delivered. "Future generations owe me one—don't you think? At least I stopped Nilo from pissing in the gene pool."

"Ray . . . don't ask me why. While you're standing there looking at all the whys the *what* runs you over like a freight train."

Even a rock in the Dirt has got some Why Behind It. Igneous e.g. or Sedimentary. I did not Respect his Answer so I asked him again.

Newberry broke open his silver razor. "I know this is going to be a shock to you my friend but listen—everybody who owns a refrigerator thinks he's civilized. It's just a trick Westinghouse pulls on us. *I* know we never moved out of the caves. Caves & clubs before and now we've got streets & houses & guns."

A perfect Point I can Remind him we have also got Laws!

"I'm not saying it's a *deep* philosophy Ray,' he said, "but it doesn't have to sound deep to be right. Look at it this way. Cavemen had campfires. A little flickering light poking out of all that darkness around them. A teensy puff of heat in the path of the Ice Age. Something they made to scare off wild animals & the ghosts of their ancestors. It's the same thing exactly."

Not exactly by me.

"No—not exactly. A campfire is better than a law. You can't roast a weenie over a law. You can quote me on that."

You said it!

I watched him peel the cowboy shirt back over the Bulge of the Mexican's Belly. "Ugh!" Newberry shimmied his shoulders, "I hate this part." And he dipped the Razor down & cut across the yellow skin 2 Cuts in a long X that met in the middle of his Stomach. So I saw what the gutters in the table had to be there for i.e. more Blood etc. drooled down them & by the Drain between his feet it dribbled into a Oildrum Underneath there.

My tongue was as dry as sandpaper but I asked him for the 3rd time in a row.

"Get Ray a glass of water," he said to Wayne. "I think there's some Alka Seltzer up over the sink." Newberry stopped cutting a minute & he gave me the Impression he was really thinking about why he is standing there in a plastic suit with 3 Corpses on the floor & 1 Corpse on the table in front of him & Human Blood up to his knees cutting X's into a dead person's Stomach with a Silver Razor. "Because . . . I think because . . . I feel *responsible*." Which was all the Thinking about it he wanted to do & he leaned down over the Mexican's stomach & cut the flesh to ribbons & dug his hand down into the Hole he made. "Yuch," was all he said, "Yucky!" and he stuck out his tongue. He fished his hand around Inside There like it was a Grab Bag.

When they started coming out I thought they were Golf Balls. He pulled them out by 2s & 3s and dropped them in a plastic bucket. I Believe he got 40 out of that particular Stomach. I drank all of my Alka Seltzer in a gulp but there is a Limit to how much Relief a person can get from Alka Seltzer in a Revolting Situation like this.

Over at the sink Wayne washed off the 40 Balls & got ready for the next batch that Newberry scooped out of the little Mexican nor I do not know how so many Crammed in there he was so skinny. It was not Golf Balls I saw by the time they got finished with the other Muchacho Wayne had 10 Dozen Rubbers all washed & dried. Every one of them was tied in a Knot and when he cut them open it was White Drugs inside White Powder that Wayne poured out very Delicate & Careful. He filled up a Dozen coffee cans.

I could only think about Dolores. This Murderer this Criminal this smiling Slave Trader this walking Perversion was her GUARDIAN! I saw how she was Helpless in his house just a INNOCENT child at his Mercy & I doubt it if he knew the

Meaning of the Word. I Doubt it if John Newberry has any Human Feelings for anybody.

"All I've got is human feelings!" He buttoned up the Muchacho's shirt over the wound his Razor sliced into him. The stump of a Artery poked up from between the shirttails. "You think I'm enjoying this?"

I will say something put a smile on his face besides 120 Rubbers full of Aspirin! What is the Difference if he says he Hates doing butcher's work but the Result of this business is his PRIDE & JOY!?

"Not for the reason you think. I'm not even happy about it. I'm just satisfied it's over. I'm satisfied everything went so well. I'm *satisfied* about it all right? Believe me I don't deserve this kind of shabby treatment from you. If you only knew the *half* of it!"

What do you Deserve for your Perverted Deeds? A Life of Luxury? I will not get a Argument out of anybody if I dare & say everything did not turn out so wonderful for those poor Mexicans!

"Oh *them*. Wayne tell Ray about this trash. Tell him the whole story before he goes off half cocked."

Wayne flapped his hand over the Cowboy Shirt. "He's Augusto Ramirez. A pimp. His specialty was little boys & girls in Mexico City. He broke them in. Showed those kids how to satisfy every kind of weird thing. Augusto wanted to move his business up here so we told him sure—no problem." He kicked the boot on the foot of the other muchacho. "That's Enrico Raul Cruz. Rico wanted to come across pretty quick on account of his wife's family. They wanted his balls for breakfast no doubt about it. He gave her the clap or something he picked up off of one of Augusto's ninas & they had a fight about it which ended up with Rico breaking her face on the back of a shovel. Broke the shovel too I heard. Nilo you know about," Wayne skipped over him & stood next to the table where the skinny Mexican boy was still laid out. "Freddy Duarte. Looks like a teenager huh? Freddy made it all the way up to 31 but I honestly do not know how he got that far. Went around with the dumb idea he was Billy the Kid reincarnated. He used to do anything anybody'd pay him to do. Got up to some pretty wild activity around Ojinaga. Showed up with a donkey

551

for a joke at some guy's Cinco de Mayo party & the guy told Freddy he'd give him $100 if Freddy'd take his pants down right there & do it with the burro."

"I never heard that," Newberry said & stared down at Freddy. "So did he do it?"

"Not for a hundred. He got another 50 bucks outa the guy for hay. Freddy said the donkey'd expect him to buy it a nice dinner after they got done just to prove he still respected her."

Big laughs over Freddy's skin & bones. (I do not Believe this story happened. So in my book that makes laughing at him WORSE.)

"This is the most worthwhile thing any of them ever did in their whole lives," Newberry said when he stopped laughing. "Look how they sacrificed themselves for the sake of a better future."

He truly Believes this cockamamie line! For your Information Mr. Newberry a Sacrifice is something a person does *voluntary*— look it up in Webster's Dictionary if you doubt this Definition! And while you are looking there maybe you can turn to B & find me the Exact Meaning of the word BETTER how you just used it. You mean it is a better Future for *them* since now they are Dead & likewise it is a better World for the rest of us? Or you mean it is just a better Future for *you?*

"I'm not crying over what happened here. And don't tell me you are either Ray because I know you're a respectable man. *You* don't like to see the streets crawling with this kind of human garbage. You're uncomfortable that's all. Being around all of this terrible violence. It's so far from your life. I know. And I'm sorry you got dragged into it. You got involved in what I do & I hate it but this is in my life too." He flicked a glance down at the wet blood on Freddy's shirt. "*Was* in my life. From today it's all a thing of the past. I can retire from the Bureau now. I can retire with *honor*. The way I've taken care of these bodybag enchiladas goes beyond the call of duty."

Oh really? I think you want to add something to that Newberry! How about that shipment of rat poison that white gold dust you cut out of their Hides? How far Beyond does THAT Business go?

"All the way & back again! It's *raw material*. That's all it is. Did you ever hear the expression What's Good for General Motors Is Good For the U.S.A.? It all trickles down. That's what it means. I can trade this dumb powder for Real Estate. I've done it already. For this piece of Real Estate we're standing on right now. Acres & acres of it for a few dozen coffee cans of this stupid junk." Newberry shook a couple of the cans in the Air like they were a pair of Maracas. He gripped them Tight & said, "It's just a beautiful thing when you're on the right side of the Law of Supply & Demand. Listen to this. I raised a loan on this land big enough to build 300 houses. Which means jobs for ditch diggers bricklayers carpenters & electricians plumbers & interior decorators. Orders from lumber yards wallpaper manufacturers & hardware companies. It means 300 new telephone customers & maybe *900* new telephones. Plus regular work for Japanese gardeners & Mexican pool cleaners. Brand new suburban streets in the middle of the desert! And good houses. Quality houses I'm talking about that'll attract young families into New Plains. So please don't think the only thing I'm interested in here is a personal profit you can measure in dollars & cents! Goddamnit Ray—I'm building a whole new community!"

Let Freedom Ring! God Shed His Grace On Thee! John Newberry does not want me to Think he is a person who LIES to poor MEXICANS & uses their BODIES & when he gets done with them just THROWS THEM AWAY like they are Garbage—& TRADES DRUGS for his personal PROFIT & laughs about his CRIMES all the way to the BANK! He wants me to RESPECT him for it!

"I don't know why you've got a *problem* with this Ray," his Voice squeaked on that word. "Have you got something against the idea of free enterprise?" I told him just his. "Remember that first time we met? We talked about John F. Kennedy. Do you remember that?"

I remember everything.

"What did he say at his inauguration—Some People See Things The Way They Are And Ask Why. I Dream Of Things That Never Were And Ask Why Not." Nor he did not stop & let it rest there I had to listen to a American History Lesson on top. "Where would we all be today if Cornelius Vanderbilt or Henry Ford stopped what they were doing & asked themselves why? Or if Standford had 2nd thoughts about building a railroad! John D. Rockefeller—J.P. Morgan—Andrew Carnegie—you know these names? You've heard of these men?"

Al Capone—Meyer Lansky—Lucky Luciano—La-dee-doo-dah!

"The work I did today means I can provide something very valuable. Something precious for the future. I'm not talking about New Plains now I'm talking about my family. Not just food & shelter for them. I can do a lot more than that now. I mean *security* Ray. I can protect them from their worst worries. I won't let them worry about *losing* anything. No uncertainty about tomorrow. My kids can have their own houses right here. I can come visit my grandchildren in New Plains! In 20 or 30 years. For now I'll just enjoy the peace of mind I screwed out of the world with hard work & Yankee ingenuity. I'm not complaining. That's life all over isn't it. If you want to do anything that makes a difference you've got to get down in it & get your hands dirty."

Newberry you talk about this Repulsive Business like it is a Lollipop Factory you hammered together by candy cane nails & chocolate planks in the middle of Gingerbread Wood! What about the way your work ends up with DEAD PEOPLE at your Feet! What about all the Laws you broke not to mention the Supreme Commandment?

"Laws come last. They always come after. Lawyers come sniffing along in the footsteps of real pioneers. You think you'd be living in your cozy apartment on Pecan St. if it wasn't for the U.S. Cavalry a hundred years ago shooting hell out of the Apaches? Everybody sacrifices something."

I point out EVERYBODY EXCEPT JOHN NEWBERRY!

Watch his face go Pale & his eyes go sad from this Wound I made in his Sensitive feelings. When he can choke down his Emotions & think of the right words he holds up his hands for me to see them in the plastic gloves with a web of Blood on both sides & wet crumbs of Freddy's stomach sticking to his fingertips. "Look what I'm willing to do for my loved ones."

*
554

Newberry told me very Proud & Satisfied how a year from now he is going to adopt Dolores so she will be his Daughter by Law. I am happy for him I am happy for her etc. & blah blah blah if he wanted a regular conversation out of me so what I gave him. My Inner Thoughts belonged to me & all of them crowded in my Mind like gray clouds piled on top of each other. His cockeyed version of the Story of our Country for one thing. As if Apaches never scalped anybody! And in spite of the scalping they did who gave them special Indian Reservations to live on *for free*? Nor they do not have to pay Income Tax down to this day so my Apartment does not come into it. If he can twist the Facts of American History so easy by his Ignorance or Because of the hole in his head where his Conscience should be then he will twist anything. So the other heavy cloud that rolled in was I could not be near Dolores & Protect her from his selfish Influence.

He made me sit in the passenger seat of my own car he even held the door open for me as if I was a weak Invalid. "Buckle up for safety," he pointed at my seatbelt. I clicked it shut around me then Newberry pulled it tight. "Don't want to lose you," he said.

I did not think about Nilo's corpse lying in the back of the Raymobile or the Cowboy Shirt either. Only when I turned around & looked out the back window to check & see how close Wayne was Behind us I could not Avoid my eyes from the bloody Sight. I put my window down all the way & the hot Air blasting in blew some of the meat smell away or thinned it out at least. I am guessing here but I think somehow Newberry got used to the smell of Dead people & when he saw the sour look on my face he tried to Distract Me by cheerful Conversation. Mainly his Topic was The Worst Is Over if he told me once he told me 10 Times, "This is the last thing we've got to do." It did not Encourage me nor it did not take my Mind off of the meaty aroma in the car so here is another Lesson of Life for the books—You Can Not Avoid Your Senses. So I leaned my head out of the window & I only smelled the dirt of the Desert & I only heard the Air roar around my ears.

I saw on the Front Page of the Examiner (yesterday?) some Boy Scouts found the 4 Corpses 9 Miles North of Deming, N.M. but when we pulled over at the time I did not Know this Exact

Location. Newberry did not make me soil my hands & help him pull Nilo etc. out of the Raymobile. Also Wayne handled the Remains of the 2 other Mexicans he had in his trunk he rolled them out of their trash bags on the Ground. They dragged them all off the road a few feet into the dry weeds.

In the back of my car they left Blood Stains plus the dirty blanket which they wrapped Nilo in. "What am I supposed to do with this?"

"Get rid of it," Newberry shrugged at me & he peeled off the top part of his plastic suit. He sat down on the edge of the front seat in the open door & kicked his legs out of bottom part. "I'd burn it somewhere," he advised me. (I Believe that is what Happened to the plastic Radiation suit because the last time I saw it Newberry stuffed it down in a trash bag & Wayne put it in the trunk of his Buick.) He pushed his open hand in front of me to shake man to man. "Good-bye Ray." I Refused him I was not in the Mood for Good Manners. "Can you open up the glove compartment for me? There's a rag in there." I only did this so I did not have to look at him. He used the rag to cover his fingers when he popped the Hood Release. Wayne was around the front with a wrench in his hand & he leaned in over the motor.

"What's he doing to my car?"

"He's not doing anything to it," Newberry said. "We're just taking your spark plugs out."

"I don't even know where the hell I am! I'm in the middle of the Sahara Desert out here! This is fine. This is what I expect. I was wondering when you were going to get to me—"

"Before you give yourself a coronary Ray calm down a minute. I just want to make sure I know where you are for the next couple of hours. I'm going to drop one of them off every 100 yards or so. We'll even leave you the wrench. Won't we Wayne?"

Wayne shut the hood & stood next to Newberry. "What?"

"We'll leave Ray the wrench."

"Of course."

"I don't know from that!" I said. "The guy at the gas station puts in my spark plugs!"

"Easy as pie," Wayne said. "They just plug in."

"Oh fine," I said & I dug the Gun out of my jacket pocket. "You can throw this out too." Newberry pressed it back by the flat of his hand so I threw it out of the window to Defy him.

Newberry went out into the weeds & brought it back. "C'mon Ray. Only thing to do is giggle and give in." He wiped it off & Pushed It Back in my pocket. "This way you always know where it is."

"You mean you do."

"Uh-huh. Right. And that way I can guarantee nothing upsetting is going to happen. Hold on to it Ray. So you can sleep at night." He got out of my car & poked his head inside when he shut the door. "I think you should check the pressure in the back tires. Felt like we were fishtailing a little bit." As if those were his Final Words to me as if he was Sure this was the End he turned around & walked over to Wayne's car.

"Newberry!" I jumped out of the Raymobile my shout all of a sudden stopped him in his Tracks.

"What are you going to do Ray? Hit me over the head with the wrench?" He started to climb inside but he looked over his shoulder to say, "You don't do things like that. You're too tender hearted for the bare knuckle stuff. Go home Ray. You don't want to see me again."

I did not think of a Strong Comeback until they pulled away so I ran behind them a few steps straight into the ball of dust Erupting on the road in front of me. "I'M STICKING TO YOU LIKE NAPALM!" is what I Warned him & I swore it on my Honor up to the clear blue Sky.

I was picking up spark plugs for 3 Hours. I am not a Mechanical Wizard so I do not Apologize it took me 1 More Hour to figure out how they go in. This Activity tuckered me out so I did not step on the gas right away I did not drive off in Hot Pursuit I sat down a minute. Think Think Think.

A person believes in JUSTICE so what can he do & answer Newberry's crimes? Every Deed attracts some Deed back by its own Gravity so I ask you what kind of a Answer does a respectable man throw back at a KILLER & a PERVERT the NATURAL ENEMY of Decent Life? What is the Right Answer when you meet a dishonest F.B.I. Agent who betrayed his Pledge of Allegiance also cheated on his Wife at the same time when he smuggled Paying Customers over the U.S. Border on his Mexican girlfriend's back—and who led her on by his Masculine Power so far she ended up with a Baby Girl to feed—furthermore a man who did not Regret the terrible way this Beloved Woman got strangled to Death because the only thing that matters to him is coming out On Top—On Top of more Death by his Own Hands & by his Precautions nobody can ever Prove he was in 100 Miles of these Crimes—instead he will use all of his Powers to plant Evidence on a Innocent member of the Public & fix him with a phony File etc. & besmirch his Good Name beyond Repair & twist everything that happened so far *to save his own skin* & Blame it all on somebody he can keep under his thumb or he will make them squirm under his Bare Knuckle! I am asking you what is the Answer to John Newberry who can do this & then drive back to his little house in Dallas in time to eat dinner with his beautiful Family?

You want to hear my Answer?

I fired up the Raymobile & drove it in Newberry's tracks all the way on that back road I only Thought about him the Whole Time. I Followed his Trail until I got to the Interstate. IF HE IS GOING EAST THEN I WILL GO WEST. I WILL GO AS FAR AWAY FROM HIM AS I CAN UNTIL I FALL OFF THE END OF THE MAP.

Oh yes I was coming to a Conclusion—

A person keeps his eyes on the Good he Pledges his Body & Soul & this Interrupts his Mind so he forgets how close he is to the evils of Life. Too much Good will Hypnotize him & make him too Tender Hearted & he will be looking at the flowers & butterflies when Evil is waiting to Ambush Him. Nor the Good he sees will not Protect him either it does him Mortal Harm.

I go back to Science here & quote you Isaac Newton's well-known Law—Every Action Makes A Equal & OPPOSITE Reaction—by my Personal Experience I will say this Law applies to Human Deeds the same. Look at the Christians of then & now. Look at Israel today & look at Germany. Look at me & John Newberry. Ergo here is the last Lesson Of Life that persons with Good Intentions will learn—while you smile very Brave & whistle a happy tune they sneak up behind your back & they Know you do not have padding on your Vital Areas. It is not the Truth if you believe Honesty & Suffering etc. will always come out on Top of selfish rotten bastards for by my Experience I dare & Say it is the Opposite.

I left my old Beliefs behind on my way out of New Mexico when I went past the Welcome To Arizona sign I told them Good Riddance. Altogether I did not stop driving I went 23 Hours Non-Stop. I did not want to sleep nor I did not stop thinking about John Newberry I could not shut off the Radio playing in my Mind. Mainly the Idea coming back was how he is my Superior i.e. if Good Intentions make us all weak then Bad Intentions make us Strong. Thank you Newberry for teaching me the Facts of Life when I am 66 Years old!

I am all for Crime now I am thinking about all the Good which you Criminals do in the World! You Killers who let us know how Delicate Threads hold up every Life. You Thiefs who show us we have to lock up our money & Real Estate to treasure it. You Cheats & Liars who make us Doubt every Word we Hear. You Pimps who Remind us how we come out of meat & the most Beautiful Desire which comes over a man is only Meat in Motion. You Perverts who teach us the low Truth about how humans Behave when nobody is looking. I will join you! I will do the Human Race a favor! I will Achieve this by my own Strength & Willpower! I will do the Worst Thing I can think of & wake you up with it so nobody will get Hypnotized by the shiny Idea there is something Good alive in the World some Power to help you some Friend to Defend You. Then you will not be so Helpless when somebody else sneaks up behind your back. I thank you Newberry for you made me into the man who I am today!

Now Howard Silverstein comes back for a minute so I can say Good-Bye to him before I disintegrate into Death.

GOOD-BYE MR. SILVERSTEIN!

"Ray I'll be honest with you. You showed some promise in the beginning. How old were you then—18 or 19? That's youth for you. And then look what happened."

"What *did* happen? Tell me what. Please!"

"The usual thing," says Mr. Silverstein in this moment. "Promise. Then less promise. A little less every year. I knew after the '39 season you didn't have anything bigger in you than The Green Ray. I watched you hit your peak in 1939."

"You mean I was never any good after that?"

"So-so."

"Just so-so? I was on for 6 more years."

"You weren't as special as you thought you were. Nobody said we were looking for Alfred Lunt to play The Green Ray."

"I'm sure I had talent. At least I'm sure of that."

"Medium."

"I'm having trouble accepting this."

"You want me to lie?"

"I was a good actor." I want to Nail Him Down & egg him on to Answer me. "I made The Green Ray come alive. Lamont Carruthers said so."

He jiggles his hand in the Air. "A One Note Samba. I'm not saying you didn't put some oompf into the part. You did. Plenty of oompf. You always had that. That's why I liked you."

"If you liked me so much then how did I end up on the street?"

"To tell you the truth you got to be a rope around my neck. You turned into a sad embarrassment," he sighs at me. "You want to know how bad it was? By the end you were starting to remind me of one of those dwarfs that Spanish kings used to have cartwheeling around the throne room. You were just pathetic."

"Your Majesty!"

"But *you* saw it like that. And I saw what was on the cards Ray. How could I let my people think I had anything to do with a freak? A real piece of resistance that last night!" I Wince from this Memory of it. "You wanted to jump around like a monkey on a chain. Fine. Excuse me if I didn't want to look like your organ grinder."

"In other words . . . "

"In other words you made me look bad in front of my friends. You were more trouble than you were worth."

"Is that all that ever mattered about me?"

"What else?"

"Who I am deep inside."

"Not interested." He starts to go. "It's not just me. Who has the time these days?"

"Wait! What you're saying is *terrible*. You're saying you judge everything completely by how it looks on the surface!"

"Most people are like that."

In the middle of Arizona in the middle of the night I laid my lead foot on the gas I made the Raymobile eat up the Miles. *I hope John Newberry is thinking about me in this Moment let him wonder about the state of my Mind.* I am going away from him & I ACCEPT EVERYTHING COMING UP! Everything is the same after 5 Seconds. The neon signs going by. The billboards. The coffee shops. The dotted white lines on the Road I pass by. I Know the things of this World for instance a Sight or a Sound comes for 5 Seconds & then—BOOM!—the next thing they are a Memory Behind Me. What do I have to think about you if I do not want? So I hope you are thinking about me Newberry Because now I close the lights on you & instead I am going to think about Bernhardt Grym—

GOOD-BYE BERNHARDT!

"My darling! Come here! Can I kiss you?" I watch him make a reach for me & then he Remembers the Rules. "No," he says very Disappointed, "I can't."

"That's the sum total of all your feelings Bernhardt?"

"Well . . . "

"Oh there must've been something else you felt about me," I can Hear myself practically Begging Him.

"There was something," Bernhardt is ready to tell me. "Your *aroma*."

"*Besides* the physical I mean."

"Your aroma of TRAGEDY! What a bouquet you had on you. What a bloom! You want to know why everybody else avoided you? A whiff is all ordinary people can take. You could clear a room in 30 seconds. But I want you to know Ray—it *attracted* me."

I Ponder this point over & I think it is Correct. I think this is the side of me that embarrassed Howard Silverstein so much. My tragic Aroma.

"You were born with it my boy! From the minute that one sperm out of billions & that one egg out of millions met to make you—you knew the sad truth in your tiniest cells . . . there's no pleasure on Earth that lasts longer than a touch & that's really all you can hope for."

"There! You said it. HOPE for," I jump in here. "I gave people hope. *I* did that!"

"You're not on the radio now."

"It's still the same thing. At least I ran my life by ideals. For 66 years I didn't compromise once."

"Show me the big rewards. Show me all your achievements. Tell me why you never got your arms around anything actually worth having in your life! No family. No house. No respect. I don't want to be too cruel about it my dear but you never even owned a washing machine."

"So sometimes it was false hope."

"If you can tell me the difference between false hope & real hope," Bernhardt drips his Next Words out, "I'll marry Yasser Arafat." I laugh out loud at this nor I can not come up with any kind of Answer to his Question so Bernhardt Says, "You're at the end of a 66 year old daydream now my dear darling. Look how it was—every once in a while some little improvement flew up & roosted in the shabby gables of your life. Like when the Mason Examiner paid you $10 for that article about the dinosaurs. Red letter days like that. Your name in the newspapers!" he mocks me.

"Yes."

"A milestone you thought."

"It was."

"It was the ratty trick your own life played on you over & over *to keep you going* for 66 years. You can blame it all on that idiot-boy hope of yours. It's been cheering you on from one dismal disappointment to the next. Clapping for your comeback!" Now he is fading away from me & the Last Thing I see of Bernhardt is his lordly nose he jerks it up into the Dark Air. "But my dear! Don't let me discourage you. Where would drama be without tragic lives like yours?"

I will not Waste any more of my Time & go back again now I do not want to go back at all but I Claim I am not a Coward. I am going Backwards to go Forwards Before I get to California I have to clear my Mind.

GOOD-BYE DAVID ARCASH!

"I finally want to tell you how much you absolutely disgusted me," I am happy to say Out Loud.

"I was glad to do it," says David. "Was it my general attitude or was there something in particular?"

"Are you interested?"

"About that much." He holds up his pinky fingernail.

"Then I'll tell you David. The way you treated females. It was revolting. It revolted me. The way you picked them up & threw them away like a dirty tissue." (I feel a big Relief already to say this in plain Words)

"Perfect," David comes back, "that's a perfect comparison. A woman & a dirty kleenex. The only difference is at least a kleenex is clean when you pull it out of the box." He lights up a cigarette & drags in a lungful of Smoke Before he has Anything Else to say. "You think I don't know what attracts a woman? It's obvious that you don't so I'll spell them out for you—Good Looks Money & Success. They come & they go Ray. It's all a temporary arrangement."

"At least I know there's some Justice in life sometimes," I tell him. "When I see how you ended up so miserable. Broke & broken down & deserted."

"It just proves my point."

"It proves what happens if you behave like a barnyard animal! You only had three ideas in your head your whole life. And only one at a time—what to eat when to sleep & who to f—!"

"Oh c'mon Ray! Say the word. Say the whole goddamn word!" I will not say it I stick to my Principles. "That's you all over. Act like you're too delicate to stand the sound of it."

"It's not delicate. It's standards. High ideals isn't something a sea slug like you can appreciate."

"A minute ago I was a barnyard animal. Now I'm a sea slug."

"I demoted you lower. If I could think of a living thing on a lower level I'd put you down there."

"You amateur," he laughs at me, "Mr. High & Mighty. Low is the only level there is." He flicks his cigarette butt out the window. "Everything else is in your imagination. And how did you end up with your high aims?"

"Not like you."

"*Exactly* like me." He leans back & looks me over. "You want to hear what women don't like about you?"

"From the expert."

"You said it. It's not your unappetizing face. It's not your pathetic bank account. It isn't even because you blew your only chance of success. You scared them away with that over-active radioactive mutant imagination of yours. It's as ugly as a hairy wart on the end of your nose. Tell you what Ray—you scared Annie right into my arms."

"Oh sure. That's what I did. Because I had the nerve to think out of everybody I was going to be the one who could make a future with her. Make a permanent life with her. Tell me what's so ugly about a good intention like that."

"It must be because women get pregnant & have babies. They're the ones who know what a crock romance is. They watch it go from this—" he cradles his arms, "to this . . . " David points at his old face then he points at mine. "If it's temporary it's beautiful pal. If you know how it just dies."

564

"My emotions for Annie never went. I've still got them with me." I try & Swallow with my Dry Mouth. "I don't want this conversation anymore. I had beautiful emotions," I say. "And high hopes. I'm not ashamed I did either."

"Whatever you say." David shakes his head, "You don't look very happy about it."

"I'm not happy."

"You never aimed low enough."

GOOD-BYE ANNIE!

"What did I do? Tell me what on Earth I did to deserve such a disrespect from you?"

Annie is sitting Behind Me I think I can see her face Reflecting in my window. Bars of light on her hair roll over & under her curly blonde Perm when she turns her head. She leans forward & her Voice screws into my ear—

"You embarrassed me."

"By what? By giving you nice presents?" She nods me Yes nor she does not stop nodding nor I do not Stop for a Breath. "By buying you lunch? Or a dinner once in a while? By calling you up on the telephone? By treating you like somebody special when you gave me a chance to? For chrissake Annie—just because I singled you out of the crowd?"

"Lucky me." She twists her Knife in, "You treated me like you were the one who was special Ray not me."

"The only thing I thought was special about me was how you made me feel. I peeled back my own skin to show you! Out of everybody I just wanted you to know about the tender feelings I had."

"You never gave me a choice," she laughs at me her hard laugh it Sparkles for a second like Splinters of Glass. "You cornered me with all that flowery attention. For the last time Ray for once & for all—I didn't want the honor!"

This mistake Depresses me if it was only flowery Attention to her so I hasten & Correct this Idea. "It was ENTHUSIASM Annie! I was *enthusiastic* that's all. I thought women appreciated

565

it when a man shows some enthusiasm," I say. "But you ignored my gestures. You let me know I fit in with you like a pygmy in a basketball game."

"You selfish crumb! It's all my fault?" Annie slumps back out of the Light & she has a lot more to say to me now I can not see her face so Clear. "Every move of yours came with a fish hook in it. You bought hundreds of flowers to show me what a passionate man you are. I hated it after dinner in a restaurant every time you made a grab for my hands across the table. Every little squeeze snapped in like a electric shock & between them there you were waiting for me to squeeze you back. Why didn't you take the hint when you couldn't get me on the phone anymore? How many dumb excuses did you have to hear from me before you got the message? If you're still thinking that my sister forgot to tell me you called or I lost your phone number listen to this—here's the real reason: I didn't want to talk to you. And you didn't stop pestering me. You sent letters to me every week & I don't even remember half of what you wrote in them. Those newspaper clippings. What did anybody discovering the planet Pluto have to do with you & me? Here's what: it was a trick to get me to pay attention to you. What embarrassed me the worst was any time I had to see you in the studio the next day after I got one of your letters. The way you watched me walk down the hall just waiting for me to say something."

"I couldn't give up on you so easy," I tell her & I try & say what else I Meant. "It was beyond enthusiastic really."

"You're right," she beats me to it, "you were *desperate*."

"Si si. He's a desperate kind of a man. A starving kind of a pen-dey-ho sometime. I think so."

GOOD-BYE AMELIA

"You lost me."

"You lost me," Amelia says she is not coming at me very Angry but she is Disappointed about it I think. "It's such a bad time & I find out I can't depend on you. By Tres Osos I know what a soft kind of a man you are."

566

I think this Opinion is not 100% Fair since I was blacked out in her bed at the time. Or what did she die thinking? All the time Nilo was kicking her around the kitchen I was hiding in bed with the blankets & pillows piled on my head?

"He was in your bed?" Annie has Trouble with this Idea.

"I took him there," Amelia says nor she is not Embarrassed by this Fact.

"Did he kiss you? Did you let him?"

"Si si."

"Eewy!"

"And more with him."

Annie wrestles this thought into her head this picture of a real woman who takes my Manhood Serious. "He French kissed you you mean? With his tongue in your mouth?"

"Si si."

"Eew! He's got such fishy lips!"

"I don't let him kiss me so much," Amelia lets the Truth come out. "He's no very bad for a lover. I took worse men in my bed."

"I might be sick," Annie turns very chalk white.

"Out the window," I say & I open it for her. Such fresh Air blows in & hits my face it wakes me up. "What does all this business about my lips matter so much? How I look is not the sum of my life! So what so I'm all left feet in the mattress dancing department. Is that the only thing you can judge a man by?"

"You think you know somethings better."

"Yes! I think you should judge me by my good qualities more! By how I think you should protect little children from evil influences. How I think you have to help the helpless & defend the defenseless. And give hope to the hopeless. Why don't a man's principles matter to you at all? I didn't leave mine on the floor under your bed Amelia I had them inside me if I was asleep or awake. I wasn't the man who made love so cheap to you—remember me?"

"You don't make a difference to me now. Hm?" Amelia's brown face Sinks Down in the brown Dirt. "What you think is nothing. Only what you do is something."

I can tell you something about the sporty Women in those

shorts they wear in Los Angeles, Calif. & the way they tie up their shirts in the Calypso manner it is a very attractive Sight to a man's eyes. I do not have the Appetite to slow down here & linger on them I just want to make a Point here the Geography affects them in this sporty manner Because the wild canyon is all around them. It is the same even if it has a Highway going through it from End to End even if it has a House in every cranny it is the same Wild Place Underneath. A house or a Trailer Park can not hide the Prehistoric ground. The bends of the asphalt go up in the Direction of the curves of the hill & the fences tip-toe around the edge of the Sharp Ravines down below. That canyon did not get buried under Civilization it is the same place Underneath as it was in Ancient days when lizards & insects had it all to themselves. They are still there too. Unless a Earthquake crumbles it into the Pacific Ocean in the Future or some other Act Of God rubs it out I know the lizards & red ants or whatever will still be there when dirt clods & weeds cover up that asphalt 10 Feet thick.

So this Wildness I think comes out in the Fashions they wear in California especially the Women with the short pants etc. they wear them in the street & Expose themselves as much as they can i.e. the Prehistoric Elements underneath call out to their Skin. I would like to learn if the Women who live out there React Different I would like to do more Research & investigate my Theory but now it is too late to go Back. I can say it was too late Before because here is what I am thinking when I drive by them in my car—*I do not count with the living anymore & what is the difference what I do I am gone already . . .*

"You're not dead yet Reuven."

GOOD-BYE PAPA!

"It's just a formality," I say. "I can't *affect* anything in my life!"

Papa sits down next to me he has to catch his Breath. "Reach over & close the window Reuvie. It's coming in cold. It's safer if you shut it." I make him Happy & close it all the way now I can Hear what he has to tell me without Interferrence. "I'll tell you how dead feels. I'll tell you what death is Reuven it's when you don't have a choice anymore. When you lie down like a lump on the floor & you don't have a choice about what happens to you. I call that death. Everything else is life."

"Papa."

"What is it Reuvie?"

"I'm suffering terrible right now."

"A person has to suffer if he wants to achieve his aims."

"But I'm suffering and I didn't even achieve a washing machine."

Papa shrugs. "A person has to suffer."

"It seems to me . . . I used to know . . . I could tell the difference between . . . what they did & what I did . . . "

"Will you snap out of it! Stop daydreaming out the window & concentrate. Think! Think! Think! I don't mean about young women in shorts either—concentrate on what's under your nose Reuven! Concentrate on what you can still do."

I look the other way & wipe my cheeks on a damp kleenex nor I do not look back at him.

Papa stops the silence he comes over again, "You always ignored what was obvious in front of you. The little things you need to pay attention to once in a while so you don't end up in the kind of sorry mess you can't reverse. You forget about the simple things you can do that make a big difference."

I offer him this Apology which I owe him for 40 Years: "Papa I'm sorry from the bottom of my heart we missed each other so long. I'm sorry I just dropped out of your view."

He hits the roof. "As usual! You can't change a minute of what happened between you & me. Oh this is typical! You get into these predicaments because by the time you finally pull your head down out of the clouds it's gone too far already and then you can't do what you should've done before!'

"I wish I could wind the clock back. I don't know what else to say to make things all right again."

"I'm not staying in this deathtrap with you," he says. "Now you're on your own."

569

"Wait Papa!" I pull him back very Strong. "You mean those are your final words? I don't want it to end this way!"

"I'm going Reuven."

"I should've trusted your advice more . . . I should've treasured your love more . . . I should've stayed where I belonged with you & Mama . . . I should've lived back East . . . I should've known my human limits . . . "

"You should've put air in your back tires."

A wiggle from the rear end of the Raymobile & the Alarm Bells started ringing in my ears—& the next second the wheels swerved out from under me & the road turned into Vaseline—I went skidding sideways around a curve downhill—the back whipped around it spun me straight into the powdery mountainside & Bounced me by my front bumper—I Punched my Brakes with both feet but I did not stop spinning I got pulled by the rear Backwards across the other Lane & crashed into the fence *out of control*—I ripped right through it & then the Force of Gravity took over—

I am plunging down into the rocks & bushes & like a idiot I am trying to steer in a Straight Line! with my fingers wrapped around the wheel going white & my molars locked together the Raymobile is sliding down like a bobsled—rocks cracking under the axles & the skinny bushes slapping the windows & plastering my windshield—all I can see is Black Smoke from the motor & a spray of Steam when the hood peels off & the whole car Rolls Over so I am going down 100 M.P.H. on my Side—the shrieking & squealing of metal tearing comes on top of the smell of Burning Rubber & when I plow into the gravel at the bottom I am not happy I Survived that bumpy ride I am scared I am going to get Burned to a Crispy Noodle—my seatbelt is jammed tight it hangs me there in the front seat—

It is a good Ford buckle but it did not stand up to a screwdriver + Panic so I did not get burned to a crispy noodle I Survived in 1 Full Piece which is not how the Raymobile ended up. My dear car my dear Friend ended up very Pathetic on its side in the Dirt like a crashed Bomber which left broken pieces of its Body stuck in the bushes Up Above. A hubcap & the exhaust pipe over here the side mirror & rear bumber over there. And my door was on the ground a few feet away in the water of the gully where I Landed. Here & Now I pay my final Tribute to that Beautiful Car let me put it like this: I have a tear in my eye when I tell you the Raymobile Died so I could Live. *It was a Honor to drive you over rough miles & smooth ones.* Rest In Peace!

Likewise I sat down for a rest to catch my Breath but I did not get 1 Minute of Peace. The Sight of my car's door torn off like a chicken wing hit me bad enough but Worse I saw how somebody's dirty hands tampered with it. Where the plastic lining got scraped back Underneath that ripped up skin a $100 Bill was flapping in the Breeze. I do not think the Ford Motor Co. stuffs money inside Station Wagon doors on the Assembly Line! So I Investigated Further & I Examined. The more I pulled back the edge the more I saw of them in there. I stopped counting when I had $5,000 in my hands plus something Extra—grimy white powder I will say a nice Sample from Newberry's traveling drugstore. You could not get rid of it all if you used a Professional Strength vacuum cleaner on it 24 Hours Non-Stop.

Maybe it Penetrates right into your skin when you Touch it I think so Because I Felt funny from then I almost Fainted. My head & my stomach started aching me terrible but my Senses did not go. I saw the Gun barrel poking up from under the back wheel & this worried me all of a sudden if a Child would find it & play with it how Dangerous it is so I dug it out then & there I took it away with me.

And I picked up my briefcase out of the mud too & a few pages of my Official File I found them floating in the brown water then I got the Idea how dangerous this Item is even more. I.e. danger-ous for me Personal in this Situation because how do I Explain it to a normal person passing by? How do I explain it so Joe Public would Believe who I really am & I do not know from Guns nor I am not a fugitive from the F.B.I. la-dee-doo-dah I am the Victim of Tragic Circumstances Beyond My Control! How am I supposed to Explain all the Facts on the spot if all the Evidence on the spot is piled up so high against me? Who is going to ask about the *background?*

CONGRATULATIONS NEWBERRY!!! YOUR PLAN WORKED PERFECT SO FAR!
You made me do things against my Will you made me go against my Good Judgment. You made me do what you wanted me to then you had me in your Power. YOU MADE ME THINK LIKE A CRIMINAL!

I did not hang around & stew in my Sorry Juice I did not wait for the Police to pull up & find me beside the Scene of the Accident I got away from there as fast as I could climb. Up the other side of the canyon all the way up to the boulders on top of the rim wherefrom I saw the saddest Sight of my Whole Day. Oh my long lost Raymobile! Oh my Aches & Pains! When I looked down Below & I saw all the broken pieces flung around behind it like trash & garbage I felt so Sore. Around my Rib Area especially. At every Breath I forced in & out I thought I was going to split apart like a nut in a nutcracker which is a sure sign of a Internal Injury. Nor I could not move any further my Condition was the same as my Raymobile lying in its Final Resting Place this time I knew I lost it permanent Amen.

Nor the nutcracker of my Injuries did not finish with me there I can still feel it pressing in the same way around my head. The sharp pressure cutting in. I can see the same Sight in front of me not the Raymobile anymore torn up in little pieces it is the trash & garbage of my manly Confidence. I Lament how I lost this part of my Life I Lament how it left me so Sorry. How I am not Strong enough I am not Smart enough I am not Good enough I am not above Low Desires. I am not above Revenge and now I defeat my own Purpose. SOMEBODY MADE ME SUFFER THIS WAY & I WANT SOMEBODY TO SUFFER LIKEWISE!

Off the side of my eye I saw the black & white Police car pull over in front of the Hole in the fence where I Crashed through. And a Ambulance parked there also a tow truck & in a minute you had 6 or 7 Persons going down the slope. They went down sideways standing up like surfers on a Dirt Wave. The Officers crawled all over the Car Wreck to Search for the Driver & when they found those Bloodstains from the Mexicans on the back seat I watched them very Close. It got Frantic around there all of a

572

sudden with them running up & down & lowering a Stretcher down on a rope & more Searching for Survivors.

A slice of cold Air caught me from the shadows folding in & I ducked down in it. I sat there & shivered & Choked on what I wanted to shout & Tell Them. About the Bloodstains in my car How they Got There & the nauseating Crime I can Describe down to the last Detail Because I was there when such a bastard you would not believe by the name of John Newberry *who is in the F.B.I. yet*—OH YES! tell it to the Judge!

Instead I stayed put where I was out in the open in the freezing cold but the Idea of a warm Police Station did not Tempt me it did the Opposite it made me keep away & Suffer. It ashames me in this late time of my Life now the Police are not my partners anymore they are my Enemies.

What fat Tears I Cried in my shirt! I clamped my hand over my mouth & I held it there for a minute so no one should hear me & spot me in such a feeble Condition. "Help . . . help me . . . help me . . . help . . ." I kept my Voice down that way I kept it to myself Because whoever can Save Me from this can Hurt Me More. "Ooh-hoo . . . help me . . . ooh-hoo . . . " those Words did not leak through my fingers they only bubbled on my lips but I did not stop Crying I did not hold in my Tears I let the sticky rivers come rolling out.

You can say I overdid the Excitement you can say I overdid it on the Physical side. If you are a Doctor who is Reading this you will Diagnose by my Symptoms it is just Exhaustion nor I do not deny the fact I was Pooped Out on all Fronts but what I am saying is it goes beyond. This goes beyond the Physical Facts.

I Felt every Muscle in my Body let go at the same time and then the Numb Feeling of my Bones vibrating inside me. I sank down where I sat & I started to shiver from the Power of it my hands dropped by my sides in the dirt like 2 Dead birds. I did not hear a Sound anywhere around me I do not think I was completely in the Land of the Living because the only Sight in front of me was the endless Ocean & the bonfires of the Sun shrinking on the other side.

Ergo you can Answer Me it was a Optical Illusion on my part

SO WHAT I do not care what you say about it. If you are a Psychiatrist I can hear you say it came out of my delirious Imagination will that kind of easy idea help you sleep better? Or if you are a Scientist you can Explain it to me by the Curve of the Earth plus a disturbance in the Atmosphere la-dee-doo-dah etc. but I Know by my Personal Experience what I saw when that sheet of clear Light Flashed in my eyes & sent cold heat roaring through me I know I honest to God witnessed the Green Ray—

Such a Green Fan of Light spread out over the whole Surface of the water how could I miss it? As fast as I could Blink it lit up the entire Ocean. And this is not a Freak of Nature that came out of nowhere it is as Real as I am! As old as the Air! The Green Ray did not change in a Million Years it goes back further even Before any person was on the Earth to see it. The same thing as I saw it is the same as it was on the first time it Appeared. And when the worldly Conditions are right & it comes back it is going to be the same thing again if anybody is Alive to Recognize it or not. For The Green Ray stretches out the same way over the long dead & the yet to be long dead. Amen.

A Black Smirch would be on my Conscience if I Killed Myself before I wrote down this Marvel. And likewise a Smirch on my Reputation if I Ignored the Vital Message it shined out to me in the beautiful clear green Light I saw aiming back East.

I just went over & opened up the front window again I am getting a little hot under the collar but I am leaving the venetians down. By this Arrangement I can keep my Defenses going & still get a nice Breeze in the room. Plus I can Hear if anybody is sneaking up the stairs from the Pool Area or if he is coming in by the Garage.

So far it is Normal out there for 4:09 A.M. no Activity in the driveway but he must be in Mason somewhere. I am guessing here but I expect Newberry any minute from now. He is going to walk up to my front door & break in on me like a burglar Because in his worked-up Condition I doubt it if he planned any further

Strategy in Final Detail. Ergo I am 100% Sure he will not be in the Mood to wait a minute & listen to me like a Sensible Human Being. I Know how he enjoys jumping to Violence so I Regret I am not going to get a chance to explain What Happened to him.

I am not Bing Crosby so I can say WHO CARES if I Lied to a Nun. By my Recent contacts I come to the Conclusion Nuns do not Regard the Discoveries of Science to the full they do not Recognize the Seeds of the Universe. At Mt. Holyoak which they tell me is *the best in the state* they do not Teach those children about the Theory of Atomic Particles or even the shape of the Solar System is minor next to their Official Views! I Admit I have a personal Grudge against them going back 350 Years i.e. I will Never Forgive for how they made Life so miserable for Copernicus and the way they treated Galileo of Italy. They made him Deny the Truth of his own Mind when he was the only person who knew the Facts of the universe. Instead of the Earth revolving around the Sun they Believe in sins on the Conscience of a little girl.

The Chief Nun who met me in her office gave me a cup of coffee & a few Butter Cookies on a plate with a Doily a very polite Gesture since I did not even ask for a drink of water. My View is I rated the De Luxe Treatment for being a Interested Party who came down in person to show a little Concern about the level of Education they practice there. And she did not have to open her mouth to let me know how Serious she felt about this Topic she took it completely Personal as if she was the Voice of Mt. Holyoak & the bricks & plaster were her skin & bones.

When I went in she was standing in the middle of the room about as Solid as the Heavy Furniture in there. She pushed her chin up & gave me a sharp Hello without a shake she kept her hands folded in front of her. This Pose made me think of the wooden Maidens carved on the front of sail ships with her Nose in the Wind. The dry smell of old carpets & Books came off her

575

dresses which I Sniffed when she swished by me & settled down behind her desk.

"Bishop Kinney's been here all morning," she ended this bulletin on a Sharp Sigh. "And he just left so I'm a little behind right now."

"We used to say it's better to be a little behind than a big ass-ss-ss," which Unfortunate Word very quick I choked off into a hacking cough & lucky for me that was when the door pushed open & my Coffee & Cookies Arrived so I do not think she was paying 100% Attention.

Her Assistant Nun also handed her a stack of papers & folders which she started shuffling while she talked to me. "He delves into every tiny detail here. I don't know where he gets the energy." She glanced up with a smile full of Satisfaction. "Even if we are his favorite. Sorry. You started to say something."

"Nothing at all," I got out of it. "What was he busy with today? I mean His Holiness."

"Chilli," she said on top of a change in her Expression that made me wonder if my fly was open. "The 4th Grade is making chilli for Saturday. It's their turn to make a hot lunch for the deprived children in the area. Bishop Kinney is a real expert on chilli con carne."

"Did the 4th Grade pass the taste test?"

"Not enough chilli peppers. Those boys & girls are mostly Mexicans over past State St. and they're used to it being a lot spicier."

"You should've put Dolores in there. She knows all about Tex-Mex."

She flipped open the cover of Dolores's school Record & ran her eyes down the top page. "Dolores isn't in the 4th Grade yet. She . . . " Her eyes flicked up at me & then back down to the paper before she said, "I try to get to know every one of our girls down to their little white cotton socks and your niece has only been here a few days." This was a polite Apology from her but I shook my head & waved it away. "You know we've put her back with the 7 year olds."

My sip of coffee went Cold in my Mouth. "But she's as smart as anything! She can read like a pro."

"I explained it to your brother on Monday."

"You did?" I took it in. "I'm just surprised you didn't put her with the 10 year olds *at least*."

"We have some catching up to do with her. She hasn't really been in school much as she should've been. For a smart 8 year old. By her age our girls have already had their First Communion."

"They have?"

"Of course."

"Is that the regular schedule or do you accelerate here?"

She shook her head she did not Understand Me. "I'm sorry. You want to know about her schedule?"

I nodded, "Mm."

"Sister Veronica teaches 2nd Grade. You may want to talk to her. Since Dolores is new at Mt. Holyoak we're beginning at the beginning with her. She's never been instructed in confession before," she put it to me very Blunt, "has she."

"Her mother never brought it up. I'm not sure."

"It's one thing you don't have to worry about. I'm happy to say your brother was very definite about it."

"He's a very definite kind of person."

"It's usually the mothers who get involved more with the 7's & 8's. Dolores is lucky she's got a daddy who wants to give her so much of himself."

"You think so?"

"I don't mean as a substitute. I just mean Dolores must feel a little lost away from her mother. It's a shame."

"That's what it is." I could only stare at the floor.

"Separations are always harder on the child. I hope I don't sound bold saying this now. I said it to Mr. Newberry. He thinks there's every chance she'll come back to the family again."

"I doubt it very much."

"It can't be as hopeless as you think." She tried to rub her Optimism off on me.

I used the Excuse of swilling the last drop of cold coffee around in my cup so I did not have to Answer her Before I had enough

Breath to. I swallowed the brown mouthful & put my empty cup back on the tray between us & I said, "Her mother's dead."

A instant pink rash of Embarrassment flushed up to the surface of the Nun's face & her throat. Her tongue stuck to the roof of her mouth then she peeled it loose to ask me, "Isn't she in Mexico?"

"Amelia's buried there."

"Oh the poor man!" She was thinking of Newberry now such a Proud person such a Sorry Widower who did not want this Tragedy to brand Dolores like a Charity Case at Mt. Holyoak— or Mark Him either so he just told her "separated" which is strictly speaking True oh yes. In a few seconds of Contemplation I saw her Understand him & Forgive him (which I am glad to say is against MY particular Religion!) then she blinked her Worry away & Came Back to me.

Except in the lull she did not know how to drop the Matter so I kept the ball rolling from My Side. I counted out all the bills I still had left over from the $5,000 out of the Raymobile—after the airplane ticket + the Rent-A-Car + my new seersucker suit it came out to $2,315 even.

"Nothing tremendous," I said. Then I took back the $15 off the top of the neat pile. "Sorry. I need this for gas."

My generous Surprise Donation took the personal heat off our Discussion & it gave her something else to Concentrate On. "It's . . . well thank you . . . it's . . . I'll send this to the Registrar . . . to Sister Therese."

"I know you didn't ask me but I'll tell you something about that. I'd like to think I'm involved in Dolores's education," I said. "To help her life along the right path."

She was still dwelling on the Previous. "I'll get you a receipt."

"You don't have to do that."

"It has to be done anyway. And then you can deduct it from your income tax." She grabbed a pink financial pad off her In tray & wrote out the necessary.

"You can mail it to me in care of my brother in Dallas. John's in charge of all my legal business now."

She was still Scribbling she held her eyes down on her Work. "How many years are there between you and your brother?"

If it was Small Talk it was the kind that made me Nervous. So I came half-way clean. "We're not altogether brothers. Not by blood. More like step-brothers. It's a complicated story." I nudged the Discussion back on the Right Track. "Can you explain it to me step by step why Dolores is back with the 7 year olds doing this communion business? In my opinion I think it's better for her this year if she learns about some other subjects first and gets to the religious side later. When she's more sure of herself. Did she tell you how interested she is in fossils?"

"You know what happens when you build on sand Mr. Newberry."

"No. What?"

She let out a Breath. "You *really* don't have to worry about her," she said & I could practically Feel Her reach over & pat me There There There the same way a Bronco Buster calms down a jittery Horse. "We won't rush her. Dolores is learning at her own speed. She already knows her Hail Mary in Spanish and she only trips over a few of the words in English. We'll get her there in the end." And she stood up on that Final Note but it was still Ringing in my ear & I sat like a Mule I did not take the Hint.

"Please Sister. I just want to understand it step by step. I don't want to go away with the wrong idea about how you're teaching Dolores in this school," I said & I asked her to Pardon my dumb yen to hear about all the daily Details.

I do not know if the Pope commands all Nuns to act Patient toward the idiots & numbskulls of this World but if he does then I owe the man a Favor. Because she did not lead me out the door she sat down & pulled her chair in & opened up like a flower. "If I can pull a few strings for the sake of Mt. Holyoak I'm not ashamed to tell you I'll pull with the best of them. I'm sorry if it's St. Cecilia's loss but I persuaded His Grace to send his brother to us this year." She let this Joyous News sink in & then she Announced his name to me. "Father Peter. The author." I hummed & hawed. She Reminded me of his Name again & furthermore acquainted me with the fact Channel 2 made a Christmas Cartoon Special from his children's books.

"I missed that show," I said.

"He's a real Pied Piper to the 2nd Grade," the Sister Nun told me. "I've seen him with Dolores and *honestly* I think there's something special going on between those two. Father Peter was in Guatemala for a year so his Spanish is beautiful."

"It's what's between them that counts."

"He's bringing her on so beautifully you can see a change in Dolores every day. I'm sure she knows what a very very important year this is for her. Believe me Mr. Newberry she couldn't do better than Father Peter Kinney for her instruction. It's a gift he's got. He can make children understand what it *means* to make their First Confession and how it *feels* to present their conscience to God."

"There. You said it in a nutshell Sister. It's what I've been trying to say. She's a terrific girl. You can skip over all that business with her & put her in the age group where she belongs. It's a waste of time to go into her conscience. What's there? I can vouch for her all the way. I know her background. She's a terrific girl."

"Will you be back in June for her First Communion?" she asked me & I Knew this was a set-up. So I just said I hope so. "I hope so too. You don't want to see her in church just repeating words she doesn't mean. Or standing in front of us all in her pretty little gown going through the motions. I'm sure you want her to know there's more to being here than singing along with Jesus Wants Me For A Sunbeam."

"I'm not saying she doesn't get up to the normal kind of shenanigans Sister. But her conscience. I mean what's in her conscience she should be ashamed of?"

And I heard how Mt. Holyoak did not build so much Excellence on Modern Ideas & Liberal Ways. I heard how Dolores has to Recognize how God does not appreciate it when she is Bold. Or when she keeps Secrets or tells them. I stopped listening to every word when that Nun started spieling about how many of her girls went off into Holy Orders & how many married Senators &

Congressmen la-dee-doo-dah but I had another Idea on my Mind which I presented to *her* Conscience all right—

"Can I ask you to put my donation into a certain area?"

"It depends what you've got in mind. I can tell you right now that nothing too exotic ever survives His Grace's budget meetings."

"I want you to put it into microscopes."

She Laughed for once & it Surprised Me it was a Warm Laugh she gave me. "Up till now it's just been between our missionary fund & our building fund. But I'll make a note," she laughed again. "Microscopes for the high school from you."

"Then Dolores can study science here."

"Of course she can. In the 8th Grade. In a few years."

"By then it's too late," I said but now she was up & walking over to the door she stopped Concentrating on me so I did not Expect any Reply when I kept talking. "By then her ideas are already settled in . . . " nor I did not get a Argument from her either.

She allowed me to take a peek at Dolores in her Class I looked at her through a little window in the door. Since she was in her Uniform sitting in the row in the middle of all the other ones it was not so easy to pick her out. Until I saw the side of her face the round line of her cheek it is the same round line of her Mother & I never Recognized Before how much she Reminds me of Amelia.

I had to stand back & let those girls pile out of the room. As soon as Dolores saw me she pushed around the ones who clogged up the door & blocked her path. "Uncle Ray!"

I bent down & we Hugged each other so Tight we did not want to let go but when the Sister Nun joined our party I kissed the top of Dolores's head & I straightened up.

"Dolores can I hear your Hail Mary?" she smiles down.

Out of the side of my mouth I Encourage her, "Your teacher said I could take you out for lunch if you can do it perfect."

"Let your Uncle Ray hear how you learned it from Father Peter."

"Then we'll go get a hamburger & a chocolate malted."

Dolores follows this Conversation over her head like she is Following the Bouncing Ball. Finally she looks straight ahead of her into the Empty Space between us & starts off, "Hail Mary mother of . . . "

A Correction from above, "Full of grace."

"Hail Mary full of grace the Lord is with thee. Hail Mary . . ."

"Blessed art thou."

"Blessed art thou among women . . . and blessed is the fruit of your womb Jesus."

"That's very good," I say also I break out in a soft round of Applause. "How's that?" Now I get a silent Correction from her. "I mean how is it so far?"

"Go on Dolores. I want to hear the rest," & she starts her off again. "Blessed is the fruit of thy womb Jesus."

"Jesus," Dolores joined in. "Holy Mary full of . . . "

"Mother of."

"Mother of . . . "

"Holy Mary mother of."

"Holy Mary mother of God pray for us sisters now . . . "

"Pray for us sinners now."

"Pray for us sinners now . . . and when I . . . "

"In the."

"In the . . . "

"Pray for us sinners now and in the."

"Pray for us sinners now and in the hour of our dead."

"Hour of our death. Not dead. Of our death."

When Dolores recited the whole Poem over again with No Mistakes it choked me up Hearing such a thing. How they can plant the worms of those Ideas to dig into her tender Conscience. I Apologize if it is Blasphemy to you but it is a Disgrace in my Opinion. What does a little girl have to know from Sin & Wombs & Death?

"You like going to school there doll? With Father Peter and everything?" I took my eyes off the road for a second so I could see her face in the rearview.

I definitely saw her shake her head No definitely I saw her do that. I Double Checked & made sure of her Feelings I asked her the same Question over again. Dolores did not stop shaking her head & this time she said very clear the word, "Nuh-uh."

If she answered me Yes in any form I would pull into the next coffee shop or whatever & stick to the hamburger plan According to what I told the Sister Nun. But my Innocent Question led to another one. "Do you want to stay with me instead?"

She scooted up to the edge of the seat. "I have to go back to Mt. Holyoak."

"Not if you don't want to." I got a Brave Feeling from telling her which Encouraged me I am not in the Wrong. "You don't have to go back there sweetheart."

"Yes I do Uncle Ray," she slumped back & kicked her feet up on the back of my seat. "I have to get my purse."

I did not slow down or turn around I put on the gas. I told Dolores to Lie Down all the way on the back seat until we got out past the City Limits of Santa Fe. *I will buy her a brand new pink purse* I was thinking—& 100 Silver Dollars & a Dozen Lucky Fossils I will start everything from the Beginning with her—

JUSTICE is in my hand once & for all! What I can do is make her Life better for her in every way which is in my Power. Especially in Education. I would teach her Geology how she can read the Story of the Earth from layers in the ground. The Painted Desert is a good place for that Lesson. I would teach her about Charles Darwin and how Human Beings Evolved from Africa. I would teach her about the Big Bang & The Law Of Gravity & E = MC² etc. as much as I can Explain about the Galaxies and other Wonders of Nature. I would play her my records of Jack Benny also Burns & Allen. I would play her Duke Ellington and other great Band Leaders for instance Artie Shaw. And I would read her from the works of Arthur Miller and the great William Shakespeare. I would tell her what Events happened in the World Before she was Born I would tell her about the East Coast. I would tell her what I was doing in Philadelphia when I was her age leading up to when I went to New York City. I would tell her all about my days on the Radio.

"I'll show you what the Green Ray looks like in California. It's out of this world," I twisted around & said over the back of the seat. The Sight which met my eyes made me lose my grip & Swerve halfway off the road—Dolores already Stripped her Clothes Off & she threw out her skirt & her jacket before I found the right button which put up her window. She moved over to the other one & threw out her stiff shirt & her shoes & socks Laughing Her Head Off with all the windows going up & down Because I can not find the correct buttons to stay a jump ahead of her. So my little Angel is perched up on the arm rest in the middle of the back seat in her Undershirt & Underpants informing me we just went past a A & W Root Beer place & how she needs to go to the bathroom. "Can you hold it a few more minutes?" She nods Yes she can. "Good girl," I Congratulate her & I concentrate on my driving so I do not run a Red Light or go 1 M.P.H. over the Speed Limit.

I consider what Dolores did was a normal shenanigan for a 8 Year old girl Ergo this is not a case of Discipline. A decent Father has to make 100 Decisions a day like that & for the Good of his Child he should be present at all times so he can Judge what is Correct. He has to be in Sympathy. I do not Defend my Mistakes over her but when you add it all up you will come to the Fair Conclusion that I would be a better Father than John Newberry—

Here is more JUSTICE in my hand. Furthermore what I can do is make *his* Life *worse*. I let him know Exactly how it Feels when somebody he cares for Disappears. When another man takes her away without his Permission. I Sincerely Hope he was sick in his stomach when he Heard about it & pictured how it Happened. NEWBERRY NOW YOU KNOW HOW COLLAPSED INSIDE A PERSON CAN FEEL WHEN YOU EXPECT TO HEAR HER VOICE & INSTEAD YOU HEAR THE SOUND OF A EMPTY ROOM . . .

Diet is the main thing to Consider when it comes to a growing Child. In spite of the beautiful Adobe Buildings I Doubt it the meals at Mt. Holyoak are very Nutritious. Going by the boiled smells of the Cafeteria I would say they Rely too much on creamed corn & diced carrots. So I was only going to stop over at Pecan Street to pick up a few Necessities & make a hot Dinner for us. I bought the best chicken plus fresh vegetables my favorite dish. I believe the market I went to was a Safeways or Food King. One of those or a Garden Basket in Las Cruces I believe cash register Number 8. I Plead with you go & find the Check-Out Girl she will Vouch for how beautiful Dolores acted with me & vice versa. That girl helped me pick out a cute T-shirt with a goofy bumblebee on it for Dolores to wear. This time I Regret nobody from the F.B.I. was around to take a snapshot I could show you how fine we were together.

I walked in the front door of my Apartment & I got a Welcome from the ripe smell of dirty laundry from the basket in the bedroom. It clung on the stuffy Atmosphere as heavy as fog only you know what it did not smell terrible it was my own Aroma there. Look how much a person's home is Enshrined on his Memory down to every Molecule even if he Rents! Also by the dirt accumulation I admit 2 Weeks without Mrs. Roderiguez really shows but if it is not so Neat & Tidy so what. If it is not so Spic & Span in every corner so what it means a Human Being lives here. I know where every Item is & how it got there my stamp is on everything.

Dolores did not follow me in on my heels she stood next to the door when I went in the kitchen nor she would not Budge Further. She waited for Permission on the Border of my Domain. So I tugged her very gentle by her hand & shut the door behind us.

"You want to go to the bathroom doll?" I showed her where it is & she made me leave the door open then I left her alone so I could get the chicken started.

On my way over I slid the chain on the door & when it locked in it told me *This is my place in here & the rest of the World is outside.* Except this is a False way to think. It is only a thin door separating nor it is not a Vacuum in my Apartment. The Air seeps in & my Aroma leaks out so to say Troubles will enter likewise I Believe. They Follow a person they come in at the Same Time. You can forget about what is done & what is doing but you can not get away from the rest of the World nobody has that level of Protection.

Dolores found me up to my elbows washing the chicken in the sink. "No more toilet tissue," she planted her feet & made this Announcement.

"You mean you used up the end of it or you didn't have any?"

"Didn't have any."

"Did you go Number 1 or Number 2?"

"Number 1."

"Tell me if you need to do the other. I'll go borrow a roll from nextdoor. You wash your hands?" She nodded she did. "Let me see."

She held them up I should Inspect them & they were damp so I wiped them off on a dish towel. And while this was going on she twisted around & took a look in the sink. "I don't like chicken," she said.

"You'll like it the way I make it," I said. "Let's go in the livingroom a minute."

"Can I watch T.V. until the news is on?"

I fished out a National Geographic the Special Anniversary one with the Children of Every Continent pictures Dolores could enjoy to herself. "I want to rest a little while in my chair. Let's keep things quiet O.K. dear? No T.V. right now."

I dropped the venetians so nobody could spot I was back in temporary Residence & I landed in the warm seat of my green leather armchair. It fits every bulge & lump of my Physique I forgot it is so Comfortable to sit there as if it is the lap of a lovable giant. I Forgot I was so Pooped from head to toe. So much I hardly moved a aching Muscle I just sat there staring at the dust Particles that shook out of the slats of the blinds I watched them Dance & Float in the layers of pale Sunlight.

"Look Uncle Ray," Dolores spoke up & she was pointing at the window.

A sharp scare Stabbed Me in the stomach when I looked over & then it faded fast—Newberry is not going to climb up a ladder & come in by the window! He is not going to dangle down on a rope from the roof! I went back to Touching the smooth brown

586

Patches on the arms of my chair where my palms Wore Off the Color.

"Why does it do that?"

"What?"

"Why does it do that Uncle Ray?" Now she was pointing at the sparkling Dust with both hands.

Even if you are too pooped to pop you should give a Child your sincere Attention so they never have to guess how much they matter to you. "They reflect the light. See?" I leaned over & patted the Upholstery & another spray of dust spread out in the Air. "They're practically microscopic those little particles."

Dolores watched so close I think she was trying to pick out a lonely Speck of that Dust & follow its Movements. She held her hand up in the stripes of light coming in over the sofa. "Those are sunbeams," she said & she was 100% Sure of this Scientific Fact.

"I'll tell you something interesting," I said. "You want to know a unbelievable thing?"

"What?"

"It takes 8 minutes for each sunbeam to come here from the sun. It has to go 93 million miles from the surface of the sun to the surface of the Earth."

"Oh."

It is another thing to get a Child to give you sincere Attention the same especially if they have something as Fascinating as Dust Particles to look at. "They reflect the sunlight," I tried again. "That's what happens with the moon at night. It's the same reason why we can see the moon. Moonlight is really the light from the sun reflecting down."

"Oh."

I think she did not appreciate the Information $\frac{1}{2}$ as much as she was enjoying the Ballet of the Dancing Dust. She slapped the cushions to bring up some more & a thin cloud puffed out around her. Rembrandt could paint a Masterpiece if he saw Dolores through that fuzzy light.

A sneeze squeaked out of her which swirled the dots of Dust into crazy Orbits & this Effect made her Laugh Out Loud. (I believe Atomic Particles travel around in very similar lines. Those Quarks for example. I wonder if Household Dust is where Scientists got the Inspiration at first?) So who am I I should tell Dolores what she should Appreciate? Let her enjoy the Beauty if she wants—

So I joined in on her level I Patted Out some more which Floated in & out of the shadows now you see them now you lose them. "You can see where the light is," I showed her. But I did not Ruin the Fun & tell her how Dust does not Defy Gravity forever it all settles down on the T.V. tray & on my hi-fi eventually so Mrs. Roderiguez has to wipe it up again on a Damp Rag. Nor I did not add the part about what they are those Particles—dead skin cells flakes of Human Dirt & hairs wings of insects & living mites etc. which look Revolting if you see them up close la-dee-do-dah I did not Interfere further I let her enjoy the stupid game of it.

Dolores played the cushions like a tom-tom & the dust swarmed all over it swam in the Air. She Breathed it in & Coughed it out & she was laughing Hysterical the whole time. Even when it turned into more Coughing than Laughing we kept on drumming my sofa to the Jungle Beat. In this time it only sounded like a tickle caught in there a Dry Cough just a little feather in the back of her throat.

I got her a cup of water from the Sparklets but she was hacking too hard to drink it. She choked out a few words which cut into me like a buzz saw. "I need my medicine." Her mouth popped open then she tried to drag in a Breath & said it again very Frightened, "I need my medicine!"

"Oh Christ honey," I rolled her over in a hurry so I could pat her & try to keep her Windpipe clear. "I don't have any medicine. We don't have your medicine here."

Now her coughs came from deeper down nor she could not talk all of a sudden. Her eyes were floating in tears & open so far it was like she was trying to Breathe with them too.

"Oh Christ. Oh honey." I heard her lungs whistling & in 5 Seconds Dolores's face was hot & red. And the most Terrible Pain I Felt was her fingers pinching my arm so hard to get me to Help

Her. I would Breathe for her if I could I would squeeze Medicine out of My Skin!

By my Memory this is when the Choking started this is when it sounded like both of her Lungs were trying to squeeze out of her mouth to Reach the Air. She folded up on the floor kicking her feet in every Wild Direction. I was watching a Tantrum of Pain & Panic in front of me a wounded animal trapped in a net nor I was Not Strong Enough to rip her Loose. When I reached to hug her she pushed me away but that was her Body taking over for itself Dolores did not Know what she was doing anymore only Fighting for her Breath. So I let my Instincts guide me when I saw her face turn blue & she was giving up then I jumped in—

"No!" I shook her shoulders & laid her down straight—I was crying over her "No! No!" & I tried to Remember step by step the Kiss Of Life. I pushed my mouth down over hers & blew a Breath into her and she lay there Limp. I tried it again but her lips did not stay open they got very slippery from the Mucus of her nose & eyes so I did not have a Airtight Grip & when I blew in again by some Convulsion she bit me very hard & cut my tongue (I hope that Explains how the Blood was on her face & all over my shirt).

I did not waste time & wait for a Ambulance instead I picked Dolores up & ran with her in My Arms all the way. I ran 6 Blocks in 5 Minutes flat. Jesse Owens could not run faster to Dr. Godfrey's.

"Help me!" I broke in on him & that was all I had to say.

The shocking Sight of us did not slow him down he put Dolores right away on the table with a Oxygen Mask she was in the best of hands. He worked on her to his Utmost he gave Dolores the highest care. I did not want to be in there I wanted to stay out of his way Because in a Medical Crisis what counts is Know-How not Worry & Tears So I was outside the room when I heard him tell Miss Petersen, "They don't have to hurry. Tell them there's no emergency."

It is my Honor to say Dr. Godfrey is a Friend of mine above & beyond the fact he is my Doctor. He did not pepper me by Questions about Who? What? When? Where? Why & How? he let me get away with the Short Version of Events. My Explanation was simple: i.e. I was just taking care of Dolores for a few days. I told him how she was at Mount Holyoak. I told him Before that she used to live with her Mama in Mexico. So I did not hand him any Lies in the least I only left a few Blanks for the sake of saving my Breath. Hereby I urge whoever is in charge of the Investigation please you should give Dr. Godfrey a copy of this he Deserves to hear the whole Story. Thank You.

I wrote down John Newberry's details on a prescription pad (ha ha! a Fatal Dose of Medicine!) and I said, "If I know him he'll want to make his own arrangements."

Doctor Godfrey looked at the name & number but he did not rush & dial it. "Stick out your tongue." His Diagnosis was I got a nasty bite but a band-aid is out of the question.

"I tried to give her the kiss of life," I answered him even if he did not ask. "I didn't know what else to do."

"You did the right thing Ray. You did the best thing you could in the circumstances." He patted my arm he leaned back in his chair. "Did you know she was asthmatic?"

"Usually she's got her medicine with her in a little bag. But since she's at Mt. Holyoak the nuns don't let her have it with her uniform," I said the way I Remembered it. "So it got left in her room when I picked her up."

"Where's her uniform now?"

"Now?"

"If you want me to tell her father. Or do you think you can?"

"No. Tell him . . . tell Mr. Newberry he can find me at home. I'll go back to my apartment and wait for him."

"Whatever you want Ray," his Voice maybe was a little Infected by my own Sad Tone. "You spend 31 years in this business & you think sooner or later you'll get used to it. Y'know when Mrs. Calusco had her accident I went down to the hospital. You were around when that happened weren't you? Around the time I sewed your scalp up."

"I was around."

"How old was she? In her 90s or something."

"She was 92 I think."

"That's right. She was 92 years old. And I thought what a tragedy it was."

"It was," I nodded.

"It was a horrible accident but . . . 92 y'know? Anyway. I still think it's awful. But it's a lot worse when I see a child go. It hits me harder. It does. I swear to God Ray when it stops affecting me like this that's the day I'll retire."

From where I sat it looked like every Muscle in Dr. Godfrey's face was straining under his Skin & holding back a Wave of terrible Emotion. He said, "Some strange things have been going on around here lately," & it was how a family priest talks to a nervous wreck out on a skyscraper ledge.

"Like what things?"

"Maybe you missed all the excitement. It's funny," he stopped he broke off looking at me. "That little girl who was in the newspaper. Incredible story. I didn't believe it really happened. Not like the paper reported it."

I snapped my fingers & tapped my forehead. "I know who you mean. Whatsername. The little girl in the liquor store."

"You were around for that. Good." Dr. Godfrey loosened up from the neck down but the strain was still on his face. "Ray—"

Before he had a chance to say Ray what I hoisted myself up out of my chair but a icy spider web of pain gripped my chest & I dropped back down. Dr. Godfrey bent over me then I asked him, "Is it cold in here?"

"Do you feel nauseous?"

"No . . . uh-uh . . . am I going to?"

He unbuttoned my shirt he lifted up my Undershirt & shook his head very grim over the Sight he saw. All of my Bruises all of my souvenirs my Black & Blue splotches my cuts & my raw red scabs my sagging Body so Punched Up that way. "Where have you been Ray?" My mouth locked tight by its Own Will & I feel he saw my Desperate look which warned him back. He tugged my Undershirt down again he stayed next to me while I buttoned up. "I've been missing our conversations. I read something interesting in the A.M.A. Journal about Chinamen last week. Chinamen pay their doctors when they feel healthy and they stop

591

paying when they get sick. You think that kind of arrangement could ever catch on in this country?"

I Admit I stopped concentrating on Chinamen before he got to the end of the sentence my Mind already slipped off to another Subject. "Maybe you can tell me something. But if you can't then don't make up a nice answer just to make me feel better all right?"

"Ask me."

"Is there any medical proof of what a soul is?"

"Depends what you mean."

"I mean did any doctors ever do the research to find out if it's real or not. Maybe you ran across some article about it in a specialist publication. If any brain surgeon might've discovered a shred of evidence the public doesn't know about."

"I don't think I've read any report like that. I don't keep up on all the literature though," he made a joke out of it.

"I just wondered."

"Unless you mean studies on brain waves. There was somebody in Europe I think about 15 years ago. A neurologist in Sweden or Switzerland who was doing something on that."

"That's it. Brain waves. Mental energy. That makes sense."

"It's voodoo science Ray."

"Wait a minute! Brain waves would fit in perfect with this kind of a theory. There's electricity in every brain cell. Every thought is a spark of electricity."

"You'd get a bigger charge from a nylon carpet."

"And you can't destroy electricity. So therefore—"

"I hate to tell you this Ray but a little electric eel swimming in the Amazon generates more voltage catching a bug for lunch than Ludwig van Beethoven's brain did when he wrote the Ode To Joy."

"It's different in here," I drummed my fingertips on my head, "it isn't just electrical instincts. It isn't just chew & swallow in here. Human beings evolved different from fish! The sparks in my brain are *ideas*. They're *memories*. My individual personal brain waves and . . . and if that doesn't add up to something like a immortal soul then you can tell me what *does*!"

"Nothing does." He shook his head very low.

"Oh that's a deep argument. You convinced me. I'm convinced."

"Who said it's a deep argument? I'm not *superstitious*. I'm not *sentimental* about it. I think souls are imaginary creations."

"If it's so imaginary then where did the idea come from? The ancient Egyptians had the idea also the ancient Greeks. And 2,000 years before that the Hebrew people took it for granted everybody came with a soul inside them. And before that too. In China."

"People always want to deny the facts of life. In particular . . . how it's so short & final."

"That doesn't prove a person doesn't have a soul. I think it proves he does." I Ignored my Chest Pain when I got up this time I did not mind it.

"You're right," he said, "it doesn't prove anything."

"Everything real in the world starts out as something imaginary in somebody's mind," I answered him from the door. "A building does. A baseball game. A mathematical equation which is more imaginary than anything else. Take $E = MC^2$ — it's only imaginary but it's something real in the world too. You see it everywhere you look."

"Keep working on it Ray. It's a promising theory. I wish I could believe there actually is something else . . . standing between the grind of our lives . . . and this mortal fear I've got . . . that there's no point to a single minute of it . . . " Dr. Godfrey wiped his damp forehead on the heels of his hands. "But you can't really say anything like that has much of a survival value . . . can you."

Anything that is made you can not Destroy it either Matter or Energy it can only Change. This is a Scientific fact this is a Law of Nature. Ergo when I use my Gun this time my manly form is going to change so much you will not Recognize it. All I have to do is fire a Bullet now & that is The End of me.

So What I am very happy about this eventual Idea. By me Death is only the End of one thing & the Beginning of something else nor this is not just Wishful Thinking either. There is plenty of Evidence & Data on this Theory there is plenty of Proof from the realm of Science.

Look at a banana. From a green bud to a yellow piece of fruit to being brown & rotten just a stain of starch & sugar Molecules. That is the Life Cycle of a banana. Or a boulder for instance. Time will grind it down into a pile of sand on the Beach. Or even my dear Raymobile started out shiny in the showroom & now it is a junkyard rustbucket. Nothing in the world can avoid this Condition every Item you can name has to Disintegrate in the earthly Oxygen.

And look Beyond besides. A Human Being is small potatoes compared to the Stars and a Star does not last Forever. The Sun is going to boil down to its smallest Parts at a certain time. Down to its Molecules & Further down to its Atoms and that tradition applies to a person the same.

I consider this amazing Fact & I am Calm all over. How I am made out of Atomic Particles from the opening day of the Universe. The cells of my Flesh & Blood they are just a new Arrangement of the original Atoms that blew out of the Big Bang! I have the Seeds of that giant Explosion in every part of my Body those violent Atoms are buzzing in my trigger finger right this minute. (Maybe this is the Explanation of Violence in the World it is just the Past breaking out of us. We can avoid it like we can avoid our own skin or a Earthquake for instance how can you avoid a Act of God?)

Nor the Stars can not escape their Doom so why should I? A Star will repeat the Past when it runs out of gas—BOOM!—it Collapses it Explodes it Disintegrates & sprays out its mortal Remains in every Direction but that is not the End of the Story. Clouds of Stardust float out in Empty Space and then the Effect of Gravity takes over.

Some Particles cling together by Magnetic Force & roam into the Gravity Field of another burning Sun which Attracts Them & turns them into the core of a new Planet. Or other Atoms will attach in the right Conditions in the Cosmic Dust & ignite each other and then there is the core of a new Star. In the Future new

Stars will cover the sky in new Patterns which is a Sight I Regret I will not live long enough to see.

Dr. Godfrey you are Wrong about how a person has to End Up. When I Perish you will look at my Remains but I will not be in them. Now hereby I request you should take care of the Necessary. You can bury what is left of me or maybe better you should Incinerate Me. It is quicker for all Concerned including me. Like the Old Saying goes—"It's your funeral!" so here is how I want it—

1. DO NOT let anybody who does not Know me on a Personal Basis speak about the Ups & Downs of my Life. Just because a man is a local Rabbi it does not mean he is a bosom buddy of every Jewish person in the area.
2. DO NOT cry Ooh-Hoo over me how I am just a helpless Victim of these sad Circumstances. Just enjoy a quiet minute of Remembrance—e.g. how I showed you how to beat a professional at Pinochle.
3. DO NOT wear a black suit!! Wear your nice off-white & your Tropical tie the one with the Hula Hula Girl.
4. DO NOT worry too much about my Absence because the Atoms of my Being are going to Survive. What you will see in the mahogany box is NOT who Ray Green was!!!

You know I wish I could think so Clear when I was in your office Before. My Mind was in such a shock then thinking about Dolores by pushing her face out of my Thoughts. Now I can concentrate a little better & I can tell you what I meant on the Subject of Souls. Here is my personal Conclusion—

I Believe a Force is inside every Event in my Life in every different Sensation—what I heard & saw what I said & did every Past Episode which stays in my Mind and 1 by 1 they all add up I will say the same way Microscopic coral animals add up to a Reef. Everything I remember. The Atoms of my Being. I Preserve them all together in my Brain Waves I Believe my Soul is located there. (Write to that Doctor in Sweden! See if his Research agrees with my Idea!)

It is a Medical Fact when I die my Body will lose its grip from head to toe nor my Brain will not have any Strength left. So it can not hold in my individual Atoms anymore & they will rise out fly apart & travel up into the Air & Beyond. Up there they circle around in the Gravity Field of the Earth & all of my Particles will mix into the Millions of Millions which rise out of other people's Lives.

The argument in the kitchen with Mama & Papa about the turkey in 1938—The Sight of Annie walking down the hall in the Liberty Building—When I ran into Amelia in the Blackout—My Voice of The Green Ray saying, "Captain—I can't *wait* to get my hands on Horvath!"—When John Newberry poured me a cup of coffee at his kitchen table that morning—all of these Specks of Time will float & Sparkle up Above. In the solid black of space around us they reflect the Invisible Light.

By the Law of Gravity those Particles will Attract each other & join up like a strand of beads in a new Combination different Atoms of different Human Beings. I do not know how many have to be there but when they Weigh the right amount together they form a new Soul. Which is heavy enough & Gravity pulls again it pulls the Soul back down to Earth.

Newberry I THANK YOU for this wonderful chance to come back to Civilization! I feel like a new person just thinking about it! So hurry up already I want to go.

Furthermore when you broadcast Radio Waves they travel out in Space forever non-stop. According to this Idea all of the Episodes of The Adventures Of The Green Ray are still going strong!

I hope by some Possibility they can change the course of a few Human Particles before they return. Thereby I can still be a Healthy Influence on young people. For instance my fearless Example of manly behavior when I followed the Clues I knew had to lead me face to face with Lionel Horvath for the Final

596

Time. How I acted to the uppermost degree I did not shrink I Fought Him to the End.

I remember what is going to happen—

I hate him. I Know what the only Item was between them I know what Connected her to him. MONEY.
MONEY is the Electricity.
MONEY is the blood of the world.

Blue skies smiling at me Nothing but blue skies do I see

Here he is. I can hear him outside down below by the Patio Chairs. Coming up from the Pool Area. I thought so.

This is the Climax of my Life & I am sitting on the floor in my pyjamas with the barrel of a loaded Gun in my mouth & a rotten bastard maniac tapping his silver razor very polite on my window asking me if I could please come to the front door! Well FUCK ending up this way FUCK being his Helpless Victim! The *hell* I am going quietly! I am coming to the door all right!!
I AM COMING BACK————